HEATHER FOXTON

THE ROBERT STYLES AFFAIR

13
ELEMENTS

For more information on the adventures
of Heather Foxton, visit:

Instagram

Amazon Author Page

To Piers, wouldn't be it not were it were it not for Foxy here for you . . .

ALSO BY M.N. SMITH

Heather Foxton
The Secrets of Godolphin Park

Heather Foxton
The Hyderabad Siphon

THE ROBERT STYLES AFFAIR

M.N. SMITH

13
ELEMENTS

First published in 2022 by 13 Elements

Copyright © M.N. Smith 2022

Interior illustrations copyright © M.N. Smith 2022

The right of M.N. Smith to be identified as the author of
this work has been asserted in accordance with the Copyright,
Designs and Patents Act 1988.

*This book is a work of fiction and, except in the case
of historical fact, any resemblance to actual persons, living
or dead, is purely coincidental.*

13 Elements, c/o: writingheatherfoxton@gmail.com

A CIP catalogue record for this book is available
from the British Library.

ISBN 978-0-9927378-5-6 paperback

Cover design and layout by
chandlerbookdesign.com

Front cover images:
Main image of Hong Kong street / Sean Foley
Other images:
andrey_l/Shutterstock.com | Mia Stendal/Shutterstock.com

Printed by
Amazon Kindle Direct Publishing

The publisher supports the Forest Stewardship Council® (FSC®), the leading
international forest-certification organisation. This book is made from acid-free
paper from an FSC®-certified provider. FSC® is the only forest-certification scheme
supported by the leading environmental organisations, including Greenpeace.

This book is dedicated to the most
incredible women in my life.

My wife, my daughter and of course
my mum.

For never giving up in aspiring to be more
than some might wish you to be.

And finally, to the fabulous city
of Hong Kong for giving us so
many wonderful years.

'Success is not final; failure is not fatal;
it is the courage to continue that counts.'

– Sir Winston Churchill

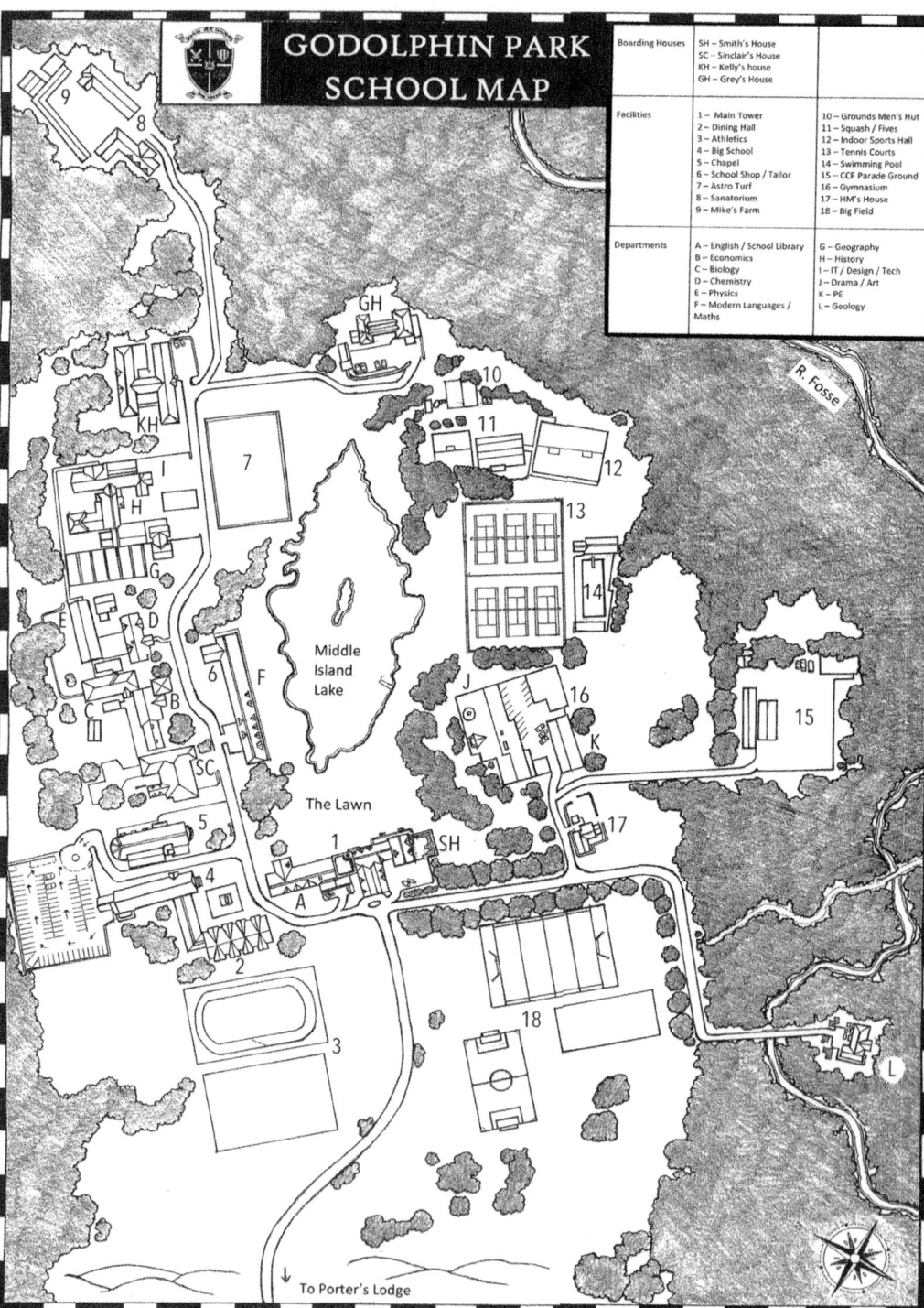

GODOLPHIN PARK
SCHOOL MAP

Boarding Houses	
SH – Smith's House	
SC – Sinclair's House	
KH – Kelly's house	
GH – Grey's House	

Facilities		
1 – Main Tower	10 – Grounds Men's Hut	
2 – Dining Hall	11 – Squash / Fives	
3 – Athletics	12 – Indoor Sports Hall	
4 – Big School	13 – Tennis Courts	
5 – Chapel	14 – Swimming Pool	
6 – School Shop / Tailor	15 – CCF Parade Ground	
7 – Astro Turf	16 – Gymnasium	
8 – Sanatorium	17 – HM's House	
9 – Mike's Farm	18 – Big Field	

Departments		
A – English / School Library	G – Geography	
B – Economics	H – History	
C – Biology	I – IT / Design / Tech	
D – Chemistry	J – Drama / Art	
E – Physics	K – PE	
F – Modern Languages / Maths	L – Geology	

R. Fosse

GH
KH
10
11
12
7
13
I
H
14
G
E
D
Middle Island Lake
J
16
6
F
15
K
B
SC
The Lawn
5
17
1
SH
4
A
2
18
3

To Porter's Lodge

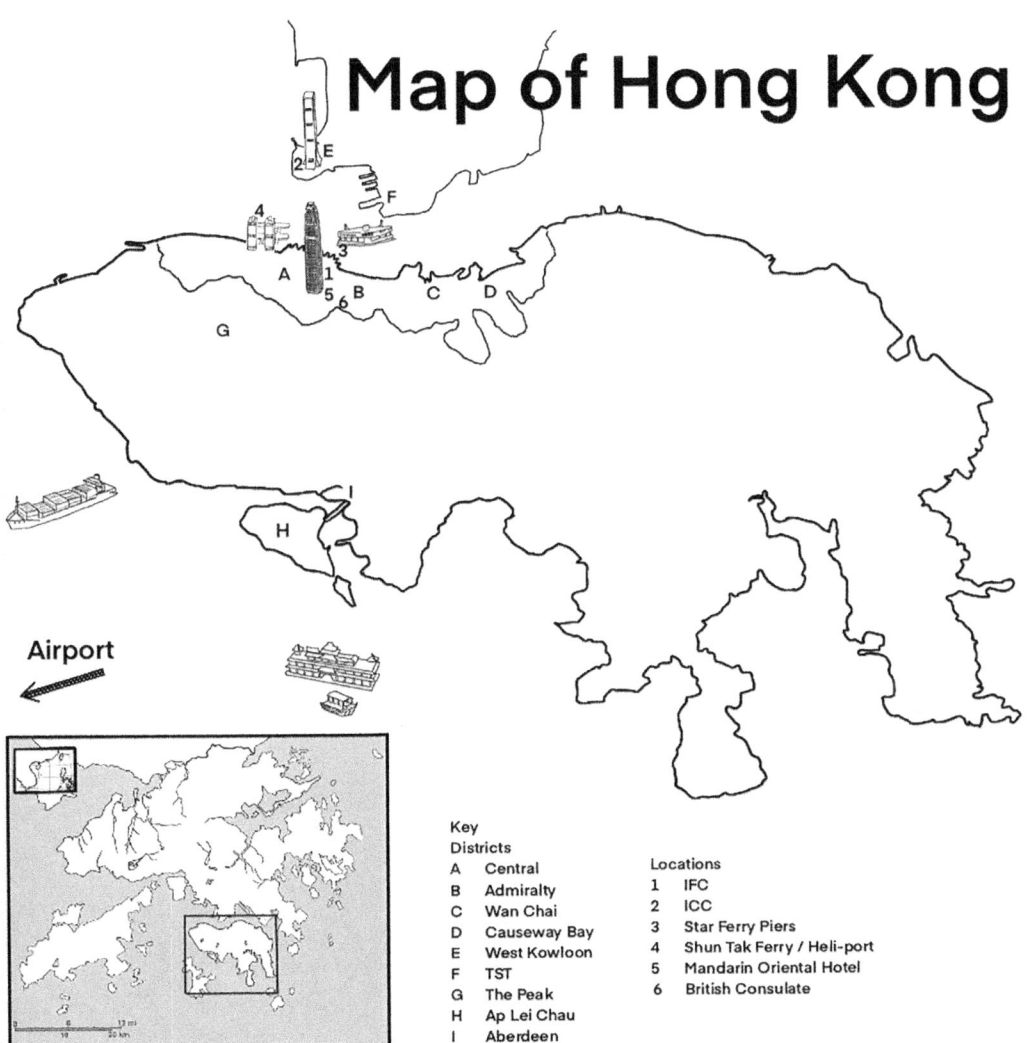

Map of Hong Kong

Airport

Key
Districts
A   Central
B   Admiralty
C   Wan Chai
D   Causeway Bay
E   West Kowloon
F   TST
G   The Peak
H   Ap Lei Chau
I   Aberdeen

Locations
1   IFC
2   ICC
3   Star Ferry Piers
4   Shun Tak Ferry / Heli-port
5   Mandarin Oriental Hotel
6   British Consulate

CONTENTS

THE GOODBYE TO INNOCENCE

Ever notice how the movies like to make out that killing someone will mess you up? Hollow you out with remorse, like deep down. All that emotional blah, blah, blah. As if that would make you sound more human, more acceptable to polite, conservative society.

Yeah, right!

Let's dispel with that little misconception right here, shall we? Utter bollocks. Don't forget, this is the same lot who almost universally advocate that car doors can stop bullets. So, yeah... Truth is, killing another person is largely a matter of circumstance. In that sense it's a bit like the truth itself. Especially in the spy game.

The reality is if someone has every intention of killing you, then you either slot them first or you can kiss it all goodbye. Don't you just love the English language for offering up such wonderfully colourful military slang, like the verbs "to slot" or "to waste" as euphemisms for the slightly more morally unpleasant "to kill"?

Anyway, here's the rub. Afterwards, you feel almost nothing. Relief, for sure. And a mad adrenaline high, which sharpens everything. Your senses, perceptions, the importance of those closest to you.

Curiously, I've found that the closer you get to death, the more alive you feel. Sounds contrived, right? But seriously, I assure you it's true. And, weirdly, it also makes you feel older. More mature. Or maybe that's just me. But there's none of the soul-wracking guilt you'd expect. Not like if you'd just knocked some poor git down in the road in your car.

That said, I get not everyone would see it like this. The average person in Civvie Street would probably be appalled by this. But no doubt they've never been in this position. And if they had, would they have had the nerve to do what's necessary and stay alive? Probably not. So, game over.

Fact is, and no one likes to admit this, but life's cheap. The events of last term were a major wake-up call for me in that regard. About just how little regard some have for others' lives. Take Sam, bludgeoned to death in an Indian open-air laundry. Or Michael O'Leary, rich and powerful as he was, shot without a second's hesitation and buried in the woods. Even Alex's dad, billionaire and super-connected, again, slotted like an afterthought. The casual disdain with which such fatality was dished out was shocking at first. But it highlighted to me the things that are worth fighting for in life, and how hard we must fight to protect those we love and the things we care about. Because in the absence of fierce resistance, the animals and the fanatics out there would simply burn all of it down.

I find it kind of amusing that were Daniel Craig to be believed, it takes two kills before double-oh status is awarded.

Yeah, right! Though he wasn't wrong about the second one being considerably easier. To date, I've chalked up four on behalf of HMG, and yet no one from the government's offered me anything. When I asked, they told me that there is no actual licence to kill. Talk about crushing disappointment! I honestly thought it would be like some kind of laminated card that they hand you in some fancy, clandestine ceremony. Welcome to the club sort of thing. Yeah, right.

Apparently, there's a very good reason for this and it's that killing people is technically illegal in pretty much every country in the world. Collating the necessary international agreements to let spies slot whoever needs slotting would be a diplomatic horror story. The international driver's licence programme it isn't.

Instead, I've simply been informed, all hush-hush, wink-wink, that when it becomes necessary, it's just best not to get caught. And that's mostly because the other thing that's illegal in nearly every country on earth is spying. Pity, because I quite liked the laminated card idea. But maybe therein lies the reason why it's not so scary or daunting. Killing people, I mean. Because there's virtually no consequence in my world for it. No notion of impending justice looming over you. Just don't get caught. We really do live in the age of impunity.

I sometimes wonder why I wasn't more shocked by all of it at the time. Like I was back when I saw Robert Pemberton-Smythe get killed. And it's not just me. I mean even Milly, my best friend and less than enthusiastic companion on most of these insane adventures, says the same thing. She figures stuff was happening so fast that there was no time to register any of it properly. I'm not so sure. More likely what they're teaching us at this crazy spy-school of ours is actually rubbing off on us. Their obsession that we focus on the mission – ignoring all distractions, compartmentalising our emotions, all cold and calculating – may be closer to the truth. Churchill once said everyone in this game has a corkscrew mind. He probably wasn't wrong. Perhaps you've got to be slightly 'different' to even get into a school like this. Let alone the full-on other government services, or OGS as we call them. Common sense would say we should've been way more perturbed by all of it. Frankly, I'm perturbed that we weren't perturbed.

I guess it's like they say: if you want to get people's attention, you're just going to have to push some boundaries. Well, you know what having several red files under your belt does? It makes people suddenly take you a whole lot more seriously. Your standing in the world becomes much more cemented and their trust in you rises, and along with that comes even more responsibility. And then so too comes greater insight into what's really going on. Which is kind of exciting. The irony being the more you know, the more you realise how little you knew. All in all, it's fair to say things have come along quickly since the Jungfrau observatory.

Espionage, as I'm discovering, is about as clear as muddy water. Nothing new there, some might say. But things are changing quickly at the moment. People say that even back in the Cold War, when things got pretty murky, the fundamentals were still there. People generally knew who the good guys and the bad guys were. More or less. Well, excluding a few blokes from Cambridge and all that. But it's essential that the cause is clear to all. That we're pointing in the same direction. It's the foundation underpinning your whole sense of right and wrong; what's permissible and what isn't. It gives everything context and helps you live with the things you've done. Because there's context and justification. The greater good and all that.

It's when these fundamentals blur – when espionage gets too close to politics, when interests cross or diverge – that things get opaque, and the very concept of right and wrong gets distorted. And then one's sense of purpose and the rules of engagement begin to derail, too.

Now, if that isn't bad enough, it's something else entirely to discover that the enemy isn't even who you thought it was. That they've been hiding at the very heart of your own side all along. That's when things really begin to come apart at the seams.

And that's exactly what happened when we got involved with a man called Robert Styles...

CHAPTER 1

COLLATERAL DAMAGE

Notting Hill, London

As the landlord of the Prince Edward calls for last orders over the din of his crowded pub, the polished wooden front door, with its colourfully etched windows, eases open and an amorous couple spill out laughing onto the pavement at the corner of Prince's Square.

There they stand for a moment, swaying unsteadily in the muggy evening air, the young man's arm draped familiarly around the attractive blonde's shoulders. He gathers his bearings and then, less than convincingly, points and slurs, 'It's this way.'

'Are you sure?' she giggles in a clipped accent, considerably more at home in this refined, well-to-do area of West London, with its regal Victorian mansion blocks and exclusive little gated gardens, than his.

Landed was his first impression of her when they had accidentally collided at the corner of the bar earlier that evening. Definitely landed, he had concluded, as she instinctively responded, 'Oh, I'm dreadfully sorry!'

He hadn't even been afforded the opportunity to apologise and insist that it had in fact been solely his fault. Of course, had it been anyone less attractive, he might not have been so conciliatory. But he had immediately noted that she was on her own, with a freshly poured glass of wine which had barely been touched, so best, he thought, to err on the side of hopeful caution and be nice.

Besides, around here, in this part of London, where one could never be too sure whom one had just bumped into, it only took one poorly judged, overly aggressive response to the wrong person, typically a journalist or someone who knew journalists, and before you knew it, there'd be an embarrassing story in tomorrow's paper. A story his boss would view very poorly indeed. Partly because cabinet ministers have a near pathologic aversion to their personal assistants bringing any form of disrepute on the government, the department or them personally. Especially now, at a time when the government was suffering embarrassing leak after embarrassing leak on a weekly basis.

A playful slap on the arm from the stunning posh girl rouses him from his momentary slip into work mode. He smiles flirtatiously back at her.

'Well, are you going to take me home?' she whispers emphatically. 'Or am I going to be left here, adrift and alone, on a cold night?'

'It's May,' he laughs. 'It's well hot.'

'Take me to bed, and I'll show you what hot really is,' she teases seductively.

Still barely believing his luck, he pulls her closer, kisses her, and they set off, walking the few streets to his flat.

Could fate have possibly smiled upon him any more tonight, he marvels to himself as they meander along the quiet residential streets. First the posh blonde got stood up by a girlfriend. Then, rather than leaving in a justifiable huff, she approached him after their inadvertent collision and asked if she could join him in his corner, given that, as she had observed, he was clearly alone, and the only other person she even vaguely knew in the pub. And, as she had playfully noted, tapping away on a laptop all by himself was no way to spend a Friday night in what is supposed to be the most exciting city on earth.

In his defence, he had pointed out that this was largely because he had only been in London for six months, having recently left university, where he had studied political science and English. That explained the relatively few friends in the capital, he added quickly. The work, he noted, was because his boss's boss needed the first draft of an important government speech for first thing Monday morning. The pub, he explained, with its stylish interior, floor-to-ceiling bookcases and secluded corners, offered him the inspiration he needed. Her arrival simply presented a welcome distraction. Without pausing for a beat, she had tossed her bag past him and sidestepped in to take the empty seat before he could even offer it up.

It only takes a few minutes of laughter-filled conversation before they arrive at the signature pastel-coloured terraced house in Notting Hill where he rents a second-floor flat with two university friends. Both of whom, he reflects gratefully, are back up in Nottingham, visiting family for the weekend.

After fumbling the key in the lock on his first attempt, he finally gets the front door open and lets her in with a small triumphant exclamation. Once in the apartment, he turns on the living room light and gives her a quick, pointed tour as to where everything is.

'And the bedroom,' he says with deliberate emphasis, 'is down there. Last door on the right.'

'And the bathroom?' she asks playfully. 'I feel like a bath.'

With a big grin, he points to a door at the very end of the same corridor.

'While I start that, why don't you go and open a bottle of wine?' she suggests as she saunters off down the long hallway, towering in her high heels. As she passes his bedroom, she glances in with interest, noting his style to be more mature than she'd guessed. Her eyes dart left and right, taking in items of particular interest.

Once in the adequately sized and tastefully decorated bathroom, she takes a customised metal bath plug with an inverted ball-link chain from her handbag and bends to fit it in place, ensuring the chain goes first, snaking down into the drain below. Satisfied, she makes for his bedroom and removes the small hi-fi system from atop a chest of drawers and returns to the bathroom. She places it up on a shelf overlooking the bath, connects it to a spare extension cable which was coiled up in the corner outside the bathroom and plugs the extension cable into the socket just inside his bedroom door.

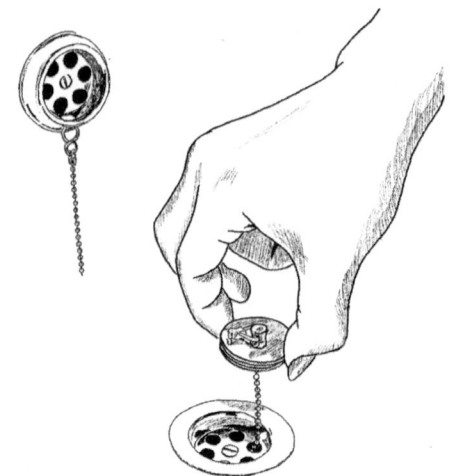

He reappears at the far end of the corridor just as she bends to turn on the large, chromed taps. Glancing backwards, she smiles, ensuring her movements are slow and deliberately overemphasised, making the hem of her skirt ride up provocatively. With the temperature set, she tells him to put down the bottle of Chardonnay and the two glasses. Grinning, he eagerly obliges and closes the door. Turning back to her, he watches with studied interest as she lights the five candles arranged around the bath. It is not lost on her that their presence here, in an all-male residence, probably has more to do with their usual Friday night seduction techniques than any real interest in relaxing baths. Clearly, she isn't the first.

She pours a generous helping of bubble bath into the water and, for good measure, drops an entire bath salts effervescent ball in after it. Then, heading towards the door, she tells him to call her when it is nicely full.

'Where are you going?' he asks.

'That's for you to find out,' she says with a coquettish dance of her eyelashes.

When he finally calls her, she returns wearing less than before. A lot less, he notices with rising excitement. Her skin has an incredible exotic caramel tan. And she has undone her hair, letting it down so it now falls in stylish waves over her bare shoulders.

'Wow, you wear that to the office?' he says with a whistle.

'A girl's got to have some fun,' she replies, sipping the wine he offers her, before giving him an exhibitive little twirl. Gone are the smart but conservative work clothes and all that remains, affording what little modesty it can, is a pair of sheer, deep-red silk thong-cut briefs with black French Leavers lace trimming. Up top is a matching silk push-up bra embellished with double frastaglio embroidery to boost her chest into an even more eye-catching commodity. And it certainly works.

A simple yet elegant garter belt holds up the dark stockings stretching down to the patent black stilettos that clack commandingly across the tiled floor as she circles him, modelling the lingerie.

Taking a sip of the wine, she holds his gaze, casually leans forwards and loosens the towel he wrapped around his waist in her absence. Dropping it to the floor, she gently eases him down into the foamy bathwater. Once he is fully in, she puts a foot up on the edge of the bath, giving him a view she knows he will appreciate. With her free hand she makes to undo the first of the suspender straps. Stopping short, she smiles seductively down at him and whispers, 'Close your eyes.'

Grinning, he eagerly obliges. But while his mind's eye conjures up the torrid fantasy of what he hopes is to come, he does not see the playful expression vanish from her face. Taking another sip of wine, she nonchalantly reaches for the small hi-fi. With a precautionary step backwards, she drops it emotionlessly into the water near his feet. The effect is just as she hoped for, notwithstanding the occasionally unpredictable outcome of introducing electricity to water. But her precautions pay off nicely.

With a long, triumphant sip, she pirouettes smartly, all signs of tipsiness miraculously gone, and fetches her elegant black Chanel handbag. From it she takes her phone and opens a device locator app. She then logs in to it with account details copied across from a notebook app. And then, like an actor at the end of a scene, all false pretence suddenly drops away and her English accent takes a very sudden shift south.

For when she next speaks, it is with a strong and unmistakeably French accent.

'Well, shall we find out where you put it zhen? Oh, wait, I'm sorry, you can't because you're dead, aren't you...?'

Laughing, she presses send and smiles as the account's linked handset begins ringing. Smiling at the faint, muffled noise coming from the far end of the corridor, she follows it into the living room. There, she takes a pair of surgical gloves from her bag and slips them on as she homes in on the back pocket of a rucksack lying near the front door.

'Zhat was easy,' she says as she opens the phone's SIM tray and removes the tiny plastic card from within. Placing it on the floor, she presses down on it with a stiletto heel, cracking the circuitry.

The handset goes into her handbag, for proper disposal later. After washing her wine glass, she dries it and returns it to the appropriate kitchen cupboard. Once back in her office attire, she takes a slow, considered walk through the apartment, wiping down the few surfaces she touched with a specially treated microfibre cloth which is guaranteed to remove fingerprints and any residual forensic evidence. Returning to the bathroom, and with extreme caution, lest she touch any spilled water, she leans over the still figure and blows the candles out.

'Right, luhver, I 'ave to go now.' With a blown kiss and an amused tutting, she adds, 'Ze pleasure was all mine.'

Gathering her bag, she makes for the front door, where she stops and focusses intently. With eyes closed, she absentmindedly rubs fingertips to thumb pads, as one might after eating salted popcorn. Finally, confident there is nothing which could lead investigators to any conclusion other than that of death by misadventure, she opens the door with gloved hand and slips down the stairs.

She walks quickly around the next corner, the emphatic clack-clack of her heels dramatising her movement in the near silence of the empty street. Just beyond, on a road already determined to be free of cameras, she climbs into a large black Range Rover which is waiting at the kerb with its engine idling patiently. Once she's in, the driver accelerates away before she can even close the door.

'Well?'

She laughs.

'Good. How did you do it?'

'In zhe bath,' she replies coolly, reaching round to put her seatbelt on.

'Bit risky,' the driver notes.

'Not when zhe landlord cuts corners and doesn't adhere to UK electrical wiring standards. Does no good if zhey only fit residual-current devices on zhe bathroom circuitry. Why don't zhey think about someone using an extension cable?' she adds. 'Of course, eet helps zhat London's water is zhis hard, what with all zhat calcium and magnesium een eet from all zhe chalk and limestone around here. All zhose minerals and *zut alors*, super-conductive water. None of zhis "pure water ees a bad conductor" problem. Ah bath bomb helped, as did zhe sweat on ees body.'

'You're a nerd, you know that?' the man chuckles beside her.

'But really eet was zhe lazy, cost-cutting landlord who killed eem. Had 'e got ground-fault interrupters fitted on all zhe sockets outside, 'e'd probably be fine. Zhey'd have noted zhe leakage of current from zhe circuit and quickly killed eet. But eet was an old bath, and eet still 'ad all zhe old copper pipes. None of zhis modern plastic piping crap in zhe bathroom. And zhat metal plug...' She tuts reproachfully as she takes a clear ziplock bag from her handbag. 'Closed circuit. *Au revoir, mon chéri.*'

With a callous grunt, the driver nods and turns onto Bayswater Road, keen to get back into central London and away from the crime scene as fast as possible. With a grateful sigh, Nicole pulls the uncomfortably warm blonde wig from her head and places it inside the bag, which she then tosses onto the back seat. Ruffling her natural dark flowing hair, she smiles and reaches for her phone.

'Eet's me,' she says as the man answers at the other end. 'Eet's done.'

'Good,' the stern voice replies. 'Take it this is a secure call?'

'*Oui.*'

'Good. I also take it you have seen the news?'

'About zhe British ambassador to Washington?'

'Indeed. Another embarrassing leak.'

'Why would 'e make such comments about zhe US president in 'ees dispatches?'

'Who knows. Overconfidence, I imagine. But this is even more embarrassing than the last leak. The foreign secretary is going to pay for it this time. Her response was just golden. The stupid cow. Now, I'm wondering if this might not also present us with another opportunity?'

'Perhaps… And what about all zhem at zhat irritating leetle spy school of yours?'

'Now, now, be nice, my angry little French friend,' he chuckles. 'Their involvement played into our hands even better than we could ever have imagined. Had they not intervened, it would not have brought half the embarrassment it has to the government. That said, I was of half a mind to have Stampard deal with the Foxton girl at the time.'

Nicole glances momentarily at the driver, all too aware what that would have resulted in.

'So why didn't you?'

'Yeah, why didn't you?' the driver calls.

'I want to be careful,' the man replies. 'There are too many people watching her career with interest. For all sorts of reasons. She is also dangerous. This girl kicked a one-hundred-and-ten-stone man off the top of a damned mountain, shattered another's larynx and cooked a third in a bloody deep-fat fryer explosion. And what happened to our man Banovic is anyone's bloody guess. She said he fell through the ice on that lake. For all I know, she could have gutted him and left him there for the wild animals. Nothing but a savage. A God-damned genetic mess in the making, that one. There's nothing I'd like more than for Stampard to throw her off a cliff, but that would be giving in to emotion, and at this critical juncture in our plan that would just lead to mistakes.

'No, I have a far better idea. We need to deal with Styles next. He's the final straw. And if in the process we can also thoroughly discredit that lot, and their embarrassing mistake of a school, too, then so much the better. No, we handle this right, and she and her idiot friends will hand us victory on a damned silver platter. Just you watch…'

CHAPTER 2

USE OF LETHAL FORCE HAS BEEN APPROVED

Central London

How things change, I marvel to myself. A little over three weeks ago, standing on a frozen lake, I told de la Praudiere, the director of operations for Offensive Clandestine Services, the UK's second most covert intelligence service after MI13, to take his job offer and get stuffed. Yet now, somehow, I'm working for them. Well, sort of. Because like most things to do with OCS, everything is unofficial. Completely deniable. Never happened. Nothing to see here. Move on type of stuff. Which is exactly how I imagine tonight will be reflected in the official record – if indeed there is to be a record.

Thrusting my phone into a pocket of my cargo trousers, I cross my arms despondently and sink back into the seat, properly irritated now by the incessant drip-drip of messages from my ex-boyfriend. Tonight held so much promise and was pitched to me as a perfect opportunity for redemption, if such a thing is possible in my world at this stage, but now Alex's last message, begging to see me, has sent my mood off entirely in the wrong direction. If anyone is guaranteed to push me off Happy Hill, it's him.

The jovial, balding taxi driver has the radio on, and an appropriately late-night groove drifts into the black taxi's spacious rear cabin. I can't help but sigh at the unnecessary complication which Alex Pemberton-Smythe continues to add to my emotional life, despite us having broken up months ago. That was when he arrived back at his family's massive country estate, arm in arm with a whole troupe of exotic dancers. If that's what they even were. The fact that my friends and I had just broken into the house and were at that point hiding in the grounds is entirely irrelevant to my current view of who was at fault that night.

An incessant light drizzle flecks the window and distorts the bright, giddy lights of the West End as they pass by outside. Not that there are many people on the streets. In fact, peering closer, it's clear that much of the city centre is almost deserted.

'Been like this since the attacks,' the taxi driver notes sourly, reading my thoughts. 'No one wants to take the risk anymore.'

'Yeah, can't say I'm surprised,' I reply, picking up a copy of today's *Metro* which a previous occupant has discarded on the opposite seat. After all these weeks, the headlines remain stubbornly laser-focussed on the attacks. Not entirely unexpected, considering they constitute the worst terrorist incidents the UK has ever seen. I unfold the paper and the chaos, carnage and untold emotional toll of that day are clear to see, captured yet again in a series of images and graphics that have become nauseatingly familiar by now.

'I can't believe they still put all this in here,' I say, holding it up.

'Not like there's much else to write about,' the driver reflects. 'Is there?'

'Suppose not.'

'Mind you,' he says, eagerly capitalising on the opportunity for a chat. 'You kinda have to admire the sheer nerve behind it. I mean, you gather up a bunch of disparate, maligned, lunatic fringe groups and let them loose all at the same time. But all over the place, and mostly miles from the nearest armed-response units or military bases. Don't get me wrong, it's bloody dreadful and all, but smart, too, if you think about it. I'm amazed no one had done it like that earlier.'

'Not sure the thirty-three hundred people they killed that day would be so complimentary,' I say ruefully.

'No doubt, luv,' he stresses. 'No doubt. But can you imagine the planning it took to get Muslim extremists, white supremacists, anti-Semites and a whole host of other fruit cakes to act simultaneously across dozens of cities, towns and villages?'

Privately, I would prefer he didn't continue with the grim post-mortem which I fear is coming. Annoyingly, I remain silent.

'And what do you get?' he asks rhetorically, stopping to turn into a side road. 'Like you said, luv, three thousand, three hundred and seventy-two people killed by those bastards. London was bad enough, but at least the cops managed to get to them here pretty fast.'

'Not fast enough.'

With an acknowledging grunt for the hundreds who lost their lives in the capital, mostly to indiscriminate bombs and roving groups of machine-gun-wielding lunatics, he continues: 'But those poor towns in the Midlands, and up north and down south-west. What must that have been like? I heard those bastards took their time, just going from place to place. All casual, laughing and joking. Like they had all the time in the world. Supermarkets, cinema complexes, even hospitals and schools, would you believe?'

'They probably knew the likely response times,' I suggest knowingly.

'Probably right, luv. Probably right.'

Nodding grimly, he begins an enthusiastic monologue, much like a news presenter might, recanting how thousands of people were shot, stabbed, clubbed to death or blown up in an unrelenting orgy of violence that lasted almost seven and a half hours from the first explosion in Leicester Square to the last terrorist being gunned down in the frozen food aisle of a supermarket in Tiverton, Devon.

Each dreadful story from that day resonates for me with a hard, dull echo of self-recrimination and blame. If it isn't Amala Aziz and her twin four-year-old girls, stabbed to death in a playground on the outskirts of Manchester by a knife-wielding twenty-three-year-old skinhead with a swastika tattooed on his neck, it's Bill Hensley, a seventy-two-year-old retired chef from the West Indies, executed without remorse by an Afghan refugee whilst tending to his front garden in Bognor Regis. Amazingly, I don't know anyone personally who died that day, but I feel equally responsible for every single death.

'Not too surprising, then,' he says, 'that the country is this messed up now, is it? You gotta wonder, don't you, what the press thought they were up to afterwards. Like running all those inflammatory stories wasn't going to kick things off. How could they not see them race riots coming with stories like that?'

'I think they're still going on,' I add glumly.

'Right you are, luv. Right you are. Like what were they thinking, publishing some of those stories? 'Specially those e-mails from those Muslim and Nazi groups. Red rags to a bull, those were. Not that social media didn't make a worse mess of a bad situation. So can't say we was too surprised that it all kicked off in Oldham. Didn't expect the hate to spread as badly as it has, though. Who'd 'ave thought we'd see nothing but cars on fire and riots left, right and centre night after night on the news? And where's the government in all this? Bleeding PM's as quiet as a mouse. Begging for calm. Like some kind of soft, bleedin' 'eart liberal. Fat lot of good that's done, 'as it?'

'I'm sure they're trying. You know, behind the scenes, I mean,' I note, less than convincingly. For while I know, certainly better than most, just how stretched the security services are, I can't help but also be a little disappointed in the weak, slightly appeasing response from Number 10. It's one thing to try not to inflame a situation; it's something else entirely to lay blame almost everywhere but where blame is actually due.

'Still, useless so-and-so. The country needs real leadership. Not someone who's too afraid to upset a bunch of minorities and say what needs to be said and do what needs to be done. At least there's a few of them making the right noises, though.'

'You mean Forbes?' I ask with a dark laugh, recalling the recently leaked audio recording of the minister of defence's speech to a group of senior army officers. A closed-doors speech that was clearly not intended to be made public.

'Bet that caused a lot of embarrassment, that did,' the cabbie chuckles. 'PM can't have been happy about that. Then again, news is full of dissent in the ranks. Whole bloody lot of them at each other's throats in Westminster. And what does the PM do? Blames the whole thing on a collapse of morality and patriotism. Rather than coming down like a ton of bricks on the communities who bred that bunch of animals, what's he go and do? Sets up a new ministry for morality. Having a larf. That said, that bloke he brought in...'

'Robert Styles, you mean?'

'That's the one. Telling you, if the PM had come down 'alf as hard on those behind the attacks as this one 'as on drugs and prostitution and civil disobedience, reckon we wouldn't be in the bloody mess we're in. It's barely a government, is it? He's been defeated twenty-three times on that new anti-terror legislation he's tried to push through. That cabinet of his is hopelessly split. That last vote – how'd you go and lose by two hundred and forty votes when you're meant to have a bleeding majority in the Commons? Largest single defeat in government history, wasn't it?'

Smiling privately to myself, I can't help but muse at the times I would so love to let the uninformed in on just how hard the ceiling has come down on those found to have been involved. But then there's the Official Secrets Act.

'Dunno,' I reply blithely.

His enthusiasm isn't dimmed by my ambivalence. Everything he recants is merely what's been deemed palatable enough for public consumption. But secretly, the reality is so bad that they've even gone and operationalised MI13. Certainly not 'just' a training establishment anymore, I reflect as I think about how ever since we returned to school for the summer term, it's become commonplace to see individuals, and often teams of pupils, dispatched on some operation or other. And while most of my friends' 'field trips' are considerably less adventurous than what I have been asked to assist with tonight, it all goes to show how strung out the authorities are in the aftermath of the attacks.

The task of finding the surviving culprits who fled, not to mention their backers, has fallen to the intelligence services. The police, for their part, are completely overwhelmed in their efforts to quell the riots, defuse the racial hatred, and prosecute those behind the waves of civil unrest and revenge attacks which still grip the country today.

However, what tonight calls for is a slightly different skill set and temperament to what most of my friends can offer. Which is why I've effectively been seconded to OCS, as and when they come calling. And while the few jobs they've given me so far were purely covert sneak-and-peak gigs, tonight promises to take things to a whole new level.

As if aware of my thoughts, the driver glances back.

'So, why are you even going to this place, then?' he asks with obvious concern. 'Even the police barely go there. Ambulances and social services quit that estate a long time back.'

For a moment, I can't help but question whether he is a genuine cabbie, or an OCS plant testing me. Sighing at the paranoia, I shrug and reply, 'Just seeing some old friends, I guess.'

'Well, you be careful, luv, 'specially this time of night,' he advises. 'Dunno what kind of friends you have there. All sorts of undesirables hanging around there. Drugs and guns. Gangs. Couldn't have picked a worse estate to go to, if I'm being honest. If you're heading to the tower blocks, best not go in the front way. There's a quicker way in, round the back. Most people don't use it, coz it adds seven minutes' walk to the shops and the Tube.'

'Cool, I'll bear that in mind,' I reply with a smile.

The scene that greets us as the taxi finally comes to a halt isn't what I expected. An array of parked police cars illuminate the surrounding area in a dizzy dance of flashing blue lights. It seems the Met has brought considerably more to bear than just beat cops. I spot several armed-response units, a command vehicle and several senior officers milling around. Not a good sign, either, is the number of ambulances parked farther on, all with their rear doors open, waiting expectantly.

'Really not sure about this plan of yours,' the cabbie says dubiously as I pay him through the small gap in the Perspex divider.

'Yeah, I know,' I reply, and step out regardless onto the pavement. To my left, kept safely back behind hastily erected police cordon tape, stands a large crowd of onlookers. Glancing around, I retrieve my phone, ready to redial the caller from earlier, when a tall, slim, bespectacled man, who looks distinctly out of place in a neighbourhood like this, dressed, as he is, in a three-piece suit, makes his way towards me.

'Miss Foxton, I'm James Holland. A pleasure to see you.'

'Admiral Holland?' I reply in an appropriately hushed tone as he extends his hand in greeting. 'I didn't expect to see you here. In fact, I thought the whole point was that we don't meet. Things must be really screwed up for the head of Offensive Clandestine Services to be here in person.'

'Miss Foxton,' he replies equally quietly as his eyes dart left and right, gauging all those around us. 'That is something of an understatement. As you must have been told earlier, this is rather urgent.'

'Yeah, they said,' I reply as he takes my elbow and leads me away from the gawping crowds. 'What's happened?'

'All a bit of a mess, really. I'll fill you in on the walk,' he says as we approach two police officers who are standing beside a police car, its lights on, blinking and buzzing frenetically. Beyond them, another police-tape cordon blocks any further progress along the residential side road.

'Who are you?' one of the policemen asks.

'We're OGS,' Admiral Holland replies flatly. From his suit pocket he brings out what looks like a police warrant card.

'You what?' the younger of the two constables enquires, peering at the badge. The more seasoned policeman rolls his eyes and sighs.

'It means other government services. Best not to ask. You'll never get a straight answer. Simple vernacular for "it's classified".'

Sighing, he lifts the cordon tape and waves us on past.

'OCS, OGS, you'd think it's fricking espionage with all these abbreviations,' I joke once we get out of earshot.

'Indeed,' Admiral Holland replies. 'Actually, I'm curious. Why does everyone call it Services? I hear so many people make it a plural.'

'You mean OCS?'

'Yes, and OGS.'

'I don't know. That's what Abbott called it. In fact, come to think of it, that's what everyone calls it. Well, not that I know many people who know about it, but those who do all call it that.'

'My point exactly. But it's not. I mean, that was never the original intent. It was always mean to be the UK's Offensive Clandestine Service. Singular.'

'Sounds better as a plural, I think. Besides, it's not like there's a lot of reference data out there. Try searching for it online. Nothing. And you don't exactly get issued with letter-headed paper, do you? So how are people to know?'

'You've tried searching for it online?'

'And you haven't?' I ask, bemused.

'No. I don't want to add it to anyone's search library.'

'Fair point. Won't do it again. So, what's all this about, sir?' I ask, as we turn into a side road that runs adjacent to the estate.

'As you know, since the attacks, the intelligence services have dug into every part of the organisations involved. Of key interest, besides where their financing came from, was where their weapons originated and who supplied them. We quickly noted that many of the groups used the same equipment. Millbank eventually identified from a number of sources a former Liberian army officer called Major Alford Konunga –'

'Doesn't exactly sound Liberian, does it?'

'Good catch. Consider the internet search faux pas forgotten. Family was originally from the Congo. Since leaving the army, he's popped up from time to time in all the fun places to take the family. Zimbabwe, then back to the Congo; later Timor-Leste, Angola and a whole list of other failed states shattered by petty conflict and war. VX peg him as –'

'Sorry, VX?'

'Vauxhall Cross. Do try to keep up.'

'Duh, sorry. My bad. Anyway, you were saying?'

'Six pegged him as a key supplier of arms and equipment in many of those conflict zones.'

'Wow, he sounds just lovely. So, besides the fact that he clearly never made the shortlist for humanitarian of the year –'

'Nor the long list, either.'

'Yeah, that too. So, what's our beef with him?'

'We like him for being the singular supplier of arms and munitions to all the groups involved in the attacks.'

'Seriously? One supplier for all of them? That's kind of unusual, wouldn't you say?'

'Ordinarily, perhaps. But possibly not if it was all a centrally coordinated effort, as your discovery at the top of that mountain suggests.'

'Yeah, well. Apparently, not everyone sees it like that. Plenty of people seem pretty pissed at me for the delay in getting the information home.'

'Wouldn't be too concerned about any of that,' Admiral Holland says calmly.

'Really? Because apparently top of the list is the home secretary.'

'Wouldn't worry about politicians, either.'

'You think? She kind of made herself pretty clear. You say don't worry about it, but it's not exactly fun to go through all that and then get back only to be greeted by an absolute bollocking from someone like her.'

We walk on, and he listens calmly as I recount a story that still irks me every time I think about it. Barely had I arrived back in the UK when I received a phone call from an Indian-sounding lady who curtly informed me that she was the British secretary of state for the Home Department. Thereafter followed an epic torching. My view, or any input from me, for that matter, was not sought. Admiral Holland listens with an amused smile as I rant on.

'So, not only was it all my fault because I was too slow to send the list of recipients back, but now I had the blood of all those who died on my hands, too. Can you believe she said that?' I exclaim as we cross the road and make for a railway bridge at the far end of the small street. All the houses are identical: semi-detached with small, scrappy patches out front separated from the pavement by two-foot-high brick walls.

'And then she goes, "It seems as far as you're concerned that the standard rules of engagement rather don't apply. Because of what? Because you're special?" And in a really sneering tone. I tried to say that wasn't true and asked what she would have done. Guess that was a mistake, because then she screamed at me not to speak back to her. What a class bitch, right? She said I should have sought advice from base before I did anything. I tried to tell her that sometimes you doesn't have that kind of luxury in the heat of the moment. That sometimes it comes down to instinct, nerve and, well, a bit of luck.'

'How did she take that?'

'Blew up again. Something astro. Started screaming how I'd got lucky. How my typical dumb-arse teenage mentality makes me think I have invincibility on tap. How I can't tell blind luck from skill. Blah, blah. She said I lack forethought and patience. And that my failure cost the country three thousand lives. And that I should have myself a nice day, and then she hung up.'

He laughs.

'That's kind of the story I heard, too. But it was the redacted version. What happened after that?'

'Nothing. She never called back. Big surprise there. But half an hour later, you called.'

'Ah, the whim of coincidence.'

'Yeah, right,' I scoff sarcastically as I recall the conversation that dramatically changed my Easter holidays.

'Hello,' I had said, wearily picking up the phone, not really in the mood to speak to anyone. But rather than finding someone else keen to take a cheap shot at me, I listened as a softly spoken, clearly public-school-educated man began speaking.

'Miss Foxton, I presume this number is your MI13-issued handset and that you have the secure settings turned on?'

'Yes...' I replied cautiously.

'Good. Now I believe a few months ago you were introduced to an associate of mine. A Mr de la Praudiere.'

'Oh God,' I mumbled, already wishing I hadn't answered the call.

'Glad to see DLP ingratiated himself with you so well. It's a special skill he has: making friends. World class,' the man had joked. My silence probably wasn't encouraging. Yet still he continued. 'And I believe he contacted you again a few days ago?'

'He did. And I told him to –'

'Yes, I heard.'

'I'm sorry. *Who* is this?' I asked.

'My name is Admiral Holland. I am the senior services head of OCS. DLP reports to me. As I am sure you heard, OCS is British military intelligence's elite clandestine operations unit. As you may also have been told by Mr Abbott, it was a splinter group from the main intelligence organisations set up during World War Two to fight the Nazis. It pottered about in Oman and Indonesia for a bit, then in Northern Ireland with the Det. Fourteenth Intelligence. Then a few years ago, Russia's GRU Unit 29155 began active operations in the UK. Like us, they are an ultra-secret unit, also with about twenty operational officers, all of whom have hands-on combat experience and come from a wide variety of backgrounds. However, their role's centred around counter-intelligence, counter-terrorism, subversion, disinformation and covert sabotage. They were involved in destabilising the Crimea in 2014. They undertook similar campaigns in Moldova the same year. Were part of a failed coup in Montenegro two years later and were reportedly involved in Russian doping-related operations in Switzerland in 2017. We suspect them of the Novichok radiation poisoning in Salisbury back in 2018. Their increasing involvement in the Western political scene made the Establishment begin to realise that we might need to up OCS's game a bit to counter groups like that.'

'Cool. And how does this relate to me?' I asked, absent-mindedly channel surfing to find a good movie to watch. 'Today's already turning out to be a pretty crap one, so if you don't mind, could I ask what the point of this is?'

'If you have a few minutes, I'd like to make you a more reasoned offer than DLP did. And potentially improve your day a little in the process.'

'What? By joining OCS?' I enquire with an amused laugh.

'Bear with me. It's not as stupid as it sounds. OCS operates with an exaggerated model of MI6's decentralised organisational workforce strategy. Basically, teams that you trust but never actually meet. It means you can help us as and when we might need it. Most of the time you'll remain at Godolphin Park, doing what it is that you do there with Thirteen. However, from time to time, especially considering the events of the last few days, the Directorate of Requirements and Production, who run the operational side of the service and assist in coordinating our activities, may identify things for which you are uniquely skilled to assist with.'

Laughing, I asked what skills those might be.

'Well, what you may not know is that Section Seven of the Intelligence Services Act, 1994, allows the foreign secretary, who oversees us, discretion to make exceptions to general law, typically including theft, bribery and so on.'

'You're after the stuff I do with Cabal?'

'Partly. What you need to understand is that the security services, be it Five or Six, typically don't get their information by breaking open a safe in a foreign embassy while the ambassador's reception is underway, or by seducing a prime minister's daughter on the foredeck of a yacht in Monaco harbour. Instead, they earn their keep by persuading people with access to information that we want to give it to us. That means the key character element at the heart of their recruitment efforts is empathy. A crushing blow to James Bond fans, I know. They value the ability to understand people, get what they desire most, appreciate what makes them tick, so they can then play on that and exploit it.

'Now that's all well and good, but there are times when the only way to get what we need *is* to break into the ambassador's safe or seduce the politician's daughter. And for all that there's OCS. We're a very small organisation, but we're quick and nimble. And unless we make a total dog's breakfast of something, we tend to get left alone by the powers that be. That kind of self-autonomy also gives the government plausible deniability. Whereas Five and Six like to peek in through the cracks and slip away with what they need before anyone notices, we tend to kick the door off its hinges.

'The question you now need to ask yourself is where you see yourself fitting in. Personally, I for one would imagine that a girl who kicked a rugby-forward-sized man off a twelve-thousand-foot-high mountain would be quite a good fit with us. Because, putting it bluntly, Heather, we're in a pretty tight bind right now, and we could do with the help.'

'You know, it was only eleven and a half thousand feet up,' I corrected him, fighting hard to stop an excited little smile from invading my face. 'But back to your point,' I noted in thoughtful reflection. 'I guess I'm getting the sense that I might not be entirely subtle enough for SIS.'

'Well, in fairness to them, kicking thugs off mountains and finishing off some of the worst scum of humanity out on frozen lakes isn't really their mission.'

'Okay, fair enough, but practically speaking... well, maybe more hypothetically speaking, when people do fall off mountains, surely there's got to be consequences, right?'

'Not if you don't get caught.'

'Jesus, you sound like my dad. I'm just surrounded by all these glowing role models, aren't I?'

'Tell me the flaw in that logic? Take Switzerland. Sure, the Swiss were mildly ruffled that they had to deal with several DOAs, but they know all too well who these people were, and none were Swiss, so they're only going to get so annoyed at what looks like affirmative action by a foreign power. And if you really need an answer, then there's always the Third Directorate, which are the MI5 guidelines that give immunity for those who commit serious crimes in the service of national security.'

'Seriously?'

'Well, within reason. They weren't drafted with any written limitations, so you join the dots. It's more academic than a real-world option. The intelligence services would never tell either the victims, the police or the CPS about these incidents. They'll be concealed so they never come to light.'

'But they only apply here, in the UK, right?'

'You do know that espionage is illegal pretty much everywhere, right?'

'So, it's really back to "don't get caught".'

'Pretty much, yes.'

'Then I imagine you'd never submit a Participation in Criminality form?'

'A PIC! Now you're just teasing me. We leave Millbank to be burdened with that sort of mindless bureaucracy. We've no desire for the Investigatory Powers Tribunal to know what we're up to.'

'So, you want me to seduce some PM's daughter on the bow of a yacht?' I laughed. 'Because the safe's easy.'

'Would you have a problem with that if we did?'

'I don't know,' I replied. 'I guess the thought never occurred to me.'

'We work in a morally opaque world, Miss Foxton. No place here for people with rigid and inflexible morality.'

'Yeah, I'll bear that in mind.'

'So, are you in?'

'Am I even allowed to answer that?' I asked.

'C took some convincing, as did Gambon, but as far as we're concerned, if you're interested, then you're coming to work for us. And to hell with everything you heard from the home secretary.'

'Okay, I guess it sounds like a laugh.'

'Good. Then welcome to OCS.'

And that's how the call had ended.

I am brought back to reality as the admiral stops beside a black Jaguar parked at the side of the road, just beyond the railway bridge in a resident's parking bay.

'I'm amazed I didn't get a ticket,' he remarks with relief.

'Yeah? Says you. I'm more impressed it's still here, and not on bricks with those nice alloys long gone,' I add glibly.

'Right? So, tonight's situation,' he says, chuckling. 'Five have it on pretty good authority that this chap Konunga is in there as we speak. In the estate. He came to visit either his cousin or his brother or his stash-house, they're not sure. Trouble is, they stupidly put it out to the police, who then tried to go in and get him. The first wave got beaten back by a bunch of kids with bats and bricks. So, wave two went in.'

'Guess they really want credit for the arrest. A bit of good news amidst a sea of shite?'

'Probably,' he says. 'But then it turned ugly. The arresting officer got shot. We don't know if he's alive or not. Another got hit fleeing the estate. Both are still in there. Several others were wounded but made it out, and an exchange of fire broke out the moment SCO19 arrived.'

'Great. So now you've got a stand-off between local gangs, drug dealers and the Met's Specialist Firearms Command. Oh, and in there is also a guy with the keys to a fricking arsenal of weapons, and the skinny on perhaps who organised the attacks.'

'Abbott and Cabal are right. You catch on quick. That said, De la Praudiere's still livid about that stunt you pulled with the homeless girl.'

'Yeah okay, guess I'm not too surprised about that one. But it was still the right thing to do.' Smiling, I add, 'So, what do you need me for?'

Lifting the boot of his car, Admiral Holland glances down at a small arsenal of guns and tactical gear within.

'Oh... I see.'

'SCO19 may well be told to stand down to avoid a slaughter. And it does us no good either if some over-psyched firearms officer wastes this guy Konunga. But the moment they pull back, he's gone. So, we can't wait.'

'Fine, where do I find him?' I ask as I glance around to check there's no one watching from behind net curtains before I eagerly browse through what the admiral has brought with him.

Opening a tablet, he walks me through the estate's blueprints to show where they believe the arms dealer to be. An aerial photo shows the block with the flat's location marked. Stairwells, communal areas, exits and entries are all marked too, as are the spaces where the Met's reconnaissance drones place most of the troublemakers. He transfers the details to my phone. Not that I reckon I'll get the luxury to consult them once I'm in there. Instead, I commit them all to memory. Picking up a Sig Sauer P229, I turn to him and smile.

'Used to have one of these.'

Looking closer, I rummage through the bag of pistols, ammunition and assorted magazines.

'Heard you lost it in the snow somewhere, if I recall? Wasn't it one of ours?'

'Whatever. Oh look, you've also got the nine-mill version. I prefer it to the point-four oh.'

'Really, why's that?'

'Coz the forty's a heavier round and is therefore slower.'

'Oh good, you're not full of crap, after all.'

'Yeah, thanks for that.'

'You're welcome. Try not to lose this one. Now, listen up. We want this guy before the Met gets him, understand? Word of caution, though. HMG has no desire to see this situation deteriorate into a bloodbath. I would like to keep the EKIAs to zero. By stealth and guile please.'

'Okay. No enemies killed in action. Got it. But someone in there getting hurt, that wouldn't be a huge problem, would it?'

'People get hurt in places like this all the time.'

'Exactly, right? But what if they're, like, really offensively hurt?'

'Doubt the world's going to be too upset. The objective is the target. Whatever it takes, understand? Lethal force is still available to the security services under extraordinary circumstances, like when there is a credible danger to the UK and its citizens. That aside, I'm obliged to tell you this. If we can avoid fatalities, that will help a lot. Attracting a lot of unnecessary attention tonight does us no good, especially the type of attention which comes from ill-fated government-sanctioned actions.'

'And that's why you opted for the largely non-lethal arsenal which we see before us, is it?' I add sarcastically, pointing to the car's boot.

'Was that sass?' he says with a raised eyebrow. 'Because it sounded a lot like how my daughter talks to me.'

'No,' I reply with mock sincerity.

'Hmm. One thing, Foxton,' he says warningly as I fill the pouches on a tactical belt. 'All joking aside, be careful. I don't particularly like this plan. There are a lot of unknown variables, and some thoroughly unpleasant people in there. For God's sake, keep your wits about you.'

'That's what the Sig's for.'

'All I'll say is no complications, please.'

'Now, by complication you mean... what exactly?'

'Some fool gang member throwing your corpse off a walkway on live TV.'

'Okay. Yeah, I'll try.'

'Good. Think you'll blend in okay dressed like that?'

I glance down at my choice of clothes. A pair of grey Dior Air Jordan basketball trainers, black military-styled cargo pants, a dark-grey T-shirt and a black denim jacket.

'Yeah. It'll do. You said casual, nothing that stands out. I reckon the clothes are fine. But seriously, you sure I'm the right person for this?'

'Frankly, I'm not sure there is a "right" person for *this*. But right now, you're the best person. I go and send some bloke from the Regiment in there, just as the Met's kicking in the estate's front door, and it doesn't bode well. You're the perfect age. Far less chance anyone will challenge your being there.'

'*Less?*' I laugh. 'Great.'

'At least I know you can take care of yourself. You've shown you can think on your feet and give worse than you get,' he says. 'Though your taking that Sig concerns me.'

'I know. It concerns me, too. Mainly because you only had two magazines for it. Oh well, I guess it'll just have to be enough.' Laughing, I slap my thigh. 'Oh, that look is priceless. Relax, Admiral, it'll be fine. Trust me. One question, though. It's a tower block, right, and he's on the eighth floor. Now, assuming the Met coming in pisses them off something royal, how am I to get him out?'

'Ideally, via the stairs, I suppose. But there is rope in that bag. Take a couple of carabiners. But that's a last resort, understood?'

'Got it.'

I toss two black padded rappelling harnesses into the bag. 'Gloves, Foxton?'

'Ah, yes. Good point,' I smile, adding climbers' gloves to the bag. 'Do you drive around with all this stuff in here all the time? I mean, how often do you find the need for scuba gear?' I ask, pointing to a buoyancy vest with an air tank attached to it.

'You'd be surprised. You never know when things could go south and you need stuff like that.'

'Okay, out of curiosity, if it does all goes pear-shaped in there, am I going to get another pissy call from the home secretary telling me how I single-handedly pitched the country into civil war?'

'Hopefully not. Look, forget her. She had a bad day. That's all. Took it out on the wrong person. But now you work for us. I'd call that progress, wouldn't you?'

'Still, she blames me!'

'Politicians come and go. Those of us fighting the long fight know what happened, and that's all that matters. We win some and we inevitably lose some. The trick is to win more than we lose, and to make sure we win the big games. We lost that day. Is what it is. But we ensure we win the war.

And nailing this bastard tonight will go a long way towards that. We need him alive. Got it?'

'Yeah, all good.'

With a nod, I snatch up one last case containing a tiny helicopter drone and its controller and drop it into a black canvas bag where I have the rest of the gear I may need. Inside, there is an infra-red sensor-scope, flash-bangs, an electro-discharge net – something I've read about and am gagging to try – and a rappelling gun. Last, I take a breaching device, designed to assist with getting through a locked door. All equipment which may well come in handy this evening.

'Right, well, bye then!' I call as I set off towards the rear of the estate.

In a bid to avoid the heavily manned police roadblock which has been set up farther along the road to control access to and from the estate, I head into the neighbouring houses' back gardens, vaulting a few fences to reach a point where a property backs onto the estate's perimeter wall. From here, it's a simple wall-jump down to the road which winds around the rear of the estate, connecting the back entrance, clearly illuminated by the flashing light show from the police cars, to the main cluster of towers, where hopefully my intended target still is.

To call this place disadvantaged would be to grossly miss the point. It appears to have been all but forgotten by the government, the local council and anyone else who could have made a difference. But equally clearly, it's not all one-sided. The people who live here don't appear to be helping themselves, either. A line of big green wheelie bins have been toppled over to spew their rotting contents out across the road, ripe for the local foxes to tear apart. The estate's reputation means the chances of the bin men venturing in here are low.

Lighting on the estate is also sporadic at best, with no end of blown bulbs and vandalised streetlights rendering much of it a dark and dangerous landscape. My intent is to attract as little attention as possible, which is why I left the tactical vest and other blatantly paramilitary equipment in the car's boot. I doubt that look goes down too well around here. The multi-pocketed belt is about as much as I'm willing to risk.

Packs of feral-looking youths roam the estate. None have any greater sense of purpose than the next group; all look bored, clearly waiting for the police to lay siege to their estate. Something which, when it comes, is all but guaranteed to rile them into an aggravated, baying mob. So, just the kind of place that a lone female should be wandering around in the dark.

Walking quickly across the undulating patches of over-grown lawn that circle the main estate buildings, I give a badly vandalised children's playground a wide berth. But not wide enough to avoid a string of lewd comments from a group of five boys loitering there in the shadows. Lookouts, I suspect, ordered to keep watch for police coming in the back. Ignoring them, I press on towards the buildings. Glancing back warily, I'm reassured to see none pay me any more attention. Confirmation, if it was necessary, of my suspicion. With a sigh of relief, my heart calms a little and I continue with a renewed sense of urgency towards the first of the grim-looking tower blocks. Getting into a scrap with a bunch of these kids is the last thing I need.

Common sense would make most people stick religiously within the lit areas. Instead, I opt for the dark swathes and make good time crossing the open communal areas and the first outer car park. The noticeable absence of normal people in these areas, even at this time of the evening, speaks volumes about the palpable sense of unease hanging over the estate. A place where community spirit clearly collapsed a long time ago. It would be impressive if anyone here actually even knows their neighbour's name. In one sense that's good, as it's unlikely anyone would know I don't live here. On the other hand, I remind myself not to underestimate teenage boys' ability to talk about every girl on the estate. A new girl here could well stand out as badly as a guy in the wrong football shirt. Fresh meat, I muse grimly.

From the edge of the grassy area, my destination is now clearly visible, rising up amidst a sea of equally ugly, squat concrete slabs. It's drab and unappealing, even from a distance, and is so poorly lit due to the amount of broken street lamps which border the concrete car park out front that it looks derelict.

I come to a stop and frown as a new, even more unappealing problem suddenly presents itself. Approaching from this direction requires use of a sunken underpass to reach the main towers. Low, wide and uninviting, it resembles a gaping black mouth into the underworld. Most of its strip lights are out of order. It's amazing to think anyone would go through here in broad daylight, let alone at this time of night. But use it I must, or I will have to scale a strange collection of outbuildings, bin shelters and hedgerows to get to the car park on the other side. Something guaranteed to be noticed and draw attention.

With a long sigh, I begin down the ramp towards the entrance. Keeping my face down, I glance up and note a cluster of figures congregated halfway through the tunnel. From here they are merely silhouettes. I stop and hesitate, sidestepping out of sight. My heart races and feels like it is beating somewhere near the back of my throat. Nearly all of them have their hoods up; some are smoking, hunched over and conspiratorial. Bursts of loud, leery laughter echo within the confined concrete space. Each of them exudes the same brooding, malevolent body language. Their obvious desire for hostility sends adrenaline flooding my bloodstream.

A variety of options race through my mind. Would they even let me pass without interference? Unlikely. And if it gets nasty, how many can I fight off at once? Certainly not enough to stop this getting messy. And shooting someone now or lobbing a flash-bang at them would alert all the other roving groups like a bloody air-raid siren.

Suddenly, an idea occurs to me. Casting caution aside, I set off at a sprint into the tunnel, waving my arms frantically.

'Oi,' I shout, running straight toward the large group of boys. 'There's a buncha rozzers comin' in o'er the fooking wall back there!'

Stopping twenty feet short of them, I bend forward, supporting myself on my knees as I pant, out of breath from the short exertion, and point in the direction from which I came.

'Muh-fucka,' the nearest boy exclaims, hurriedly throwing his half-finished cigarette to the ground. 'C'mon,' he shouts excitedly.

In the half light, with long strands of tussled hair hanging over my face, none of them even bother to give me a second look as they race off down the tunnel towards the promise of confrontation.

'Innit...' I mutter to myself with amused relief. Wasting no time, given that they could return at any moment, I run through the rest of the tunnel and emerge up into a car park that has clearly seen better days. The scattering of beer cans, broken glass bottles and loose litter continues the trend I have already seen everywhere else. But the three burnt-out car hulks here amplify the sense of hopelessness for the estate. Quite why people would gleefully trash the place where they live like this is beyond my comprehension. But trash it they have, and no one has seen fit to spend any resources fixing the place up.

Across the car park, a group of men emerge from one of the stairwells and begin gathering up some bricks from a pile by the wall. Never a good sign. I reach into my bag and take out the tactical radio. Time to find out what is going on. Tuning the radio onto the UHF2 band, I delicately adjust the frequency knob between 380 and 400 megahertz until the encrypted digital emergency channel comes through clearly. Despite the coded chatter, it becomes clear the Met is now coming back in for its wounded officers. If distraction were ever needed, then this will be it.

Taking a seat on the bonnet of one of the burnt-out cars, I cross my legs, draw the bag closer and open the case for the tiny surveillance heli-drone. After a furtive glance left and right, and then over my shoulder to ensure no one is creeping up on me, I power it up, open the controller handset and wait for the camera feed to appear on the small screen in its centre. Then, hunching over the device, I increase the power and the five-inch-long helicopter rises above the car. Directing it via small controls on the handset, I send it up towards the top floor of the tower block. The tiny buzzing sound is quickly lost behind the approaching sirens. From the screen I see the drone climbed faster than I expected and before I know it, it has cleared the top of the block, offering a view over the flat roof above and a sea of old television antennas.

Reducing the climb, I bring the drone back down to the eighth floor's open walkway. I angle the tiny joystick forward and the drone begins moving along the walkway. Doorway after doorway slips past on the right-hand side of the screen until the drone reaches flat 8G. There, I bring it to a hover. Nothing looks amiss, but for a second someone pulls a window blind aside and a face darts an apprehensive look outside. They seem not to notice the small heli-drone, and the blind drops back into place.

From the video feed it appears the first police raid came to an embarrassing halt twenty feet short of the door to 8G. There, surrounded by a group of men, some with handguns, and another with a sawn-off shotgun, lies one of the two missing police officers. It's impossible to see where he has been wounded, but wounded he is, and at this rate I don't give his rescuers good odds of getting to him without a nasty firefight ensuing in the stairwell.

Time, I think, to check the route needed to get there. Eight floors up, the small drone responds quickly and intuitively to inputs on the controller, and it manoeuvres nimbly along the walkway and into the darkened stairwell.

Like the open-air walkway, the tower block's stairwell is an equally grim visage of peeling paint and vandalism. Graffiti adorns nearly every inch of it. Better, more vibrant art occupies the larger patches of wall, while more amateur attempts, most of which have run badly, cover any space not worthy of the higher-quality vandalism produced by the estate's more talented artists.

Floor by floor, the drone descends, relaying everything it sees back to me. On some floors, groups of armed men have gathered, all exhibiting a clear desire to welcome the incoming police with the same sense of communal greeting as was shown earlier this evening. None notice the small drone buzz past their landing.

Over the radio comes the order everyone's been waiting for, myself included.

'All teams, this is command. Teams one and two, you are green to go. Three and four, hold back and await further orders. Let's go get our brothers back.'

The small drone finally appears at the bottom of the stairwell. With a press of the auto-land button, it quickly crosses the car park and settles softly again on the car's roof. Folding the rotors back in on themselves, I return it and the controller to the box, and then the box to my bag. Then I slide off the bonnet and make for the back of the tower block. The stairwell is a lost cause.

Passing by two men hiding in a recessed bin shelter and armed with baseball bats, I smile and wave, to which they merely nod and resume their wait for someone they don't like the look of to wander past. I stop approximately halfway along the back of the building amidst a poorly maintained flower bed, which is now just a large weed garden, dotted with hundreds of cigarette butts. Peering up, I take a few paces back, retrieve the rappelling gun from the black bag hanging over my shoulder and aim it towards the roof. Pressing the release button results in a loud pneumatic hiss and a good kick backwards as the hook fires up, trailing its thin but sturdy cable behind it. It sails up and over the roof. Now for a bit of luck. It needs to catch on something that offers a good, strong anchor. Which it must do, because it doesn't come back down. I depress the retract button halfway down. The electric motor hums softly, and the spool winds back in slowly until the cable goes taut. Tugging on it hard, I find there is no give, so I walk to the wall and then put all my weight on it. Still no give. It's about as good as it'll get. Affixing the rappelling gun to a carabiner on my thick nylon belt, I brace a foot up against the wall and fully depress the retract button.

The resulting high-torque tug lurches me from the ground and I have to quick-step it not to be pulled off balance and slammed awkwardly, face first, into the rough surface of the brick wall. Walking fast, I keep pace with the rapidly winding spool and quickly ascend floor after floor. The higher I climb, the less faith I find I have in this stupid idea. The only thing that gives me comfort is the fact that the cable is laid static over the roof's parapet and is not being dragged over the rough stone. Nonetheless, I find myself quietly swearing as the ground gets farther and farther away from me.

By the fourth floor, I am past caring. A failure now and there's no surviving a fall from this height anyway. The seventh floor brings a small measure of comfort that I am almost there, and come the eighth I make a hurried grab for the ledge to heave myself up and over the top. Reaching down, I turn the electronic motor off before it begins to drag me across the rough tarred roofing. It takes a moment to disconnect the spent grappling hook cartridge from the gun's barrel. I attach the spare, which I also brought along. Just in case.

My eyes follow the unspooled wire, and I balk at just how lucky I was. The grappling cable appears to have snagged on one of the larger television aerials, which has been bent sideways by my weight during the ascent. Likely the only thing that saved me from plummeting down into the sad flowerbed below is the fact that the larger aerial requires a stronger than average floor fixing.

'Not good,' I grumble as I make for the far side of the roof. If my estimate is correct, I should now be directly above 8G.

There's a crackle of static over the radio and a whispered voice reports, 'Team two has recovered Harrison. On our way back to the paramedics. Found him on the south lawn, near the front car park for tower one.'

'Good job, Two. Team one is heading to tower three for Stevens.'

'Roger that. Two's coming round the back of tower two. We can see tower three dead ahead. We'll come up the back stairs.'

Glancing over the edge of the tower into the car park far below, I try to work out where the police are coming from. Not that it matters much. Unless they intend to shoot every aggressor they encounter, their rescue has imminent failure written all over it. Removing the coiled thirty metres of climbing rope from the shoulder bag, I thread one end through my carabiner and tie it off securely around a cluster of protruding rebar that sticks up a foot from the roof.

Pulling it taut, I step into one of the abseiling harnesses and carefully edge down the side of the building's external pillars. At the eighth-floor walkway, just below, I slip in behind a pillar and lower myself silently to the floor. Sniffing, I detect an unmistakeable whiff of urea in the air.

Just lovely, I think, casting a grossed-out glance at the offending corner. I hurriedly pull the loose, dangling rope back up from outside the building and tuck it neatly up against the wall, well out of sight.

Peering around the concrete pillar, I see the same cluster of men from earlier guarding the landing area by the stairwell, near to where the wounded policeman lies slumped against the wall. It's clear that his weapon and radio have been taken by one of the men. I carefully unclip the figure-of-eight carabiner. Taking the IR scope from my bag, I edge back in behind the pillar and extend the flexible keyhole viewing tube out and bend it to the left. The monochrome screen shows in detail the long walkway, with doors on the right, one after the other. To the left is a chest-high wall. My options are limited. Approaching the front door to 8G from here is impossible without being seen. Zooming the viewer in, it seems to me that only three men are properly armed. One probably with the cop's sidearm. Their general lack of firepower in the face of a police raid leads me to suspect these men are not protecting the African arms dealer, or else they would likely be hefting considerably more weaponry. It might be the case that they're not even aware of whom the police are actually after.

However, it's clear the police made it up to the eighth floor on their first visit, so their interest definitely lies up here. Even this lot can't be so thick as to have missed that. Then again, in a place like this, half the people on this floor are probably of interest to the police. Either way, strangers suddenly appearing from behind pillars eight floors up, especially those dressed in dark clothing, tend not to get warm welcomes.

From the wounds to his leg and shoulder, the policeman looks in serious need of medical attention. His odds if left unassisted aren't great. The incoming assault team's chances of getting up here quickly aren't great, either. I fear this mission of mine may well turn into a rescue as much as a kidnapping. My only option, therefore, lies in speed, because any prolonged engagement up here will only result in a swarm of pissed-off, less-than-friendly types pouring up the stairs, looking for a fight. It's best everyone is long gone before that happens.

I startle as a sharp crack emanates from somewhere down below. Turning within the small, recessed space offered by the pillar, I peer over the wall to see a burst of flame light up the base of the building. Several incoming police officers, all in full siege kit, are forced back by the unexpected explosion and resulting burst of flame that spreads across the pavement, licking at their legs. A second Molotov cocktail follows a moment later. It looks to have been thrown from one of the middle floors. It, too, bursts into flame. A barrage of bricks rains down on the police's raised shields. Amidst the unfolding chaos below, most of the men on the walkway, of which I now count six, cluster excitedly to the wall and peer over, yelling hate-filled abuse down at the retreating police.

With a deep breath, I prepare myself mentally for what's to come. Then, shouldering the unfolded stock of the electro-net discharge weapon, which resembles a kind of stubby grenade launcher, I step out into the walkway. Advancing rapidly towards the gang members, I wait until I'm so close that I can't miss and there's zero chance of the net snaring on walls or ceiling.

All are enjoying the entertainment below too much to notice my approach to within ten feet of them. In their defence, they are not helped by the thumping, persistent base that pounds from inside flat 8G.

I drop to a kneeling position, steady myself and fire. The stock kicks back aggressively and with a loud bang it discharges a rapidly expanding blur of movement in their direction. They spin as one, looks of shock rippling across their faces. But the net has already fully expanded into a square wall of incoming fine wire mesh. An instant later, the leading edges snag on the first man. The trailing corners whip in from all directions, aided by weights at the end of each, snaring man after man within their clutches. None are fast enough to escape it. Barely have they registered what's happened before an invisible wave of high-voltage electricity surges along the trailing wire that's connected to the gun's built-in battery, tasering them into one shuddering mass of falling bodies.

'Oh my God,' I exclaim in exhilaration. 'That was pretty sick.'

Closing the gap, I pull the Sig from my thigh pocket and bring it to bear against the leader's forehead.

'We'll be taking that, thank you,' I whisper, sliding the fallen Glock 17M away from him with my foot. He remains too stunned to resist. Only his eyes track me, full of surprise and seething anger. A second and then a third semi-automatic pistol, a Beretta 92 and a Browning Hi-Power, are given up equally quickly. One more weapon than I expected. I stuff all of them into the black bag. The shotgun I toss back along the walkway, towards the pillar. Lastly, I snatch up the policeman's fallen radio.

Grabbing the back of his padded vest collar, I drag him away from the group, which is starting to come around again. Very quickly they begin to realise the problems caused by being entangled in a fine metal mesh. Having propped the wounded constable up against the wall, I remove the largest object from my bag, the breaching weapon.

'Who the hell are y –' the policeman begins.

'Hush,' I say, handing him his lost radio. 'Best you tell your mates not to bother with the stairs. They're a lost cause. Back in a sec. Hang in there.'

Without waiting for a response, I make towards the door of 8G, cautiously ducking low, because the element of surprise is now long gone. Near the weathered blue front door I stop, pocket the Sig, unfold the front arms of the breaching device, take aim squarely and pull the trigger. Four explosive blob cartridges fly out and affix with a wet splat to the four corners of the door, roughly where hinges and dead bolts might be on the other side. Aiming at the lock, I pull the secondary trigger and a fifth blob splats over the keyhole. Each blob connects back to the breaching gun via a thin trailing wire. Releasing a side catch just above the forward handhold, I let the wires unspool and quickly move backwards and away from the door, and crouch near to where the policeman sits watching, shocked and slightly bewildered.

'Always wanted to say this,' I grin, ducking away from the front door. 'Fire in the hole.'

With a press of the only other button on the stock, there come five instantaneous sharp cracks and the door rips inwards with a muffled blast.

'Right, see you in a second. And watch those gits, will you?' I say, placing his gun on his lap. My Sig remains where it needs to be: in my right-hand thigh pocket. 'Any of them so much as look at you the wrong way, waste them. Understand?'

No one has attempted to leave the flat, so it's either empty now, which would be unfortunate, or, more likely, an ambush awaits. Given that I have no desire for Admiral Holland's concerns about my getting thrown off the walkway to come true, speed and surprise will be critical. Taking several flash-bangs from the bag, I stuff one into my trouser pocket. Pressing up against the rough brick wall, between the front window and the doorframe, I pull the pins and throw both grenades in left and right, deep into the front room and adjacent kitchen. They explode almost the moment they leave my hands, filling both rooms with blinding, deafening blasts. The window behind me shatters out of its frame in large, jagged shards.

Sig in hand, I take a deep breath and duck low into the front room. Quite what I intend to do to if I come across anyone as I turn the corner into the living room is still unclear. The decision is forced on me as a man lurches towards me from the smoky cloud hanging in the air. He has his hands to his face, clearly disorientated. The lizard brain, deep within me, instantly classifies him as less than life threatening. Grabbing his shirt, I swing him around and send him flying out through the gaping doorway into the opposite wall, where he cries out and falls to the floor. At which point he becomes the policeman's problem.

Pivoting on my heel, I keep the Sig low, down at waist level, and dart a glance into the kitchen. It's empty, and half destroyed from the flash-bang. Ahead, at the end of a small corridor, is a closed door. It doesn't appear to be reinforced; however, on second glance I notice a peephole fitted in its centre. Not a good sign.

Cursing, I dart low and forward-roll across the living room. With my last flash-bang in hand, I snatch a pillow from the threadbare sofa and toss it down the hallway towards the peephole. Without delay, I accelerate down the corridor after it, crouched low, Sig in hand. The moment the pillow touches the peephole, blocking the light, it explodes in a shower of feathers as a shotgun blast rips through the thin wooden door. The shot hisses past angrily above my head.

There's no time for rational thought. My right hand squeezes off three shots through the wood, down low, where they are likely to either cause leg wounds or simply scare, but without accidentally wasting the very person I came here to get.

A wailing cry comes from behind the door as I leap up into the air, like a high jumper, flat and horizontal, with my legs tucked in, only for them to explode out to full length as I reach the door.

Momentum and the savage two-legged kick combined takes the flimsy door clean off its hinges. The shooter's face takes the full force of the blow on the other side, and he's smashed down beneath the fallen door. The last flash-bang flies in as I fall back to the corridor floor, eyes and ears covered by my hands as the grenade detonates. Without waiting, I follow it in, low with rapid darting movements.

Jumping down, I stamp hard on the door, snapping it over the fallen man. Tossing his sawn-off shotgun aside, I turn to see another man, dark and aggressive, stumble unsteadily into the nearby wall. Grabbing his collar from behind, I wrench him off his feet and swing him in a savage arc that sends him reeling across the room into a television set over in the far corner. He and the TV fall to the floor in a messy heap.

Before me, concussed, bleeding and hopelessly disorientated, is a large, lanky African man in his mid-fifties. Stumbling sideways, he falls over a low coffee table. He swears aggressively in a language I don't understand, but the gist is clear enough nonetheless. He rises again, before falling backwards across a sofa, which is the only other piece of furniture in the room. The rest is piled full of green plastic military packing crates, the type typically used for weapons and munitions storage. I spin left, then right, covering the room with the outstretched Sig, ensuring no other surprises come leaping out from the darkness at me.

The man on the sofa matches the description and the old photo which Admiral Holland showed me on the walk to his car.

His brain is still trying to comprehend the speed afforded me by several billion pounds' worth of covert, illegal, British government-sponsored genetic engineering. But this is a man obviously familiar with violence. His hard, unflinching face makes that clear.

Smirking, he lunges sideways for a short, stubby, fully automatic Mac 10, which is lying on the left-hand side of the sofa. My brain races. Holland will freak out if I shoot him. Dropping low, I launch upwards, pirouetting over the broken coffee table in an aerial cartwheel to kick the rising weapon from his left hand as I land in a crouch before him. Grabbing his hand, I jab the barrel of the Sig hard into the base of his left deltoid. He cries out and clutches at the juncture between his bicep and tricep. Clearly, he is more familiar with dishing out violence than receiving it.

'Evening, Major Konunga,' I say pleasantly, stepping back a couple of paces. 'Awfully sorry for barging in like this, but there are some people who would like a quiet word with you, if that's alright?'

'You broke my arm!' he snarls.

'Oh, don't be such a drama queen,' I scoff, glancing away to ensure neither of the other men are displaying any intention of becoming a problem. 'It's a dead arm. I need you mobile, not crippled. Right, let's go.'

Flipping him over, I slip on a fast-tightening nylon wrist restraint and yank him to his feet. With an aggressive push, I get him moving towards the front room. As we pass through the doorframe, he suddenly lurches sideways and tries to jam me into it. Taller and heavier than me, he sends me stumbling off balance. Cursing, more in irritation than anything, I swiftly holster the Sig in my right thigh pocket and twist back towards him. A savage gut punch folds him in half, eliciting an unhealthy-sounding retching cough. Sidestepping him, I grab his belt and collar and deadlift him horizontally up to shoulder height. Then I viciously slam him face first into the wall. Stepping back, I drop him to the floor.

'C'mon,' I hiss, pulling him to his feet. Somewhere in his head, it must be dawning on him that his next act of stupidity might well see him getting launched over the balustrade outside.

Once out on the open-air walkway, I push Konunga down to the floor and offer an outstretched hand to the wounded police officer.

'Time to go, mate. Else it could all go to the dogs pretty quickly up here.'

The shouting is not far away. Clearly, it's not his colleagues coming to get him.

'Doesn't sound like we're getting down that way,' he replies grimly, pointing to the stairwell.

'Yup. Come on, up you get,' I say. 'It's going to hurt like a bitch, but there isn't a whole lot of choice right now, okay?'

Grimacing, he takes my hand and pulls himself to his feet. With a groan as his full weight bears down on the wounded leg, he grunts, 'Still want to know who the hell you are. You don't even look old enough to be out of school.'

'Yeah, well, less you know the better.'

I glance to my right, as one of the netted men shouts, 'Up 'ere!'

Sighing, I scoop up the net launcher and depress the charging button. Five seconds later, when the small LED turns green, I calmly push the discharge button again. A collective shudder ripples through the snared huddle, making their teeth chatter as their bodies convulse for a couple of seconds.

With the approaching shouts getting louder from within the nearby stairwell, our options are indeed quite limited. It's either the rappelling gun or the coiled abseiling rope over in the corner. I reach down for the piton gun and lean out over the walkway wall. Frowning, I realise it's not a great angle from which to fire it up and over the roof.

The car park below now resembles some kind of post-apocalyptic pitched street battle. Not only have the police arrived in force, but so too has every disenfranchised youth from across the estate with a desire to engage in an armed stand-off with them. Several vehicles are ablaze, including two police cars. Fire covers large patches of tarmac as a result of earlier petrol bombs. The bin shelters are also on fire, sending flaming rubbish soaring up into the air. There it floats, smouldering, amidst clouds of tear-gas which hang lazily in the still, blackened air. More police are dismounting from two newly arrived black vans. Hooded figures dart from doorway to doorway and from behind cars to unleash a fusillade of bricks and bottles in the direction of the advancing wall of police.

'Jesus, what a dog's breakfast,' I mutter, rolling my eyes.

I release the hook's reel a few feet and hurriedly wrap the loose cable several times around the nearest concrete pillar and attach the grappling hook to it, securing it in place. The police officer realises what is coming and begins to protest, claiming it to be impossible in his condition. Ignoring him, I fasten the rappeler to his duty belt, which I gauge sturdy enough to hold him. Grabbing him by the armpits, I heft him up onto the wall.

'Okay, look here. This button,' I say urgently, tugging the cable to ensure it has a firm anchor. 'You need to lower yourself. Press this to descend. Release it to stop. Got it? Now, he goes first. If he tries to duck in onto another floor, or do anything stupid, you put one through his leg. Got it?!'

Turning to Konunga, I pull him to his feet.

'You hear that, Major? Dick me around again, and if he doesn't slot you first, I fricking well will. Better not be afraid of heights.'

Konunga is unfazed and stands his ground defiantly, his expression a perma-sneer. I can feel his confidence rising as the running footsteps and shouting get closer. Sighing, I pull the Sig and aim it at his thigh.

'Move. Towards the end of the walkway. I'm not going to play with you. Move now, or I chuck you over and say you jumped.'

The estate's thugs may be getting closer, but they're not close enough to save him. And he knows it. Grabbing his shirt, I pull him to where the coiled rope lies on the floor behind the pillar. With the pistol aimed at his hip, I cut the plasti-cuff with a small knife from the bag. Then I toss a harness and a pair of gloves from it to the floor before him.

'Just so you know, they said "alive". They didn't say unharmed. Hope your rappelling skills haven't got too rusty?'

Swearing at me, he reluctantly steps into the harness and fastens it. I take the rope and wrap it several times around the stone pillar, securing it firmly to essentially create a new base fixture. Then I weave the end of it through my carabiner and toss the rest of it at Konunga. With gloved hands, he takes it, threads it through his and climbs up onto the wall. His old military skills are still there. Sitting on the edge, he swings his legs over and locks the rope in place between his shoes. Wary, in case he tries to use his weight to suddenly tighten the rope, to which I am also attached, snaring me against the pillar, I quickly mount the wall and toss the loose end of the rope down towards the car park below.

Gripping the rope, he slips off the wall, holding himself in place with tension through the carabiner. As I crouch beside the pillar, the rope goes taut through my carabiner, too. I hold on and watch as the two men begin moving down the outside of the building. The police officer twists around as he releases the spool, whereas Konunga's descent is more graceful, with small, measured bounces as he releases the rope.

Ducking to look back around the pillar, I see the first men appear at the top of the stairwell, baseball bats and hammers in hand. They get five seconds to advance along the walkway before I toss the last flash-bang from the bag amidst them. I slip off the wall as it goes off, and hurriedly drop down the rope as anguished cries ring out from above.

Descending a floor with each bouncing jump, I fight the jerky tension in the rope caused by Konunga's weight below. It's manageable but makes the abseil more challenging. I expect him to jump in on each floor as he passes, but each time he glances at the policeman, who is clearly in considerable pain, and each time he thinks better than to try it. I am impressed that the PC can keep the pistol aimed in his free hand whilst controlling his descent with his left. At the third floor, Konunga peers up towards me. He is greeted by the sight of the Sig pointed directly at him. It seems to be enough to dissuade him from whatever last-ditch plan he was hatching.

I reach the ground a few seconds behind them and immediately cover Konunga, who now poses the greatest risk. I reckon he'll either try to run or call for help. Neither is a good option. The rioters have thankfully all fled, either back into the building or across the carpark, where a pitched battle is taking place near the front of one of the other towers. Discarding my harness, I grab the policeman by his body vest and drag him backwards while keeping the gun trained on the African major. Spotting a cluster of six heavy-duty nylon double-cuff zip ties on the policeman's belt, I snatch them off and approach Konunga.

'On your knees. Now.'

As expected, he is less than obliging. He must know it is now or never. I help him down by kicking the back of his left knee from behind, and he lurches towards the ground. Then I fix three sets of zip ties around his wrists. Yanking his shoes off to a string of indignant protests, I slip another three zip-ties over his ankles and pull them tight. Then I kick him sideways onto the grass. The surrounding darkness, chaos and noise offer enough distraction that no one has noticed us yet. Returning to the police officer, I hear he is radioing in his location.

'You need to get them to secure that top-floor flat pretty much immediately. You understand? There's a fricking arsenal in there. You do not want that crap out there on the streets. Do it now. Put the call in. I don't want you forgetting when the paramedics rock up and start sedating you.'

Clearly unused to being ordered around by anyone other than a senior officer, the policeman sheepishly takes to his radio again and relays the message.

'How long before they get here?'

'Not long,' he says, pointing. The first hint of a smile breaks through his grimace of near constant pain. Approaching from the tunnel on the other side of the car park we see a group of police with shields raised. They quickly start in our direction.

'Good. Well, so long, policeman,' I say with a wave and run back to Konunga's wriggling body. Bending, I ignore his hurled insults and heft him up onto my shoulder.

Together, we set off across the car park, darting between burning cars and avoiding the debris that has been rained down from the various walkways overhead. We skirt past the police and head back down into the tunnel. Thankfully, it's clear. Emerging out on the other side, I see a group of youths face down in the wrecked playground, a team of police standing over them, all with their backs to me. The darkness gives me the chance to run across the fifty metres of open lawn and reach the wall behind the overturned, and now burning, wheelie bins.

Konunga curses at the indignity of being unslung from his firewoman's lift and hefted up onto the top of the wall, before being unceremoniously pushed off to fall the seven feet into the soft, earthy flower bed which I remember to be on the other side. I hop over and quickly text Holland to say that I am on my way back.

Three gardens and several more high fences later, we re-emerge on the quiet residential street. Behind us, the police roadblock is still in place, albeit with considerably more officers now in attendance. I hurry across the road towards Admiral Holland's sedan. Clearly not expecting me to emerge with a six-foot-tall man slung over my shoulder like a sack of potatoes, he hurriedly steps from the car and, with a mildly alarmed look, opens the back door.

'Good God, did you carry him all the way?' he says, helping me to shunt the furious major across the back seat.

'Pretty much,' I reply, sighing with relief to be free of the wriggling weight. 'Afraid I had to toss him over a couple of fences. But there's some good foliage back there. So he shouldn't have broken anything.'

'Almost feel sorry for the bastard,' Admiral Holland chuckles. 'And I'll be having all that kit back, thank you very much. It's not cheap.'

With a sigh, I open the boot and drop what I have left in the black bag into it.

'Just so you know, you're missing a rope and a few other bits and bobs. Maybe the cops will find some of it back there somewhere,' I say as I slam the boot and step up onto the pavement.

'As if we would ever admit we were here,' he says. 'Now, I took the liberty of ordering you a black cab. It should be waiting for you back where you arrived. Get in. I'll drop you off.'

'Sure, thanks,' I reply, and climb into the front seat. The admiral forces Konunga's feet into the back seat and slams the door. As we reverse and turn around in the leafy suburban road, I ponder aloud:

'You know, I reckon you could've easily called some guy up from the Regiment to do this, and they'd have done it just the same. Kind of got me thinking. See, I reckon the reason you didn't want any of them involved was nothing to do with age, or the likelihood of standing out in there. Nor was it anything to do with being able to punt rugby players twelve feet. I reckon you just don't want anyone else to know you have this guy. But calling Hereford would've involved at least half a dozen people. Probs more, right? That's why you came to me. And that's why you're here, and not some staffer.'

He shoots me a quick sideways glance. And just for the briefest of moments, a wry smile appears. Saying nothing more, he accelerates down the terraced street and stops at the end to let me out amidst a sea of flashing blue lights and sirens.

'Guess I'll be seeing you,' I say.

'Unlikely,' he replies with a quick wave. 'But we'll be in touch.'

Laughing, I close the door and watch as the car drives off past dozens of police officers. I can't help but be amused at the irony that all remain oblivious to the restrained, struggling man slung across the back seat passing just feet from them.

Side-stepping through the milling crowds, I glance at my watch. It's ten fifteen already and high time I got myself home. Godolphin Park's weekend leave is short enough as it is. I expect my parents might like to spend at least a little time with me before I go back, late tomorrow afternoon. As if on cue, my phone begins vibrating in my pocket. I needn't guess who it is. Sure enough, the screen announces an incoming call from my dad.

'Pumpkin. Did you have fun?'

'Hey, Papa,' I say, amused at his ham-fisted attempt to sound laidback when he clearly isn't. 'Don't worry, it was a tame night, I promise. A movie, pop-corn, lots of chatting. Just a chilled girls' night out.'

'What kind of a father would I be if I didn't worry, huh?'

'I know. But Dad, I'm seventeen. I can take care of myself.'

'That's debatable. So, am I going to get to see you? I've barely seen you since you got back from school.'

'Yeah, I know. I'm sorry. I'll be home in, like, twenty minutes.'

'Great. You hungry?'

'Ha, you know me. I'm always hungry. So, sure, I could have a bite.'

'Chinese?'

'Yeah, okay, Chinese takeout sounds good. Tell you what, how about we shove a movie on?'

'Sounds good, Pumpkin. I'll go find us a bottle of something nice.'

'Perfect. Okay, I think my taxi's here. See you soon.'

Hanging up, I slip my phone into my pocket and smile as I realise I forgot to return the admiral's Sig Sauer.

'Ah, too bad,' I exclaim, and wave at the taxi which has just pulled into the road.

CHAPTER 3

THE UNORDINARY ORDINARY

Canary Wharf, London

'Heather,' someone shouts again, rousing me from my sleep. For a few fleeting seconds, my mind is unsure whether the events of last night actually happened or if it was all just a vivid dream.

'What?' I groan as I roll over and pull the duvet over my head.

'Come here,' my father shouts from somewhere nearby in the duplex apartment. Sighing, I squint against the bright sunshine streaming through the open curtains and look at the bedside table to see the time on my phone, which is charging there. The small notification light is blinking. I reach for the handset, bring it under the duvet and scroll through my new messages. With a tap, I open one up from Milly.

How did it go? it reads.

Typing back, I write, *Not bad. We got him. Doubt many will hear about it tho.*

That's fab. Nice one. Was it scary?

Got a bit sporty at times.

Tell me all l8r! she quickly types back.

Yeah laterz...

'Heather! Will you come here,' my father calls again. 'Get up. It's almost lunchtime.'

'Jesus, *what*?' I exclaim under my breath as I cast the covers aside and make my way sleepily towards the door. 'Can't anyone get any fricking rest around here?'

I pad across the hallway, still in my pyjamas, and poke my head in around the doorway of my parents' bedroom. Light and airy, like most of the apartment, it looks like it came directly from the pages of some interior design magazine.

'Yeah, Dad?'

He is sitting on the edge of their bed, staring thoughtfully at the mobile phone in his hands.

'Just got off a call with a partner at that hedge fund I told you about. The ones who want me to go be their chief operating officer. It's tempting. I mean, it could be quite fun, I think. Certainly challenging, and way more lucrative, which will be good. Better than the B of E.'

'Well, that's good, right? I mean, I don't know much, but even I can see you aren't that happy there.'

'Well, the pitch was promising. But it all just kind of turned out a little different from what the job description said it would be.'

'Not being funny, but you did seem pretty bored from the start. Maybe a change is a good thing, right?'

'I suppose. Then again, I did get that India trip out of it. So that's something positive.'

'I guess. Anyway, you called?' I add, keen to discover what was so urgent that my sleep had to be interrupted.

'Oh, yes. Where's my Endurance?'

'Your what?'

'My Endurance. My watch. Where is it? Pretty sure you had it last.'

'I dunno. What's it look like?'

'It's black. Has a compass around the bezel. Bright-orange strap. Can't exactly miss it.'

'Oh, you mean this?' I say, feigning ignorance, as I hold up my wrist.

'That's it. See, this is exactly what I'm talking about. You just don't respect my stuff.'

'That's not true. I respect it a lot. In fact, I really like it, too. It's super light.'

'Yah, because it's made of titanium. Now, give it back. I want to wear it.'

'What am I going to wear, then?'

'What do you mean?! I've bought you two nice watches recently. You can't keep raiding my watch drawer all the time.'

Grumbling, I roll my eyes and unstrap the watch. As I hand it over, I can't help but glance down into his open watch drawer, and immediately I hone in on a new addition.

'Oh, hello! Who are you?' I exclaim, reaching out to pick up the new addition to his collection. 'Another Bremont! Dad, haven't you got enough of these? Wait till Cruella del Maison sees that. She's going to shoot you.'

'Come on, that's unfair,' he sighs. 'And mean. Take it back.'

'Okay, I'm sorry. Doesn't mean it's not true, though. Must say, I like this. A lot,' I add, gently turning the matt-finish desert-tan pilot's watch over in my hands. The face is appropriately plain and rendered in a silvery-sand-like colour. The knurled anthracite case band is finished in a grippy metal styling. 'This is so me!'

'Uh-huh,' he mumbles, already resigned to where this conversation is going. 'It's one of the ones they test with the ejector seat people. Hence the little yellow and black second hand counterweight.'

'It's silly light,' I observe, flashing him a questioning look.

'Titanium, too, I think.'

'Colour's nice. Suits my complexion, don't you think? What is it? Like some kind of pale desert-sandy tan. I dunno.'

'Think they call it savanna,' he replies.

'Yeah? Might swap the rubber strap out for something else, though. Not sure yet. Oh, look. You've got a matching NATO strap for it. That's perfect.'

'I'm sorry. Since when did you think it was yours?' he splutters. 'I quite like this, I'll have you know.'

'Oh, please, Papa. Please! Promise I'll stop raiding your watch drawer. Like, for ever.' Pausing for a second, I fix him with a questioning expression. 'Does Mum know you bought another one?'

His expression sours.

'What she doesn't know won't hurt her. Besides, I don't need another argument.'

'Oh no, seriously! You two still fighting?'

His ambivalent shrug tells me all I need to know. Frowning, I can't help but ponder whether their marriage would be better had I had never come into their world. It's an usually vulnerable view for me to take, or to give the time of day to. No doubt these insecurities are amplified by the recent discoveries I have made around my adoption. It seems clearer and clearer now that my biological mother had little choice but to give me up. Whatever happened after Genesis, I doubt doing black ops stuff with a new-born baby was much of a viable option.

Quite what the circumstances of the adoption were, I still have no idea. But it's become clear to me that she had little choice in the matter, and the same could probably be said for my adoptive mother. A fact she has reminded me of more and more since I hit my teens. Come sixteen, the animosity went up exponentially, and it certainly hasn't got any better recently. If anything, her general frostiness to everything has got worse of late. Then again, maybe I am being too sensitive. Perhaps their problems are all due to something completely unrelated?

Would they argue less if my dad was earning what my mum clearly thinks he ought to be bringing in? This apartment and their nice, fancy lifestyle certainly can't come cheap. Quite when she became so permanently conditioned to all the high-society parties, holidays in Como, airport lounges and business-class flights, all the trappings of a dual-earning, high-income household, I don't know. But a combination of low interest rates, a flagging economy, numerous stock market slumps, Dad's decision to accept a lower-salary job at the Bank of England – something he's clearly working hard to remedy – and the fears associated with being high-paid, senior employees who aren't getting any younger all seem to have combined to take the humour and fun out of their relationship over the last few years.

Changing the subject, I hurriedly say,

'Too bad, I'm sorry to hear that. Anyway, so about the watch. Seems a shame for it to sit in the box. You know, in the dark. Like, all alone…'

'Oh, go on, then,' he sighs.

'Awesome. Thanks, Papa. You're the best. You know, you'd think the amount you buy from them, they could give you, like, a membership or something. At least a discount. Or maybe invitations to freebie events. You know. That kind of thing.'

Sighing, he says resignedly, 'Okay, how do you know about it?'

'Know about what?'

'About the boutique invitation next weekend.'

'What invitation?'

'It cracks me up when you play all innocent like this. I can see right through it, you know that?'

'No, seriously… I actually don't know what you're talking about.'

'Like I believe that. Alright, I'll play along. There's an event at their London shop next Saturday, showcasing some tie-in with a company that makes jet packs.'

'Jet packs for what? For people?'

'Yeah, like real-life Iron Man kind of thing.'

'Seriously?'

'Yeah,' he replies with a chuckle. 'Real-life jet-fuel backpack, with turbines on each arm. And they chuck out something like a thousand horsepower through them.'

'That sounds sick. Can I come?'

'You're back at school tonight.'

'True, but I can always just nip back up next Saturday. Sure Mr Lander won't mind. Come on, Dad, it sounds fun. Don't be a killjoy.'

'We can talk about it. If you're good, maybe. Now bog off. Leave me in peace.'

'Sure thing, Papa,' I grin. 'But can I change this strap for that NATO one you've got lying there?'

'Fine...' he mumbles, grudgingly handing me the strap and a spring-bar removal tool.

'Cheers, Dad.'

'Oh, and Heather,' he calls as I reach the door. 'Do me a favour, will you, Pumpkin. Put on some proper shorts. I don't need to get it in the neck for not having pointed it out before your mother sees you like that.'

'Like *what*?' I exclaim in mock indignation. Peering down, I hoist my T-shirt a fraction and smile innocently. 'You mean my pants?'

'Sweetheart,' he says, walking into the bathroom. 'Even in Brazil they'd know better than to call those "pants".'

'Yeah, alright, fine. Love you, Dad!' I call over my shoulder as I retreat to my bedroom with my new favourite watch.

*

Even though the first exeat of term was only a day and a half, it still felt like a proper break from school. And Saturday night's extracurricular activity made what would otherwise have been a boring weekend, sitting at home – given that I didn't keep in touch with any friends from my old school – quite exciting.

The taxi ride back to Godolphin Park is fast, as the dark country lanes are typically quite free of traffic, and we pull in through the school gates less than twenty minutes after the train arrived at the little rural railway station nearby.

It still amazes me that the British Secret Service has managed to run a clandestine facility as large as this, spanning a huge country estate, effectively in plain sight of everyone, for over a century. Even the taxi driver has no idea, or else he probably wouldn't have been able to resist prying. In London, cabbies are always telling you what the building is *really* used for whenever they pass by either MI5's Millbank or SIS's Vauxhall Cross.

After paying him, I grab my Louis Vuitton holdall and dart across the car park into the back of the house. I ignore the excited little buzz that grips the small group of first-year boys sitting at the bottom of the stairs as I approach.

'Hi, Heather...'

'Alright, Heather?'

'Want to join us, Heather?'

My fleeting smile disappears the moment I squeeze past them and dash up the stairs.

'It's like a fricking "run the gauntlet of horny thirteen-year-old boys" down there,' I exclaim as I walk into our study, tucked away nicely all the way up on the third floor. Milly, my stunningly bright and equally pretty Nepalese roommate, glances up from the huge book she has her face buried in, clearly pleased to see me but also disinterested in my observation.

'You smile at them. That's your problem,' she says, going back to her speed-reading. 'It just encourages them. As far as they're concerned, they all think they're in with a chance.'

'Yeah, fat chance,' I scoff. 'But I can't be rude.'

'Rich coming from someone who –'

'I swear, if anyone else mentions me kicking someone off a mountain, I'll...'

Laughing, Milly closes her book.

'Yup, that one's going to stay with you for a while. Okay, I'm done. Going to get ready for bed.'

'Okay. Hey, look what I found,' I say, proudly retrieving the Sig Sauer from my bag.

'Oh, not another,' she sighs. 'Really?'

'Oh yeah. The rate I'm racking up pissed-off people,' I exclaim. 'Need all the help I can get.'

'Do you really?' she replies sarcastically. 'Did the last one help you? Blow anyone's head off with it, did you?'

'I sense you don't like guns. That's okay, I hate guns, too.'

'You're so full of it,' she laughs. 'I don't hate them. I just don't want them around me. You're more likely to shoot yourself, or me, than anyone else. But it's more than just that. Guns didn't get us out of all the messes we've got into, did they?'

'Is that rhetorical?'

'What do you think? My point is, you got us out of most of those messes. As you rightly should have, given most of them were *your* fault, but I'll let that bit slide. I know you're having a bit of an on-off crisis at the moment, but you really shouldn't. You always say it yourself: you either make it or you don't.'

'Do I?'

'Yes, you do. And you don't need one of those things to sort out your problems. Whatever you think of yourself at the moment, after that telling-off you got from that silly, silly woman –'

'The home secretary.'

'I am personally offended to have to refer to someone like that with a title. You have to stop questioning yourself. Wasn't your fault. I know it. Everyone here knows it. You need to know it. Anyway, lecture over. I'm tired. Was a busy weekend. So, go shower, then tell me all about last night. Can't wait to hear about it. Sounds absolutely insane.'

'It or me?'

'Probably a bit of both,' she smiles, and makes for the door, toothbrush and paste in hand.

'Hey, wait for me. I'm coming,' I call after her as I grab my wash bag from my shelf and my pyjamas from beneath my pillow.

*

Interestingly, we are barely a quarter into the summer term, and despite the school essentially being on what can only be described as a war-footing, the atmosphere is even more chilled and laidback than it ever was.

No one seems to care or comment on the numerous pupils constantly disappearing on some nefarious activity or other for one of the main intelligence services. The UK's war on terror has rapidly become business as usual at Godolphin Park. Such deployments no longer generate any of the excitement or gossip that they used to.

Most are to assist MI5's various surveillance teams, whose old remit to conduct counter-espionage operations against foreign targets was rapidly expanded to counter what feels like a mass uprising of home-grown terrorists, imported would-be jihadists, far-right racists, the generally disenfranchised and no end of fruitcake fringe groups, most of whom have been financially disadvantaged by the mess the economy is in, and all with an axe to grind against the government.

That's not to say the school is a big, rosy picture of harmony and communal peace. Far from it. The one noticeable source of tension curiously stems from a decision taken over the holidays to merge A-School – which comprises the original training facility, established back in 1919 when the school was first set up to train promising young boys and girls, generally from the upper classes, to develop the requisite skills for an eventual career in espionage or the foreign service – with the newer, more secretive B-School – which was established around the time of the Second World War to recruit pupils offering more specialist abilities and, as Churchill put it, the corkscrew mind suited to live operations.

From what I understand, all the parents of A-School pupils, typically being either landed, connected to or already within the Establishment's upper circles of trust, know about the school and its 'real' purpose, and are often the ones responsible for sending their children here in the first place. However, parents of pupils in B-School are often unaware of the school's true purpose.

Of course, there's a very good reason for this: most normal parents may well accept the idea of their children benefiting from an education, no matter how unorthodox, if it is readying them for a career in a prestigious area like foreign service; however, few would ever agree to something that involves their children taking part in live operations.

So, while A-School was always an almost open secret, albeit with a heavy marketing slant towards the Foreign Office rather than Five, Six or GCHQ, B-School remained firmly in the shadows. The government's offer of a top-class public-school education, typically free of charge thanks to the scholarship offered, usually swings the deal without too many questions being asked, and that's how must of us in B-School got here.

Had the teachers got their way, I expect they'd have tried to limit social interaction between the two schools, and to a degree they certainly tried, with segregated buildings, delineated houses, clever timetabling and a general culture of secrecy. The best they achieved was ensuring that what went on in B-School tended to stay in B-School. But the reality is, friends talk. And enough of what happened leaked across the wall.

But now that the two schools have been merged and the full reality of what B-School does has become common knowledge, an edge of resentment has crept in. First of all, A-Schoolers naturally asked why they weren't selected for B-School, where the real action 'clearly' was. And B-Schoolers, like us, looked on in horror as the likes of Victoria Farabee-Peacock and her snooty friends were allowed in. Soon, a lot of former A-Schoolers began asking why so few of them were being tasked with live operations. The typical response was that training was required. Except training never materialised. So, very quickly everyone started wondering what the point of the merger really was.

Clearly, resources were stretched, so compromises were required. As far as the teachers were concerned, action was taken and capacity and capability were restored. Except, the repercussions are still being felt, as Milly and I discover when we walk into the breakfast hall, just across the road, early the next morning. Our eyes widen at the sound of a screaming match in progress.

'You've got to be kidding me,' I exclaim as we join the queue of bemused onlookers lined up at the food counter. At one end of the hall are my friends from B-School who for the most part are either in Smith's or Kell's, the houses founded by Sir Mansfield Smith-Cumming and Vernan Kell, respectively the founders of MI6 and MI5. Most of the shouting, accusations and insults, however, are coming from the nearer tables, which are filled generally by members of Sinclair's and Grey's, the two larger houses founded by Sir Hugh Sinclair and Sir Edward Grey, respectively the then director of naval intelligence and the then foreign secretary.

'I'm amazed how many people didn't actually know what was going on down in ETS,' I whisper to Milly as she begins loading her plate with fried eggs, bacon, pork sausages and baked beans.

'I know,' she replies. 'Me, too.'

The stream of overtly racist abuse reaches new heights as a group of Grey's upper-sixth stand to shout across the hall at a group of Kell fifth-formers.

'I'm British, you idiot,' one of the Kell boys yells, standing, too. 'My parents were born in Pakistan, but I'm as British as you.'

'Yeah, you tell him, Sanjiv,' Milly whispers under her breath.

'And where were they when all this was going down, huh, Patel?' retorts a red-faced Sinclair upper-fifth-former. 'Probably in their takeaway, watching it on the news, cheering on the attackers.'

'Oh, for the love of donkey,' I mutter under my breath. 'You've got to be kidding me.'

'You racist, privileged prick,' Sanjiv shouts back.

Shaking her head, Milly adds a yoghurt and turns to find a table, preferably, I hope, away from all the acrimony.

'Look,' calls one of the larger Grey's upper-sixth boys, whom we all know to be the school's first fifteen hooker. Like most of the rugby team, he feels he is unquestionably in the right. Smirking, he taps his friend's shoulder and points at Milly. 'There's another one. Come to help your jihadi brothers, have you?!'

'I'm from Nepal, you retarded moron,' sighs Milly. Turning to me, clearly flustered, she adds, 'Do you think stupid people know when they're being stupid?'

'Not when they're being *that* stupid,' I laugh.

'Oi, got something to say, you traitorous slag?' the team's hooker shouts, this time at me. 'Whose side are you on, huh? B-School bitch.'

'Mate, it's not worth it,' cautions another rugby player beside him. 'From what I hear, that Paki-loving psycho will gut you right here using a sodding spoon if you're not careful.'

I smile warningly, not entirely adverse to the idea. With an irritated glance, I look over at Farabee and her friend Candice Hardcastle, whose physique would be well suited in the first fifteen's scrum. Beside her is Farabee's number-one spineless bum-pal, the red-haired Augustus Cole. They are huddled together at the end of the Grey's bench, clearly relishing the exchange. As if telepathically, I can almost hear the nasty side of Farabee's mind change gears.

'Brace yourself,' I mutter to Milly. 'Here she comes.'

'Well, you know why that is, don't you, boys?' Farabee croons in her clipped Queen's English. The Grey's table turn as one to look at her. 'Because they're shagging,' she exclaims, pointing accusingly at us. 'They're lovers!'

Beside me, Milly tenses noticeably. It's not lost on me that very few people know about her relationship with Anabel, our fellow lower-sixth housemate from Hong Kong. For Farabee, it was just a typically baseless insult, thrown without regard to achieve maximum offence and public embarrassment. To Milly, it must be a very close shot across a very sensitive bow. As she flushes red, I step forward protectively while maintaining an amused smile.

'I just realised what it is, Farabee. You're jealous,' I laugh.

'What? Of going down between her smelly legs!' she fires back. 'No thank you.'

Setting my tray down, I round on her, all humour gone.

'Why are you always so fricking radioactively nasty to my friends?' I shout across the dumbstruck hall. No one moves. Loaded forks hover in mid-air; mouths hang open, frozen, as eyes dart left and right. The entire room waits apprehensively, no doubt many secretly hoping the school's first homicide will unfold before their eyes, here in the dining hall.

Fuming, I yell, 'You know what? Screw you, Farabee.'

Snatching a tablespoon from the nearby cutlery container, I advance aggressively towards the Grey's table, sending a wave of concern rippling along the bench as each person shunts backwards in alarm into their neighbour.

'What the hell is going on here?!' booms a deep voice from the far end of the hall. We all turn to see Richard James, a tall, athletic-looking upper-sixth-form prefect, standing there with an incredulous expression. 'What is wrong with you people?'

'They started it,' Augustus Cole calls, pointing at the SH and Kell tables.

'I don't care,' Richard shouts, advancing towards us. 'Have you all missed the bloody point? Do you even know what's going on out there? A bunch of animals killed three thousand people, and here you lot are, at each other's throats. It's bloody unacceptable is what it is. And what were you going to do with that?' he exclaims, pointing at the spoon in my hand.

I shrug my shoulders and toss it into the used cutlery bin. Farabee immediately takes this as Richard having sided with her, which is irritating but not surprising. In truth, his interruption was welcome, as I really had no idea what I was going to do with the spoon other than give her a fright. Gallingly, she flashes a smile at him, the likes of which even an irate prefect can't ignore.

'Start working together, for Christ's sake,' he shouts. 'Because we either win united or we die divided.'

'Come on,' I say, taking Milly's arm. 'Let's go find a table at the other end.'

Sighing, she agrees and follows me.

'For what it's worth,' I say, leaning closer as we get out of earshot of the others. 'I think you smell great.'

Even in her fit of fury at Farabee, Milly can't help but let out a small laugh.

'Oh, stop it,' she giggles.

*

Once breakfast is over, we casually make our way back to SH and trudge up the stairs to see our friends. We walk into the boys' study to find them laughing in fits of disbelief. *The Avengers* is playing on the large computer monitor that they have set up on the desk before them. Both have their feet on a pile of beanbags. Their room is in its usual state of disarray.

'I can't believe they got away with that,' Nigel exclaims.

'Ai,' says Luther. 'No one knows what it means.'

'No one knows what?' I ask, treading carefully through the scattered field of computer components and other electrical items.

'Loki,' Nigel says, still amused. 'He just called Black Widow a mewing quim.'

'Huh? Is that rude?'

'Er, yes,' Milly replies emphatically, casting a reproachful glare at the boys.

'Really?'

'It's old, medieval slang for girly bits.'

'Seriously? How did they put that into a superhero movie?' I ask.

'Probably because most people have no idea what it means,' Milly replies, rolling her eyes in exasperation at the grinning boys. 'It was smart scripting. Probably appealed to the writer's sense of humour to slip it past all the studio execs.'

'How do you spell it?' I ask. 'K-w-i-m?'

'No,' Milly says, less than impressed to have been dragged into a discussion like this. 'It's q-u-i-m.'

'Oh, thought it would be like when I abbreviate "know what I mean" in a text message. Like an acronym.'

'Sadly, no on both counts,' she sighs without bothering to look around. 'Not only is the spelling wrong, but also truncating "know what I mean" is not an acronym. It's an initialism.'

'What's the difference?'

'An acronym's a proper spoken word.'

'Oh…'

'Sorry, so it's kind of really confusing, especially if you're a boy,' Nigel interjects. 'If all these words are bad, then what are you meant to use to refer to… to a girl's… you know?'

'Honestly, is vagina really so bad?' Milly wails, putting her head in her hands.

'Well, there's so much choice,' I exclaim, relishing the opportunity to make her squirm a little. And if I can embarrass the boys in the process, then so much the better. 'I mean, sure there's always that, but it's a bit clinical, don't you think? Why not pussy or fanny? Or if you really want to add a bit of sass, how about vajayjay?'

'I cannot believe we are having this conversation,' Milly groans.

'Why, what do you call yours?' Nigel blurts out, before realising it wasn't the best line. He looks at Luther awkwardly, who sniggers in amusement as his roommate's cheeks redden.

'Yeah, you just keep digging that hole for yourself, Bromhead,' I laugh. 'You're doing great.'

'Sorry, I don't mean personally… You know what I meant. Like, what's an okay word to use? So we don't… you know… offend anyone?'

'Well, you can try to avoid the insulting ones,' I suggest patronisingly. 'Twat, beaver, anything with a "ge" sound in it. Minge, flange, that kind of thing.'

'As long as you avoid the "c" word,' Milly says, finally giving up and joining in. 'It's so…'

'Damn, if you don't have the words for it, then it must be bad,' I note, giggling. 'There you go, boys. Best avoid that.'

'If you say so,' Milly sighs.

'Anyway, can we help you?' Nigel asks, desperate to either change the subject or get back to their film, which remains paused on the screen.

'Yeah, we actually came for –'

'In truth,' I interrupt, pointing at the paused monitor, 'I'm kind of impressed. I was half sure we'd walk in and find you two watching porn.'

'Oh, do leave them alone,' Milly groans.

'Nah,' Luther drawls. 'Honestly, it's all got a wee bit boring.'

'I'm sorry, did I just hear you right?' I laugh. 'You have an entire internet of depravity out there, and you're bored of it?'

Nigel shrugs ambivalently.

'What ye lasses don't understand,' Luther says, leaning forward, as if what's about to come might be hard to grasp, 'is that the limits of pornographic deviancy are not defined by the stretches of imagination, but rather the limits of human physicality.'

'Ew, what does that even mean?' Milly exclaims, shuddering, aghast.

'Means that eventually one can see everything there is to offer, and then it becomes boring,' says Nigel, with all the disinterest of someone reading a shopping list.

'Jesus Christ,' I splutter. 'You're not even eighteen and you're already bored by porn! What the hell's wrong with you two?'

'See,' Luther says, turning to Nigel. 'Men. Totally misunderstood.'

'Yeah, and it's everywhere,' Nigel complains. 'From morning to night, it's all that comes through on my phone. After a while, it just, I dunno, gets same-same.'

'I can't take this anymore,' Milly stammers. 'Come on, Hev. I just want to go and read a book, and not have to listen to all this.'

I follow her out into the corridor, chortling quietly to myself.

'Those two are unbelievable,' she groans.

'Yeah,' I reply absentmindedly. 'You know, quim's a great word. I should use it more often,' I ponder aloud, amused by my own thoughts.

'You're so sad at times, laughing at your own jokes,' Milly grins. 'Please don't tell me that's what you're going to start calling yours now?'

'Why not? It's kinda unique and appeals to my sense of humour.'

'Your slightly twisted sense of humour, more like,' Milly adds teasingly. 'I can't believe I'm surrounded by people who only have sex on the brain. What is wrong with all of you?'

'What's wrong with you for not having it on your mind all the time?' I counter.

'Who says I don't?'

'You did, just now!'

'No, I think about sex loads. But I also have other stuff on my mind. Like interesting stuff.'

'Uh-huh. And I don't?'

'You just named your bits. WTF?'

'Maybe you should give yours a name, too.'

'Oh, would you stop,' she exclaims, marching on towards our study, evidently appalled.

Sniggering, I follow her in.

*

To call what we do here "lessons" would be to miss not only the point but also the subtlety of the school's end goal. Because rather than aspire for an accumulation of knowledge only for it to be regurgitated come exam time and then promptly forgotten, MI13's goal is to produce officers for whom the skills of espionage are so honed that they have become embedded in the mental and physical muscle memory of each pupil who passes through the school.

In practice, this means rotations, as they loosely term classes here, are structured in a recurring cyclical fashion. Rather than working through a set curriculum from start to finish over the two years, MI13 teaches the basics across all the main disciplines required, returning to each in turn again and again, adding more and more knowledge and capability with each cycle. Having now been here long enough, I am finally beginning to see the logic and benefits of this unintuitive and unorthodox teaching style.

What it also means is large periods of free time, during which recently acquired knowledge is allowed to sink in properly without immediate interference from additional lessons, which could muddy the mental waters.

A few days after the breakfast hall fiasco, the whole SH lower-sixth find ourselves with just such a free morning. It's a welcome opportunity for our small year group to take over the tiny library – recessed off from the busiest part of the house, on the ground floor at the end of a short corridor, opposite Mr Lander's study – and relax.

I walk into the cosy little mezzanine-style room to find Milly and Anabel occupying one of the deep brown-leather sofas. Nigel and Luther look equally comfortable in two mismatched armchairs near the bay window. By the far wall, which is lined with bookshelves, are the two newest members of our year group. James Barger and Nick Blanchard both joined completely unannounced barely a week into term, which might be considered odd in most schools but apparently is commonplace here.

Then again, my joining was equally sudden, but then there was a reason for that. Sufficiently freaked out after a failed attempt by Chinese agents to acquire the several billion pounds' worth of proprietary genetic engineering I carry around with me every day in my DNA, the government decided this was a pretty good place to stash me. Something I am, for obvious reasons, keen to keep secret. If that was my reason for coming here, I wonder what James and Nick's is. So far, we haven't managed to find out. Neither seems particularly remarkable. Not in comparison to Milly, say, with her photographic memory and insane grasp of complex mathematics, or Anabel and her uncanny grasp of languages, or Luther, who hacked the NSA when he was barely twelve, or even Nigel, for that matter, who made his first computer at about the same age. In fact, so far we haven't seen anything which suggests what the new boys' talents are.

Both are of medium build with mousy brown hair and are mildly geeky. They've been friendly enough so far; affable might be the nicest way to describe them. James is from Yorkshire and is the more opinionated of the two, always with a provocatively contentious view to share. Nick, on the other hand, is the more laidback, usually staying silent and just observing.

'Hey,' I call to no one in particular as I sink into the seat by the large bay window, draping my legs over the armrest. Milly is reading aloud from a book.

'So, seems Godolphin made most of his money through railways, shipping and racehorses. But in the late 1890s he struck it lucky with gold. That's why he moved to British Columbia. But he missed this place so much that he paid a small fortune to have an identical duplicate house built near

Victoria, which was only a boat ride away from Vancouver and Seattle. How crazy is that?

'Says here he sold the house in 1906 to the governor of British Columbia and moved back to England. In 1919, as his health deteriorated, he donated this place to the British government, and we know the rest of the story, right? Doesn't say it here, but I wonder if that could've been Spanish flu? Interestingly, that's the same year that they set up the Government Code and Cipher School, which was the forerunner to GCHQ. In 1940, the Canadian house was sold to the Canadian armed forces. And *that's* how it got used in that movie, Nigel.'

Oblivious to what they are talking about, I glance to my left and peer out onto the house square, a bright, leafy, fenced-off area of grass where a few members of our house are kicking a rugby ball about.

Looking around the room, it dawns on me that somehow I seem to have become the odd one out. Not in a bad way, mind you, but more noticeably now than before. There is Anabel and Milly, sitting close together, but not so close that suspicions could be raised. In fact, the lengths to which they go to conceal their relationship is almost comical, if it didn't say so much about their insecurities.

Then there's the inseparable little clique that is Nigel and Luther – the tall, lanky white Somerset boy and his short, squat, somewhat rotund Afro-Scottish roommate who have been besties since the lower-fifth. Their nerdy, introverted, genius tendencies immediately cemented their bond of friendship. And lastly, the two new boys, who, despite having only known each other for about a month, have clearly formed a friendship.

The realisation that they are all essentially paired up, in some sense of the word, leaves me somewhat as the loner of the group, not on the outside but definitely orbiting it. That would probably bother me more if I wasn't so comfortable being an only child.

'So, Nigel, back to what you were saying,' Anabel says, glancing at him over her newspaper. 'Then what happened?'

'Nothing,' he replies, downcast. 'She looked at me weirdly and then laughed. That was it. Then she just ran off after her friends.'

'Sorry, what did I miss?' I ask.

'Nigel asked Hannah Murphy to go with him to the social at Dearbourne Grove next weekend,' Milly announces.

'Oh, Nigel. Why would you ask a girl to come to a social with you?' I say. 'Those things are complete cattle markets. Everyone's getting off with everyone. It's a target-rich envi-ronment. You don't need a date. Last one they held here in Big-School, I heard the fifth-formers clearing up afterwards found nothing but used condoms in that area behind the cur-tains where the pianos are kept.'

'Eww, how gross is that?!' Milly shudders.

'That's what I said,' chimes in Anabel. 'Well, the cattle market bit. I didn't know about the piano area. That's pretty grim.'

'It's hopeless,' Nigel sighs. 'I'll never find a girlfriend.'

'Aye,' Luther adds, equally depressed. 'Dinnae ken what we's doing wrong.'

'Trying too hard, mate, from the sounds of it,' James offers without looking up.

'Well, how am I meant to get one if I don't try?' Nigel protests, looking around, confused. 'I mean, if I do nothing, no one notices me.'

'Aye,' Luther adds, nodding thoughtfully. 'Gie's us an idea.'

'Just be yourselves,' Anabel suggests.

Seeing this conversation will head in circles, I pick up a magazine and ask, 'So, what's gone wrong in the world today, then?'

'More riots in Hong Kong,' Anabel notes from behind her newspaper.

'What're they pissed off about this time?' I ask.

'Loads of things. China mostly. New security laws. Police crackdowns. That sort of thing,' she replies. 'Hong Kong's an awesome place, but housing's the most expensive in the world. Public healthcare is pretty so-so. Schools are expensive, and salaries are still low. The government has so much money, but it doesn't spend it right, and it's in bed with all the property tycoons. Whole thing's a big game of cahoots.'

'Got a good one here,' Milly announces. 'Seems a disgruntled palace employee just leaked that the royal twins Stephanie and Henry were conceived through IVF after all, and on the NHS. And that's just a day after the health minister categorically denied the rumour.'

'Woops. Bet they can't be pleased about that,' Nigel comments. 'The government, I mean. Let alone the palace.'

'Honestly, I'm not sure it makes that much difference, not after all the other leaks recently,' Nick Blanchard says laconically, finally joining the conversation. 'It's been one embarrassing story after the other. How many ministers have had to resign from the cabinet so far? I can't keep count. After that leak, bet he's the next one to go.'

'They've certainly lost enough of them, that's for sure,' Nigel notes. 'And the government seems paralysed. The PM's too afraid to act for fear of more protests or further fall-out.'

'Seems the only thing he did do was to appoint that bloke as the minister of civic morality –'

'Robert Styles, you mean?' Milly interjects.

'Yeah. Don't you mean the Ministry of Morals?' James adds with a laugh. 'What a joke. You think some guy told to look after overseeing the fight against prostitution, pornography and civic obedience is really going to help stem the massive home-grown terrorist problem we clearly have? Where's the bloody SAS when you need them?'

'Doesn't exactly help when the PM blames the attacks on a collapse of morality and patriotism in the country, does it?' says Anabel.

'Resignations left and right, scandal, gossip and inept failure all around,' James adds, getting into his stride. 'Any surprise, then, that the PM's been defeated on no fewer than twenty-three occasions on the new anti-terror legislation? Christ, he leads a cabinet that's hopelessly split, a party that's crippled with disagreement and a country that's just as deeply divided. I mean, that last vote was the most emphatic Commons defeat in history. Nah, the PM's terror law is finished. He lost by two hundred and forty votes – that's not a defeat, that's an absolute buggering.'

'Still, like him or not, the guy's got himself a pretty meaty remit,' Nigel says, looking down at an article in the *Times*. 'They're calling him the ethics and morality tsar. He's just managed to get his fingers into the Home Office as well, influencing how policing is done, how magistrates and even High Court judges rule on cases. Pretty clear he's already tinkered at the Department of Education –'

'Oh, don't even get me started on those sex-ed and morality classes we've got to do,' I exclaim. 'What a total waste of time.'

'Are you surprised though? What with all the wokest rubbish being spouted around at the moment,' Milly sighs. 'See, look right here, this is exactly what I mean,' she adds, as astonished as she is irritated, holding aloft the *Daily Mail*. 'What is it with so much of today's perma-offended youth? So quick to attack. So woke, but unable to show any humour at all. All trying to outdo each other with post-modernistic crap gleaned from whatever enlightened, liberal, socialist nonsense they're OD-ing on. Iconoclastic turd-pouring from every orifice in modern woke society. Hatred and vitriol everywhere...'

'You crack me up!' I say, laughing out loud, like the others. 'You got all that from reading the *Daily Mail*?!'

'Let me see,' Anabel chips in, peering over. 'Oh, that column. Yeah, not surprised. Woke central, right there.'

'Erm, okay, here's an interesting one,' Nick says. 'Remember that thing in Switzerland. When was it? Like Easter time or whenever. Three blokes killed at the top of that resort. What they thought was some Mob hit?'

My ears prick up, as do Milly's.

'Yeah? What about it?' she asks neutrally, glancing at me from the corner of her eyes.

'Seems the Swissies just dropped the case. No reason given. The attorney general declined to comment. That's kind of weird, right? They're questioning the decision. Calling it a cover-up.'

'Dunno,' I mumble, trying to sound as disinterested as Milly looks. 'Guess they had their reasons.'

'Anyone keen to do any of those extra classes this term?' Milly says, conveniently changing the subject. 'Belle's going to take the psychology course, aren't you?'

'Yup,' replies Anabel. 'Thought that sounded quite interesting.'

'Remind me, what's on offer?' I ask, putting my phone aside for a moment, and looking at Milly.

'Oh, well, I imagine you'll be keen on stuff like parachuting, aviation, or maybe scuba diving. Was actually keen to try the scuba diving myself, if anyone's interested?'

'Yeah, I might be,' I reply, nodding.

'Yeah, that sounds fun,' Nigel adds.

Standing, I look down at Luther and ask, 'What sayeth yee, my Carib-English pork chop friend? Wanna come learn to scuba dive?'

'I gottae see how much work they send me from Cheltenham. Between classes, I mean. I want tae go up there again for the summer placement in a few weeks. A wee bit o' work for them cannae hurt. I'll let you know, okae?'

'Jesus, you can't call people that,' Milly gasps, horrified.

'Why not?'

'What do you mean, why not? Because it's... it's just wrong!'

91

'Is not!' I exclaim. 'It's a term of endearment.'

'Luther,' Milly protests. 'Say something!'

'Havenae a problem with it. I'm jus' tryin' tae read mah book.'

'You're hopeless,' she laughs. 'Telling you, as a British girl of colour, it's just wrong.'

'God, you're right,' I exclaim, realising my mistake. 'It should be Carib-Scottish pork chop!'

Milly groans and hangs her head in despair.

'You're just teasing me now, aren't you?'

'A little, yes,' I reply with a smile. 'Besides, last term you called him Porky or Porkins.'

'I did not,' she exclaims, appalled. 'I called him Porkchop.'

'Oh my God, same-same,' I splutter.

'But different,' Anabel adds, laughing.

'I can do that,' Milly says. 'I'm brown. You're white.'

'What a load of bollocks,' I laugh. 'Didn't you hear…? Technically, I'm colour-blind.'

'Wasn't Porkins an X-wing pilot in the original *Star Wars*?' Nigel asks, disinterested in our bickering.

'Aye, how did they get away with that?' Luther mutters, shaking his head.

'I know,' says Nigel. 'Only fat bloke in the whole Rebel Alliance and they call him Porkins.'

'You sure it was an X-wing?' Anabel asks, clearly looking to wind them up.

'Yeah, no doubt,' Nigel replies emphatically, falling for her hook completely. 'Battle of Yavin was all X-wings, wasn't it?' he says, looking across at Luther. The resigned shrug he receives sends him diving for his phone to check.

'So, whatcha say, Luther?' I ask. 'Are you offended?'

'I dinnae ken,' he replies with a carefree shrug. 'What you gotta understand, white girl, is we don't care, because we know black people make this look cool.'

'Make what look cool?'

'Life,' he says with a teasing grin.

I roll sideways in fits of laughter.

CHAPTER 4

KNOWLEDGE IS POWER

Godolphin Park School – Location Classified

The unexpected militarisation of MI13, when it comes over the following weekend, is swift and deliberate, and coincides with the formal completion of A-School's merger with B-School. It heralds several major changes, the first of which affects the school uniform.

'You upset you missed that drinks thing?' Milly asks as we walk into Godolphin Park's Espionage Training School early Monday morning.

'Nah, no big deal,' I reply, shrugging. 'Though my dad won a prize in their raffle. He said he'd take me along.'

'What is it?' she asks keenly.

'You wouldn't believe it,' I laugh. 'It's totally nuts.' Leaning closer, I whisper into her ear.

'No way!' she blurts out. 'Isn't that, like, crazy dangerous?'

'Probably.'

'Rather you than me,' she mutters, unimpressed. 'When is it? Next Saturday? You really think you can get Lander to give you a day pass by then?'

'Sure. I mean technically it's an acquired skill, right? Like flying. This term's all about new skills, isn't it?'

'Yeah, good luck with that,' she scoffs derisively. 'It's a jolly, plain and simple.'

'Yeah, I know,' I giggle.

As requested, we head towards the back of the main hall. Behind a trestle table stands Frank Sable, the director of ETS, and an elderly member of staff, Mrs Richards, who handles much of the administration. Surrounding them are piles and piles of large brown boxes.

'Well, how could this happen?' Frank asks incredulously, scratching his head.

'I don't know,' the nervous-looking, bespectacled lady replies. 'I can only think someone ticked the wrong box on the purchase form. Maybe they didn't know what captain's eggs were?' she suggests, fidgeting with the hem of her knitted woollen pullover.

'O...kay, what have we got here, then?' I ask, keenly peering into the nearest open box.

Tutting, Mrs Richards quickly scurries off with an armful of black clothing, which she sets down on the next table, sufficiently far away from her irritated boss. Atop each pile she has assembled are a pair of black boots and a matching tactical belt.

'What's all this, sir?' Milly asks Frank.

'Wait your turn,' he snaps, hands on hips, as he stares at an open box. Sighing, he turns to us.

'Alright, Butterworth and Foxton,' he says, picking up a clipboard. He finds our names and crosses us off, then walks to one of the open boxes and begins selecting various items, checking sizes as he accumulates two large piles. One by one, he carries them over and sets them down on the table before us.

'What's all this?' I ask.

'New ETS uniforms,' he replies, irked at being asked the question which dozens of pupils must have asked already this morning.

'Why? What's wrong with this one?' says Milly, looking down at the smart grey-and-black blazer and skirt combo we currently have.

'Probably nothing,' he replies wearily. 'But some bright spark somewhere thinks this will bring a renewed focus to what we do here. The old one remains for school events, and classes up in the main blocks.'

'Uh-huh,' I mumble as I riffle through the pile. Replacing our current choice of loafers, brogues or heels are two lightweight pairs of black combat boots. Below them are three identical sets of black military utility tops and matching cargo trousers. Black socks and a wide black nylon utility belt finish off the radical change in uniform.

'Who designed this?' Milly asks, unimpressed. 'Hugo Boss?'

'Don't let too many people hear you say that,' Frank chuckles.

'Oh, I don't know,' I comment, holding each item up for closer inspection. 'I kind of like it. Must have cost an arm and a leg,' I note, spotting a familiar trident-like logo on each item.

'Yeah, it is very you,' Milly sighs, shaking her head in despair. 'What a waste of money. The old one was fine.'

'Yeah, well, war on terror,' Frank replies. 'Cheque book's open, I guess.'

'And those?' I ask, pointing to the first box, which Frank and Mrs Richards were apparently so upset about. Inside are piles of dark-blue baseball caps. Each has a grey portcullis icon front and centre, flanked by text which reads 'MI XIII'. Topping and tailing the logo, in bright-yellow curving text, are the words 'Military Intelligence and Section 13'.

'New caps,' Frank mutters irritably. 'But they screwed them up. They weren't meant to have the yellow leaf patterns embroidered on the peaks. So the order's ruined. Typical.'

'Oh, I dunno,' I comment. 'Quite like it.'

'Yeah, but you don't hold the rank of captain in the navy, do you?' he points out patronisingly.

'As if anyone's going to care,' I reply blithely.

'Can I see?' says Milly.

Frowning, Frank hands her one from the top of the box.

'Very naval in style, aren't they?'

'Old man's retired navy,' Frank replies. 'Style was his choice. Which is probably how the eggs got on all of them. Except they're not even admiral's eggs, they're captain's eggs. So even that's wrong. Typical. Imagine someone forgot to uncheck the box after placing his order.'

'Gambon?' I query.

'It's admiral or professor,' he sighs. 'Choose one, but at least give the man some respect, Foxton.'

'Oh dear,' Milly says, turning over the cap. 'That's embarrassing. They're all customised.'

Sure enough, on the back of each is embroidered the designated wearer's surname in yellow lettering.

'Oh, that I gotta have,' I exclaim, keenly rounding the table.

'Oi,' Frank complains. 'Those have to be sent back.'

'Okay, that'll make mine even more unique,' I reply, digging into the box. I quickly reach surnames beginning with the letter F and triumphantly pull mine out. Before Frank can tell me to put it back, I already have it on.

'Galls me to say it, but it kind of suits you,' says Milly.

'Oh really,' I reply excitedly. 'See, Mr Sable? Even more reason for me to keep it. Saves you having to reorder me one. Can I keep it?'

'I'd prefer not.'

'Would you really force me to give it back, sir?' I coo, fluttering my eyelashes at him.

'Oh, you are so shameless,' Milly groans, slapping my arm.

'Isn't that the truth,' Frank grumbles. 'Honestly, I don't care. But you can't wear it here, understood?'

'Sure, sir. Promise!'

'Oh, and Foxton,' he sighs. 'Cabal asked me to show you something. Got a minute?'

'Sure, sir. What is it?'

'A surprise, of sorts. All I'll say is, he finally managed to shift that ruddy car of yours from the car park.'

'O'Leary's Jag? Oh no!'

'Still can't believe you brought that silly thing back here, of all places,' says Milly.

'Where else was I meant to leave it?' I protest. 'I couldn't exactly dump it at my parents', could I? And the guy had no family. There was nowhere for it to go.'

'Maybe the police managing the murder inquiry might have wanted to get their hands on it?' Milly exclaims as we make our way into the stairwell and down to the parking level.

'Quite,' Frank says, leading the way. 'Anyway, you'll be glad to know he traded it for something slightly, and I emphasise the word, less obnoxious. Though I still cannot believe you talked him into it. The man should have his head seen to. Pandering to you like this.'

We emerge into the brightly lit underground car park and make our way between the vehicles towards where the unmissable Jaguar had been parked. In its place is a large, boxy, aggressive-looking black SUV.

'Oh my God,' I exclaim, rushing towards it.

'He swapped it for *that*?' Milly exclaims, folding into fits of laughter.

'A Mercedes G-Wagon?' I cry. 'Wow, I mean, it's insane...'

'It looks like something a gangster would drive,' Milly cries, wiping tears from her eyes.

'Not far off,' Frank admits. 'Apparently, Cabal traded it with some Russian he knows in London. Former Spetsnaz chap, I think.'

'Where's it now, then? The Jag, I mean.'

'Probably in a forty-foot container on its way to St Petersburg with forged papers, I'd imagine,' he chuckles. 'Is what it is, Foxton. Deal with it. Look on the bright side, he could've got you a Fiat 500.'

'I'd have liked that,' Milly says.

'I don't dislike it,' I exclaim, peering at the name badge. 'It's a Brabus V8, right? In black. What's not to like? Looks mean as hell. I'm just amused he traded it with some Russian mafia type is all. Typical. This thing's probably hotter that the old one.'

'Not my problem,' he replies. 'Shouldn't have nicked it in the first place, should you?'

'Where's the keys?'

'You get them once you've sorted out the licence, registration and insurance.'

'How am I mean to do that?'

'Not my problem, either. Right, enough of this waste of my time,' Frank says, making for the stairwell. 'You two also need to swap your iSpies for the new model. Can you please do that before classes start?'

Realising we have likely pushed our luck too far with a rather stressed Frank Sable, we obediently follow him back up into the main hall, and approach a member of the technical staff, who is setting pupils up with new mobile phones.

'Your current-issue handsets, please,' the technician says, holding out his hand impatiently. 'We're retiring the old ones.'

'Why?' I ask as I rummage in my rucksack for the iSpy.

'You're the last group using these,' he replies. 'They're simply too expensive to keep up to date as a proprietary platform.'

'But what about all the cool secret stuff on it?' I ask.

'Gone. Too expensive and too problematic to maintain. Besides, the service is moving away from secret towards covert. Big difference.'

'What he's trying to say, Foxton,' Frank Sable elaborates from the next table, as patronisingly as before, 'is that operating in plain sight, using obfuscated language, over publicly available comms apps and channels is actually more secure than encrypting everything.'

'Who thinks that?' Milly asks a little pointedly.

With a shrug and a knowing smile, he puts his hands in his pockets and says, 'Put it this way: the best crypto in the world's pretty useless if a foreign power has the keys.'

'Do they?' she asks. 'Have the keys?'

'Well, that's the question, isn't it,' he replies. 'How would you ever know? Either way, relying entirely on algorithmic crypto in this day and age is a risky strategy. Safer to obfuscate content in a way that no one'll understand it if they aren't on the inside. Apples meets bananas at Christmas Square means nothing if you don't know what each word stands for. Encrypt a message and anyone who can break the code gets to read everything you've said. Why do you think some parts of the government have begun using typewriters again?'

'Okay, I suppose I get it,' Milly admits grudgingly.

'Hey, don't for a minute think that negates what you do,' Frank assures her. 'We're talking about in-the-field comms here. Not the container's protection. Hands down, British Intelligence has one of the most robust, iron-clad networks out there. That'll always remain completely dependent on strong algorithm-driven security. But we're talking about operating procedure here. Besides, this is cheaper. Way cheaper. Issuing you all with commercially manufactured handsets means we pay for none of the R&D. Just leave the old ones with Steve and he'll transfer the contents to the new one, okay? Just choose which one you want.'

'Whoa, is that what I think it is?' Nigel exclaims, arriving in the queue behind us. 'I didn't think they were out yet.' He points to the handset Steve has just unpacked.

'They're not,' the technician replies. 'But government customers can get advance orders. All we do is add a hydrophobic layer to waterproof all the internals and they're good to go.'

'Which one is it?' Nigel asks, peering closer. 'Oh, cool, it's the seven-inch touchscreen one. I heard they've got awesome zoom lenses.'

'Oh, they do,' Steve says enthusiastically. 'It's a periscope zoom. Really something. Here, let me show you.'

Milly and I smile as Nigel pushes in between us to get a better look. Rather than hang about, we walk on to the last table. While we wait in line to be issued with what appears to be a regular pair of reading glasses, Milly turns to me.

'So, you reckoning on any more field trips down here this term to dig into your mum again? You know, just mentally preparing myself for the very real possibility of getting expelled. Planning ahead. That sort of thing.'

'Nah, you can relax about that,' I say with a smile. 'I'm not so fussed anymore. I kind of know enough, know what I mean? And honestly, I've been living in her shadow for long enough. I'm kind of tired of it. It's time to start living my own life.'

'Oh, I'm so glad to hear that,' she gushes, laughing with relief.

'No way!' Nigel exclaims, joining us again. He gently eases past and peers at a pair of the glasses. 'Are those what I think they are?'

'Is it just me getting a weird sense of déjà vu?' Milly laughs.

'These things are wicked,' he exclaims, ignoring her good-humoured jibe. 'Can't remember who makes them, but they're the first user-friendly wearable glasses-cum-computing interface I've seen. Done well, I mean.'

Scowling at his inability to use plain English, I pick up a pair and turn them in my hand.

'Arms are a bit bigger than usual,' I note.

'Yeah, figures,' Nigel says as he edges closer. 'Let's see. Try putting them on.'

He hands them back. Obliging, I do and give a long, low whistle.

'Whoa, they have, like, a whole heads-up display on the lenses. That's nuts,' I exclaim.

'Lemme see,' Milly urges, taking them off my face. 'How do you control them?' she asks, searching the arms for buttons.

'You use one of these,' the techy on the other side of the table explains, holding up a plain silver ring. 'Put this on your non-dominant hand, probably your ring finger. Looks like a normal ring, like a wedding band, right? But it's a touch-sensitive surface. Move your thumb on it, like a trackpad, up and down. That sort of thing. Like a mouse mat. Pretty intuitive once you get the hang of it.'

'What? We all get one of these?' Nigel asks, unable to hide his excitement.

'Looks like it,' the technician replies, pointing at the piles of boxes behind his table.

'How do they charge?'

'In their case, like a pair of headphones. Out of the case, they'll get you through a day with serious use.'

'What can they display?' I ask. 'I mean, what do we use them for?'

'Well, they display basic information, like time and day, compass heading. That sort of thing. Or you can see messages on them, or respond by selecting from pre-written responses or using voice-to-text, if you prefer. It also links to your maps application, and some other functionality on the new phones you're getting,' the tech explains as he begins setting pairs up for Milly and me. 'But it gets smarter than that. Put them on and someone can talk to you through them. The tips of the arms have bone-conducting speakers. So you can hear their voice, but no one around you can hear what's being said.'

'They are so cool,' Milly gushes, trying the demo pair on again. 'What colours do they come in?'

'They only come in the one style, but you can have either black or tortoiseshell frames.'

*

The sky is astonishingly clear. A rich, textured azure blue, with barely a cloud in sight. Up high, stretching lazily across it, a lone contrail marks the route of an airliner cruising overhead at high altitude. It reminds me of what I did this past weekend, having pestered Mr Lander so badly for a Saturday pass that he finally relented. I wish I was back up there, zooming through the air, free as a bird, thanks to the prize my dad won us.

The gentle breeze which wafts across Big-Field offers the only respite from the strong midday sun, which beats down and makes all of us curse whoever thought it would be a good idea to swap out the old school uniform for this new all-black head-to-toe military get-up. No surprise, then, that in the week since it was introduced, it has already picked up a good number of uncomplimentary nicknames.

'Oh, but just wait, because it gets so much worse,' Milly cries, reading from a document as we make our way from SH to ETS.

'Oh great. Here we go.'

'It says they want to effect a transition across all year groups to more practical application classes, with less theory and study-based teaching. But first they need to establish a level-set for everyone.'

'What's that even mean?' I ask, looking as confused as all our friends who are walking with us.

'What it means,' Milly says, talking to the five of us, 'is that before they'll teach us anything more on this term's formal curriculum, they want to recap half of the more basic stuff, like a level-set of sorts.'

'Like what?' Anabel asks with an irritated sigh. 'Knew this whole A-School thing would be a pain.'

'For us, they want to go back over topics like 'History of Intelligence' and 'An Introduction to Agent Recruitment'. And A-Schoolers will start from scratch on the more practical sides of surveillance and that sort of thing.'

'Great, talk about waste of time. Haven't they learnt all this?' Nigel protests.

'Possibly,' Milly replies. 'Maybe it's more for us? Who knows, perhaps they spent more time on all the theory than we ever did? Anyway, check this out. So, after all that, they've added a new class called "Acquisition of Information and Manipulative Influencing Skills".'

'That sounds a bit more fun,' I say. 'Maybe it's not all bad after all.'

'Kind of makes you wonder, though, what they're really after, doesn't it?' Anabel says, deep in thought. 'Are they really trying to prepare us for a career in government service, as they've always claimed, or are we just a here-and-now resource to use in their new war on terror? The curriculum's beginning to look a little schizophrenic.'

'You're not half wrong about that,' I add ruefully.

Barely half an hour later, we settle in for the first lesson of the day. Class sizes have doubled from what they used to be, making the atmosphere noticeably less relaxed. Unperturbed, the headmaster strides into the bright, modern-looking class-room, which has multiple wall-mounted screens set between large pinboards that are covered with large-scale maps of certain troubled parts of the world. As one, the class rises.

'Be seated,' he announces. 'And welcome to today's refresher course on the history of intelligence. Espionage, as I sincerely hope you never have to discover for yourself, is not a game which humours fools or tolerates mistakes.'

Pacing the aisles between our individual desks, Professor Gambon quickly captures the class's attention as only he can. Perhaps it is his quiet, soft voice, or the golf club which he clasps firmly behind his back.

'One rarely gets to learn from mistakes in this game. That's half the reason MI13 was set up in the first place. When you're out there, you only get one chance. Make a mistake and you're either dead or blown, which amounts to the same thing. All you have is the tradecraft we teach you here, and whatever natural intuition you have. The stakes are high. Covers can be blown by the most minor of mistakes. But let's recap a few things, shall we?'

Turning in my chair, I let my eyes drift across the room and am dismayed to see Farabee-Peacock and her friends sitting towards the back of the class. Sensing my gaze, she swivels her beady eyes towards me, and beneath the desk her middle finger rises in defiance. With an eye-roll, I turn back to the headmaster.

'It's fair to say history has shown that the first rule of intelligence must be to never seek confirmation for something you already believe. Examples might include Hitler's certainty that D-Day would come at Calais. We knew he was thinking that, so we simply helped him believe it even more. It went so far as creating a wholly fictitious army near Dover, under General Patton's command. Or Bush and Blair's belief in WMD. Trouble was that the intelligence community helped support that view. Or Andropov's belief that the West would launch a pre-emptive strike. If you refuse to let the intelligence lead you to a conclusion, but instead force it to tally with what you already suspect, then it can only lead to problems.

'All too often people only want to prove what they already suspect. It's human nature. Let the politicians have their views, I say. But the intelligence services must never pander to those views. If you look at the structure of SIS, you see it's deliberately designed to try and avoid the issues of the past. To that end, it establishes a firm delineation between requirements officers, or R officers, who determine the government's requirements needs, and production or P officers. We know what data we want to get hold of. So, the targeter identifies people we believe are likely to have access to that information. The case officer cultivates the agent, and hopefully secures the documents or information we're after. All that's left is for the R officer to then work with Whitehall to validate the information. And based on what we get, the politicians then determine government policy.

'Sounds simple. Organisational impartiality. But it hasn't always been that way. Classic case in point would be the story of Joseph Beppo, the head of Germany's Luftwaffe intelligence in the Second World War. He was so focused on telling his boss, Goering, what Goering wanted to hear that he left out anything contradictory, regardless of how critical it might have been. He would repeat how Germany would win, that their planes were superior to the RAF's. He based his reports on the flimsiest of information. Calling it intelligence would be an insult to the word. He was not interested in the facts one little bit. And of course, the rest is history.'

'Headmaster, could you spend a bit of time covering the WMD case?' Victoria Farabee-Peacock asks, much to several people's surprise, mine included. In fact, I am confident it is the first time I have ever heard her engage in class. Now that could be because we have, fortuitously, shared few classes before this.

'Well, of course,' Gambon replies, pulling up a chair and easing down onto it. 'To understand the issues that took place, one really needs to understand the contextual history. The US failed to prevent Nine-eleven because no one in US intelligence took Islamic terrorism particularly seriously as the Cold War ended. And by the time they did, it was all too late. As a result, when the time came, they had no agents in Bin Laden's camp. Not entirely surprising, really. After decades engaged against the might of the Red Army and the cunning of the KGB and the GRU, one could be forgiven for not taking a bunch of disenfranchised youths in the Middle East particularly seriously. They had virtually no one learning Arabic. Their microphones were all pointed elsewhere, and no one was doing any analysis, either.

'Come Iraq, they had largely the same problem. As we have discussed many times in the past, if one has no insight into what is going on, then when an informant does come along, you might be more willing than normal to clutch onto the source with both hands and brush over any concerns that in other circumstances would raise some serious alarm bells. Which brings us to the agent known as Curveball.

'The scene set, along comes this chap, who walks into the German BND claiming to have been part of the Iraqi biological weapons programme. The Germans, however, quickly began to doubt him. He had a bad attitude, and his demeanour soured the longer the debrief lasted. But despite their suspicions, their reports did not reflect this change in confidence. Which was less than ideal, because his product was shared across the Five Eyes Intelligence Community, and soon the US's Defence Intelligence Agency began buying into what he was saying. Come Nine-eleven, the BND were done with Curveball, and the Americans grabbed him with both hands.

'Now, in fairness, his technical knowledge of the Iraqi weapons programme was indeed impressive. But by early 2002, we too had for the most part lost faith in him. Sadly, his technical knowledge meant there were still some people here in the UK listening to him. Bear in mind that no Brit or American had ever actually spoken to this chap. Everything was based on the German debriefs. But once he gave eyewitness evidence of Saddam's mobile biological warfare units, the ball started rolling too fast. Come the 2003 State of the Union speech, Bush made the public claim that Iraq had mobile weapons labs. Worse, he then ordered General Powell to address the UN. That was, let me think, yes, had to be February 2003. People trusted Colin, and no one was listening anymore after that.

'A few days later, weapons inspectors raided a site that Curveball claimed to be a bio-weapons facility. Turned out to be a seed-processing plant. All the samples they took came back negative. But Bush had run out of patience. The weapons inspectors were pulled out, the deadline passed and off we went to war. It was like the Guns of August all over again, because despite people's individual scepticism, we as a group, the intelligence community I mean, failed to be alert to the dangers of only choosing information that aligned to our political masters' views. Sadly, it was only later that we realised this fool, Curveball, was a sex-obsessed drunk, a liar and a fraud who got his information from the internet.'

Standing, Gambon shrugs, points at Farabee and says, 'Good question, FP.'

'Nauseous' barely comes close to describing my visceral reaction to hearing the headmaster compliment her, of all people, in such a familiar tone. Milly rolls her eyes at me and mimes putting her fingers down her throat. Which makes me laugh out loud. Quickly stifling my outburst, I offer a mumbled apology.

Scowling, Gambon retrieves his golf club. A sure sign the lesson is getting back on track.

'Well, that there was about as textbook a failure of intelligence as one can get. So, let's look at the other side of the equation. The Battle of Midway is a prime example of the benefits of good military intelligence on the part of the Americans, and the very real cost of poor-to-none on the part of the Japanese. It showed the difference one person could make. An intelligence officer called Edwin Layton, a man so deeply immersed in the practices of the Japanese Imperial Navy that he recognised one code word out of a sea of code words and tied it to another piece of information that told him the Japanese were in fact talking about the island of Midway. And the rest, again, is history, as were the four Japanese aircraft carriers that got sunk in a single day as a result.'

'Don't forget one particularly eagle-eyed pilot,' a boy at the back chimes in.

'Quite so,' Gambon chuckles. 'Quite so. It was a team effort, after all. Any other instances anyone can suggest where intelligence has turned the tide of conflict?'

'What was that operation where they dumped a body at sea with fake invasion plans?' an Indian girl at the front asks.

'Good example. Yes, Operation Mincemeat. Any others?'

'What about the CIA sending Stingers to Afghanistan?' says a boy from Kell.

'That might be muddling military action with intelligence. As well as confusing myth with fact,' Gambon notes. 'The reality was the Politburo had already decided to withdraw before those missiles arrived. And the Stinger missile was a delicate bit of kit. Humping it over the Hindu Kush on a donkey meant most were broken by the time they arrived. I think they began to get through in September '86, and the Red Army began withdrawing in November. What we never knew was the state of things back in the Soviet Union at the time, and it was far worse than we thought. Things were already falling apart in the outer republics. Red Army troops were routinely getting shot in the streets. Moscow needed its army back, and while the missiles may play well for Hollywood, they had little impact in reality.

'I mention these stories,' he says, 'because an intelligence officer who is a student of history can learn a great deal from the successes of those who came before them, as can they from mistakes others made. And the most tragic will always be mistakes made in good faith that ended up costing lives. Take the death of CIA base chief Jennifer Matthews in December 2009. She was blown up by a Jordanian doctor called Humam al Balawi. The CIA believed him to be a terrorist informant. At the time, they were very short of informants, and therefore desperate for them. So desperate, in fact, that they completely fell for the idea that this man, whom they barely knew and had not even done a full background check on, would work for them. Try to imagine that they wanted him so much that he was not even searched when his car arrived at the desert military camp where they had agreed to meet.'

'Why, sir?' asks a girl sitting two seats behind me. 'Wouldn't that be standard operating procedure?'

'Ideally, yes. But they were probably too scared of potentially offending him. That's how desperate the CIA was to get someone inside al Qaeda. Of course, the moment he was close enough, he detonated his bomb and killed nine people. Seven were from the CIA, waiting to greet him. They had even baked him a cake. It would be a mistake to judge them. We are not in their shoes, but we can learn from the past.

'The deeper lesson to take from that case would be to remember that the moment you take your eye off a developing issue, you're likely to end up on the back foot and playing a painful game of catch-up. Had Western intelligence given more credibility to Islamic fundamentalist groups, things might have turned out very different. Now, if the latter half of the twentieth century was a fight between superpowers, democracy versus communism, and the first part of the twenty-first century a fight against Islamic fundamentalism, what do you think the fight of the future will be? Anyone?'

'The way things are going, looks like another fight against the new superpower communists,' a boy at the back jokes. 'China?'

'Possibly,' Gambon notes, shrugging his shoulders. 'Certainly can't be discounted. But we've done all that, the large superpower facing off against one another. That's simply political power-play. Maybe the only secrets left to find there are about getting an insight into the bigger picture. What is their long-term goal? And we know how to do that. So, think, where else could issues develop? Where else should we apply our intelligence-gathering capabilities? If it's just information that a government wants, then they might as well subscribe to Reuters or Bloomberg. If you are to truly deploy these very specialist capabilities, where ought we to do that? Who has secrets nowadays, if it's not other governments anymore?'

'Companies and corporations,' suggests Milly. 'They're the ones with the information others want. Whether it's software, medical breakthroughs, vaccines, advances in crop research, that sort of thing.'

'That's true. Remember how everyone thought some governments were trying to hack into Covid vaccine research?' Anabel adds.

'Is that to suggest that governments don't wholeheartedly trust companies?' Gambon replies with a crooked little smile.

'Yes,' Milly replies emphatically.

'Oh, this will be a good chat,' Gambon chuckles, inching his chair forwards.

*

Several hours later, as the bell rings, the class decamps again and heads silently across the hallway to another, larger classroom, where we take our seats at identical desks and await the arrival of the next teacher.

'Tired, are we?' Frank Sable calls as he enters the room. 'Been a long day of people talking at you, has it? Well, let's see if we can't make this one a little more interactive, shall we?'

He is greeted by a less than convinced murmuring.

'Excellent, well, let's start by addressing the question raised at the end of last session. Torture and the forced extraction of information versus the voluntary giving of it. Does it really get results?'

Stepping to the screen at the front of the class, Frank turns it on and cues up a scene from the film *Taken*. He dims the lights. On the screen we see a man strapped to a wooden chair in a dingy, poorly lit room. A tall man approaches and stands, looming over him. Protruding from the captive man's thighs are two thin metal poles. The ends are connected by wires to a makeshift rig which is wired up to the room's light switch. At each refusal to answer a question, the tall man flicks the switch, sending the bound man into screaming convulsions. The single light bulb dangling in the centre of the room flickers.

Pressing pause, Frank turns to us.

'So, here we have former CIA man Liam Neeson in search of the people who took his daughter and applying the necessary pressure to some lowlife scumbag he knows to be involved.'

He smiles and presses play, and Neeson says, 'You either give me what I need, or this switch stays on until they turn the power off for lack of payment on the bill.'

'It's a great line, right?' Frank chuckles. 'Now, despite what the TV and major Hollywood movies would have you believe, what we've discovered is that this kind of stuff just doesn't work. Unfortunately, for the people who just want to get to work on their enemies with a pair of pliers and a blowtorch, a far better option could be to treat them humanely. When we train some of the people who do this stuff for the army and the security services, a lot of them are surprised to hear that employing people skills, building a rapport, sharing stuff with the person they are seeking information from have a statistically better chance of success than ripping a fingernail out every time you get an answer you don't believe.

'The catch, of course, for anyone in this game, is that this message has clearly not got out yet to every tin-pot dictator, two-bit banana republic secret police or organised crime cartel who're still getting all their ideas from straight-to-streaming B-movies.

'If this fact was more widely acknowledged, British and NATO forces could dispense with all the resistance-to-interrogation training we give our people. But we still make pilots, Special Forces and other trainees go through all that in RTI courses, including roughing them up, depriving them of sleep, making them stand naked in uncomfortable positions for hours, sexual humiliation, no food, no water, shouting and abuse, for hour after hour. The guidelines say only name, rank and number can be offered up.'

'You didn't have to do that, did you?' Milly whispers, turning in her seat.

'Yeah, bummer, I missed out on that part,' I laugh. 'They only do that at the end of the SF Selection. Pity. Sounds fun.'

'I hope you're not serious.'

Smiling, I redirect her attention to Frank Sable.

'Sir,' a boy at the front says, raising his hand. 'But does that… Let me rephrase. How can that have any bearing on or prepare anyone for what's really likely to happen at the hands of the really nasty people out there?'

'Honest answer. It can't. And frankly, it may well be badly out of date. Now, the question asked last week was what to do in such a situation. I am not sure there is a good answer. Don't get into such a situation may be the simplest one.

'That said, I remember speaking to a guy from Delta. He was telling me about a chap called Michael Durant, one of their chopper pilots shot down over Mogadishu by Somali rebels in the late nineties. Now, they didn't have fancy psychological programmes or high-tech interrogation techniques. They just beat the crap out of him and kept him tied up on a mouldy mattress in a bombed-out house downtown. But this guy made efforts to befriend his captors, make them see him as a person and not as an enemy. And you know what? He survived and was released.

'Trouble with RTI is, it simply breaks you, which then sets a precedent that it's okay to break. Worse, it conditions you to think it's them versus me. And maybe it is. But that removes the possibility of hope. Worse, it deludes you into thinking you can withstand the worst out there. Well, the callous application of blow torches, pliers and Black and Decker drills will quickly put an end to that kind of thinking. It's also been shown that soldiers who go through it have a worrying tendency to then copy those very same interrogation techniques when dealing with their own prisoners.'

'Sounds cheery,' Milly mutters sarcastically.

'Yeah,' I reply. 'Tell me about it. Just hope we never end up in that position.'

Frank moves to the front of the class, cleans the blackboard and clears his throat to get everyone's attention again.

'Right, moving swiftly on, let's quickly cover the rest of the topics I want to talk about today. Firstly,' he says, consulting a piece of paper on his desk, 'I'd like to go back and cover several aspects around agent recruitment, if you don't mind?

'Hopefully, you're all familiar enough with history by now' – he smiles teasingly – 'to appreciate that MI6 didn't have a whole lot of success in the First World War. In fact, they recruited no one in Germany during the whole conflict. Now, that may not be too surprising. They were only set up in 1909. But by the time of the Russian Revolution, ten years later, Admiral Sir William Hall, the then chief of naval intelligence, realised that trying to go it alone with a bunch of cavalier-type rogues laying their hands on information was producing hardly any product of value. So, British Intelligence decided they needed to outsource intelligence gathering to agents, insiders and locals who could betray their own side and give us what we needed to know.

'For this reason, today's Security Service and Secret Intelligence Service focus on the recruitment and running of agents to collect information, rather than conducting operations directly against foreign enemies. Certainly more than they used to. That more active role is now largely outsourced to groups in UK Special Forces, such as the Increment, or E Squadron, which is the UK SF attachment to MI6.

'So, if we want to understand best practices in running agents, we need to appreciate the problems. The first and most important concern has to be the inherent irony in all of it. Think how patriotic most people in the intelligence services are. And then consider that much of our work is asking others to betray their friends and colleagues. And if they are successful, we celebrate them. But if one of our own should ever dare to betray us, we ostracise them, destroy their life and brand them a traitor against England –'

'Aye, and what about wee Scotland?' Luther calls from the back.

'All right, quiet,' Frank calls, hushing the laughing class. 'Calm down. Yes, very good, Mr Glasgow. Now, where was I?

Yes, double standards. The point is, we must never forget the personal risk we are asking of those who work for us.

'The second problem with agents and their product is the inherent disbelief it is all too regularly met with. Often the better the product, the greater the disbelief. Spies, by their very nature, are treacherous. If they can betray their own side, what makes us think they're being honest with us? You see the irony here? An agent comes in with an astonishing piece of information. It either reinforces what we suspected or it completely contradicts our thinking. Which is the easier to believe?'

'The first,' Milly blurts out, hand in the air.

'I'd agree. Problem with the second scenario is that it's often hard to believe. Worse still if we can't corroborate it in any way. So, all too often it's rejected. Maybe the agent had access to the only proof. The more sensitive the information, the fewer people will ever see it, making it even harder to prove. How often do you think a politician will take a punt on a single unverified piece of information and take a firm stance internationally on it? Hardly ever. Far too risky. Chances are they will be made to look a fool. Therefore, getting multiple unconnected agents to corroborate the same information is critical, or else all the effort is often in vain.

'Okay, let's go back to the agent recruitment bit, because despite its problems, it's still absolutely vital. The aim, of course, is to hone in on the personal weakness a would-be agent has. Maybe it's anger, resentment, jealousy at something around them that's wrong, or maybe they are sad and lonely. All these are fine, and frankly desirable. What we don't want, almost ever, is an ideological agent. Those ones are almost impossible to trust, because how can you ever verify a state of mind? Claiming a point of view, especially a political one, is the easiest lie in the world. Well, after "I love you", perhaps. Far more desirable is the agent who wants something tangible. Political change is pretty thin as a cause to betray one's country, and dangerous for us.'

'So, what are we looking for, sir?' a boy at the front asks.

'Money's a good one. And usually the most honest driver. Or perhaps a new life in a new country. Far better to move to the Lake District than try to achieve political change in their dump of a home country. Maybe they want a partner. Who knows? But these are real motivators.'

'Sir, don't you think that some people might actually love their home?' asks a Sinclair lower-sixth-former on the other side of the class. 'They may just dislike the current leaders?'

'Okay, fair point. I use it more as a rule of thumb. I say beware the ideological agent, but sometimes you might be right. Perhaps this is where your own judgement comes to the fore. How much you trust them should be directly linked to who they are. Someone junior I would be sceptical about. The more senior they are, perhaps the more frustrated they are –'

'Even within our generation?' Nick asks. 'Seems most political unrest gets caused by university students.'

'Not untrue,' Frank acknowledges. 'But how many uni graduates are in a position to encounter highly classified materials?'

'Okay, I guess that's a fair point,' Nick says.

'Moving on,' Frank continues. 'Family issues can also play a large part in securing an agent. As can the simple human desire to stay alive. Go back to the troubles in Northern Ireland. Take Gerry Adams's family. Did any of you know his father was a paedophile?'

The blank looks around the classroom confirm Frank's suspicion.

'Well, read up on it. And when you do, you'll also discover that so too was his brother, who abused his own daughter. What you won't read about is the extent to which the Adams family cooperated with British Intelligence. And they were not alone. Don't forget, the then prime minister, Margaret Thatcher, had already invoked a shoot-to-kill policy –'

'Sorry, sir,' I joke, 'but as opposed to what? A shoot-to-miss policy?'

His withering look makes me regret the pun immediately, and I sink into my seat, embarrassed. Still, it garners a few sniggers from around the classroom.

'How could that policy have been legal?' Milly interjects, unimpressed with my attempt at humour. 'I thought the government doesn't sanction assassination outside of war.'

'Admittedly, the British government's official position was that our forces were neutral,' Frank explains. 'And our involvement was only to maintain law and order in Northern Ireland. But at the same time, Miss Butterworth, "legal" is whatever the government of the day says it is. Let's not forget that the Holocaust, apartheid and slavery were all technically legal in their time. So, here's a question for you. Given that an open shoot-to-kill policy was in effect, and against both sides, I should add, why were so few senior IRA leaders taken out by the security services?'

Again, Milly raises her hand, wiggles her fingers enthusiastically and blurts out an answer: 'Could it be because most of the leadership was basically on our side?'

'Interesting theory,' Frank notes. 'Go on...'

'Well, if they informed on their own side, perhaps in return we didn't kill them.'

'Well, in that case you'd have to ask, who was working for whom? Because that sounds ominously close to a quid pro quo.'

The class remains silent for a moment as the possibilities dawn on us.

'Well then, why did the troubles go on for so long?' another pupil asks.

'Ah, now there you might need to consider a very different theory. Any ideas?' smiles Frank.

'Sir,' Milly says, raising her hand again. Without waiting to be acknowledged, she continues, 'Maybe it was a deliberate strategy on behalf of the government?'

'Go on, Miss Butterworth.'

'Well, sir, I've read about people saying that fighters need to get old before they'll ever grow tired of all the killing and the fighting...'

'Go on. Because that's a very different proposition to your first one.'

'Yes, sir, I know. But if you keep assassinating everyone who comes into a leadership position, won't new, more energised people just fill their places? The IRA would never have got tired. Maybe Thatcher chose not to remove their leadership because she figured the people in place would eventually grow weary of losing friends all the time and would eventually decide to give up?'

'It's another interesting theory. Novel, too, to imagine politicians playing the long game. But interesting, nonetheless. Can you give me an example of the alternative strategy, Miss Butterworth?'

'Most obvious one, sir, would be America's strategy in Afghanistan and Iraq. How they handled their whole war on terror after Nine-eleven. It looks like they didn't stop to consider the fact that Islamic terrorism would never tire so long as there was no one left alive long enough at the top to get tired.'

'Excellent analysis. So, class, the first part of your homework this week is to argue which of the two theories is more plausible: Miss Butterworth's theory that we held back from assassinating the IRA's upper echelons in order to achieve a long-lasting peace, or her theory that their top leadership was spying for us. For hand-in at the end of the week, please.'

A good few pupils, most of whom came from A-school, glance around at Milly with irritated frowns.

'Right, so let's talk a little bit about the value of the agent in these modern times, shall we?' Frank says as he settles on the corner of his desk. 'The Cold War was all about information discovery, disinformation and, on occasion, understanding what the Russians were thinking to prevent some disaster of misunderstanding. But the war on terror is all about preventing acts before they can take place. But against this kind of ideology there is no deterrent. I mean, there's nothing in Western justice systems' arsenals that scares these people. So, we need to get an insight into their organisations. Assassination programmes have splintered these groups into tiny, disconnected little pockets. Now, perhaps we get lucky and receive a tip-off. More likely, something comes up in electronic surveillance. But the general rule of thumb is that we'd never trust a single human source. We'd want it supported by some other evidence, right? Because if we get that, then we can begin trawling the historic archives of signals intercepts which we hoover up day in, day out.'

'Sir, is it true we're limited by what the government's priorities are, or could the service pursue interesting leads independently?' a Grey's boy asks.

'Absolutely right. Pursuing avenues unrelated to something on the requirements list is forbidden without specific approvals. I'm mindful of time, and I have a few more bits to get through before we break. So, let's imagine we are now accumulating the supporting evidence we need to back up an initial tip or intercept. This is where an agent can really be worth their weight in gold. An insider can also give us the necessary context to ensure we're reading things right.'

'But, sir, unless someone wants to betray their own side, how can we persuade them to help us?' the same boy asks.

'Jeremy, if I give you all the answers, where's the creative thinking we want to inspire in you?' Frank asks pointedly. 'The only way to develop new ideas is to think of them. Rehash the same old strategies time after time and soon you'll be stale and ineffective. Anyone, any interesting ideas about how you could apply the necessary pressure on would-be agents to help us?'

'Why wouldn't you target people who have immigration violations in their immediate family?' Farabee suggests.

Trust her to come up with something like that, I muse cynically to myself.

'That's one option, for sure. Either way, let's not kid ourselves that this is easy. It has certainly become harder,' he says. 'Back in the day, the first item we asked of any potential recruit was a copy of their organisation's internal directory. But nowadays, splinter terrorist groups don't even have these.

'So, we need to take things slowly. Developing good intelligence takes time. We need to nurture the resource. We can't push them, bribe them or threaten them. The best agent runners build a real, meaningful rapport with their agents. If the handler doesn't care about the agent, it's not going anywhere.

'But never forget, there is danger here as well. While SIS has been lucky in terms of not losing a single career officer in the field since the end of World War Two, handlers must never forget that an agent could betray them and the case officer at any moment. Years of close relationship could all end one random Tuesday afternoon with a bullet to the head in an alleyway. No warning. Bang. It's a fine line, always keeping one's wits about you, getting close but never too close.'

Glancing at his watch, Frank begins gathering up his papers.

'So, in conclusion, before the bell goes... What we've covered has really focussed on recruiting agents, managing them and getting them to provide the information we need. But then it's critically important to escalate the information as soon as possible. Because, as the age-old adage goes, intelligence does not exist until it is successfully delivered.'

'Sir, do you have any good examples of where the service didn't escalate critical information quickly enough?' Farabee asks.

My head turns sharply, my interest piqued as to why she would ask that. Despite her thin, insincere smile, I can't tell if it is a deliberately pointed question or just coincidence. Farabee couldn't possibly know about what happened in Switzerland. Could she? Then again, her father is high up in the Civil Service, so anything's possible. Sighing, I sink into my seat and cross my arms petulantly. Glancing backwards from her second-row seat, Milly gives me an awkward little shrug. Offering little more than a frown back, I turn to look out the window and watch a lower-year class going about their close-quarter combat training out in the middle of the main ETS hall.

*

By the time we trudge into the final class of the morning, in one of the older, less techy wood-panelled classrooms in the main history block, for Civics, Morality, Relationships and Sex Education – or CMRSE as the government have decided it be termed – morale is pretty much at rock bottom.

Everyone is tired of being lectured. Barely anyone amongst the old B-School crowd is talking anymore, all clearly unhappy with the new speech-heavy content of classes. Perhaps with the exception of my friend Milly, who seems to be relishing the more fact-based study. She scuttles up beside me with a broad smile. It only grows bigger as she sees how bored I am from my peeved expression.

'Why are you looking so happy?' I ask as we take our tablets out and lay them on the rear-most bench in the classroom.

'Come on, it's not completely uninteresting,' she says. 'Sure, it's been a bit slower than the usual, more practical classes, but it's still interesting.'

I shrug, and then scowl as Farabee passes by the bench in front of us, sticking her tongue out between a V made by her fingers.

'Are you sure it's the content,' Milly sighs, 'or the fact that we're now lumped in with that lot?' She casts a sour look at Farabee and friends as they take their seats at the far end of our bench.

'Bit of both, I guess. I've been getting nothing but pissy looks and crap from them all morning.'

'Yeah, me too,' admits Milly.

'Sod it, maybe we just have some fun with them,' I suggest.

'Oh dear,' Milly replies. 'Please don't do anything stupid.'

'As if I would,' I scoff dismissively.

'Alright, now I'm concerned. Should I just move to another table?'

'Course not. It'll be fine. Promise.'

'Heard that before,' she says with a grimace.

'Just think that if she's going to make up stuff about our sex life –'

'We don't have a sex life!' protests Milly a little too loudly.

Ignoring the few curious glances that attracts, I continue, 'Duh, you know what I mean. Point being, if she's going to do that, then we can make up stuff about hers.'

Thanks to the newly formed Ministry of Morals, we now have these additional classes imposed on us, as does every school across the country apparently. They were designed to address the supposed rot at the heart of society which apparently drove so many disenfranchised young men and women to do what they did in the attacks. Of course, it misses the point completely, yet still, week after week, we must endure it. The curriculum requires classes to cover STIs, contraception, pornography, miscarriages, sexual harassment, consent and LGBT issues. I imagine their hope was these classes would address the most basic principles behind an orderly society, including manners, ethics and inter-racial relations. Curiously, they miss the mark on nearly every count.

'I tell you, this guy, Styles, is literally making friends everywhere,' a student says sarcastically from the table in front of us. 'My mum works in government, and she says he's forcing changes all over the shop, including at the Ministry of Justice, the Department of Education, the Home Office and the Department for Digital, Culture, Media and Sport.'

'That's what you were saying, weren't you?' I say, looking at Milly.

'Shh, here comes the reverend,' she whispers.

Well in his sixties, the school's chaplain is an affable enough man with a bald crown, little grey tufts above his ears and a warm, caring demeanour. His job used to be simply to look after the school's chapel, and coordinate Sunday morning services and those held for major festivities. But as he once taught Religious Studies at a former school, the headmaster thought him the ideal member of staff to teach this class. A job I imagine he resents, because shortly into each class – most of which tend to advocate an abstinence-filled, teetotal lifestyle devoid of pornography, drugs and debauchery – someone will eventually grow bored and sow the first seeds of disruption, after which productive teaching typically comes to a grinding halt and pandemonium ensues.

Today, I find it's my turn, and so after a few minutes I can't take any more of it. Milly stiffens noticeably as I slowly raise my hand and groans in fearful anticipation as I clear my throat.

'Yes, Miss Foxton?' the reverend says hesitantly.

'Thank you, sir. What I was wondering is, if this is about sex education, could we maybe talk about things which are more relevant to our debauched, promiscuous lifestyles? Like, I dunno, slut shaming, abortion, virginity and maybe masturbation? Things that we should all really know more about and which the boys should probably understand a lot better?'

'Just because you don't understand it,' Farabee drawls from the end of the bench, 'doesn't mean we are all as sheltered and naïve as you.'

'No seriously,' I continue. 'I mean, I read an article about how when you masturbate, it can clamp tight all by itself down there?'

'Oh Jesus,' Milly groans, hiding her face in her hands beside me. 'Please don't do this to me.'

'I'm not kidding,' I exclaim, unperturbed. 'I mean, what's that about? There might be people here who get that but have, like, no idea. They might be thinking they have some weird condition. Did you know it even has a name? Get this. It's called vaginismus. I mean, who knew, right?'

'That's enough, Miss Foxton,' warns the reverend. 'Class, kindly all turn to page fourteen in your –'

'Are you serious?' a girl blurts out from two tables away.

'Yes, for real. No joke. It's, like, a totally legit thing.'

'Right, that's quite enough,' the reverend calls.

'Listen to the reverend, will you!' Farabee hisses from a few seats to my left.

'Please, sir,' I continue, now unable to stop myself. 'I just think it would be great if we could cover real-world stuff that we're actually concerned about with sex and relationships. You know, like whether getting repeatedly bugger-battered up your bottom can make you incontinent? I think, Victoria, didn't you said you were worried about that earlier?' I note, glancing innocently towards Farabee-Peacock with mock concern.

'Enough,' the reverend shouts.

'You bitch!' Farabee hisses and throws a pencil at me.

It misses, and I dissolve into fits of laughter as the smirks and giggling, which had been poorly hidden until now, erupt into the open and the classroom descends into chaos.

'I hate you,' Milly giggles beside me.

CHAPTER 5

TABLES TURNED

Godolphin Park School

Over the next few weeks, my deteriorating enthusiasm for the back-to-basics curriculum results in an uptick in ever more disruptive, puerile humour. And I am not alone, either.

Interestingly, the reverend, whom I discover from Frank Sable was formerly the regimental padre with the SAS, is the one least annoyed by it all. In fact, I'm beginning to think his astonishingly feeble efforts to rein us in are his way of spicing up lessons he knows to be dead boring, as he has little option other than to adhere to the mandated curriculum set by the Ministry of Morals. I notice with amusement that he clearly refuses to reprimand me, or any of the others for that matter.

Less enthused, perhaps not entirely surprisingly, is Victoria Farabee-Peacock, who as the weeks pass, oddly, seems to have fewer and fewer comebacks to my increasingly sordid sexual insinuations about what she does in her spare time.

'Don't get me wrong,' Milly says, stifling a giggle as we cross the main ETS hall between lessons, 'but suggesting VFP's closer to her parents' horses than the RSPCA would approve of might be going a little far, don't you think?'

'I'm sorry, VFP? Seriously!'

'I know. It's just easier.'

'Okay, maybe that was a little bit over the top,' I concede, 'but she's a big girl. She can handle it. Besides, it's not like she didn't sow the seeds.'

'No argument there. But honestly, I'm actually not so sure she can handle it much more.' Seeing my quizzical expression, Milly quickly adds, 'Hey, just saying is all.'

'Why, what have you heard?'

'Not much. But you must've noticed she's stopped firing back at you in the last week or two.'

'Yeah, so?'

'It's Farabee. Don't you think that's odd?'

'In truth,' I reply, 'I haven't given it all that much thought, really.'

'All I'm saying is, I don't think Grey's is exactly filled with the sweetest of people.'

'True, but they're all pretty tight.'

'Are they?'

'What? You saying they're teasing her?'

'Who knows? But just look over there,' Milly says, gesturing as we reach the next classroom. Across the way is a group of Grey's sixth-formers, including Augustus Cole. 'Who's missing?'

'Okay, so she's not there. So what? Maybe she's off with her boyfriend?'

'Perhaps. But then again, perhaps it's everything. And if the rumours are true, her new boyfriend is in Sinclair's. Maybe dating outside of Grey's is seen as poor form?'

'Not incestuous enough, you mean? Maybe. Dunno. But you seriously think they're latching on to all the bollocks I'm coming up with in morals class and taking it for a spin?' I ask, unconvinced. 'I thought she was their little queen ring-leader.'

'Appearances might be deceptive. They're all a bunch of turds, after all. And the verbs you've coined are quite catchy, truth be told. I still giggle at the bugger-battered one. Though it's pretty grim if you think about it. Farabee's a bitch, for sure. But she's also a fairly sheltered bitch. Maybe she doesn't have good comebacks to your urban gutterishness. Maybe she's looking a little vulnerable now the tables have been turned. Or others see a chance for the top spot.'

'You make them sound like a pack of hyenas,' I laugh. 'Eating their own.'

'Wouldn't be too far off, would I?'

'Foxton,' comes a bark from behind us. 'Butterworth.'

We turn to see the headmaster stalking towards us, accompanied by Frank Sable. They appear to have come from the staff common room. Frank beckons impatiently.

'Oh, God, what now?' I mumble. 'Hey, remind me about the whole Farabee thing later, okay, because I'm intrigued.'

'Sure. Why?'

'Well, because while she may be a prize turd of the highest order, we shouldn't turn into what she's been to us all along.'

'Agreed. Moral high ground. Got it. Right, now what's gone wrong here?' Milly says under her breath.

Both adults look distinctly unamused, and we walk towards them with a mounting sense of trepidation.

'Come this way, you two,' Gambon says humourlessly.

Sharing a meaningful look, we follow them in silence down a long hallway towards the headmaster's office. For a room with no windows, it is still remarkably light and airy, decorated as it is with a thick, cream-coloured, plush carpet, a few table lamps and a large standard lamp amidst a scattering of pine furniture. Sitting in one of the armchairs is a distinctly average-looking man whom neither of us have seen before. His creased, off-the-hangar suit looks like it has been worn all week.

'This is Mark,' Gambon says, making the necessary introductions. 'He's from the Security Service. He has a couple of questions for you both.'

Seeing our shared look of concern, Frank says, 'Relax, you're not in trouble.'

'Yet...' Gambon adds with a smirk.

'Excellent. Yeah, thanks, Frank. Let me give you some background quickly,' Mark says, opening his tablet up on the desk. 'I have been informed by those who ought not to be named that you know this chap Konunga,' he says, bringing up a familiar photo.

'Yeah, you could say we've bumped into each other before,' I reply with a little smile.

'Great, well, once your Major Konunga was in custody, we interviewed him, and as part of a plea deal he gave us some answers. Amongst them was a name, that of a former member of South African Special Forces. According to Konunga, this man was the central linchpin who brought all the various splinter groups together. Konunga imported the weaponry and this South African, a Colonel Tanner, acted as the middleman who connected all the groups together and arranged the dispersal of weapons out to each of them.'

'How did you get him to give up the South African?' I ask with a raised eyebrow.

Mark glances at Gambon for a hesitant second, and then simply says, 'We appealed to his sense of right and wrong.'

Over by the door, Frank chuckles dryly, and the MI5 man continues.

'Anyway, long and short of it is, we finally apprehended Tanner trying to leave Heathrow yesterday afternoon. He was taken to a police station in central London and held there pending an arraignment hearing before a local magistrate.

'Technically, the police could only detain him for twenty-four hours without charging him. We were going to have a senior officer approve a further twelve hours' detention. Ultimately, we wanted a magistrate to grant an additional ninety-six hours. Catch here was whether he could be held on terrorism charges or not. Only Konunga's evidence identified him, and beyond that we had little else to hold him on for longer. Any good lawyer worth their salt would have shredded any request to hold him for the full twenty-eight days permitted for terrorist offences without more evidence.'

'Okay, so, err, why are you here?' I ask.

'We need you to watch something,' he says, waking his tablet and bringing up a multi-feed video playback. 'See what you make of this.'

'When was this?' Milly asks, leaning closer.

'About four hours after Tanner was arrested.'

The MI5 man presses play and all four grainy, paused video clips come to life. Top left is a view of a reception area. It appears to be within a large police station. Next to it is a fixed view down a long, plain corridor. Bottom left is an interview room, and bottom right, a view across the street, presumably outside the police station.

Shifting my chair for a better view, I watch as the video begins. Mark directs our attention to the reception area feed. Directly below the camera is the duty officer's counter. Beyond that lies an open area of linoleum-tiled waiting room. A line of plastic chairs stretches along the far wall. Only two are occupied. At the far-right-hand side are the police station's glass front doors. Little is happening. In the bottom-left feed, a man is shown into the interview room and handcuffed. He appears large and formidable in build.

'That's Tanner,' Mark notes.

In the bottom-right video, a man and a woman approach the station's front doors. Solicitors would be my first guess. Both are smartly dressed and carrying briefcases. The woman is wearing a pencil skirt suit, a crisp white shirt, dark stockings and black high heels. The man is also wearing a suit, with polished black shoes. He holds the door open for his female companion and in they both walk, apparently mid-joke, laughing in amusement at something. The woman has long wavy hair and is wearing large dark sunglasses.

The man is clearly well known by the duty officer, who waves amicably as if his arrival is a regular, everyday occurrence. The male solicitor signs the visitors' log while talking to his female companion, who rests against the counter with her back to the camera. Absentmindedly, she passes a piece of paper across the counter and speaks very briefly to the duty policeman. Then she also adds her details to the log, but her face remains hidden from the camera's view by her falling hair and the angle of the shot.

'What am I meant to be looking for?' I ask.

'Just wait,' Mark says quietly. 'It's coming.'

The video continues. Both solicitors gather their possessions and are directed towards a security door on the left-hand side of the waiting room. There they pause for a moment before being buzzed in. As they step through, they appear at the far end of the corridor video feed. We watch, unsure what it is we are meant to be looking for, as the two solicitors follow a female police officer along the corridor towards the camera. Again, the camera fails to get a good look at either of them, as both have their heads bowed in conversation. But then the man looks up casually at the camera as they approach.

'I'm still not getting the point of this,' I say, folding my arms as boredom begins to set in.

'Almost there,' says Mark.

The solicitors stop below the camera, and for a few seconds they talk casually. The policewoman points the female solicitor to an adjacent door before turning to the man.

'She's just told the woman that her client is in that room, over there. She says she'll be back in a moment with the investigating officer. Now she's taking the man to another interview room, where his client is, and saying that she'll be right back,' Mark says. 'Okay, so off they walk, and then...'

The female solicitor idles in the corridor for a few seconds before approaching the interview room door. From inside the interview room, we see the door ease open. She steps out of view from the corridor feed. The interior camera is placed high up, far above the door, looking across the table at the well-built man. Tanner has a short, crew-cut hairstyle and is wearing a tight-fitting grey T-shirt which emphasises his muscular arms and chest. He looks distinctly unimpressed and bored.

The woman in sunglasses leans into the room, as if to ask a passing question, as her hand slips into her briefcase.

Tanner barely has time to react before two dark blotches suddenly appear on his chest and he slumps backwards.

'Whoa, whoa, whoa, what happened there?' I exclaim. 'Rewind it.'

The absence of sound on the recording gives it an oddly discombobulated feel. Talking a further half step into the room, the woman braces the silenced pistol with her left hand and puts another round front and centre into Tanner's forehead. A large dark splatter suddenly splashes across the wall behind him.

With her hands clasped together in shock, Milly leans forward and points numbly at the screen. Slightly calmer, I stand still, staring at the paused image with a peeved expression. The deeply cynical part of me had just been waiting for it to happen, whilst my optimistic side had held on to hope that I was wrong. Cynicism wins again.

'Great,' I mumble darkly as the gun is returned to the briefcase. As Tanner's brains begin their slow slide down towards the skirting board, the mysterious assassin darts a cautious look out into the corridor. Nothing happens. No alarms go off and no one comes running. Instead, walking calmly, the woman strides back along the corridor, buzzes the door and paces quickly across the waiting area.

'That's where she tells the desk officer that she forgot her case file in her car,' Mark says. 'Back in a second sort of thing.'

We watch together, speechless, as she leaves as calmly as she arrived. The last view of her shows her climbing into a dark four-by-four that came around the corner just as she exited the station. All very neat and coordinated. Within seconds, the vehicle has turned the corner and is gone.

Sighing, Mark leans forwards and turns off the video.

'Are you fricking kidding me?!' I exclaim, gesturing at the screen. 'And what? Tell me they got a licence plate?' One look at Mark gives me my answer. 'Oh, you've got to be joking. How? I mean... That guy was our only lead.'

'Sounds like motive enough to want him out of the picture then, I'd say,' Dr Gambon comments from behind his desk.

Turning to Mark, Milly asks, 'What did the male solicitor say? He clearly seems to be familiar with the shooter. Surely he knows who she is!'

'He swears he met her five metres from the front doors.'

'Seriously! Look at them,' I splutter, pointing incredulously at the blank screen. 'They could be fricking dating by the way they're carrying on.'

'CCTV corroborates his version,' Mark adds with a frown. 'Camera outside the station has her getting out of a Range Rover and making a beeline to join him as he approached the doors. He's adamant that he's never met her before, and nor does he recognise her from anywhere. He claims she approached him and said they'd met previously at a recent law-firm party. He was too embarrassed to say otherwise, so he played along. That bit there, where they were laughing, is where she told a joke about a partner at her firm who had got drunk at the party. He claims to have no recollection of that, either, but admits he was at the party in question.'

'But you could just pull that stuff off social media,' says Milly.

'I'd expect so,' Mark agrees.

Taking a deep breath, Milly rewinds the video to where the woman leaves the station.

'Okay,' she recaps, 'so clearly she isn't a solicitor. It looks like their meeting was coincidental, but we're betting it wasn't.

She needed a distraction, and he offered the solution. Appear friendly with a solicitor the cops know and her credentials are all but established. Her ability to build a rapport in five seconds with a total stranger suggests either an uncanny gift or some real tradecraft –'

'Aha, the very word I was hoping for,' Gambon exclaims, clapping. 'Now, what did we just witness? A revenge hit for some nefarious misdemeanour this man Tanner perpetrated at some point during his time as a roving mercenary in some of the world's nastiest conflicts? Or was he silenced because certain parties were getting concerned about what he might tell us about the planning for the attack? Now, before you answer that, ladies, let me tell you an enlightening little story which may have some relevance.

'Back in World War Two, the Royal Airforce undertook an exercise to examine all their returning aircraft in a bid to understand where they had been damaged. They plotted all of this in a big diagram, marking the spot where each plane had been hit by enemy fire. And when they finished, they had amassed several very dense concentrations of damage. But there were a lot of areas also with no marks at all. These heavily damaged areas, they said, were where the planes needed to be reinforced the most, as that was where they were being hit the most. But then a mathematician called Abraham Waid, some Polish chap, pointed out that the damage was only being observed on planes that made it back safely. What they should do was armour the areas on the diagram where there was no observed damage. Because those areas, he said, were clearly where if hit the plane would not survive. Back then, they called this survivorship bias. It's a human logic error whereby people focus on the things right in front of them while they should be looking at what is not so obvious. My question, therefore, is what do you two make of this?'

'Play her arrival again,' Milly says, turning to Mark. 'Okay, first thing is the hair. Look how immaculately styled it is. It's nine in the morning. Who does that every day?' Milly gestures to her own wavy mass of hair. 'I'd say that's a wig. The sunglasses, again, more of the same. Deflect and distract. What accent did she speak with? Is she a Brit?'

'Nope. American, going by witness accounts,' Mark replies.

'Probably fake,' I mutter cynically. I peer closer and frown.

'Go on, spit it out, girl,' Gambon says, leaning forward.

'Look, call me nuts, but I figure there's all sorts of weird connected stuff going on here. Like, go back to where all this started. Pemberton-Smythe connected us with that French cow Nicole, right? Pardon my language. But we always reckoned on there being someone, or some group in the background, pulling the strings, right? I mean, someone clearly ordered her to slot him, right? She didn't seem the type to do it just for a laugh. But we don't know who. But when it all went to the dogs, they called her in to waste Pemberton all over his lovely carpet. And we know there was a connection between Pemberton and O'Leary. And when it came time to cut O'Leary out of the picture, they called in that dickhead Banovic and that French cow again. We know Banovic was clearly connected to that Swiss banker at the observatory who channelled all that money to the various groups in the attacks. But Banovic is out of the picture now, thankfully. These groups led us to that arms dealer in East London. He promptly fingers this South African guy. And now almost immediately after they pick him up at Heathrow, a nondescript woman strolls into a police station and slots him with two in the chest and one in the head. Which is the exact same thing that happened to Pemberton-Smythe, by the way.'

'You think that's *Nicole*?' Milly exclaims.

'It's an interesting theory,' Gambon notes, peering intently over his half-moon glasses at me. 'And exactly what I was thinking. So, is it her?'

'Hey, look, your guess is as good as mine,' I reply. 'The video's kind of grainy, and she does a nice job of not giving the camera a good front-on view. Who knows? Maybe.'

'Isn't it strange,' Milly says, thinking aloud, 'how you can get hi-def video from the surface of Mars, but we can't even get clear video from a CCTV a few miles away?'

'Police station cameras don't cost quarter of a million quid,' Mark offers sarcastically.

'Foxton, focus,' Gambon interrupts. 'Is it her?'

'Sorry, sir. Look, it could well be. Height looks about right. As does build. Those huge glasses hide a lot of her face, as does the hair. But the odds are on our side, right? She does seem to pop up whenever their plans, whoever *they* are, hit a snag. Shoes are definitely her style.'

'Okay, that I agree with,' Milly laughs.

'Less than scientific, but I have to say it concurs with my analysis,' Gambon says. 'You've both seen her before, and on multiple occasions. If anyone could confirm the theory, it would be you. Thank you, girls. That will be all.'

As we leave, we overhear Mark comment, 'Well, this all hinges on your idea that these events are connected. Issue I have, as do a lot of people up in London, is that it's all rather tenuous. Fact is, Gambo, not to put too fine a point on it, you have no motive. There's lots of what and when, but very little why. Serial killers leave more of a pattern than this. Until that changes, people will continue to take the product coming out of your shop with a pinch of salt.'

'He's not wrong,' Milly says with a frown, closing the door behind us.

'Yeah, tell me about it. What was that story of his all about? Was that just the most random thing ever?'

'It felt like it, right? But nothing Gambon does is random. What's he trying to tell us? I assume it's a warning of some kind about taking the wrong actions based on what you think you can see but that's actually wrong because you're not seeing the whole picture.'

'How's that meant to work? Now we're into known unknowns.'

'Actually, I think he means the unknown unknowns,' Milly replies.

'So, what aren't we seeing?'

'Beats the hell out of me,' she sighs.

*

For much of the rest of the day, the startling update from MI5 is all Milly and I can talk about. That is until Anabel bursts excitedly into our study just after eight in the evening. By this time, Luther and Nigel have already finished their prep assignments and joined us. Collectively, we look up, intrigued, as Anabel sinks down onto my roommate's bed beside Milly.

'Do spill,' I urge, seeing the excited look on her face.

'You're not going to believe this,' she begins. 'Juicy gossip. They just took Richard James up to the san.'

'Oh dear,' says Milly. 'What happened to him?'

'Think it's more like, what did Farabee do *to* him?' she sniggers, clearly amused.

'Well, do tell,' says Milly. 'This'll be good.'

'Apparently,' Anabel says excitedly, leaning forwards to share her news, 'Farabee went over to' – her voice drops conspiratorially – 'shag him, but she got a bit rough and tore his...' She giggles incessantly. 'His...'

'Yeah, go on!' Milly urges.

'... his foreskin.'

'Eww,' both boys say loudly, recoiling in horror.

'Seriously?' Milly snorts. 'How?'

'Well, I don't know,' Anabel cries. 'How do you think?'

'Wait,' I exclaim, laughing. 'Richard James, as in the Sinclair upper-sixth-form guy?'

'That's him,' Anabel says, nodding.

'The school prefect?'

'Yup.'

'The guy who stood up for Farabee in the canteen, back whenever it was?'

'Yup.' Milly nods.

'See, no good deed goes unpunished,' I quip.

'Yeah, that's got to suck,' Nigel adds sympathetically. 'Wow, I mean, no girl's worth that, right?'

There is a moment's pause as we remember just whom we are talking about here. Then, as one, we fall about laughing.

*

News travels fast, which is ironic given that one of the school's primary goals is to instil a culture of secrecy in its pupils. The following morning, upon taking our seats in the first class of the day, the reverend steps up to the rolling blackboard and pulls it down in search of a clear space upon which to write. However, much to his irritation, and the class's amusement, what rolls around from the rear of the board is a very graphic, albeit slightly amateur manga-esque chalk drawing of a girl and a boy in what looks like the aftermath of last night's unfortunate accident.

Crude it might be, but it's enough to send the class into fits of laughter. All eyes immediately search for and hone in on Farabee, who has frozen, a mixture of horror and seething anger welling up behind her reddening face. As the reverend hurriedly wipes the offending image off, it becomes clear who in Grey's is driving the recent anti-Farabee sentiment, as none other than Candice Hardcastle walks past her and tauntingly tears a sheet of paper slowly beside her ear. Victoria doesn't look up or react in any noticeable way but quietly fumes, glaring at the table top. Laughing, Hardcastle stomps off, clearly proud of herself.

'What's that all about?' I whisper.

'Not sure,' Milly replies. 'Heard it was something to do with the summer placements. Hardcastle wanted VFP to get her into the Foreign Office or something like that. Seems her dad said no. Didn't like the look of Hardcastle.'

'Can't say I blame him.'

'I know. But the rumour is, VFP didn't even ask him and just said no.'

'Well, that'll do it.'

Looking Farabee up and down, I notice she is not in her usual strutting high heels today, but rather a pair of plain black loafers. She seems diminished in stature as a result – not just shorter but less intimidating, too. And significantly less confident.

'Oh, how the mighty fall,' Milly reflects gleefully, leaning in so not to be overheard by anyone.

'Yeah. People love to tear things down, don't they? I can't help but watch with kind of mixed emotions, though, don't you think? On the one hand it's way overdue poetic justice –'

'Amen,' Milly says emphatically.

'Yeah, but on the other hand, everyone's human. And I remember how my friends turned on me after that whole mess in Morocco. Just like that. It wasn't vicious or hateful, but being abandoned by those we thought were our friends hurts, right? Whoever you are. Admittedly, I hadn't been Queen Bitch to half the planet, but even so I remember how isolating and hurtful it was.'

'Oh my God, are you actually feeling sorry for her?'

'I don't know. Maybe a little. Look at her. She has no idea how to deal with this. It's kind of sad, and a little pathetic, too.'

'Serves her right. And I'm not so sure she's that vulnerable. Probably just staying quiet while she privately schemes on how to pay Hardcastle back with interest.'

'Yeah, maybe...'

Bouts of sniggering continue throughout the lesson as the reverend drones on in his usual patronisingly moralistic monologue. One that will likely continue without pause until the bell finally goes. Cautiously, people cast quick, judgement-filled glances back at Farabee from time to time. She makes a stoic effort to ignore all of them.

Nonetheless, the under-trodden are getting bolder, I realise.

The final straw comes halfway through class when the reverend begins to write on the board. Candice Hardcastle turns quickly and, with a venom-filled sneer, flicks a fountain pen directly at Farabee. Her aim is undeniably good. A splash of vivid red ink sprays across Farabee's face in what looks like some kind of horrific arterial gush.

'Oh, Richard, what did I do?' Hardcastle hisses cruelly.

A hushed, deathly silence falls over the class; all eyes are on Farabee as Hardcastle stares on challengingly, clearly proud of herself. Up by the board, the reverend continues, either unaware of or simply not interested in what is happening behind him.

Slowly, Farabee looks down emotionlessly at the larger splatter of red ink that continues down across her crisp white shirt.

'Bet she wishes we were in ETS today,' Milly whispers, captivated by the thought of what could now happen. 'Wouldn't show on the black uniform.'

Suddenly, Farabee's chin and bottom lip wobble, ever so slightly, and an unexpected burst of emotion wells across her face. I can't tell if it is seething anger or a sign of imminent tears. Hardcastle sniggers and turns back to face the front, confident nothing will come of it. Amazingly, Farabee holds herself together, stands tall, gathers her bag and then heads towards the door without so much as asking for permission to leave.

'Yeah, keep walking,' Hardcastle sneers under a poorly disguised cough. 'Turn left at the end of the driveway.'

'Oh, lay off, will you?' I exclaim with an exasperated sigh.

'Piss off,' Hardcastle hisses. 'As if you care.'

'She may be a prize bitch, but you're an arsehole, Candice,' I fire back. 'Yeah, sure she gives it out, but at least it's verbal. And anyone can dish that back if they want. But you, you enjoy physically bullying people because you're bigger. So yeah, while I hate her, I hate you more.'

'Like I care,' Hardcastle replies dismissively, turning to cast glances left and right along her bench of fellow Grey's lower-sixth for support. Interestingly, most avoid her gaze. In a huff, her shoulder slump and she sits fuming in silence.

As the class settles back into order, the reverend continues as if nothing has happened. Few speak for the rest of class. Beside me, Milly stays ominously silent and simply gazes thoughtfully out the window and across the sports pitches. I expect she is not particularly happy that I defended Farabee. Not that I would call it that. But her body language is rigidly tense. Privately, I would hope she understands why I told Hardcastle to lay off. Realistically, though, that's unlikely. But if we don't heal, nothing good can come of it. Surely? Or so I'd like to think. Perhaps that's hopelessly optimistic. And I realise most of my housemates would probably call me naïve. And maybe I am. Though I'd prefer idealistic. Not that I'd argue the point, not after the years of misery Farabee has subjected them to.

When the bell finally goes, a mind-numbing thirty minutes later, the class trudges out, bored and evidently keen to escape. I hang back and wait for Milly. She smiles awkwardly and hugs her books tightly to her chest as she heads for the door.

'Hey, please don't be cross,' I say softly as we emerge outside into the fresh air. 'I can't stand Hardcastle, that's all.'

'I'm not annoyed,' Milly says, stopping to turn to me. 'Just conflicted.' Then, with a sigh, she glances past me, perplexed. 'What the –'

'You!' comes an accusing scream from behind me. I turn to see Farabee emerge from the bushes that press up against the exterior brick wall of the old teaching block. Intrigued, we watch in fascination as she delicately extricates herself from the bush and carefully steps through the flower bed towards us.

'So you know, I don't need your help,' she snaps bitterly.

'What are you doing skulking in the flower beds?' asks Milly.

'I am not skulking.'

'It kind of looks like you are,' Milly replies, more defiantly than usual. 'And from the look of your shoes, I'd say you've been skulking in there for quite a while. Were you waiting for *us*?'

Ordinarily, Milly answering back would have been rewarded with a venomous blast from Farabee's notoriously sharp, icy tongue. But not today. Instead, Farabee simply scowls, clearly aware that she was, indeed, skulking in the undergrowth. Finding her thoughts, she jabs a well-manicured nail at me.

'This is all your fault,' she hisses.

'How can it possibly be *my* fault?' I retort.

'You gave them the idea that people could give me crap.'

'Oh, spare me the bollocks, Victoria. You've spent the last four years spewing the nastiest, most racist and belittling crap to my friends. Worse, you made all those gits whom you called friends think it was alright. And now someone comes along and stands up to you, and as a result your pack of feral friends turns on you. And you think it was *me* who gave them the idea!'

'Whatever,' she snaps. 'I don't need your sympathy, either. If you don't think I can deal with something like this, then you are sorely mistaken.'

'For a second there,' I laugh, 'I almost thought I saw a glimmer of humanity. A touch of vulnerability. Something that might even make you, dare I say it, potentially likeable.'

'Tolerable might be closer to the mark,' Milly notes flatly. 'At a great arm's length.'

'Don't be stupid,' Victoria replies with the faintest hint of a sideways smile.

'I saw that, too,' I reply as I wander off with Milly, partly amused and deeply intrigued what she will now do to pay Hardcastle back with interest.

'Don't for a second think this means I like you people,' she calls after us.

'We wouldn't dream of it,' Milly shouts back. 'And the feeling's mutual, by the way!'

Laughing coldly, Farabee disappears back into the bushes.

'You know, just when I thought I had her totally sussed out as fitting in the perma-bitch bucket...' Milly says, staring back at the swaying bushes, still perplexed.

'Yeah, you're not wrong there. If there's one thing this place isn't short of, it's weirdo onion characters. The hard-to-read ones who just keep shedding layers.'

'Well, she's a snob. Landed family, huge estate, lady of the manor type,' Milly reflects. 'Who knows what's going on in that over-privileged, calculating mind.'

CHAPTER 6

HIGHLY UNORTHODOX

Godolphin Park School

S ubmissions for our lower-sixth summer-term placements were submitted two weeks ago, just before half-term began. Since everyone returned to school after a welcome week off, the sense of excitement has grown, almost feverishly so, until all anyone is able to talk about is where they hope to be assigned and where they hope not to be assigned.

All the recent fretting, the hushed conspiratorial gatherings at meal times, the tension – which was especially palpable this morning at breakfast – has been leading up to this moment. The announcement.

An air of nervous anticipation hangs over the ETS hall. The entire lower-sixth is present, arranged in orderly rows, all facing front, watching, as the headmaster reads off assignments from a long list.

Many are off to Legoland, as he amusingly refers to MI6's headquarters. Another large group are off to Box 500, as he calls MI5. Some are bound for the Foreign Office. Unsurprisingly, Farabee-Peacock is in that group. Hardcastle isn't.

Nigel will go to Hanslope Park, a large country estate in Buckinghamshire. He is giddy with excitement as he quietly describes with relish a fabulous old country manor surrounded by leafy parkland and barbed wire. I soon understand why he's so excited, for it's where Q Branch is based. His smile disappears when Dr Gambon jokes about how he has great faith that Nigel can help improve Q Branch's IT help desk.

What I did not realise was just how many people lend MI6 their country estates when they are abroad for extended periods. But, as Gambon explains, going wildly off topic and disappearing down a mental rabbit hole, it makes sense. Not only does it significantly reduce the service's fixed real-estate costs, but it also provides the landlord with a tenant who can reliably keep squatters and New Age travellers off their land while they spend the summer in the Bahamas or the winter in Niseko, whatever it may be.

Not surprisingly, Luther is off to Cheltenham, just as he had hoped. His grin is almost as large as Nigel's when he finally realises Gambon was joking about the help desk.

And while many others get the assignments they wanted, some don't, like Candice Hardcastle, who receives a posting with naval intelligence, on live operations somewhere in the North Atlantic on a task force frigate.

'Wow, there's the payback you were looking for,' Milly whispers. 'You know she gets really seasick.'

'Who, Hardcastle?'

'Uh-huh.'

'That's actually pretty funny. Knowing Farabee, bet she's sorted it so they bunk her in the worst possible place on the ship, like as high up as possible, where the lurching from side to side will have her almost permanently in the toilet.'

'Isn't the naval term the head?'

'Who knows. Maybe. How long's it for?'

'Ah, long enough, I reckon,' Milly muses.

As we listen, it becomes increasingly disconcerting that neither Milly's, Anabel's nor my name is mentioned. And when Gambon finally lays his list aside, we three glance questioningly across at each other.

'That can't be good,' Milly notes.

'Telling me,' I reply, peering left and right to see if anyone else was left out.

It appears not.

'Right, that's it, everyone,' Gambon announces. 'Buses will begin arriving for the station run at midday. Collection is outside Big-School. Promptness will be appreciated. Please collect your itineraries and train tickets from Mr Sable before you leave.' He points to the back of the hall, where Frank is standing at a table covered with large brown envelopes.

'You think it's a mistake?' I ask Milly as Anabel walks towards us, an equally troubled look on her face.

'Doubt it,' Milly says, smiling at her girlfriend. 'Nothing happens by accident around here.'

'Did I miss something or were none of our names called?' Anabel enquires.

'Yeah, we were just discussing that.'

'What do you think that's all about?'

'Good question,' I reply, pointing at the long white corridor which leads to the lift to the geology building, far above. 'Now what?'

We watch as a noticeable commotion ripples along the queue of pupils gathered near the mouth of the tunnel waiting to collect their envelopes from Frank. The line parts and a tall, suited man strides into the hall.

'Holy crap!' Nigel whispers behind us. 'What's the minister for defence doing here?'

'That's Forbes?' I exclaim.

'Do you actually watch the news?' Milly asks.

'Don't start. Just didn't recognise him is all.'

In person, Guy Forbes is a lot bigger than he looks on TV. Both in terms of height and girth. But he carries his almost Corleone-esque bulk with relative ease. In fact, it only makes him more intimidating than his notorious reputation would suggest. For while his public persona is classic politician, serious but smiley, there's no shortage of hearsay and rumours within MI13 about his unpredictable character behind the scenes: sometimes gruff, resolute and menacing, at other times dry and pointed, and on occasion slight in manner and almost invisibly passive aggressive. His reputation for delivering curt, career-ruining nods of dismissal to those he deems inferior to himself or who fail him is legendary. Humour is virtually unheard of. Yet occasionally, when the constellations begin to align with whatever scheming Machiavellian plan is on his mind, rumour has it one might just be lucky enough to see a wry, crooked half smile creep in.

'Right, are we doing this?' Forbes says loudly to Gambon as he marches stiffly across the hall towards the headmaster. 'Where are they, then? I don't have all day. Chop-chop, Gambo. PM wants me back in London by early afternoon.'

His voice is a deep, rich baritone, albeit with a dangerous edge of authority. His accent oozes privilege, betraying a public-school education and a lifetime of being surrounded by people from similarly landed backgrounds. Eton, most likely.

Sighing, I push thoughts of Alex from my mind. Forbes's words are deliberate and purposeful. He peppers his speech with mid-sentence pauses which hang, empty, ominous and threatening, before he launches into his next thought.

Pointing to us with an unenviable scowl, Gambon hails us over.

'Miss Foxton, Miss Butterworth, Miss Heathcote-Wong. This way, if you please.'

'Oh, that can't be good,' Nigel comments. 'You guys must have really screwed up this time.'

'Yes, thank you, Nigel, for being absolutely no support at all,' Milly mutters dryly. 'Come on, let's see what this is all about.'

'Yeah, Nige,' I add. 'Sometimes you really have the social skills of an out-of-date packet of ham.'

The joke elicits a short-lived giggle from the three of us, before we resign ourselves to what promises to be a spectacular roasting of epic proportions. Forbes watches us with an appraising eye as we approach. His stare lingers on me for a fraction longer than might be considered polite.

Then, turning to Gambon, he says, 'Right, thank you, Headmaster. I'll be needing a private word with your pupils. We'll use one of those classrooms over there.' Looking at Anabel, he adds, 'I take it you are the China expert in this little group. Good, well, lead the way.'

Darting a glance at Gambon, I see that an unchaperoned meeting was not part of the plan. Nonetheless, his clear irritation registers as nothing more than a faint flicker in the eyes before composure returns to his face. Smiling, he points the way but doesn't follow.

'Sir, our names weren't called for the –' Milly begins, only to be quickly cut off.

'Yes, we'll discuss that later,' Gambon replies. 'Best deal with this first.'

Once inside the room, which looks out across the hall, Guy Forbes closes the door, sighs and points to the seats closest to the teacher's desk. I ease myself down onto a chair, as do Anabel and Milly. Amusingly, we all cross our legs at the same time. My grey uniform pencil skirt with its high side slit which is perhaps an inch closer to risqué than is conservative rides up accommodatingly. As I glance at Forbes, my brain does the calculations, rapidly gauges the angles, considers the view and quickly concludes there's a better than average chance he can see a little too much. I rise briefly, tug the skirt down emphatically and settle again, repositioning my crossed leg at a lesser, more considered angle.

All the while he keeps his eyes on me, unblinking, in a studied, almost challenging manner. Then, for a second, he smiles in amusement and chuckles. It irks me that he already knows more about me than I'd like.

Outside in the hall, the bell chimes, denoting what would usually be the end of the second class of the morning. Today, it sounds more like the last call for a departing train.

'I appreciate this might all seem a little unorthodox,' Forbes begins, 'but sometimes this is just the way things have to be. Fact of the matter is I'm here at the behest of the PM. He's in a bit of a pickle, you see, and he needs your help.'

'Sorry, can I just ask…' Milly interrupts cautiously, glancing at Anabel and me, '… are you sure you have the right people? I mean, what could the *prime minister* possibly need *our* help on? Surely he has the entire government at his disposal, doesn't he? I mean, especially for really important things, which I assume this must be, you know, given that it requires a senior cabinet minister to come personally?'

'You must be the algo-cryptologist?' Forbes replies with a trademark wry, crooked smile. 'The brains of this little operation, I hear. Well, this is called plausible deniability. I'm sure you understand how sensitive this facility is. Direct association between the prime minister and it in any way, especially through a personal visit, could be reputationally problematic. He has enemies everywhere. And as you can tell by the series of incessant bloody leaks, someone is actively trying to destroy him, and possibly the government. Fact is, we don't know who to trust anymore. Many of these embarrassing leaks concerned highly sensitive issues which were known only to a very select group of key people. It may mean members of the security services could even be involved. And over the last few months, several high-profile, often very embarrassing stories about members of the cabinet have hit the press. Including myself, I might add.'

'You mean the potential closure of that big naval shipyard up in Scotland?' Milly asks.

'Which was absolutely untrue,' Forbes stresses, wagging his finger, suddenly every bit the voter-engaged politician. 'It was a management restructuring. Nothing more. Another media half story.'

'Sorry. Just asking.'

'Let's be clear, shall we?' says Forbes as he drapes his suit jacket over the back of the teacher's wooden chair. Sitting on the other side of the desk to us, he continues, 'Everything that's going on, all the effort, everyone pulling out all the stops, is for one purpose: to find out who was behind the March Massacres. The potential fallout if we get it wrong or fail could be colossal.

The very survival of the government might be at stake. So, let's not mince our words. Collectively, we – the entire intelligence and law-enforcement community – failed to stop the single most deadly terrorist attack in the UK's history…'

He pauses, but his eyes momentarily drift in my direction and immediately I know what he's really saying. A look of pitying consolation and then it's gone, too fast for the others to notice, but the implication hits home hard. I am to blame.

He continues quickly, looking away again.

'Thousands dead, even more wounded. A nation tearing itself apart in sectarian reprisals. Law and order stretched to breaking point. It's not hard to imagine the military being called in soon to bring order to the chaos. Which is largely why the PM recently appointed me as deputy prime minister. Now, if we don't find out who was behind this, we could be looking at a collapse of the whole system. There needs to be a bogeyman, you understand? The nation demands it. But that's a totally different problem to what I came here today to discuss with you three.'

'How can we help, sir?' Milly asks, edging forward like a keen journalist at a press conference.

'Right, well, just between us, let me ask what you three make of all these highly damaging leaks in the press? A number of them have resulted in several key ministers having to resign, which has weakened the government significantly. I suppose what I am asking is, what if all of it is connected?'

'You think there's a single person behind all of them?' Anabel asks dubiously.

'Possibly,' he replies, shrugging. 'If that's true then whoever is behind all of this is smart, no doubt very clever, and completely politically motivated.'

'Oh good. For a moment there I thought you were going to ask us to find out who's behind the attacks?' I exclaim with relief.

'No, Ms Foxton. Half of the intelligence services and most of the police forces across the country are working on that. Instead, what I have been asked by the PM to request your assistance on, the three of you, is in finding out who is behind these leaks. They must stop, you hear? They are undermining confidence in the government and hindering our ability to handle the situation. I won't say any more, because I don't want to influence your investigation with spurious suspicion or conjecture.'

He chuckles, and part of me wonders whether he hasn't already succeeded in doing exactly that. The suspicion is already planted, whether we like it or not.

'Now, that said,' he continues, 'if finding the culprit leads us to even bigger discoveries, then so much the better, wink-wink, nod-nod, if you get my gist. But for now, concentrate on the leaks. Let's agree to continue this conversation when you've found something a little more substantial than an old politician's natural suspicion, shall we?'

'When should we do this?' Anabel enquires. 'We start our summer placements in literally a couple of hours. How do we fit this in with that?'

'No, this *is* your summer placement.'

'I'm sorry. Is that official?' Anabel asks.

'Oh, yes. All agreed with your lot here.'

'Okay,' Milly says, firing an intrigued look in my direction. 'In that case, do you have any ideas who might want to hurt the prime minister?'

'Given the subject matter behind most of the leaks, logic suggests it could be a government minister or a senior civil servant. And therein lies the problem. If true, this could hurt the PM, badly. Especially if it's a minister whom he appointed. And right now, that's not what the party, nor the country needs. Now, if this proves to be the case, then given the potential connections such a person might have within the intelligence community, you can see why we can't approach any of the main services. Too likely it could leak. However, you are all so far outside of that circle that we can be pretty sure they won't have feelers here. That makes you three the best resources we have to work on this. You know what's going on, and I suppose you also have powerful motivation to see this through.'

'Sorry, I don't understand what you mean?'

'Oh, yes you do, Ms Butterworth. While no one will say it to your faces, especially yours, Ms Foxton, the fact is that success here will go a long way to redeeming MI13's reputation in certain circles after the fiasco in getting those lists out of Switzerland.'

Before any of us can interrupt, he raises his hand for calm and restraint.

'Now don't misunderstand me. I'm not trying to play on anyone's guilt here, and I can only imagine how it must feel. And so you know, I heard about the home secretary. Bang out of order. No one could have known the importance of those lists. So, no one's getting blamed, even if some are specifically looking to assign blame. Understand? That said, people will talk, and knowing what they're saying can give the necessary motivation to put them firmly in their place. I assure you, cracking this will do that, in a very profound manner.'

He sits back and smiles beguilingly. On the face of it – if it wasn't so obvious that we are being completely manipulated and in such an underhand manner – this appears to present the opportunity for redemption, and a fun placement, also. But it is redemption for something I don't feel was our fault. Nonetheless, I am keen, as I imagine are Milly and Anabel, to get something important to work on. Even if all the pressure we'll be under makes me nervous about screwing up, again.

'Okay,' I reply with a sigh. 'Where do you want us to start?'

'Well,' Forbes says, reaching for his briefcase and removing from it a bound Manila folder. 'My assistant and I put this together for you. It's a little rudimentary and is based upon those whom we think *could* have had access to information that was leaked. You'll see it is collated in chronological order. There are notes in there about the associated briefings or internal memos that were held or circulated in the weeks prior to each leak. It was done quite quickly, so it may not be complete. But it's a start.'

He holds up a piece of notepaper.

'This has log-in details for the cabinet office server, which you'll need. From there you can see what briefing papers went to whom, and when. It might take a bit of digging but should give you the whole picture. Additionally, in the dossier we have cuttings of pretty much every leak. For the most part, these relate to the breaking of each story which led to a minister's resignation. We omitted reprints. In nearly every case, each one was first published by a single newspaper. So maybe there's something in there that will help.'

Shrugging, he slides the folder across the table.

'How do we contact you if we find something?' Anabel asks as she picks it up, examines the first few pages and passes it to Milly.

'You can message me on my mobile. Typically, my days are filled with back-to-back meetings, so responses may not be the fastest. But I'll give you my card.' He lays it on the desk and scribbles another number on the back using a Houses of Parliament-branded biro he retrieves from inside his jacket pocket.

'One rule, though. Speak only to me or my private secretary. And his details are also there, on the back. No one else. Under any circumstances,' he stresses, holding the parliamentary business card back threateningly until we agree with nods.

'Good, because loose lips sink ships.'

With a laugh, he rises, gathering his jacket.

'And what if we find out who it is?' I ask. 'Like, what then?'

'Then we'll see,' he replies with a dismissive wave of his hand. He glances at his watch and makes for the door, mumbling to himself as he goes.

'Right, best be off, then.'

He doesn't look back. After a moment's contemplatory pause, all three of us rush to the viewing window and watch as he hastily departs, as loudly as he arrived, shouting an insincere goodbye to no one in particular.

'What do you make of that, then?' Anabel asks, grinning widely.

'Good question,' I ponder aloud.

'Quite. But how interesting was that?' Milly comments thoughtfully. 'Come on, let's go find Gambon. See what he has to say.'

By the time we find the headmaster, the fleet of buses have come and gone, whisking the rest of the lower-sixth off to their various placements all over the country.

'Feels odd to be the only L6 left in the whole school, doesn't it?' Anabel says as we make our way towards the headmaster's whitewashed house nestled within the school grounds not far from SH.

'Sure does,' says Milly.

The quaint little thatched cottage is surrounded by thigh-high, white trellised fencing. Ivy envelops much of its walls, and several neat little flower beds encircle it, arranged between well-maintained patches of lawn.

'Let's see what his take on all this is,' I say, flicking the latch on the wooden gate. The front door opens before we are halfway up the short garden path.

'Come on in,' Dr Gambon mutters, waving to us. 'This'll be interesting.'

'Ha, that's what I said,' Milly squeals excitedly to us.

We settle on one of the sofas in his cosy front living room. Flocked teal wallpaper covers three walls. The fourth, over towards the kitchen, remains unpainted, stark and white in contrast. Photos of the headmaster's family and friends adorn the mantelpieces and bookshelves. A host of unusual decorations are dotted liberally around the room. Above the fireplace hangs a framed revolver set in a glass case. Ornate gold-and-black Arab headgear sits on a shelf near the front window, beside a photo of a man in sunglasses atop an enormous camel. On the corner desk sits a graffitied lump of broken brick. Piles of books, mostly hardbacks, are stacked beside the sofas, on coffee tables and near the window alcove. Large, thick, intimidating tomes, including various editions of *Jane's Fighting Ships* and the *Dictionary of American Naval Fighting Ships*, sit nestled amongst books on fleet tactics and biographies of renowned admirals. A large collection of maritime maps litters the living room floor.

'Doing some spring cleaning,' he explains. 'Couldn't trouble you for a cup of tea, could I?' he asks, looking up at me as he settles into one of the two mismatched armchairs on the other side of the central coffee table. 'I seem to remember your knowing where my kitchen is.'

'Know where your whisky is, too,' I reply.

'Not that you get to have any this time.'

I grin and leave my friends befuddled at the overly familiar exchange. The kettle has just boiled, and a teabag lies waiting beside an old green cup. Once I set it down beside him, I ease myself into the remaining armchair and relax.

By the time we finish briefing him on our strange meeting with the minister of defence, Gambon is leaning forward keenly with his fingers steepled. Lost in thought, he peers out the window into his front garden. We sit in silence until he speaks. When he does, it is slow and measured.

'Do you feel like they already have a suspicion about whom it could be?'

'Possibly, sir,' Milly replies. 'We have yet to look through what he's given us, but it does feel like their suspicion is already focused on a small group.'

'Yes, it does, doesn't it? It is always ominous when the security services are asked to prove what sounds like a foregone conclusion. I prefer more open-ended questions.'

'Sir, you must know Guy Forbes,' says Milly. 'What do you make of him?'

'He's a narcissist,' Gambon replies unflinchingly. 'He sees everyone as being here to do his bidding. To orbit him in a holding pattern until such time as he has need of them. The irony of it is, if you go back through his career, it's never actually stood against him. He's flip-flopped from flamboyantly delivered broken promises to outright lies and backstabbed his way up the political totem pole. Yet none of it has stopped him from becoming this country's defence minister.

He's known to have run roughshod over friends, family and those who work for him. Collateral damage, he'd call it. So, be aware, won't you?'

'Great. Just what we need,' I sigh.

'His political view is pure threatism, not that that is a real word, but it serves to describe him well. He sees powerful, determined and destructive forces out there who want to destroy the UK. I suspect he sees himself as being surrounded by complacency and people incapable of understanding these threats or summoning the necessary courage to combat them. He sees it as his duty, therefore, to use his position to tackle these threats quietly but aggressively. Like Dick Cheney, Forbes has fooled a lot of people into thinking he's just a government technician with no real agenda. Far from it: he has ambitions. And big ones. Those not alert enough may miss what he's up to.'

'So, how do you recommend we approach this assignment, sir?' Milly asks.

'Well, the assignment is a good one. From a practical perspective. But make sure to maintain your objectivity. Go through the materials he gave you. Trust it, fine, but verify everything, understand? I recommend you tackle it in two stages. First, go through all of it and draw out the connections to whittle your list down. See if anyone stands out. And then, if someone does, then we dig deeper. But be mindful of two things. The first is to ensure you don't fall into the trap of trying to make the facts fit any pre-imagined outcome. And the second is to ensure you do not get caught. Defence minister or not, this is highly irregular. These are cabinet members, don't forget: the people he's insinuating are the source of the leaks. None of whom got where they are without breaking some eggs. So, be careful. There's hypothesis testing and then there's accidentally giving credence to a foregone conclusion and impacting real people's lives. But that's life in a blue suit, I suppose,' Gambon notes dryly as we stand to leave.

'Sorry?' says Milly.

'Doesn't matter. Old navy saying, Ms Butterworth, old navy saying. One thing, though, which struck me as curious…'

'Yes, sir, what's that?'

'His office requested you three. Specifically. By name.'

We stop near the door.

'Now why do you reckon they did that?' Pausing, he smiles, and then adds, 'Rhetorical. But worth bearing in mind, no?'

*

With summer placements now underway, it means no formal classes anymore for us. That combined with a significantly quieter espionage school has afforded my friends and I no end of free time in which to plunge headlong into our very secret and potentially contentious assignment.

Given the project's sensitivity, we opted for going old school, as Milly amusingly called it, and have assembled a row of large mobile whiteboards in an unused storeroom at the far end of a long corridor at the very back of ETS. This part of the facility was a later addition and is constructed from hastily poured concrete slabs. As a result it is cold, poorly heated and rarely used. But it is far enough away from the main hall to all but guarantee that no one will stumble in on us by accident. While it is enough for our needs, it does somewhat lack that homely feel. All bare concrete walls, harsh overhead strip lighting and desperately in need of a spring clean.

But once the dust, cobwebs and general grime were swept away, we soon filled it with folding tables and connected the power up to run the computers, printers and other equipment which Milly demanded we have. Anabel brought a music speaker, and I liberated a coffee machine from the lower-level pantry. With music playing and coffee flowing, we got to work.

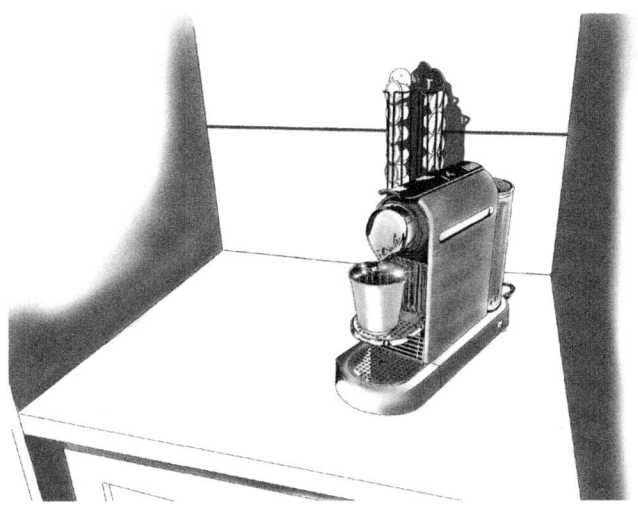

On the whiteboards we have stuck each of the various newspaper leaks in chronological order.

'Reckon we're better off doing this in sweeps?' Milly suggests as the last one is taped into place. 'Each sweep gets more granular and more nuanced. That allows us to analyse all this in a more structured way. But maybe we get lucky on the first one; I mean, you never know.'

With no objection or better ideas offered, that's what we do. As the days pass, favourite playlists are quickly identified and the coffee machine gets a near-constant workout; after half a week, we begin to hear complaints that there are no more capsules left in any of the ETS pantries. The white-boards gradually accumulate more and more Post-its and printed pages, until they resemble evidence boards from a TV detective series.

Milly's initial optimism that our first sweep could glean us credible insights into possible perpetrators is quickly dashed. Looking over the various major leaks which the government suffered, we find no single person who stands out as an obvious candidate. Nor can we find anyone who might have directly benefited from all the leaks. Several members of the cabinet and a good number of senior civil servants are potential suspects for each leak, given that they stood to gain politically from it, whether by way of the embarrassment it caused to those directly involved or because the leak resulted in resignations which in turn opened up positions for them.

But trying to find a single person who stood to gain from all proves to be a false trail. After a week of futile searching, we finally decide to move on to phase two, which requires the in-depth evaluation of all government papers, briefing notes, internal bulletins and committee agendas associated with each leak in a bid to identify those who had access to all. The credentials which Forbes shared with us work first time around. Printer cartridge quickly replaces printer cartridge and the large Xerox in the corner of the room churns out documents on a near-constant basis for hours every day.

'This is one sure-fire way to kill whole forests,' Anabel complains grimly as she removes another large stack of cabinet briefing documents, interdepartmental memos, white papers, ministerial consultations and formal legislative proposals.

The only thing that saves us from being driven insane by the needle in the haystack problem facing us is the fastidious attention to detail and near-obsessive levels of bureaucratic fervour which the civil service applied to their paperwork. What initially looked like a horrendous and unmanageable volume of documentation is rapidly made comprehensible thanks to the rigorous governance applied to their activities, which includes proper document versioning, formal meeting attendee registers and clear distribution tracking lists for all formal cabinet office bulletins and memos, not to mention the fastidious notetaking and action tracking we find in the meeting minutes.

Yet despite this, the sheer volume of materials stored on the cabinet office server is daunting, and the time it takes to sift through and cross-reference all the relevant documents consumes our every waking hour. From early in the morning until late at night, day after day, the three of us pore over the original source documents that must have been the golden source for a large proportion of the leaks. We cross-reference ideas, swap suspicions and share conspiracy theories each time we suddenly have a new brainwave about the source of the leaks.

Many names we can immediately remove from the list, as they were either not privy to certain documents, missed briefings or did not attend meetings. Others we cross off when we analyse their movements, based on the private calendars they each filed with the cabinet office, such as when they had been out of the country or in their constituency on critical days.

Yawning, I realise I have lost track of what day it is because we have barely left our makeshift bunker. However, I do know that I'm drinking my fifth espresso of the morning when Milly leans back with a puzzled frown on her face. Rubbing her eyes, she looks round at me.

'So, here's the problem. Actually, there are two big problems. The first is that the list is still just too big. These documents were often circulated to the whole cabinet. And then there are also all the private secretaries, the staff in the cabinet office, secretaries and a whole list of people.'

'Not exactly helpful, is it?' I reply with a sigh.

'Not really. I mean, they call these sensitive documents, but the distribution circles for these briefings are not exclusive. Really think we're going to have to come up with something else.'

'Okay,' I say. 'And the second problem?'

'Well, that's the fact that these leaks were about a whole lot more than what was in these cabinet briefing papers. Sure, a lot of them concerned confidential information related to government policies, ministerial mistakes, expense claims and so on. But there's a lot juicier stuff, too, that had to come from somewhere else entirely. The private affairs. The offshore trusts. The embarrassing skeletons in some of their closets. That stuff was in none of these documents. In fact, a lot of it was what you'd think would be private. And it wasn't discussed in meetings, either, that I can see. So, how did it get leaked along with all the embarrassing government policy stuff, like Forbes's proposed closure of that Scottish naval shipyard? No, this is clearly someone with not just really good access to information but who was also privy to a lot of gossip.'

'Agreed,' I say. 'And even though the leaks were published in a number of papers, that doesn't necessarily mean it wasn't the same person behind the whole thing.'

'I don't disagree. Guess the point is,' Milly explains, 'if we only use the documents Forbes gave us, then we'll never get the full picture, because the rest of the leaks had to stem from sources we'll never know. So, we're always going to have a gap.'

'Stop a sec. I just noticed something,' Anabel says from her table, which is covered with newspaper articles. For a few moments she furiously riffles through the stacks of paper before her, making marks here and there with a yellow highlighter, before slumping back with a triumphant smile. 'I don't know why I didn't spot it sooner. It's so obvious now. Remember when we plotted out where each story first appeared? And remember how there was no real pattern to which newspaper they appeared in?'

'Yeah,' I reply. 'The stories leaked in about half a dozen newspapers.'

'Slightly less, but basically right. And the lead journalist was different on each story, right?'

Milly and I both nod, intrigued as to where Anabel's thoughts are leading.

'But on every story, there's a second journalist credited. I've just checked and checked again. His name's always in a much smaller font, and often noted at the bottom as a contributing reporter, usually buried as far out of sight as possible, several pages back at the end of the continued article. But here's the thing: it's the same guy on every one of them.'

'Seriously?' I exclaim, rushing to her desk. 'Let's see.' Sure enough, skimming through the stapled cuttings she has assembled, I see that one highlighted name appears on all of them: Jeffrey Pelt, collaborative reporter. I look at Milly.

'What's a collaborative reporter?'

'I could make a guess.'

'I've never even seen anyone credited as that,' I say.

'Don't pretend that you read newspapers,' Milly giggles.

'Oh, that's harsh...'

'... but true,' Anabel sniggers. 'More seriously, though, how can one person work for that many newspapers? I'd figure if say you work for the *Guardian*, it's not like your work would ever appear in the *Times*, is it? So, how's this guy able to do it in the papers that broke these stories?'

Tapping her pen on the table, Milly pauses for a beat, and then asks, 'Who owns all those papers?'

'Give me a sec, I'll find out,' Anabel says, returning to her computer screen.

'Because the only logical thing I can think,' Milly says, looking over at me, 'is that the leaker went to a journalist he or she knew, and for whatever reason the people who own all these papers then spread the stories across a number of their newspapers.'

'Why bother?'

'Good question. Increased circulation across all your papers? Or maybe to make it look like there were more people leaking stories than there actually were. Maybe to make it look worse than it was. Or to cover for the fact they only had one source. Who knows?'

'Yeah, maybe,' I concede. 'Guess it appears more newsworthy if it looks like there are problems everywhere. Just publishing them in one place might not attract the same attention. Or it could look like the paper has a beef with the government.'

'Looks like you're right,' Anabel confirms, pointing to her screen. 'They're all part of the same media consortium. Albeit in some cases pretty well hidden through a weird ownership structure. Not impossible to find, but not blazingly transparent, either.'

'Which one?' Milly asks.

'International News Corp.'

'Is that the Australian one? The one Rupert Murdoch set up?'

'No, that's just plain News Corp.'

'Wow, imaginatively named, aren't they?' she laughs, rolling her eyes. 'Given they're both media companies with loads of creative people working for them. Okay, and who owns International News Corp?'

'Some guy called Wilson Irving. Correction, Sir Wilson Irving.'

'Sounds vaguely familiar. Who's he?'

'Just reading up on him now,' Anabel mumbles distractedly as she scans down the internet page. 'Seems he started out with property investments. But also inherited a ton, which I guess always helps. Landed family. House of Lords. Big estate up in Norfolk. Owns social media apps, magazines, news outlets and a film production company. Oh, he also owns W1 London FM radio.'

'Okay, so he's fairly minted,' I summarise with mock ambivalence. Seeing Anabel's troubled expression, I ask, 'What's up?'

'Well, something just occurred to me. And it's a language thing. So come here. Have a look at all these stories. There's a problem with them. It's subtle, but it's there alright. It's the collaborative thing that bugged me. I've been reading them over and over, and I noticed something. You'd imagine that any set of stories written by different journalists would be quite different in style, right? Even if you had the same assistant helping on each story. I mean that sounds fair, right?'

Milly and I both nod.

'But that's not what seems to have happened here. Because I'm pretty sure the same person wrote all these stories.

Each paper has its own house style, right, and offers up a different political slant. Some are a bit more tabloid, whereas a couple are more formal in style. And even though the stories are written in the style of the paper in which they appeared, they're full of little telltale signs that suggest they were written by the same person. Punctuation, turns of phrase, syntax, that kind of thing. Little quirks of written language.'

'You think this Pelt guy wrote *all* of these stories,' I say, 'and the papers just assigned a random lead journalist as the named primary on each story to make it less obvious?'

'Well, each of them is a political correspondent in their own right, so there's nothing wrong with that,' Anabel replies. 'But essentially, yes.'

'That's interesting,' Milly ponders, sucking intently on the end of her yellow-and-black pencil. 'Okay, wait a sec. We already have a shortlist of sorts with about half a dozen members of the cabinet on it, yes? And that eyes-only bulletin which only went to cabinet members ruled out all the permanent secretaries and support staff. So, we have the final names of those we know received all the relevant briefing papers and were privy to the information underpinning the policy-related leaks.'

Holding her finger in the air as if it will somehow stop her losing her train of thought, she walks to the whiteboard and from memory writes the names onto it.

'I suppose we might as well take the prime minister off,' I suggest. 'I mean, it's unlikely he's trying to sabotage his own government.'

'Perhaps,' she replies. 'But he's a politician. Who knows what warped intentions they have? Let's leave him for now and scratch him off if the evidence points towards someone else.'

'Yeah, okay. Oh, please let it be her,' I exclaim, pointing to the home secretary's name. 'Fate couldn't be that sweet, could it?' I laugh.

'Not exactly a fan of hers, then?' Anabel asks.

'Oh, don't even get me started on her. Winds me up to even think about it.'

'Right, well, err, moving swiftly on,' Milly says with an amused smile. 'I have another idea.'

'Go on,' I say.

'Cool, so I think we can change how we approach this. Until a minute ago we thought either the "leaker"' – she makes air quotes – 'was spreading their leaks all over the place to cover their tracks or that the government had several leaks. Which is what it looked like from the dossier, didn't it? All random and unconnected. Which is why we focussed on the underlying documents and who had access to what. But now that Belle's spotted this subtle little connection –'

'We go after the journalist,' Anabel interrupts excitedly.

'Yay, real spy stuff,' I laugh.

'Exactly,' Milly says, beaming proudly at her girlfriend. 'We concentrate on this Jeffrey Pelt guy and see where he leads us.'

'Sweet,' I exclaim, rubbing my hands together excitedly. 'What can I do?'

'Nothing,' she says. 'There's something I've wanted to try for a while. And we don't even have to leave the room.'

'Oh...'

'Don't be down,' she says reassuringly. 'I promise this will be so much easier, and a whole lot scarier. I'm actually kind of excited to try it.'

'Oh, is this that thing you were telling me about?' Anabel asks.

Milly giggles excitedly, clapping her hands, and darts a playful, adoring look at Anabel. She quickly outlines her plan, which compared to her usual plans is fairly simple, even if slightly morally questionable.

First, we need to find which newspaper in the media group primarily employs Jeffrey Pelt. Once done, it then takes Anabel less than two minutes to persuade that paper's news desk to give us his mobile number by claiming to have an important tip which he would doubtless be interested in but is too sensitive to send by e-mail.

With his mobile number in hand, it takes Milly less than three minutes to take control of his phone using a Smurf Suite application.

'So even though his handset is not being used right now, I can still send it an activation code,' she explains, 'which won't light up the screen or appear in his notification tray. But it gives us a remote link to his phone, and now we can sift through whatever's on it. And he has no idea. Kind of cool, don't you think?'

'Kind of scary,' I reply, quickly checking my own phone. 'So, we can go through all his apps, documents, messages and files from here?'

'Yeah, that's kind of concerning, isn't it?' says Anabel.

'Oh, that's not even the worst of it,' Milly gushes. 'This'll let me turn on his microphone or camera, and we can listen in on whatever he's up to. And he'll never have a clue, either.'

'Can anyone say, bye-bye, privacy,' Anabel comments grimly. 'Who needs to bug anyone anymore?'

'Wait, so the guy could be... like, you know, in the toilet, and...'

'Yup.'

'Eww, that's so gross,' I exclaim.

'Trust your mind to drop straight to the sewer,' Milly sighs.

'Try his e-mail first,' Anabel suggests. 'Maybe he names his source. Let me find who his editor is. Perhaps we'll find something where they mention the name?'

'Okay, let's try that,' agrees Milly.

A quick search brings up several recent e-mails, and Milly soon finds a chain between the journalist and an editor in which Pelt responds to a question from the parent company's general counsel confirming that all his meetings with his key source were done in person and that no electronic communications were ever exchanged.

'Well, that's a bummer,' she mutters, and reads on but is unable to find a name.

'He goes on to confirm that if the paper was ever sued or issued a court order, there'd be no electronic records that could be seized, and all his handwritten notebooks are stored somewhere safe.'

'Complicates things slightly, don't you think?' says Anabel.

'Yeah, well,' I reply, glancing at my phone as it begins vibrating furiously on the desk. 'I'm sure we'll… Hang on, let me see who this is. Yeah, hello?'

'Any news?' the caller barks.

'It's fricking Forbes,' I whisper, covering the handset's microphone. 'Oh, hi,' I reply. 'How can we help?'

'Any news?' he repeats, irritation creeping into his voice. It sounds like he is outside in a busy street. I hurriedly explain what we have done so far and run through the shortlist of potential names that we have.

'So, the problem is reducing the list further.'

'Hmm,' Forbes ponders moodily.

'But,' I blurt out, wary of his reaction, 'we've just found out that there was one reporter involved in all these stories, regardless of which paper published them. Which is weird. And that he always met his source – and it sounds like there was just one source – face to face.'

'Have you tried Sentinel?' he shouts against the wind.

'What's that?'

'Don't they teach you anything at that school of yours?!'

For an awkward moment, as a hot, prickly heat washes over me, I stammer for a response.

'What's Sentinel?' I whisper urgently to my friends.

'I know what it is,' Milly says. 'But we don't have access.'

'Okay, we know what it is,' I reply with relief. 'How do we get access to it?'

'My PS can get you that...' The line crackles and Forbes can be heard puffing with effort as he climbs into what I assume to be a London taxi, judging by the pitch of the engine I hear in the background. 'Houses of Parliament,' he orders and slams the door. As the taxi accelerates, he adds, 'It'll be sent over to you.'

With that, the line goes dead.

I turn to Milly with a questioning expression.

'It's a security application,' she says. 'One used by the government, members of the Royal family, people of strategic national importance, that sort of thing. It allows the security services to monitor where these people are at all times. It's a transponder they carry with them. Well, it was. The first generation were radio signal emitters. Today they tend to be loaded onto mobile phones which get issued to key people. But it's separate to GPS location.'

'So what?' I ask. 'How's it help us?'

'Well, I figure what he's getting at is that Sentinel still works even if the user turns off their normal GPS. Now, assuming Pelt didn't turn off his location settings on his phone, we could cross-reference his movements around the time of each leak with the Sentinel data for each of the potential suspects. I mean, I'm no expert, but that makes sense, wouldn't you say? At least worth a shot, no?'

'Seems he's already sent it through,' Anabel says, peering at our shared mailbox. 'That's quick.'

'Yeah, really quick,' I agree, watching over Milly's shoulder as she opens the e-mail to reveal a hyperlink, username and password.

'Okay, well, let's give it a go,' she says. 'See what we see.'

A palpable sense of excitement grips us as she logs into the system, and we quickly realise the potency of the information contained within it.

'While I do this,' she says, 'couldn't go grab me some lunch from the food hall, could you? I'm starving.'

Half an hour later, we return to find her waiting, desperate for food but with an enormous smile across her face.

'It took some digging,' she explains cheerfully as she keenly tucks into the large portion of cottage pie we brought her.

'And...?' I say enthusiastically.

Laughing, she points at the screen, and squeals, 'Come take a look.'

We gather around behind her as she explains what we are about to see.

'A while back, Five designed a program that tracks suspected terrorists and other POIs, which means –'

'People of interest, right?'

'Wow, you do listen in class. I'm impressed,' Milly says,

looking up at me with a teasing smile. 'They took that Covid contact tracing app and modified it to track instances of proximate contact between people's mobile devices, showing when the owners were in close contact. I took that and loaded up the movements of this Pelt guy from back when these stories were coming out thick and fast.'

A thin red line appears on the map of London, resembling a child's frenzied scribble.

'That there's all his movements over that period. Pelt's, I mean. Now watch when I load in the Sentinel data for each of the remaining possible candidates.'

In the same manner, several new darting lines appear, all in different colours.

'What a mess,' I laugh. 'How are we going to make sense of that?'

'We don't have to,' Milly says, grinning. 'This is where it gets really interesting. Are you ready? Oh my God, I'm so excited. Watch this!'

With a few taps and some clicks on the mouse, numerous black circles appear on the screen.

'Those,' she explains, 'are the instances where his phone came in close enough proximity to one of the ministers' phones. Now, I apply a statistical model over it, and we whittle down anything irrelevant.'

She selects a few options and parameters, and many of the lines disappear.

'What happened?' asks Anabel.

'I removed all the days when there was no contact.'

'Not sure that's much better,' I joke. 'I mean, look at it. What a dog's breakfast. And there, that cluster. What is that? Is that Westminster?'

'Yeah, but Pelt's a political correspondent, isn't he?' Milly notes. 'It's not exactly a surprise for it to register proximity to many of the ministers in or around the Houses of Parliament. Here, let me put an exclusion zone around it. That will leave us with just where they crossed paths out and about, which is more likely the case if you wanted to meet a journalist for an off-the-record meeting, wouldn't you think?'

The scribbled-upon-map suddenly becomes considerably less complicated. All that remains is the journalist's original red line and two additional lines, one green, the other blue, representing the last remaining possible candidates.

'So, each of those little red flags that just appeared is what?' I ask.

'Ah, they represent a moment in time when Pelt was in the necessary proximity to one of the potential leakers.'

'Still leaves quite a lot, though,' I note. 'Both lines cross with his a lot.'

'Who's left?' Anabel asks.

'Just her favourite person in the whole wide world,' Milly replies, pointing with amusement in my direction, 'the home secretary. And the minister of morality.'

'Oh, please, God,' I exclaim, clasping my hands together in prayer. 'Let it be that cow!'

'Can we whittle it down anymore?' Anabel asks.

'Yes. We need to bear in mind that they could have just passed each other by coincidence. A small world and all that. But see what happens if I tell it to only flag where they were in proximity for a prolonged period. Say more than five minutes. Watch this.'

With a press of a button, the trace map is simplified yet again, leaving considerably fewer tracked movements.

'Seems they were both meeting this guy,' observes Anabel.

'True,' I say. 'Any chance you can check what dates these meetings were? I mean, is there any pattern between them and when the stories actually broke?'

'Yay! I was waiting for one of you to ask.' Grinning hugely, Milly claps her hands, giddy with excitement. 'Check this out!'

With an enthusiastic punch of the enter key, a series of dates appear in a newly tabulated grid which appears on the right-hand side of the screen. Beside it, Milly opens another spreadsheet in which she has entered the dates of all the recent leaks which we could find.

'What do you see?'

As Anabel and I lean closer, Milly is unable to contain herself and blurts out, 'Styles met Pelt almost exactly two weeks before each news article was published. It's almost uncanny. And that's true for the ones that concerned matters recently discussed in cabinet, circulated in briefing materials and of a highly sensitive, personal nature.'

'Seriously?' I groan in disappointment. 'I was so hoping it would be the home secretary.'

'Look on the bright side,' Milly giggles. 'Who says it wasn't partly her, too? She certainly met with Pelt often enough, but nowhere near as often as Styles, and not on a timeline as correlated to the stories' publications. Watch this. These are Styles's movements on the days when he met the journalist. There's no doubt. Each time it was for about half an hour.'

To prove the point, Milly shows us their movements on each key date, drawing her finger across the trackpad to scroll across the map of the city.

'Stop, wait, go back,' I exclaim, pointing. 'I thought I saw something weird.'

'What?' Milly asks, rewinding the timeline.

'Not sure. It looked like Styles's location jumped. Wait, go back further. No, maybe it was the previous day. Yeah, okay, so stop. Watch here. He's in the Houses of Parliament. Looks like for most of the day, and then… see, right there! His signal. It literally jumped to Notting Hill.'

'Yeah, odd,' Milly murmurs, rewinding the movements again. 'You're right. It disappears and a second later pops up over there. Who knows? Latent signal interference, maybe?'

'Could he have taken the Tube, perhaps?' asks Anabel. 'Westminster to Notting Hill –'

'Perhaps,' I reply. 'Would be Jubilee, change at Oxford Circus for the Central line, or District and Circle all the way around. But it's not quick. Not that quick.'

'You think people like this take the Underground?' Milly says, smirking.

'True. But you never know. Either way,' Anabel concludes, 'glitchy program or not, it's still pretty concrete, isn't it?'

'You're right. It is,' I note, wagging a reproachful finger at the screen. 'But I'm kind of surprised, though. That pattern. That routine. I mean, it's like… fricking careless.'

'A little too careless,' Milly ponders thoughtfully.

'Yeah…' I nod, as I get up and head for the coffee machine again.

CHAPTER 7

ON GOVERNMENT SERVICE

Godolphin Park School

'Good God, I don't believe it. And… you are sure?' the minister for defence finally grumbles after a long, drawn-out pause, during which the full ramifications of our report finally sink in. 'This is very serious stuff. The man's one of the PM's closest allies, for Christ's sake.'

'We redid it three times,' says Milly, casting a nervous look at Gambon, Anabel and me.

'I can second that,' Gambon adds, leaning forward across his desk to speak into the phone. 'The analysis is sound. Based on the facts available, which we have gone through numerous times, it stacks up.'

A long, awkward silence follows. Gambon smiles and turns to look out of his large window, down towards the lake in the distance. The setting sun streams in through it, bathing his quaint, classically furnished office in a rich, warm glow.

'Known the man for years,' Forbes finally mutters. 'Heavens knows everyone talks in this place. Whether to gain allegiances, trade information or just to confide in another MP for support

or advice. But this… this is wholesale sabotage of his own party. How could he? How damned foolish. There goes any hope
it was just some disgruntled staffer, or a permanent undersec-
retary with a dignity at work gripe. Someone we could just
retire quietly. No fuss. No embarrassment to the government.'

'That said, sir,' I note hesitantly, 'we should point out
this is all based on ELINT. We have no actual direct human
intelligence available to substantiate it. That would probably
need to be the next step, just to be sure.'

'Who could I possibly ask to do that?' Forbes complains.
'He's far too well connected within the services. The man
plays golf with the deputy director general over at Five,
for Christ's sake. He'd know we were onto him before the
damned surveillance team was even selected. Besides, we've
gone to war on a lot less than this. Why not stop now? Surely
this is enough.'

Another uncomfortable pause follows. Silently, I gesture
at my friends and shrug questioningly at Gambon. He holds
up a finger.

'Hold that thought,' he says, unmuting the speakerphone.

'Why would he do this?' Gambon asks. 'Motive. Where
is it?'

'Bloody good question,' Forbes mutters. 'If I had to sink
to black humour, I'd joke and speculate he was so morally
offended by his cabinet colleagues' conduct that he wasn't able
to control himself. Morally compelled to sell them out. God
knows. But I see where you are going with that thought. We
need motive, I suppose. So then, this next stage surveillance,
what did you have in mind? And why can't you lot do it? Isn't
that half of what you do anyway? And you have your whole
summer placement free. What do you say, Gambon?'

'Well,' the headmaster replies. 'The girls are right. Unless one digs into Styles's life a bit more, we'll never know for sure. We could certainly do some field work into what's going on. It might give some sort of additional context and could confirm the suspicion unequivocally.'

'Well, I have no qualms over that,' says Forbes. 'Now, thinking down the road for a moment. What happens if we find we need to save the government from added embarrassment at a time when it can scarcely afford more scandal? What if we need to... how shall I put it... make the problem surface somewhere else?'

'Slippery slope,' Gambon replies, casting us a wary look.

'I hear your concern, Headmaster. I'm not saying, prove he isn't the source. God forbid. What I mean is... well, let's just get to the bottom of this mess, shall we, and then we can decide what to do next. Do whatever you need to do. Just keep it all very hush-hush. Report back when you have something. How's that sound?'

'Copy that,' Gambon replies with a bemused smirk. He mutes the phone and turns back to gaze out across the rear lawn.

'Swans are here again,' he observes quietly, pointing towards the lake.

'So, we're agreed?' Forbes barks. 'Timing is of the essence. I don't need to tell you the pressure the PM's under.'

Unmuting the phone, Gambon says, 'I think we have a good strategy. Leave it with us.'

'Much appreciated,' Forbes mumbles gruffly, and the line goes dead.

For a moment we each sit in contemplation, pondering over the call.

'What did you make of that, sir?' I ask, finally breaking the silence.

'Interesting...' Drumming his fingers on the desk, Gambon casts a look back down towards the lake and the bevy of swans. Then, turning slowly back to us, he says, 'Build on what you have. Dig into this chap, see what stones you can turn over. Forbes's joke about moral compunction is amusing enough, but I want to understand the why. Let's see if there is more to it than that. I expect you'll need to base yourselves up in London. Best secure charge cards and kit from Mr Sable. But watch your expenses. I don't want to see invoices for a new Mercedes or anything daft, understood?' His eyes focus emphatically on me.

'Sir, I don't know where you get your ideas.'

'Yes, I bet you don't,' he grunts, rolling his eyes. 'And make sure you sign for any kit you need. But do it very quietly. If so much as a whiff of this odious undertaking ever gets out, it will not shine particularly favourably on the service, or this institution.'

We all nod agreeably, fighting to conceal our excitement at this sudden turn of events. To say that our placement, if it can even be called that, just became considerably more interesting would be an understatement. Taking a card from his desk drawer, he slides it across the desk.

'You have my number. Keep me posted...'

*

The English are generally renowned for a few things: inventing afternoon tea, originating sports and then losing at them, having a notoriously dry and sarcastic sense of humour and, last but not least, being able to moan almost incessantly about the weather. While most will never change, the latter is at genuine risk, given the very real threat of climate change.

These last few years, British summers have turned out to be almost Mediterranean in nature. I am sure we will soon begin complaining about the heat. But for the three of us it offers the perfect excuse to escape the confines of our gloomy bunker and decamp to the grassy slope overlooking the lake. There, amidst a scattering of picnic blankets and beanbags, we establish a new base of operations, with our laptops, more battery packs than we know what to do with, a mobile wireless hotspot device, several thermos flasks full of Milly's homemade Cuban lemonade, a chiller box stocked with cold cuts, cheeses, fruits and breads from the canteen, and a speaker that punches above its weight, streaming music from our phones.

In this perfectly idyllic setting, we lounge, often in just our bikinis and sunglasses, lathered up, at Anabel's insistence, in nothing less than factor-fifty sun lotion, researching the increasingly interesting Right Honourable Robert Styles, MP. As the rest of the school labour on inside classrooms, we slowly cook out on the lawn under the sun as it meanders its long, lazy arc across impossibly blue skies.

Uninterrupted, we make good, steady progress, shielded from the school buildings by a dense copse of trees. It is only because of the ever-present possibility of being stumbled upon by overly curious lower-fifth-formers that we grudgingly accept the inevitable tan lines and retain our bikini tops – just in case.

We begin in the members' section of the UK Parliament website, where Styles's contact details, both in Whitehall and in his South Staffordshire constituency, are given. Below that we find enough high-level information to begin a bio on him, including an overview of his parliamentary career, including all his election results, roles, posts, voting record, motions, questions and even an official portrait photo.

Our ensuing trawl through the open-net and social media sites builds nicely upon that. However, even those have their limitations, especially given that our person of interest is obviously cognisant of his public image and has therefore been extremely careful to cultivate it. Publicly available records are soon exhausted, forcing us to turn to government sources. Education records, a marriage certificate, a divorce certificate, years of tax returns and what few personal financial records we can find add more meat to our growing biography.

What quickly emerges is a picture of a man who is clearly very guarded about his private life.

Despite our focussed efforts, which are admittedly interspersed with occasional bouts of pure sunbathing, putting together a full and detailed bio proves significantly more challenging than any of us imagined. But after almost two weeks of work, we reach the point which Gambon told us would eventually arrive. That point beyond which the only information of interest left to discover is that which can only be uncovered by direct observation and focused surveillance.

'Well,' I say with a resigned sigh as I close my laptop and cast a last glance at the mid-morning sun. 'I guess it's time we go and tell him what we've found.'

'Yeah, suppose so,' nods Milly. 'I've really enjoyed this, though. It's been so chilled.'

'Well, you certainly have a nice tan to show for it. That's for sure. Meanwhile, I've barely gone two boxes along on the paint chart, from brilliant white to, like, off-bone,' I laugh, 'while you two've gone to the complete other end of it. So frickin' unfair.'

My friends grin as we gather all our things up, don shorts and T-shirts, and amble back towards SH. After depositing everything but our laptops in our studies, we make our way through the quiet house, out into the main school block corridor and up the curved stone stairway to the headmaster's office. His secretary has us wait outside while he finishes his last meeting before ushering us in. I am less than thrilled to see Mr Cuthbert, the deputy head, who has never warmed to me, seated off to the side beside a writer's bureau, hastily finishing off notes from what I can only presume was their last phone call.

'Take a seat, girls. We'll be with you in a flash,' the headmaster says, turning back to the deputy head. 'Reckon if we can get agreement on that, then that should pretty much close the issue off and we can be done with this farce for another year.'

'Certainly hope so, Headmaster,' Cuthbert replies, screwing on the cap of his black resin fountain pen. 'These blasted Ofsted people just don't know when to give up.'

'Indeed. Right then, bureaucratic nonsense aside,' Gambon says with a comically raised eyebrow, 'I believe you three have come to tell us interesting things about a certain member of parliament, have you not? Or have you finally had enough of chargrilling yourselves out there?' he says, pointing towards the lake. Seeing our shared looks, he laughs.

'Angles, girls. And elevation.'

'Yeah, well, moving swiftly on,' I mutter, clearing my throat.

Bemused, Gambon motions to the sofas in the centre of the room, where we take a seat. Cuthbert remains where he is. His distinctly unimpressed expression suggests we should have changed into our school uniforms before coming up.

'Regale us with your findings, then.'

Taking turns, we hurry through the backstory on Robert Styles. Anabel delivers a brief on his childhood and education, noting that we will return to the latter later, because there's something interesting there. I then take over and skim through his time at Cambridge and his short-lived career as a lawyer, before he switched tack and entered parliament as a junior minister in his mid-twenties.

'Suppose it helps when your father is close friends with the Conservative Party chairman,' Gambon notes dryly.

'Didn't do him any harm,' I add. 'Because it didn't take him long to get appointed parliamentary secretary to the Treasury and chief whip. After that, he had a stint as secretary of state for education –'

'And unto his hands did we cast the fate of the nation's education,' Cuthbert mutters. I glance from him to Gambon and back again, waiting to see if they have anything else to say. When both remain silent, I continue.

'And that brings us to the terrorist attacks.'

'Which is where I pick up,' Milly says, edging forwards enthusiastically. 'In the aftermath of the attacks, he was tasked to establish the Ministry of Ethics and Morality. To say it's come along fast would be an understatement. But critically, it hasn't just grown, but it's also accumulated power and influence very rapidly. Which has resulted in what some observers euphemistically refer to as spectacular mandate creep. As it stands, he now has an undisputed hand in crafting the nation's education curriculum, as well as influencing guidance that's issued to the courts and magistrates, drafting codes of conduct as regards policing, and a say in a host of other policy areas technically overseen by other, older ministries. And he's everywhere. On TV, in magazines and in the press. He and the ministry's spokespeople are on breakfast shows, radio programmes and social media, all spouting messages of morality and social harmony whilst encouraging minority assimilation into the UK's culture.'

'Clearly failed on that one, didn't he?' Cuthbert sneers. 'Bloody country's tearing itself to pieces.'

'Can't deny the man's achievements, though,' Gambon says. 'He's young, if one can call mid to late forties young nowadays. He's charismatic, energising and photogenic. Not many politicians are on the covers of *GQ* and *Esquire*. Nothing would surprise me if he isn't the next PM. So, I can see you three have left all the juicy stuff to the end, haven't you?'

We smile and the others look to me.

'Okay, guess it's my turn again. You already know about the Sentinel stuff, which proved Robert Styles met the reporter who worked on each of the leak stories exactly two weeks before each one broke.'

Both teachers nod, Gambon patiently, Cuthbert slightly less so.

'But here's the thing. They went to the same university.'

'A couple of years apart, admittedly,' Milly interjects. 'And not only were they both in Trinity College, but we found a ledger showing they were both in the same debating society.'

'Well, I'll be damned,' mutters Cuthbert darkly.

'There's more,' Milly adds, smiling apologetically at me as she opens her computer and scurries over to place it on the headmaster's desk. 'A few months before all these stories started breaking, we found there was a large one-off payment made into Robert Styles's bank account from an offshore holding company. Unfortunately, we can't see who the ultimate beneficial owners of it were, but... well, there we are.'

'That's no small amount,' Gambon whistles, beckoning Cuthbert over.

'You do know he comes from old money, Styles does,' the deputy head notes. 'Regardless, having that sum appear in one's bank account could help grease wheels and encourage someone to do something stupid.'

'Tell them about the China stuff,' Anabel urges.

'I'm sorry... the China stuff?' Gambon repeats, leaning forward with interest.

'Okay, so this is where things get a little speculative,' I say. 'But there's enough coincidence here to make it potentially quite interesting. Why don't you tell them?' I say, looking at Anabel. 'I mean, you found it.'

'Okay,' she smiles. 'Remember when I said there was something interesting about Styles's education? When we first came across it, we didn't think a whole lot of it. But the more we dug, the more a pattern started to emerge –'

'Potentially emerge,' Milly adds warily.

'Yeah, it's speculative, but... well, just hear this,' I say, glancing excitedly back towards Anabel, all too aware of the ramifications of what we are about to insinuate.

'So, after he left Eton, he went to Cambridge,' Anabel explains, 'But after that Robert Styles won a place to go and study at the Peking University in Beijing. This was back before it was even a thing. As a result, he speaks fluent Mandarin. Also, that's when he met his wife –'

'Ex-wife,' Milly adds quietly.

'Yes, sorry, ex-wife,' Anabel corrects herself. 'Except they still live together, apparently. She's from Hong Kong. They studied together. Perhaps coincidental, but it's worth noting that the media group which published all these leaks is part of a Chinese state-owned media consortium. Anyway, in going through all Styles's expense accounts filed with the Houses of Parliament, we found that he frequents a Chinese restaurant near the Langham hotel in London. Often after work hours.'

'Point being?' Cuthbert interjects. 'Because so too might half the country's MPs. Frequenting one's local Chinese take-away is almost a prerequisite to live in the UK.'

'That's true,' Anabel says. 'Except this is not his local. In fact, he neither lives near it nor works near it. But what really makes *this* one interesting is that it is located very close to the Chinese Embassy and is a known haunt for Chinese Embassy staff including... Are you ready for it?'

'Oh, do spit it out, girl,' mutters Cuthbert.

'... including their clandestine services teams. Five taps this place as one of their favourite hangouts, which is saying something in a city like London.'

Pursing his lips, Gambon frowns and glances at Cuthbert.

Laying her notes hesitantly in her lap, Anabel looks with uncertainty from adult to adult. A silence falls over the room. Cuthbert drums his fingers slowly on the desk and glances back at the headmaster with a peeved expression. Laughing nervously, Gambon leans back in his plush leather office chair and sighs.

'There's a rather considerable gap between conjecture and truth, but one that can be bridged with the smallest of facts. What we're missing here is fact. The man is probably the closest advisor and confidant to the prime minister. It's one thing to suggest that he leaked these stories because he's some kind of puritanical, ethics-driven fiend. The Minister of Morality and Ethics simply unable to stand by and see these transgressions get brushed under the carpet any longer. Almost understandable, I suppose. In the public interest. Integrity meets irreconcilable conscience. But it's something else entirely to suggest he's acting at the behest of a foreign power. Especially "them". The former is just poor judgement. The latter, an act of treason. Now I suggest it would be prudent to be rather more assured of this assertion before anyone outside this room gets so much as a whiff of it, understand?'

'Well, then maybe now's a good time for us to head up to London,' I suggest, 'and see what Styles is really up to?'

'Ms Foxton, I believe you're right. Do keep something in mind, though, won't you? And that's to remain laser-focused on staying objective in your thinking. Let's be very careful about setting out in search of facts that support a theory, shall we? I know we say this again and again, but that's because it is so crucial. Let the facts lead you to proper conclusions. Otherwise, the intelligence is flawed from the outset.'

'Are you sure about this, Headmaster?' Cuthbert asks warily, wasting no opportunity to glare at me with his dagger-like eyes. 'This is most unorthodox.'

'That it is,' Gambon admits dryly. 'But necessary, I fear. I am not yet sold on the Chinese angle. But I find that deposit into Styles's account coupled with these tenuous observations sufficiently concerning, even at the hypothetical level, to warrant a closer look, wouldn't you agree?'

Burgess Cuthbert mumbles something inaudible and quick-ly changes tack.

'No argument there, Headmaster. But at the same time, it might be prudent to impose some appropriate governance and oversight in this instance. Mandatory reporting windows, local supervision and clear rules of engagement which, frankly, should prohibit any direct engagement with the minister.'

'Well then, what's the point of even –' I blurt out before Gambon cuts me off with a raised hand.

'Yes, yes, there will be plenty of time for all that good stuff,' he says calmly. 'How do you propose we approach this, then, Burgess?'

'Frankly, I'd hand it off to the appropriate counter-espionage teams up at Millbank. Let them sort it out. A mess like this only leads to awkward problems.'

'Oh, great, we're back to this cr –'

'Language, Ms Foxton,' Gambon cautions. 'And respect.'

'Yes, sorry, sir. I apologise.'

'Not to me,' he sighs, pointing in exasperation at Mr Cuthbert. 'To Burgess.'

'Sorry, Mr Cuthbert.'

Nodding in satisfaction, the headmaster continues.

'I don't disagree, Burgess. All good points, and you're not wrong. But at the same time, it also strikes me that this could be a fantastic in-the-field learning experience, and when we get down to brass tacks, that is what the school is here for.'

'But the risks, Headmaster...'

'Manageable, I hope. Now, I presume all three of you will be part of this little venture?' Gambon asks, turning to us. 'Your skill sets are sufficiently complimentary, and you've amassed enough time in the field between yourselves to give me sufficient comfort that you won't make a complete balls-up of it.' Fixing us with a deeply appraising look, he leans forward across the desk. 'Do try not to balls it up, won't you!' he implores. 'Given how this is shaping up, it would be for the best that the PM's right-hand man does not discover that HMG is spying on him.'

'We'll bear that in mind, sir,' I reply as we rise from the sofas.

That doesn't appear to reassure him greatly.

'What she means, sir,' Milly quickly stresses, stepping in front of me, 'is it will be absolutely fine.'

'I jolly well hope so,' Gambon grins, casting a sideways glance at Mr Cuthbert. 'Oh, one other thing, girls, before you go. Mr Sable is launching a new class this morning for some upper-sixth-formers. If you can fit it in before you head off to London, your feedback would be interesting. What with the rest of your year group being otherwise occupied. We're thinking of adding it into the wider curriculum, so the more feedback, the better. In fact,' he says, consulting a timetable on his desk, 'if you head over now, you should be able to make it in time. Then see Mr Sable, kit yourselves up and get on with it.'

We nod and leave quickly before he changes his mind about letting us off the proverbial leash.

As we rush down the stairs, Milly mutters sarcastically, 'Why do I get the feeling it will be far from absolutely fine?'

'You're such a sceptic,' I exclaim. 'Always assuming the worst.'

'And not without good reason,' she says emphatically. 'You think I like almost always dying whenever I step outside with you?'

'Well, you do it quite well. I always assumed you liked flirting with death.'

'I don't want you flirting with anyone,' laughs Anabel. 'Least of all the Grim Reaper.'

'*Yeah*,' I add, swatting Milly humorously on the shoulder in mock rebuke. Giggling and jostling each other playfully, we make our way through the bustling crowd of fifth-formers who are changing classes and walk out of the main school building, across the otherwise deserted Big-Field and along the long, straight road that cuts deep into the woods, until we emerge into a clearing, in the centre of which stands the baroque-styled sandstone geology block nestled in an immaculately landscaped garden.

'Ah, take it in while you can,' Milly sings, closing her eyes and inhaling deeply. 'We're not going to get this kind of peacefulness up in London,' she says, spinning around joyfully on the grass with her arms outstretched. I nod. She's not wrong. And for a calming moment I, too, stop and close my eyes, listening intently to the birdsong and the gentle rustling of the wind through the trees' branches.

'Come on, you two. Hurry up!' Anabel urges from the top of the steps, where she is holding the large wooden front door open.

'Oh dear, now she's starting, too,' Milly jokes.

Once inside, we take the lift down to the basement complex which houses the school's main espionage training facility. There, at the end of the stark white access corridor, we see a hastily made sign which reads 'Acquisition of Information & Manipulative Influencing Skills'. A hand-drawn arrow below points towards the facility's main auditorium. We arrive just in time to see Mr Sable leaving the stage to take a seat at the very back. Interestingly, well over half the upper-sixth audience are female. The lights above the tiered rows of folding seats dim.

Up on the stage at the front, illuminated beneath the bright stage lighting, are two people.

'Great, thank you,' the man begins. 'As you heard, my name is Roger Aynesworth, and I am the former foreign affairs correspondent with the *Times*. Together with Ms Sophie Darlington-Sorbet here, I will introduce you to a new module about passive information extraction.'

Milly leans in and whispers to Anabel and me, 'That can't really be her name, can it?'

'This game, who knows?' I reply, fixing my gaze on the slim, elegant woman standing before us. She has long, luscious brown hair, a finely curved figure and model-like proportions. At a guess I would put her in her early thirties, even if she looks ten years younger. Good genes, I ponder with a wry smile.

'I mean, look at her,' Milly says. 'Bet you she's some MI6 honey trap. That, or some high-society socialite –'

'I say ultra-high-end escort,' Anabel whispers.

'Oh my God, what are you two like?' I joke. Surreptitiously, I take my phone out and do a quick internet search, grateful for whoever ensured there's a signal down here, so far underground. Angling the screen towards my friends, I whisper, 'Nothing. She's a ghost.'

Milly nudges me and points to the stage.

'... so, while I was indeed born in Devon,' Darlington-Sorbet says calmly in a clipped upper-class accent, 'Frank exaggerated somewhat when he said my phone book is full of princes, sheiks, billionaires and politicians –'

'Not by much,' Frank calls cheekily from the audience.

'Okay, maybe this much of it,' she admits, gesturing an inch-wide gap between thumb and forefinger. Tossing her head backwards, she laughs disarmingly, and I find myself shifting in my plush velvet-covered seat as I realise how uncomfortably captivated I am by the adoring smile which she gives him. It's just as overtly sexualised as the rest of her movements, yet in no way does she come across as slutty or inappropriate. Somehow, it seems effortless, and as calculated and considered as a ballet dancer's movements or, perhaps more accurately, a cat stalking its prey.

As she lectures, casually pacing the stage, it becomes obvious that she can turn that alluring charm on and off at will. And going by the way she holds the adoring gaze of her fellow presenter, not to mention that of every boy in the auditorium, I imagine it must be a devastatingly effective weapon when employed deliberately.

'How the hell does she do that?' I hiss under my breath. Neither of my friends respond. Frowning, I turn to see them gawping, slightly open-mouthed, as she slowly paces about, her tight pencil skirt tautening with every step, accentuating her toned thighs and backside, as her skyscraper heels clack commandingly on the wooden stage.

'... that said, the rest of what Frank mentioned – and I apologise to all the boys here – is true. This session is probably more for the girls. Not that you should leave, because understanding this and being able to recognise it when it happens to you is key.'

'Agreed,' Frank says, rising to address the wider audience. 'Always good to be mindful of the tricks that may well be used against you one day, lads.'

Reaching for a bottle of mineral water, Darlington-Sorbet nods, takes a slow, considered sip and settles onto the high barstool in the middle of the stage. Smiling, she lets her eyes drift across the audience, registering us properly for the first time. An air of calm washes over her and the carefully maintained dance of movement finally disappears. An unexpected seriousness replaces it.

'Look around. What do you see?' she asks, blunt and to the point. 'I imagine you see a world in which despite years of effort, gender inequality still reigns. Of course, it would be wonderful if that were not the case. But it seems we still live in a world where most of the most powerful, most senior and most influential people in government and business remain stubbornly male. Now, while that may well seriously piss you off,' she says, holding up a well-manicured finger, 'it also offers up a world of great potential advantage to the female of the species. If only one knows how to employ the assets you've been given to maximum effect...'

For what could well be the first time in any school lecture, I sit up, fascinated by what the lecturer has to say. Beside me, Milly sniggers silently to herself at the sight of this. Giving her knee a punitive flick, I shake my head and listen on as Sophie Darlington-Sorbet begins speaking about the role women have played in espionage over time.

'Of course, it's no surprise then that generally speaking women attract less attention than men. And even when we are noticed, it's usually for very different reasons. Threat and suspicion are not the underlying catalysts. For that reason, women are so much more adept at befriending a target's wife or children in a way a man never could. Such abilities should never be underestimated or squandered as a potentially rich source of information. But all this pales in comparison to what can be achieved when a man is either looking for or hoping for good company, if you know what I mean.'

Several of the boys' sniggers are short lived, as dozens of cutting stares from girls in the audience turn their way.

'Now, I think I can honestly say that there shouldn't be a girl in this room who is surprised at how even the most intelligent and careful people can show an unnerving tendency to be woefully indiscrete if they think they are talking to an attractive but dumb and beddable woman. Worse still if they think she is inconsequential and not a part of their world. This false sense of security comes in part because they think women like that won't cause trouble for them. Nor will they socialise with people with whom they themselves socialise, and this can't be clearer than when such men, and, I hasten to add, some women, too, are dealing with a prostitute.'

Anabel flicks us both a questioning look. I put a finger to my lips. This, I don't want to miss.

'However,' she continues, wagging a cautious finger. 'And here comes the point. Men like this are generally not stupid. They may do things some consider to be stupid, but they themselves are not stupid people. Flinging oneself at someone in a position of power achieves nothing. Getting laid, almost for sure. But little else, I suspect. And that's because if a man does not respect you, he will give you nothing more than what he wants to. But he'll certainly take whatever appears to be on offer. The real trick is to lure someone into revealing more than they want to, and you do this by targeting his ego, vanity and innate desire to impress. And more often than not, his natural competitiveness. That takes skill, manipulation and cunning. A female who knows more than a man will often spark his desire to regain the upper hand. And once you get him there, it's simply about manoeuvring him onto the topic you are really interested in.

'Now, I'm not saying it isn't a delicate dance. Overplay your hand at any point and his defences may spring back up, and you'll quickly find yourself out of the game and likely under all sorts of suspicion, which brings its own risks. That's not to say that the careful application of sexuality can't hurt. Sometimes a bit of playing with your hair or a subtle wetting of the lips can give some added incentive, but the challenge or enticement you must pose has to be cerebral and not physical. If you dress like a tart, a man will secretly assume you don't value yourself highly, so why should he? If he thinks you're just looking to get laid that night, then he may assume you do it regularly, and then all he sees is used goods, and the idea of going where all those other men have already been will likely devalue you in his eyes. Is that astonishingly unfair? Of course. But this isn't an ethics class. We are dealing with the reality of the world. And the reality is, as a spy, if he takes you to bed simply because you're pretty, he might not assign great value or worth to you cerebrally. Which means he'll betray nothing confidential to you.'

'Sad, but probably true,' I whisper to Milly.

'Well, I have no intention of finding out, thank you very much.'

'That must be nice.'

'What?'

'Being able to say that there are skills or assets you could bring to bear, but which you won't for moral reasons.'

'You seriously saying you'd shag someone for information?'

'I don't know.'

'You sure about that?' she asks with a raised eyebrow. Before I can answer, she smiles, pats my leg sympathetically and nods towards the stage.

'There's no better way to hone this than by practice,' says Darlington-Sorbet. 'I can lecture you till I'm blue in the face and it won't help. So, girls, we're going to go and practise. Starting tonight. Specifically, at a dinner being laid on at the Royal Military Academy Sandhurst. I want you to spend the rest of the day reading up on the British Army, Sandhurst and so on. You will each be sitting next to an officer cadet whose age will be close enough to your own, and I want you to get as much information as you can about the academy, their class, people's names, who their instructors are, et cetera, et cetera. If you can find out when and where they are next going on exercise, for example, you will have compromised their operational security, and all of them should know better than that. I don't care what tactics you use to get the job done. But remember what I said earlier about self-worth. Make up your backstories, whatever. It's up to you.'

Nodding, she looks across to the former *Times* correspondent.

'Roger will now take you through a very different suite of skills aimed at getting people to divulge information they shouldn't. Most of which are not as passive, subliminal or manipulative as those I just described. And these, you'll be glad to hear, boys, are applicable to both sexes.'

'Oh, pity,' I whisper. 'That could've been quite fun. The Sandhurst thing, I mean.'

'For you, maybe,' Milly replies. 'But I have no desire to sit next to some cadet and rub my leg up against his under the table in a bid to get him to divulge information which I could just as easily get lying in bed with my laptop. Besides, we have work to do, and ours isn't a training exercise.'

'Yeah, okay. Fair enough. Can we at least just listen to the rest of this?' I ask.

Glancing at her watch, Milly sighs reluctantly, turns to Anabel and nods.

*

With bags packed as best we can in anticipation of a trip that has a very real chance of turning into an open-ended stay in London, we order a taxi to the station.

Once there, Milly's scandalised look puts an end to any ideas I had about getting us first-class tickets. Frowning, I ask for regular tickets instead.

'You're such a snob,' she rebukes me as we head to the platform.

'Ugh,' I groan. 'As if anyone would care.'

'I care,' she says forcefully. 'Integrity means something to me.'

'It's all me-me-me-me-me,' I chant, laughing. 'Besides, it's only wrong if you get caught.'

'I'm not listening to you,' Milly says, turning away with a disbelieving shake of her head. 'I'm not getting into trouble because of you.'

Limited services due to nationwide industrial action means the train which eventually arrives is half its normal length and already full. Which means we're left standing between carriages, near the toilets, for the fifty-five minutes it takes for the countryside to morph into urban sprawl and the train to finally pull into London Waterloo.

'That... that's why I'm a snob,' I finally fire back, pointing emphatically as we disembark onto the bustling platform.

'Okay, yes, fair point,' Milly concedes, rolling her eyes grudgingly. 'Still, I'm glad we're finally here. This is exciting.'

She's right, of course, for while the journey was unnecessarily uncomfortable, a distinct sense of freedom accompanies our arrival in London.

'Me, too,' Anabel replies, as we make for the long line of black taxis waiting outside the station. 'Where are we going to stay?'

'Oh, just some little place I found online,' I say, hefting the bags, one after the other, into a cab.

'That doesn't exactly inspire me with confidence,' Milly replies, climbing in.

'Trust me. It'll be fine. And perfectly located for what we have in mind,' I assure them.

When we arrive in the narrow back street just around the corner from Green Park, Milly glances nervously across at me and then peers out the window again with an increasingly uncertain expression.

'Wait, you booked us into a five-star hotel?'

'Yup, but it's only a boutique hotel.'

'In the heart of Mayfair.'

'Uh-huh.'

'Are you insane?'

'Nope, but some might debate that.'

'You have any idea how expensive this must be?'

'Yup.'

'And that doesn't bother you?'

'Nope.'

'B... but...'

'Hey, it's not our money,' I reassure her soothingly.

'You guys have no idea what five-star hotels really are,' Anabel smirks knowingly as she opens the door and steps out onto the kerb. 'You should see some of the insane resorts we have back in Asia. Like in Thailand, Bali or the Philippines. That's different-league luxury. Wait until you ask where the pool or the spa is. Bet they'll look at you like you're smoking something.'

'Yeah! See, Mills, it's all relative,' I say playfully. 'Which makes this, like, middle of the road. So, it's fine.'

'This is not middle of the road,' she exclaims.

'I know,' I grin. 'Welcome to Flemings Mayfair. I couldn't resist. Not with a name like that. It's so us.'

'Looks nice enough,' says Anabel appraisingly.

'I can't believe you're siding with her,' Milly moans. 'We are in so much trouble when the bill goes through.'

'Better to ask for forgiveness than for permission,' I advise as I extend the handle of my suitcase.

'That is so the wrong spirit.'

'Yeah, whatever.'

'I hate you.'

'And you know what?' I reply, laughing. 'I don't take it personally.'

The taxi pulls off down the street, leaving us to look up at the brown brick building with its whitewashed lower level. Stretching the width of the first floor is a bright white strip with the hotel's name embossed across it in big, raised gold letters. Several flags drape lazily in the gentle breeze.

'It's better than being back at school,' says Anabel.

'I suppose that's true,' Milly concedes.

Once we have checked in, we are escorted from the small, dark lobby with its striking black-and-white-tiled floor, and shown to our rooms, which are all up a floor and along a few cute, narrow, winding corridors. As she peers into hers, Milly turns to me with a slightly disappointed expression.

'We all have singles?'

'Yes, genius. That was what they had. Or would you prefer Gambon and whoever does Thirteen's accounting to see that two of us slept in the same room?'

'Ah,' she exclaims, pursing her lips.

'Yeah. See, sometimes I can think smart, too.'

'Okay, good thinking.'

'I'm in the third from the end,' Anabel adds with a grin.

'Great, good to know,' I call, giving her an overemphasised thumbs-up. 'Just I'm not the one who needs to know.'

Milly slaps my arm playfully and blushes brightly.

'Right, how about we all go sort our lives out,' I suggest, 'and then maybe meet in the lobby again in thirty minutes?'

As plans go, what we come up with over the next two hours, as we meander along the intermittently shaded paths of nearby Green Park, is admittedly less than robust. That's mainly because, as Milly and I are all too aware, well-laid plans don't usually last very long. So why bother? But it's also because we're not entirely sure what we are even looking for. Irrefutable evidence that the Right Honourable Robert Styles is indeed the single source of all the recent leaks that have embarrassed the government and called into question its competency to govern? Definitely. Are we trying to determine whether a quid pro quo was established by that rather large third-party payment into his account? Possibly. And lastly, if so, might that not suggest an ongoing and complicit arrangement between Styles and the Chinese government, or agents operating on its behalf? We have no idea. But in fairness, it's not like anyone has given us any formal guidance, either.

'Don't you think that's, like, really weird?' Milly asks as we settle onto a park bench on a long, deserted stretch of pathway adjacent to a big, open patch of grass.

'Not really,' I reply dryly, peering around in curiosity to see where we are in relation to the spot where I was first introduced to the secret world in which I now live. That was so many months ago that it feels a lifetime has passed since then. 'I never heard back from OCS, either. Seems there's a pattern developing with this lot.'

'Maybe it's some kind of misguided adult fixation on plausible deniability?' suggests Anabel.

'Maybe.'

'Well, whatever it is,' I say, 'we have a plan of sorts. Let's just see what comes off it.'

'Agreed,' says Milly. 'Worst-case scenario, we find nothing.'

'Gotta have faith, Mills. I have a feeling we'll easily find something.'

'You always have a feeling,' she sighs. 'And that's usually when it all goes horribly wrong.'

'Yeah, yeah, whatever. So, go on. Might as well call Forbes's number. See if he can fix you up to get into the Ministry of Morals. That'll be a start.'

Nodding, Milly dials the number we were given and waits patiently as it rings. It only takes two rings before a loud voice barks, 'Yes!'

With a gasp, Milly sets the phone to speaker mode and we all hurriedly cluster around her.

'Mr Forbes,' she stammers. 'It's us.'

'Who's us?' comes the gruff reply.

'From Godolphin Park.'

'Ah...'

'You said to call if we needed anything.'

'Yes...'

'Styles.'

'What about him?'

'Well, we need to get into his ministry building tomorrow...'

'Should I ask why?'

'Probably best you don't,' I chip in quickly.

'Quite. The abattoir owner doesn't concern himself with the opinions of livestock.'

'Kinda think he might if he were one of the livestock,' I mutter with a puzzled expression.

'I heard that.'

'Can you get us in?' I ask.

'Just the building, or into his office itself?'

'His office would be best,' Milly replies. 'But if there's an outer office, like where his staff or his PA sit, that would work, too. I need to ID his phone so I can upload a zero-click, zero-day exploit onto it.'

'I'll pretend I know what that means. Fine. I will have one of my staffers deliver some interdepartmental document or whatnot. You can tag along. How long do you need to be in there for?'

'Only a couple of minutes. But I need to have about a minute undisturbed.'

'Very well. Then I will have my staffer require a signature from Styles. While he does that, you get your minute or two left outside.'

'Thank you,' Milly says, beaming widely.

'Good. Are we done?'

'Yes, that was all –'

The line cuts, and we are left staring at the phone in wonderment.

'You think he's just deliberately rude?' Milly asks as she slips the handset back into her pocket.

'Nah, bet it's a requirement for the job,' I joke.

'Well, at least that bit's sorted,' Anabel says. 'Now you just need to go back down to school to pick up your car.'

'Tell me about it,' I grumble. 'What a hassle. Wish we'd thought about that before we left.'

'I know. Well, lesson learnt. Look, why not head back down now?' Milly suggests. 'Least then you can be back for dinner.'

'Suppose so. Okay, fine. Can one of you look for where I can park it before I get back?'

'Yeah, we'll talk to the hotel,' Milly says. 'Least this way we can tail Styles by car and foot when he leaves the Houses of Parliament or his ministry. No way we could try hailing taxies and not lose him.'

'Agreed. Even though I'm not entirely sold on the idea that the car's subtle enough for what we're thinking, but hey.'

'True, but it's better than nothing. Could you imagine trying to remain inconspicuous in that thing you stole from O'Leary?' Milly mutters under her breath.

'It can't be stealing if he was already dead when we took it.'

'You know, I question your morality at times,' she laughs. 'Besides, you're the only one with a car, ill-gotten or otherwise, so we're kind of out of options.'

'Yeah, fair point. I guess the drive up will be fun. I've barely got to use it so far this term. So, I'm not complaining.'

'Certainly sounds like it. You did sort the insurance and registration?'

'Yeah, both sorted. Just don't ask how.'

'Oh dear,' Milly groans. 'Knowing you, you'd have persuaded some poor schmuck to take it out in their name and put you as a named driver.'

'Oh my God, how did you know? Did Mr Silverman tell you?'

'No, I just know you too well. How did you persuade him?'

'Think he's trying to impress Professor Summerfield. I said he could use it to take her out.'

'Shut the front door. No, you didn't!' Milly scoffs. 'That's so funny, and so wrong as well. Hope you paid him.'

'Yup. And saved a fortune.'

'Shameless.'

'You know,' Anabel notes in amusement. 'I'm not even slightly jealous when I say you two really are like an old married couple at times.'

'We are so not,' I laugh, pulling a hair scrunchy from my pocket. 'Anyway, I'll see you both laters, then,' I add as I get up, gathering my messy, windswept hair into a ponytail.

And there I leave them, nattering energetically, all by themselves on a park bench in the middle of Green Park on a lovely sunny day. Slipping my earphones in, I set off on the trip back down to school to pick up the Merc, which we really should have thought about bringing before we even left.

*

I have just returned to my room, having parked the G-Wagon for the night in its usual space around the back of Down Street's 'abandoned' Tube station, only three streets away from where the hotel is. It's been left there every night this week, as the hotel has no parking of its own. So far, no one seems to have objected. The absence of tickets or a clamp each morning can only mean the area is either out of bounds to parking wardens, given that OCS have their London base of operations in the old Tube station beneath, or London's parking attendants are having a staffing issue.

Ideally, having just had another whole day behind the wheel, I would have liked the chance to lie down for at least a few minutes, but it's not to be as a gentle knock comes at the door.

'Hey, they're on. You coming in?' Milly asks, poking her head into my small hotel room.

'Yeah, cool. Give me two secs,' I reply, making for the equally compact bathroom. I pull the thick, cosy white dressing gown from the hook, kick off my jeans and wrap the gown around me, over my T-shirt. Then, having slipped into the pair of equally comfortable hotel slippers, I grab my room key from the bedside table and literally ten seconds later knock on Milly's door. Anabel answers with a grin and hurriedly beckons me in.

Milly is lying on her bed, her tablet propped up on a pillow in front of her. Anabel scrambles on beside her, while I pull the room's only armchair towards the bed and bend in low to see the camera.

'Hiya!' I call with a wave at the split-screen video image. 'How are you boys doing? Did you miss us?'

'Hey, Heather,' says Nigel, waving.

'Aye, we miss you,' Luther moans dramatically. 'But they're keeping us busy up here in Cheltenham, so...'

'How's it been?' Nigel asks.

'Yeah, not bad,' I reply, easing myself onto the edge of the bed to see properly. 'We've been at this guy for a while now.'

'It's been fun, though,' Anabel adds. 'We've had him under surveillance for most of the week. Pretty routine so far, just rushing around like you'd expect a member of parliament to do.'

'How do you know where to pick him up each day?' Nigel asks. 'I mean, you can't be on him all the time, right?'

'Ah, that was a bit of pure Milly genius, right back on day one,' I reply.

'Wasn't that hard,' she scoffs, blushing self-depreciatingly. 'I figured we'd have that problem. Amazingly, Forbes helped on that one and sent us a copy of Styles's agenda from the cabinet office. He even helped me get into Styles's Westminster office on false pretences. Allowed me to get within range of his phone. Sable sent me one of those cellular detector apps, and I used that to scan for all the mobile signals pinging in his office. There were only three. And then I just waited outside and watched as each came and went –'

'Aye, until ya ken which one was his. Smart, that,' Luther nods. 'Course, we coulda done it faster, but that works, too.'

'Yeah, so now we have a laptop here monitoring his movements,' Anabel explains.

'It's meant we're constantly on the go,' I add. 'Tailing by car. Oh, I am so glad to be driving again,' I gush. 'And the guy driving his government Jag... hold on, sorry, his Jaaaag, likes to put his foot down any time he can. Which makes it a laugh and a half –'

'For you maybe,' Anabel adds, rolling her eyes. 'The two of us are pretty much living in fear as loony driver here throws that tank of hers around like a race car trying to keep up.'

'It's not that bad,' I protest humorously. 'Though probably doesn't help that I have it in sports mode all day –'

'See, that's what I mean,' exclaims Milly.

'Anyway, stop knocking my car, or else you two can both sodding walk tomorrow.'

'If only we could be that fortunate,' says Milly, clasping her hands together and gazing pleadingly skyward.

'Yeah, right! Anyway, how about you guys?' I ask. 'How's it up north?'

'Loads of fun,' Nigel replies. 'But I'm only in Norfolk. Luther's, like, almost back in Scotland.'

'Am not,' he exclaims. 'Cheltenham isnae that far north. Not that any of you soft southerners have a clue.'

'It's north of the M25. Case closed,' I laugh. 'So, how's it slumming it on that massive country estate, Nige?'

'Oh, love it, Heather. It's like a retreat. Except we spend all day knocking up all sorts of wicked tech. Almost don't want to leave. How're you guys splitting up all the work?' he asks. 'Are you all on him all the time?'

'Well, we kind of split it, with me always in the car. Milly covers him when he's on foot, and if he heads onto public transport, Anabel goes in after him. And it works well, right?'

'Yeah, but tomorrow,' chimes in Milly, 'will be a big day. It's our first Saturday up here on Styles-watch. So, we've no idea what it could bring. Maybe he'll go and do something a little more interesting than what he's been up to all week.'

'We can only hope,' sighs Anabel.

'Yeah, we're going to try a bit of divide and conquer. So, I'll stay on Styles,' says Milly. 'See where he goes and what he gets up to. I've kind of got the hang of how he moves around now, so it's easier that way. Hev's going to have a go at the journalist, Pelt.'

'Reckon we've got nothing to lose,' I say. 'I called him on Wednesday posing as a journalism student from the London College of Communication and asked to interview him about handling sources.'

'Aye, and whit de ye know about journalism, huh?' Luther laughs.

'Nothing. Don't need to. We know the whole book about running intelligence agents. Same-same, but different.'

'And what're you up to, Belle?' Nigel asks.

'Nothing,' she says with a deeply contented smile. 'I've been on trains, buses and the Underground all week, criss-crossing all over London, trailing around after him. I don't think any other MP uses public transport like this guy, even the minister for transport. And then there was that trip up to his constituency in South Staffordshire on the train. After all that, I'm going to have a lie-in. But in the afternoon, I'll head over to meet a professor of Chinese Political Studies at SOAS university. He advises the government on their China strategy. I want to get a better understanding of a few things Styles was up to when he was in China. Might give us some better insights.'

'Here comes her Bayesian inference stuff,' I groan, covering my eyes in mock defence. 'Isn't that what you called it?'

'Oh dear,' Milly sighs, slapping my arm. 'Such a science philistine. This is the bit that makes you a lousy intelligence officer. You're all gut instinct, fire from the hip, ask for forgiveness afterwards –'

'It's worked pretty well so far.'

'I question that,' she retorts. 'I'm with Belle –'

'You don't say,' I giggle immaturely.

Smiling, she takes a calming breath and continues. 'I'm also with her when it comes to establishing alternative hypotheses. Just because something looks clean-cut, doesn't mean it is. I think her exploring other options and possibilities is a good use of time. And she should get her sleep. Come on, I think it's time for bed. Busy day tomorrow.'

'Yeah, that's cool,' I say. 'Hey, boys, it was awesome to see you. I gotta go have a shower, though. I feel well skanky.'

'Can you get off my bed, then?' Milly laughs, pushing me off.

'Yes, Mum,' I say, slipping off the bed. Blowing them each a kiss, I add, 'Time to love you and leave you. Happy trails, boys. Right, I'll see you downstairs at oh eight thirty tomorrow morning, okay, Milly? While Sleeping Beauty there lazes her way through the morning.'

'Jealousy doesn't suit you,' Anabel coos softly as she snuggles intimately against a colossal white pillow.

'Yeah, tough gig you have there,' I drawl sarcastically and throw a cushion at her. She squeals and takes cover beneath the duvet.

After a second round of goodbyes, I gladly return to my room for a desperately needed shower and the comforting solace of my bed.

*

The large, chunky Garmin fitness tracker that I wear on my left wrist counts some twenty-seven thousand steps, and given how my feet are aching, I should probably have worn a more suitable pair of shoes for a whole day of walking around town. With a grateful sigh, I sink slowly onto the low wall outside the hotel and let my shoulders slump.

It's just gone seven in the evening. The light hasn't started to fade yet, but it surely will within the next hour or two. The narrow road is busy with tourists. My eyes dart from one to the next, taking each of them in, noting what they are wearing, whether anything looks amiss about them and whether I have seen them before. I smile as I catch myself at it again and turn in the other direction, trying to relax. The top-hatted Flemings hotel doorman tips his brim politely and helps a couple of guests into a taxi. Absentmindedly, I flick the screen of my phone, checking again for new messages. Nothing.

Frowning, I scan up and down the road, trying to work out which direction Milly will approach from. Tapping my foot impatiently, I look back through the most recent messages and the same buzz of excitement washes over me. My eyes hone in, once again, on the message that has given me stomach butterflies for the last thirty-four minutes.

Yay… Got him!

Despite the rapid-fire pestering that ensued, Milly steadfastly refused to elaborate, jokingly citing section twenty-six, paragraph five, and insisting she would fill us both in when she returned. I roll my eyes again at her lame Bond joke and sit back, slowly rotating my ankles while I wait. Not that I have to wait long, for a few moments later she rounds the corner from Piccadilly into Half Moon Street.

Hurrying to meet her, I call, 'Hey, you!'

'You crack me up,' she says, giving me a quick hug. 'You really aren't good at waiting, are you?'

'What can I say? I'm excited to hear what you found.'

'I bet you are. You heard from Belle?'

'Only that she's running late with her professor friend. They've caught up with some other bloke the professor said they should also go speak to. She'll be back later. Told her we'd meet in the bar.'

'Oh, you did, did you? Why am I not surprised? Personally, I think it's some kind of miracle we haven't been in there yet. What with you being here.'

'Oi, you insinuating I have a drink problem?'

'If the shoe fits,' she replies teasingly. Then, laughing, she glances down at my Dior X Air Jordan Ones and smiles.

'Talking about shoes, are those things actually comfy?' she asks, pointing dubiously at the grey-and-white, high-cut basketball boots. 'I'd imagine they can't be that comfortable?'

'Nah,' I scoff dismissively. 'They're like walking on cushions of air. Why do you think they call them *Air* Jordans?'

'You do know how much they're worth, right?'

'Sort of. Funny you mention it, I had some Arab lady try to buy them from me earlier.'

'Oh yeah. How much?'

'You don't want to know. You'll think I'm mad.'

'Oh no, I already know you're mad. We all know that,' she laughs. 'Then again, you probably didn't buy them, either, so...'

'Well, okay, that's true. My mum got them, but they don't fit her, so yours truly is foster-homing them. What I meant was, I figured you'd think I was mad to take them out of the box, let alone wear them.'

'You are! That's a given. But nowhere near as mad as the people who're willing to shell out that much to buy them second-hand. Anyway, that aside, I suppose they are kind of cool, even if not slightly to my taste.'

'You do know it's our generation buying these things, right?'

'When have you ever heard me say I associate with "our generation"? I'd have worn flip-flops if I could've. Your feet must be well foisty after being in them all day.'

'Why, thank you,' I sigh. 'They're actually all Italian leather, I'll have you know. Which is breathable. Besides, this isn't just a trainer. It's a homage to the original AJ-one, which admittedly came before Tinker Hatfield, but were still a cool design. Just these have all the Dior trim thrown in, like inside on the strobel line and below on the sole.'

'I don't even know what half of that means,' Milly sighs, shrugging her shoulders. 'I imagine it concerns Michael Jordan somehow.'

'Wow, you're sharp.'

'Piss off. That's usually my line. Can't believe you stole it.'

'You're welcome. Come on,' I say, putting a guiding arm around her shoulder, keen to sit down properly. 'Let's get a drink.'

'Manetta's bar, ladies?' the doorman enquires as we approach the hotel's front entrance.

We nod.

'To the back of the lobby,' he says, pointing. 'Down the stairs and someone will show you in.'

We thank him and make our way inside, where the concierge staff greet us warmly.

'Plausible deniability,' I whisper as I take my fake ID from my purse, ready to be asked for it the moment we enter the bar.

'Some upside, I suppose, to being schooled at a place with printers that spit out government-quality identification,' Milly admits grudgingly as she, too, gets hers ready. 'I doubt the DVLA would even be able to tell the difference.'

'What difference?' I giggle. 'They're generated through the DVLA's own system.'

At the bottom of the stairs we are met by a smartly dressed waiter in a waistcoat and bowtie, before being escorted along a small corridor into a long, thin bar with subdued lighting, chestnut panelling and large convex mirrors at both ends. Polished rose gold dominates any space not already given over to aged wood, dark leather or lush grey fabrics. Adorning the walls are numerous vivid portraits of famous authors.

'Oh, this is so my kind of place.'

'What, back in the 1930s?' Milly asks, bemused.

Ignoring her, I glance to our left and see there's already someone sitting on one of the red-and-black bar stools. Turning, I point to the far corner, where several opulent grey-velvet sofas line the wall.

'We'll take that one, please.'

'Certainly, madam,' the waiter notes, nodding agreeably. He peers quickly at our proffered driving licences, nods and leads us across the bar. Each table has several supple, black, upholstered leather chairs arranged around it. A few are already taken, but it's still early, so the bar may well fill up later. For right now it is ideally quiet for what we need to discuss.

Behind the bar, another smartly dressed young man gets to work readying a plate of snacks for us as the waiter presents us with the menu. The bar nibbles arrive half a minute later.

'You know, this place inspired Agatha Christie's *At Betram's Hotel*,' Milly says, reading from the first page of the leather-bound menu. I nod absentmindedly, my eyes roaming the sumptuous room.

Milly quickly orders 'A Portrait of a Young Man', inspired, she notes, by the James Joyce novel.

'Jesus, you're actually drinking,' I joke quietly, noting it is made from Woodford Reserve bourbon. 'You rebel.'

'Well, I couldn't resist, if truth be told,' she whispers excitedly. 'It would be a tragic waste of such a romantic, literary setting not to indulge, wouldn't it?'

'Not going to get any argument from me on that one,' I mumble as I flit through the menu, before selecting a rum-heavy cocktail called 'Three Lives', inspired by someone I've never heard of called Gertrude Stein. Milly despairingly sinks her face into her hands and mock-weeps at my ignorance.

She glances up and, seeing my purse-lipped, unimpressed expression, laughs and begins recounting her day, pounding the pavements of London in pursuit of Robert Styles, a man who clearly also favours public transport on the weekends, as he ticked off a number of accumulated errands.

'Suppose I'm fortunate he didn't ask for his official government Jag –'

'Jaaaag,' I chuckle to myself as I set to work on the cheese and charcuterie board. 'I kind of miss that silly car.'

'I don't,' Milly replies emphatically, peering at her phone, which just pinged. 'Actually, you go first. She'll be here in a few mins. Then I can tell you both what I saw.'

'Ugh, can't believe you're making me wait even longer. Swear you're enjoying this. Okay, fine. So, Jeffrey Pelt. The guy's, like, Mr *Guardian* Reader through and through. All Ted Baker, with a worn leather satchel and Onitsuka Tiger trainers. I met him in this cute coffee shop in Notting Hill. I said I was doing my dissertation on the art of nurturing sources. He seemed to buy that. Anyway, we spoke for a bit about how he gets sources to trust him. He went on about Chatham House rules and stuff like that. Never disclosing his sources. Blah, blah, blah. About letting them tell him more than they wanted to by remaining silent after the main interview, so they feel obliged to speak more.'

'Sounds like an intelligence debriefing.'

'Doesn't it. Anyway, after I ran through all my questions, I turned to his recent successes, and especially the government leaks pieces. Don't think he was too keen to talk about them in detail, but we kind of went back and forth discussing it, but very hypothetically. Like where the best places to meet an informant are, or the best times, all that kind of stuff. But get this. He seemed genuinely surprised to hear the papers all credited him on those stories. He said he hadn't read the articles. Can you believe that?'

'Maybe,' Milly says thoughtfully. 'You hear actors say they have never watched their own films, or authors say they never read their book again after it was published. Why not the same for a journalist?'

'Perhaps. Anyway, that aside, the interesting bit comes in what he said next, which was the oddest thing.'

'What?'

'Well, so, he started talking about how he and his contact for the government leak stories met on a number of occasions, as we know, and always in quite public places, like coffee shops. He said they would always sit in the corner, where it was easy to spot someone watching them. And then, like a bit of an afterthought, he added that often sources fail to make meetings for all sorts of reasons, but this one was good: he said she only failed to make one meeting.'

'I'm sorry... *she*?'

'Yup. That's what he said. I mean, there were quite a few people there and there was music playing, but I'm sure of it.'

'Well, if I had to trust anyone's hearing...' Milly says, smiling.

'I suppose. Anyway, what do you think?'

'Maybe he said it deliberately?'

'Maybe. But there was more. When he started discussing all this, his whole manner changed. Like his body language. He kept looking at the exit and touching his face. I noticed he also repeated himself a few times and kept overemphasising the reliability of what he was saying. All "to be honest" and "to tell you the truth". That kind of thing.'

'Well,' she ponders aloud. 'Those are classic telltale signs a person's lying. But adding the "she" bit would be a pretty sneaky deflect and detract.'

'I know. It was just such an afterthought kind of comment.'

'Well, it's the perfect way to do it, isn't it? Don't forget, the guy's a journalist. He isn't your friend. Why would he be all rah-rah about protecting his sources and then give away their sex? He might have sounded all blasé, but maybe it's totally deliberate?'

'So, you still think it was a man?'

'That's the thing, right? Who knows now?'

'Jesus, it's so fricking corkscrew,' I groan. 'Messes with your mind. Now I don't know what to think. Was it an accident, or a deliberate "throw me off the scent" comment?'

'It's not for us to guess. It's like Darlington-Sorbet said: the best way to feed an enemy agent information is after you've shagged him, when you're both just lying there in bed, all relaxed. Even better if you're smoking a fag, because it looks even more of an afterthought.'

'I'm surprised you remember that,' I grin as our drinks arrive.

'Hey, just because I remember it doesn't mean I want to do it. Besides, I don't smoke.'

'This is so messed-up,' I mutter with a sigh, stirring my glass. 'Good tradecraft says we at least have to consider if what he said might actually be true. Ever think about that?'

'That's my point. File it away, and we come back to it if the facts change enough to make it a serious possibility. But take the facts as they stand. Experienced journalist. Knows all the tricks. Maybe he was selling you a red herring. Maybe not. Maybe it was a slip of the tongue. But truth is, we know how unreliable human intel can be. So, maybe ignore it, because on the other hand we have all the signals intel, which categorically puts Styles right there with him each time. I'm more willing to believe that than get swayed by what could be deliberate misinformation. Or maybe you simply misheard.'

'Okay, fine. Let's file it away. Hey, look, here she comes,' I say, pointing as Anabel enters the bar.

'*Bonjour*!' she exclaims, slumping down onto the sofa next to Milly. She casts a quick, wary look around and then gives her a quick peck on the cheek.

'I don't know why you two are still so careful,' I say, taking a sip of my drink. 'I doubt many people give a toss.'

'I think you'd be surprised,' Anabel replies, reaching for the drinks menu. 'See we're hitting the hard stuff. Wow. Okay, I'm game for that. I'm exhausted after all that.'

'You and us, too,' says Milly. 'Get a drink, then I'll tell you what happened today.'

Once Anabel's Long Island Iced Tea arrives, we wait for the waiter to return to the bar before leaning in excitedly across the small glass table.

'Long story short, the morning was completely uneventful,' Milly begins. 'And pretty much a total waste of time. He did his dry cleaning. And took it himself, which is surprising when you see the house he lives in.'

'We talking really silly?' asks Anabel.

'Totally silly. Just wait till you see it. Anyway, then he met some political lobbyist for a coffee in Sloane Square. Bus and Tube there and back.'

'How'd you know they were a lobbyist?' I ask.

'I took a photo of them with the truly insane zoom lens on this thing,' Milly says, picking up her phone, 'and ran it through the facial software. She's some construction industry lobbyist.'

'Interesting, given that he's the minister for morality, wouldn't you say?' says Anabel.

'True. Something else to bear in mind for later, I guess,' Milly says, glancing at me. 'But what was of real interest was when he went to get lunch. So, go back a bit. First, he heads down into the Underground and he takes a train to Westminster, where he heads into his offices for a bit. When he comes back out, he has a briefcase with him. But then he ducks back into the station and takes the Jubilee line up to Green Park and changes onto the Victoria line to Oxford Circus. He then walks up Regent Street, past the Langham, and heads into his favourite Chinese takeaway.'

'Kidding,' says Anabel. 'Who goes that far for Chinese?'

'Oh, please,' I exclaim. 'You're always saying how you can't wait to fly back to Hong Kong for dim sum. And that's, like, seven thousand miles!'

'Ai-yah, that's different,' she laughs.

'Anyway,' Milly giggles, 'I waited across the road, near a coffee shop. He came out a few minutes later with a couple of plastic bags full of those Tupperware containers. You know, the usual takeaway boxes. Took me a second to notice he didn't have the briefcase anymore.'

'For real?' I whisper, leaning forward excitedly.

'Yeah. For a sec, I was tempted to go in and see if it was there.'

'So, what did you do?' Anabel asks, leaning in equally close.

'Well, I just followed him. I mean, what option was there? So, back we went, past the hotel and on towards Oxford Circus. It was only when we got into the station and he was approaching the barrier that he suddenly stopped and turned. I was pretty much right behind him, and he practically spun and slammed right into me.'

'Jeez, you're kidding,' I laugh.

'He barely even noticed me. He just hurried back to the takeaway.'

'Was the case still there?'

'Yeah, because he came out all relieved with it a minute later, waving and smiling to the owner inside. And then he hailed a black cab and headed home again.'

I sit back and take a deep breath.

'What do you make of that, then?'

'On the face of it,' says Milly, 'it could be exactly what it looked like. Busy man forgot his briefcase by accident.'

'Yeah, maybe,' I note, sceptically. 'On the other hand, it kind of smacks of Oleg Gordievsky, don't you think? Like how he smuggled documents out of the Soviet Embassy, wandered around the corner at lunch and dropped them off to be photocopied, before returning the originals before anyone noticed they were gone. What if that's what Styles was doing?'

'Like a twist on a classic dead-drop,' Anabel ponders aloud. 'The accidental drop?'

'Suppose it makes sense,' says Milly. 'I was keen to see what you both thought. I didn't want to jump to conclusions. I mean, it would certainly have been long enough for whoever to scan whatever was in the case and have it ready again for pick-up. And to anyone following him, it would just look like an accident.'

'Which is what it's meant to look like,' I add. 'I know it's stating the obvious, but the question then has to be whether the man has anything to hide, in which case the application of tradecraft is definitely the nail in the coffin –'

'True,' says Milly and she takes a slow sip and shudders at the strength of her drink. 'Of course, the real question is why?'

'Hopefully, that's what we get to find out.'

'Yeah, or we simply discover,' Anabel butts in, 'that it's entirely accidental and nothing more than coincidence.'

'Right,' I say, 'which means the only option is to follow him some more. If the trend continues, then it's clear. I say we start now, tonight. Set up around the corner from his house and wait for him to head out. See where he goes. Who does he meet with? I mean, if he dropped something off to them today, who knows whether it means there could be a follow-up this evening?'

'Now that's thin,' Milly says, rolling her eyes.

'Maybe, but not totally beyond the realm of possibility. Besides, what've we got to lose? It's not like we have big plans or anything.' I look encouragingly at each of them in turn. 'C'mon, let's finish these drinks and then get ready.'

*

By the time we have all showered, changed into suitably dark clothes, charged our phones and arrived back down in the lobby, it is just gone eight p.m. As I take a seat in the corner, my phone rings.

'Hey, Mr Sable,' I say, answering it.

'Quick one. You may be interested to know GCHQ just called, asking if we authorised the tracking of a cabinet member's personal mobile device.'

'Oh, really? You mean the Sentinel tracker information we requested? What did you say?'

'No, I mean the thing Butterworth sideloaded onto his phone. Said it was part of an authorised training exercise.'

'Cool. Think they bought it?'

'Who knows? Probably not. Either way, best keep a lookout for Five, just in case they come sniffing.'

'Thanks, Mr Sable. I'll let the others know.'

'Good. How's it going?'

'Getting interesting. Let's put it like that.'

'Interesting as in theoretically challenging from a training perspective, or interesting from a "we may have a problem but just don't know how big yet" perspective?'

'Potentially the latter.'

'Right. Well, I'll let the HM know. Just in case. Happy trails, Foxton. Try not to get into trouble.'

'Yes, sir. I'll be sure to bear that in mind.'

Chuckling, the head of ETS hangs up, just as Milly and Anabel walk into the lobby. I quickly fill them in on Frank Sable's warning.

'Okay, should we quickly check Styles is still at home?' I ask Milly.

'He was last time I looked.' She glances again at her phone and nods. 'Still there. Good, let's go then.'

The doorman hails us a taxi and we all hurriedly bundle into the back.

'Corner of Tufton Street and Great College Street, please,' says Milly.

'Like you say, Miss,' the driver calls back, and the cab pulls away from the kerb. 'Sherlock Holmes fans, are we?' he asks in a deep-set cockney accent.

Puzzled, I glance at the others and reply, 'Why do you ask?'

'Just where you're headed, and at this time of night, too. Not a whole lot there other than lots of expensive houses. But see, that whole area, it's one of the last parts of London that still has the original gas lamps to light it up at night. It's a special kind of light. Gotta see it ta know what I mean. Not as bright as all them modern electric stuff. More mellow, if ya know what I mean. Some of them are up to two hundred years old. Means they film a lot of the Sherlock films and TV shows around there. Real *Hound of the Baskervilles* type stuff. Charles Dickens's London. Barely changed in two hundred years. Only thing missing is the mist like fog ya used to get.'

'Really,' I say. 'I had no idea.'

'Not many people do. If you're interested, there used to be about fifteen hundred of 'em in London. The old gas lamps, I mean. Few years back, some plonker in a van managed to reverse into one outside St James's Palace. And get this, week later, the same twerp went and did it again. Can you believe that? So, now's there's only a thousand, four hundred and ninety-eight of them,' he says, laughing to himself.

'How do you know all this?' enquires Milly.

'Ah, trade secret, luv. I could tell you, but then I'd have to kill you.'

Every sense in my body sharpens. I fire the girls a questioning look.

'Five?' I mouth silently.

Both shrug. Milly raises a cautious finger. The silence creeps on, two seconds, three seconds... getting awkward.

'Nah,' the driver finally says, chuckling. 'So, coupla months back, I had the bloke who's in charge of the city's lamp lighters in the back. Interesting geezer. Only five of 'em left in London. Picked him up from Buckingham Palace. He was laughing at how his team aren't allowed into Parliament for security and all, but they wander in and out of the palace every coupla weeks. Funny place, England, innit?'

The conversation falters and we ride on in silence. Before long, we pass the Houses of Parliament, before heading on towards Millbank.

'Righty-ho,' the driver calls as he turns across the oncoming traffic and enters a dark road. To our right is a long stretch of medieval-looking wall with trees overhanging it. A row of three- and four-storey houses makes up the left-hand side of the street. All are dimly lit by the scattering of gas lamps which, as the driver described, cast a lovely warm, albeit dim, cone of light around the immediate area. The gaps between posts remain unlit. Towards the very end of the road it becomes so dark that the buildings are barely silhouettes against the midnight-blue sky.

'You weren't kidding about this area, were you?' Anabel notes.

'Nope. Welcome to nineteenth-century London.'

Chuckling, the driver pulls to a stop. After paying, we climb out onto the pavement. Once he's gone, the road descends back into darkness.

'You just wait till you see Styles's house,' Milly says excitedly, leading the way.

'Just check he's there still,' I reply. 'Would suck if he's gone out in the meantime.'

'No, he's still there,' she confirms. 'Come on. It's literally just around this corner.'

We walk on and turn left into Barton Street.

'You just wait,' she says. 'It's something else.'

Judging distances in a road this gloomy proves challenging, but there appear to be about five or six houses or buildings on the right-hand side, with perhaps a few more on the left, all with good-sized frontages and black wrought-iron railings. Beyond them, the road bends to the left, disappearing from sight.

'Styles lives at the far end,' Milly says quietly as we pass beneath two trees growing from the pavement. 'Not the one dead ahead, but the one next to it. On the left. Number twenty-one Cowley Street.'

As it comes into view, she points to the Grade 2-listed building. It is a tall, three-storey, brown-brick building with a basement level and a dormered mansard sloping tiled roof.

'Holy cow, does he own all of it?' I ask.

'Yup, apparently so.'

'Damn, he must be minted.'

'Think that's putting it charitably.'

'It must've cost a fortune.'

'You're not wrong,' says Milly. 'Think he paid several million quid for it. At least. Average is about three to five mill around here. I checked. The neighbouring house, the one at the end, looks like it could be some Royal Society of some kind. All ornate pillars and balconies. Even has a flagpole jutting out the front.'

'Some neighbourhood,' Anabel mutters.

Whistling lightly under my breath, I suggest we get closer and do a subtle walk-past.

'Yes, because this is so subtle, isn't it?' Milly sniggers. 'Late as anything, and three teenagers just wandering down Millionaire's Row. Yeah, dead subtle.'

'It's fine,' I assure her. 'Hardly anyone's even got their lights on. No one'll notice.'

As we approach the bend, Styles's terraced house comes fully into view. The only external illumination comes from a single streetlamp located almost directly outside the house and two small porch lamps set either side of the ornate black-and-white front door. Their glow bathes the lower floor in a focussed cone of warm light. The building's windows all have similarly whitewashed frames. Ornamental wrought-iron railings cover those on the ground floor, providing a semblance of security. The house has an otherwise featureless frontage, made up entirely of the same brown brick as its neighbours, typical of so many well-to-do nineteenth-century London homes. Inside is in darkness, save for two windows on the second floor. As we turn the corner, we all jump as the neighbour's basement-mounted security light bursts to life, illuminating the whole front of the house, and much of the street, in a stark, white light. Cursing, we scurry on.

'You see anything inside?' Milly asks.

'Not really,' I reply.

Anabel also shakes her head. 'Perhaps it's best we set up farther along the road, maybe where it gets dark again?' she suggests. 'And wait and see what happens.'

With no better alternatives, we slink back into the shadows of a brown, arched doorway belonging to the last house on the street, from where we have an unobstructed view of Styles's house, now some forty metres away.

The wait is slow and tedious. Minutes tick by with a frustrating lack of urgency. Small talk soon dries up and boredom sets in. The first hour eventually passes, and with no sign of movement from Styles. Standing becomes uncomfortable. Feet begin to ache. Backs stiffen. The second hour quickly takes on a feel of torturous boredom, and eventually we find ourselves sitting in a row next to each other on the entrance step, our backsides slowly going numb from the cold, hard stone.

I am about to suggest the other two go for a walk to alleviate the boredom when I notice movement on the second floor of the building opposite us.

'Heads up,' I say, pointing. 'Someone's coming down the stairs there.'

The others look up as the ground-floor lights come on, followed, a second later, by the light in the entrance hallway.

'Turd, someone's coming out,' I blurt out.

'What do we do?' stammers Milly.

'Act sort of pissed,' I whisper urgently. 'We can't look like we're just loitering here. They're bound to call the police.'

Milly and Anabel look at me blankly in a moment of uncertainty.

'Just do it,' I hiss, this time more firmly. 'We cannot get arrested for lurking like idiots!'

Taken aback, they giggle nervously and hurriedly stand. Anabel takes the lead and quickly assumes character. Together, they stumble backwards into the wall, where they put their heads together and giggle conspiratorially.

Sighing in exasperation, I take my phone from my pocket, activate the screen and hold it to my ear, just as the opposite front door opens and an elderly couple emerge. They immediately stop and stare at the darkened doorway in which we are standing. The man takes a protective half-step forward. Clearly movements in the shadows around here are cause for concern with the locals.

'No, wait,' I laugh, easily loud enough to be heard across the road. Stepping out onto the pavement, I crane my neck to look up at the building looming high overhead. 'No, we're outside. Just come down and let us in.' I allow for a brief pause, then add, 'Okay, put Sally back on the phone...'

The couple close the door on the other side of the road, and with a final curious glance in our direction, carry on up the street.

'Who's Sally?' Anabel giggles.

'How the heck do I know?' I reply, smirking, as I watch the old couple turn into the next side road. 'That was close.'

'Too right,' Milly sighs. 'We probably should have had a better cover story for hanging around here like this.'

'You're not wrong,' I admit. Then, smiling, I add, 'Once you come up with something plausible, I'd love to hear it.'

'Yeah, bet you would. Hey, check this out. Styles's mobile phone just went dead. Signal's gone. Think his battery died?'

'Who lets their battery die at home?' Anabel asks. 'There's always a charger lying around, surely.'

'Hang on,' I say, raising a hand for silence. 'His door's opening.'

Light spills onto the street, and for a moment a figure is silhouetted in the doorway. I edge the others back a little into the shadows and watch in fascination as Robert Styles closes his door and locks it behind him. Then he slips his keys into his outer jacket pocket, dons what looks to be a farmer's peaked cap and sets off at a brisk pace along Cowley Street, towards us. He is dressed in jeans and a Barbour jacket, with the collar turned up at the back. He takes the same road as the old couple and slips from sight.

'Right, come on, let's go,' I say urgently.

We emerge into the street and run across it.

'We've got to keep eyes on him,' Milly warns as we reach the corner, just in time to see Styles turn left at the end onto Great Peter Street. 'There's no fall-back plan now, not with his phone off.'

'Wait a sec,' says Anabel. 'Does it strike either of you as odd that he turns his phone off tonight, but kept it on every time he went to meet that Pelt guy?'

'Well, maybe he thought he could explain away meeting a journalist,' theorises Milly. 'Especially a political journalist. But who knows what he's up to tonight. What if he's meeting a member of Chinese intelligence?'

'True,' I say hesitantly. 'Though, it's a bit of a leap…'

'Okay, fair point. But what,' Anabel speculates, 'if he's just having an affair or something?'

Milly and I stare at her for a moment.

'Then our whole theory goes up in smoke,' I say. 'And is it really an affair if you're divorced –'

'But still living together,' Anabel notes. 'Something which just strikes me as weird.'

'Either way, perhaps best if we split up,' I say. 'Less chance he'll spot us. I'll bet you he turns left and heads up towards Westminster station. If he'd wanted a taxi, he'd have called for one. Reckon he's on foot tonight. Tell you what, why don't you both beeline it back into Great College Street and then head towards Abingdon Street Gardens and follow him from there. I'll stick with him here for now.'

'Which is Abingdon Street Gardens again?' Anabel asks, pulling out her phone.

'It's back where the taxi turned into the Sherlock Holmes neighbourhood,' I explain. 'Where all the journalists always do their pieces to camera with Parliament behind them.'

'I know the one. It's not far,' Milly says, pulling on Anabel's sleeve.

'Cool. I'll call you and let you know what he's up to if he goes another way.'

As my friends depart in a rushed walk, I hang back, peering around the corner at the back of Robert Styles. He quickly passes the Institute of Economic Affairs and Great Peter House. At the end of the road, he stops, looks left and right and then glances warily over his shoulder. I stay hidden but note his caution with interest. Satisfied, the MP turns left onto Millbank and quickly crosses over onto the other side of Abingdon Street, closer to the Palace of Westminster. With a safe enough gap established, I set off after him, staying on the left-hand side of the road.

Making good time, Milly and Anabel soon message to say they have reached the gardens. From there they quickly spot Styles. Staying within the confines of the gardens, they keep pace with him, while I hang back far enough not to be noticed. There are surprisingly few people on the streets for a Saturday evening, and Styles walks fast, soon reaching Parliament Square Garden, where he crosses over again to pass by the statue of Sir Winston Churchill. As he does, he tips his hat.

It is a strange detour, I think, because then he crosses back over the road again towards the gated entrance to the Houses of Parliament. At some point he has put on a pair of glasses, further disguising his appearance. He does not acknowledge the police officers milling about near the gates, and quickly crosses at the zebra crossing, before passing the closed Tesco Express located beneath Portcullis House. With a final cautious look back in all directions, he darts into the entrance of Westminster Tube station.

The three of us hurriedly regroup and follow him in as innocuously as possible, hanging at least twenty feet behind him. Using different turnstiles, we follow him onto the descending escalator and calmly ride it down into the bowels of the cathedral-like Underground station. With its exposed rock- and concrete-clad walls, metal walkways and industrial piping, it reminds me of what the Batcave might look like, albeit with all the lights turned on.

Ahead of us, we can still see Robert Styles. Two groups of late-night commuters walk between him and us, hopefully masking our presence somewhat. He heads into the Jubilee line and waits for a southbound train to arrive; there's one due in two minutes.

We use the next tunnel to gain access to the platform and stay a safe distance farther along it, casting only occasional glances at the electronic schedule board above him. But it is not the timing of the inbound train which interests me but rather his demeanour. While he seems calm, neither happy nor anxious, it does not look like he is simply on a night out. The late departure means he would only catch the second half of most restaurant's last seating. All West End shows got underway at least an hour ago. And pubs only have a short while left before they close. And who arrives at friends' this late? Frowning, I ponder what he is up to. Skulking around the Tube at night in a poor attempt at a disguise when surely a government car is at his beck and call seems curious.

We hear the train approaching well before we see it. A pre-emptive blast of hot air signals its imminent arrival.

A moment later, the familiar illumination from the headlights lights up the tunnel's mouth, before the train thunders into the station, accompanied by its strangely high-pitched whine and the rattle of the rails as it decelerates to a halt. The doors hiss open and the ritual of letting passengers off before boarding plays out along the length of the platform.

We wait until Styles gets in before hurriedly following suit, stepping into the brightly lit carriage at the opposite end to him, just in time before the beeping noise of the doors and the whoosh as they close.

We ride on in silence, seeking to attract as little attention as possible. To that end we sit several seats apart. The carriage bumps and rocks its way noisily along the winding tunnel. A steady gust of wind streams in through the open window at the far end. All too aware of what's purported to be floating around in these tunnels, I avert my face from the draught and turn in the other direction, to peer up with disinterest at the string of adverts above the opposite windows. Quickly boring of posters for accident claims lawyers and upcoming entertainment events, I let my eyes drift to the headlines of the newspaper being read by a businessman sitting next to Milly. The same paper which she is also clearly reading out of the corner of her eye.

As the train pulls into the next stop, the tannoy announces our arrival at London Waterloo.

'Change here for the Northern line, Bakerloo line, Docklands Light Railway, Waterloo and City and southwest rail services.'

With a flick of her eyes, Milly directs my attention to where Robert Styles was sitting. Following her glance down the carriage, I see he has stood up and is now waiting to get off the train through the carriage's far doors. At once we stand and disembark with the other passengers alighting here, and join the slow procession meandering along the platform towards the connecting tunnels and the exit. Allowing ourselves to be split up amongst the other commuters, I deliberately hold back and let Milly and Anabel – both of whom are several inches shorter than myself and therefore less likely to draw his attention – to take point, following closely behind Styles as he boards the first of several escalators that take us higher and then higher still up through the station's many levels. Until, finally, he leads us out into the main concourse of Waterloo Station.

Dialling Milly, I drift off to the right of where I can see them walking. She picks up quickly.

'This place is a fricking nightmare to follow someone,' I mutter, sure to keep an eye firmly on the fast-moving MP's distinctive cap. He meanders across the station, then through several shops but without paying attention to anything within them. Then, unexpectedly, he exits the large WHSmith, turns ninety degrees and heads back into the Underground.

'Oh, hello,' I exclaim. 'Now, is it just me or is this beginning to feel a lot like someone who doesn't want anyone to know where he's going?'

'Good, it's not just me, then,' Milly jokes. 'What's he up to?'

'And where's he going?' Anabel adds.

'Heads up. He's going down again,' I say. 'Let's keep on him. See where he takes us.'

'Chinese Embassy most likely,' Anabel mutters.

We hang up the call and proceed through the turnstiles and down another series of escalators into the stiflingly hot underground passages. There, on the northbound Bakerloo line platform, Styles boards another Underground train. Milly and I hang a carriage back, while Anabel boards Styles's. This journey does not last long, either. And shortly thereafter he disembarks at Piccadilly Circus. Again, we join another slow procession of late-night revellers as they troop up the stairs and through the long, winding tunnels, past the billboards, posters and advertisements that line the walls and escalators. With puzzled expressions, we follow him up and out of the station.

'Hey, hey,' I say, gesturing for Milly and Anabel's attention. 'This is getting a little too weird. Best we hang back. It would suck for him to spot us now.'

Piccadilly is heaving. The chaos, fear, paranoia and general sense of unease which has gripped so much of the country these last few months since the attacks seems nowhere to be felt here.

'You wouldn't think people were getting gunned down here in their dozens not long ago, would you?' Milly says, shaking her head sadly.

'Life's gotta go on, I guess,' I reply grimly.

'Yeah, and people forget fast,' Anabel adds. 'Sometimes I don't think people want to remember.'

We walk on, reflecting on ways the country has changed since the attacks, while up ahead Robert Styles makes a beeline towards and then across an equally busy Leicester Square. There, to our amazement, he heads back into the Underground and takes the Northern line down to Embankment, where he takes the long route through the tunnels to the District line.

'This is starting to get boring,' Anabel notes with a yawn as we board another carriage.

'Too right,' I mutter. Muffling a yawn of my own, I glance through the connecting doors to the carriage in which Styles is seated. The familiar beep-beep-beep sounds throughout the train. Suddenly, and with surprising speed, Styles leaps to his feet and squeezes out through the doors just as they close.

Cursing, I lunge for the door nearest us, but too late: I fail to reach it in time and instead smash forcefully into it, to the consternation of the people standing near it.

'What the hell?' Milly cries.

'Shit! We let our guard down. He fricking scarpered,' I sigh resignedly, slumping against the door as the train pulls away and rapidly gathers speed with its familiar accompanying whine. We can only watch in frustration as Styles hurries off towards the opposite platform.

'How?' says Milly with a frown. 'Do you think he saw us?'

'I'd be impressed if he did,' replies Anabel. 'We were pretty careful, especially as it was only the three of us.'

'Agreed,' I add. 'I suspect he was going to do it at some point regardless. His patterns were evasive from the start.'

'Larger teams would've been prepared for that, though,' says Anabel. 'Someone would have remained on the platform. Just in case, right?'

'True,' I concede. 'What do you think?'

'Question is, who did he think would be following him?' Milly replies. 'Journalists? I mean, possibly, but the paparazzi aren't the KGB. You know they're there. Cameras and flashes and everything.'

'Could the Chinese be following him?' Anabel speculates quietly. 'If he's on their leash, surely they'd want to keep an eye on their asset.'

'Perhaps, but then why would he give them the slip?' I ponder.

'Hev's right,' says Milly. 'If he's working with them, or for them, then it's not them he was looking to give the slip to tonight. It has to be someone else he's avoiding.'

'But who then?' says Anabel.

'I don't know. But your first guess would have to be Five's counter-intel teams, right? Makes sense if he's playing for someone else. Maybe now's when we call Gambon,' Milly suggests firmly.

'Yeah, I think you're right,' I say, taking my mobile out. 'Let's get off at St James's Park. We'll call him from there.'

CHAPTER 8

A MEETING OF MINDS

Maida Vale, London, NW8

'Did you even try to brush your hair this morning?' Anabel asks as we turn into yet another quiet, tree-lined residential side street full of large detached and semi-detached houses, many of them Georgian and all of them gorgeous.

'Not really,' I reply. 'We were in a rush.'

'You know, I don't think I have ever met any girl who takes less interest in her appearance than you.'

'Oh, that can't be true. I take loads of interest in my appearance.'

'No, you don't. You hardly ever wear make-up. I don't think I have ever seen you paint your nails, and your hair, well, the less said about that mop the better. You could do so much with it.'

'Anabel's right,' Milly sighs. 'So, where exactly are we going?'

'Apparently, it's where Gambon and his mates sometimes meet for Sunday morning brunch when he's up here,' I reply, happy to change the subject. 'Some cosy little pub tucked away in leafy suburban northwest London was all he said.'

'Well, he got that bit right,' she says, gazing at the street's large houses. 'And how much farther is it?'

'Yeah, not far,' I reply, glancing at my phone. 'Says it's just around this corner, and then diagonally on the other side of the road.'

'You said it was only a five-minute walk.'

'No, I didn't. Gambon said it was five minutes from Maida Vale Tube.'

'Oh...'

'And how long's it been since then?'

'I don't know. I didn't think I needed to time it.'

'Who exactly are we meant to be meeting there?' asks Anabel.

'Search me,' I reply. 'All he said was to be here for midday. And that we'd discuss it all here. Not on an open line,' I add, grimacing humorously as I recall the minor dressing-down I received for saying a little too much on the phone last night. 'Okay, turn right here. This is Grenville and Clifton Hill. Should be right across the road.'

Sure enough, just a little farther on, on the other side of the road, we spot a gallows-like sign hanging over a thick hedge. It reads 'The Clifton – public house'.

'Cool, that's the one,' I announce, pointing at the light-brown-brick three-storey building which is shielded from the road by several trees and a high hedgerow. A small side road beside it leads to the back of the building. Halfway down it, beneath a sheltered doorway, we spot the main entrance. As we head towards it, a call comes from the other side of the hedge.

'High-beam, we're in here,' calls out a voice I don't recognise.

'Oh, for fark's sake,' I sigh. 'Will that sodding name ever go away?'

Peering through a break in the hedge, I spot Gambon sitting with two other men at the beer garden's farthermost picnic table. All three have their backs to the far-end hedge, giving them a commanding view of the terraced area. Theirs is the only one of the half dozen tables with a large sun umbrella above it. Which might be why the others remain unoccupied. Gambon waves us over.

We step up into the small patioed front garden and walk over to join them. Sitting to Gambon's right is a distinguished-looking, grey-haired man, slightly younger than our headmaster, with glasses and a checked flat-peaked cap. One very similar to Robert Styles's. He smiles as we approach. To our headmaster's left is a far younger man, perhaps twenty years their junior, with fuller dark hair, in jeans and a T-shirt, who is trying hard to hide his amusement at some shared joke.

'I genuinely thought that was her operational name,' the man in the cap protests as he rises to greet us. 'Is it not?'

The younger man shakes his head with an embarrassed little smile.

'I sure as hell hope not,' I say, shaking his hand as I slide onto the bench opposite them. 'It's more the nickname from hell. Thank you, gits from Hereford.'

'Oh, someone from down there gave it to you?' the elder man enquires, retaking his seat.

'Don't ask,' I sigh as Milly and Anabel climb in on either side of me. 'Desperately trying to get it to go away.'

'Ladies, may I introduce Sir Martin Hargreaves,' Gambon says, gesturing the man to his left with the flat-peaked cap.

'Chief of SIS,' Milly adds quickly. 'Otherwise known as C.'

'Correct. And his chief of staff, William Sanders.'

A short round of introductions and handshakes follows, after which the younger man passes us a food menu and goes inside with our drinks order.

'We're just waiting on two others to join us,' says C, glancing at his watch. 'Should be here any minute.'

'What are you doing in London, sir?' Milly asks the headmaster.

'As chance would have it, I've been invited to a meeting of the Joint State Threats Assessment Team in Whitehall first thing tomorrow morning. So, thought I'd come up for the weekend. Catch up with some old faces.'

'Sounds fun. What is it?' I ask.

Gambon looks at Milly, directing the question to her.

'The JSTAT was set up in 2017,' she replies without thinking. 'It's composed of senior officials from the intelligence agencies and key government departments and was set up in response to the threat posed to the UK from foreign intelligence agencies.'

'Oh...' I comment, cursing silently as I probably should have known that.

'What's being discussed, sir?' says Anabel.

'China mostly,' replies C. 'And a bit of Russia.'

'Why, what's China done now?' she asks.

'More like what haven't they done,' C says with a dry chuckle. 'Take it you saw that the US Defense Secretary said in an op-ed piece for the *Washington Post* over the weekend that China has been running tests in the hope of creating biologically enhanced soldiers.'

'I hadn't heard that,' I reply, glancing emphatically in Gambon's direction.

'Thought you'd be interested in that one,' C says with a smile.

'What kind of tests were these?' I ask.

'The data's pretty thin at this point, but I wouldn't be surprised if the source lies close to home, if you get my drift. By which I mean I wouldn't be surprised if those samples taken by the people at Pemberton-Smythe's quickly found their way back to the mainland. The PLA has certainly shown historic interest. It would be surprising if an unrelated group were also interested at the same time. Quite what the connection between both parties is, however, remains anyone's guess.'

'Money and power?' Milly suggests sarcastically.

'Probably,' Anabel sighs.

'I'm curious, Ms Heathcote-Wong,' C says, turning to face Anabel. 'What's your take on where this could all be going?'

Surprised to be asked, Anabel shuffles in embarrassment, sliding her hands beneath her thighs.

'Well, nowhere good,' she begins hesitantly. 'That's for sure. I mean, only last week, US officials came out saying that China is now the single greatest threat to the planet economically, militarily and technologically. So, the rhetoric is certainly ratcheting up on all sides. Which is interesting, given America's apparent desire to sign that trade agreement with China.'

'Ah, the duality of international relations,' C notes with a smile. 'On the one hand, the US continues to come down super-hard on what they call Chinese plans to rob, replicate and then replace commercial competitors globally. On the other, they seem as keen as always to form a better trade agreement. All the while viewing many of China's top companies as merely a thin layer of camouflage for the party's underlying interests.'

'Doubtlessly so,' adds Anabel as she reaches for the food menu. 'Everything with China has to be seen through the lens of what they're trying to achieve. The way they see it, China needs a strong centre, which in their eyes means the party. Throughout their turbulent history, whenever China was weak in the centre, what resulted was chaos and upheaval. Achieve a strong centre and you get a happy and prosperous China. The question your committee needs to ask itself is whether that will satisfy them. Or will it just make them flex their muscles and bully everyone to get things their way?'

'Perhaps the prudent global response,' C suggests, as his chief of staff returns from the bar, 'is to hope for the best but prepare for the worst.'

'Agreed,' says Anabel. 'But they're a long way ahead of the West. For years, the CCP has been at it to change the international world order through all sorts of different channels. They want to reframe the world's view of China in a more favourable light, tarnish their critics and generally undermine the world's ability to counter China's rise.'

'Not doing a particularly good job of some of that right now, are they?' William Sanders comments.

'Depends on your point of view,' Anabel counters. 'They've been fairly successful at enlisting a lot of very pro-China supporters. They have all sorts of strategies to achieve this. In China, you'll hear a lot of terms getting bandied about, like *heishou*, strategies for dealing with hostile enemies, and *biaotai*, which is about securing declarations of allegiance, especially from foreigners, which they then publicise to validate the CCP's standing. They've done a pretty good job in getting Western corporations to pressure their governments on matters relating to China. They have invested significantly to bring large parts of the developing world into their corner. Often through loans, debt, security provision, all that sort of stuff.

People could write books about all the different strategies they are employing. In fact, I think people have. There's a very good one you should try called *Hidden Hand*, if you're interested.'

'I might just try that,' Gambon notes, amused at Anabel's lecturing such senior intelligence officers.

'It's all about the party,' Anabel stresses. 'You know the PLA is not actually the national army of China, right? It's the military wing of the Communist Party. And for the party, the most important thing of all is the concept of face. Losing face, suffering embarrassment or humiliation, all that stuff, is, like, so bad over there. People go to silly lengths to avoid it, even just socially, never mind politically. And on a national scale, like in China, it can drive the entire political agenda. It's old-school and clichéd, I know, but the old Sun Tzu expression "to know your enemy, you must become your enemy" is so true. China wants to be the top global superpower. But mainly to cement prosperity, security and peace at home. Because that's what they've kind of promised their people.

'Their biggest fear is the house of cards comes down and they face a collapse of support for the party back home. Chinese history, don't forget, is basically three thousand years of the rise and fall of one dynasty after another. They've made all sorts of promises on this front, and here comes the face bit, because not making good on those would be, like, so embarrassing.

'And then comes the making right of historical grievances. China has a really long memory. And in its recent history, which they'd view as the last several hundred years, they've basically been humiliated by pretty much everyone – the Russians, the Brits, the Americans, half the European nations, and on and on the list goes. But certain things stand out. The Opium Wars, for instance. And related things, like the British and the French burning down the Summer Palace in Beijing in the early 1860s. That probably still pisses them off big time. Admittedly, it was in response to the Chinese imprisoning and torturing members of a delegation sent to negotiate with the Qing dynasty leaders. But who's counting that?

'And as far as China's concerned, they're only doing exactly what they saw all the other big, rising empires do over time. The Greeks, the Romans, the Brits, even the Russians and the US more recently. Rigging markets, bully-boy tactics, blah, blah. Just do what you want and sod what people think. The real joy for the Chinese right now is how fragmented and divided the West is. They know they can keep pushing the boundaries and no one'll do anything. And by the time the West wakes up and sees how far the line's been pushed, China won't care anymore. Say hello to my twenty-four carrier battle groups. That sort of thing.'

'Perhaps you should be there at the briefing tomorrow,' C laughs. 'I'm sure you could deliver all this better than whoever they've got lined up for it.'

'Guess it doesn't help that the Russians keep testing the fences, either,' I say, keen to make up for not knowing what tomorrow's committee is.

'Well,' Gambon replies, 'the Russians have been trying to rig elections and interfere in foreign political events for as long as I can remember. Tried it with Thatcher after she came to power in '79. Part of the reason behind her dislike for the miners. Had nothing to do with her being a snob. Truth was, their union was being financed by the KGB. That the Swissies blocked the payments was irrelevant as far as she was concerned. And it's never stopped. The Russians' efforts have merely evolved over time into these new groups they deploy to achieve much the same ends, like that new Sandworm unit, 74455.'

'The ones who attacked the Ukrainian power grid,' C says, nodding.

'And Macron's presidential campaign in France at about the same time,' Gambon adds. 'Then there was the Olympics in Korea and Japan. Hillary Clinton's campaign, too. They're also the ones who attacked our investigation into the Salisbury radioactive poisoning.'

'The joke is, we know who they are and where they are,' William Saunders says as a waiter arrives with a tray laden with craft ales and soft drinks. 'Perhaps we should just knock on the door of twenty-two Kirova Street in the delightful Khimki suburb of Moscow and just ask them to stop?'

'At times, Bill, one is almost tempted,' C says. A moment later, two men with dark hair walk into the beer garden. Both could be in their forties. One is dressed in chinos and a striped shirt with a blue cardigan draped over his shoulders. The other is in jeans, a shirt and a Barbour jacket.

'Well, this is impromptu,' the cardigan-wearing man exclaims. The two late arrivals quickly take hold of the nearest wooden bench and drag it over to join the end of ours.

Gambon quickly introduces the cardigan wearer as Mark Scorecroft, the cabinet secretary, who he says 'heads the Civil Service, is a senior advisor to the PM and is in charge of overseeing the intelligence services and their relationship with the government'.

'That there,' he adds, 'is David Young, who's the DCIS, or director of counter-intelligence and security.'

Introducing ourselves, we shift up a little and make room for everyone to fit onto the combined benches.

'Are you lot with Six, too?' Scorecroft asks as he eases himself onto the bench next to us.

'Not exactly,' C interjects before any of us can answer.

'Oh,' the cabinet secretary replies, intrigued.

'It's funny you call it Six still,' Milly says before he can ask more.

'Part of the culture, I suppose,' Scorecroft replies. 'I know it's technically obsolete, and you'll never see it on the office stationery, but it does have a certain ring to it, don't you think?'

'Certainly part of the culture,' C notes. 'Part of the brand. It's what people recognise. Adds to the cult of British intelligence. One that's been carefully crafted since the time of Kipling's *Kim*. Bond merely drove the dagger home, so to speak.'

'Must have irritated a few people when the Security Service went back to using the old MI5 name, didn't it?' Milly asks.

'Would've been helpful had they told us,' C replies, nodding. 'Would frankly have been better had we both done the same thing. But there we are.'

'I can imagine,' David Young replies. 'Oh, by the way, did you ever manage to get that clock of yours fixed?'

'Ha, eventually yes, thank you, but you wouldn't believe the hassle,' C groans, rolling his eyes.

'What's that?' I enquire, cheekily interrupting what's clearly a private conversation.

'Last time we were having coffee,' the DCIS replies, amused, 'C, here, gets a panicky call from his secretary saying his clock has stopped and asking whether he has a number for anyone who can come service it.'

'What's this for? Your watch?' I ask.

'If only,' C sighs, picking up his phone. 'No. Outside my office on the leadership level, I have this rather large old grandfather clock.' He scrolls quickly and turns the handset around to show us a photo of a standing clock that must be about seven feet tall, made of solid oak. It has a square top and an open glass front through which we can see the mechanical complexity within. 'It's got great history but is an absolute pig to service, because there really aren't that many people around who know how to service a hundred-year-old clock –'

'That took some work,' C's chief of staff reminisces painfully.

'Let alone many for whom we can get security clearance to come into the building,' Gambon chuckles. 'I'm so glad my old problems are now your problems.'

'Yes, thank you, Gambo, for that heartfelt sympathy,' C drawls sarcastically, putting his phone away. 'Had it not been made by Cummings, I'd have tossed the bloody thing out the first time it went wrong.'

'Still have the chair by the desk for those quiet chats?' Gambon asks.

'Wouldn't do without it,' C laughs.

'If not with Six, are you with Five, then?' Mr Scorecroft asks, still clearly puzzled who we are, given our present company.

C and Gambon chuckle. I cast a look at our headmaster, unsure if the cabinet secretary is even cleared to know about Godolphin Park.

'Tenacious as always,' Gambon says, reading my thoughts. 'No, they're with me.'

'Ah, with you,' the cabinet secretary says, catching on. 'That's a little unusual, isn't it? I didn't think you had an operational capability. I thought it was purely a training capacity down there.'

'Well, recent events have somewhat strained resources,' interjects C.

'I can well imagine.'

'Which means for certain particularly talented individuals,' Gambon explains, casting a smile in our direction, 'some light operational experience is now coming their way. If Cheltenham had their say, Ms Butterworth there wouldn't be here right now.'

'And a pity you missed our earlier conversation with Ms Heathcote-Wong here about China and current international affairs. I can see where your talents lie, young lady,' C adds.

Embarrassed, Anabel blushes, lays her menu down and climbs up from the table.

'I'll go get some food,' she offers.

'Good idea,' says Milly, rising to join her. 'What do you fancy?'

'We ordered when we arrived,' Gambon replies.

'Can I just get the chicken Caesar salad, with bacon and croutons?' I ask, glancing quickly at Anabel's menu.

'Nothing for us, thanks,' the DCIS says. 'We can't stay long. Lunch with the PM, I'm afraid. But we'll come get a coffee,' he adds as he and the cabinet secretary head inside with my friends.

Once they have gone, C turns to me and asks, 'So, what would you have said if he'd asked where your talents lie?'

'Err...' I begin awkwardly.

'You don't need to answer that,' he laughs. 'If you were going to say good genes, you'd largely be right, but it's not the answer I was thinking of.'

'How so?'

'I think it's fair to say I have a pretty sound nose for what makes a good operative. The best, I've found, are those who've been living double lives for years before they were ever recruited. Homosexuals, people with deep secrets. People like you, in fact.'

'In what way me?'

'Well, I knew your mother, you know,' C says. 'Your biological one, I should add. Long time ago, of course. So I understand why you're different. I imagine you never knew any of the history when you were growing up. And probably a good thing, too. But you knew you were special, didn't you? Different to your friends. I expect that made you conceal a lot. That sort of experience makes one mentally fast on one's feet and tends to help one mask the tells of deceit well. People love to mystify what it takes to succeed in this world, but I think it's as simple as that. In fact, I'd say, and don't let this go to your head, but you may have all the makings of a model spy. And that rather unique blood cocktail of yours is just the icing on the cake.'

'I don't... I don't really know what to say to that.'

'I think you do.'

'Yeah, right,' I scoff depreciatingly. 'Honestly, I still can't quite get my head around all of this. It is pretty mad.'

'Interesting that you still find it so challenging to accept,' Gambon comments. 'But I suppose as if one's teenage years aren't hard enough, having all this on top can't help. Perhaps we take it for granted at times how challenging this may be for all of you, let alone with what *you* have to deal with. Not exactly a classic childhood, I suppose.'

'I could add, Ms Foxton,' C says, casting a pre-emptive look at the pub's door, 'that while the circumstances of your very real lineage have been made into something of a cliché by the movies, it's actually nothing more than an evolution of something that's been progressing since World War Two, when German troops were issued Pervatin during the invasion of France, which is basically methamphetamine.'

'Yeah, I heard about that somewhere,' I say. 'Wouldn't they go for something like three days straight without sleep?'

'That was about the sum of it,' Gambon says. 'Of course, that it also caused recklessness and a dangerous lack of empathy probably wasn't top of the Wehrmacht's list of concerns, but it gave them a superhuman mindset for those few critical days.'

'I suppose,' I ponder out loud, 'if you think about it that way, perhaps it's not such a stretch to see how several decades later, what with leaps in science and so on, building on the concept like Genesis did wasn't actually that incredible.'

The conversation ends abruptly as Anabel, Milly and the two government men return.

'What did we miss?' Milly asks keenly, slipping in next to me.

'Not much,' I reply. 'We were just talking about how the quality of MI6 referrals correlates to the referee's age. Like, for example, how someone close to retirement may not be a good judge of a candidate in their twenties.'

'Is that so?' says the DCIS, nodding.

'And I rest my case,' C says, looking emphatically first at me and then Gambon. 'Well, now we're all here, perhaps you three best tell us about what you found out over the last few days.'

Taking turns, we recount the recent events that began with Guy Forbes's unorthodox request that *we* uncover the source of recent government leaks. And how initial findings narrowed the list down to Robert Styles. The five men listen intently and without comment. Though it is obvious the cabinet secretary is less than thrilled that a member of the cabinet was put under surveillance by the country's security services.

'I don't disagree with your conclusions,' says C finally. 'If a member of the cabinet is indeed found to be in the service of or aiding a foreign power, then this government will be in the biggest political scandal since Profumo.'

'Worse,' the DCIS interjects. 'Since Philby and his bloody idiot friends.'

'Agreed,' Gambon adds. 'And these kinds of thing have an unnerving habit of coming out eventually. We absolutely need to know for sure. Then we can take the necessary steps. So, not a word of this to anyone, clear? Should the press find out, then we're truly buggered.'

'Yeah,' I sigh despondently. 'More good news.'

'It's still concerns me that Forbes came to Thirteen with this,' C says. 'That is unusual, especially in that he requested you young ladies by name. I know he was aware of you, Heather, at a high level. But not your friends here, surely. What's the angle?'

'Literally summed up what I've been thinking since his visit,' says Gambon. Tapping the table pensively, he adds, 'Motive. That's what I want to understand.'

'Who, Styles's?' the DCIS asks.

'No, Forbes's.'

'Interesting, why? It's not like putting a stop to the leaks is so unreasonable, is it?' he replies. 'I agree the approach was odd. But not the oddest thing I've seen from him.'

'Styles is the more interesting to me,' says the cabinet secretary. 'I've seen some nefarious stuff in my time, but deliberately sabotaging your own government at a time of national crisis, that beggars belief. To what possible end?'

'Tell them about the drive,' the DCIS says.

'What drive?' asks William Saunders.

'I must stress the confidential nature of this,' the cabinet secretary says, dropping his voice, 'and that it must not go beyond this group. It took a while for us to see the pattern. As you know, after results of a general election are known, as a new government is inbound, the new PM submits a list of the candidates he or she desires to make up their first government. The Security Service pulls the files that they have and assembles a dossier on all of them for the new PM. In it is all the bad news, all the skeletons and so on that the PM ought to be aware of before giving out ministerial portfolios. It started back in the fifties and sixties, when there was a real fear that the communists might infiltrate a sympathiser into government. It's handed over on a zip drive, which the PM then keeps safely.'

'That we know. But not sure I like where this is going,' C groans.

'I expect you can guess what's coming,' says the cabinet secretary.

'Oh dear, when did he lose it?' asks C, shaking his head ruefully.

'A while back. It was kept in the safe at Chequers. One evening –'

'Wait! That's what *it* was?' I blurt excitedly. 'I was there when they found out the safe was empty. Well, not on the day itself. But soon enough after. It was a training exercise –'

'They always are,' the DCIS mutters ruefully.

'The issue here,' the cabinet secretary adds, 'is that the leaks came in the exact same order as they appeared file-wise on the drive.'

'But how would Styles have gotten hold of it?' Milly asks.

'We don't know how it was taken,' Mark Scorecroft sighs. 'Very few people knew the safe's combination. And when is anyone's guess. The PM hasn't consulted it for a good while.'

'So, you think Styles got hold of that memory stick and then used that in combination with all the info he was getting in cabinet to discredit his peers?' Milly hypothesises.

'Would explain how he knew the details that were never in their briefing papers,' Anabel surmises.

'Agreed,' I say. 'But how do you know the PM didn't just give it to Styles? They're close, right? Minister of morality and all that. Could you call it a "need to know to do his job"? And then maybe he lied and said it must have been nicked, like that night when we cracked the safe. Maybe so he didn't have to admit he had given it to a friend who probably wasn't cleared to see it, technically speaking.'

'It's a good theory. Anyone want to go ask the PM?' C chuckles.

'Okay, fair point. But either way,' I continue, 'now it's just a simple question of whether Styles did it purely for personal political gain or at the behest of a foreign power –'

'Like the Chinese?' suggests Anabel.

'Exactly.'

'Well, I am loath to speculate,' Scorecroft says. 'But it might be worth noting at this point that on Friday, Styles's office filed travel plans for him to visit Hong Kong in a couple of weeks' time.'

'Well, that has to be the clincher, surely?' I exclaim.

'It doesn't look good, I will admit,' says C. 'But as I am sure you will have been taught, jumping to conclusions where the data does not support the view is best to be avoided.'

'Yeah, I'm pretty sure the headmaster mentioned something about that,' I reply with a smirk.

'Good. Well, we need some answers,' C announces. 'Did the travel itinerary give indications as to what the purpose of the trip would be?'

'I'd have to check to be certain, but I think it was listed as a personal visit, for family reasons,' the cabinet secretary says. 'But there was some official business, if I recall correctly.'

'Suppose it makes sense,' Anabel chips in. 'His wife has family there.'

'If you could check, Mark, that would be good. In the meantime,' C continues, 'it would be prudent to keep an eye on Styles. If the trip is for family reasons, then he has no reason to meet anyone there in an official capacity. Curious time to go, though. It's China's front garden and in the grips of yet more protests and riots.'

'Seems to have been like that since the yellow umbrella troubles of 2014,' Gambon says grimly. 'Not likely to get much better any time soon, either.'

C glances at his watch and then ponders for a moment.

'Douglas, what are the chances you could spare these three young ladies for a few more weeks, till we can get to the bottom of this whole curious affair?'

Dr Gambon glances at us and then at the reigning spymaster.

'The lower-sixth still have several weeks of summer placement left. So, time is not the issue. What you're proposing is no small assignment, though. There are considerable risks involved. Least of which is getting spotted by the minister himself. And not much support out there if things unravel.'

'I completely agree,' C stresses. 'All I am thinking is to go out there and keep an eye on him. Watch him when he has no formal commitments. Much like what you have done so well these last few days here in London. Just to see whom he meets. If all he does is go for family meals and take the Star Ferry to go shopping in Kowloon, then you get a nice trip out of it. But if he meets, let's say, people of interest, especially anyone from the other side,' C says, raising a finger. 'Well, that might just give us the insight we need to begin applying the necessary pressure to ease him out of the cabinet.'

'Certainly better than confronting the man with hearsay and unfounded allegations,' the cabinet secretary agrees.

'It sounds fun,' I say, grinning at Anabel and Milly.

Neither answers. I glance around to see the reason: a server is walking towards the tables with a large tray laden with plates and cutlery. She sets everything down and wishes us an enjoyable meal.

'Best we be off,' says the DCIS, glancing from his watch to the cabinet secretary. 'Need to be at Number Ten for one p.m. We'll let you all work out the logistics. Suffice to say, mum's the word for now.'

The men shake hands with everyone at the table and then quickly walk away from the beer garden. A moment later, two car doors slam and a powerful vehicle pulls away from the kerb. Tucking into my salad, I look expectantly at my friends. They both nod, but with perhaps less enthusiasm than I might have hoped for. Anabel looks decidedly conflicted.

'It could be kind of fun,' she suggests with a less-than-certain shrug. 'My only worry is that the city's in a bit of a mess right now. We might not notice it, but –'

'Agreed. We sure about this?' Milly asks, possibly hoping that someone will quickly come to their senses and put an end to what I imagine she thinks is not the smartest of ideas.

'You're perfect. We can't ask any of our own people to do it,' C's chief of staff says. 'Dispatching live operational intelligence officers in pursuit of a current cabinet member on Chinese territory comes with all sorts of problems. But with you, we could call it a training exercise.'

'They are technically on their summer placements,' Gambon notes.

'Exactly,' Saunders exclaims. 'Even better. We can claim it was limited-scope live practice foreign-assignment training – should anything happen that requires explanations.'

'Of course, we wouldn't let you go in cold,' C stresses. 'We would ensure you received the same kind of foreign-placement training all our Foreign Office staff and armed forces personnel receive. We just need to make sure that everything runs smoothly and that there are no unforeseen complications.'

The chief of MI6 glances at me. The meaning is obvious. In an instant, the hitherto forgotten spectre of my own recent failures in Switzerland return to me with a sharp, resounding slap, draining me of confidence and enthusiasm.

'Yeah, look,' I sigh, deflated. 'It's flattering and all, you know, that you think we should do this. But they're right. Maybe going out there isn't the best of ideas right now.'

Laying his knife and fork down, C fixes me with a tolerant smile.

'You know, people who are good at something have usually failed more times than any beginner has even tried.' Pausing, he takes a considered moment to cut his steak. Starting to chew, he adds, while pointing his steak knife at me, 'Is this sudden deflation because a certain so-and-so gave you a hard time? Someone who's never been in the field herself, never at the sharp end of the spear. You think that her view somehow carries the requisite weight to make you doubt yourself? Because of what? Because she has a fancy title? The number of idiots I've seen pass through government ministerial posts is, frankly, astonishing.'

'Well, it's…' I sigh, frowning. 'It's…'

'Let's be blunt, shall we, Heather? All the would-haves, could-haves in the world are just hypothetical recriminations. They have no place in our work. People in this business make the best calls they can, often in crappy circumstances. But hear me when I say, doubt kills. When I realise I have made a mistake, which I do, frequently, I find it's worth remembering that in 1788 the Austrian army mistakenly attacked itself one night and in the process ten thousand men lost their lives. Perspective, Foxton, perspective. Now, I assure you, what happened over there in Switzerland was not a screw-up. Either believe me or don't. But let's be clear, shall we: you need to stop doubting yourself. You're strong, fast,' he says, counting on his fingers as he goes. 'Senses like a damned cat and, thanks to your childhood, you have a suitably secretive nature. Frankly, few people are as suited to live operations as you. You need to get your head around this, understood?!'

'Okay, I'll try.'

'I think what the chief is saying,' Gambon adds, 'is that we have complete faith in all three of you. We would not suggest it otherwise.'

Glancing at the others, I shrug. Both Milly and Anabel give me "What do you think?" looks.

'Screw it,' I laugh, stabbing a large piece of grilled chicken. 'If you put it like that. Sure, why not?'

'Good, then that's settled.' Turning to his chief of staff, C adds, 'I want a new code word created for this little venture.

That way we can limit the number of people with access to the product that comes from it.'

Nodding, William Sanders consults his phone for a moment and then looks up.

'How about Operation Rust?'

'That'll do. Now, rules of engagement,' C says, suddenly more serious. 'No engaging with Robert Styles. Under any circumstances. If he does contact agents of or those affiliated with the Chinese government, you will disengage immediately and board the first flight out of the city. Under no circumstances will you engage those assets in any way, shape or form, understand?'

We nod.

'You said we need to do some training,' Anabel says. 'Where will that be? Up here in London at VX?'

'The Office, you mean,' C asks with a chuckle. 'No, definitely not. You know, one day when they sell that place and everything's declassified, I think people will be surprised what it's actually used for.'

Anabel asks what he means, but his reply is merely a cryptic smile.

'So, where do we go for the training?' I enquire.

'Somewhere far more appropriate. In fact, probably our most important facility. Lovely place. Nice and quiet. Down on the coast. One of my favourite places to go. I always take the quarters above the gatehouse. Wonderful break from the city.'

And with that, C returns to his steak.

'How's the food by the way?' he asks innocently.

*

Given the narrow window before Robert Styles departs for Hong Kong, the spymasters ask if we can reach the training facility by nightfall so that we can join the scheduled classes due to begin first thing tomorrow. That means very quickly getting our affairs in order: namely, checking out of the hotel, returning to school, packing for a few days' training and then reaching the facility. All in less than six hours.

Milly and Anabel are keen to get going as fast as possible. However, there are a few errands I want to run before I leave London, given that I don't know when I will be back. We therefore decide to split up, with Milly and Anabel returning immediately by train. I will drive down later and meet them at school for the onward trip to the training facility.

Their comments from earlier have been playing on my mind. Whilst not particularly susceptible to peer group pressure, their observations about my appearance struck a note for some reason. Perhaps when I was younger I might have cared a bit more. But then, around the age of twelve, my mother began with her pushy attitude to how I looked and dressed. Given that I was now a young lady, and should look the part. To the point that even going to the shops felt like we were about to do an editorial photoshoot. Like anyone, my natural reaction was to push back and rebel against her. The result is the slightly tussled mess I see in the mirror each morning.

Perhaps my friends are right. Maybe I should make more of an effort, but only because I want to, and not because I am being pushed to. With an accepting shrug, I head off across the West End to fit in a few desperately needed treatments. This includes getting a facial, sorting my brows and having a full-on mani and pedi session at a place I know.

It's only afterwards, when I'm standing on the pavement outside the nail salon, that I pause momentarily amidst the bustle of passing tourists to consider whether there is anything else I need done near here. For a moment, I even debate getting a bikini wax done, but quickly decide against it. Amusingly, I immediately feel proud of my decision. For some reason, the thought of getting one done just seems to conflict with my current state of mind. I don't know why. But oddly it does. So, no thanks, not today. Besides, as I think about it, why would I want to go back to essentially looking like a child, just as I am about to head off on an adventure that feels properly grown-up and mature? There seems a right contradiction there. And, Sod's law, I bet we don't get within a mile of a beach in Hong Kong.

As I dwell on my thoughts, which strike me as surprisingly profound, I find myself sinking into a curiously melancholy reflection. It dawns on me that perhaps my problem is I haven't actually made my own self-esteem for a while. Others have. Like my mother. Peers at school. Or strangers, like the sodding home secretary. Or social media, smart marketing and the endless stream of porn that is sent mainly by boys at school on a near daily basis. All constantly pressurising us to conform to someone else's ideal. It doesn't help to find myself seeking validation from boys I am interested in. Like Alex. As a result, I am constantly emotionally undermined by my desire for a relationship. For closeness and intimacy. And yet somehow my relationships all seem to go wrong. Is it my fault? Is my parents' deteriorating relationship my fault as well?

Being reasonably self-conscious, I'm aware of my hormones and their occasional effects on judgement. As a result, I always try to remain cognisant of the risks of seeking affirmation from others. Especially boys who're just past puberty. I'm not so foolish as to think any boy my age is even slightly ready to settle down – as much as that pisses me off. But Alex felt different. Maybe that's what all girls like to think. That somehow we're different. That maybe boys will change for us. More foolish thinking, I realise.

The problem with generally being quite the optimist is that sometimes it only takes a small, innocuous comment to upset the emotional apple cart and sink me into a spiral of doubt and introspection. Perhaps it is because when criticism comes I am often unprepared for it and don't know how best to respond. Sometimes my instinct to retaliate or defend myself fails me and instead I find myself looking for merit or truth in the accusation or criticism. Which is what happened with the home secretary's criticisms. I mean, technically it *was* my fault that delays occurred getting the information out before the attacks. And that was a mental speed-bump I found insurmountable. Of course, constant chiselling like this is not constructive, or healthy, but to then have had one's confidence so utterly shattered by a total stranger, a senior government figure, is galling. And I have had far too much time to dwell on it. No wonder it has so badly undermined my self-esteem recently.

But then some of C's words of encouragement come back to me, and a small, warm feeling of confidence begins to rise deep within. His words are infinitely more credible than hers or, for that matter, my own sense of insecurity. And the strength they instil in me is unlike anything I can muster myself.

Confidence begins to surge through me again, and a crazy idea comes to mind as I look at the next shop window. For a moment, I'm conflicted, unsure if I have the nerve to go through with it. Making it back to school in time to meet my friends won't be possible. But their earlier comments bring a devious grin to my face. Quickly, I call them and arrange to meet them in Gosport later. Because this I must do. With my mind made up, I walk excitedly into the reputable West End hair salon.

CHAPTER 9

1MTE

Gosport, South Coast, UK

As expected, my self-indulgent detours in London delay me by several hours, but the ensuing mad thrash back down the A3 towards school not only tests the national speed limit, but also narrows the gap considerably and keeps a large grin plastered on my face for the whole journey. A frenzied ten minutes of packing, and it's straight back on the road again.

I make good time and am only an hour behind my friends as I reach the outskirts of Gosport, down on the south coast. Waiting at a set of traffic lights, I run my fingers affectionately across the grained black-leather dashboard as BTS's Butter pumps from the very expensive, high-end sound system its previous owner saw fit to have installed.

'I love you so much,' I laugh. Smiling, I glance at my phone and reopen the note from our headmaster.

Girls,
      Your destination is MTE *(no. 1 military training establishment)* at Gosport. Located in Fort Monckton, it is the most important

establishment in SIS's property portfolio. And for the next few days, the field operations training centre will be your home. For background, it is where we teach basic and advanced field training to operational personnel and where we do liaison training with SAS/SBS. We have several courses on this week, one of which you three will join.

Gambon.

Following the sat-nav's staccato-like instructions, I soon find myself approaching the coast on a narrow stretch of isolated road. Open grassland lies on either side. I message the girls, informing them of my imminent arrival. Then, tossing my phone onto the passenger seat, I pass a lone road sign at the side of the road which reads:

Smiling, I accelerate on towards the fort, which resembles something between a low-lying medieval coastal fort and a prison. It is surrounded on three sides by acres of grassland which provide a healthy perimeter. On the far side lies the sea. A zigzagging high stone wall snakes around the entire facility.

As I pull up to the barricaded guardhouse, a sentry wearing a plain, unmarked blue uniform steps out and requests my ID, as well as the confirmation documents I received from an anonymous looking e-mail address shortly before departing GPS. Once he's satisfied that I am who they were expecting, he waves me through another metal gate. A high, castle-like perimeter wall encircles the inner facility. The short stretch of road takes me across a sunken, grassy moat which might once have been filled with water to a second, more intimidating barrier gatehouse. Above it is a roofed building with windows overlooking the approach.

After clearing another round of security checks, during which I have to explain all over again why my appearance is now so markedly different to the photos they have on file, I am finally waved on through into a long, triangular-shaped parade ground cum car park. There, a similarly uniformed security guard points me towards the parking spots closest to the low-slung wing where we will be housed.

Two-storey buildings surround the car park; older ones crafted from large blocks of Purbeck stone sit alongside newer ones made from light-brown brick.

My friends emerge out into the car park as I pull up into a free parking space. Turning off the air-con and radio, I breathe a deep sigh of relief to finally be here and open the door. The air is wonderfully crisp and fresh, with the heady scent of the sea infused into it. I can just hear the waves breaking on the beach beyond the main building. Overhead, seagulls hover effortlessly in the wind and squark shrilly.

'Whoa,' Milly exclaims the moment I climb from the vehicle. 'What happened to your hair?'

'Yeah, I know, right,' I reply, grinning as I examine the reflection of my radically new haircut in the rear window. Gone is the long, tussled mess of old. In its place, an elongated pixie bob: short at the back, a shaved undercut on the sides, but airier and more textured on the top, with a long, side-swept fringe on the right-hand side.

'Wow, the top's almost pompadourish,' she exclaims excitedly, moving closer to hug me in greeting. 'There's enough product in there to keep a collapsed soufflé upright.'

'Well, it's certainly a bit of a butch-up, isn't it?' Anabel says, smiling, as she too embraces me. 'Kind of looks like a Roman legionnaire's helmet.'

'It does not,' I exclaim, aghast, pulling away in mock offence.

'I'm definitely getting slightly gay vibes,' Anabel whispers excitedly to Milly, deliberately loud enough for me to hear.

'Yeah, don't go getting any stupid ideas,' I fire back, emphatically jabbing my thumb at myself. 'It's just more practical, if I say so myself. Especially if we're headed off on a mission. I figure it's blind luck that I haven't had my hair grabbed or used against me more up till now. This is just more practical, but at the same time looks like I mean business, don't you think?'

'Oh, it definitely shows that,' Milly laughs. 'You sure you aren't secretly embracing some kind of bold new identity?'

'Hanging around with us a little too long?' Anabel enquires flirtatiously. 'We rubbing off on you? Coz it kind of looks a bit like, how shall I put it... a bisexual bob.'

'It does not,' I laugh. 'Do you even know what a bisexual bob actually looks like?' I fix her with a playful pointed look. 'Yeah, my point exactly. And just so you know, this is called a long pixie.'

'It's kind of Brie Larson Captain Marvel, don't you think?' Anabel teases, turning to Milly. 'Is that's where she got the idea? I bet it is.'

Scowling, I stoop to pick up my bag.

'Jesus, the crap I have to put up with. Besides, I never do anything fun or exciting with my hair. I figured, time for a change. A whole new Heather. Besides, the rate this mop grows, it'll be half grown out by the time the summer hols start.'

'Rather you than me,' Milly laughs. 'If mine grew that fast, I'd cry.'

'And be penniless broke,' Anabel adds.

Nodding, I look around and take in our surroundings properly for the first time. A small look of concern ripples across my face.

'God, what have we got ourselves into this time?'

'If I recall correctly,' Milly says, pulling a comically thoughtful expression, 'wasn't it you who said this was a good idea to the chief of MI6?'

'Yeah, whatever. Didn't hear any of you objecting.'

'As if. This place is something else,' says Anabel excitedly. 'We really are in the black world now.'

'Telling me. They almost turned me away at the gates. Said I didn't look anything like my photo anymore.'

'That's so funny,' giggles Milly. 'But you do look really different.'

'Come on. I gotta dump my stuff. Let's walk. Tell me all about it as we go.'

'From what one of the instructors was telling us earlier,' says Milly as we set off, 'there's a couple of very cool flat, grassy areas at either end of that long building. Over on the sea-facing side. Nice views, apparently.'

'I bet,' I reply, breathing in the fresh sea air deeply.

'This place is, like, two hundred and something years old,' Milly continues. 'There used to be a castle here, but they dismantled it back in the reign of Mary Tudor. Or somewhere around that time. Most of this used to be an army barracks, I think. Rooms seem pretty standard. Kind of Ikea. But comfy enough.'

'Good. So, who comes here? I mean, Gambon said they use it as a training facility for Six.'

'Everyone we've seen so far is kind of... how shall I put it?' Milly says, looking at Anabel for suggestions.

'Reticent?'

'Yeah, that's a pretty good word for it. They all look like SIS Intelligence Branch.'

'Agreed,' says Anabel. 'Haven't seen anyone who looks military yet. Nor any General Service officers.'

'The ones I've met,' I say as we reach my room, 'you'd never know they were. Not from looking at them, anyway.'

'Suppose,' Milly replies. 'Anyway, it's an early start tomorrow, as we have quite a bit to cram in. Did you also pack for Hong Kong?'

'Nah, was in too much of a rush.'

'Not surprised,' says Anabel, gesturing to my hair.

'See you also had your lashes and a mani done,' observes Milly, ever the eagle-eyed friend.

'Would have been criminal not to. When's the next time I'll be able to? Besides, I figure we'll have to go back via school when we head to Heathrow. I'll pack then. Coz I meant to ask you what to wear anyway.'

'Sure,' says Anabel. 'Tomorrow?'

'Yeah, that's fine,' I reply. 'An early night might not be such a bad idea.'

After bidding them goodnight, I am only too glad to quickly shower, change and then pass out almost the moment my head touches the pillow.

*

Breakfast in the fort's mess, early the next morning, is a rushed affair. With a takeaway cup of coffee in hand, I hurriedly follow my friends across to the main block, where we are to receive a short briefing from the base commander before joining our course.

We are met at the ground-floor entrance by a bespectacled man with a comb-over which fails to hide the fact that he is, in essence, bald. He's neatly dressed in a navy-blue, ribbed woollen jumper and beige slacks, and is holding a clipboard. After noting our names, he nods and gestures we should follow him up the stairs to the first floor. Halfway up, Milly stops and points quizzically at a long metal pin mounted on the otherwise bare wall.

'Sorry,' she says. 'What is this?'

Smiling, the bespectacled man comes back down a few steps.

'Oh, this old thing. Wasn't this on the staircase up to the accommodation level? Didn't even realise they'd moved it. It's from the Telemark raid during the Second World War. When we destroyed that Nazi heavy water plant in Norway. This is one of the rods that controlled the flow of water. Or something like that. There's lots of great stuff like this dotted around the place. Right, shall we?' he says, gesturing the way.

At the top of the stairs, we follow him down a long corridor to the entrance of a room set up with a semi-circle of tables and chairs arranged in its middle. Multiple flat-screen TVs cover the walls. The décor, like in the rest of the facility, is modern and relatively minimalist.

'Dave, the people from The Office are here,' he announces.

'Good, show them in, please, will you, mate,' someone within the room replies gravely with a Yorkshire accent.

'He'll see you now,' the man says, showing us in. Sitting near the window, finishing off some paperwork, is a bearded man in jeans and a well-fitting red T-shirt. He glances up momentarily, then goes back to what he's signing, before coming back to us with a more considered look.

'Oh, good Lord,' he exclaims, pointing at us in disbelief. 'I know they say this is a young person's game, but you've got to be joking.'

Rolling my eyes at the comment, I drag a chair away from one of the tables, swivel it around so that it's back to front and sit down. Sighing, I turn to my friends and say sarcastically, 'Everyone's a bloody comedian today.'

That gets a few laughs, especially from the bespectacled man, who is still standing in the doorway. With a glance back at Dave, the base commander, I reply, 'You ever consider that if *you* don't believe it, then chances are, neither will anyone else?'

'She has you there, mate,' the man by the door calls with a chuckle. Turning, he heads back into the corridor. We can still hear him laughing as he retreats down the stairs.

'That's a nice sea view,' Milly says, walking to the windows, from where she is afforded a panoramic view of the small beach directly below and the Solent beyond. A short way along the coast is the entrance to Portsmouth harbour. An Isle of Wight ferry sails slowly past outside in the channel.

'Can we get down to the beach?' Anabel asks.

'Bet we can find a way,' I say, joining them to have a look.

'Right, you lot. Take a seat. This will be real fast,' Dave announces, walking over to close the door. 'So, first things first, welcome to 1MTE. A couple of ground rules for you three. You've come at a bit of an awkward time. We're currently running our normal new recruit course, which lasts for six months. Allows us to finish all the background screening while they're here. I need to warn you, though, none of them use their real names here, and discussing details of one's personal life is prohibited. Chances are, few of them will ever see each other again. So, I need you lot to stick to this, too. No trying to get their names or anything from them while you're here, okay?

'As for your names, we don't want you using them, either. So, from here on out, you're Doris, Betty and Mildred,' he says, pointing to me, Anabel and Milly in turn. 'Understand?' Ignoring our less than impressed looks, he continues, 'If indeed you need to use names. "Oi, you" should suffice. We have you down for the Basic Foreign Posting course, in which you'll be covering kidnap protection, escape and evasion. All the good stuff that Foreign Office types get briefed on pre-foreign deployment. What's complicating matters a little is that thanks to a brilliantly mistimed refurb programme the MOD is doing down at the Lines, we're running the SAS's Counter Hostage Training Course here, too.

'Make no mistake, we'll go hard on you. They may be simulations, but we want to make them as real as possible. I want you all to understand what it feels like to be in the trenches. Because if you don't understand this, then you're not going to be able to respond in those few critical moments when it all hits the fan for real.'

Pursing his lips, he pulls three folders across the desk and opens Milly's and Anabel's first. He skims through them, nods and then comes to mine. Upon opening it, a scowl fixes itself to his face.

'Well, well, what have we got here, then? Redacted, redacted, redacted. Black marker everywhere. Fat load of use this is. Might as well be empty. Oh wait, look. Does say potentially aggressive temperament. Well, at least there's something here we can work with…' Sighing, he tosses my folder aside. '…so long as you remember to channel it. Moment it controls you, you're buggered.'

'Thanks. I'll bear it in mind.'

'Make sure you do. We don't get many second chances. Says here you three are heading off abroad in a few days and they want to avoid complications. Take it that means something to you?'

'You think they mean Pemberton's home?' I ask my friends.

'Homes,' Milly corrects me. 'It's pretty much been a disaster at nearly all of them. Oh, and in India, too, I suppose.'

'Yeah, and don't forget the top of that mountain,' Anabel adds, trying to hide an amused grin.

'Yeah, you're right,' I sigh. 'In truth, it's pretty much all been a bit of a royal screw-up. I don't even know why we're being sent to Hong Kong.'

'Speak for yourself,' giggles Milly.

'And no locations, either, please,' says Dave, tiring of our immature banter.

'Okay, sorry,' I say. 'It just seems kind of weird, right, that despite our track record, they keep sending us on these fieldtrips. Don't you think?'

'Seems someone up there either really likes you or really hates you,' Dave notes in amused exasperation.

'Yeah,' I reply. 'Because that's just the kind of clarity I love so much about all this stuff.'

'Well, if you three really want to see what a royal screw-up is, keep watching,' Dave says, pointing out the window at a green civilian helicopter on final approach to land in the grassy area by the north-west bastion. 'Because here come two of them in person.'

*

'Holy crap,' Anabel exclaims in a hushed whisper of excitement as we leave the briefing room and descend the stairs on our way towards our first session of the day. 'The royal twins are here!'

'Come on, it is kind of cool,' Milly gushes as she stops by a window and strains for a view across the car park, desperately hoping for a glimpse of the new arrivals who emerged from the helicopter half an hour earlier.

'Okay,' I admit grudgingly. 'It is kind of cool.'

'Jesus, you're so blasé,' says Milly. 'Did you hear what he said? Prince Henry and Princess Stephanie. They're here! Where we are. In this base. Like, right now.'

'Er, yes, I was there, too. For their annual security refresher training. Yes, I know.'

'Do you know what that means?'

Fixing her with a look that hovers between complete disinterest and abject sympathy, I sigh and say, 'Yah, I'm just not that excited.'

'Why not?!' Anabel demands.

'Coz I doubt they'll let us within a million miles of those two.'

'Why?' she says, disappointed. 'They're our age. Maybe they'd like to hang out.'

'Well,' Milly reflects. 'She may not be wrong. I guess the whole point of them being here is to prepare for what happened to Princess Anne back in the seventies.'

'What was that?' Anabel asks.

'Oh,' I interject, 'some nut-job handyman ambushed her car in one of the London parks one night. Shot her driver, shot the copper with her. And tried to kidnap her.'

'Whoa, I never knew that,' Anabel exclaims. 'How do you know all this?'

'She knows everything,' I reply with an eye-roll.

'Fair point. But how do *you* know this? You usually have no clue.'

'That's harsh. Take it back,' I laugh. 'My point is, if the whole reason for them being here is to keep them away from the plebs of society, you seriously think they'll let us lot anywhere near them?'

'I don't know. Maybe. I mean, aren't they always in London's swankiest nightclubs? Or at big parties at friends' country estates? That sort of thing?'

'Yup,' I reply. 'Or at least that's what rumour control says.'

'Maybe they're freaked out after the attacks?' Milly suggests.

'Well, can we at least try to see if we can spot them? Maybe over there, where all those people are?' Anabel asks, pointing across the car park to where a crowd has gathered.

'Can't hurt,' says Milly. 'Let's do it at lunch. We're busy till then,' she adds, glancing at the paper timetable. 'Come on. It's this way. We have an introduction to basic foreign posting and then, at ten thirty, we have a session on how to avoid getting snared by foreign agents or killed by terrorist groups. We really sure we want to go on this trip?'

'For sure,' I exclaim. 'It sounds a laugh and a half.'

'You and I have very different senses of humour.'

'What do you think?' I say, turning to Anabel.

'Oh, I don't really care. I'm just glad to be going home again.'

*

By the time we leave our classroom, from where we have watched the growing commotion all morning, and make our way across the main car park, it's with distinctly different thoughts. For Milly, the morning was filled with an endless list of reasons why the upcoming trip to Hong Kong is nothing but bad news. Tales of Terry Waite, an Anglican Church envoy, kidnapped in Lebanon and held for four years, not to mention the dozens of cases of diplomatic staff killed, wounded or turned by the enemy whilst serving abroad, have done little to ease her concerns.

Anabel, on the other hand, genuinely doesn't seem to care anymore, which is genuinely surprising given how cautiously she usually behaves at school.

For me, while the content covered in today's classes was sobering, it wasn't scary. Perhaps because this whole mad adventure started all the way back with my own attempted kidnapping. It was reassuring to hear that when it came to fight, flight or freeze, my response was the best option on the table, and I didn't hesitate then, so what's there to worry about now, after all the training we've had?

During the morning, all the cars were moved to a secondary car park, outside the fort's main wall. Mine included,

I note. Two thirds of the space created was then turned into a large, open training area. Freshly applied yellow tape denotes roads, and several old cars, all of which have seen better days, as well as a few black Range Rovers are parked in the middle of the new mock streets. The far end of the car park is now dominated by a hastily erected two-storey wood-framed building, which is crude but effective. It was assembled from prefabricated sections offloaded from a series of long, flatbed lorries which have come and gone all morning. Large, flexible rubber tubing connects many of the rooms to industrial-grade extractor fans. Reams of cabling leads from the building to an innocuous white van parked around the side of the makeshift building.

'What on earth have they built here?' Milly asks, casting a look up at the crude, boxy structure.

'I think I know what it is,' I say as we approach. 'So, down in Wales, some of them were telling me about something called a killing house.'

'See?' Milly exclaims with an exasperated flap of her arms. 'What did I say about this just getting worse and worse!'

'It's to practise hostage rescue stuff. Storm the building. Gas, guns, live ammo. That sort of thing. But, like, the whole nine yards. Rubber walls to absorb the bullets. Fans to clear out gas and smoke. You know. Fun for the whole family.'

'You realise our idea of fun is vastly different,' Milly notes sceptically.

'Guess they video all of it?' Anabel comments as she peeks into the open van as we pass by. 'Thing's full of CCTV screens.'

We make for a patch of grass set off on the side to sit down and watch while we have our packed lunches from the canteen. Within seconds we are approached by a severe-looking man in a green, heavily ribbed woollen jumper with shoulder epaulets and elbow pads.

'Do you lot have clearance to be here?' he asks, consulting his clipboard.

'I don't know. Do we?' I reply, glancing at my friends.

'It's alright,' calls another man from beside one of the nearby Range Rovers. He's equally serious looking, but is dressed in black fatigues, combat boots and full assault kit. 'They're fine. Not SIS.'

'Interesting,' I ask, thinking aloud. 'Why would you not want anyone from Six to watch this?'

'Standard OpSec,' Clipboard Man replies before heading off across the car park.

'They're still doing the background checks after all,' Anabel suggests.

'Yeah, maybe.'

The man who's wearing fatigues – who could well be an officer, but it's always hard to tell with the Regiment – pauses and looks over in our direction again, but this time more appraisingly than before. He tells the soldier he was talking with to hold that thought and walks the fifteen feet to where we are sitting.

'So, you're the one, huh?' he says, nodding slowly. 'Heard about you on Pen y Fan. One of the lads said it was like getting overtaken by Captain America.'

'Yeah, right,' I scoff. 'Bit of an exaggeration. That sodding mountain almost killed me.'

'Way I heard it, you kept pace with some pretty serious blokes on the DS. Guys who weren't tabbing with twenty-five kilo Bergens. So, not that much of an exaggeration.'

I shrug and lie back on the grass.

'Yeah, maybe. Anyway, so what's going on here, then?' I ask, squinting up at him.

'All sorts,' he replies, turning towards the activity. 'The lads in black are Regiment. Most of the rest are SO14 Royal Protection Group, with a couple of blokes from the Special Escort Group. Those two on the bikes. Anyone who looks homeless is probably an SAS instructor.'

Laughing, I peer past him and take in the scene. While the soldiers appear to be standing around, casually waiting for something, there's a distinct vigilance to their mannerisms. All are armed at the thigh with 9mm Glocks and across the chest with short, stubby HK MP5s. The two uniformed police motorcyclists remain off to the side, chatting idly, sitting astride their all-white, powerful Honda 1200cc police motorbikes. Both bikes appear to only be equipped with blue flashing lights, with no sirens. The Royal Protection Group are given away by their more formal attire, all slacks, ties, suit jackets or blazers, not to mention the ubiquitous transparent coiled earpieces that each has in.

Little happens for a while, so we stay where we are, munching our lunch, enjoying the simple pleasure of the clear blue sky and warm sun, while preparations continue all about us. Vehicles are moved into position, teams are briefed on their roles and equipment is checked, and then checked again. A few metres away, two soldiers sit idly on the kerbside, joking quietly about what to expect. We listen intently as one of them recalls a story about a time when Prince Charles and Princess Diana were at Hereford doing very similar training.

'... and then,' one of them laughs, 'a sodding frag grenade set her hair on fire.'

'Get it right, Steve,' the man standing over us scoffs. 'A smouldering frag landed in her hair, singeing it. That's all. But in fairness, kudos to her. I heard she had it trimmed, right there and then, so no one would notice. More than can be said for half the VIPs who go through this.'

'Heard Thatcher was hard as nails,' the second soldier asks. 'That true?'

'Steely-eyed missile lady, that one was.'

'Any of them ever get properly hurt?' I ask.

'Not yet,' the officer replies with a smirk. 'I heard Prince Charles got a little concerned for a while, sitting there, waiting for the room to get breached, and scribbled out a note in case it all went pear-shaped. It's in a frame down at the Lines. Know it off by heart. Pretty hilarious. Goes, "Should this all go wrong, I, the undersigned Prince of Wales, will not commit B Squadron 22 Special Air Service Regiment to the Tower of London."'

'That's funny.'

'Yeah. It is.'

'Sorry, what's the aim of all this training?' asks Anabel.

'Mainly just to get them familiar with what it might feel like if it does all go pear-shaped. Like if they were ever taken hostage. For us, it's vital they know how to react when we come. The last thing we want is for a hostage to panic and run into the line of fire. We need them sharp and alert, ready to move the moment one of the lads grabs them. Hope is, once they've been trained, they'll know to either remain still or hit the deck when the flash-bangs and bullets start flying.'

*

'Right, lads,' the official-looking man with the clipboard calls from the middle of the car park. 'Look alive. His and Her are on their way.'

Glancing to our left with differing degrees of excitement, we see a group of people emerge from the whitewashed building which spans the front gate access road. Leading the entourage languidly making its way towards us are the prince and princess, both of whom are dressed in black boiler suits. In person, they are taller and slimmer than expected. Both have very dark, almost jet-black hair, which makes their pale complexion all the starker in contrast. Neither is unattractive, but of the two the princess is by far the more striking.

'Don't exactly travel light, do they?' Anabel whispers.

'Well, one needs one's personal private secretary, security team, hairdresser and valet, doesn't one?' jokes Milly.

'Apparently so,' I reply slightly scornfully.

The origin of the pronoun joke soon becomes clear as the royal guests turn. Each has a respective 'His' or 'Her' stencilled in white across the shoulders of their black overalls.

After calling the group to order, the man with the clipboard respectfully beckons the day's VIPs over to a trestle table, beside which are two foldaway wooden chairs.

'Your Royal Highnesses, if we could get the pre-exercise briefing out the way, we can progress to the live portion of today's schedule.'

'I guess there's something you don't see every day,' Milly musses as the prince and princess settle down for the briefing surrounded by a large semi-circle of heavily armed, humourless soldiers and wary-looking personal protection officers. We listen in as the coordinator runs through a few safety guidelines and the schedule for the afternoon, before handing over to the SAS officer with whom we spoke earlier. He is finally introduced as Major Cedric Elroy, the senior officer present.

'At its simplest,' Major Elroy begins, stepping forward from the crowd, 'there are three options in any conflict situation: fight, flight or freeze. For obvious reasons, freeze is bad. Our aim today is to train the freeze reaction out of you as much as we can. That will leave you with two options: fight or flight. Each has its place, depending on the scenario. For everyone here, especially the security detail, some of the riskiest moments will come when their Royal Highnesses either arrive or depart a venue. As far as Your Highnesses are concerned, it is the decision of your protection officers whether to push you back into the car and evac, or make for the building. Less straightforward is the royal walkabout. In those instances, your protection detail will generally always try for quiet and discreet, rather than the heavy-handed presence favoured by our American friends. Nonetheless, our hope is that it never comes to them having to intervene.'

'And everyone's home in time for tea,' one of the troopers calls cheekily.

The resulting ripple of laughter quickly dies down as the man with the clipboard looks around with a scowl that could unnerve even the strongest of heart.

'Which just leaves fight,' Major Elroy adds, smirking. 'A strategy that's more dependent upon your instinctive responses than help coming from anyone else. How you respond when someone grabs you, lunges for you, ambushes you or rams your vehicle, or worse, will have a very direct bearing on whether you even make it home for tea or not.'

The talk goes on to cover the order of exercises that will be run over the next few hours and what each is intended to achieve. All that we are missing, I think to myself, is a proper picnic as we settle back and watch the afternoon's entertainment unfold. Dressed in civilian clothes, members of the SAS take on the roles of overfamiliar members of the public and would-be attackers, putting the royals and their security detail through a variety of ever-worsening scenarios.

Vehicular ambushes followed by frenetic bursts of offensive driving by the police drivers soon turns into a training session where the twins themselves are taught to drive tactically, using their car as a battering ram to escape being pinned in. And while it seems to come reasonably easy for Prince Henry, the same couldn't be said for his sister, Princess Stephanie.

'Is it me or do you get the distinct feeling she's not really enjoying this?' Anabel asks quietly as the princess misses her gear selection again, catching reverse and lurching the large four-by-four to a violent and shuddering halt. At precisely the moment when coming to a dead stop was the last thing she wanted. The nearest SAS man calmly steps up to her open driver's side window, raises his pistol and shouts, 'Bang" loudly enough for everyone in the car park to hear.

Visibly flailing around with rage behind the wheel, she screams an ever louder and more energised high-pitched tirade of colourful expletives, most of which are directed at the vehicle's gear selector.

'What you reckon, sibling rivalry or she really doesn't want to be here?' I ask.

'Who knows?' Milly grins. 'But she's got a temper. Oh my God, did she just thump the steering wheel? This is too funny. We should have brought popcorn.'

By this time, most of the vehicles are no longer in the best of shape, with many banged-up and dented, several with wing mirrors hanging off and one retired with steam gushing from a ruptured radiator. Those still operational are returned to their starting positions and the exercise is rerun.

Once again, the soldiers ambush the princess's car, before opening fire with paintballs at the front windows, killing the driver and security officer in the passenger seat. And because she forgot to lock the back doors, the attackers have them open before she can even reach the driver's seat. Forced to her knees in the open street with her hands behind her back, the princess is once again summarily executed in broad daylight.

'Okay, let's come back to this one later,' Clipboard Man calls. 'In the interest of time, best we move on to the royal walkabout scenarios.'

Vehicles are moved off to the side, a line of crash barriers is brought forward and assembled, and participants take their assigned places, with soldiers as the baying public masses desperate for a glimpse of the royal visitors. The royals are to emerge from their chauffeur-driven car and, in the company of their aides and ever-wary security detail, are to approach, greet and then move along the line with a swiftness that keeps them on schedule whilst trying not to look rushed or uncaring.

We watch in fascination as the royal siblings step from the car, smile, wave a classically wrist-flexing swish of the hand and then advance towards the mock crowd. Some pass across recently gathered sticks as stand-ins for flower bouquets, others ask for selfies, some share stories about how meeting them is a lifelong dream finally come true. And on down the line they progress. At every moment, we expect one of the soldiers to pull a weapon and put a pretend round through one of their foreheads. And clearly the princess also expects this. Her moves are staccato, erratic and highly cautious.

But soon they reach the end of the line, unmolested and still alive.

'Okay, back to start positions,' the man with the clipboard calls. 'Let's go again.'

Twice more the walkabout is rerun. And each time nothing untoward happens.

'What a waste of time this is turning out to be,' Princess Stephanie huffs moodily to her brother loudly enough to be heard as they take their start positions yet again. Even we, sitting twelve feet back on the grass, are beginning to lose focus and drift into private conversation.

Her piercing shriek, when it comes, jolts us alert. We all jump up and jostle to make sense of the commotion unravelling before us. Someone appears to have a firm grip of her arm and is pulling her over the police railing. Her brother appears to be laughing, several feet behind her. Her security detail run in from all directions to aid her. Her personal assistant, who was beside her, has reeled backwards in fear and shock.

'Fight back, Your Highness,' the man with the clipboard calls futilely.

The affronted, frozen look of panic on her face is, for a second, slapstick funny, and I can't help but burst into laughter. Unfortunately, my amusement coincides with the exact moment the man standing before her decides to step aside, affording her a clear, unobstructed view of my friends and me.

'Uh-oh,' Milly blurts out, turning away innocently. I watch in scorn as she and Anabel both take a step or two away from me.

'Get off me,' the princess screams at the soldier, who now has her almost completely over the barricade. 'I said, get off me!'

The soldier, however, continues, probably assuming her newfound anger is all just part of the roleplay. But the princess has visibly disconnected from the exercise and is no longer struggling but instead staring at me with a highly accusing, deeply pissed-off look.

'Something you want to contribute?' she shouts.

All around the car park, people begin to realise she is no longer engaged, and hesitation dulls their enthusiasm for the make-believe. Some of the soldiers in the crowd turn to see to whom she is speaking. Finally, even her attacker realises something is amiss and loosens his grip. She wastes no time in snatching her arm back and rubs it in irritation before turning back to me.

'Do you think you can do better?' she calls in a dismissively superior tone.

'Pissed her off now, haven't you!' Milly whispers, still pretending to look at something on the opposite side of the car park.

'So it seems,' I reply under my breath.

'If you have something to say, say it to my face,' the princess shouts. Standing beside her, aides and members of her protection detail share wary, uncertain looks.

'No, please,' she gestures disingenuously. 'Enlighten us as to how you think it should be done.'

'Guess the rumours are true,' Anabel mutters, still looking in the other direction. 'She's a bitch alright.'

'So it seems,' I reply, all the while holding the princess's gaze.

'Your Royal Highness, perhaps we should –' her closest aide begins, only to be cut short by a curtly raised finger.

'No, they all want me to pull back and drop down if someone grabs me. But it's not that easy. The attacker has the advantage.' Pointing angrily at me, she adds, 'If she thinks she can do it any better, then be my guest. Come up here and show everyone.'

'Yeah, that might not be such a great idea,' Major Elroy says, glancing in my direction.

'No, I insist,' the princess argues. 'The audience think they can do better. One should let them show us.'

'Honestly, I really have nothing to offer,' I reply, shrugging awkwardly. 'You're doing way better than I ever could.'

'Oh my God, stop staring at her like that,' Milly hisses. 'Are you trying to piss her off?'

Amusingly, that is exactly what happens. And clearly my response only exacerbates matters.

'Nothing to offer, Your Royal Highness,' she adds pointedly. Curiously, I note, she didn't offer the same helpful correction to the major standing beside her. Looking down her nose at me, she adds, 'Disrespect as well as insubordination. Well, go on, then. Do as I say.'

Sighing, I turn to Milly and Anabel, unsure how to respond. Neither knows where to look, which makes the whole exchange suddenly even funnier. It seems so petty. Unable to keep a straight face, I turn back to the now fuming princess and laugh.

'Seriously, Your Royal Highness,' I protest with a smile, 'I really don't think I could do any better.'

Princess Stephanie spins confrontationally as two soldiers a few feet behind her snigger briefly.

'Care to share what is so funny?' she snaps. Both look deeply conflicted.

'It's just... I... I can't believe she's being so unbelievably rude to you, Your Royal Highness.'

Vindicated by this damning judgement, the princess rounds

on me. Behind her, the trooper grins broadly. While I don't know him, he clearly knows me, which likely means he's heard what happened while I was on Selection.

'Indeed,' she shouts, evidently on the verge of launching another scathing broadside in my direction. I am almost relived when the tension is suddenly broken.

'Right, err, everyone,' Clipboard Man calls loudly, pointing to his watch. 'We should, well, yes, err, let's all move on to the next exercise, shall we?'

'Yeah, good call,' Major Elroy adds quickly, rolling his eyes while politely pointing the way towards the makeshift killing house.

Perplexed, Princess Stephanie eyes me suspiciously as she is led away.

'Well, you handled that well,' Milly laughs, quickly appearing beside me.

'My thinking exactly.'

'I was joking.'

'You don't say,' I scoff, folding into fits of laughter.

'Cheers for that,' Anabel sighs. 'There goes any chance of befriending them. Down in flames goes that plan.'

'Sorry,' I say with a sigh. 'My bad.'

'Pretty typical,' Milly reflects. 'I mean, things always do go down the U-bend for us, don't they?'

'Only half of which is my fault. Probably less than half, if I'm being honest. The rest is bad luck and fate.'

'Yeah, right,' Anabel scoffs. 'Either way, best we head back to class. We have another session starting in a few mins.'

'What's it on?'

'Data protection whilst outside the UK,' she replies, glancing at the timetable.

'Great. Oh well, come on then,' I say. 'Maybe we can come back out here later.'

'What, so you can piss her off some more?' Milly says sarcastically.

'Yeah, this time we'll bring popcorn,' Anabel adds with a roll of her eyes.

*

The moment the royal twins enter the fort's mess, just before teatime, the princess's hawk-like eyes rapidly scan the busy room and quickly narrow in on us, sitting off by ourselves on the far side.

'Uh-oh,' Milly mouths quietly, pointing subtly. 'They're here. That's surprising.'

'Isn't it?' Anabel agrees, before a shadow of consternation falls over her face. 'She's coming this way. Oh dear. You've done it now, Foxy. She looks really ticked-off.'

Out of the corner of my eye, I cast a look across the mess hall. Sure enough, the princess is approaching fast with long, confident strides. Her expression is indeed far from happy. Pretending not to have seen, I only look up as Princess Stephanie arrives at our table, arms folded. She takes a wary look around to see how many pairs of eyes are on her. Noting her audience, she smiles sweetly.

'Who do you think you are?' she says quietly, flashing me a wonderfully disingenuous smile. 'I don't appreciate being made to look stupid.'

'My apologies, *Your Royal Highness*, I don't see how I did.'

'Your sniggering made me look foolish. You insinuated that my best efforts were somehow sub-par. I will have you know that fighting off a fully grown man who has the advantage and likely all the motivation needed is less than easy.'

She casts another wary look around. Then she turns back to me, her chummy demeanour contradicted by the venomous delivery of the words she spits out in a witheringly patronising clipped rebuke.

'But I suspect that's not what you think, is it?'

'Hey, like I said earlier, I really had nothing to add. Not like I could have done it any better. Honestly.'

'Oh, I beg to differ. In fact, I suspect your reaction would have been very different indeed. I'm not sure that many of the others clocked it, but I certainly did. And it begs a question. Who the hell are you and what makes you so special? No, wait, don't answer that,' she says, holding up a silencing finger. 'I'm going to make a guess. To begin with, you're certainly not important. That much is obvious because I have never heard of you. And you are not with the trainees from MI6, because they are not allowed to socialise with us. So, what's that leave? You're not friends or family of anyone who works here. So, I speculate that you are something else. You and your funny friends here. The fact that you are even here means you must be HMG in some capacity or other. And they don't exactly send people from the Inland Revenue here, so that means you are from the shadowy side of things. Which is interesting. But what's really interesting is how some of the people around here handled you earlier on.'

'Oh yeah, and how was that?'

'Delicately. Unusually delicately. You see, the thing is, people like this lot, with whom my family socialise regularly, are not inclined to treat many people quite so delicately. The more senior members of the Firm, absolutely. But beyond that, I've noticed it's only those they either respect or fear who get that sort of deference. Now I didn't sense fear, but there was a wary respect. So, I have to ask, why? Why you? Why a teenage girl? I reckon there's something about you that makes you rather special, even by their standards, or else the only reason they'd give you a second glance would be to perv. I know normal. I see it every day. And you're not it. They were worried about what you would do if you had been stood in earlier today. Weren't they? Now why would that be? Why would they not want anyone to see your reaction? No, don't answer me,' she snaps, cutting off my intended protest at this belittling monologue, which is beginning to get tiresome.

'And the two jokers standing behind Cedric clearly knew of you, too. I don't imagine many teenage girls become a talking point around the barracks of Hereford unless they either wear exceptionally little on Instagram or have done something extraordinary to win themselves that kind of genuine respect. And the only thing the SAS really respect is outstanding physical achievement. Normal girls are generally not the ones putting in those kinds of performances. So that can only mean one thing. You're not normal. So, the only logical conclusion is that you are *abnormal*. It then stands to reason that you must somehow have abilities beyond most people's. And that kiss-my-arse, I don't care haircut you're sporting suggests you clearly aren't that concerned about what people think of you. That kind of arrogance is impressive, even by the standards of the circles within which I move. So, it must be justified by something. Which brings me to my last point. You are here. Normal people don't get invited here. Put all that together and I am led to one conclusion.'

She leans in closer, smiling craftily as she does so lest anyone around the mess suspect our conversation is anything but the friendliest.

'I think you are part of some sort of military programme. I'm not sure what yet. Some sort of enhanced skills thing, I would guess. Drugs, maybe? Some kind of other medical enhancement thing? The conspiracist in me would love to speculate that it's something outrageous like genetics. But whichever way, I think the signs are all there. And I think some of this lot know it, too.'

She straightens up, folds her arms and stares down at me emphatically, waiting – unblinking and clearly impressed with herself – for my answer. I can't tell if she's serious or just taking one huge, provocative punt. Regardless, to be presented with my past in such a blunt way is a bit of a slap across the face and it momentarily takes the wind from my sails. Her conclusion can only be the result of her being either surprisingly intuitive or astonishingly lucky.

'You're sharper than you look,' I begin, measuring my words very carefully. 'Let's just say, for a moment, that you're right. Don't you think it's a bit rich you giving me crap for my genetic heritage?'

'Excuse me?!' she retorts.

'You heard,' I reply quietly so only she can hear me. 'A bit rich coming from you. The way you put it. It's a little condescending, don't you think? I mean... twins. C'mon, nowadays, that's basically a euphemism for IVF. I'm willing to bet neither you nor your brother would be here if it weren't for someone in a white lab coat playing around with a couple of test tubes. Perhaps your little theory isn't so far from the truth. Does it matter? Sure doesn't give you the right to get in my face, being all superior and all, just because of the family you were born into. I'll be honest with you, for me, personally, that doesn't carry a whole lot of weight. Sure, it makes you fortunate. No doubt. And privileged? Definitely. But superior?' Pursing my lips, I slowly shake my head. 'Not to me, you're not. So please, do me a favour. Knock it off with all the attitude, seriously, before someone says something really stupid and this all gets way out of hand.'

'Excuse me?!' she replies, this time far more indignantly.

'Come on. Stop with all the "put the other person on the back foot" kind of comments. It's starting to do my head in. Look, I honestly have no issues with you. Not with you or your brother, or anything to do with your family. Yeah, okay, I did think your attempt at fighting off an attacker who means you nothing but ill earlier was a fricking joke. Maybe I shouldn't have laughed. But looking at the world you live in, it wasn't surprising.'

'I will not be spoken to in this manner by a... a commoner!'

'Jesus, will you listen to yourself?' I exclaim, standing up, noticeably more confrontationally. 'Seriously, keep it up and...'

Despite the overwhelming urge to suggest that her misguidedly superior arse might well end up getting kicked all the way out into the car park, I refrain and let my expression communicate the intention instead. At this, one of the royal protection officers steps forward and places his hand dangerously close to my chest, holding me back.

'I'll have you know that openly threatening a member of the royal household is an offence.'

My eyes narrow into a hawk-like focus that lingers on his hand for a moment, before moving slowly along his outstretched arm, up to his eyes. There they stop, affronted and annoyed, before traversing across the room to Major Elroy, who is warily easing himself off the table corner on which he was perched. Scowling, he hurries across the mess towards us and arrives just in time to lay a calming hand on the protection officer's shoulder.

'Geoff, mate, yeah, let's not do this. Best everyone calms down before someone gets hurt, alright?'

I shrug, nonplussed, and step back with an open smile.

'And with all due respect, this may go a whole lot easier if you just apologise,' he says. For an irritated second, I think he is talking to me. The words 'No fricking chance...' are already forming on my lips when I realise he is looking directly at Princess Stephanie.

'I will not,' she snaps indignantly.

'I believe it would be for the best,' he says firmly. 'This place is about forming allegiances and camaraderie, not sowing division or settling scores. Your choice, your Royal Highness. Otherwise, there's a very real chance this'll get badly out of hand. And if it does, there's not a damned thing anyone in this room will be able to do about it, short of shooting her. No offence, Geoff,' he adds, looking at the security officer. Then, sighing at the princess's reluctance, he shrugs. 'Just saying, coz the last person this one had issue with got thrown off a sodding mountain.' Seeing my intrigue, he adds, 'What can I say? Friends in high places.'

'Kicked,' I add, smiling. 'He was kicked.'

'Fine,' Princess Stephanie mutters, eying me with intense curiosity. 'I'm sorry for questioning your questionable genetic lineage.'

Every word is laced with reluctance, but they bring a smile to my face.

'Good. Now you,' the major says, rolling his eyes and turning to me.

With a laugh, I look at the princess.

'And I'm sorry for insinuating that my boot might end up kicking your overprivileged and equally genetically questionable arse.'

'Oh, Jesus Christ, you two're as bad as each other,' the major sighs. 'Sodding well deserve each other, you do. Go have a damned beer together and get over it.'

With that, he walks off to buy his police officer friend a drink, and probably explain the narrowly averted PR disaster – or certainly as much of it as he is allowed to.

Turning to the princess, I realise I should probably make up with her. In the far corner, over near the bar, I see her brother, who is clearly amused at what may well have been one of the more exciting exchanges he's witnessed in a while. As it turns out, I needn't make the first move. The princess does it for me.

'He's probably not wrong,' she notes resignedly, watching the major walk off. 'That said, I'd be interested to hear about the man on the mountain. I am intrigued now. It sounds ever so exciting and such a very different life to what I am used to. One doesn't get to kick that many people in the palace, despite what the news likes to report.'

'Too bad,' I reply with a sideways smile. 'Probably best, then, that they don't let someone like me in, isn't it?'

'You can say that again,' she laughs. 'I think you would intimidate some of the people there.'

'Oh yeah, why's that?'

'Because I bet you could probably bench-press most of them, or snap them in two if the thought occurred to you.'

'Best people don't piss me off, then, isn't it?' I add with a raised eyebrow.

'Indeed. What do you say to that drink, then?' she asks, gesturing at the bar in equal amusement.

'Thought you'd never ask,' I exclaim. Glancing at Milly and Anabel, who are looking on with comically wide eyes of amazement, I whisper, 'You two coming?'

'Oh, alright, then,' Anabel replies, and she and Milly rise faster than I have ever seen either of them move before.

'What takes your fancy?' Stephanie asks.

'Dunno. Something strong.'

'Bit early for that, isn't it?' she says, glancing at her watch in judgemental bemusement.

'Yeah, well, it's kinda hard for me to get tipsy otherwise. Bummer, but *c'est la vie.*'

'Fast metabolism?' she enquires.

'Something like that,' I reply with a resigned sigh.

'Uh-huh. Because clearly that's what no girl would ever want, is it?'

'Yeah, okay, fair point. Anyway, c'mon. My shout.'

'Really?'

'Yeah, sure. I mean, you're probably not even allowed to carry money, are you?'

*

Considering the identity of our drinking companions, it shouldn't really have come as a surprise that the two mess staff on duty would be less than enthusiastic about evicting us come closing. Which simply means we completely lose track of time, laughing and joking far longer into the early hours of the morning than any of us planned.

The result is several pairs of bleary eyes come breakfast the following morning. And that's the few of us who even make it to breakfast. The twins arrive a few minutes after me, while my friends are nowhere to be seen. Taking a seat in the far corner, off by themselves, they wave weakly and then fetch coffee. Lots of it. Stephanie is wearing sunglasses, like some kind of media-shy celebrity, and saying very little. Her brother appears to be taking no end of amusement from how rough she clearly feels. Which must be better than my friends, who still haven't made an appearance by the time I finish my third coffee.

As I set the cup down, I sense someone approaching behind me. Stiffening slightly, I glance down to my right to see a pair of combat boots come to a stop. They are well polished, but not to a squaddie mirror shine.

'So, if I had to guess,' I venture, without looking up, 'I'd say Major Elroy…'

'What gave me away?' he says, taking the empty seat opposite.

'Dunno. Figured it had to be someone who respects the military enough to use polish, but not to the point that it's too spiffy. Kiwi Parade Gloss finish that isn't.'

'Right, so what have they got you up to today?' he asks disinterestedly.

'Oh, who knows? More of the same, I guess. Honestly, I haven't looked. I figure "how not to get arrested while abroad". Or something like that.'

'Good to see you're taking it seriously.'

'I know, right?'

With a raised eyebrow, he looks down at my leg, which is twitching energetically in a rhythmic bouncing movement beneath the table.

'Don't you ever sit still?' he asks. 'You're one of those people with way too much energy, aren't you? You'd do my wife's head in. Anyway, was speaking to an old buddy of mine last night. Someone who did Selection with you –'

'Oh yeah, who's that?'

'Like I'm going to tell you. Point is, he had a lot of good stuff to say about you. If you can believe that. And this isn't someone who has a whole lot of good things to say about most people.'

'Okay, I think I know who it is.'

'He told me a story about how you RTU'd some A-hole by booting him halfway across the dorm. That true?'

'Okay, now hang on –'

'Apparently, the formal report noted it was just under twelve feet from the side of the bed to the wardrobe...'

'Yeah, whatever.'

'Suffice to say, that bit got redacted from the record. Anyway, what are you up to at fourteen hundred today?'

'Dunno. Why?'

'He said we should make sure to show you a good time.'

'If it's who I think it is, I doubt that.'

'Okay, so I'm paraphrasing.'

'What did he really say?'

'That we should shove you into the killing house. Get you to experience a breach at close range without ear defenders.'

'God, so thoughtful. I'm touched,' I drawl sarcastically. 'With friends like that, who needs enemies?'

'Yeah, I thought so, too.'

'Go on, what's the catch?'

'None, actually,' he replies, smirking at my distrust. 'Usually, there's a security clearance required for this kind of thing. But in your case, getting vouched for by guys like this carries weight, if you get my drift.'

'Yeah, bureaucratic hurdles weren't really what I meant. I was thinking more about how this could go badly wrong for me, personally. You know, live ammo, getting shot. That kind of thing.'

'So glass half empty,' he says, shaking his head reproachfully. 'Trust me. It'll be fun.'

'Yeah, right. You guys are lucky no one forces you to publish how many people get hospitalised or die in your training programmes. Okay, I'm up for it. I can't believe I always fall for this crap. Let me check something. Fourteen hundred, right?'

Reaching for my phone, I call Milly. After an amusing twenty seconds listening to a string of abuse for having woken her, I get my answer. Laughing, I hang up.

'Okay, we're free,' I reply.

'Good. Then meet us at the killing house. We're doing some hostage rescue breach familiarisation for your new friends over there. You get to see them poo themselves.'

Smiling, I turn to look at the hungover twins.

'Seriously? Reckon you're missing a trick. I mean, the state they're in... Why wait till this afternoon? You should do it this morning. Flash-bangs going off right next to your head. Just what any good hangover needs.'

'Friends like you, who needs enemies?' he notes with a devilish grin.

'Oi, that's cold.'

'But not wrong... Right, fourteen hundred. Don't be late.'

With that, he playfully slaps the table, rises and sets off across the mess to the main exit, where several of his fellow soldiers are waiting expectantly.

*

Which is how, several hours later, I come to find myself standing, arms folded, in the darkened corner of a poorly lit, medium-sized, rubber-clad room. The door opens and four soldiers drag in the royal twins, both of whom are blindfolded, and unceremoniously dump them down onto chairs set either side of a small, square table in the centre of the room. Two adjustable desk lamps sit on the table, plugged in via a snaking extension lead that disappears off beneath the main door. Glancing at my watch, I note it is now almost a quarter to three. The siblings' agitated demeanour suggests Elroy's troops have done a pretty good job over the last forty minutes of putting the fear of God into them.

Eight full-size mannequins are arranged haphazardly around the room. Five are standing, and the remaining three dummies are positioned behind and off to the side of the blindfolded hostages on small stools. All have targets affixed to their chests and faces.

A low-wattage, naked lightbulb hangs at the end of a threadbare cable directly above the table. It sways gently in an imperceptible draught. Henry and Stephanie turn from side to side, angling their heads backwards in a bid to get a glimpse of their surroundings from beneath their thick blindfolds. Neither says a word.

My instructions from Major Elroy were unflinchingly clear and delivered in the typically no-nonsense, blunt military style I sort of miss from Selection.

'No matter what happens,' he said, 'in absolutely no circumstances are you to even consider moving from your corner or saying anything.'

So here I stay, pressed into the corner, to the right of the doorway. Not two feet from me stands a cheap, badly chipped plastic mannequin clutching a wooden Uzi.

We all flinch as the door is noisily thrust open, and Elroy and one of his sergeants burst into the room. With unnecessary force, Elroy slams it closed again behind him, making the twins recoil in fear. Together, the soldiers advance towards the two visibly nervous captives. Their hobnailed boots clack noisily on the makeshift wooden floor. Elroy swats the light bulb, sending it swinging back and forth, making fast-moving, eerie shadows dance around the room.

The tough-love treatment continues for a few minutes. Elroy flicks a few bemused smiles in my direction as he leaves the two young royals in no doubt about what is going to happen to them. It's wonderfully imaginative, thoroughly unpleasant stuff. Most involves their being filmed while someone with a Stanley knife slowly deprives Henry of one body part after another, all of which will then be posted, week after week, back to Buckingham Palace until such time as the British government releases some unpleasant piece of work from one of HMG's less desirable prisons. At the same time,

Stephanie, he says, laying it on thick in a low, sinister, grumbly voice an inch from her ear, will find herself assuming the role of the number one piece of local entertainment, chained to a post in a goat pen on the dusty outskirts of some far-flung village somewhere in the Middle East for the amusement of anyone passing by. Videos of which, he adds, will find their way onto YouTube.

Even though I know this is a training exercise, with obvious limits, he plays the part so unpleasantly that the line quickly blurs and I almost begin to believe him, too. To her credit, Stephanie retains her stoic posture and composure. Like me, they must also know this is not what they are really here for. That bit is yet to come. Having witnessed Abbott and Lennox perform a breach of Pemberton-Smythe's home office a while back, I have a vague idea of how the Hos-ex might unfold.

When it comes, it is loud, fast and brutal. It begins with El-roy glancing at his watch before nodding meaningfully to the other soldier, who then swats the low-hanging bulb, sending the crazy shadows back into action. Together, they yank the twins' blindfolds off. The royals get but a second or two to blink and get their bearings as the soldiers take three fast steps backwards to press themselves up against the back wall. Then Elroy starts his stopwatch the same instant as the door disappears in a blinding flash of light. The dynamic entry has begun.

Two objects fly into the room. Knowing what they are and having an idea of what comes next is no preparation for the real thing. Even with hands clasped over my ears and my eyes clenched shut, it's impossible not to recoil backwards as the flash-bangs detonate in alarmingly close proximity. Barely are my eyes open again than the first black-clad, respirator-wearing assaulter enters the room. Menacing as hell, he takes the second of disorientation afforded him to analyse the room, differentiating terrorists from hostages, determining who is armed and who isn't. With weapon raised, he steps forward quickly, allowing two, three, then four spectre-like figures to appear from behind him amidst the smoky haze.

Without pause, they fan out into the room, radiating ill intent. The instant they are clear of the doorway, staccato bursts erupt from each silenced muzzle in a choreographed, muted frenzy of phut-phut-phuts. All hit their mark, mere feet away from the two soldiers and the two royals. My new friends cringe backwards from the double assault on their senses. Despite knowing what was coming, I can't help but flinch also as three rounds slam into the dummy beside me. Even with their suppressors, the weapons' sharp retort is shockingly loud in the close confines of the rubber-tiled room.

The impacted bullets clang noisily into the collection trays below each target, and with a tinkling of shell casings still bouncing haphazardly across the floor, two soldiers round the table, snatch the bewildered and disorientated royals from their seats and drag them towards the door. They are all gone faster than I thought possible.

Blinking with amazement, I cast an amused look at Major Elroy as he stops the timer. With a slight swaying Indian head wobble, he smiles and comments, 'Yeah, not bad, I suppose.'

'Not bad!' I reply as my heart hammers furiously within my chest. A rush of adrenaline lightens my head as I peer intently at the nearest dummy, realising just how close those live bullets came. 'They moved like greased lightning.'

'I suppose that's a compliment coming from you. Of course, it's not as dramatic as kicking someone off a mountain, but it does the job.'

'You're not going to let that one go, are you?'

'Might do if I see what a grown man getting his arse kicked across a room looks like.'

'Now there's something I'd pay to watch,' comes an all-too-familiar voice from behind me.

'Fat chance,' I scoff without turning to look at Princess Stephanie.

'Too bad, killjoy,' Elroy says with a sly smirk as he and the junior soldier walk past me. 'Your Highness, time for that debrief, I think.'

'As you wish,' she replies.

'And who let you back in here?'

Turning around quickly, she hurries from the killing house, followed by the two soldiers. With them gone, I find myself alone with just the dummies. The last of the smoke is being sucked from the room by the whirring extractor fan. But the thick stench of cordite remains. Sighing sympathetically, I turn to the nearest plastic dummy.

'Just not your day, is it? Oh, I'm sorry, what was that? You want to know what it feels like to be kicked across a room?' Folding my arms in contemplation, I turn to look emphatically at the doorway and add, 'Right, come on, then, you bastard!'

Out of the corner of my eye I see two faces peer around the shattered doorframe. Their expressions of excitement turn to frowns of disappointment as they see me waiting for them.

'Ha, knew it,' I exclaim. 'You just can't help yourselves, can you?'

'Such a crippling disappointment, you are,' Stephanie sighs. Glancing at Elroy, she says, 'Looks like we really need to go now. Bar, six o'clock?' she asks, raising her eyebrows.

'Absolutely,' I reply keenly.

'Marvellous, see you then.'

As their footsteps grow fainter, I turn back to the dummy and smile.

'Bet you thought you'd got away with it, didn't you?'

With a swift lunged kick, I launch it viciously across the room. It clears the table and flies into the far wall, where it falls, broken in half, to the floor.

'Whoopsie,' I mutter, momentarily embarrassed. Unsure what to do about the shattered dummy, I hurry, giggling, from the room. When I step out into the sunlight, it's to find Major Elroy, the two royals and three other soldiers standing beside the white control van, which is parked adjacent to the killing house.

'Well, now I've seen everything,' the major says.

'Oh yeah, why's that?'

He gestures me over and points into the van. In curiosity, I approach to find they have all been watching a CCTV feed from inside the killing house.

'Oh, bollocks,' I sigh. 'Forgot about that.'

'You have to teach me how you did that,' Stephanie gushes.

A nearby shout makes us turn in interest. One of the Regiment's PT instructors is walking energetically across the car park towards the breach team, who have begun to pack up their gear. He is in a white T-shirt and red sports shorts.

'Right, lads,' he calls. 'Who's up for some phys?'

'I'll come,' I shout back eagerly before others can answer.

'Yeah, I meant anyone but you!'

'Oi, that's discrimination!'

'Ego protection, more like,' Major Elroy teases loudly. 'I suspect the sergeant there is concerned about his men's morale should you beat all of them.'

'Right,' the PT instructor exclaims indignantly. Pointing at me, he adds, 'You, back here in ten in PT kit.'

'You're on,' I call back.

'Guess we'll see you in the mess when it opens,' Princess Stephanie suggests.

'Too right.'

'Try not to embarrass them too much,' the major jokes, gathering his phone from the van's dashboard. 'Now, how about that debrief?' he asks the royals. 'There's a few things we need to cover off.'

*

After a thoroughly amusing PT session, I hurry back, shower and then head straight to the bar for what turns out to be another epic get-together with our new friends, who seem genuinely keen to hang out with others their age, much to the displeasure of their minders, whom we suspect secretly view us as bad influences.

I wake even earlier than usual on the morning of our last day. Instead of going for a run, as I have done on the other days, I decide to head up to catch sunrise on the grassy, flat area set above an old, fortified gun emplacement at the far left-hand end of the base's sea-facing building. I arrive, slightly bleary-eyed, only to find the princess already there. A faint glow is just visible above the western horizon. In the distance, the first hovercraft of the day thunders off on its way to Ryde on the Isle of Wight.

'Morning,' I croak hoarsely. 'Oh dear, you don't look very happy. Is it just the fact that it's only Wednesday or are you still upset they ran out of Prosecco last night?'

'If only it was that simple,' she sighs, passing me her phone as I settle down beside her. I scroll back up to the top of the open internet page and begin skimming the news story, and the source of her misery quickly becomes clear.

'They for real?' I exclaim.

'Them and every other bloody British tabloid.'

'Where'd they get these pictures?'

'Where didn't they get them?' she sighs despondently. 'Clearly some "friend" was all too willing to provide them. Most likely in exchange for a hefty cheque.'

'Who's the girl in the photo? If you don't mind me asking.'

'Who knows?' she groans. 'It was late. I'd had a bit too much to drink. I thought we were alone. But hey,' she exclaims dramatically, 'guess we weren't.'

'How bad is this?' I ask.

'Well, it's everywhere,' she replies. 'Every paper now has it. It's all over social media. The bloody vultures are circling properly now, aren't they? Ugh, and it's about to get so much worse.'

She gestures beyond me. Turning, I see her brother step up onto the grassy rooftop.

'Wouldn't believe who I've just had on the phone,' he says, striding over nonchalantly. Remaining standing, he stares down at his sister. It's hard to tell if his expression is one of sympathy or frustration.

'Oh, I can very well imagine,' Stephanie replies with a pained expression. 'Papa, or one of the minions?' she asks.

'I do so wish you wouldn't call them that,' he sighs.

'So, the thing you need to understand about our family,' she says, speaking only to me, 'is the rather cold and cruel streak that runs through the Firm.'

'The Firm?' I repeat, unsure of myself.

'Yes, that's what we call the whole apparatus that surrounds our family.'

'I do wish you wouldn't talk like this in front of strangers,' Prince Henry says, finally sinking down onto the grass.

'Strangers...?' I repeat.

'Okay, that didn't come out as I meant it to,' he says, his brow furrowed. 'But in our world, trust is a nebulous concept. Chances are, those pictures were taken and leaked by someone we've known for years. You know what I mean. No offence intended.'

'None taken.'

'Like you think she will speak to anyone?' Stephanie adds. Her tone is neither angry nor humouring. 'She probably has more secrets than you or I put together, I expect.'

Her brother shrugs and runs his hands wearily through his hair. Turning back to me, Stephanie is about to continue when Milly and Anabel also reach the top of the steps.

'Wow, you two are up early,' I call.

'Didn't want to miss sunrise on our last day,' Milly replies.

Now Stephanie continues: 'Clearly, it's not lost on you that we tend to be resistant to outsiders. I suppose that much isn't hard to see. But there's also a staggering refusal in our family to act with anything approaching parental affection.'

'Oh, now come on. That's a bit harsh,' Henry protests.

'When will you stop making excuses for the inexcusable?'

'Sometimes I just don't know where all the venom comes from,' he says, shaking his head.

'Okay, well, then why don't we start with what must be sacrificed in the name of duty? Huh, how about that? And then maybe we can talk about what any normal person would consider a fair return. You know, as opposed to the vicious savaging that we get the moment we do anything human. Jesus, God forbid.'

'What do you mean?' I ask as Milly and Anabel complete the cross-legged little circle.

Glancing out to sea, Henry sighs.

'It's a low blow, but what she means is if you want to understand my life...' he says, before pausing to consider his next words. 'Well, it goes a little like this. I basically have to wait for my father to die before my life has any meaning.'

'And I,' Stephanie adds dramatically, 'have to wait for my father and my brother to die before mine takes on any meaning. Which is unlikely to happen, so I get to have fun while he sits in waiting, like a good boy. Except, if I do ever have fun, it's bound to end up in the papers, and then I find myself subject to considerable and somewhat unpleasant judgement.'

'Which is why, if I ever do become king,' her brother adds teasingly, looking at his sister, 'perhaps the very best thing you could do is to go and take a nice, long holiday somewhere very quiet, so we can avoid the tabloids crawling all over the palace for the transition period.'

'That's just charming,' she scoffs.

'Does it bother you?' I ask them.

'Not really,' Henry replies with an ambivalent shrug. 'Should it?'

'I don't know. Maybe.'

'Well, it has rather been my destiny since birth. A bit late to take issue with it now, wouldn't you say?'

'That's a fairly level-headed way of looking at it,' I say. 'In a sense, it's a little like how I am beginning to feel. Like there's this big, looming destiny that's been with me since I was born but is only now starting to come over the horizon.'

'Steph did mention something about having a theory.'

'Figured you might,' I say to her.

'Seems our lives might not be so different after all,' Henry notes with a sideways smile. 'Each with destinies ordained to one degree or other since birth. Ours to be played out in the full glare of the public spotlight –'

'And yours in the shadows,' Stephanie interjects, speaking to me.

'Yeah, you might not be wrong about that,' I sigh.

Shrugging, Henry adds, 'I meant to say that ultimately we're a family, like all other families, with high moments, celebrations and a fair few lows. We have similar problems to everyone else. Petty rivalries, disputes, you know, what have you.

There's completion between siblings, naturally. But for us the stakes are just a lot higher.'

'It's an interesting view,' Stephanie says sarcastically.

'Not really. Take yourself, for example, Heather,' he says, ignoring his sister's jibes. 'I bet you've amounted to more than your parents ever imagined you would. Not being disrespectful, but most teenagers our age probably go to school, go home, do homework, go round their friends', have a shag, get pissed, go to sleep, repeat.'

'Kidding!' I laugh. 'Mine haven't got a clue what we're mixed-up in.'

'Okay,' Stephanie says, puzzled. 'Odd, but fair enough. Well, for us, we'll never achieve anything more than what was already ordained for us at birth. But because of the order of ascension, I will likely never become monarch. So, all this, and for what? It's easy for people out there to judge. People with ordinary lives, lives which aren't scrutinised to the ends of the earth. They probably think we are all just about entitlement and privilege. But it's easy to miss that we're also trapped, if you like, in this very odd little bubble. What people miss is the order in which the service goes. Take what you three obviously do. They call it "on His Majesty's service", right?'

'Secret Service,' Milly jokes.

'Quite. And from where we sit, I'd say we are all serving the people of this country, too. Whether for trade, tradition, tourism, pomp or glamour. Sure, once upon a time, we may have been an institution of absolute power, but now in order to survive we need the support, or approval even, of the country.'

'And how do you think you're doing on that front?' Anabel asks.

'Not great,' Henry admits with a sigh. 'A few years back, for some reason, a lot of the old-guard advisors left.'

'Retired,' Stephanie adds bluntly. 'And not exactly through personal choice, either, if you catch my drift.'

'Yes, fair point. They tried to bring in some new, more modern people. Some spin doctors from the government. PR types. That sort of thing. But seems they didn't go down too well with some of the older members of the family. Wasn't really our problem. We were too young to really care or notice, wouldn't you say?'

The princess nods.

'But they tried to bring in all sorts of controls. Some desperately needed discipline. And then they all got fired for it. And now there are just a bunch of rah-rah-yes-men who offer no challenge. And Daddy's so busy kinging, he isn't really running the household much anymore.'

'Guess it doesn't help that your dad gets one inept government after another,' says Anabel.

'Yeah, well. Pretty much a family rule not to comment on that.'

'I bet,' Milly laughs.

'Does anyone else think this is getting way to serious?' I laugh. 'Anyway, changing the subject, I never finished what I was saying last night in the bar. The point I was making, albeit badly, was that it's best not to hit anyone with a clenched fist.'

Taking the princess's hand, I curl her fingers into a fist.

'Just asking for broken bones. Only the first two knuckles are directly supported through the metacarpal and the arm's bones. The other two can't take the load and are prone to breaking. Way better to hit with the heel of the fist, like a hammer blow. There's strength and rigidity in that. And even the average person –'

'Are you calling me average?' the princess asks with a raised eyebrow.

'Pretty much, yeah.'

'Okay, fine. I'll let that slide. But only because you're showing me all this.'

'Uh-huh. Anyway, point being, do that and even the average person can transfer four newtons of energy that way. That's enough to hurt in anyone's book if you land it in the right place.'

'Really not sure teaching her this is the best idea,' Henry says cautiously.

'Why not?' the princess exclaims. 'We've basically got an expert here. Why wouldn't I have her teach me this?'

'Oh, no, please don't say stuff like that,' Milly groans. 'You'll make her unbearable.'

Laughing, Prince Henry glances at his phone as it pings with the arrival of several messages.

'Oh dear, time to go, it seems,' he says resignedly. 'The chopper will be here shortly.'

'Typical. Just as I was beginning to have fun,' Stephanie sighs, taking her brother's offered hand so he can pull her up.

We, too, stand, equally sorry to see them leave. Shrugging wearily, Princess Stephanie leans in and briefly kisses me on the mouth. It is neither rushed nor overly deliberate, but it lingers just a fraction longer than normal embraces. She quickly gives Anabel and Milly a similar kiss. When she pulls away from Anabel, she emphatically licks her lips.

'Laters, bitches!' she says playfully. 'You're all gorgeous. I'm going to miss you so much. But there's royalling to be done.'

'Well, maybe one day our crazy paths will cross again?' Milly says keenly.

'Yeah, I hope so,' Stephanie replies. Smiling, she adds, 'And no is your answer.'

'But we didn't ask anything,' Milly says.

'I can hear you thinking it,' she says, grinning. 'The press are all alluding to it. But they miss the point in their rush for the angle which sells the most papers. Life's simply too short and the opportunities too fleeting not to take advantage of them when they arise. Doesn't mean anything about me as a person, or my preferences.'

With that, she turns and strides confidently off towards the steps, waving over her shoulder as she goes. In the distance, a helicopter banks gently and begins descending towards the open space where we saw them first arrive. Her brother shrugs, mildly embarrassed, and waves goodbye. Then he turns and follows his sister.

For a moment I stand totally still, as dumbfounded as I am amused and intrigued, and I find myself gently touching my lips in fascination. Curiously, an odd, lingering sense of touch remains. It's still there long after she has disappeared from sight.

'Ha, don't like it too much,' Milly giggles. 'But I'd say we could all notch that up as having just got off with a Royal.'

'Oh, shut up,' I sigh with a roll of my eyes.

CHAPTER 10

EASTWARD BOUND

In Transit

Our new friends are not even over the horizon when an urgent telephone call from C comes through to announce that our own stay in Gosport must also come to an abrupt and premature end, a whole day early.

'Styles has moved up his flight,' he shouts over the loud whistling of the wind. 'He flies today. Can you hear me alright? I'm walking to the office. Doctors are telling me to watch my cholesterol. Now, I believe you know Hollis?'

'Yes,' I reply.

'Good. He will be your primary point of contact from this end while you're over there. Understood? And when you arrive, hook up with our local man in Hong Kong. He's been told to expect you and has your details.'

'Okay, got it.'

'Right, then best you all get back to that school of yours. Pack, sort your lives out. My assistant will book your flights when she gets in. Good luck. This should be fun. Chat when you're back.'

With an excited look, I turn to my friends. As one, we jump up and race back to our rooms to gather our belongings. Ten minutes later, we are passing through the facility's gates again in the Merc.

*

'You know what the most amazing thing is?' I say as we pull into the underground car park beneath the geology block barely an hour later.

'What's that?' Milly replies. 'Besides us not getting stopped for speeding.'

'You know, you're close. What I was going to say is there wasn't a single comment the whole journey about how fast we were going.'

'Yeah, I suppose,' she replies.

'Something's changed,' I note, climbing from the high vehicle. Pointing, I add, 'You two have changed.'

'Don't know about that,' Anabel says. 'What I do know, however, is that we all need to change, and pretty quickly, too, if we're to make the flight.'

'You're right,' Milly exclaims, checking her watch. 'And we need to repack.'

*

Like Milly, I am almost finished carefully packing my case – a battered, sticker-covered Rimowa – with layers of neatly rolled clothes when Anabel bursts in.

'Sorry, one more thing,' she announces breathlessly. 'Forgot to mention it's best to bring an umbrella. It could be either really sunny or really stormy and rainy. Tough to know, this time of year.'

Frowning, I reach into my wardrobe and look at the only umbrella I have. The snag is, it's not exactly compact. Pulling the classically slim umbrella out by its curved, hardwood handle, I clear my throat in embarrassment and then point the tapered metal ferrule at them.

'Err...?'

'Oh, wow,' Milly says, glancing around. 'That is a very bright-yellow umbrella. Bit unwieldy, isn't it?'

'Okay, so I nicked it from my dad, ages back. Just never used it here,' I sigh, seeing their looks. 'It's actually quite light, but you don't have anything smaller, do you?'

''Fraid not,' says Milly. Anabel also shakes her head and laughs.

'Take it, they'll love you over there. Yellow umbrellas were kind of the symbol of the anti-government protestors.'

'Oh great,' I reply, tossing it onto my bed with a shrug. 'You all packed? Because we should probably get moving. Or we really will be late. Wow, I can't believe I'm being the responsible one. What's wrong with this picture?'

'Okay, fine,' Anabel moans. 'Wait, you're seriously going to wear your MI13 cap?'

'Yeah,' I reply, dropping it into my backpack. 'Why not?'

'Because it has military intelligence written all over it – like, quite literally.'

'Yeah, you sure that's such a good idea?' Milly cautions.

'Hell yes! Because, as we found out in one of the first sessions at 1MTE, Article twenty-nine of the 1907 Hague Convention states that spying involves clandestine action, right?'

'Yeah...' Milly says uncertainly.

'So, soldiers or agents of the state who are not in disguise but who penetrate enemy lines cannot be considered as spies.'

'True,' she admits. 'But that means they would need to be wearing something that clearly identifies who they are. Else it could be considered a disguise.'

'Exactly, like a uniform.'

'Well, yes, that or the equivalent.'

'And what would you call this, then?' I exclaim, pointedly flapping my cap at them. 'Seriously, like anyone would ever believe it. People are more likely to *discount* you as a spy if you wear something like this than become suspicious.'

'That is some arse-backwards logic,' Milly sighs.

'But curiously, it might actually work,' Anabel laughs. 'Because it's so arse-backwards, most people would never believe anyone could be so bold or stupid as to –'

'Exactly,' I blurt. 'Everyone will discount it. But if we get arrested, they can't do us for spying, coz we fricking said so, right here. I mean, if you think about it, the most successful espionage exploits were always the most unorthodox and outlandish ones.'

'Sorry, I don't disagree with the logic, but you're not actually planning on getting arrested, are you?' Anabel asks with concern. 'I mean, please don't.'

'I'll try not to. So, umbrella, yes or no? Is it too on the nose? What do you think, Belle?'

'No more so than that sodding cap of yours.'

'Cool. Done. We should probably get a move on, then.'

'Alright,' she laughs.

'And make sure you don't forget your passports,' I add. 'As in plural.'

'Yes, Mother,' Milly replies, rolling her eyes.

'Seriously. And make sure you take the right ones. We don't need anyone rocking up with their real passport.'

'Good point,' Anabel exclaims, dashing back towards her room.

'Still got to get used to having different names,' Milly says as she chooses the right passports to take on the flight.

Having laid my wash kit in the suitcase, I add a cocktail dress across the top, fasten the elastic straps and ease the upper lid closed. I flick the combination lock wheels, set the case upright and grab my cap, umbrella and weathered, olive-coloured Sandqvist-Bob backpack, which I'll take into the cabin with me. Within it, I have a novel, my tablet, a pair of noise-cancelling headphones, a small make-up bag and all the other little items I like having with me on flights.

'Right, you coming, or shall I see you downstairs in Mr Lander's private side?'

*

The conversation doesn't last long. Whether through tiredness, boredom or just the desire for some peace and quiet, both my friends are soon fast asleep. Glancing back from the minicab's passenger seat, I see they are resting against each other and, amazingly, holding hands.

Smiling privately at the touching sight, I lean my head against the window and drift off into thought, lulled by the gentle rhythm of the car. Save for the classical radio, which the cabbie has on low, we drive on in silence. Outside, the trees blur past hypnotically and the rolling fields slowly give way to small towns and villages.

Growing up an only child, I only ever had to contend with my own reality. One of the biggest surprises to have come from all our training is how fascinating it is to immerse oneself into other people's mindsets. To see things from another's perspective allows me to view the world through very different lenses.

As I glance back again at my two best friends sleeping happily behind me, it occurs to me that I have never really taken the time to stop and see things through their eyes. Perhaps to do so would take such a fundamental shift in mental perspective that I have never found the necessary combination of time, focus or incentive to achieve.

It isn't helped by the fact that the world seems to be gripped by a near constant assault on some part or other of society, demanding it either empathise more, sympathise more, better understand or be more tolerant towards some other marginalised and historically repressed group. These often rabid campaigns tend to follow lines of gender inequality, racial inequality or sexual or gender identity, and have now become so numerous that I have almost lost track.

Quite whom these anger-filled tirades are being directed at sometimes confuses me. What compounds the confusion even more, besides the naturally vague nature of these typically social media-driven assaults, is that having opened the door for debate, the originators of these movements are then usually completely unwilling to hear any view that differs from their prescribed hymn sheet. Any hint of a different opinion is typically met with the full force of today's wokest cancel culture. And anything other than complete agreement with the sentiment behind the assault of the day results in an absolute avalanche of hate-filled venom coming from all directions. So, because they don't want debate, sometimes the best thing to do is just to ignore their message entirely. And instead of opening our minds and empathising with the very people whose worlds are considerably more complicated than our own, we do the opposite, and shut it out because there is simply too much noise.

I realise that's probably what I have done with my friends. Because I can't honestly recall ever properly considering what being gay must be like. Or how it could change my view of the world. Of course, it wouldn't change everything, because I don't see sexual identity as the be-all and end-all. Not like some people, who let it dictate everything from the rhythm of their speech to their choice of clothes, mannerisms and, sometimes, their whole social circle. That, I think, may be a little excessive. But if it makes them happy, then it's none of my business. And maybe that's the better approach for the perma-offended out there, too. Simply live and let live. After all, what right does anyone have to tell another whom they can and can't love?

Glancing back, I realise with a sudden pang of sadness that this is perhaps the first time I have ever seen them even holding hands. In fact, it's the first time they've ever even alluded to being in any sort of relationship in public. Not that I'd call the backseat of a minicab particularly public. And now the dull ache of yearning for intimacy of my own suddenly rises deep within me. Pushing it swiftly aside, I return to my earlier train of thought.

I imagine getting placed in SH must have been a bit of a schadenfreude moment for them. On the one hand it must have been great, because they met each other in a house with people liberal enough and sufficiently open-minded not to give them crap for their relationship. On the flip side, however, with Mr Lander as their housemaster – a man so ridiculously in tune with everything happening within his house that effectively nothing 'untoward' can ever happen – it became a relationship they struggled to make the most of.

As a result, they mastered the art of camouflaging their intimacy from nearly everyone, including, for a long time, the others in our year group. It seems it was only after my arrival that they loosened up a bit. And not by much. No wonder, then, that the prospect of this trip is so exciting to them.

If they're lucky, they may even get a shared room this time around. And if what Anabel says about Hong Kong's hotels is anything to go by, they should be able to do it in style, too. I'm just glad that at least the trip may offer them the privacy I expect they must be desperate for.

*

Thankfully, none of our passports get as much as a second glance when we make our way through a very busy passport control. As we head on towards security, a new group message comes through via our encrypted messaging app from an unknown number. It informs us that Robert Styles is due to depart on the Cathay Pacific flight leaving an hour after ours. It is signed simply 'George'.

'It's a Hong Kong number,' Anabel says, peering at my phone. 'Reckon it's the Six guy out there?'

'Could be,' I speculate. 'Guess we'll find out.'

'At least it gives us enough time to clear immigration, get our luggage and then find a good spot where we can follow him from,' she notes. 'The airport's so efficient we could be waiting a while for him to come through. Interesting he's flying Cathay and not BA.'

'Maybe he's cashing in old air miles,' Milly jokes. 'Let's just hope his plane doesn't overtake ours.'

'Hey, don't tempt fate,' Anabel replies. 'That would be just our luck.'

The scale of the security screening operation at Heathrow is always something to behold. It is not just the number of scanner machines, but all the frenetic activity that surrounds each of them: the tray-delivery conveyor belts, the small army of blue-uniformed security staff milling about, the tubular body scanners and the hordes of bustling passengers, all funnelled into this one concentrated area beneath the cavernous, arched roof of Terminal 5.

Once clear, with laptops repacked, shoes back on and wallets, passports and phones all in their rightful pockets, we head towards the nearest departures board, which, thankfully, shows that both flights remain on schedule.

Whether C's assistant deliberate intended to book us all into business class or whether it was merely a costly oversight on her part, perhaps due to her habitually booking her boss into it, none of us know. Nor, frankly, could we care less.

Instead, we make an excited, hasty, giggling beeline across the departure terminal, and up several escalators to the rarefied comfort afforded to those willing to shell out quite this much for an airline ticket. We stand on the threshold of the lounge with wide grins and bated breath as the people in front of us are admitted. The refined luxury that lies within will certainly afford a considerably more comfortable wait than usual before our flight is called.

'How cool is this,' I say, keeping my voice low, as I hand over our boarding passes and passports to the lady behind the front desk.

'I know,' Milly exclaims even more excitedly.

'Shh. Else people will think we're lounge virgins or something.'

'But your parents are pretty minted,' Anabel laughs as we take our documents back and head straight to the bar. 'I'd have thought you were well used to all this.'

'Yeah right. My dad insists the best I get is premium econ. He says it's better I don't grow up a spoilt brat who thinks that kind of lifestyle is to be expected. But even then, The Devil Wears Prada gives him all sorts of hassle about wasting money on me like that. She'd shove me back in steerage if she could. That said, I suppose I did get business for that trip to India last term.'

'Love it how you call it steerage,' Milly says. 'I've never been business. This is insane. Don't know how I will ever be able to go back to the regular departure lounge after this.'

For obvious reasons, given our destination, not to mention the purpose of the trip, it was deemed advisable to issue us all with new travel documents for alias identities. As was explained to us by Mr Lander, as we hurried through his private living quarters on the way to meet our taxi, the given names in each were chosen to be as close to our real names as possible, so that if someone accidentally uses a real name, observers may well assume they misheard.

The other benefit of travelling on cover passports is they come with new dates of birth. Dates which we were asked to choose on the drive up from 1MTE to ensure we don't forget them. No one objected when we added a year to each, bringing us all out on the safe side of eighteen. This lack of pushback from MI13 means that once we are comfortably settled at the bar, it only takes a cursory glance by the barman at the details page within each passport before champagne begins arriving in a steady stream of refills. With nothing else to do but wait, we finally relax and enjoy the experience to the full, with jokes and laughter that get increasingly louder and more raucous with each top-up.

Boarding is swift and efficient, with none of the soul-sapping queueing typically experienced back in economy. Instead, we arrive at the gate fresh from the chilled extravagance of the business-class lounge and are immediately waved on past the long line of dejected-looking passengers standing in the huge queue, which stretches the length of the boarding lounge and is moving at the pace of a snail. We grin excitedly as we are directed to the left upon entering the aircraft. The wonderfully spacious and refined business-class cabin is light, airy and calm in all the ways the back of the plane will never be.

My friends have the rearmost two seats on the right-hand side of the fuselage, Milly by the window, and Anabel beside her on the aisle. With barely a glance at my boarding pass, the immaculately presented steward points me, with an award-winning smile, to my seat, which is perfectly situated for gossip and chit-chat directly across the aisle from them.

The flight is less than half full, and business slightly less than that. The seats in front of my friends remain empty, as are the pair before me. By good fortune, no one turns up to take the seat beside me, either, so the moment the doors close, it immediately becomes a dumping ground for all my carry-on gear, including my backpack, noise-cancelling headphones, water bottle, neck cushion, half-finished and very battered copy of *The Deathly Hallows*, and all the other odds and ends I typically lug onto flights.

Shortly after the seat-pressing thrill of take-off, inflight meals arrive. This far forward, they are consumed with an actual sense of enjoyment, helped in large part by the relative comfort afforded by larger tray tables, crisply starched tablecloths, chilled metal cutlery and an impressive selection of alcoholic beverages.

Trays are soon cleared, movies played and drinks drunk – and I notice my friends indulge themselves almost as much as I do. Which, for them, is impressive, given that neither has ever been much of a drinker. But indulge they do, and especially Anabel, above whose seat the call sign comes on with unfailing frequency. Each time a steward quickly appears to top up her champagne. Eventually, movies finish, trips to the toilets are made, flight socks donned, seats reclined, lights dimmed, inter-class curtains closed – and the cabin sinks into a comfortable darkness as we soar on towards Asia and the mystery that is becoming the Right Honourable Robert Styles.

Slumping back into my three-quarter-reclined seat, I let out a long, happy sigh and close my eyes. Then, with a groan, I realise my headphones are still on the seat beside me, where I left them when I went to brush my teeth in the oversized WC located just behind my friends' seats. The effort of turning around and reaching for them defeats me and I remain where I am, struggling to summon the energy.

The plane jolts heavily, and a moment later the co-pilot comes on the intercom.

'Ladies and gentlemen, the captain has turned on the fasten seat belt sign. We are now crossing a zone of turbulence. Please return to your seats and keep your seat belts fastened. Thank you.'

I open one eye and notice, across the aisle, Milly and Anabel giggling and talking in barely inaudible whispers as they snuggle up closer together. My eye closes for a second as Anabel casts a cautious glance around, before tossing her flight blanket loosely over Milly's lap.

'Shh, shunt back a bit...' she whispers excitedly. Her voice, which isn't slurred yet but might well be with another glass of champagne, drops and I miss the end of the sentence. Whatever the muffled suggestion, it provokes a dramatic change in her girlfriend's demeanour.

'No!' Milly hisses, genuinely alarmed. Firing wary, craning looks around the cabin, she tries to fend off Anabel's approaching hand. It takes me a second longer than my ego would have liked to realise what is going on. Less than impressed by my staggering naivety, I am as surprised as I am intrigued. It's bold and adventurous. Even if I was asleep, which they must clearly assume to be the case, this seems a bit risqué. Especially for them, given that neither has ever shown themselves to be particularly adventurous, and certainly not quite so forward. I mask a smile and can't help but surreptitiously watch through the hanging curtain of hair which obscures my face from view. For a fleeting moment, my conscience rears up, deeply uncomfortable with this, but the tenaciously curious part of me quickly wins.

'Loosen your trackies,' Anabel suggests.

'No. Are you nuts? We'll get caught. And arrested,' Milly protests in a barely audible whisper.

From the soft rustling of fabric, it sounds like her protests do little to dissuade Anabel, whose determination elevates her in my estimation with every passing moment. I just catch sight of her right hand snaking in under the blanket while she looks in the other direction as innocently as possible. Milly wriggles awkwardly and clearly tries to push the invasive hand off and away again.

'Just go with it,' Anabel urges. 'Don't fight it.'

'No, please don't do this,' Milly groans through gritted teeth. 'I won't be able to stay quiet.'

'Best learn quick, then,' Anabel whispers, all breathy and seductive.

A near-silent curse from Milly suggests Anabel has successfully made it past her tracksuit's drawstring.

'Jesus, stop!' Milly hisses. 'We'll get caught.'

'Not if you stay quiet, we won't. Open up,' Anabel instructs more authoritatively than I've ever heard her. At the same time, she leans in and nuzzles Milly's neck through her loosely hanging hair.

A sudden, sharp intake of breath from Milly as her body goes rigid suggests Anabel has breached the sanctity of her knickers. Cursing, Milly squirms and slumps a little further down in her seat.

'Nice,' Anabel whispers, and her hand begins to move rhythmically beneath the blanket. Milly's breathing picks up pace. I can't believe they are doing this, just across the aisle from me, in an open cabin, with at least half of it full. It must take considerable effort for Milly to muffle her almost but not entirely inaudible moans. The curse of above-average hearing means I am not spared any of the sordid details as their enthusiasm gets the better of them.

Barely thirty seconds later, Milly grips Anabel's arm and, in hushed protest, whispers, 'Stop. I can't take it. Don't.'

Unfazed, her girlfriend does the complete opposite and ups the pace.

'No...'

'Mile high club, here we come... quite literally,' Anabel whispers. 'You really want to stop me... pull it out.'

I smirk at her humour and notice that Milly releases Anabel's hand and brings her own up to her face, whether out of shame or to silence herself, I don't know. Anabel leans in closer across the seat divide and brings her left hand to rest on Milly's chest, which she then squeezes slowly through the hooded training top, eliciting a more noticeable response. Barely still in control, Milly turns and presses her face to Anabel's. In response, Anabel does something which, frustratingly, I can't see, but which sets Milly's mouth in a big frozen O-shape.

Even from my seat, I can feel the inevitable only moments away. Suddenly, Milly jerks beneath the blanket and clamps both her hands between her legs, pinning Anabel's in place. She turns and buries her face into Anabel's neck as her body shudders for several seconds. I dare not move, as fearful of my spying being detected as they were of being caught in the first place. Even as her stifled moans subside, Milly keeps her face buried in the nape of her girlfriend's neck. It's a good minute before she finally looks up and quietly mouths, 'You're mad, you are.'

'I know,' Anabel responds confidently. 'But that's why you love me.'

As they huddle together in whispered intimacy, I take a deep breath and roll over onto my other side, where I remain still and stare at the armrest for a good moment with a wide-eyed grin of disbelief. Slowly reaching for my headphones, I realise it is high time for sleep. Settling myself snuggly, I try desperately to rid my mind's eye of what just happened, lest the image of Milly biting her bottom lip in those final intense moments returns to me in my dreams.

I'm not successful.

CHAPTER 11

FRAGRANT HARBOUR

Hong Kong

With the last of my breakfast cleared away, I can finally stow the tray table and focus on finishing the rest of my movie in peace. The all-too-familiar pop in my ears signals the beginning of our descent even before the pilot comes on to announce it. That comes a minute later, resulting in my screen freezing and an irritating banner appearing that says 'Announcement in Progress'.

'Ladies and gentlemen, as we start our descent into Hong Kong, please make sure your seat backs and tray tables are in their full upright position. Make sure your seat belt is securely fastened and all carry-on luggage is stowed underneath the seat in front of you, or in the overhead bins. Thank you.'

The movie restarts, but only to pause again ten seconds later as the same announcement comes on, this time in Chinese. Scowling, I wait for it to finish. When it does, I huff in annoyance as the film pauses again for yet another announcement.

'This is your captain speaking. We have made good time on our flight today. We are in a short holding pattern for a few minutes to let a few planes ahead of us land. But we expect to land on the northern runway 25R on time. For passengers on the left-hand side of the aeroplane, you will see good views of the city. Just to let you know, it is a balmy thirty-one degrees today in Hong Kong, with eighty-two per cent humidity. Light westerly winds, and with the chance of rain later in the day.'

As the same announcement comes on in Chinese, I give up and turn off the screen, too irritated to bother continuing the film. Making a mental note to try to finish it off on the return flight, I get up and make my way to a vacant seat on the left-hand side. As I peer out at the thick layer of clouds below us, yet another announcement comes on.

'Ladies and gentlemen, we have just been asked to inform you that there is currently in progress a peaceful and orderly demonstration in Hong Kong International Airport's arrival hall. Protestors can be identified by the yellow T-shirts they are wearing. Airport staff are on standby to navigate you around the sit-in.'

I glance across at Anabel with a raised, questioning eyebrow. Nodding, she gets up and approaches. It's hard not to see her in a very different light this morning.

'What can I say?' she sighs, sinking into the vacant seat beside me. 'Same-same, but different. They've been at this again and again, these kinds of protests, for as long as I can remember.'

'Who are *they*?'

'Mixed bag. Mostly students, but these recent protests have got a lot wider support from everyone else.'

'Is it just China they're pissed about?'

'Mostly, and that's all the media focus on, but there's also a lot of annoyance at the local government, which they see as just being Beijing's puppet. They're annoyed about schools, hospitals, housing, wages, pollution, lockdowns, you name it. I love Honk, but it's got its fair share of real-world problems. And most are felt far more acutely by the locals than the ex-pats.'

Frowning, she shrugs resignedly and points out the window. 'Welcome to Honkers.'

The huge airliner has just dropped out from the clouds, revealing a breathtaking sun-bathed vista below. Light puffs of stark-white fluffy cloud drift below us, casting faint shadows on the calm emerald-green sea. A scattering of small rocky islands dots the otherwise featureless scene slipping past beneath the plane. When the main island of Hong Kong comes into view it, too, is largely covered in the same thick layer of dense deep-green vegetation. Off in the distance, several huge bridges seem to connect some of the outer islands to the heavily built-up New Territories, which lie between Hong Kong Island and the Chinese mainland, some thirty miles to the north. Excitedly, Anabel points towards a long double-arched bridge.

'See that bridge? The one that looks like a floating butterfly? I think the whole thing's made of steel. They built it in China and floated it down here.'

'Why would you build a bridge out of metal?'

'Strength, maybe? Possibly to stand up to local typhoons better. Not sure really.'

'Can you drive main battle tanks at speed over tarmac?'

'I bet you can. God knows what it does to the road surface, though. So, probably not.'

'Maybe that's the reason, then.'

'You're so cynical. But probably not wrong.'

Without warning, the city appears. There is no build-up, no gradual urbanisation, not like most major metropolises with outskirts and suburbs. Instead, within the space of a few metres, dense sub-tropical jungle morphs into the most insane, hyper-built-up landscape imaginable. Almost every building is a high-rise tower, some set off by themselves but most grouped in clusters. All appear at least a dozen storeys tall, probably well over thirty in most cases, and here and there a skyscraper is far higher than that. Snaking expressways, crowded with tiny, toy-like vehicles, meander along the northern edge of the island and between the buildings.

Separating the island from the denser, even more heavily populated New Territories lies the busy waterway of Victoria Harbour. Crisscrossing it, leaving thin, white, frothy wakes behind them are all manner of vessels: dredging barges, skiffs, pleasure boats, old Chinese junks, larger commercial vessels and what appear to be two black go-fast boats plying their way at speed across the wide harbour. Farther out, a few colossal container ships lie at anchor near the larger, more outlying islands.

If it was even possible for the buildings to get taller, they do, and by a considerable factor, as the Central downtown area finally comes into view. Here the towers are clustered even tighter together, and unlike the more nondescript outlying residential areas, these buildings have true individuality, with elaborate façades; many are clad in the neon branding of major finance companies or Fortune 500 corporations, or emblazoned with brightly coloured Chinese logos which I don't recognise. All appear to be trying to outreach their neighbour to soar higher into the sky. And all this amazing architecture is crammed before the gently curving backdrop of Victoria Peak, which looms tall and jagged, high over the city.

'Hey, meant to ask, do your parents know you're coming?' I say to Anabel. 'They do still live here, right?'

'Yes and no. Or is that no and yes? No, they don't know, and yes, they still live here,' she replies, smiling. 'See, it's kind of tricky. They pretty much know what GPS is. Well, certainly that it has big connections to the Foreign Office. But it just seemed too much of a hassle to tell them I was coming, coz then they'd want to know why. Or they'd be worried because of all the problems here now. Worse, they'd say, come stay at home. Either way, it would just be awkward and a pain.'

'Yeah, I guess. Maybe better this way. We don't know what's going to happen.'

'True. And this way, staying wherever they've put us, we get to go explore the city properly ourselves when we aren't on Styles,' she adds eagerly. 'I can't wait to show you both around.'

'I think I love this place before I've even set foot in it,' I say excitedly. 'It looks totally nuts.'

'Yeah,' Anabel says with a knowing smile as she gets up to return to her seat. 'It is.'

Glancing back out of the window, I find it strangely unfathomable that the city below is in the grips of the worst social unrest in its history. Before we flew, I took a moment to read up on its history, from the umbrella revolution of 2014, from which stems the city's connection with yellow umbrellas, and the ensuing cycle of civil unrest.

When COVID-19 struck, there followed a period during which China slowly, almost imperceptibly, began making inroads on a number of social rights in the city by enacting patriotism laws and various other ordinances through which it could prosecute behaviour it deemed undesirable.

Thereafter came changes to electoral law, further limiting who could stand for public office in the territory. For a while, it almost seemed like things might quieten down a bit, but it was a false peace.

Several weeks ago, for whatever reason and without any warning, the National People's Congress Standing Committee launched an onslaught of ever more egregious initiatives, all designed to erode what was left of the city's old civil liberties, including an assault on press freedoms, increased censorship across social media, daily headline-grabbing interference in the courts and wholesale replacement of the school curriculum to reflect the party's view of history and world order.

The result, not entirely surprisingly, was an immediate return by students to the streets. Mini cities of tents and makeshift shelters sprang up to occupy large tracts of Central and other districts across the harbour, like Kowloon and Tsim Sha Tsui. An accompanying logistics effort by anonymous donors also kicked off, with stocks of bottled water, instant noodles, various other supplies and support being delivered regularly to the protestors.

Rumours were rife of foreign government support, but nothing was proven. With its major road arteries into and from the city effectively blocked, traffic ground to a halt and was diverted awkwardly into surrounding back streets, causing general irritation and inconvenience to all. And for a few weeks, the city simmered in frustration at having been sunk back into the kind of deadlocked chaos most had hoped was behind them.

But then, in a misguided bid to disband the thousands of entrenched students, the authorities launched a miscalculated and disproportionately ham-fisted response. Fleets of riot police vans descended on the camps. A small army of overzealous riot officers with shields and batons led charge after charge against the students. Then came water cannons and CS gas.

The ensuing violence captured the attention of the world's press. Across the globe newspapers and magazines published images of protestors clad in yellow T-shirts and sporting stylised, grinning, moustached 'V for Vendetta' Guy Fawkes masks, standing defiant, silhouetted by the police lights against a backdrop of drifting clouds of tear gas. Footage of blood-soaked teenagers, many of them girls, being hauled away without care or concern by aggressive riot gear-clad police officers energised much of the wider Hong Kong community, which until then had remained largely neutral.

And so began the mobilisation of a full-scale mass civil revolt, with frequent riots and pitched battles ensuing between the beleaguered local police and an ever-increasing number of demonstrators.

And this is what we have come to visit, I muse quietly to myself as we descend towards the airport below.

*

'Hey, almost forgot,' Milly says as we rise from our seats the moment the engines have wound down and the seat belt sign goes off. 'Don't turn on your phones yet. They might have a man-in-the-middle phone mast here at the airport.'

'A what?' I ask, leaning in towards her.

'It's like a phone mast the PLA could have set up here. Instead of everyone's phone pinging the proper Hong Kong Telecom masts on arrival, they all ping the PLA's mast instead, which then downloads software to everyone's phone while it onward-connects them to the main mast. But by then it's too late, and they've got you and can read everything on your phone.'

'That's freaky!'

'Smart, though. Anyway, keep it turned off until we're well clear of the airport. And then we'll set up a private Wi-Fi network between our phones, so our close-quarter comms don't even go over the internet. Very hard to detect, and even if they are, the contents are all encrypted. I'm also going to set up a steganography app on all our phones. That'll allow us to add important stuff into a digital image. Basically, it gets concealed within the image, and we encipher it and then transfer the data securely. If they can break that, I'll buy them a drink.'

'Okay. Good call,' I say as I stuff my belongings into my backpack. 'You know, there's a certain irony about all this, isn't there?' I say with rucksack in hand as we make for the now open door. 'I mean, for ages everything was all about keeping me as far away from the Chinese as possible. And now look, here I am strolling right into their back yard.'

'Kind of makes you wonder, right?' Anabel replies with a shrug as she sets off hand in hand with Milly up the disembarkation tunnel and on toward the arrivals terminal. I watch them from behind with a bemused little smile as I recall the in-flight entertainment I saw last night.

Grinning at the prospect of what the trip promises, I set off to catch up with them.

*

As a Hong Kong permanent resident, Anabel is afforded the privilege of passing straight through the automated fast-track immigration channel, while Milly and I join the meagre queue of tourists lining up at the few passport control desks that are even open.

'Guess tourism is a little down at the moment,' Milly whispers quietly.

'You can say that again.'

While the line moves quickly, the airport's back-of-house moves even faster, because by the time we get into the baggage hall, our luggage has come through and Anabel has already hauled it from the carrousel and onto a trolley.

'Reckon there's any point us waiting here for Styles?' I ask.

'On second thoughts, doubt it,' Anabel replies. 'Better, I'd say, to go dump our bags, get sorted and be ready to be on him once he's on the go. He also has to do all that faff. No point us wasting time waiting here.'

Agreed, we set off together. Customs clearance is uneventful, and after buying three local SIM cards, which I insist on paying for with cash, we head out into the arrivals hall. Unsurprisingly, no one is waiting for us on the other side of the barrier. Instead, we follow Anabel through the modern terminal, giving the baying hordes of protestors a wide berth, and outside to the taxi pick-up point. The heady blast of thirty-degree heat which hits us takes me aback.

'Oh, wow,' I exclaim. 'It's like standing under a department store door heater in wintertime.'

'Just on full blast,' Milly adds.

'What's wrong with you?' Anabel scoffs, sighing in blissful pleasure. 'This is lovely. Aw, feel that. Bliss.'

A moment later, the sweat-inducing humidity, which is already in the upper levels of tolerance, hits home. Thick and dense, the air has a palpably damp feel to it. Which is exactly how my clothes feel within a couple of minutes.

'You're not even sweating,' I exclaim, peering closely at Anabel's forehead.

'I'm Asian. We don't sweat.'

'I thought that was a myth.'

'Nope, it's true,' Milly replies with a happy smile.

'Can see I'm going to be having several showers a day if it stays like this.'

'Oh, poor Heather,' Anabel laughs, waving for a taxi. 'It's not even ten in the morning yet. Wait for midday.'

A glossy red-and-white, boxy-looking Toyota Crown Comfort pulls into the space before us. Numerous Chinese character stickers adorn the bodywork. As we approach it, the left-hand rear door and the boot pop open. I manage to find space to fit our luggage amidst the assorted clutter within the boot.

Once in, Anabel, who is squashed between Milly and me, gives the driver our hotel's address in Cantonese. Nodding, he flips the 'taxi for hire' flag on the dashboard down and puts the car into gear using the steering wheel-mounted selector, before pulling away into the heavy traffic.

'Still don't know how we ended up in a hotel on the Dark Side,' Anabel mutters.

'What's the Dark Side?' asks Milly.

'It's what islanders call the New Territories. Basically, anything on the other side of the harbour. The joke is, islanders never go over to the Dark Side. It's very local.'

'Is that true?' I ask.

'No, not even slightly. But somehow the name stuck. Though there are some gweilos who've probably never been there. But they're missing some of the best bits of Honk. Some really great bars and restaurants over here.'

'What's a gweilo?'

'Means white folk, like you. Okay, that's a bit harsh,' she laughs. 'It's really just local slang for a foreigner. But mostly Westerners. Sort of translates as ghost man.'

'Should I be offended?'

'Not sure. I don't think Hong Kong's ever figured out if it's an insult or a term of endearment.'

'Come to think of it, pretty sure you told me that once,' I reply, gazing out at the approaching city as its real scale becomes apparent. This truly is a city of concrete, glass and steel, but on architectural crack. 'Seriously, how did they manage to fit this number of silly tall skyscrapers into such a tiny area?'

'I know, right?' Milly says, craning her neck for a better view. 'You ever think how quaint everything back home feels in comparison?'

'All the time,' replies Anabel. 'Cracks me up how there's hardly any buildings taller than five floors. Feels weird. Just Europe in general. It always feels so small every time I come back after the hols.'

As we head deeper into Kowloon, the roads get considerably narrower, the buildings older and more run-down, and in some cases borderline dilapidated. Just as I am about to comment that the city certainly doesn't feel like it's on the ragged edge of civil unrest, we round a corner and everything suddenly changes. The road is deserted. Litter and debris are strewn everywhere. Smoke hangs lazily in the non-existent breeze. High above, the morning sun beats down mercilessly on the city. As a result, heat radiates up from the tarmac in a shimmering mirage. A burnt-out shell of a police car has been abandoned, half mounted on the pavement. Flames lick the scorched bodywork. Below it, a circle of fire still burns furiously, perhaps from a blown tank or a petrol bomb. A scattering of masked people dart from doorway to doorway, creeping up the road towards police lines which can be seen in the distance.

'Guess we found our riots,' Milly notes as Anabel leans forward to speak to the driver. He hurriedly puts the car in reverse and backs us away to take a different route.

Seeing that our local SIM cards are now activated, Anabel places a call to the number we were told to contact upon arrival. What follows is a short, one-sided conversation during which she does a lot more listening than talking.

A minute later, she hangs up, and says, 'That was someone called George Clementine –'

'Like the orange?' I ask.

'More like a satsuma, but a bit smaller,' Milly laughs without looking around. 'The guy who messaged us in London.'

'Seems he's the local head of station here,' Anabel adds. 'Anyway, you want the good news or the bad news?'

'Let's go good,' Milly replies.

'There is no good news.'

'Ugh, okay... well, how about the bad?'

'First bit of bad news is, Styles also just landed, and they had a consular car collect him, purportedly to take him to the consul general's house, where he's meant to be staying...'

'O-kay,' I say hesitantly. 'Sense a "but" coming…'

'… but he changed his mind and has opted instead to go stay in a hotel in the centre of town.'

'Great. What else?' I ask.

'George said we need to come to the consulate once we're settled into our hotel to sort a few things out.'

'Is that really such a great idea?' I ask. 'I mean, maybe it's best you don't come to the consulate, Belle. Last thing you need is to run smack bang into one of your parents.'

'I suppose.'

'They ever seen a picture of you?' I ask Milly.

'Possibly,' Anabel replies. 'Hard to be sure.'

'Okay then, not worth taking the chance, either. I go alone. Unlikely anyone knows me there. Let's keep you both out of sight.'

'Agreed, might be better,' Anabel concludes.

'Good. Now the hotel thing…'

'Yeah, why's that so bad?' Milly asks.

'Because,' Anabel explains, 'the plan was that someone in the consul general's condo was going to inform us whenever Styles was about to go anywhere. That's how we were going to get a bead on his movements. But now we're going to be pretty much blind to that. It was stupid to book us into a hotel this far from the island.'

'Which one?' I ask.

'Which one what?'

'Which hotel is Styles staying at?'

'Seems it's the Mandarin Oriental.'

'Is that good?' I ask. 'I hear good things about them.'

'Is it? Err, yes,' Anabel replies sarcastically. 'Which is probably why he's staying there.'

'So why are we staying here?' I ask, pointing out at the entrance to the Kowloon Shangri-La, outside of which the taxi has just stopped.

'Probably because it was booked by someone who's got no clue about the city or its geography,' Anabel replies. 'I expect someone muddled up the name. There's another one on the island, right opposite the consular building, which would make way more sense. Reckon they confused it with this one over here.'

'Okay, screw it,' I say, turning to her in earnest. 'Tell the driver to take us to the Mandarin Oriental.'

'Are you kidding?'

'Nope. Deadly serious. C'mon, let's go. It'll be a total waste of time us staying here, so far away on the Dark Side.'

'Unbelievable. You're such a snob,' Milly exclaims. 'What's wrong with this place?'

'It's not where Styles is staying. So, we're not staying here, either.'

'Can we even make that decision?'

'Yeah, because he's at the Mandarin. Anabel, is there a problem with it?'

'Oh, God no! It's amazing. Problem only comes when it's time to settle the bill.'

'Solved,' I sing airily, pulling my purse from my bag and waving my government-issued charge card.

'We don't even know how long we'll be here,' Milly sighs. 'Someone is going to freak if we take a hotel like that.'

'Better to ask for forgiveness than permission,' I reply, deadpan. 'Besides, you really think the Shang and the Mandarin are going to be that different? Seriously, it doesn't matter whether he's at the consul general's or this new hotel, we might as well be back in London for all the good being stuck all the way over here's going to do us. This thing only works if we're close to him.'

'I suppose,' Anabel admits.

'Now do you understand what I mean when I say we always get into trouble with her around?' Milly says, jabbing her thumb in my direction. 'Just wait for the reaction when she submits the expense claim.'

'No complaints from me if we're going to stay at the MO,' Anabel giggles happily, leaning forwards eagerly to speak to the driver.

Anabel's enthusiasm turns out to be well founded. That much becomes clear the moment our taxi pulls up outside the sheltered front entrance of the Mandarin Oriental.

Established as the very first of the chain all the way back in 1963, the luxury hotel sits on the eastern fringe of Hong Kong's central business district, a stone's throw from some of the city's largest and most prestigious shopping malls and corporate headquarters. Two smartly uniformed Indian doormen approach to help with our luggage, and escort us into the lively, upbeat main lobby. Inside, the hotel is clad in swathes of light and dark marble which are tempered with lashings of warm-feeling hardwoods. Large, open seating areas mix classic Western hotel styling with local Cantonese influences and traditional Buddhist decorative touches.

Once checked in, we exchange our spare key cards so we can come and go as we please into each other's rooms. With Anabel and Milly overjoyed to be in a king room together, I get one for myself, farther down the hallway on their floor.

I slip my passport back into my travel wallet, to join the other cover passports within. For the avoidance of confusion, this one, which is just for hotel identification, has a small round sticker on its cover with the letter H noted on it. Correspondingly, the one for the flights has a letter F. A third for the consulate has a corresponding C on it. Hopefully, multiple identities used across a variety of undertakings will break the chain of potential identification. Or so goeth the theory.

'Can you dump all my stuff in my room?' I ask, pointing to my suitcase and backpack. 'I'm gonna go meet that George Clementine guy over at the consulate. See what that's all about. Maybe you can figure out where Styles is staying and how we can get some kind of warning system going for when he decides to head off anywhere.'

'Okay, I'll let George know you're coming,' Milly says. 'Guess we see you later, then.'

'Yup. Keep your phones on, just in case,' I add with a cheery wave as I head for the main doors.

*

The standard taxi drops me off at One Supreme Court Road in Admiralty, directly outside the British consulate building. The sprawling, light-sandstone complex looks colossal from the outside, bigger even than many embassies I have seen. By mistake, I first approach the entrance to the British Council, which I discover occupies the adjacent building to the one I am looking for.

Turning, I spot a lone man sitting on a bench on the other side of the road. For a moment he looks up at me over his newspaper. It is a quick look, but enough to rouse my suspicions. Considering the area, it seems a strange place to sit. Especially out here, in the heat and the sun. Glancing left and right along the road, I note the bench doesn't seem to be part of the large hotel situated directly opposite. Nor is it where a bus or taxi might pick someone up from. And given the time of day, it seems a strange place to sit down for a rest, especially as there looks to be a large, foliage-heavy park at the far end of the street. Of course, he could just be waiting for a friend. There's always that possibility.

Donning my aviator sunglasses, I walk up the hill towards the correct entrance, flicking a scrutinising second look at him as I pass. It all but confirms my initial suspicion. Bespectacled, and with a trim fawn-coloured beard, he appears to be wearing a farmer's-style checked peak cap. Perhaps I missed something, or have these just seriously come back into fashion? The coincidence that it looks to be almost the exact match of the one C had isn't lost on me. His attempt to return to his newspaper and begin reading it again seems forced and does little to alleviate my suspicion. I pause at the incline that would take me around the building and on towards the main entrance, and then turn with a sigh, walk back down the hill and approach him. Smiling widely, he folds his paper and looks up expectantly.

'Afternoon,' he says jovially. 'Seems someone has their wits about them today. That's something, I suppose.'

His accent is British, but any local inflection has long been lost by what I imagine has been a career spent more abroad than at home. Besides the cap, which must stand out like anything around here, his shirt is a light, loose cotton, as are his beige trousers. I note with interest that he opted for rubber soles with his scuffed brown-leather brogues. A smart choice. Considerably grippier than smooth leather. And prudent, too, I suppose, given that Anabel forewarned us that nice shoes rot here especially fast if they get wet.

'Mr Clementine, I presume?'

'Call me GC,' he adds, extending a hand.

'Hi,' I reply, shaking it. His grip is firm, but not intimidating. 'If you are who you say you are, then I presume you know who I am?'

His grin broadens further.

'Tradecraft's on full throttle today, isn't it?'

'Can't be too careful.'

'No, you can't, High-Beam,' he says. 'No, you can't. Good flight?'

'Yeah, not too shabby. I assume I have C to thank for ensuring that pain-in-the-arse nickname made it all the way over here?'

'That would be telling,' he laughs. 'Well, I wanted to catch you before you went inside the hornets' nest.'

'You make what awaits sound so appealing.'

'Well, pressure's on, I'm afraid. And not everyone around here is so happy about it. Hong Kong's always been a bit of a playground for our lot. But nothing like this. Lately, it's turned into an absolute espionage hotbed. Everyone's here now: the Yanks, the Russians, the Israelis, the Frogs, us. I even bumped into some of the chaps from Portugal a couple of days ago. All buying information and sowing disinformation. Vested national interests on overdrive, you might say.'

'Seems we've arrived at just the right time, then?' I laugh.

'Don't joke,' he replies with a mischievous grin. 'This place is a powder keg just waiting to go off. I got a call from your man Gambon yesterday. Interesting chap. First time I've spoken to him. Forewarning me of your arrival and briefed me on what you're up to here. Sounds a bit of a wild goose chase if I'm being honest. Anyway, he asked if we could provide whatever assistance might be required.'

'Okay, well that's good to know.'

'Also asked me to tell you to try not to bugger things up.'

'Sounds about right.'

'Good. Come on, then. Let's go see if the CG's ready to see you. Take it your friends aren't coming?'

'Nah. Left them to sort things out,' I say as he leads me off towards the staff entrance. 'So, how come everything's going pear-shaped here, then?'

'In a nutshell, this is the early staging front for the ideological clash of the twenty-first century. The fight between freedom and democracy and repression and communism. Right now, everyone's hedging their bets as to what happens with China. But I figure you want the abridged version. So, I suppose it starts back when the Soviet Union properly collapsed. Cheyne, Wolfowitz and others in the US drafted something called the Defence Planning Guidance. It was a plan that envisioned a post-Cold War era in which there was only one superpower: America. Their plan was to prevent the emergence of any rival. But what you're seeing here, playing out in the streets down there, is just that very scenario. China has arrived, and it wants Taiwan. But it also wants to reshape the world order in line with its view of things. Step one seems to be to get HK and Macau, while it works behind the scenes to erode international diplomatic recognition of Taiwan. Well, Macau's basically in the bag. Bringing this unruly little place to order seems their next priority, because going for Taiwan now would be problematic. Unsurprisingly, the US isn't so keen on letting that happen. And everyone else is here for the scraps. So, there's a lot to play for.'

We pass through security, where they take down the details from my other passport, again with a different name and date of birth. Once cleared, GC leads me across the lobby to a lift. As we wait for it to arrive, he stretches out a hand.

'Let's have a look at that.'

I hand him my passport and he examines it briefly before passing it back with a crooked smile.

'Nice,' is his only comment as he steps into the lift.

We get out several floors up and cross an open-plan office area filled with desks, each of which is equipped with one of the largest monitors I have ever seen.

'What the heck are these?' I ask, peering in interest at the closest screen. 'They're huge.'

'Tempests.'

'You what?'

'Tempest screen protectors.'

'Uh-huh. What's so special about them?

'Stops people stealing information by tapping the electro-magnetic emissions from the screen.'

'You can do that?'

'Yeah. Come on, let's see if the CG's free.'

'Sure. What's her name?'

'Claire Swallows.'

'For real?' I snigger. 'Bet she had a hard time of it at school.'

'Typical teenager,' he chuckles. 'Mind in the sewer. How do you know she isn't named after a type of bird?'

'Come on. It's kind of funny. Anyway, why do we need to see her?'

'She likes to know what's going on.'

'Yeah, you know what? In all honesty, I'd kind of prefer not to meet her. Less people who know we're here, the better.'

'Don't worry. It'll be a quick in and out, if I know her. Best not to say anything.'

When we arrive at the consul general's office, her assistant asks we leave our phones and then waves us in.

'Never know who's listening,' George says.

'Great. That fills me with confidence,' I reply.

The CG is at her desk, on the far side of a large, tastefully decorated office. She is an austere-looking middle-aged woman with a humourless expression and a dull, uninspiring bob of a hairstyle which shows signs of grey peeking through. Her clothes are equally bland and uninspired. Clearly, she didn't decorate the office, for it is full of strong, vibrant Asian influences, including Vietnamese paintings, Thai silk cushions and delicate wooden ornaments which complement the largely cream-coloured furnishings. A large Union Jack stands off in the far left-hand corner. Directly behind her, high up on the wall, is a framed photo of the monarch. Standing next to her, behind her desk, is a young Asian man wearing a nicely tailored suit who may or may not be in his early to mid-thirties. It's hard to gauge. On the desk before them lies a manila folder, which the CG closes and hands back to the man as we enter.

'This is excellent work, Sam,' she says, looking up at him with a smile. 'Presume this has already gone back to Vauxhall Cross?'

'No, ma'am. I will run it by George first,' he says quickly, pointing towards us.

'If you must. Ensure it is added to the Red Book today.'

'Sorry?'

'As opposed to the blue one,' George says, chuckling beside me. 'Intelligence goes to Number Ten in two cases. A red one from Six, a blue for GCHQ. The cabinet secretary then sifts through them and puts the best stuff into a striped case called Old Stripey for the PM's attention.'

'Yes, of course,' Sam says, bristling noticeably at being shown up like this. 'I'll ask for it to be added to the PM's briefing.'

'Excellent,' the CG replies. 'Have them mark it as "Top Secret and Personal, UK Eyes A". I'd prefer it wasn't widely circulated at this point.'

'Will do, ma'am.'

'Good, then I'll also get a summary to the China Desk at FCO when we're done here.'

'Yes, ma'am.'

'Anything interesting?' George asks, casually strolling into the office.

The young intelligence officer bristles a little, perhaps at having his moment interrupted. The CG settles back into her chair, crossing her arms and looking peeved. It's immediately obvious the two of them don't exactly see eye to eye.

'Well, yes, as a matter of fact,' she replies somewhat icily. 'One of Sam's contacts just gave us some very insightful views on those troop movements across the border. Didn't I ask you to look into that well over a week ago?'

'Apologies. It's on the list, I assure you. It's just a rather long list at the moment.'

'That's what I keep hearing,' she says, casting a somewhat snide sideways glance at George before looking more favourably at the younger intelligence officer. 'Keep this up and we may well be looking at a new head of station soon.'

Ignoring the dig, George beckons me in. He gestures that I should take the chair beside the one into which he eases himself, across the desk from the CG. I remain standing and casually look around her office.

'What's all this?' the CG asks, pointing at me. 'I see office attire has taken a day off.'

Peering down at my choice of white tank-top vest, cargo shorts and Palladium desert boots – a look some might consider inappropriately casual, given the surroundings – I smirk in amusement.

'Yes, sorry, we just arrived, Mrs Swallows. Or should I call you Madam Consul General?'

Ignoring me, she turns back to George.

'Truth be told,' she says sarcastically, 'considering the product that's come out of your so-called sources these last few weeks since I took over, I might as well have walked outside and looked up and down the street. I'd be about as well informed as anyone. Frankly, I don't know what you do with all your time, Mr Clementine, but gaining us a cunning insight into the mindset of the enemy it is not. Would that be a fair appraisal, Sam?'

'Well, it's a complex situation out th –' the younger officer begins, shooting an uncomfortable look at George. His half-heated defence is cut off almost immediately.

'Well, I'll take that as an affirmative,' the CG interjects bluntly. 'Because it's not like anyone can say the intelligence budget is money well spent around here, is it?! Except for you, Sam.'

Comically, George remains smiling, which appears to antagonise her even more. Glancing at Sam, I sense he might be enjoying this as well, but for very different reasons. While outwardly his expression remains stoically neutral, there's something of a glint in his eyes. I suspect he's enjoying the sight of his boss getting scolded like this by the CG.

Sighing, she leans forwards, fixes George with a stern look and says, 'So, here's what I want from you. I want intelligence. Real, solid intelligence. Product that gives HMG a tangible strategic advantage in the pissing match that's going on out there. Something that's sufficiently impressive to stop this situation from degenerating into some biblical fuck-up-the-arse for British interests. I have no desire to see this impressive career I have built derailed by your ineptitude and laziness. Do I make myself clear?'

Smiling disingenuously, George removes his cap and rubs his hand through his hair, tussling it. Turning to me, he says, 'Madam Consul General, I'd like to introduce you to Ms Nichols here. She's just in from London and is here in relation to the matter I notified you about last night.'

'Well, I haven't got to it yet. So, you'll have to humour me.'

'Right, well, this relates to efforts to determine the source of the recent government leaks back home.'

'And how's this got anything to do with Hong Kong?'

'In a nutshell, one of the primary suspects just flew in, and Ms Nichols has been tasked with keeping an eye on the individual.'

'Sorry, who would we be talking about here?'

'That would be the Right Honourable Robert Styles.'

'Hang on,' she says, firing a withering look at George. 'You've sanctioned HMG to put the sodding minister of morality, close friend and advisor to the PM and potentially the next bloody PM, under surveillance? Surveillance to be run out of *my* consulate. And when exactly were you thinking of running this past me?'

'If it's of any help, my orders came from the Ministry of Defence,' I add, hoping it deflects blame from George.

'I'm sorry, and where exactly are you from?' the CG asks with a distinctly patronising tone.

'She's with our friends at one north of twelve,' George replies cryptically.

'Christ, don't tell me you're one of Sloan-Sinclair's lot!' she exclaims with a roll of her eyes. 'Jesus, that's all we need.'

'Is that a problem?'

'Not to be too blunt about it, Ms Nichols, but quite possibly, yes. We're on a bit of a knife edge here, if you hadn't noticed, with the half the bloody PLA massing at the border. I don't need some child coming out here to play spy in my city and fouling things up. This isn't some sort of work-placement opportunity. Now listen here, Clementine, MOD aside, I want you to watch her like a bloody hawk. One step out of place and it's straight onto an aeroplane out of here. FCO calls the shots. Do I make myself clear?'

'Crystal.'

'In fact,' she continues, 'on second thoughts, I'd be a lot happier if Sam acted as primary liaison.'

'With all due respect, ma'am, I'd prefer if the operations of my depart –'

'Objection noted. But I think there are more pressing matters for your personal attention. Babysitting seems insultingly below your experience, doesn't it? Given what's going on out there. No offence intended, Nichols.'

'Oh, none taken,' I gush insincerely.

Her expression barely flickers. Pursed-lipped, she keeps her withering gaze locked on George. Adopting a deeply condescending smile, she adds, 'It might be good experience for your junior officer. Even you must admit that his securing a high-level source deep in the Chinese administration was a coup for your department. In fact, if I recall correctly, it's your department's only notable achievement of late.'

'There are still some bona fides to establish about Hornet, ma'am,' George adds. 'I wouldn't put too much stock in the source yet.'

'Sour grapes, George? Oh, how unbecoming.'

'Just a healthy dose of professional scepticism accumulated over a long career doing just this.'

'Yes, well, the benefits of that wealth of experience are still to be seen. And you, Nichols, whatever your name is, I want regular updates to Sam. Nothing happens without his approval. Clear?'

I nod and shrug noncommittally.

'I have things to do now, so I need my office. Sam, if you'd be so good as to keep me informed of what's going on?'

'Of course, ma'am.'

The CG draws some documents closer and begins flipping through them, marking certain pages as she goes. Our welcome clearly outstayed, George rises to leave. Dithering for a second, I turn back to the CG.

'I'm sorry, is that it?'

Without looking up, she nods brusquely and waves dismissively for me to also leave her office. Only too happy to oblige, I spin on my heel and walk briskly after George, who is halfway to the lift by the time I catch him up.

'Well, er, that was interesting,' I say with a raised eyebrow. 'Patronising, but interesting.'

'Waste of time, don't you mean? Where's Sam?' he asks, handing me my phone back.

'Looks like he stayed behind with her.'

'There's a surprise. Ambitious little turd. They almost deserve each other, those two.'

'I don't like being judgmental, but I couldn't help but get a weird kind of vibe from him. Dunno why, maybe it was the suit. A little too try-hard, you know what I mean?'

'Yeah, well, listen to those vibes. I don't know in his case, but they've saved my arse on a number of occasions.'

'One thing's for sure: she doesn't like you.'

'Well, I bet she just loves you now, after how you emphasised her name like that.'

'I don't know what you mean,' I reply, fighting a smirk.

'Yeah, right. Is what it is, though. Sadly, one has to respect the title, if not the person.'

'Suppose. So, what's her story?'

'Bit of a mixed bag. She's only been in country since the beginning of the month. But hit the ground running. Very good at managing up, or so it seems. And likes everything to be green. No problems here sort of thing. Which is fine, if that's your style. Just a little hard when the country is coming apart at the seams in front of your eyes. Right now everything's glowing red, and she's not too happy about it.'

'Is that why she thinks you're hesitating in escalating stuff to her? That sounded like what her gripe was.'

'Baked therein is the assumption that I have something worth escalating.'

'True. But that would then imply you're not very good at your job,' I reply. 'Way I see it, if C and Gambon trust you enough to tell you stuff, then I reckon they rate you, else they wouldn't tell you diddly squat. And if that's the case, then I guess you probably are good at what you do, which means you must have sources all over the place. Only conclusion then is that you're just not passing it up through her. Just curious why that is?'

'Chatham House rules?'

'Of course.'

'I kind of get concerned when someone seems keener to pass information in any direction where it might gain them some sort of advantage than they are to handle it with the necessary care it deserves to protect our agents.'

'Well, that sounds fair. And it's good to know.'

'Just your usual politics. You know how it is.'

'Are you kidding?! I'm still in school. What do I know?'

'Not your average school, though, from what I gather.'

'I don't know what you mean, Mr Clementine.'

'I bet you don't.'

'Was that a test?'

'It's all a test,' he replies with a sly smile. 'Right, enough of all that. Let's go find my car. Time I take you on a field trip. Give you the lay of the land.'

'Cool. I'll let my friends know.'

'While you're at it, best let them know about this,' he says, handing me a printed sheet of paper.

'Is this what I think it is?' I ask, stopping for a moment to skim-read it. 'Styles's itinerary?'

'Declared itinerary at any rate. What he does to fill in the gaps is your problem. But these are his official engagements filed with the consulate, and those from his private calendar.'

'Love to know how you got this. Seems he has a dinner tonight at the China Club,' I observe. 'It says "with friends". This China Club place, is it nice?'

'I'll say. Top-notch private members' club.'

'We'll need to be there. How do we get a table at this short notice?'

'I can try to call them and see.'

'Anyone here a member?' I ask. 'Or anyone you know?'

'The CG is.'

'Good, we'll use her name. Say it's for her niece and two friends.'

'I like that,' he grins. 'Nice and cheeky.'

'I presume it's expensive.'

'So-so. She'll notice it on her bill though.'

'Yeah, well, sod her if she can't take a joke.'

As we cross the car park, I text Milly and Anabel, telling them to get ready for dinner at 2000 hours.

'Hey, this is cute,' I say, pressing send as we reach a red Volkswagen Golf.

'Not exactly the word I was hoping for, but thanks. You drive?'

'Yup,' I nod as I climb in.

'Oh yeah, what do you have?'

'Merc G-Wagon.'

'Piss off! How did you afford that?'

'I didn't. By some freaky chance I came into possession of a really nice Jag. But the former owner – deceased, I should add – was inconveniently connected to the attacks back home, and we couldn't have the government implicated through association. So I had a former French Foreign Legion mate trade the Jag with some ex-Spetsnaz guy.'

'Oh, Jesus. I don't even want to know.'

'Yeah, I know, right? Best forget I even told you. So, where are we going now?'

'We'll go for a quick trip around the island, through Central, Mid-Levels and Soho, and then across to Happy Valley and Causeway Bay, before heading over the harbour through the Eastern Tunnel, through TST, into Kowloon, past ICC, back through the Western Tunnel, then around Pok Fu Lam to Aberdeen, the south side, and back well in time for you to prep for your dinner. Sound good?'

'Sure does.' I beam excitedly.

Seat belt on, George loads his music and drives out of the car park to join one of the few expressways not blocked by protestors. We have only been driving for a couple of minutes before he glances in his rear-view mirror and grins.

'What do you see? We being followed?'

'Sure are. Three cars back. Blue sedan in the right-hand lane. Keeping their speed constant. Been seeing more and more of it this year. They must have a lot of guys down here to run this kind of operation against everyone. It's beginning to feel like it must've back in Moscow during the Cold War.'

'Keep it steady a sec,' I say. 'Wanna see if I can get a shot of them.'

'What for?'

'I dunno. Might be useful later.'

'Go for it. But be subtle.' Glancing at me, he adds more seriously, 'Hey, I get this all sounds fun and exciting, but just remember something, yeah?'

'Sure, what's that?' I say, craning round to zoom in on their number plate and snap off a few shots.

'Just don't forget, out here, on the front line, we're essentially on a war footing at all times. This stuff can get very real, very fast, yeah?'

Nodding, I close the camera app and check my phone for messages. Still no response from either of my friends. Scowling, I edge it into my pocket, and concentrate instead on GC's tour and getting a better understanding of the city's layout.

*

Upon finally returning to the Mandarin, several hours later, I give George a cheery wave and run up the stairs into the hotel's opulent lobby. I make a hurried beeline through the usual early-evening shuffle of guests, businesspeople and meandering tourists, and on towards the gilded lifts, located at the back of it. Frustratingly, there is still no response from my friends. I thrust the key card against the lift's reader to select our floor. As the doors close, I can't help but mumble, 'What's the sodding point of instant messaging if no one sodding well messages you back instantly?'

With an energised stomp, I march down the corridor towards their room, determined to get a good reason for their failure to reply. Halfway there, my phone buzzes. For a fleeting second, I hope it's them. As annoyed as I would be to find they had gone to sleep, I can't help but be concerned for their wellbeing. I need to make sure they are safe, and that nothing untoward has happened in the meantime. Instead, it's a message from GC, which says:

Dinner confirmed. 8pm. Booked under the name Elizabeth Bowen-Jones.

Glad that something is going right, I use my friends' spare key card and ease their door open. Catching myself with a rueful smile as I pocket the card, I ponder: since when did sneaking around like this, making as little noise as possible, become the new norm?

Just as I am about to close the door and loudly announce my presence, I stop and cock an ear in curiosity. The main room appears empty, but the shower is on. Straining, I hear muffled noises coming from the bathroom, just up ahead on the left. There are two voices. But it's not conversational. Curious, I slowly close the front door and tiptoe along the darkened hallway. The bathroom's substantial wooden sliding door is almost closed, with but a gap of a few centimetres left through which to peek.

My eyes narrow.

Sleeping they weren't.

The shower has been on for a good while, that much is clear, for the whole bathroom, including the mirrors and the glass shower door, are heavily steamed up. But not to such a degree that it's impossible to see what is going on. Both my friends are in the generously sized shower together. While the steam affords them some modesty, it's not enough, and I find myself watching, intrigued.

Anabel's eyes are closed, her head tossed back and her arms outstretched to steady herself against the shower's glass walls. Despite the mounting sense of unease which grows the longer I watch, I find myself helplessly transfixed as Milly steps into view behind Anabel who, being more generously endowed than us, has a noticeably pendulous energy about her as she writhes in the spray. My heart thumps aggressively and I swallow hard as one of Milly's hands comes around to roam across her girlfriend's upper body, while the other moves down between her legs and settles there amidst the foaming bubbles. In response, Anabel's mouth hangs open in a long, silent cry that never comes.

With a final concerted effort, my conscience finally triumphs and I sneak back to the door, albeit reluctantly, and let myself out into the hallway. There I stand for a moment, wide-eyed and incredulous.

Once back in my room, I kick off my shoes, toss my bag and phone onto the bed – where they almost bounce off the other side – grab a bottle of water from beside the TV and slump down with a sigh into one of the big armchairs near the floor-to-ceiling windows.

Sitting in silence, I glance at my watch and debate how much longer to give them. Finally, I consider calling their room, but instead find myself staring at the handset, overcome with a sudden and unexpected yearning for affection of my own. Frowning, I replace the phone and idly drum my fingers on the receiver as I turn to look out at the brightly lit fairground on the other side of the multi-lane carriageway which runs past the front of the hotel.

As I watch the people milling around the Ferris wheel, roller coasters and various colourful fairground rides and attractions, I can't help but imagine what it must feel like to be wanted and desired. How I crave the comfort that surely comes from having someone special in my life. Looking around the otherwise empty room, I sigh deeply and try to push the sound of my friends' intimate laughter from my mind.

All I achieve is to realise, with a glum frown, that if all the action and excitement were taken from my life, what's left doesn't make me happy.

With that, I snatch up the phone and dial their room.

*

'Just like we were taught, remember OODA,' Milly says in a hushed whisper as we step from the lift into the China Club on the thirteenth floor of the old Bank of China building, only a few blocks from the hotel. 'Observe, orientate, decide, act.'

'Can start with the orientate bit over here,' I say, pointing to a club directory pinned to the right-hand-side wall of the cosy little reception lobby.

'Okay, so this floor's almost entirely the main dining room. One up, looks like a bunch of private rooms and the Long March Bar. Top floor's more private rooms and a library.'

The interior décor of the opulent members' club is pure 1930s Shanghai, with lashings of varnished wood and swathes of elegant soft furnishings. The walls are crowded with contemporary Chinese art. Virtually every free space, shelf or table top plays host to some form of antiquity from a bygone era. Dominating the lobby is an impressive art-deco sweeping staircase, which winds around to the upper floors. Just beyond it lies the entrance to the main dining room.

'I do love this old Shanghai tea house vibe they're rocking here,' Anabel gushes. 'It's so classy.'

'Certainly makes you forget you're in the middle of this crazy bustling city,' says Milly.

'I know, I can't believe how busy it is out there,' I note. 'It's like half the city couldn't give a toss about what's going on.'

'Yeah, personal space is a pretty alien concept here,' Anabel laughs.

'What time did your friend say Styles was getting here?' Milly asks.

'Eight, I think.'

'Shall we go in?' says Anabel.

After taking our names and glancing at the reservation notes, the maître d' leads us across the surprisingly busy dining room towards our table.

Like most of the guests, we have made an effort. Anabel is in a lovely silvery high-necked silk cheongsam with a skirt split up the side. Milly has opted for an equally fitted classic little black dress, while I have chosen a signal-red, low-backed party dress with an attention-grabbing thigh-high side split.

Here again, the décor is heavily inspired by pre-revolutionary 1930s Shanghai art-deco styling. In one corner sits a large Bosendorfer grand piano. The chairs, tables, flooring and large cylindrical pillars in the middle of the room are all made from the same warm, dark hardwood. The contemporary Chinese wall art here has been infused with a smattering of flashier pop art pieces. Ornate Chinese lanterns are suspended in between the vintage ceiling fans. Our heels clack embarrassingly noisily on the original wooden flooring as we are led past groups of diners towards our own marble-topped table, set against the far wall. Each of the three place settings has a garishly coloured menu placed beside it. From here, we have a commanding view of the entire restaurant. Within seconds, one of the immaculately uniformed waiters arrives to fill our cups with green tea. Like the others, he is wearing a Mao-style white uniform, with silver buttons and flashes of red on the cuffs and collars.

Barely have we sat down when Anabel says, 'Oh, wait. He's here.' She gestures towards the entrance. 'Err, hang on…'

'Jesus, don't look round,' Milly hisses, 'but he's coming right towards us.'

'Who?' I ask.

'Styles. With the waiter.'

'Uh-oh. That can't be good.'

'Think he's rumbled us?' Anabel asks with concern.

'Dunno. Best assume otherwise,' I instruct. 'Just play dumb.'

Turning just as they reach our table, I look up with surprise.

'Sir,' the maître d' begins, looking at Robert Styles. 'I should introduce you to these young ladies. Miss Bowen-Jones is the niece of Claire Swallows, your very own British consul general, based here in the city.'

Smiling broadly, I realise GC did exactly as I suggested to get us a reservation. Dabbing my mouth with my napkin, I buy a couple of crucial seconds to think, then I place the napkin slowly on the table, stand and shake his hand. My brain scrambles for words as my friends gawp up at the MP with barely comprehending looks of surprise.

'Miss Bowen-Jones,' the maître d' says, 'this is the Right Honourable –'

'Right Honourable Robert Styles,' I interject with a nod. 'Yes, indeed. I recognise you from the TV. And from the Mandarin. It seems we're all staying in the same hotel, as chance would have it.'

'Really, what a small world,' he exclaims jovially. 'Funny, Claire didn't mention her niece would be here.'

'Oh, don't take it personally, Mr Styles,' I laugh. 'We don't anymore on our side of the family. In fact, I'm impressed if she remembers any of us, except at Christmas. But that's family, right?'

He laughs an awkward, stuttering laugh of uncertainty, before wishing us an enjoyable evening and moving on swiftly to a table four away from us, in the centre of the restaurant, where his guests are already waiting.

'That was close,' I sigh as I sit back down. 'That's my fault. I suggested GC say that to nab a table here.'

'Well, now Styles is properly going to remember us, isn't he?' Milly says with a frown. 'And worse, he knows where we're staying. Great!'

'Good. Perhaps best he does,' I reply. 'Think about it. Now he thinks he knows who we are. So, if he sees us around, he'll naturally discount it way more than he would if he had no idea who we are. Especially at the hotel. Even better, he now also thinks the CG's family is a touchy subject, so hopefully he's tactful enough not to mention it to her. Just in case he puts his foot in it.'

'Wow, you figured all that out in... in, like, two seconds,' Anabel exclaims.

'I guess.'

'That's impressive,' she says. Then, smiling sarcastically, she adds, 'You know, with skills like those you could be a spy.'

'Yeah, cheers. Thanks for those few kind words.'

'Ha, and if that didn't work you could always be a model in a dress like that,' Milly jokes.

'Oh, shut up, both of you,' I scoff.

Milly takes a moment to set up her iSpy, standing it against the flower vase in the middle of the table. By carefully zooming the camera in on Styles and his companions, she focuses the hardware optimised audio microphone on them. Thankfully, there is no one behind us whose curiosity will be piqued by the strangely placed handset. She presses record and leaves it to transcribe the conversation.

'Good, let's hope that works,' she says, picking up her menu. 'We can go through it later.'

'Tell me about your afternoon,' I say. 'Then I'll tell you all about the cow of a consul general.'

'Pretty uneventful, wasn't it?' Anabel says, looking innocently at Milly. I fight the urge to smirk at the irony of her comment. 'Seems Styles got himself a right cushy upgrade, though. When he arrived, they said he was being upgraded to a swanky suite.'

'Nice if you can get it,' I muse.

'You're telling me,' Milly gushes. 'I had a look at pics of it on the internet. It looks huge.'

'Did we get eyes and ears on it?'

'Yup,' Anabel replies. 'Got a tiny camera in the hallway, with a view of the door. And we slipped a sticky mike in under the bottom of his door. Should give us sight and sound for a few days.'

'Just hope it doesn't tug off on the carpet when he opens the door,' Milly says, her brow furrowing at the thought.

An arriving waiter distracts us, and we fall silent to let Anabel order a wide selection of Chinese delicacies. As he departs, I hurriedly call him back to add a bottle of champagne.

'*Meh*, is what it is. About the bug, I mean,' I conclude with a shrug. 'So, do you want to hear about the right piece of work we've got running the consulate?'

Both nod enthusiastically. So, for the next few minutes I recant, with vivid detail and sarcasm-laced impressions, the afternoon's meeting with the CG, and the ensuing tour of the city with George.

Our food soon arrives, as does the champagne, and we eagerly dig into the veritable feast Anabel's ordered.

'Oh, this bubbly goes down so smoothly,' I sigh pleasurably. 'Doesn't this have all the hallmarks of being a really tough gig?' I add jokingly.

'Going down a bit too smoothly,' Anabel comments, licking her lips. 'So smoothly, in fact, that I need a pee. Don't scoff all the crispy roast pork. Leave some for me, won't you?'

As she walks off towards the exit, I turn to Milly, gesture at Styles and say, 'What do you make of what he's up to?'

'Not much, honestly. I'm watching the transcribed audio. Seems they're just old friends of his. Well, him and his ex-wife, it sounds. Lot of "What have you been up to?" and "How's Susie?". He seems keen to tell them about life in politics and Whitehall gossip. But this doesn't read like any sort of clandestine meeting, certainly not one with reps from north of the border.'

'Yeah, well,' I say, glancing around to look again at Styles's Western dining companions. 'Would've been too good to be true, I guess.'

'Doesn't mean we back off, though,' Milly stresses.

'Oh no, absolutely. I just doubt tonight will produce much of interest on that front, that's all.'

I refill our glasses and take another helping of the succulent roasted Peking duck. My attempts to pick up a slippery hargow dim sum from the bamboo steamer with my chopsticks has Milly in fits of laughter. She stops abruptly as Anabel hurries back to the table.

'Quick, come with me,' Anabel urges in a hushed voice. Touching Milly's hand, she adds, 'Babe, bring your bag.'

Turning, she hurries back across the room as quickly as possible without attracting undue attention.

'Now what? Reckon she can't find the bathroom?' I joke, standing to follow.

'Search me. C'mon, let's go see what's up,' Milly says, grabbing her handbag. Pointing at her phone, she adds, 'I'll leave this here. Should be safe, right?'

'I guess.'

Together, we follow Anabel out of the restaurant, and up the winding marble and wood staircase. We catch up with her on the top-floor landing, where she signals for us to remain quiet and accompany her down the hallway. At the end, she opens a small door and waves us through. Hoisting up my dress, I take a large step up to find myself on a small open-air rooftop balcony. My friends quickly follow me out. The balcony is long and narrow and runs alongside the club's cosy-looking library, which is partially visible through several small, metal-framed windows.

'Why are we up here?' I ask.

'You will not believe who I just saw walk in and head straight up here,' Anabel whispers conspiratorially, pointing at the library. Without waiting, she excitedly continues, 'Give me one of those acoustic thingies you have in your bag. This is too weird to miss.'

Hurriedly, Milly delves deep into her handbag and, after some searching, pulls out a small plastic box. She hands it to Anabel, who quickly extracts a tiny earpiece and a button-sized round disc. Slipping the paired earplug in, she steps over to the nearest window and presses herself up against the adjacent wall. Carefully, she slips her hand out and presses the disc up against the glass, where it remains unobtrusively affixed in the corner of the bottom-most pane. Quickly moving away, she re-joins us at the balcony's ledge.

'Who's in there?' I urge.

'There were three of them going up the stairs,' she replies haltingly, listening in at the same time to the conversation taking place inside. 'One's the number two in the Hong Kong police. While it isn't, like, entirely strange to see someone like that here, he was with the PLA's HK garrison commander, which is a bit odd, and another guy whose name I don't recall but whom I'm positive is the PLA's new head of irregular warfare and special operations.'

'How'd you know?' I say.

'I remember seeing an article about him in some Chinese army paper.'

'Interesting little clique,' I note with a raised eyebrow.

'Too right. Especially given what's going on at the moment.'

'You sure this is such a good idea?' Milly asks nervously. 'I mean, what if they catch us? We'll properly be in a mess then.'

'Who dares wins?' I reply with a shrug. 'A group like that… seriously, this is too good to pass up. Even if it comes to nothing. Call it a training exercise.'

'Knew you'd say something like that. Okay, fine. Can't say I'm so happy about this, though.'

'Shush,' Anabel says. 'Let me get a line on what they're up to.'

As she listens in, Milly and I edge sideways to get an oblique view into the room. The three older men who just entered are dressed in casual civilian clothes. They are in the midst of greeting a small, bespectacled, balding little man in a badly fitting, threadbare suit who appears to have been waiting for them in the library. Standing in the far corner is another man. Considerably younger than the others, he is dressed entirely in black and has short, neat hair and a humourless expression.

He remains largely still, watching and scrutinising everything. His eyes rove the room, taking in each of the older men with a predatory alertness. And when he does move to greet them, it is with a calculated deliberateness that the others lack. Ten seconds' observation is enough to tell me he's bad news. His lifeless, sinister eyes are enough to send a cold shiver down anyone's back. Killer's eyes.

A scattering of small table lamps cast a warm glow over the small library. The man whom Anabel identifies as the PLA's head of special operations, takes a large armchair beside the fire. From his pocket he takes a cigar travel case and he sets to work snipping the end of a cigar and lighting it with an industrial-looking blowtorch-like lighter. The local garrison chief and the deputy police chief choose the two-person Chesterfield directly opposite him. The sinister man in black lays his phone on the table and remains standing, tall and erect, off to one side with his hands clasped behind his back.

'What do you reckon?' I whisper to Milly. 'Career soldier?'

'That, or really bad haemorrhoids.'

The slightly malnourished little man in the cheap, shiny suit takes the sole remaining armchair. He hugs his worn briefcase tightly to his chest and remains silent. With my phone's impressive zoom lens, I reel off a few close-up shots as a waiter causes a distraction by delivering what look like brandies to each. The stern-looking man in black declines the wide-bodied, bulbous little glass and glares at the waiter, encouraging him to make a hasty retreat. The nervous staff member scurries for the door and hurriedly closes it behind him, leaving the men to their discussions.

'Okay, so from the gist of it,' Anabel whispers a few moments later, once they have begun talking in earnest, 'the guy with the cigar says he's just come from Beijing. He says the powers that be are growing tired of these insolent little protests going on down here. He says it's beginning to hinder the bigger plan. And that it must stop. He says they should all take this to mean action is required, and within days, not weeks. He says there is a major protest planned for this coming Sunday which must be disrupted at all costs. Otherwise they will just grow in size and confidence. Several million people taking to the streets is simply too much. There's only so long that these images can be fobbed off back home as protests against the West for its interference in Hong Kong. He says he's here to tell them enough is enough.'

'Well, that sounds all sorts of ominous, doesn't it?' I note quietly.

'Yeah,' Anabel replies with a furrowed brow. She gestures for quiet as she listens intently.

After a couple of minutes, I tap her arm expectantly. She waves me off, deep in concentration.

Finally, she says, 'Okay, this is some serious stuff they're talking about. They're spit-balling ideas like sowing unrest into the upcoming protests. Or infiltrating Chinese soldiers and sympathetic Triads into the protesters' ranks. That way they can deliberately escalate things by over-running the police lines and inciting the mob to attack the PLA base.'

'Yeah, because stuff like that always ends well,' I drawl sarcastically.

'Exactly,' adds Milly. 'An attack on the military would give the army carte blanche to move in and quash it once and for all, wouldn't it?'

'Probably. Sounds like they want to engineer some kind of armed insurrection,' Anabel continues. 'Cigar guy's telling them that whatever happens, it needs to leave the international community with no option but to agree that direct intervention by the Chinese government is required. Now they're debating whether that means targeting foreign corporation staff. But the copper isn't so sure. He says it'll mess with the economy too much. Better to let the gweilos think it's still safe for them here, else their companies may panic and relocate to Singapore or Dubai. PLA man's saying they'll all eventually go of their own free will anyway, especially once the plan becomes clear, so what difference does it make? The copper's arguing with him now, saying their bosses have too much invested in this city in terms of stocks and property. He doubts they'll want some rash, ill-considered or misdirected thuggery sending all of it into negative equity. Cigar guy's getting irritated. Says it's this kind of spineless inaction that's got them into this mess in the first place.'

Suddenly, Anabel curses. 'One of them says they saw movement out here. Someone's coming.'

'Okay, quickly, over here,' I say, pulling them to the edge of the balcony. I bring them in close and extend my hand out in front of us, clasping my phone at arm's length, ready to take a selfie.

'Smile,' I say, just as the door opens and the man in black peers out. He fixes us with a suspicious stare as I glance backwards over my shoulder to frame the shot. 'Hang on,' I say. 'Don't move. I'm trying to get that building with all the lights in. Oh, hey, you couldn't take a picture of us, could you?' I call, as Milly and Anabel giggle and pull faces for the camera. With disdain, he steps back inside and closes the door, leaving us to breathe deep sighs of relief. Milly and I shoot enquiring looks at Anabel.

'He says it's just a bunch of stupid girls doing Weibo. Nothing to worry about.'

'Well, either way, it's a good picture,' I comment in amusement. 'C'mon, best we keep well out of sight. They notice us again, they may not be so dismissive.'

Moving farther along the balcony, we let Anabel continue her eavesdropping. I run off several more bursts of photo shots as I pass the last window.

After a few moments, Anabel looks up, puzzled, and says, 'It all just got really weird. Like they're suddenly conversing in code. The little man with glasses is now talking. But he's got an odd accent. Can't place it. They asked him if these plans don't work, would his proposal? He says yes. It would certainly give them reason enough to ban the protests. But he says things could get out of control. Sorry, his Mandarin's not great. I'm struggling a bit to make sense of what he means. He says it could cause chaos, which could spread to the mainland. At least, I think that's what he said.'

'What could? The protests?'

'Not sure. Hold on, Hev, maybe. The main man says they'll consider it. But that the viability of the ervamectin protocol's critical, whatever that means.'

'*Ervamectin*?' Milly queries. 'Could he have meant Ivermectin?'

'Who knows? Maybe...'

'What's that?' I ask.

'It's a microbial drug used to treat parasite infections,' says Milly. 'Typically in less-developed places with poor-quality water supplies. But what's that got to do with the protests?'

'Dunno,' I reply.

'Interesting, though. He's asked the small guy in glasses to stay in the city for a few more days. See how things go. Okay, sounds like they're wrapping up. Come on, best we go,' Anabel urges as she removes the earbud and slips it back into its case.

'Shall we take the bug?' asks Milly.

'No, leave it,' I reply. 'Too obvious to remove it now.'

Keeping to the shadows, we slip past the windows and dart back inside. Thankfully, drawn lace blinds inside the library's double glass doors mask our passing.

'C'mon, hurry up,' I urge as we jostle one another down the stairs.

'I am, I am,' Milly hisses. 'Not everyone can move in heels like you can.'

Once back down on the thirteenth floor, I glance up and see the group of men begin their descent.

'Hey, huddle in close,' I instruct, manoeuvring to get the staircase lined up behind us. 'I want some proper face-on shots as they come down the stairs. This we have to mail in.'

Closing up beside me, my friends hug in tight, sucking in their stomachs and making an exaggerated fuss of carefully arranging their hair. Selecting the front-facing camera, I line the shot up, strike a pose and begin taking photos the moment the men walk into view, high up on the landing behind us. Together, we giggle, pulling faces, some serious, some playful. I take shot after shot in rapid succession, all focused on the scene behind us. Laughing, I finally stow my phone in my handbag and lead the way back into the restaurant. We pass the men at the bottom of the steps without so much as a glance. And none of them pay us any interest, either.

Our food is long since cold. So, with little appetite left after what we have just witnessed, we call for the bill so we can leave as fast as possible to update Sam. While stiffing the CG for dinner would be amusing, it would only lead to awkward questions, which we don't need.

'Shall we tell George as well?' asks Milly.

'Oh, I will. But the CG was adamant that Sam be our primary contact. I expect she doesn't entirely trust George to tell her stuff. So, we have to brief her snitch first. But I'm only going to send the photos to George,' I add pointedly.

'You know snitches end up in ditches,' Milly giggles.

'That's hilarious,' I exclaim. 'I've never heard that before.'

'Funny, right?' she says with a grin.

'Well, probably best not to irritate her on our first day,' Anabel notes as a waiter places the bill on our table and quickly departs again. 'Technically, she could kick us out if she wanted.'

'Don't disagree. Like George said. Is what it is. Okay, so who is this guy? The one with the cigar?' I ask as I count out the required number of hundred-dollar bills and lay them inside the leather folder.

'It's a pretty new post within the PLA,' Anabel begins as we stand and make for the door. She continues once we are alone in the lift. 'Historically, Chinese spec ops were just direct-action forces. They were never into unconventional warfare, like counterinsurgency, hostage rescue or psy-ops. But that's all changed recently.'

'They any good?' I ask.

'Depends what you mean by good. Put side by side with US, UK or Israeli special forces, they are years behind. They just don't have the same strength in their non-commissioned ranks. Take the SAS –'

'Oh yes, we know them well,' I joke.

'Exactly. Most of their creativity comes from within the NCO ranks, right?'

'Yup. Amusingly, if you can believe it, their nickname for just that kind of roots-driven planning is a Chinese Parliament.'

'Ha. I never knew that. Anyway, point is, the PLA just doesn't have that strength, mainly because their view on conscription versus volunteering is different. And the party's overly cautious view of the military doesn't exactly help, either. It's easy for them to steal and copy military tech, but almost impossible to copy culture without the right environment. I heard that's what this guy is trying to do. As well as all sorts of other nefarious stuff that we can only speculate about.'

'Don't need to speculate too hard,' says Milly as the lift doors open. 'Think we heard enough of it upstairs.'

'I'm still curious to figure out who the guy with glasses was,' Anabel comments as we step onto the pavement of the small side street. 'Perhaps send Sam a voice message. That's probably about as much as we can do for tonight, I reckon.

I mean, as crazy and coincidental as that just was, it's not why we're here. Perhaps it's best to leave it to Six?'

'Agreed,' I say, walking a few metres away to record a rapid debrief message. As I watch it slowly egg-time and send, I look around absentmindedly to admire the spectacular city looming high overhead on all sides. It seems so much brighter by night than anything we're familiar with back in the UK, where a combination of less-powerful streetlights and an absence of illuminated buildings on this scale sadly renders most British cities comparatively gloomy in comparison. Once the message is gone, I send the same message, along with the photos, to George. Turning back to my friends, I ask, 'Well, now what?'

'Now, we go clubbing,' Anabel blurts out excitedly. 'Styles isn't doing anything exciting tonight, or at least it doesn't seem like he is. There's this place I've missed so much. Come on, you'll both love it.'

The club she has in mind is barely a three-minute taxi ride and is tucked away at the end of a narrow, almost invisible alleyway, the entrance to which is hidden between an ice cream stall and a kebab takeaway. The meandering passage leads us down between high rises on either side until we reach a small courtyard, in which a bouncer's station has been set up. A short queue of people is lined up before it, and one by one people are receiving a stamp to the hand and being let past.

'This is Drop,' Anabel announces. 'This place is an institution. I only started coming here in the Christmas hols, but it's so much fun,' she adds with a deeply rebellious look.

'Why's it called Drop?' I ask.

'Not sure. I always thought it was because everyone's always dropping pills in there. But it could just be because everyone dances until they drop. Who knows?'

'It's a gay club,' I observe neutrally, taking in the couples queued up in front of us as well as some of their outfits.

'Some nights,' she says. 'Sometimes not. Guess we got lucky tonight.'

'I'm game,' I reply, catching Milly's questioning look.

'You sure?'

'Of course. Why not?'

'I dunno. I mean, you could end up spending half the night fending off interested girls.'

'Yeah, somehow I doubt it,' I reply.

Anabel laughs. 'With a hair style like that –'

'Yeah.'

'– in a place like this…?'

'Sure, it's fine,' I scoff, waving them off dismissively. 'I can handle it.'

'Uh-huh, really,' Milly says dubiously. Turning to Anabel, she adds, 'This'll be interesting.'

As the queue shortens, I find myself increasingly intrigued – not by the club itself, but rather by my two friends and the blossoming that is happening before my very eyes. Both expend so much energy in managing the anxiety that seems to come from what they are going through. Both are highly emotional, sensitive and intelligent individuals. But they have always been so afraid of what being in an openly gay relationship should look like, or mean. Worse, they seem genuinely scared about how it could come across to others. And yet since arriving in this vibrant, slightly mad city, much of that fear seems to have suddenly fallen away. For perhaps the first time ever, they are holding hands in public. In front of us in the queue, two men, barely older than us, share a kiss, and no one around us seems to care. I can't help but notice that Anabel and Milly move a little closer as a result. I fight to hide my smile. It's lovely to see.

The basement-level club is a dark, heaving sweat fest. The frenetic strobe lighting gives it an additional trippy vibe. The thump of the sound system's base reverberates through my body. There's a small, square-shaped, neon-lit bar in the centre and the dance floor wraps around this; then sofas line the walls. At the far end is a raised platform on which several more tables play host to larger parties.

The meagre size of the club coupled with the number of people they've let in means there is barely any room to move. The result is everyone pressed up against their neighbours. Just moving through the pumping crowd proves to be a slow process. Given the temperature outside, even at this time of the evening, clothing is on the minimalist side. And every touch results in the same damp stickiness.

Finally, with generous gin and tonics in hand, we head for the dance floor where, surrounded by increasingly amorous couples, things rapidly degenerate. Before long – fuelled by another round or two of drinks – the dancing becomes ever more brazen, and I come to find myself sandwiched between my friends, dirty dancing style. I upend my drink and dissolve into hysterics as both press themselves close, gyrating energetically up against me.

'Oh, Jesus,' I cry. 'I'm nowhere near pissed enough for this. You two crazy cats are too much for me.' Extracting myself from the sweaty grind-fest, I gladly make for the bar for a very large glass of iced water.

*

When we finally emerge out into the balmy night air several hours later, all three of us look sweaty, dishevelled messes. It takes a few seconds of blinking to acclimatise to the lights in the courtyard.

'Oh my God, what a total cattle market,' I exclaim, relieved to finally be outside again. My ears still ring, and I know I am talking louder than necessary. 'Was everyone just getting off with everyone in there? And I had no idea how many people would be doing drugs quite so openly in the toilet. God, I feel so naïve.'

'Told you coke's huge here,' Anabel laughs.

'You don't say!'

'But interestingly, you don't see a whole lot of hash. Though the local kids do have a bit of a problem with ketamine and meth.'

'Isn't that like a vet's anaesthetic?' Milly asks rhetorically. 'As in what they use on large zoo animals?'

'That's the one.'

'Jesus. And the club wasn't that bad,' Milly says, looking at me. 'Even if it did get a little fluid towards the end.'

'Fluid...' I smirk. 'That's one way of putting it. I walked into the toilets at one point to find two guys having sex in the cubicle. I mean the door wasn't even shut properly. And then there was another couple doing drugs off the sink top, and getting off with each other as I washed my hands.'

'You caused quite a stir,' Anabel notes. 'Not many tall, blonde gweilo girls in there. Certainly not as tall as you.'

'You don't think I noticed! Not that I get what the big deal is. There were loads of hot, pretty girls in there.'

'And none of them caught your eye?' Milly ventures with a sideways glance.

'Oh, would you look at the time,' I mutter as I walk off down the passageway. 'It's almost breakfast.'

'Oi, that's unfair,' she shouts after me. 'You didn't answer the question. And it's still early!'

'Woohoo, look who's getting all adventurous,' I call back.

As I reach the end of the alleyway, I stop suddenly as half a dozen rowdy Westerners come rushing down the adjacent steps from Hollywood Road.

'Holy crap,' one of the men calls to his friends. 'Let's move. Come on, girls.'

'Have you seen the size of my sodding heels,' one of the girls fires back in a thick Manchester accent. 'We're trying...'

'It's totally out of control,' another shouts as they rush past and make for Lyndhurst Terrace, which will take them on downhill towards Central.

'What's going on?' Milly asks as she and Anabel catch up with me.

'Dunno, but it doesn't sound good.'

Unable to resist, I climb the short flight of steps in curiosity, sidestepping another rush of people fleeing past me. When I reach the road, I stop and turn. Beside me, Anabel's horrified expression sums the situation up well.

'Oh, I've got a really bad feeling about this,' she gasps.

'You and me, too,' I exclaim as I survey the carnage before us. Gesturing for Anabel and Milly to follow me, I lead them along the road towards the chaos unfolding in the centre of the road junction, barely fifty metres away.

A small police car has mounted the pavement on the other side of the road and is now ablaze. A group of five men in yellow T-shirts and black trousers have just dragged the occupants, a male and female police officer, up to a nearby broken shop window. Two of the men are now in the process of urinating on them. Both officers appear to have been disarmed. The male officer was clearly roughed up during the scuffle. The other three yellow T-shirt clad men are hurling stones at a second police car parked farther up the road. Its occupants can just be seen sheltering on the far side of it. Their windscreen is already shattered, as is the roof-mounted light bar. Pedestrians are fleeing in all directions.

'I'm sorry, this can't be a coincidence,' Anabel says, surveying the spontaneous mini urban riot.

'Yeah, you might be right,' I reply, glancing cautiously up and down the street. 'Looks like it's just these five men. I dunno, girls, is it just me, or does this all look just a little too organised for student protestors? C'mon, let's get a few good shots of these guys.'

As we step into the road to approach the men, a large, powerful police motorbike with vivid yellow-and-blue-chequered livery roars around the corner with its lights, mounted both front and rear, flashing frenetically and its siren blaring loudly. Close up, it's a dizzying assault on one's senses.

Before the rider can deploy his stand or unholster his sidearm, two of the men tackle him from the bike, bringing it crashing to the ground with them. Together, they drag him out from beneath it. The larger attacker, who has the first officers' guns tucked into his belt, swiftly pulls the cop's weapon from its holster, while his accomplice rips the helmet from his head. Then the larger protestor kicks him savagely in the face. Crying out, the fallen police officer curls into a ball, before the two men begin giving him a fearsome beating.

'Oh, this is just bollocks!' I announce, gesturing for Anabel and Milly to stay back. 'He's buggered if no one does something, and quickly.'

Common sense would ordinarily caution me against getting into any kind of altercation in four-inch heels, but I see few other options. The closest police officers remain huddled for shelter behind their battered car, a good twenty-five metres away. The unmistakable warbling of sirens can be heard nearby, but not close enough to be of help.

Cursing, I run into the road, landing on the balls of my feet, and swiftly close the gap to the most dangerous of the yellow-shirted men: the one with the three guns in his belt. His senses are sharp, as are his reflexes. A civilian he most definitely isn't. His head whips around as I approach, and before I can grab his belt to fling him into the kerb-mounted burning police car, he launches a snap punch. Ducking low, I arc my right arm up to deflect the incoming swing, before snapping it forwards in a vicious swipe that clothes-lines him off his feet and down onto the asphalt. Lunging towards the next closest man, who seems momentarily stunned at being accosted, I land a hefty kick to his solar plexus, sending him flailing backwards into a metal pavement-mounted railing. Spinning round, I grab the feet of the fallen man and flip him onto his front before he can stand up again. With a heeled foot firmly on the small of his back, I wrench the three weapons from his belt. With two dangling from my little finger by their trigger guards, I level the third revolver at the nearest men. All freeze, clearly taken aback and shocked at the interruption.

'Watch out!' Milly cries from behind me as a small white van surges past, narrowly missing me before it brakes hard. My friends waddle over comically as fast as their heels will allow, and begin filming the men, which makes them all cover their faces as they run for the van. Doors slam in quick succession, and the van pulls away as fast as it arrived.

'What the heck was that?' Anabel blurts out.

'Dunno. It was parked up over there,' Milly says, pointing along the road. 'That was all a little too organised.'

'Too right,' I say, and point at the police officers. 'Best go check they're alright.' Then, running into the road, I call back to them, 'I want to see where those guys are going.'

Darting rushed glances left and right, I frown at the absence of taxis just when I need one. The only viable option is the fallen police bike. Running up to the pair of officers from the burning car, who are wearily rising to their feet, I drop two pistols to the pavement and carry on towards the motorcyclist.

'You okay?' I ask. 'You look like you're in shock.'

His face is badly swollen, his nose possibly broken, and his left eye is already almost completely closed. Appearing at my side, Anabel bends down and peers closer to examine him. Wincing at her light touch, he nods grudgingly.

'Good, then I need to borrow your bike.' Without waiting for an answer, I reach down for the big BMW. 'Shit. I can't do it with these on.' Kicking my heels off, I bend low, gripping the handlebar and beneath the rider's seat, and heave the huge bike up with a scream of effort. 'Christ, it's unwieldy,' I groan as I realise it must weigh close to two hundred and fifty kilos.

'Do you need help?' Milly says, rushing over.

'Won't say no,' I say as I heft it up through forty-five degrees. With her help we quickly get it upright, and I swing my leg over.

'Do you even know how to ride something like this?' she asks.

'Sort of,' I puff. 'Alex kind of showed me on that silly big Ducati he had. Hand me my heels, will you? If I remember right, all I do is…'

Milly places my Louboutins in my lap as I pull the clutch on the left handlebar. Then, desperately trying to remember the correct order, I turn the key, flick the kill switch on and then depress the starter, located beside my right thumb. The engine surges to life, sending reassuring vibrations rumbling through the frame.

'Sweet, that wasn't too hard.'

'Turn the lights off,' Anabel warns. 'Else they'll spot you a mile back.' With the front- and rear-mounted red and blue flashing lights off, I turn the headlights to their lowest setting.

'Sorry about this,' I call to the injured officer, who seems more concerned with his heavily bleeding nose than the imminent loss of his bike.

'Take this,' Anabel says, grabbing the discarded helmet from the road. 'Saves you getting snapped by any cameras you pass.'

'What a team,' I exclaim, hurriedly donning the glossy white, visored helmet. 'Meet you back at the hotel,' I call.

Depressing the left foot peg, I engage first gear. But then I release the clutch too fast, and the bike lurches forward and promptly stalls. Cursing, I restart the engine and more slowly release the clutch out as I accelerate away. Within twenty metres, the engine begins revving too highly and jerky vibrations course through the frame. I curse myself for forgetting to change gears and then hurriedly talk myself through the process.

'Off throttle, clutch, shift up through neutral into second, slowly off clutch, back on throttle.'

Amazed that it worked, and that I didn't screw it up and crash, I finally begin to relax a little and enjoy the rush as the big, heavy bike responds smoothly and nimbly to my inputs. Nonetheless, I try to remain wary of the power within the large twin engine and remind myself that it'll punish me the instant I don't respect it. As I accelerate on through the heart of Soho, my mind drifts to Alex and the irritatingly fond memories I still have of him and the fun we had together. Absentmindedly, I find myself mouthing his name, and then chide myself for being such a soppy idiot.

Just as I think I have it worked out, an over-enthusiastic tug of the brake as I approach a bend causes the bike's weight to lurch forwards. Cursing, I make another mental note that the rear brake is on the right pedal and that it's there to be used.

Despite the early-morning hour, the streets are busy with traffic and the pavements full of drinkers and partygoers spilling out of brightly lit bars and clubs. Most seem oblivious to the fact there was a riot just up the street, with police cars still ablaze. Some, though, are alert enough to spot me.

A chorus of shouts, wolf-whistles and leery comments rings out as I zoom past. Given some of the shouted comments, one could be forgiven for thinking that theft of a police motorbike isn't particularly frowned upon here.

It's with relief that I finally catch sight of the white van again, held up behind a small queue of cars and taxis at the third set of traffic lights, where Wyndham Street meets Glenealy. Keeping my distance, I affix my iSpy to an empty mount on the handlebars and open the navigation app. As I wait for the lights to change up ahead, propping the bike up barefoot begins to prove painful. Leaning first one way, then the other, I carefully slip my heels back on. It only occurs to me to drop the bike back down again into first as the lights turn green.

The traffic moves off slowly. With no warning, whether through impatience or because they have spotted me, the van's driver suddenly swerves to the right and accelerates off past the slower-moving taxis in front of it. Cursing, I gun the engine, shift up and, grinning with excitement, surge out past the slower cars. When I next catch sight of their van, they have slowed a bit, suggesting perhaps they haven't seen me yet. Hanging back, I follow them along Lower Albert Road, past the chief executive's mansion compound, replete with a baying crowd of disgruntled protestors outside the entrance, most dressed in yellow T-shirts, who are being kept back behind cordon tape by a few nervous-looking police officers. Rather than a mad thrash chase, I realise the trick tonight will be to hang back, round the corner slowly and then full-throttle the bike along the next straight to catch up again, before hanging back to let them gain a lead until they round the next corner, at which point I can race to close the gap once more.

The road dips down before rising quickly into a curving overpass. It then passes beneath a messy, tangled spaghetti junction of flyovers which curl around on themselves to feed the roads heading up and down the mountain. Glancing up, I see Victoria Peak looming high over the dazzling spectacle of a city laid out below. With the wind whipping at my red dress, I take a fast turn and accelerate up the hill, merging with the traffic on the steeply inclined Cotton Tree Drive. Up ahead, the van turns off onto Magazine Gap Road and begins the journey up the long, winding road that twists its way up Peak Road towards the exclusive, rarefied neighbourhoods scattered around the Peak. The higher we climb, the more impressive the condominium residences become.

Upon finally reaching the top, the roads levels out and gets noticeably narrower and even more twisting than before. Hurtling the hefty bike from side to side now becomes a not inconsiderable challenge. Passing the Peak Galleria on my right, with its tram station, bars and restaurants, I swing the bike around a tight ninety-degree left-hand turn and accelerate up the steep climb. With the bike's headlights now turned off, I keep a considerable distance and tail the van farther and farther along the quiet street to a turning marked with a cul-de-sac sign. Hanging back, I edge around the corner and watch the van drive to the very end of it. The road is poorly lit. Here the houses are very few and far between, but all are massive, gated properties secluded behind tall trees and foliage. The van pauses momentarily and then passes through a set of electric gates and disappears along a curved driveway into the property.

With a puzzled frown, I turn off the engine and push the stand into place. Sitting back, I stare in puzzled fascination at the entrance of the mysterious darkened mansion just visible through its thick perimeter of trees. Since when did radical disestablishmentarians start living in multi-million-dollar mountaintop villas in one of the most expensive cities in the world? I reach for my iSpy and save the location to my maps app. Then I call Milly.

'Heya,' she says, answering quickly. 'Oh, good, you're still alive. How's it going?'

'Interesting. I'll tell you all when I get back. Where are you both now?'

'Back in the hotel. We didn't want to hang around for more police to arrive. We do not need our names on file anywhere in this city.'

'Yeah, good thinking.'

'Oh yeah, by the way, the cop whose bike you nicked –'

'The one whose head I saved from getting kicked in?'

'Yeah, that one. Before we left, he said his buddies went and put out an all-units bulletin for the van and the bike. He was just giving you the heads-up. Grateful, I guess, for still having his head and not having lost an eye.'

'How sweet. Well, if you were still there, I'd have you tell him to get a taxi up to the location tag I'm about to send you, because then he'd find his bike. Wouldn't need to take crap from his buddies about losing his bike.'

'I'm sure he'd appreciate that. If he wasn't probably in hospital. Did you trash it?' she asks warily.

'I find your lack of faith disturbing.'

'I bet you do. See ya in a bit, then,' she laughs, before hanging up.

After sending Milly my location, I take the hem of my dress and shunt myself up to mount the petrol tank. With the flimsy material, I wipe down the key, the handles and any other surface I touched, including the side of the helmet. I carefully dismount and take several low-light photos of the mansion's exterior. Then I begin the long walk back to the main road to try and find a taxi.

The walk is longer than I anticipated and heading downhill in four-inch heels soon becomes precarious: I take them off again and walk the remainder barefoot. The back streets are, unsurprisingly, deserted, given the early hour, and not particularly well lit, either. It takes about ten minutes to reach the main road again. Spotting a fast-approaching Toyota with its small round light on above the dashboard, I rush the last dozen feet, thrusting my arms in the air and shouting, 'Taxi!'

Thankfully, the driver stops for me. Settling into the worn, black, faux-leather rear seat, I rub my sore feet with relief and ask to be taken to the Mandarin. The ride is a strange, jerky experience as the driver incessantly pumps the pedal, accelerating and decelerating the car erratically like some kind of cheap fairground ride. Whether he thinks it might save fuel, which I seriously question, or just can't drive properly, I'm not sure. Of course, it might be a bit much to expect heel-toe shifting to match revs with the wheel speed for smoother gear changes on corners, but at least a consistent speed would be good. I smile to myself as we jerk our way all the way down the Peak towards the city.

It is with relief that I finally climb from the car some twenty minutes later in front of the hotel. With a weary sigh, I slip my heels back on for a slightly more dignified crossing of the lobby, before kicking them off again in the lift as the doors close.

Milly and Anabel must have arrived back a while ago because both are already showered and in their dressing gowns when I let myself into their room using my spare key card.

'Well, that was a laugh and a half,' I exclaim, dropping my shoes in the hall. They have the TV on and both are glued to the BBC.

'Come check this out,' Milly says urgently, waving, but without taking her eyes from the screen.

'What a total mess,' Anabel comments, turning the volume up two notches.

'... tonight's riots have been reported by many as having come out of nowhere,' the BBC's reporter says solemnly. Behind him, slightly out of focus, is a post-apocalyptic scene. Several cars are ablaze, a number of them police cars. What glass remains in the broken shopfronts behind him reflects a frenetic dazzle of flashing red and blue lights, which makes the setting even more dramatic. Thick wafts of smoke drift past in the background, giving the reporter an almost ethereal glowing halo. 'According to police reports, in a spontaneous and coordinated wave of terrorist extremism, violent groups of men appeared across the city. Their targets, the local police. All appeared to be members of the main student protest movement, who have now become known by their yellow T-shirts. Student leaders were quick to deny any involvement in these attacks, however, claiming their protest is a peaceful one. In some parts of the city, this wave of mindless violence and vandalism was met by fully armed riot police, who quickly employed the use of tear gas, smoke and water cannon trucks.

'International observers have noted this heavy-handed response may only serve to inflame matters further, drawing more protesters into the fray. As it stands, local hospitals have so far recorded some fifty-seven injured, three critically. This is Richard Wong, reporting live for the BBC, from Hong Kong.'

'Amazing how there's no mention of what happened in Sha Tin,' says Anabel.

'Why, what happened there?' I ask as I collapse back wearily across their king-size bed.

'A friend messaged me with a video of a bunch of thugs in black T-shirts attacking people near the bus station. Rumour is they were Triads who're pro-Beijing. The shocking bit is there is a police station barely five minutes away, and not a single cop turned up.'

'So, all in all, a bit of a mess, then,' I surmise.

'That's one way to put it,' she quips. 'Total fricking chaos in a major financial hub might be more accurate.'

'Okay,' I sigh, sitting up again. 'Look, I'm off to bed. It's been a silly-busy day. I can't believe we only got here this morning. But look, in a nutshell, I'm not sure these fools,' I jab my thumb towards the TV, 'are what they purport to be. I trailed them up to some silly big house way up on the Peak.'

'That's odd,' says Anabel.

'Yeah, so look, maybe tomorrow we get to work and deep-dive the people at that little impromptu shindig we stumbled upon tonight. Especially the small guy. He's the odd one out, right? Which makes him interesting. The others, we can easily guess what their role in this mess might be, even if we can't prove any of it. Can we at least try to figure out who he is?'

'Yeah, we can try,' says Milly. 'Of course, luckily we don't need to prove things beyond reasonable doubt.'

'You know, I'm curious,' I say, folding my arms. 'When you say rebel stuff like that, do you feel a natural, inherent conflict between it and your usual goody two shoes character?'

'Oi, go on, get out,' she says, throwing a cushion in my direction. 'You're so nasty.'

'Yeah, right,' I laugh, dodging it as I gather my things. 'Sweet dreams. See you both tomorrow.'

'Before you go, send me the pics you took tonight,' says Milly.

'Okay, will do. Night, then.'

*

Being an unnaturally early riser, I've finished breakfast before either of my friends has even sent their first instant message of the day. In fact, neither has even checked their phones by the time I let myself back into their room. Anabel is still lazing on the bed. Unperturbed by my arrival, she lazily looks in my direction, smiles and then unhurriedly covers herself with the sheets. I pretend I didn't see and go straight into the bathroom, where Milly is in the midst of getting ready.

'Ah, smells nice in here,' I note cheerily, sniffing deeply.

'Aw, thanks,' she replies, setting her bottle of Chloé perfume down beside the marble sink.

'Yeah, well, I may need to change all that…'

'Seriously?' she groans, looking from me to their toilet and back again. 'How can someone be both funny and grim at the same time?' she replies, disgusted. 'Why can't you go use your own bathroom?'

'Would you believe me if I said I'm too lazy?'

'No!'

'Me neither.'

With a huff and a scowl, she leaves and closes the door behind her.

'Don't take too long,' she calls through it. 'We have something interesting to show you.'

Barely a minute later, having washed my hands, I give the bathroom a single spray, high up, with Milly's Chloé, and head out to join them.

'Best not go in there for a bit,' I warn.

'You are so unbelievably gross,' Anabel exclaims, slumping back down on the bed.

'That's what I said,' Milly cries.

'Yeah, yeah. By the way, before I forget. George pinged back overnight. He also suggests we dig into that meeting a bit more, if we have time. He said he was interested in who the odd one out was. With a crowd like that, he reckons if we can work out who the little guy is, it might explain what they are up to.'

'Coincidental or what?' Milly exclaims, glancing at Anabel.

'I'll say.'

'Why? What have you found?' I ask.

'Take a look at these,' Milly says, bringing her seventeen-inch laptop to life. 'Before I went to bed last night, I loaded some of the photos we took into Six's people-finder search engine and just let it run.'

'Did it give us anything?'

'Eventually. Seems the scrawny guy has never been at the forefront of any photos we have on file, but eventually we found these. Look.'

Peering closer, I flick through the three photos that the search returned. They appear to have been taken in a factory, all stark and white, with industrial strip lighting overhead. A large crowd has gathered around a single, beaming man of considerable stature, who is standing in the centre. All those around him gaze adoringly up at him, some with tears in their eyes.

400

'Where was this?'

'It's a photo shoot from a couple of years ago back at some fish processing plant a little bit outside of Pyongyang. Somewhere down the Taedong River.'

'Go about four rows back from the glorious leader,' Anabel suggests, lazing in her thick duvet.

'Ah, and there you are,' I exclaim, leaning forwards. 'Crazy that it can find a face all the way back there.'

'Your guy's North Korean,' Anabel yawns.

'Can we be sure of that?'

'Just look at him,' she exclaims. 'He's so clearly Korean.'

'Isn't that a bit racist?' I ask, smirking.

'Oh, don't you dare say all Asian people look the same!'

'What, like all Westerners look the same?' Milly giggles.

'Exactly. But trust me. He's so Korean. And his accent isn't from the south, either,' Anabel says. 'Also, his clothes are a total giveaway.'

'Such a fashion snob,' I mutter. 'So, look, that's great. But what does it mean? That the guy's in the fisheries business? That makes no sense.'

'True,' Milly notes pensively.

'We'd need to find him here, right?' I say. 'And figure out who he really is. Why's he so important that they need to keep him around for a few more days?'

'We might have a line on that, too.' Anabel yawns again, rubbing her face sleepily.

'I sure hope we don't have anywhere important to be this morning?' I ask, watching her roll over and snuggle up to a large pillow.

'We're good,' Milly assures me. 'Styles is in meetings the whole morning.'

'So, what do we have on this guy? How do we find him?'

'Take a look at the photos from last night,' Milly says, switching to another folder on her computer.

'What am I looking for?'

'Anything that might tell us where to look for these guys. Him especially,' Milly teases, pointing at the North Korean man.

'I'll give you a hint,' says Anabel excitedly. 'Look at the second-to-last photo you took. On the table.'

'Don't spoil it,' Milly sighs. 'Let her find it herself.'

'Okay. Yeah, what is that?' I say, peering closely, zooming in on the image. 'You mean the thing lying on the table? On top of that brick of a phone he has?'

'Yup,' Anabel chimes in.

'It's like a credit card. Why wouldn't he just have it in his wallet? Do they even have credit cards in North Korea?'

'It's a hotel key card,' says Milly.

'Yah, Ritz Carlton, baby! Black card, silver lion head,' Anabel cries, unable to hold back any longer.

'You sure?'

'Absolutely,' she exclaims. 'Someone's getting a nice, no-expense-spared trip. That's for sure. Means he's just over there.' An arm emerges from beneath the duvet and points towards the harbour.

'So, let's go find out who he is.'

'Can we get breakfast first?' Milly asks, glaring at Anabel's form beneath the sheets.

'Fine, but be fast. We don't know when he might check out.'

'What's Styles actually up to this morning?' Anabel enquires as she finally slips from the bed and pads lightly, still wrapped in the enormous duvet, towards the bathroom.

'Breakfast with the consul general,' Milly says, reciting from memory. 'Then he has some meet and greet at the British Council, which takes him up to lunchtime. Then lunch at the British Club, with a who's who of the expat crowd.'

'Cool, so we have the morning at least,' Anabel calls as the shower comes on. Neither of us catch what she says next.

'Ok, well, I'm going to the gym then,' I say, then add mockingly, 'and get a swim in while you two munch croissants and sip English breakfast tea.'

'Oh, okay,' Milly replies disparagingly, giving me an exaggerated thumbs-up. 'Because that sounds so much fun.'

*

The International Commerce Centre rises from the tip of the Kowloon peninsula as a bold, unapologetic symbol – if one was even needed – of just how much Asia has pulled ahead of most of the West. It is a gleaming glass and steel skyscraper the likes of which doesn't exist in the UK, or most of Europe for that matter. Crowning out at an almost insane four hundred and eighty-four metres, it trumps the Shard in London by a hundred and seventy-five metres and affords occupants a peerless view out over Victoria Harbour, and far beyond.

'Jesus,' I exclaim, peering up in awe as we step from the lobby to get a proper view of the impossibly tall tower. 'How many floors does it have?'

'A hundred and eighteen, if you believe the lift,' Anabel says casually. 'But this being Hong Kong, with its weird tetraphobia, it actually has a hundred and eight.'

'Tetra-what?' I ask, with an amused, baffled look.

'Tetraphobia. It's a fear of the number four. No, don't look at me like that. I'm serious. There are no floors with the number four in it. So, no fourth floor, fourteenth, twenty-fourth and so on, all the way up. They just skip them.'

'Sorry, WTF?'

'So, in Chinese, the number four and the word for death are really similar. So quite often they avoid using the number four in buildings.'

'Wait, didn't you say people paid, like, these insane premiums to buy prestigious or lucky addresses here, stuff with the number eight in it?'

'Yes, because eight's a lucky number.'

'But if you buy the eighty-eighth floor of a building, which from the look of it one clearly could, they wouldn't be getting that, right? They'd be getting, like, way lower down in reality. Like the seventieth floor or something.'

'That's technically true.'

'Wow, did you just do the maths in your head?' Milly giggles sarcastically.

'Ha, everyone's a fricking comedian today, aren't they! Whatever. Now, am I right to think this is the building Lara Croft jumped off in one of those *Tomb Raider* films?'

'Yes,' says Anabel, shaking her head. 'But the geography was all wrong. They started out in Times Square, which is, like, way over there, on the island. It's in Causeway Bay,' she notes, pointing. 'But then somehow they jumped off the ICC, which is all the way over here. And they landed on a boat in the harbour, yet for some reason flew all the way over to the Bank of China building, which is that big one, way over there on the island, with the triangular kind of design stretching up it. Anyway, it's the movies.'

'Alright, c'mon,' I say. 'Let's go see if we can get some info on this mystery guest. You got everything we need?' I ask Milly.

Nodding, she pats her small handbag. Together, we walk into the large, open lobby and head straight for the recessed lift bank, where an attendant directs us to the next available car.

'That's really weird,' I say, breaking the silence as we pass the seventieth floor. 'My ears just popped.'

'Mine, too,' says Milly.

'Kind of freaky that happening outside of being in a plane, don't you think?'

'Not sure I even notice it here anymore,' Anabel replies as she watches the in-lift TV with a glazed expression. 'Too many tall buildings, I guess.'

The climb up to the hundred and third floor passes astonishingly quickly. The doors swish open onto a large, dimly lit, rectangular-shaped lobby that is luxuriously decorated with the same liberal lashings of glitzy gold, dark woods and intricately textured fabrics that we saw downstairs. Cheap looking this place most certainly isn't.

As planned, Anabel makes her way uncertainly towards the check-in desk. Milly and I beeline it off to the right, where we find a two-seater leather bench. Reaching into her bag, Milly extracts her phone and a small plastic box, which I quickly open, while she launches a specialised app on her phone.

'I still don't believe this thing,' I say, peering closer at the tiny, housefly-like drone.

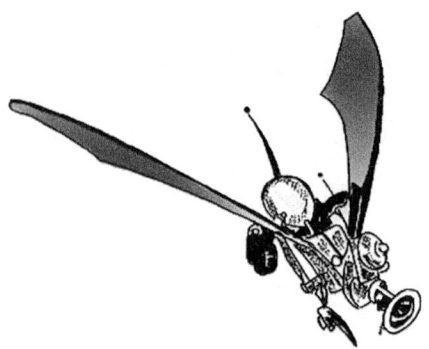

'Crazy, huh?' she notes as she powers it up. The tiny wings begin to beat and without warning it rises sharply from the box. With little movements of her fingers on the screen, she directs it up towards the ceiling, where it won't be easy to spot. Then it whips off towards the reception area. I peer over her shoulder in amazement as the feed shows a view approaching above the check-in clerk's head. A moment later, Anabel enters the frame. While there is no sound, we know from our earlier rehearsals that Anabel will start by telling him she works at the China Club, and that one of their guests left his mobile phone in the restaurant the previous evening. As planned, she takes a dummy handset from her pocket and lays it on the countertop. Clearly bored by an errand she feels below her, she idly looks around the lobby.

The clerk leans forwards to ask a question. Most likely the guest's name.

In anticipation, we know Anabel will respond that the booking was made under a Chinese companion's name. All the club knows is that they ordered the guest a taxi back to the Ritz Carlton and that the gentleman in question is Korean. Possibly from north of the border, her manager reckons, given a comment the client made about restaurants in Pyongyang.

As was almost to be expected, the clerk shakes his head, yet glances nervously around at someone standing behind him, who might well be his duty manager but whom, on closer scrutiny, does not have any name badge on his dark suit lapel. The man gives an almost imperceptible shake of his head and looks away again. The clerk's focus returns to his screen, and he stares unblinking at it for a moment longer. Milly hurriedly zooms the fly-drone's camera down at the screen.

'Got it,' she says in an excited whisper.

'That's nuts. Can you imagine espionage before all this cool tech?'

'Tell me about it.'

Glancing up, I see the clerk offer Anabel an apologetic shrug of his shoulders.

'Notice how he keeps glancing at the suited stiff behind him?'

'No. I'm trying not to crash this thing. Okay, bringing it home. Easy does it. These are twitchy little suckers.'

With the drone safely returned to its case, we get up, look at our watches and make for the lobby lifts again. We take the car after Anabel's. All in, it took us less than three minutes to secure what we came for.

Once we have both bought a coffee from a small shop recessed beneath one of the Elements shopping mall's escalators, we meet up again with Anabel, deeper within the mall.

'Guess we reckoned right,' Milly says as Anabel walks over to join us.

'Yup,' Anabel replies. 'They completely denied having anyone of the sort staying there.'

'Which is interesting,' Milly says, 'because while he was pretending not to know, the clerk had the room number open on his screen. Here.' Milly offers the phone to Anabel, who pinches and zooms in on the video.

'You notice the stiff standing behind the guy you were talking to?' I ask Anabel.

'Oh, couldn't miss him. Zero chance he was hotel staff. If I had to guess, I'd say he was Chinese Ministry of Interior Security. I reckon the last joke he ever heard was in kindergarten. See, look, I was right,' she comments, pointing at the phone. 'His name is Lee. He's definitely North Korean. They've got him on the hundred and seventeenth floor.'

'Yeah, well we have his room number,' Milly comments. 'And even better, he doesn't check out for a few more days. Now we just need to get eyes and ears into his room before he leaves. Figure who he is and maybe what they're up to.'

'Let's not leave it too late,' I say. 'Remember, they seem pretty fixated on this Sunday's protest, for whatever reason. Doesn't give us long.'

'True, but getting the room number was one thing. I don't know how we're going to get within half a mile of his hotel room though.' Anabel snorts derisively. 'Did either of you see all the guys posted at the lifts?'

'Which ones?' Milly asks.

'The ones who take guests up to their rooms. There were two security guys at each lift. Looked like secret service types. They were checking that everyone going up was a guest. I reckon they must have some high-ranking officials staying there or something like that. It's the only explanation for the heightened security presence. Trouble is, without access, we have no hope of planting any observation devices.'

'Think it's too big a risk for us to book ourselves into the hotel, even if only for a night?' Milly ponders. 'I do worry that one of us accidentally runs into one of the men from the China Club? I mean, I get it's slim, but you never know.'

'Ordinarily, I'd take the piss about you being overly cautious,' I say. 'But this time I'm inclined to agree. Too risky. Bummer that he still has an old Nokia, else we could plug into his mobile. That would be way easier, right?'

'Agreed,' Anabel adds. 'These people probably miss nothing. And the coincidence would be too much. Besides, keys are restricted by floors, aren't they? No guarantee we'd get the same floor.'

'So that rules out planting a listening device inside his room,' Milly says.

'It does, doesn't it,' I reply glumly, before the first inklings of a grin begin to form on my face.

'Oh no, I really don't like that look,' Milly sighs. 'It always comes with bad news.'

'Oh, you have no idea,' I exclaim excitedly. 'And you're definitely not going to like this one. Besides, I'm not even sure we can get what I'd need. Gotta talk to GC as soon as possible. We also need to figure which side of the hotel this guy's room faces, so we can laser it from across the harbour.'

'I'm sorry… laser designate it?' Milly stammers. 'What kind of hair-brained scheme are you coming up with this time?'

'Brace yourself. It's a little out there on the wild side.'

Sighing, Milly shrugs weakly, and says, 'Go on, then. Let's hear it.'

When I tell them, she lurches forward, spluttering coffee from her mouth. Coughing, she clasps a hand to catch the drips and sets the cup down on a bench with a look of horrified disbelief.

'I'm sorry, you're going to *what*?' she exclaims. 'Are you completely out of your mind?!'

CHAPTER 12

ROOM WITH A VIEW

Hong Kong

'Yeah, perhaps best not to ask questions you really don't want the answers to,' I reply. 'But trust me, this'll be a laugh.'

'Heard that before,' Milly says with a deepening frown.

'Got to agree,' Anabel adds, her brow equally furrowed with concern. 'It is utterly nuts.'

'Maybe…' I reply, smirking. 'Oh, changing the subject. We need to get a camera into Styles's room. We honestly don't know what he's up to in there. It worries me that he seems to be doing exactly what his itinerary states, like a good little boy. And the rest of the time he's been hunkered away in that room of his.'

'Agreed. Time to see what's going on in there,' Milly says, nodding. 'He could be doing all sorts of stuff by phone for all we know.'

'Can I leave that with you?' I ask. 'Perhaps while I go see GC tonight?'

'Yeah, that's fine,' Anabel replies. 'I'm sure we can come up with some way to get into his room. Maybe I pretend to be an aide dropping consular files off to him or something.'

'Yeah, exactly,' Milly adds. 'Something that can't be left at the front desk. See if GC can't get a consulate ID for you.'

'Good. Let's call him, then,' I say, pulling out my iSpy.

*

The remainder of the afternoon is idled away, with our bottoms getting increasingly sore – before finally going completely to sleep while we sit on a park bench in Hong Kong's botanical gardens, watching as Robert Styles, wearing a full suit and tie, reads a book all by himself on a bench in the shade of a tree.

At first, we were convinced this had all the hallmarks of a clichéd clandestine meeting in the making. We were sure he would not be here for long, not with a suit on. But then we remembered he had lived here for years and most likely acclimatised to the heat and humidity. But still, we were sure it was only a matter of time before he would be joined on the bench by whoever it was that he had come here to meet. But as minutes turned to hours and the sun crawled slowly across the blue, featureless sky, the possibility begun to dawn on us that perhaps he really was just taking an afternoon out to read a book in a park near the consulate.

When he finally rises, stretches and walks off, we turn to each other with disbelieving looks. The sun has also had enough and promptly drops behind the tallest building on the horizon.

Styles's long, lazy afternoon spent with his copy of James Hilton's *Lost Horizon* leaves scant time for me to get back to the Mandarin and meet George Clementine in the hotel's Captain's Bar. After a rushed three-minute shower followed by a frantic scramble for something appropriate to wear to a swanky Hong Kong bar, I dash out the door in a sequinned backless wrap top, a white mini skirt and high-heeled wedges.

Already quarter of an hour late, I hurry, fretting, across the gentile, wonderfully scented hotel lobby and dart down the short flight of steps into the dark, cosy L-shaped bar. It has a fabulously quaint and snug feel, without being gloomy, and emanates the relaxed vibe of an old-fashioned speakeasy. The walls are adorned with wood panelling, eighteenth-century British colonial maps and arty black-and-white jazz-themed photos. The décor appears untouched by the passing of time, with much of its furnishings likely still the original styling, from the curved bar's brass trimmings and matching foot rail to the red leather sofas and large chessboard-etched glass dividers set between the central sofas.

To the right, at the bottom of the stairs, is a small, raised stage, with a wall of exposed brick as a backdrop, on which a jazz quartet is playing. I quickly spot George through the crowd. He appears happily settled in the far right-hand corner in a large, old-fashioned leather armchair, with a vintage pewter beer tankard set before him and a plate of exotic-looking bar snacks from which he is selectively picking.

'Hey, I'm really sorry I'm late,' I apologise upon reaching the table.

'No problems,' he says, looking up with a smile. 'I could sit here for ages, just watching the world amble past. Please, take a seat.'

'Thank you.'

With a happy sigh, I sink into the opposite armchair.

'Nice shoes,' he notes with a sly chuckle as he picks a Japanese seaweed cracker from the silver snacks dish. 'What are they? Louboutins, going by those silver studs.'

'Good eye you have there.'

'What can I say? Occupational hazard, being observant. Nah, truth is, the wife has expensive taste.' Pausing, he adds, 'Of course, it's good they didn't have their usual security guy on tonight. He might've turned you away, thinking you to be a lady of the night, dressed like that.'

'Oh, really? I don't know whether to be amused or offended. I thought this outfit was pretty conservative.'

'Oh, I'm not saying it isn't. Spot on, in fact, for a place like this. No, don't get me wrong. But this is Asia. Tall blonde women are often simply assumed to be Russian. It happened to me last time I was here. They challenged my companion for just that reason.'

'No way! She must have been fricking mortified.'

'Yeah, I don't know about that…'

'How can you say that?'

'Well, because she was, in fact, a prostitute, so…'

'Yeah, not sure I want to know much more. Wait. Hang on. Aren't you married?'

'And very happily so, too. She was, how shall I put it, also seeing the Indian consul general and happened to have a very interesting line into what was going on in Kashmir between his country, Pakistan and China.'

'Uh-huh, I bet she did. Let me guess, HM Treasury helped loosen her tongue.'

'Something like that.'

'Got to say, I'm loving this colonial gentlemen's club vibe,' I say as a white-jacketed waiter appears at my side.

Without thinking, I simply order another of the chilled beer tankards. To his credit, George makes no comment, and goes up a couple of notches in my estimation. 'So, what should I know about this city of yours, then?'

'Well, the first thing you need to know about Hong Kong is this,' he says, leaning forward and rubbing his hands together enthusiastically. 'It's a morally corrosive environment.'

'How so?' I laugh.

'People do what they want here, and no one passes judgement, or tells you it's wrong. It's one of the city's main draws. You want to do drugs? Go for it. No big deal. You're married and you want to take four hookers back to the Four Seasons? No one gives a damn. Not like back in the UK, where people will socially ostracise you for that sort of deviancy. Here, it's your business. You want to ruin your marriage? Sure, your friends will be sad for you, but it's your choice. And they'll still meet you for a pint next Friday. Then again, the wife is probably playing away from home, too. So, it all balances out.'

'People do that?' I comment, wide-eyed. 'Or are you just winding me up?'

'No joke. This place, any hole's a goal.'

'Ew, that's pretty gross. Seriously, does this city's depravity know no bounds?' I reply with a grin as my beer arrives. 'That was fast. Well, cheers, George.'

'Cheers,' he says, clinking my tankard with his before taking an appreciative sip. 'No joke. Point is, this place, if you don't know who you are before you arrive, you might well end up leaving a very different character. It does things to people.'

'I don't know. I kind of find that a little hard to believe, especially at the moment.'

'Don't be naïve,' he says, chuckling in amusement. 'Despite what you think's going on out there, what with all that rioting in the streets, this place is still about two things: making disproportionate returns on investments, and the freedom to do whatever you want – as long as it's not political in nature.'

Now, I realise, is not the time for any kind of mundane filler comments from me. While I'd love to know his story, there will be another time for that. Right now, I feel I should let him drive the conversation until it's time to ask my favours of him.

'Right, so tell me about last night, then.'

Scooting forward in my chair, I take the next couple of minutes to brief him fully on what we observed in the China Club, and then this morning at the Ritz Carlton.

'So, you think there's a clandestine link between a PLA general, their garrison commander, the HK deputy head of police, and some guy from North Korea who may or may not work in their fisheries industry?'

'Yes, and a couple of other shady dudes in the mix, too.'

'What's it? The link, I mean.'

'Not sure yet. But the end goal seems to be to bring an end to all these protests. The how, we don't know. Though that flash riot we witnessed could be the start of it. But I have a plan, which is kind of what I need your help for.'

'Oh yeah? To what end?'

'The weird little undernourished guy from Pyongyang. He's the odd one out. We figure if we can get a bead on who he is, or what his thing is, then we'll get an idea of what they're up to. Now, getting to his room is a total nightmare from inside the hotel. They've jacked security up something chronic. Also, my friend thinks there's a reasonable chance that they may also have his room under surveillance, because, well, they don't trust anyone, do they? So, if it's not too much of a hassle, think you can get hold of one of these? Just short term,' I say, sliding a folded piece of paper across the table. He picks it up and unfolds it. An amused smile creeps onto his face and he looks across at me, on the verge of laughing out loud.

'Are you shitting me?'

'Why? You think it's a bad idea?'

'Bad, no. But insane, yes, even for this profession.'

'Maybe, but it's guaranteed to work, right?'

'Guaranteed to get you killed more like,' he replies. 'I've seen these guys post on Instagram. I'm not sure it's meant for what you have in mind.'

'That's my problem. Can you get it?'

'Sure, I can get it. They're plenty tied into the MOD. A formal request is all that's needed. I can have it brought in overnight using the diplomatic bag. Of course, whether I should is a different matter,' he says, taking his phone out. 'Question is, do you know how to use it?'

'Yeah, leave that to me.'

Nodding, he sends a short message, smiles and places his phone back on the table.

'Done. Fingers crossed it should be here tomorrow, all things going to plan. It is mad, you know that, right? Your plan. Then again, I don't know why I'm concerned. Technically, you're Sam's responsibility, so what do I care? Won't be any skin off my back if you end up digging into the West Kowloon peninsula like Wile E Coyote.'

'That's charming.'

'Isn't it,' he laughs, and drains the last of his beer, before ordering another. 'Speaking of that little turd, have you told him any of this yet?'

'Only what we witnessed at the club. I wanted to see what you thought of the rest of it first.'

'What I think is, you should use a drone. But what do I know?'

'We thought of that. Too difficult. Especially with the wind.'

'If I could be bothered, I'd call bollocks on that. I think you just want to give this *Looney Tunes* plan of yours a go. That's what I think.'

'I know,' I grin. 'But we need the information on this guy. Else we can't prove anything about what they're up to.'

'Just remember, Heather, no matter how cynical you get in this game, you'll never cease to be surprised at how naïve you still are when you find out what some people really want to do.'

'You don't strike me as naïve.'

'That's because I'm rarely surprised anymore by what people are capable of. I started my career with HM Customs and Excise, if you can believe it. My job was to watch and then catalogue porn films seized by Customs. So, all day, every day, I watched porn films, noting down every obscenity each contained, as each counts in eventual convictions.'

'Jeez, and people get paid to do that?'

'Apparently so,' he replies with a shrug. 'Hey, heads up. Here comes your man now...'

Feigning the desire to attract a waiter, I turn and catch sight of Robert Styles entering the bar. An observant waiter catches my eye and I signal for another beer. He nods and heads for the bar.

Turning back to George, who has the clearer view, I say, 'What's he up to?'

'Looking for someone, it seems. Okay, he's heading over to a table. Contact looks like a local chap. Young, slim, nice suit.

Polished. I'd guess a banker, entrepreneur or Chinese government, possibly. But the international assignee type. Suave and worldly. Not the dull bureaucrat.'

'Reckon it's business, politics or espionage?' I ask innocently.

'This place? Probably all three,' he replies dryly. 'It's about as discrete as any you'll find on the planet. So, who knows? Interesting, right off the bat, the guy just passed something across the table to Styles. Could have been an envelope. Styles just slipped it into his suit jacket pocket. I'll keep an eye on him. So, tell me, why the suspicion that this trip of his might not be all it's advertised as?'

'Long story,' I reply, unsure how much I can, or should, say. 'It kind of started with a need to trace where all those leaks were coming from.'

'Ah yes, all a little embarrassing,' George grins. 'Government hasn't lost that many ministers since that mass resignation about Boris Johnson.'

'Tell me about it. I guess they came to us because they didn't know who else to go to.'

'Yeah, your little set-up has intrigued me since I first became aware of it. An interesting operation. Does seem a little desperate, though. Them coming to you on something like this.'

'Yeah, I think they are desperate; Number Ten, I mean.'

'Not surprised. They keep losing minister after minister with each embarrassing revelation. So how did the minister of morality get involved?'

'Some suspicious coincidences. But long story short, we couldn't rule him out as not having been the source of those leaks. And it seems that his connection to Hong Kong, and therefore by association China, worries the powers that be.

They fear that if he is the leak, it may not be morality driven but possibly as part of a foreign plan to sow chaos in the British political scene.'

'So, you think he's come out here for some nefarious purpose, wrapped up in the camouflage of a political field trip?'

'Who knows? Guess we'll see. Does seem an interesting time to come out here, given his remit. There doesn't seem a whole lot of sense to it.'

George shrugs ambivalently. 'We'll see.'

'I guess. So how do you see all the mess panning out? The protests, I mean. What are we trying to achieve here, or the Americans?'

'Oh, that's a complicated question. Perhaps easier to deal with the Yanks. What do you know about the US right now? Because I'm not sure they know what they want, to be honest. The idiot they elected seems to be doing his level best to run their country into the ground. If you're worried about Styles being in the pocket of China, then we should all be way more worried about POTUS being in the pocket of the Russians. The man's decimated their State Department, so their grasp of events on the ground is now seriously impaired. Too many good, knowledgeable people have either been fired or quit. And I'm not sure their intelligence agencies have a clear line of sight into what Washington wants of them anymore, either. Back home, things are even worse. Which always hampers US foreign policy. Their economy is not doing so great. Almost half of their adult population are out of work. Thirty million of them have a better-than-average chance of being evicted shortly. And even though large parts of the US are starting to clock on, it may be too little, too late. It seems the nightmare scenario of the Second Amendment's heavily armed militia roaming the streets is rapidly becoming a reality.

'As I hear it, literally on a daily basis an army of protesters are facing off against federal agents in a dozen cities. And the president? Going by his social media posts, he's off playing golf most of the time, and his wife is replanting the West Wing's rose garden. This presidency's done America no favours. Their old enemies now hate them even more. Their old allies have been alienated and insulted in many cases. Most historic neutrals now hate them, too. Which, ironically, plays right into China's hands. Divide the Western allies and you're halfway there. Sadly, there's scant real leadership or strategy coming out of the White House, so best not to hold out hope from that camp until after the next election. All in, I'm not sure the US has any idea what they are trying to do here.'

'More good news,' I sigh.

'Hey,' he says, nodding towards Robert Styles. 'Man's on the move.'

Sure enough, as the waiter arrives with my new tankard, I see Robert Styles stand, adjust his tie and walk out with the slim, immaculately dressed Asian man. As they stop at the top of the steps and exchange words, Styles takes out the envelope, briefly examines its contents and nods.

'You want to see to that?' George asks.

'If that's okay? Do you want this?' I ask, pointing at the beer.

'Sure,' he says with an appreciative nod, reaching for the condensation-coated mug.

Taking my bag, yellow umbrella and phone, I make for the exit. But halfway there, I stop abruptly and turn with a smile to face a suited man sitting at the bar. How long he has been here, I am unsure. Not long, it looks like, given that his whisky has barely been touched. He looks up from the small notebook in which he is keenly writing.

'Well, hello there,' I exclaim. 'Now isn't this a blast from the past. Officer Rohner, isn't it? The man who likes to drive fast.'

The white-haired Swiss policeman turns slowly and smiles as he recognises me.

'Ah, the mysterious girl who has private planes waiting for her at airports after hours.'

'Well, you know how it is,' I laugh depreciatingly. 'Girl's gotta do what a girl's gotta do. You're a long way from home. What brings you here? Coz you don't exactly look like you're on holiday,' I note, pointing to his suit and tie.

'I retired,' he says, nodding acceptingly. Then, with a smile, he adds, 'But you know how it is. One can get bored sitting around not doing much. A friend at a Swiss law firm offered me a little on-and-off job as a private eye.'

'Sounds like a pretty sweet gig. Even if it is a bit of a war zone out here at the moment.'

He nods, but gives little more away.

'What is it?' I joke. 'Corporate espionage, or some suspicious wife back home?'

'Perhaps both,' he replies with an evasive smile.

'See, that's why everyone likes you guys,' I laugh. 'Total discretion.'

He chuckles and I bid him a hurried farewell as Styles hands the Asian man something, nods brusquely and strides off into the hotel lobby.

'I won't ask what brings you here,' the retired policeman calls after me.

'Good,' I reply, waving. 'I'd never be able to tell you anyway.'

I emerge into the lobby to find Styles standing alone in the far corner, near the main exit. He has torn the envelope into little pieces and is throwing them into a rubbish bin beside him. Then he makes for the lifts and presumably heads back up to his room. As I casually walk over to the bin, I quickly dial Milly to warn her, just in case she and Anabel are in the midst of bugging the politician's room. Irritatingly, there is no answer.

'You've got to be kidding me,' I grumble as I delve into the bin to retrieve the torn pieces, just as an enthusiastic-looking cleaner moves in towards me.

'Silly me. Dropped something I shouldn't have,' I explain, seeing her confused look. Then, with as many pieces retrieved as I can find, I ask the reception to lend me some sticky tape.

When Anabel and Milly return to their room, it's to find a note on their door with an arrow pointing down the hall towards mine. They let themselves in to find me sitting cross-legged on the floor with dozens of tiny scraps of paper laid out before me, like a lunatic's jigsaw puzzle. I look up with a grin and excitedly beckon them in.

'What are you up to?' they ask.

'That's a very good question. To which I don't have a good answer. Yet.'

'Who are they?' says Milly, pointing at the beginnings of the patchwork reconstructed photos on the floor.

'Not entirely sure. Styles binned it in the lobby, right after meeting some slick-looking dude in a flashy suit. I've no idea what it's about, but from what I've stuck back together, I think they're police mugshots.'

'What, like criminal arrest mugshots?' Anabel enquires, approaching to settle beside me. 'How odd. Why would Styles be meeting with people to talk about local criminals?'

'Beats me.'

'You think they could be reformed offenders?' she asks.

'As in what?' says Milly. 'He's trying to make some kind of example of the local correction system's reformative capabilities?'

'Honestly, I have no idea,' Anabel replies. 'You tell me. But there's a kind of logic to it.'

'I dunno,' I ponder aloud. 'This lot don't exactly look like criminals.'

'True,' says Milly. 'They look more like models, if it wasn't for the height boards behind them.'

'Not unheard of for Triad gangs to recruit local youths in their teens,' Anabel notes. 'But don't make too many assumptions about people's ages out here. Just can't tell sometimes.'

'Yeah well, I'll keep at it. See if anything turns up,' I say. 'What are you two up to tonight?'

'Not sure,' Milly says, glancing at her girlfriend. 'Maybe just an early night?'

'Yeah, sounds a plan. Oh, hey, how'd it go with his room?'

'Piece of cake,' Anabel replies. 'GC had an official consulate ID card dropped off, along with a Manila folder. I went to reception and said I was there to drop off materials from the consul general's office and that they had to be hand-delivered to his room. The duty manager took me up. I was in and out in about ten seconds. I put a camera unit above the desk, behind some kind of wooden grill. Offers a pretty good view across the whole suite. Should be good enough for sound and visuals.'

'Awesome. What a team,' I exclaim. 'And the guy didn't notice you come out with the same package as you went in with?'

'Nope. There was a copy of *Asia Spa* magazine in the folder. I just left the magazine, so it looked empty.'

'That's hilarious. Cool. Well, we're going to need to review all the footage tomorrow, or the day after, I guess. Have a good night. Tomorrow will be a fun one.'

'Oh, so can GC get what you were after?' Milly asks.

'Hopefully, yes,' I reply eagerly, crossing my fingers.

CHAPTER 13

ON A WING AND A PRAYER

Hong Kong

'Oh my God,' I exclaim, gripping Milly's arm in excitement as George leads us into his office, deep within the consulate. 'I can barely contain my excitement.'

'And you think I haven't noticed?'

'Just wait till you see this thing...'

'Oh yeah, I can't wait,' she drawls sarcastically. 'George is right. This is an act of lunacy.'

'Yeah, I know,' I say, grinning madly.

'Well, here it is,' he announces, pointing to a large plastic military crate on the floor.

'Oh good,' says Milly, shaking her head. 'I'm so glad we went for the subtle, "can easily fit in a backpack" sort of idea. Because this is definitely it.'

'Yeah, everyone be haters today,' I mumble as I flick the catches and lift the lid. 'Oh, now would you look at that,' I exclaim, taking in the raw, potent beauty of the latest Gravity Industries VTOL jet suit. 'Can you believe this thing will clock north of a hundred miles an hour?'

'Sounds like a super way of smearing yourself all over the side of a building.'

'Oh, Milly. I love you, but you're so negative. Gotta have faith,' I say, clasping her shoulders.

Pointing at the twin arm-mounted dual micro-jet-turbines visible at the top of the box, George says, 'We absolutely need that thing back. And in one piece, you understand? It costs something like half a million quid. There are a few slightly nervous people back at Vauxhall Cross right now. Got it?'

'Yeah, yeah, don't worry about it,' I reassure him confidently. 'Trust me, it'll be fine.'

'You'll appreciate that's not filling me with confidence. What's your plan?' he asks.

Nodding, I pull a seat up and sit down.

'Well, Styles is completely booked all day, so we have loads of time to sort it out, but I was thinking the simplest plan might be to set off from this side of the harbour and then just gain altitude as I cross it. By the time I get to the other side, I could be at the right height to approach the window –'

Frowning, Milly raises a finger and, with pursed lips, announces, 'It won't work.'

'Why?' I challenge.

'Mostly because of the amount of fuel you'll use climbing fifteen hundred feet. Do you have any idea? That's a simply terrible idea. You're going up as much as you're going laterally. You're better off starting from a point of altitude.'

'I'd tend to agree with that,' GC says.

'Seriously, if you're going to go through with this madness, at least start off from somewhere really high,' Milly urges with an air of frustration. 'Like one of the tallest buildings on this side of the harbour, if not the other side.'

'Maybe IFC?' Anabel suggests.

'Precisely,' says Milly, eagerly consulting a geo-distance calculator app on her iSpy. 'The straight-line distance between IFC, here on the island, and ICC, over in Kowloon, is two thousand and seventeen metres, or six thousand, six hundred and twenty feet. Okay, IFC is a thousand three hundred and sixty-four feet high, and ICC is two hundred and twenty-four feet higher, at a thousand five hundred and eighty-eight feet. Wind direction here seems a bit unpredictable, but average tends to be northerly or westerly. That could complicate things.'

'And the eddies the wind creates around these big buildings is something else,' Anabel adds. 'But the idea of starting higher does kind of make more sense, wouldn't you say?'

'Yeah, I guess making a more horizontal journey makes sense,' I agree.

'Just don't forget, it's there and back,' Milly says, putting her phone away.

'And how do we get up there?' I ask.

'Yeah, well, that could be tricky,' says Anabel. 'No one's just going to let us wander up there for a selfie, are they?'

'True,' I reply.

'Yeah, hang on a second there,' George says with a pensive look. 'I can't believe I'm getting involved in this amateur-hour farce, but I may have a line on getting up to the roof. Best just leave that problem with me, okay? I take it this will happen tonight? A little too unsubtle to do it by day.'

'Yeah, I think so. Do you think we can wait that long, though?' I ask my friends.

'Oh, absolutely,' Milly exclaims. 'Try it by day and five hundred videos of it will be straight onto the internet. Must be at night. There's no choice.'

'And we're sure this is the only option?' Anabel sighs. 'I get that it's the preferable option. Though I can't believe I actually said that.'

'Yes,' I reply. 'It means we don't have to negotiate our way past the hotel security. And more importantly, if they're as paranoid as they seem to be, then there's a good chance they're doing security sweeps of the most sensitive guests' rooms every day. Maybe after the cleaners have been in, who knows? But either way, it means if we plant a device in the room, chances are they'll find it almost immediately. However, there's way less chance if it's outside, like maybe in the uppermost corner of those high windows. I mean, who looks there?'

'And if they did,' Milly adds, 'chances are they'd discount any emissions detected as coming from outside.'

'It's a good point,' I add, secretly relieved to finally receive some support for the idea, the dangers of which are only now beginning to dawn on me for real, the more I think about it. 'We sussed out which room he's in yet?'

'Yup,' says George. 'Two down from the top, three across from the left. And you'll need this.' He hands me a small black backpack. 'Binoculars are to find his room. Targeting designator is in the bag, too. We can mark your destination from this side of the harbour. Night vision will be next to useless in a city with this much light pollution. You'll find a pair of green tinted glasses in there. They'll clearly show you where the beam is impacting. Clear as day. That'll be your window.'

'Now, last bit of the puzzle is this,' he says, taking a GoPro adhesive mount from the table. Affixed to it is a half-metre-long pole arm. 'I just need to attach this to the helmet which comes with the jetpack, so you can hover outside Styles's room and press this neat little device at the end of the pole against the upper corner of his window. It may look like a splat of bird poo, but it has a micro camera and a vibration detector hidden within it. That'll give us video and sound. There's a few other neat bits of functionality, too.'

'And we couldn't have just done this with some kind of splat gun thing?' Anabel asks. 'Like Batman used.'

'Hey, this thing's on loan,' George says, pointing at the jet suit. 'Count your blessings. Don't go believing everything you hear about Q Branch. It's not like we have an arsenal of this kit just lying around. Limited budgets and limited availability. This isn't Wayne Enterprises. Get the drift?'

'Bummer,' I groan. 'Okay, so what do I need to know?'

'Besides the fact that manoeuvring inches from a sodding high building is difficult?' GC asks sarcastically. 'Well, your real problem is the size of the device. Because it's so small, the bug can't transmit very far. Not if you expect the battery to last. Therefore, you will also need to place this relay unit close by,' he says, holding up a small black box, the size of a pack of playing cards. 'We need this to boost the transmission signal out across the harbour. It's got a bigger battery and antenna in it. This must go onto the wall, or somewhere within a metre or so of the splat. Somewhere out of sight. Understood? Otherwise it won't work.'

'Okay. Got it. So, seeing as I can't use my hands, you know, given that they're pretty much enclosed inside those forearm jet thingies, how exactly am I meant to fix that in place?'

'Yeah, so this is the bit you're probably not going to like...'

His idea takes less than half a minute to explain. But it is greeted with a disbelieving wall of silence. Deeply unsettled, I turn to each of them, looking for any signs that this is a joke. Anabel and Milly look as dumbfounded as I feel.

Finally, I glance back to George and, with a deep breath, mutter, 'Oh shit, maybe this wasn't such a hot idea, after all.'

*

As Milly eases the door to the roof of IFC open, she squeals as the unexpectedly strong wind almost wrenches it from her grasp. The moment I step out onto the narrow viewing platform on the north-west corner of the building, my hair, like hers, is whipped crazily in every direction.

It has just gone half past eight, and the sky is now suitably dark for what we have in mind. Or at least as dark as it can get in a city with the level of light pollution of this one. The daily Symphony of Lights laser show, beamed from the rooftops of forty-two of the city's tallest buildings, finished about fifteen minutes ago.

The big surprise, as far as I am concerned, is the vertigo-inducing view. This is the highest I have ever been in my life outside of an aircraft. Anabel and I set our respective ends of the heavy-duty military crate down. With a sideways grimace, I find myself swallowing hard, my throat suddenly a whole lot drier than before. Imagining this and now experiencing it are two very different things.

From our vantage point, we have a near bird's-eye view across most of the city, and far beyond to Kowloon and the New Territories. From up here, the city resembles a large-scale architect's lobby model, only in the canyons below us, the tiny cars and buses are actually moving. The whole waterfront is one long collage of brightly lit buildings. Huge rooftop corporate billboards and flashing logos merely complement the endless sea of illuminated windows and moving traffic.

Even the harbour is awash with lights, as countless small craft ply their way across the dark waters in both directions.

The queasy sensation is not helped by the banks of powerful lights positioned on the other side of the waist-high railings. All are aimed skywards to light up the row of inwardly curving, white claw-like architectural elements which rise high above the building and give it its distinctive nasal-hair-trimmer appearance.

All the surrounding towers look anaemic in comparison to this monster of a skyscraper. And none of them are exactly small, either. Even a couple of metres from the edge, the height is so much more daunting than I had expected it to be. The closer I edge towards the railing, the stronger the deeply queasy feeling in my stomach becomes. And by the time I am at the very edge, my knees have taken on a distinctly jelly-like wobble.

'Oh, Jesus,' I exclaim, gripping the rail, as a wave of intense nausea hits me. Fearing I might actually be sick at the thought of what I've agreed to, I groan weakly, 'I fricking hate heights.'

'Oh, you are kidding me, right?' Milly exclaims, looking around in astonishment. 'And you only mention this now?'

'It kind of only occurred to me now.'

'Honestly, sometimes I really don't know how you got this far,' she says, shaking her head. 'Well, either way, doesn't matter now. Coz it's a bit late, isn't it?'

'Yeah,' I mumble with a scowl. 'Seriously, what was I thinking?'

'Hey, you're the one who always ends up doing all this stupid dangerous stuff,' Anabel giggles as she begins to undo the multiple latches securing the case. 'But you sure are taking the biscuit with this one.'

'Yeah, I was wondering when reality might kick in,' George chuckles as he places a jerrycan of aviation jet fuel which he has somehow acquired beside the larger packing case. 'On any normal day, we'd have got someone from E Squadron to come up here and do something as stupid as this –'

'See, now you're just *trying* to make this even worse, aren't you?' I say with a less-than-amused scowl. Turning, I peer over the ledge, only to reel backwards with dizziness.

'Nope. There really is no making this any worse than it looks,' he replies with a smile. 'That said, there's something to be said for the old army adage that no matter how bad a situation gets, you just have to stay strong and keep on pushing. And when it's all over, we can sit down together with a nice brew and joke about how insane this all was.'

'Jesus, you sound like someone I knew down in SENTA.'

'As in Wales?'

I nod absentmindedly as I remove a layer of densely padded foam, revealing the rather menacing all-black jet pack neatly arranged within.

'For what?' he asks. 'I mean, what took you down there? You didn't do something silly like Selection, did you?' he jokes.

'Yup,' Milly interjects with a rueful shake of her head. 'Another of the acts of lunacy that our girl here has racked up.'

'Oh, well in that case, I don't know what you're complaining about. Come on, strap that ruddy thing on and get going,' he laughs. 'This'll be a walk in the park compared to that! Of course, get caught here with that thing on your back, in this political climate, and HMG will disavow any knowledge of the whole mad escapade.'

'You make it sound like *Mission Impossible*,' Anabel laughs.

'I'd say *Mission Impossible* looks relatively easy compared to this,' he replies, pointing directly across the wide, open expanse of harbour that separates us from the brightly lit West Kowloon peninsula, where the impossibly tall and frenetically illuminated ICC tower rises even higher into the night sky.

'Tell me about it,' I groan as I lift the main backpack unit from the box. George quickly begins to fuel it.

'Truth be told,' I add, 'it's best you go put that kettle on, because I'm going to need a really good cup of tea, and quite possibly something considerably stronger once this is all over.'

'Indeed,' he says, nodding agreeably as he secures the first fuel bladder nozzle. 'Right, let me get this second one as full as it'll get, too. You might as well begin getting the rest of that stuff on.'

The first inklings of a smile appear the moment I slip into the waistcoat-like tactical vest, which contains all the flight control systems and starter batteries. It clasps securely across my chest. After stepping into the padded leg loops, I quickly slide my arms through into the harness rig. With the last bladder filled, George and I heft the main backpack up. All three of them then secure it in place while I guide them from memory as to the order in which each strap is meant to tighten. Next comes the ultra-compact base jumper's parachute. Specially designed to affix to the jet pack's harness rigging, it sits front-facing – just in case the worst happens. Lastly, I pull on the matt black forearm gauntlets, both of which play host to a set of twin jet turbines affixed slightly angled towards front and rear. The robust fuel lines are bundled together with the power cables inside a tough protective tubing which connects both jet gauntlets to the main backpack.

With the requisite pre-flight checks done and all electrics engaged, I reach down for the suit's helmet, mindful not to overbalance with all the extra weight. It is snug, lightweight and made of black carbon fibre. Protruding from its front is the pole which George has rigged up to a mounting. At its end is the off-white bird poo surveillance device, which looks more like a badly chewed children's gummy sweet than anything else. George hands me the green-tinted glasses. Once I have them on, I finally slide the helmet's built-in visor down.

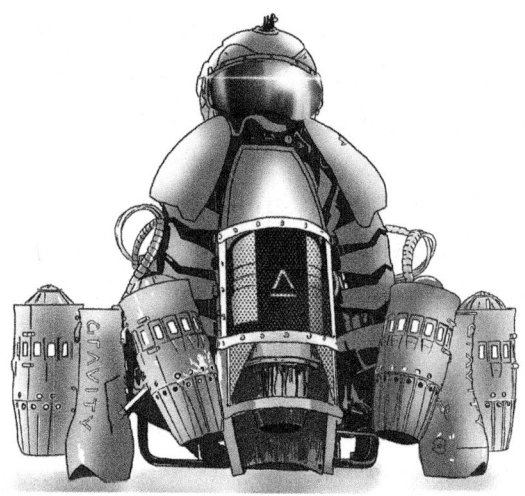

'Right, I think we're ready...'

Gripping the handle inside each gauntlet, I take a deep, measured breath and depress the ignition switch. There is a fraction of a second's pause, which affords me one last chance to reflect on the forthcoming madness. With a jolt, the engines burst to life, and I feel an immediate push of pressure up against my arms and back. The jet engines' high-pitched whine is loud, even with the padded helmet on. Despite selecting the lowest throttle setting with the clicker in my left gauntlet, a wild wind erupts around my feet, buffeting and tearing at my trousers. The wireless heads-up display appears within the helmet's visor. It takes a moment for the gauges and dials to spring to life before settling to reflect the vital flight data I need to know in order to try not to die in the next ten minutes.

Savouring the smell of the jet fuel, I take careful note of the readings for critical engine data, fuel reserves, altitude and speed, and remind myself what this trip is all about: fuel consumption. Within the matt black protective plastic casing strapped to my back are two airtight, rubberised fuel bladders arranged either side of the larger, single, slightly outward-facing engine, to direct the jet flow away from my legs. These bladders feed all five engines via blockage-resistant tubing. Within my right gauntlet, I give the throttle trigger a gentle squeeze, spiking the jets to thirty thousand revs, before letting them settle back down to idle. A digital compass oscillates in the bottom left-hand corner of the heads-up display as I turn to face ICC, setting myself on an almost northerly bearing.

Anabel and Milly edge towards the far corner of the small balcony-like area from which I am to launch. There, they begin setting up the laser target designator which will guide me to the correct window, far over on the other side of the harbour.

Nodding appraisingly, GC gives me a final questioning thumbs-up. Buoyed by the confidence the jet suit gives me, I return a massive grin and focus on the HUD readings and the sensations pulsating through me from the engines. Clicking up through the power settings, I open the throttle slightly, and feel the power build. And with it comes a rapid acceleration of my own heart rate as the gentle roar of the engines climbs to a shrill, high-pitched whistle. Great dollops of adrenaline flood into my bloodstream and I double down, concentrating on the immediate task at hand to counter the light-headed euphoria that could come from it.

Every incremental depression of the trigger results in a disproportionately fearsome increase in the growing whirlwind whipping around my legs. I am reminded again just how fast heat dissipates in air. For while the downdraught is powerful, there is almost no temperature left in it near my feet. The vibration builds, surging through every part of me. My stomach feels like it's in a washing machine, and if I wasn't clenching my jaw so tightly, my teeth would surely be chattering noisily inside my vibrating skull.

All too aware that every second the engines are on is time I won't get back later, I call to my friends, 'How much longer?'

'Almost there,' Milly replies urgently back over the radio. Five seconds later, she taps Anabel on the shoulder, who then peers one last time through a large set of field glasses and gives me a resounding okay sign.

'Last radio check,' I say, shouting unnecessarily loudly in the hope of being heard over the furious roar of the jets. 'So, you stay here until the bugs are planted, then you leave, right?'

'Roger that,' George replies, pressing his handheld radio to his ear. 'You set down wherever you can, and we come get you. Ideally, talk us to the location before you get there, so we can get you into the van immediately. Don't want you standing around on some street corner with all that gear smoking away.'

I nod and turn to back away a few paces from the railing. With the target now identified on the other side of the harbour and everything as ready as it will ever get, I throttle up and bring my arms down closer to my side. Milly and Anabel scuttle past to safety as the jets reach a shrieking crescendo.

It feels like I am suddenly in the centre of my own private typhoon. I rise onto tiptoes and, with a small push, rise effortlessly from the floor. Airborne, I immediately find myself drifting towards the building's central utility's structure, on top of which stands a single, large satellite dish. Correcting my vector, I add throttle, rising to ten feet above the balcony platform. Glancing left and right, I assure myself that I am not about to drift into one of the building's ornamental teeth-like structures, before gaining more height to counter for the drop in ground effect that will surely happen the moment I pass beyond the building's structure.

'Best get a move on,' GC says over the radio.

It takes me three long, calming breaths to quell the nervous shiver that just ran through me.

'Okay seriously, best not to look down,' I say, focussing with a laser-like stare on the blue ring of light which crowns the very top floor of ICC, far off across the harbour. 'Here goes!'

Bending forward slightly at the waist, I let the rear-mounted jet ease me out over the abyss. A giddy sense of terrified excitement grips me as I cross out beyond the precipice. Once clear of the building, and mindful not to glance down, I ease my arms back a little, then even further, adding more and more speed. It takes a few seconds for my brain to comprehend that instinctively treading air in the futile hope of finding solid ground does little to help, and finally I make them go still, closing them up together for greater aerodynamic efficiency. For a moment, I find myself marvelling at how stable this triangular arrangement of engines is.

The farther I get across the harbour, the more my confidence builds, and the more I open the throttle. The acceleration is as daunting as it is exciting. The rush of air, and with it the roar in my ears, spikes my heartrate. Within seconds, thirty miles per hour has become ninety. But with such speed comes a proportionate drop in the fuel reserve. By the time I cross the coast over West Kowloon, a third of my fuel has gone already.

Far, far below, I see cars the size of tiny models slowly moving alongside the glass-roofed mall as they approach to the base of the tower. Slowing up, I check my altimeter and note I am several floors below where I need to be. Coming to a hover – which feels utterly unnatural and somehow the last thing I ought to do, given my altitude – I am immediately reminded how susceptible to the wind this rig is at slow speeds. Drifting right with alarming speed, I hurry to correct the yaw, whilst searching for the reflective flare of the laser which will tell me where I need to aim for.

For a heart-stopping moment there is nothing to be seen. My eyes dart left and right as my brain scrambles to remember if it was two floors down and three across or three down and two across. The rapidly decreasing fuel reserve is beginning to concern me, and I have to focus to ignore the uncomfortably hot, prickly sensation that runs down my body from my scalp. Gaining altitude whilst maintaining a hover feels so much more precarious than crossing the harbour. Small jolts of wind whipping erratically around the building in invisible eddies push me left and right, and occasionally towards the building itself. One particularly forceful gust takes me to within twelve feet of the enormous glass and steel tower. Backing away hurriedly, I peer up and to the right and suddenly see the green lens flare of the laser.

'Thank feck for that,' I exclaim with a relieved laugh as I throttle up and move towards it. But the closer the building gets, the more precarious this all feels. The risk of getting blown hard into the glass, losing control and plunging earthwards fills me with dread. My earlier plan not to look directly down has all but gone, and every few seconds I can't help but snatch a fearful glance down at the four hundred metres of near vomit-inducing nothingness which my HUD indicates separates me from the concrete far below. I want to be sick at the sight.

And yet still I climb.

As I approach the designated window, I tell myself that I have this. That I have totally sussed this thing out. That it will be fine. That the few hours' practice I had weeks ago is easily enough. Besides, I have a parachute. What could possibly go wrong?

Reassured I am not.

I try to ignore the nagging knot of worry building in my stomach at the thought of what happens if I run out of fuel halfway across the harbour. My maths was never the best, but at this rate of aggressive fuel consumption, even I am able to realise that things could easily go either way. Dispelling the negative thoughts, I focus instead on the last few feet of the approach, mindful of the constant corrections needed for the wind. The room is in darkness, but there is enough ambient light to make out the outline of furniture inside. Carefully, I edge closer, determining where best to place the splat-bug device. Too far to the edge and the retracted curtain will surely block it. Too far into the centre and it will certainly garner unwanted attention.

A metre from the glass, with my finger dancing nervously on the throttle and my arms now growing weary from all the micro-corrections needed, I finally bring the helmet-mounted pole into contact with the glass at what I reckon to be the optimal spot. With a hard forwards bob of my head, I place the splat and lurch backwards, relieved to see it has stuck onto the glass. All that remains is the transponder box. Hovering six feet from the building, I glance down at the structure which George described earlier.

Running around the base of each floor is some sort of protruding external skirting board which resembles a form of vented panelling. It consists of several thin metal veins, much like the sound baffling found at airport perimeters. It juts out a few feet from the building, but even from here it does not look strong, nor a good landing spot. But as GC pointed out, there is simply no option other than to land on it if I am to hand-fix the transmitter box to the steel column set between the windowpanes.

'Oh, you've got to be kidding me,' I mumble as things begin to get properly thumpy within my chest. 'This has bad idea written all over it.'

Drifting left a little, I approach the building once again. Quite where the courage for this madness is coming from, I honestly don't know, but it dries up the moment my foot touches the flimsy panel of vents. An ominous creak underfoot just as I dial down the engines makes me lurch forward in panic to grab the metal column. The clunky gauntlets hinder me from gripping it properly. Instead, I find myself clasping on to it for dear life with the gauntlets, with my face pressed against the column. The bulky gear prevents much movement, and the head-mounted pole won't let me turn to look in the other direction. I try tipping my head back to turn to my left but am immediately overcome with a sense that I will lose my balance and topple backwards off the narrow ledge. With a groan, I realise I have no option but to gingerly slip my left hand from the engine casing and ever so slowly bring it up to unclip the pole from the forehead mounting. Tossing it away isn't an option. At this height, it could probably kill someone down below, like some sort of heaven-sent spear. And then questions will be asked. Cursing, I slip the pole carefully into my right thigh cargo pocket.

It takes a few seconds to recognise the faint, woozy sensation which has suddenly come over me, making my legs feel like jelly, as a bout of vertigo. I cling to the structural column even tighter as my surroundings spin and whirl around me, shifting on plains that make no sense.

Opening an eye, I make the fatal mistake of looking down as the wind tears at me. Suddenly, I am sweating, despite the cool breeze at this altitude. A sick light-headedness adds to my racing heartbeat and the terrifying tightness gripping my chest. In an odd moment of clarity, I realise none of my limbs want to obey me anymore.

'Oh God, I hate this,' I moan softly to myself between short, deep breaths. My whole body is now shaking, too terrified to move. 'What the hell was I thinking…?'

'How are you doing over there?' comes Milly's soothing voice in my ear. It is the first I have heard from them since I set off. And while I appreciated the lack of distraction till now, just hearing her voice sends my spirits soaring.

'Honestly, not so great,' I groan, laughing in despair as I cling to the column, eyes scrunched tightly shut. 'Who'd have thought this could be so fricking debilitating?'

'You do realise that courage isn't the absence of fear but the ability to push on through it, right?' she says softly.

'There's always someone with a smart-arse line.'

'It's no line. Seriously, I know you can do it. And you're not ready to fall off that building –'

'What, and dig in like Wile E Coyote, you mean?' I joke weakly as I tighten my grip.

'Well, let's try not to, shall we?' she replies encouragingly. 'I can only imagine how freaky it is, but this is where you dig deep and find that little bit to get you through.'

Cursing silently, I force open one eye, and then the second. Gritting my teeth, I bend very slowly and reach into my left-hand thigh cargo pocket and carefully retrieve the small black box. I realise I need to extract my other hand from the second jet gauntlet to remove the paper from the sticky pad that's affixed to the rear of the small box.

Remind me, Heather, I say silently to myself, *why didn't we go with one of the other options?*

Ever so slowly, I wriggle my right hand from the fitting, which falls to hang loosely at my side, and bring it around, squeezing between my body and the steel column to pick at the edge of the protective sticker. Fearful of the sickening lurch which looking down will produce in my stomach, I try to do it through touch alone. But without luck. The pad has such strong all-weather adhesive that no corner gives. Finally, just as I am about to give up in frustration, one catches. With a relieved sigh, I peel off the paper. Avoiding any fast movements, I press the box firmly up against the column. A flick of the small, rubberised switch on its side and a confirmatory green light appears.

Reaching sideways, I keenly grope for the opening to the right-hand gauntlet. With my hand firmly inside it and gripping the handle, with relief I repeat the process with the left gauntlet. Turning slightly, I shift my weight onto my left foot and try to turn around to face outwards. But as I do so, the panel suddenly buckles beneath me and then gives way, lurching me off balance and tipping me, screaming, out into the void. A surge of terror unlike anything I have ever experienced rips through me as I flail desperately to grip anything.

For a fleeting second, my senses are utterly overwhelmed by the speed and acceleration, the noise and rush of air, and the stomach-churning sensation as I plunge like a rock. Brightly lit windows stream past me in a frenzied blur. The wind tears at my flailing limbs. Everything, including breathing, is momentarily forgotten as my brain clouds with indecision, torn between igniting the idling engines again or hastily tugging on the parachute's ripcord. Rational thought eludes me and in an ill-considered moment of panic I ignite all five jets with a massively over-enthusiastic snatch of the throttle trigger. With a scream my fall is instantaneously arrested... before I am rocketed skyward over the harbour like Iron Man.

Stabilising myself into a hover at four hundred and fifty metres in the air, I let out a colourful string of expletives and take several deep, calming breaths to try to slow my racing heart and hyperventilating gasps back down to below coronary-inducing levels of panic.

'Woah, that was a serious pucker-up moment,' I pant.

Glancing at my fuel reserves, I do an alarmed double take and hurriedly ease forward to lose as much altitude as possible as fast as possible, lest the engines fail, or some other unforeseen idiot calamity befalls me. Better a short drop into the harbour than a plunge from this height. Raising my arms out to my sides, I bleed off altitude at an impressive rate in what is little more than a barely controlled fall, until I finally level out again approximately thirty feet above the choppy harbour waters.

The island still looks a long way away. There is no time to lose. Pitching forward, I rapidly accelerate into my return trip. Not that I am entirely convinced that a fall into this water would be any less unbecoming than a plunge from great altitude. With grim amusement, I recall a story Anabel told us about the filming of *The Dark Knight*, years ago here in Hong Kong. Apparently, or so the story went, the script had called for Batman to end up in the harbour. Naturally, the film's safety coordinators took a water sample. Upon receiving the results, the studio's lawyers hurriedly stepped in and proclaimed, 'Mr Bale is not getting into that water.' Apparently, the sample contained a veritable cocktail of unbecoming bacteria and pathogens, including tuberculosis, E. coli and salmonella. As a result, the script was promptly amended and Batman did not go into the harbour.

Of course, while things may well have improved since then, given it was a while back, I have no interest in being the fool who tries to prove the point. I'm now halfway across the harbour, and my idle reminiscence is interrupted by the unexpected appearance beneath me of two fast-moving black rigid inflatables. They are in close formation, one staggered slightly behind the other and off to its port side. The appearance of police go-fast patrol boats was not part of the plan.

Veering evasively to my right, I hurriedly try to put as much distance between myself and the boats as I can, but the high-pitched roaring whine of my turbines is still enough to be heard over their large outboard engines. Several occupants, all clad in black assault gear, crane their necks skyward. Fingers are pointed and urgent calls follow. Swerving to my left, I peer over my shoulder to see the trailing powerboat peel off and veer around in an aggressive fast turn, sending a wave of frothing water spraying outwards as it surges back towards me.

Laughing in grim disbelief at my bad luck, I throttle up and accelerate towards the illuminated bustle of the Star Ferry terminal with everything the jets can give me. But the second boat's occupants seem to have eyes on me. The lead boat appears to have come to an idled stop. Given my luck, I suspect cynically, they're calling in the sighting at this very moment.

The surprisingly choppy, white-capped waves whip past beneath me in a dizzyingly hypnotic rush as I reach the pack's top speed. Still, the rigid inflatable is worryingly fast, and while not gaining upon me, it isn't falling back, either. And so long as they have eyes on me, they can call for help to intercept me when I land, assuming my fuel even lasts that long.

My worst fears are confirmed as a new but distinctive noise joins the cacophony of mini-jet engines and multiple high-powered outboard motors that swirls around me in the darkness.

Glancing to the right, I frown at the sight of a helicopter rising from the rooftop of the Shun Tak heliport. The frown only deepens as I realise it isn't a commercial helicopter, with their usual brightly coloured livery, but rather is all black. Which can only mean military. Dipping its nose dramatically, the pilot hurtles the machine forward, out over the water, directly towards me.

'Jesus, do they just have these guys sitting around waiting to go at a moment's notice, or what?' I mutter as I frantically tilt myself left, away from the helicopter's intercept path and on towards the island. My only hope now is to get over land with enough fuel remaining to avoid the clutches of the boat crew, and to dart into the narrow confines between the skyscrapers, walkways and myriad other obstacles which this city has on offer to deter the helicopter's continued pursuit.

At this speed, I make landfall within seconds, roaring in between two of the Star Ferry piers, startling a group of string-vested amateur fishermen who have cast their rods from the pier-side into the questionable waters below. By easing off the throttle and flaring my arms a little wider, I descend to level off at about fifteen feet, before making a beeline across the busy road, over the stream of passing cars, through a ring of trees bordering a bus terminal and across the expressway beyond, towards the back side of the IFC mall. The high-pitched jets leave no small number of rubber-necking pedestrians in my wake.

Unnerved by the sound of the helicopter closing in fast, I hurriedly snatch a glance back to see it approaching with a heavy sideways yaw, albeit about fifty feet higher. In the rear, a crew member pulls the sliding door open and raises a large pair of binoculars. Snapping my head around, I angle right and dart towards the gaping mouth of the Central–Wan Chai Bypass. Six busy lanes of traffic lead down into the tunnel, which undercuts much of the island's notoriously congested roads, to emerge on the far side of Central. Banking hard, I dip aggressively down to street level to nip in beneath the elevated blue-and-white road signage.

Accelerating again, I surge into the tunnel, before slowing and swinging around to look back at the entrance. The black helicopter descends as low as the pilot will safely take it. Then, without warning, it hurriedly rises up and out of sight.

Now comes the gamble, I think, as I edge back towards the entrance. The looks I am getting from drivers as I pass a few feet above their roofs while they speed beneath me is in many cases priceless. I take the risk, and when I re-emerge from the tunnel it is to find, to my enormous relief, that the helicopter has gone. Climbing above street level again, I see it speeding towards what I can only assume to be the other end of the tunnel on the opposite side of Central, likely in a bid to cut me off from emerging there in a few minutes' time.

'Okay, where are you guys?' I shout urgently into my radio. 'I'm flying on fumes here. Might be better if I just come to you.'

Logic would have suggested that the more fuel that's burned, the lighter I would become, and therefore the higher the suit would try to push me, but this hasn't happened, so perhaps the flight control system has automatically compensated by turning down the power accordingly. A glance at the gauges would appear to confirm this. Either way, I'm relieved at having one less problem to deal with.

'Hey, yes, we're here,' Milly's flustered voice calls back. 'But we've got a bit of a problem. A taxi just hit us at the traffic lights, but what with all the stuff we've got in here, George kept driving. But there was a police bike at the lights, and he's now after us.'

'Where are you?'

'Near the waterfront. Coming past the fairground.'

'Close enough. I'll come to you. Stand by.'

Gunning the engines again, I rise up over the trees, high enough to see the distant flashing lights of a fast-moving police bike. Thankfully, the waterfront stretch is flat and largely devoid of any obstacles or buildings, offering me a clear line of sight across the multiple roadways, green spaces and communal facilities that lie between here and where my friends are. Accelerating towards them, I note that the HUD has just flashed up a thirty-second fuel warning. This is going to be close.

'I need you to pull over,' I instruct urgently. 'Like in the next ten seconds.'

'Are you sure?' Milly says, unconvinced.

'Yes,' I shout. 'You keep moving away from me, I won't make it. I'm almost dry.'

Counting down over the radio, I watch as their white van slows and then pulls over into a lay-by just outside the fairground's perimeter wall. The police bike also slows to a standstill. The cop dismounts and begins to approach the van. Surging forwards to close the gap, I descend from the sky with alarming speed. The element of surprise is still mine. My landing is a little harder than I anticipated, and I stumble forwards for a few awkward paces along the grassy roadside.

'Get George ready to move the moment I tell you,' I instruct.

Running towards the bike just as the policeman casually turns to look in my direction, I bring my right-hand jet nozzles to bear against the rubber tread of the rear wheel and blip the throttle aggressively. The rubber liquefies instantaneously, causing a sudden rush of air as the tyre deflates. Shouting angrily, he begins to run towards me. Behind him, GC puts the van into gear and rapidly pulls away from the kerb. The police officer stops and turns, shouting angrily after the departing van. Taking my cue from his distraction, I take three large strides and propel myself skywards again to soar over his head in a great leaping arc.

'Stop the van,' I call urgently.

'Stop the van!' Milly repeats even more urgently.

George brakes suddenly. Relieved, I ease off the throttle, flare my arms and descend back down to the road, just as a red fuel warning appears on the HUD and the engines wheeze and splutter. Then they go silent, dropping me the last five feet to an accompanied scream. Again, it's a poor landing, and my speed sends me stumbling into the rear of the van. The doors burst open, slamming into my shoulder, knocking me backwards into the gutter. Groaning, I look up to see my friends' nervous faces looking down at me.

'Oh no, I'm so sorry,' Milly squeals.

'All good. Let's go,' I shout, climbing into the back. Milly pulls the doors closed behind me, and George pulls us away from the irate traffic cop.

'Oh my God, what a total rush,' I exclaim as I begin unclipping the suit's straps. 'Well, most of it, at least. I mean, there was a moment back there where it all got a little sporty.'

'You don't say,' Milly exclaims.

'Yeah, we could pretty much hear everything you said over the radio,' Anabel adds.

'Great,' I groan in embarrassment, slipping from the cumbersome main pack. 'Perhaps not my finest moment.'

'Did you set the surveillance device okay?' George calls from the driver's seat without turning.

'Yup. Let's just hope it works.'

Depleted of fuel, the jet suit weighs in at about twenty-six kilos. Quickly, I have it stowed back inside its sturdy packing case.

'What happens to this now?' I ask, sitting to avoid being thrown across the interior as George turns a corner.

'First I drop you lot off back near your hotel,' he calls. 'Then I drop the van off with someone who'll make it disappear, and then we get that thing on the last flight out of here. We do not need anyone discovering it in our possession.'

'Can say that again,' I laugh.

'The good news is, it doesn't look like we're being followed,' Anabel notes, peering through the darkened rear window.

'Let's hope it stays like that,' George replies, holding up crossed fingers, as he turns into a narrow alley a block from our hotel. 'Best I let you all out here. I'm pretty sure there are no cameras in here.'

We hastily gather what we need to take with us.

'Any fun plans for the rest of the evening?' he asks conversationally. 'I suppose it's still early for you young people.'

'Not sure,' I reply, turning to Milly.

'We should probably see what Styles has been up to,' she announces, glancing at her watch. 'He tends to go out a bit later in the evening. If we're quick, we might even catch him. See where he goes, who he meets. That sort of thing.'

'Good luck with that,' George chuckles. 'Hey, before you go, have you updated Sam about what's going on?'

'Not yet,' I reply, somewhat evasively. 'Don't you guys, like, talk?'

He laughs derisively. 'It's advisable that my involvement in all this be kept to the minimum. The office is a little political at the moment, to say the least. Best if his updates come from the expected channels, namely from you. We regroup tomorrow, okay? See if tonight's little exercise turns up anything useful. You never know – occasionally you have to get lucky, right?'

*

The Notorious B.I.G.'s 'Hypnotize' blares almost too loudly from the multiple ceiling-mounted speakers. It's hard to tell if this is a bar or a club. The décor is cheap. The dingy atmosphere disguises just how cheap. Their excessive use of ultraviolet lighting serves only to illuminate the white, figure-hugging shorts and crop-top uniforms of the south-east-Asian waitresses as they dart amongst the crowd of predominantly Western drinkers.

'You know,' I shout in a futile bid to make myself heard over the music. 'Doesn't this strike you as an odd kind of place to find a serving member of Parliament like the Right Honourable Mr Robert Styles over there?'

Milly nods and flicks another glance along the length of the bar, towards the far corner table booth, where the MP has been sitting for the last half hour. Comically, he appears to have taken a page out of the amateur spy's handbook and is wearing beige chinos, a loud, short-sleeved Hawaiian shirt and a Panama hat.

'Hang on,' Milly interjects, glancing past me. 'Someone's just joined him. A Chinese guy.'

'Fit, from the look of it,' observes Anabel.

'Fit as in army fit?' I ask, avoiding looking. The two of them rubbernecking is bad enough.

'I dunno. Maybe,' she says.

Frowning, I subtly turn to look. The newcomer is a young, slick-looking local man with gelled back hair who is dressed entirely in black.

'Don't quote me,' I say, 'but I'm almost certain that's the same guy he met the other night in the Captain's Bar, when I met GC for a cheeky drink.'

'How sure?' Anabel replies.

'Hey, at this distance…'

'You think Forbes might be right and that he's up to something dodgy?' Anabel says.

'Maybe, but why would you come here?' Milly asks. 'This place is such a dive.'

'Precisely because no one'll recognise him. Or they're unlikely to, at any rate,' I suggest.

'True. I guess if you wanted to meet with handlers from an enemy intelligence organisation, this is pretty much a perfect place for it.'

'Yup,' Anabel agrees, nodding. 'Certainly loud enough that no one could possibly overhear what you're saying, dark enough that you could hand over a plasma-screen TV and no one would notice, and enough of a dive that no one would ever think to look for you here.'

'Tell you what, keep an eye on him. I completely forgot to call Sam after George dropped us off. Probs best I get that out the way before he moos and complains about us. Then we'll see where this leads with Styles. Give me a sec, okay? I'm going to pop outside and brief him on the whole Ritz Carlton thing. Back in a second.'

Stepping out onto the pavement, I find the exit blocked by a crowd of African girls idly milling around in the road. Casually glancing in both directions, I see a spot a short distance away, farther along the neon-drenched street, where there are no people – a rarity in this city. Finding somewhere with no one within twenty-five feet has proven challenging.

The call is very one-sided and over in less than two minutes. Besides a closing, 'Good, thanks for the update,' he had almost nothing to say. With an exasperated eye-roll, I head back inside.

'Hey, where did the slick-looking guy go?' I ask as I slip back onto my barstool in between my friends.

'He literally just upped and left,' Milly says, shrugging. 'Surprised you didn't pass him on the way back in.'

'Maybe I missed him. That was brief.'

'Yes, he didn't even finish his drink,' Milly notes.

'Guess it wasn't a social meet,' Anabel adds.

'Doesn't look it.'

'Long enough to hand something over, though.'

'True, but no chitchat?' I say. 'How boring. I mean, if you're going to commit treason, at least have some fun doing it, right? Like have a bit of banter.'

'Sometimes I wonder about you, I really do,' Milly sighs.

'C'mon, screw it. I think it's time to find out what this guy's really up to. Bollocks to all this shadow crap. Time to go have a proper chat, me thinks.' Signalling the bargirl, I gesture for another drink, before adding two more for my friends.

'Oh dear, here we go,' Milly groans. 'How much have you had to drink?'

'Not enough. Hey, you notice her?' I ask my friends as the barmaid turns away to get a clean glass.

'Yup,' Milly says, bemused. 'But I'm not sure she's exactly our type, if that's what you mean.'

'I don't follow –'

'I know you don't,' Anabel says with an equally amused smile. 'Milly means she's pre-op. Or is that he's pre-op?'

'What? Wait... No... Really?' I exclaim, casting a long, scrutinising look down the bar. 'Seriously?'

'Sometimes you're so naïve, it's actually quite sweet,' Milly says, putting an arm around my shoulders.

'Alright, that's enough,' I scoff, shrugging her away playfully, albeit slightly embarrassed. My drink quickly arrives and for a short, intrigued moment I hold the barmaid's gaze.

On reflection, I should probably have guessed. She looks Thai, with delicate yet slightly angular features, deep brown eyes and jet black, very straight hair. She is wearing a revealing, loose-weave, white crochet beach dress which glows in the UV-soaked darkness. It stands out in stark contrast to her tanned skin, which is visible beneath. Clearly, she isn't wearing a bra. A playful little smile dances across her face as she gazes into my eyes. It's one of knowing that someone else knows and suggests that she's effortlessly comfortable with that fact. Grinning, I laugh and take my drink.

With a sing-songy, 'Laters,' I stride off towards the MP's booth. The deep-blue, asymmetric silk dress I chose for to-night, not to mention this pair of skyscraper-high, sparkly silver heels, are bound to make an impression on anyone. Of that I am convinced. And while the dress isn't plunging, the high-cut slit up to my left hip is undeniably attention-grab-bing. And with this new haircut, success is as good as guar-anteed, I tell myself.

'Not interested,' he says with barely a glance up at me the moment I arrive at the edge of his table. Instead, he remains fixated on his phone, on which he is furiously typing.

'Erm,' I stutter, the wind torn from my sail.

Ignoring my presence, he slips the phone into his trouser pocket and signals in the air for the bill. Deeply offended by the rejection, I skulk back to my friends.

'Well, that clearly went well,' Milly sniggers.

'I don't believe it,' Anabel sighs, sliding a Hong Kong ten-dollar bill across the bar to Milly.

'You bet on it?'

'Of course. It was too good an opportunity to pass up. I said you'd crash and burn,' Milly replies, examining the bill up against a ceiling light.

'Why would you do that?' I splutter, sinking dejectedly

back onto my barstool. 'Is there something wrong with me?' I ask in puzzlement.

'No,' she replies, grinning. 'Not really. You know, besides your clingy personality, below-average looks, nice-but-dim intellect... that sort of thing.'

I give her a sarcastic guffaw. 'I am not clingy.'

'Fair point. I give you that. Horribly independent is closer to the mark.'

'Thank you. No, seriously, though, I don't get it. He was completely uninterested. I mean, he didn't even look up at me. He just said, not interested.'

'Probably thought you were a hooker,' Anabel suggests, sipping her drink casually.

'That's the second time someone's alluded to that since we arrived. But look, even if that were true,' I argue, 'wouldn't you at least show some interest? Tell me honestly, if you were a man, would you sleep with me?'

'Personally?' Milly splutters. 'I can't believe you'd ask me that.'

'Don't answer that question,' Anabel jokes with an exaggerated stare.

'Why?! What's wrong with me? Why's no one wanna sleep with me?' I exclaim with a disbelieving laugh. Lifting my arm, I cautiously sniff my armpit. 'Is it me?'

The barmaid stops before us, smiles and says, 'I will...'

'Yeah? Noted and appreciated,' I reply and empty my drink, before sliding Milly's Negroni across and taking a deep sip of it. 'But seriously, am I doing something wrong? Why would he pay me absolutely no attention?'

'Perhaps it's a good thing he didn't,' Milly notes. 'We were explicitly told not to engage with him.'

'Really want to know why they say no?' the barmaid asks.

'Well, she's my friend,' I say, pointing slightly dismissively at Milly. 'So I guess that's an okay excuse.'

'Oi –' Milly protests.

'They're both gay,' the barmaid says, interrupting Milly, as she casually dries a glass and places it up on a shelf overhead. Pointing, she smiles at Milly and then towards the doorway, through which Robert Styles has just left.

'You not the problem. You gorgeous,' the girl says. 'But make bad choice in lover.'

'How do you know I'm gay?' Milly exclaims, leaning forwards over the bar top, aghast.

'Shh, that's not the interesting bit,' I chip in, placing my hand soothingly on her shoulder. 'Go on. Say that again. What do you mean they're *both* gay?'

'You know nothing,' the barmaid laughs in an unnervingly deep baritone. 'The man there. Who just left. Who you try chat up.' She swallows a snigger. 'Bent as the River Phraya, girlfriend. You could open leggies on table and he still not interested. Phone more interesting.'

A perplexed look fixes itself to my face.

'But he's married,' says Milly. 'With kids.'

'That's what I was going to say,' adds Anabel. 'Albeit divorced... technically.'

'Then she not only naïve girl here,' the barmaid replies, smiling.

'Great, she was listening to our whole conversation,' Anabel sighs.

Ignoring her, the barmaid continues, 'Silly girls. Always thinking problem is you. World more complicated. You think he married so he straight. And you sexy girl, but he not interested, so must be you not pretty enough. Not sexy enough. Wrong. Silly girl think.'

I scowl, somewhat irked to be lectured by someone who barely looks older than us.

'You realise this changes everything!' Anabel announces.

'You're telling me,' Milly concludes, frowning. 'And could explain his odd home set-up as well?'

'If that's true,' I say, 'then we've been coming at this whole thing from completely the wrong angle since the beginning.'

'Me not wrong,' the barmaid adds confidently. 'You want come party later with me?'

'You know, as interesting as that could be, I should probably say no,' I reply, laughing hard at the offer. Naïve I may have been about Styles, but I'm not so naïve as to miss what she's really asking. 'But I will stay for another drink, though. I want to understand how you could possibly have known that just from looking at the guy.'

'Another?' the barmaid grins.

'Sure, why not?' I reply. 'After the evening I've had, make it another Negroni. I liked that.'

'Cool. Well, I think we'll leave you to it,' Anabel says, rising from her stool. 'It's getting late, and I imagine tomorrow's going to be even busier than we thought it would. We've got that march scheduled tomorrow, so we don't have a whole lot of time to figure out what's really going on.'

'Yeah, great,' Anabel sighs. 'Just as a typhoon might also hit us. More good news.'

'For real?' I ask with comically wide eyes.

'Likely they'll know for sure tomorrow morning.'

Nodding, I glance at Milly, whom I hoped might stay a little longer. But she, too, stands and smiles sheepishly.

'Oh my God, you're leaving me for her!' I exclaim, pointing comically at Anabel.

'Yup,' she replies, grinning broadly, as she wraps an amorous arm around Anabel's waist.

'Cock,' I mumble under my breath in mock rejection.

'Yes, well, I suppose you could try for that, if you're feeling in the mood,' she teases playfully, glancing at the barmaid. 'But if you want what I have, then go find your own.'

'Oh, that's cold,' I call after them as they make for the exit.

'Yeah, just like your bed will be,' Milly laughs back.

'Oh my God, where did all this attitude suddenly come from?' I exclaim to myself in amusement as I drain Milly's glass. 'Seriously starting to regret ever bringing them here...'

*

The conversation with the amorous barmaid soon becomes frustrating, as she constantly darts off to serve other customers. Eventually, as I finish another Negroni, I give up and ask for the bill, much to her obvious disappointment.

Extricating myself from the loud, sweaty bar, I make my way out onto the equally sweaty street and ease through the milling crowd, retrieving my phone as I go. Along with a couple of messages from school friends, there is one from an unknown number. Opening it, I see a message signed by Sam in which he states an urgent need to debrief me properly about what we have discovered. An address for an MI6 safe house is given. Quickly texting him back, I enquire when he wants to do it.

A response pings back seconds later.

Now

Sighing, I walk to the end of the road and flag down a passing taxi.

'Ap Lei Chau,' I say, reading out the address slowly. The driver nods and pulls out into the busy Wan Chai traffic. The twenty-minute journey to the island's south side takes us through Central, around the residential headland of Pok Fu Lam and into the more industrial heartland of Aberdeen. There, we turn off onto a dark road devoid of any other vehicles. Everything around here looks to be some form or other of industrial warehouse.

'Interesting place to have a safe house,' I ponder aloud to myself. Remembering my friends, I send them a quick group chat message to say that I have gone to see Sam for a proper debrief.

A response is unlikely, given the time. Most likely both are fast asleep by now. Braking abruptly, the driver points towards a raised loading bay belonging to a nondescript, grey, five-storey concrete building. Barely any of the floors have windows.

'Great,' I mumble as I pay the driver. Grabbing my phone, small clutch and umbrella, I step from the taxi. My door is barely closed before he impatiently pulls away. With an eye-roll, I head towards the loading bay's steps. Other than myself, there is no one else in sight. The thought occurs to me that I am not sure how much I like this. The lot is barely lit, and every shadow holds imaginary would-be attackers.

Hurrying to the top of the steps, I find an old intercom. I dial the number given in the message, press the bell button and wait for someone to answer, glancing around cautiously.

There's a click and the adjacent door pops open. So much for operational security.

At the end of a short, wide corridor is a large, battered freight lift with heavy sliding gates that need to be slammed closed before the car will rise. It has evidently been a while since they were oiled. With the fifth floor selected, I am left to ponder whether it was the bargain basement rent or the out-of-the-way location that made MI6 choose this hole as a safe house. One thing is for sure: it would take a miracle for anyone to find it by accident.

When the lift shudders to a stop at the fifth floor, I wrench the gate open to find myself staring down a dingy, dilapidated, grey breeze-block corridor. All around, whatever paint there once was has badly peeled. A deathly silence hangs over the entire building, save for the incessant dripping of water from the ceiling. As a result, large puddles have formed on the floor. Recessed side alcoves are piled high with debris from a long-since abandoned renovation. Three of the ceiling strip lights flicker erratically, casting stretches of the long passageway into relative darkness.

I would ordinarily have expected a safe house to offer good security and multiple exits. This place offers neither. Sighing, I set off in search of the room number given.

Despite my stepping carefully to avoid the assorted debris littering the corridor, including broken glass and bottle tops, my heels clack noisily on the poured-concrete flooring. As I finally reach the door in question, I instinctively turn my nose up in revulsion at the strong, bitter smell hanging in the stale air. My first reaction is that it smells like the wretched, coppery stench of dried blood. Never exactly a good sign. Especially since the last time I smelt it, things didn't turn out so great.

There is no buzzer. Frowning, I gingerly ease the heavy metal sliding door open, wincing as it squeaks noisily on old, unoiled runners. I can only assume Sam's use of the term 'safe house' was a slip of the tongue. This place has all the hallmarks of a cover front. But even that self-assuring theory is cast into doubt the moment I step inside and realise, to my bewilderment, that I have come to a meat-processing facility. The far end is entirely bathed in darkness. Only the strip lights above the area immediately in front of me are on. Their stark, clinical glare illuminates an area of white tiled flooring on which stand two large brushed-aluminium conveyor belts. Sam is sitting on the right hand one, idly swinging his legs in boredom. Looking up, he smiles. But it lacks warmth. Rather than being genuinely amicable, I sense it's rather more self-congratulatory.

A nervous shiver runs down my back and it has nothing to do with the frigid temperature in here. As I look questioningly at Sam, I become increasingly aware of a quiet, nagging sensation at the back of my mind. That oddly accurate warning mechanism honed, evolved and passed down through the millennia which generations ago served to stop people from getting eaten but is now adapted for the more unpredictable dangers of modern living. Only today it comes a little too late.

I am about to spin on my heel and run for it when the door grinds shut behind me. Standing there with a thin, icy smile of achievement is a lithe Chinese woman. To describe her as out of place would barely begin to do her justice. She is porcelain-doll pretty, with pale, luminescent skin and long, flowing, glossy black hair. Her clothes are all high-end designer couture. In her hand is a very real-looking semi-automatic pistol. And behind her stands a fat, tattooed thug in a white wife-beater vest.

'Well, that was easy,' Sam gloats, clapping his hands excitedly as he hops from the conveyor belt. 'Honestly, I don't know what SIS are teaching recruits nowadays.'

'What is this?' I demand nervously.

'We're going to ask you some questions, MI6 girl,' the woman replies coolly in heavily accented English as she walks past me to take up a position beside Sam.

'I don't suppose it'd do any good to tell you I'm not actually MI6, would it?' I offer hopefully as I try to keep the frantic, panicked thumping that has begun within my chest under control.

'You know, I honestly don't care,' Sam replies as numerous men step from the shadows all around us. In all, I count ten of them. And that's on top of Sam and the wannabe influencer standing beside him. All are local, most of them heavily tattooed. Triads, I suspect. All are older than me. Which means none are as fast as me, no matter how lean or fit they look. My only other advantage, as far as I can tell, is that none will be nearly as motivated as me to get out of here. But that's where the good news ends. For all are armed. Which is problematic. Some with large meat cleavers, one with a crowbar. The rest have smaller but equally unpleasant-looking knives. One has even opted for a box cutter. Heels and a thin cocktail dress are not the optimal attire for a situation like this. Ice hockey pads might be a better option.

A palpable, slow-burning fear wells up within me, simmering, then boiling and erupting into a hot, prickly panic. I turn as another man emerges from the shadows. The PLA's Special Operations man from the China Club. Again, he is dressed all in black, and he looks as humourless as the last time I saw him. He stands straight and erect in the doorway of the facility's management office, which is recessed off in the far corner, adjacent to the main entrance.

A cold, nervous shiver ripples through me at the sight of him, and what it means for this rapidly worsening situation. Like a dark room closing in around me on all sides, claustrophobic and smothering, the increasingly grim reality threatens to overwhelm me.

'Put the umbrella down,' Sam instructs, pointing at the conveyor belt behind me. 'You can never be too certain with old Q Branch. I'd prefer no unexpected surprises.'

Scowling at him, I place the long yellow umbrella on the belt and step back.

'Interesting choice of colour,' he notes dryly.

'Yeah, that's what someone else said,' I reply, conscious not to name any of my friends.

'Just couldn't resist another insult, could you?' he adds bitterly. 'No matter. The good thing about this place is I seriously doubt anyone else will be around to hear the screams. But always best to err on the side of caution, wouldn't you say?'

With a thin smile, he nods to a skinhead in the far corner. With a few presses of the largest green buttons on the control panel beside him, assorted machinery whirls to life throughout the facility, including the two conveyor belts, the ceiling-mounted rail-track system and two large dicing and packaging machines at the far end of each conveyor belt.

'What do you want, Sam?' I ask. My throat catches awkwardly and I force a dry swallow.

'I want to ask questions, and I want you to tell me interesting things. Like how a girl sent here to watch some errant MP managed to stumble upon something friends of mine have been working hard to keep secret? That is curious, wouldn't you say?' he asks, leaning forward. 'What we need to know is what else you know. A little birdie tells me you've been hanging out with that joke of a has-been, Clementine. He may be a useless retard, but occasionally he pulls something impressive from his hat. If we are compromised, we need to know how badly. You understand?'

'To be honest, we haven't found much more than I explained on the phone.'

'Excuse me if I don't believe you. Honestly, has no one told you not to start a lie with the words "to be honest"? Is this really amateur hour?'

'What are you going to do? You know that statistically speaking, beating me up won't give you anything useful. And torture is well known not to give accurate results.'

'Did they teach you that in a classroom?' he asks disparagingly. 'Well, let me bring you in on a little secret about the real world. You don't need any of that old clichéd stuff. You won't find anything as stupid as Chinese water torture here. It's so much simpler than that. We're just going to break you, and by the time we're halfway through, you'll be begging to give me everything we want.'

Whether it's the overwhelming quantity of adrenaline suddenly coursing through me or blind fear which hinders me from firing back some pithy, sarcastic comment, I don't know. But I find my mouth dry and my sweaty hands clutching the underside of the conveyor belt, against which I am leaning.

'You figure it out. You're a smart girl. See a lot of women here right now, do you?' he asks leerily, turning to the pretty Chinese woman. 'What do you think, Yang? Reckon by the time this lot get to their second innings, her resistance will be hovering somewhere between abject defeat and simply wanting to top herself?'

Yang stares at me with unblinking eyes. Her expression remains unflinchingly neutral as Sam continues.

'By that point, I expect you'll look like a cross between a road accident and a puddle of that white scum which accumulates in the corner of people's mouths when they're badly dehydrated. Torture,' he laughs. 'You've got to be joking. Why bother? Hey, interesting fact. Resistance is highly correlated to self-esteem. Did you know that? Use a person like a sexual toilet for long enough and the total collapse of self-esteem is all but guaranteed. It's really quite primal.'

With a slow, dull, heavy thudding in my chest, I count again the number of men here. Enough disturbing videos circulate each week at school to leave no one in any doubt as to the depravity with which men can treat members of the opposite sex. But to suddenly be faced with the prospect of a very real and very imminent large-scale assault sends me reeling to a scarily dark and recessed corner of my mind. As an ever more violent stream of images plays across my mind's eye, my chest constricts and a raw, visceral fear washes over me. Breathing suddenly becomes challenging as I take in the men: their number, their size and the venomous hatred that clearly seethes within many of them. Delicacy and respect are not what I should expect from any of these people. In a grimly dark moment of reflection, I realise it's almost amusing the degree to which we correlate our safety to something as basic as the wearing of clothing. But the more rational part of my mind, the only bit still functioning properly, realises that a flimsy silk dress and underwear is not going to offer much protection when this starts in earnest. Reaching back slowly, I feel for my clutch bag.

Other than Sam and the Chinese woman, the Triads remain half in the shadows on the far side of the two conveyor belts, just waiting. The string-vested thug has not moved from where he is, guarding the door. Near him, still standing at the entrance to the prefabricated office, the PLA man looks on with a crooked, thin smile.

Without a second's more hesitation, I lunge to my left and sprint for the darkness beyond the packaging machines. Even in heels I move faster than Sam can lunge forwards to grab me. Dashing past several large inbuilt fridges which line the far wall, I thrust open a large set of insulated double swing doors. Beyond them is a colossal storage space stocked full of rows of carcasses suspended by huge hooks from an idle ceiling-mounted conveyor belt system. The only light comes from the emergency exit signs and glowing insect traps located around the warehouse.

I slam the doors behind me and rush on deep into the macabre forest of skinned livestock. Some could be pigs, but most appear to be cows. It's too dark and I am in too much of a hurry to care much. But there are rows and rows of them, so densely packed that one could easily get lost in here.

Somewhere behind me, beyond the bloody wall of meat and bone which now blocks me from view, the doors fly open and several people walk into the vast meat storage area. Their shoes echo noisily on the solid concrete floor as they fan out. The acoustics make it hard to gauge how far away each person is. Creeping farther in, I angle off towards the right. Tiptoeing as best I can, I quickly come across a stack of packaging boxes piled up against the side wall. All are covered with a variety of colourful Chinese symbols. As hiding places go it's not the best, but at least it will allow me to wriggle in behind them and send a message.

Opening my clutch bag, my mind reels from the discovery of whom Sam must surely be working for. I'm startled by a sudden blaring noise. For a brief, alarming moment I'm confused as to where it's coming from, before I realise with horror that it's my own mobile phone. Cursing in panic, I fumble to retrieve the illuminated vibrating device. With a frantic stabbing at the seemingly unresponsive touchscreen, I try to silence it.

Barely have I declined the call – which caller ID flags as being a telemarketing call – than the boxes are torn away from in front of me. Standing there, stoic and neutral, as if he has seen all this before, is the shadowy PLA man. Glaring at me from behind him is Sam. Scowling, he clicks his fingers and jabs his thumb back towards the packaging room. Two of the Triads step forward and grab me by my arms and roughly haul me, stumbling, back into the front space.

Throwing me hard up against the conveyor, the Triads step back and retrieve their meat cleavers. As the others return to the room, the PLA man speaks in short, almost aggressive tones to Yang. Then he nods curtly to the eldest Triad and strides towards the door, which is duly pulled open by the white-vested man. He slides it closed noisily after him.

'What did he say?' Sam asks Yang.

'To get on with it,' she replies, irritated at the rebuke.

'Well, don't worry about that. We'll get the answers we want,' Sam replies confidently. Turning to me, he adds, 'You're a pain in the arse, you are. Originally, my intention was to lock you in a meat locker after this lot are done with you. Wait for a team to come and smuggle you over the border, where you can just disappear. But you know what? For that last little stunt, I have something far more appropriate in mind. But before we get to that, I thought I'd give you one last chance to do this the old-fashioned way. Some simple questions. Maybe if you can answer them truthfully, we can save you a little discomfort –'

'Ah well, then, I've got one for you,' I interrupt, realising that to keep any advantage here I need to put them on the back foot. Shaking my head, I continue, 'You really think the rest of the world will stand for it when they find out what you lot've been cooking up with that North Korean you've got shacked up in the Ritz?'

For a moment Sam glances nervously at Yang.

'I told you they knew more,' she hisses. 'This should have been handled the moment she arrived.'

'It's okay,' Sam replies soothingly. 'I can handle this.'

With relief, I realise they don't know about my friends. Which would make sense. After all, Sam hasn't met any of them, and they didn't come to the consulate on our first day here.

'Stand for it?' he replies, smiling broadly. 'How would anyone ever prove anything? One thing's for sure, whatever we have planned will put a very sudden end to anyone's desire to be out in large groups on the streets. Can anyone say where's my facemask?'

The Chinese woman fires him an irked look.

'What?' he retorts. 'It's not like she's going to be around to see it, is she?'

'You're all mad, you know that, right?' I say, looking at each of them in turn. 'You can't possibly honestly hope to get away with this.'

'Get away with it?' Sam replies, clearly tiring of the discussion. 'I think we've already got away with it. Now, let's discuss the information we need.'

'No, I don't get it,' I interrupt again, hoping to sow division. 'Aren't you meant to be the rising star of the consulate? The guy with all these amazing sources, like way high up in the Chinese government? How did they rope you into all this crap?'

'You honestly think there's merit in toiling away, year after year, risking one's life for the measly civil service salary they pay? Yeah, right. This is the easiest scam going. We've been playing them like a piano.' He points at Yang. 'Her, with her connections to Chinese intelligence, and me with my access. We simply created fictional sources, and SIS are so desperate for insights into what's going on in Beijing that they'll pay through the nose for it. Er, yes, thank you, we'll take that!'

'Wow, that's almost as funny as it is tragic,' I note dryly.

'Wake up. Can't you see what's happening here? You British fools seem to think the fate of Hong Kong is somehow yet to be determined. That you can make a difference with your idle tinkering. But you're wrong. It's already sealed. The same for Macau and Taiwan. They're all already China's!'

'But you're British. Sorry, dude, but WTF!'

'My father toiled for years in this very meat factory, before Britain opened its arms to thousands like him. Their BNO passports allowed them to make a living of sorts in your cold, grey, wet, miserable little island.'

'And you're pissed at us for giving him a passport? Wow, GC said you were a prize little turd. Guess he doesn't know you're a traitorous prize little turd, too.'

'That old fool? All he's done is hold me back and delay my advance.'

'Wow, you sound like half my generation with your bleating about entitlement. Besides, I thought you didn't care?'

'I don't,' he shouts.

'So this is how you repay them, huh? By betraying your side?'

'Wake up. If you're not with China, you're against it. You think I'm going to let all the hard work go to nothing? When China takes over, I'm not going to be one of those fools fleeing on the last Airport Express to Chek Lap Kok, expelled with their tails between their legs.'

'Yeah, okay, whatever. I can see this is pointless. So, what do you want, Sam?'

'Very simple. You're going to tell us what you know about the plans to foil the protests, and how you found out about this.'

'Well,' I sigh. 'I guess if I wanted confirmation, then there it is.'

'You think this is a joke?' he snaps, leaning forwards angrily. Beside him, Yang's calm demeanour finally shows signs of cracking. 'Let's see how much of a joke this is. Here's what we're going to do. Once this lot are done with you, I'm going to have them saw you in two. I found this little gem in a book about medieval torture. You're going to love it. We'll hang you upside down from those ceiling hooks, with your legs apart, and then we'll cut you in half. And we'll use that,' he says, pointing at an old, rusty serrated saw, some five feet long, with handles at both ends, which is leaning against the wall in the far corner.

On cue, two of the Triads step forward and pick it up. Looks of amusement spread across their faces. Clearly, this is what they have been waiting for. Without emotion, Sam points back towards the room with the hanging carcasses.

'You're going to end up just like those cows. Now, I imagine you're probably wondering how you can get out of this nightmare. Well, you can't, is the simple answer. It's a toughie for the mind to get its head around, isn't it? Fact is, what's coming is inevitable. The only question is how long it'll take.'

'You know,' I say, fighting desperately to maintain control over the mounting wave of terror welling deep within me at the prospect of being tortured by someone who's confident, has time on their side and whose only motivation is simply to cause as much pain as possible. But I can't let them see my fear. Swallowing hard, I add defiantly, 'You're all out of your fricking minds! Seriously, sawing someone in two! What's wrong with you people?'

'Playtime's over, silly girl,' Sam announces. 'This is the real word. Where people sometimes actually die for their country, and for what they believe in. Are you ready to die?'

Scowling at him, I reply, 'Seriously pisses me off that you're now the second person today to tell me I'm silly and naïve. What do you think, dickhead? Do I look like I'm gagging to get sawed in sodding two? No, not particularly. Are you ready to die today?'

'Ha, you're a funny girl,' he sneers, wagging a finger. 'But here's the difference between us. You have your silly Western intentions but lack any real backbone behind it. We, however, are committed to our cause and what we're building here. Make no mistake, we're going to get what we want from you. The genius of this is, because you'll be hanging from one of those meat hooks, all the blood will go to your head, meaning you'll be conscious throughout. I read they used to do this to witches, or those suspected of having been unfaithful. Sometimes it lasted several hours before they finally cut the body fully in half. Occasionally, just for fun, they'd stop halfway through, perhaps once they'd got down to the stomach. You know, to wait it out a bit, just savouring the agony, as the bottom half hangs open. All these fun little touches one can add, you know, to make it that little bit more personal, and so much more excruciating. Well, the good news is, we have all night ahead of us. So, yeah, I'm pretty sure you'll give us what we want the second we begin, and that'll be deeply appreciated, thank you very much, because then we can just carry on for the fun of it. Or maybe these guys will get if from you before we even start on any of that. Either way, I think I'm actually going to enjoy this.'

I can't let myself even begin to picture what he has just described. It would completely overwhelm and paralyse me. My only option is to pretend I didn't hear it and deflect and distract to buy myself time.

Fixing him with a scrutinising stare, I say, 'I'm kind of getting the sense you don't like me very much.'

'Truth be told,' he exclaims coldly, pulling up a plastic garden chair to sit on, 'I despise you. You and everything you represent. All your colonial ideals. Your arrogance and hypocrisy. Your belief that the world belongs to you, a silly little pretender island lost in the North Atlantic. How arrogant. You need us. You need our trade. You need our products. And yet what do you do? A constant barrage of xenophobic anti-China rhetoric. I think back, and it's an endless list of slights. You bombed our embassy in Belgrade. You protested during our Olympic torch ceremony. You feel you have the right to levy sanctions against us. Us! China! You complain at everything we do. We suffered a century of humiliation at your hands. The Opium Wars, the taking and plundering of our lands. Defeats to the British, the French, the Japanese, the Russians.'

'Sounds like you get beaten by a lot of people,' I observe casually, certain it will annoy him even more. 'Maybe wars just aren't your thing. I mean, are you guys sure you want to pick a fight with all those countries all over again? Coz that's exactly where you're headed with your "screw the world" attitude.'

'You think it was fair for the Eight-Nation Alliance to invade us to suppress the Boxer uprising?' he vents, increasingly agitated.

'I dunno. When was that?'

'See,' he shouts, his cool veneer slipping. 'You don't even know! You don't even know what you did in the late eighteen hundreds. And then you had the nerve to impose reparations in excess of our entire annual tax revenue. You forced us to open our ports to trade with you. And that's before we get to all the territory you took. We lost Hong Kong to Great Britain, Macau to Portugal. Large parts of northern China and Sakhalin Island to Russia. More went to Germany, France and Japan. Then, as if that wasn't enough, the British and French had to burn the Old Summer Palace to the ground. An astonishing, incredible building. A marvel of human achievement. You people destroyed the Qing dynasty and the Republic of China –'

'Oi, now hang on a minute. Pretty sure that last one was your own doing. Right before you decided to round up and kill anyone with a brain. Or ship 'em off to the fields, which was kind of the same thing.'

'Enough,' he screams.

'No, not enough,' I shout back, seeing my chance. 'I get it that everyone kicked your arse for a hundred years. I get it that the treaties that followed weren't fair. And I get it that that's humiliating. So you're pissed about all of it. Fine! But you keep saying "you" as if all that crap is somehow *my* fault. But wake up call, dickhead. I'm seventeen. I've got about as much to do with it as a fart in a frickin' spacesuit. You really think having this lot rape me and then cut me in half will serve as some kind of catharsis to ease all that pain? Fuck off! Why don't you just go home, have a wank and get over it. Because I'm going to give you diddly-fucking-squat!'

'Typical gwei-mui,' he sneers. Yet it's clear he's lost his cool. He glances nervously at Yang, and then at the assembled Triads, who appear not to have the faintest idea what is being discussed, and then tries to regain the initiative. 'You think you can talk your way out of this? Wrong. I'll get what we need from you. If we have to pull all your nails and teeth out one by one, I'll get it. Slowly sawing you in half will just be the extra icing on the cake.'

'Yeah, you keep telling yourself that, dickhead. You know what? I get it. I get why you'd betray everyone you know. Why you'd sell out. Dickless marvel like you, it's probably the only way you get any respect. But you know what I don't get? How you can't see how badly she's playing you,' I say, pointing accusingly at Yang. 'I mean, what did she promise you? Or are you just hoping all this might win you a girl like her? Because you sure ain't going to afford a girl like that on your salary. Even with the pay-offs for your fictional little stories, you'll be hard pressed to afford that frickin' bag of hers. You have any idea how much Hermès will take outta your wallet for one of those Birkins? And those LV heels don't come cheap, either. And they sure don't last long, not in this city, with the uneven paving stones around here. I'm betting half that outfit came from Chanel, too, am I right? They're using you, and you're too stupid to see it.'

'Enough,' the Chinese girl screams. 'Sam, make her talk. We need to know what she knows, and who she's told.'

'I agree. Let's get to it,' Sam says, rising from his chair. 'We'll get what we want and then what's left of you can vanish across the border, never to be heard of again. They'll spend weeks searching for you. And everything here will continue just as planned.'

'Yeah, most people have a pretty good plan, until they get punched in the face,' I mutter dryly, looking at the assembled Triad gang members. 'Are you lot really the best they have? Well, I am not impressed.' I glance at each of them in turn, all too aware that I need every second I can get to strategise as many options as possible.

'Strap her to one of these belts,' Sam orders, his patience exhausted.

'With pleasure,' Yang sings as a hoodied Triad, likely the leader, signals for a man to assist.

Multiple clashing emotions erupt within me. Chief of them is overwhelming anger. Anger at them all for their presumptuousness. Anger at myself for walking into this mess. And anger at Sam for his betrayal. Combined, it serves to push my fear and self-pity aside and clarify my thoughts. With heart hammering furiously, adrenaline coursing and hands shaking, I realise I am not ready to die. And certainly not here in this dingy, forgotten corner of a city, being shared around by these men like a piece of used meat. I may have walked in here and inadvertently brought this upon myself, but willingly lying back and taking what's coming without a fight...

Hell no!

Gritting my teeth, I resolve to myself that if these bastards want to have what isn't theirs to have, they'd better kill me first, or else I will surely kill them all.

My only option is to let go of all restraint, to allow myself to embrace the inevitable conflict on which my life will now depend without hesitation, and in doing so to disregard all rules: to cast aside all the limiting constraints of polite, civilised society and accept the darkness that lies beneath this easily underestimated veneer.

The chance for flight is long gone. So, fight it is.

First, I cannot let anything which is about to happen register on an emotional level. Second, I need to lull them into a false sense of security. The easiest option is to open the emotional tap just enough to let my exterior demeanour unravel into a façade of tear-filled emotional meltdown. As I dissolve into a sobbing wreck, a decidedly focussed, calculating awareness takes grip of me internally. Everyone around me is rapidly mapped, their movements, weapons, size and threat level all gauged as my erratically darting eyes flit from one to the next.

Everything I do now is designed to buy time. Coming apart at the emotional seams works. The edge has already left most of them. Many have taken their eyes off me. Some even lay their meat cleavers down. Their adrenaline dissipates, leaving them increasingly vulnerable to an unexpected attack. With the PLA man gone, Yang is probably the most senior person here. She must go first, followed by the Triad leader in the grey sports hoodie, who has stepped forward to watch. With them out of the picture, enough chaos may ensue to give me a fighting chance of leaving here alive.

Yang reaches out for me, with clear intent to grab me by the throat. Without warning, my crying suddenly stops and

I snap-twist sideways, my left hand grabs hers and my right shoots out, threading beneath her arm, to grip the scruff of her expensive white silk shirt. Savagely bending forwards at the waist, I wrench her off balance, bringing her face smashing down into the top of the industrial aluminium worktop. Her body crumples to the floor, blood oozing from her destroyed nose. A ripple of alarm radiates out across the room. Muscles tense, heartbeats increase, pupils focus and the adrenaline begins pumping.

The closest Triad, who was approaching to restrain me, reacts first and charges at me, swinging wildly with a metal bar. Behind him, the local Triad leader snatches up Yang's fallen pistol. Ducking and darting left, I let the crowbar whistle past harmlessly overhead. Rotating at the waist, I wrap an arm up and over his, before twisting and turning, pushing him sideways, off balance. He stumbles back into the gun-wielding Triad, impacting with him hard. A sudden deafening retort follows as the gun accidentally discharges, and with it goes the side of Yang's head, all over the floor. Her body sags limply sideways as blood gushes down her front, reddening her expensive clothes.

Rising quickly before the crowbar-wielding man can take in what just happened and swing again, I drive my elbow up, bent and dangerous, to impact beneath his jaw, snapping his head back and banging his teeth together forcefully. The heel of my left hand impacts squarely into his nose, rocking him back several more places. A final kick to his face with the ball of my right foot sends him reeling across the open workspace into a fridge door.

Shaking the shock away, the man with the gun opts to charge at me, teeth bared, war cry at full volume, with nothing but ill intent. The others remain still, all either passive observers, keener to see me take a beating from someone else, or simply too stunned by the departure of the pretty Chinese intelligence officer's face to leap into action themselves.

As I arc left, my hands snatch at the gun, twisting it savagely from his grip. Righting it in my hands, I level it to the side of his head and pull the trigger. The painfully loud retort from the pistol rouses all around from their complacency. At this range, the 9mm round passes straight through the man's head and carries on towards the fridge door, twelve feet behind him. There, it strikes the crowbar-wielding man squarely in the chest. A loud, hollow *pling* suggests it made it to the fridge after all. Both fall like puppets with their strings cut. A fraction later, everything which the passing round tore from inside the man's head also arrives in its wake. The angry splash of thick red and grey matter impacts with a resounding wet slap, before trickling messily floor-wards in great, sopping globs.

It appears I have their collective attention.

Remaining still now would be a fatal mistake. Rushing the next closest man, I leap into the air and land with my arm around his neck. Sheer power of momentum carries us on down into a squatted kneeling crouch, from where I toss him heels over head into the opposite conveyor belt. The impact drives the wind from his lungs, and a passing kick to his face with my pointed shoe elicits a pathetic mewing noise. A single round to his forehead silences him. I am up and standing again by the time the next man arrives, and well placed with a solid triangular stance to drive a punishing blow directly to his solar plexus. He staggers past me and falls face first into the worktop. The next round finds its mark in the back of his head, removing him, too, from the equation.

Another brave, have-a-go hero with a large scar across his cheek arrives to find my arm suddenly around his neck. Turning, I simultaneously bring the pistol to bear against his temple whilst kicking out, landing my right stiletto viciously into the centre of another incoming attacker's face. Something gives, and it isn't the well-made Italian heel. He staggers away, screaming, clutching at his left eye. Blood streams through his fingers. Dropping from the man, I dart back two paces, raise the weapon and fire twice. Head and chest. And down he goes. Rapidly sweeping the outstretched pistol thirty degrees to the right, I place another two rounds into the screaming half-blind man.

Grabbing a loose hessian sack from the worktop, I swish it through the air, wrapping it around the forearm of the next incoming attacker, in whose hand is clutched a particularly unpleasant-looking carving knife. Spinning, I drag the man off balance and send him stumbling out into a wide arc. Letting go, he continues and collides with another inbound Triad. With a leap, I soar into the air, delivering a withering spinning kick to the side of his head. The other incoming man receives a swift double-tap, same places. Same results. The knife-wielding man only gets a single round to the heart before the slide locks back. Without emotion, I drop the pistol and spin to deal with the next incoming Triad.

His chosen form of greeting is an overly enthusiastic right hook, which I duck away from, before snatching at his passing fist. Lunging down and to my left, I reverse the direction of his punch's travel, twisting his arm back on itself, sending him flying up into the air and over his own arm directly into the large, gaping mouth of one of the industrial meat blenders cum packaging machines that was turned on earlier. Without the necessary collection container installed, rent tatters of flesh splatter out of the back in all directions, covering the floor, wall and ceiling behind it in fleshy lumps of dripping meat.

Ducking low, I spin on my heel and shoot upwards, the base of my hand extended out fully to catch the nose of the next inbound attacker. A sickening crunch follows, and a gush of warmth sprays across my face, chest and hair. He sinks to the floor, screaming. Not keen to begin taking chances now, I snatch up a fallen meat cleaver and embed it with a vicious swing three inches into his cranium.

Darting backwards, I realise I miscounted the Triads. There are twelve of them, not ten. Not that it matters. The next man throws first one, then two and then a third wild punch before I twist under his arm, rising behind him to wrench him backwards and off balance. His head impacts the metal edge of the nearest conveyor belt. A vicious double-handed impact downwards on his collarbones breaks the neck.

Behind me, the final Triad rushes in from the sliding door, a sword in hand. Where the hell did he get that, I ponder as I bend backwards to avoid the first swing. But my evasive turn is not fast enough. He grabs my dress and pulls me sideways. The seam gives instantly, lessening his leverage but ripping the material from hip to underarm. A swift stamp down on his foot drives the needle-like stiletto though his thin trainer top and down into his foot. He shrieks and leaps back, wounded, but more irritated than defeated. The second's pause gives me the chance to lunge out, bringing my outstretched leg up to drive the heel into the front of his neck. He goes down with considerably less fight left in him than he had a moment before, as he clutches in vain at the pumping geyser of blood spraying out in great gushes with each beat of his rapidly weakening heart. I grab the fallen sword from the floor and drive it, doubled-handed, through his chest and out the back.

For a fleeting moment, I look down, unimpressed, by the torn dress that now hangs open all the way from my bra down to my waist. Irked, I turn and approach Sam, grabbing my yellow umbrella as I pass the conveyor belt.

Nervous and alone, he backs away, quick-stepping his way over bodies and a large bucket of water in the centre of the floor, towards a large blast freezer. He heaves the door open and tries to pull it closed, but I jam the umbrella into the gap and wrench it open.

The moment there's enough room to swing it, Sam comes at me with a long metal pole. I can't tell if it's anger or fear that clouds his eyes. Regardless, I dart sideways, duck, twist and lunge forwards, bringing the handle down to catch him squarely on the shoulder with such force that the umbrella's metal shaft bends dramatically. Yanking it back, I ram it into his stomach. As he lurches forwards, I slam my wrist hard into the centre of his face. My watch takes the full brunt of the impact, sending him crumpling to the icy floor, where he remains, whimpering softly.

'You bitch, you broke my nose!' he hisses, staring in shock at his blood-soaked hand. Without a word, I step outside, pick up the large red bucket and re-enter the freezer. Unemotionally, I toss the water all over him.

'Here. Something to remember me by...'

Then, after flinging the empty bucket hard at him, I pull the door firmly closed. The lever-like handle cranks downwards to engage the safety clasp. Sam's muffled cries from within win him no sympathy. The wall-mounted temperature gauge reads minus eighteen. Turning, I ponder how quickly someone might come to his rescue. Too soon, I conclude. Grabbing the fallen crowbar, I slot it in behind the handle and lunge backwards with all the force I can muster, placing my foot up against the steel door for added leverage. Without warning, it snaps off at its base, sending me flailing back messily onto the floor. Rising, I toss the pole aside with a noisy clang and turn and take in the room. It takes a concerted effort not to be affected by the scene. Instead, glancing at the time, I am relieved to see my watch is still working. Pithily, I mumble, 'Yeah, tested beyond endurance alright.'

Looking around, I realise there is positively too much evidence here to leave like this. With an irritated scowl, I begin to gather all the bodies and drag them by their feet into the second meat locker, where I pile them up in its centre. Next come all the knives and weapons, and anything that might have my fingerprints on it. These are all tossed on top of the messy mound. Fetching a coiled hose from the far corner, I turn on the tap and spray down as much of the floor as I can reach, making sure to get the most noticeable pools of blood and gore. All is flushed towards the central drain.

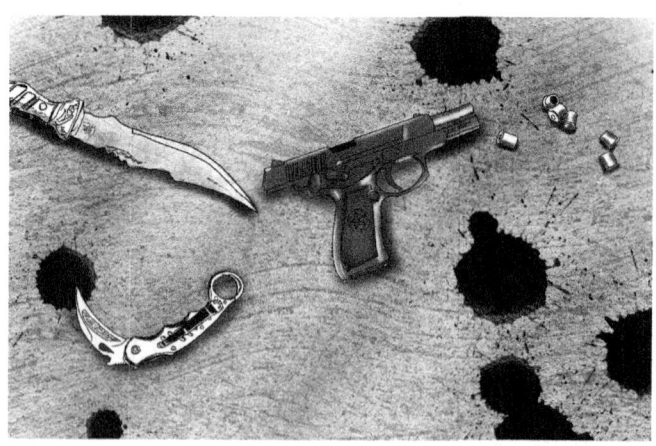

As the last of the reddened water lazily circles the drain, I notice the Birkin still sitting on the conveyor belt, where Yang left it. Amazingly, it remains blood-splatter free. With a conflicted look, I glance back into the meat locker and consider my options. A moment of indecision follows as I weigh up the choice of either destroying such wonderful handicraft or leaving the two-hundred-thousand-dollar bag untouched. The latter option comes with the catch that it only serves to make the police's task of identifying one of the bodies so much easier.

Neither choice is especially appealing. Cursing, I swipe the handbag from the belt top and march into the freezer. There, I tip its contents out onto the pile of bodies and weapons, and place my own smaller clutch bag inside it. Then, I set off in search of something that will ignite. After looking around the meat processing areas, all to no avail, I finally find some cleaning supplies, including two industrial-sized bottles of isopropyl alcohol-based cleaning product, at the back of the management office. A rummage through the pockets of the stacked pile of men quickly produces a pack of matches. All that's left is the careful application of the laws of flammable liquids.

A minute later, with a good fire raging angrily, I leave and close the door behind me. Now I just hope there's sufficient oxygen in the large freezer for the fire to burn long enough to make the coroner's job significantly tougher, but without getting so out of hand that it brings the fire department calling.

After pausing for a short moment to savour the pleasant tactile feel of the Hermès' silk-wrapped handles, I take the bag and make for the small management office, were I set about irreparably destroying their CCTV equipment. And there, much to my surprise, sitting on the next desk over, I spot a half full bottle of Scotch whisky.

'Yeah, I'll be having that, thank you very much,' I mutter, reaching for the ten-year-old Talisker. I run through the list of precautions now required. Then, retracing my steps, I use the tattered silk dress to wipe down every surface I touched, clung to or opened.

Satisfied, I turn to leave and take several generous swigs on the way down the corridor towards the lift. Each produces a harsh, peaty burn at the back of my throat. But I welcome it. For even as I ride the lift back to the ground floor, I feel the Scotch calming my frayed nerves and settling my beating heart. Myriad thoughts jostle and compete for my attention. How could I have so badly trusted the wrong person like this? Can I even trust my own judgement anymore? Worse, recalling the details of my biological mother's file from Gambon's safe, I question whether I am becoming a little too much like her for comfort. My mind spirals as I try to address each thought and make sense of my doubts and questions, whilst also rationalising all that just happened.

But as I wipe down the lift hail button and step into the corridor, it all simply becomes too much to process, and with my grasp on control already tenuous, the emotional load overwhelms me. Stopping in the hallway, I feel my composure crack. I put my hands to my face and burst into tears. But two or three gasped sobs is all I allow myself before I take a sharp intake of breath, hold it for a second and stand tall, steadying myself. A concerted effort is required to keep my emotions in check long enough to let the wave pass.

By the time I finally open the outer door, it is to be confronted by a wall of gushing rain. Bursts of lightning streak the sky and each accompanying clap of thunder is startlingly close and loud. With the ruined umbrella left behind in the bonfire, I stubbornly wipe the last tears from my face and step out into the downpour. Despite it not being cold, I noticeably shiver and realise how exhausted I am. The adrenaline is long since gone, and I recoil as a particularly violent burst of thunder and lightning explodes in the sky directly overhead.

The wind has picked up considerably, and it is now whipping at the rain, which is lashing down in great driving waves in all directions. The all-round drenching has me soaked through in seconds, and well before I even make the kerb side. But at least it takes the flecks of blood with it.

It is only when I find my hand unwilling to loosen its increasingly tight grip on the bottle's neck that I recognise the sensation for what it is. The onset of shock. Sighing, I take another deep swig. Coughing, I grimace ruefully, before sinking another mouthful.

With sodden, matted hair messily pasted across my face, I finally collect my wits enough to reach into my bag to find my phone. It's unlikely I will get a taxi here, so I will need to make for the nearest main road to find one. As I trudge through the deluge, I dial Milly. While it rings, I realise that it's true what they say: things do seem noticeably richer after a near-death experience. Colours seem shaper, even on a dark, gloomy evening like tonight. Time feels a more precious commodity, one not to be squandered, and friends take on a significantly more tangible importance. I notice a more energetic spring return to my stride as I realise I get to go home now and see my friends. I make a mental note to make sure I tell them how much they mean to me when I see them, and how important they are in my life.

'Hey,' I announce when Milly finally answers.

'Oh, it's you,' she laughs, clearly drunk, I realise. Something I would love to be right now, if only my overactive metabolism could just slow down enough for me to get properly pissed. Two large swigs follow in quick succession.

'What time is it?' she asks as I cough and splutter. Maybe necking Talisker is not the best idea.

'Don't ask.'

'*Ai yah*. It's late.'

'You speaking Canto now?'

'Guess it's rubbed off on me. Hey, you okay? What's up? Where'd you go?'

'Who is it?' I hear Anabel ask in the background. 'Is it Hev?'

'Yeah.'

'Tell her to come round. We miss you, Hev,' she shouts.

'I miss you too,' I reply quietly, as I relish the water pouring down my face.

'She alright?' Anabel asks, now closer to the handset. 'She sounds down.'

'You alright?' Milly repeats. 'You sound down.'

'Yeah. No. Maybe. I dunno.'

'That doesn't exactly sound convincing. What's up?'

'Let's just say thing's kinda got a little too real. I just met with the PLA and a bunch of Triads who wanted to ask me a few questions.'

'Shut the front door!' Anabel exclaims.

'For real.'

'How? I mean why?' Milly blurts out.

'We've clearly stumbled onto something. Something they want to keep real hush-hush.'

'Who were they?' Anabel asks.

'A mix. Chinese intelligence. Local Triads, too,' I reply. 'But that's not the worst of it. The guy at our consulate was in the PLA's pocket.'

'Which guy?'

'Sam.'

'Sam! GC's number two?'

'Yup.'

'What? How?'

'Well, he and his Chinese intelligence handler cum wannabe girlfriend just had a crack at me.'

'WTF,' Milly exclaims, suddenly less slurred than before. 'Tell us everything. Are you alright?'

'Yeah. Shocked is all. Guess it's like they say: in this game, it's the person who doesn't at least consider the ultimate betrayal who's ultimately betrayed, right? Anyway, that's getting a little deep. I gotta stop thinking like that. Anyway, git's now in a meat locker, and has been for a while. The bucket of water I chucked over him probably isn't helping.'

'You think?' Anabel giggles.

'Whatever. Screw him. Anyway, tell you everything laters,' I say. 'Gonna try to find myself a taxi. Desperately need a drink.'

'We'll call room service,' Milly laughs. 'Stock up.'

'Cool. Be seeing you in a bit.'

*

Finding a taxi during a rainstorm proves challenging, but eventually one passes by, and I am dropped off outside the hotel some twenty minutes later. Holding my torn dress in place, I saunter innocently across the lobby, barely attracting more than a courteous nod and a 'Goodnight' from the reception staff.

Up on our floor, I make for my friends' room with a euphoric sense of relief. Bleary-eye tired and a little drunk, I fumble for a moment with their spare key card, before finally letting myself into their room. Both are sitting in the armchairs near the window. Two half-empty champagne flutes and a bottle of Prosecco occupy the small round table between them. Milly is in her pale-blue pyjamas, Anabel a fluffy white hotel bathrobe.

'Oh my God. I'm so glad you're safe,' Milly cries, rushing towards me. She throws her arms around me and squeezes me in a tight hug, unfazed to come away soaked. 'We were so worried.'

'Yeah, so was I for a bit there,' I choke, surprised by the intensity of her embrace. 'Tonight was a little sporty, if I'm being honest.'

'Did they hurt you?' Milly asks, her voice a little slurred. A glance at the Prosecco bottle shows it's three-quarters gone.

Setting the empty Talisker on the sideboard, I reply, 'Thankfully no, but they certainly wanted to.' I'd like to think I sound completely sober and lucid. That much whisky, however, and I know that's probably not the case.

'I can't believe it,' she gasps, her face a creased mask of concern.

'Milly, you know why I love you so much?' I say with amusement. 'Because even now, after everything, this stuff still shocks you.'

'Oh my God, is that blood?' she asks, peering at me in alarm.

'Yes, but not mine – thankfully.'

'What happened?'

'You don't wanna know,' I reply as I step into their bathroom to wipe the last flecks clean.

'Is this going to be a police problem?' Anabel asks.

'Who knows? Laws are basically guidelines at this point. Not sure I really want to dwell on it right now. Maybe tomorrow?'

As I return to their room, my eyes drift to their open bottle and then down to my hand, which is still trembling slightly.

'I could seriously do with some of that right now.'

'I'm so glad you're alive,' Milly gushes, rushing to fetch the bottle for me. As she returns, she notices the torn dress. 'Oh dear,' she says, examining the long tear. Peeling the fabric aside, she checks for any injury. As she delves around inside the ripped material, her fingers lightly graze the side contour of my chest, sending a surprisingly wanton charge through me. I hold still, hoping it might happen again. But it doesn't. Instead, she steps back and hands me the bottle.

'Don't stop. That felt nice,' I laugh, before flushing with embarrassment that I said it out loud. Quickly, I take several long pulls from the bottle, emptying it.

Looking up with a sympathetic smile, Milly rises to tiptoes and plants an unexpected kiss on my lips. Hurriedly, she pulls back, leaving me frozen in surprise. No words come. My brain stalls, unsure how best to react. Sensing little obvious objection, and clearly emboldened by the alcohol coursing through her, she leans in and her lips make contact with mine again. But this time they linger longer, full and embracing of my mouth. Time slows and the turmoil in my mind falls away, leaving a simple clarity about my own mortality, time and living a life with no regrets.

'What are you doing?' I ask softly, slowly pulling away. It's a question of curiosity and not, I notice, of rebuke. With a smile and an amused shake of her head, Anabel removes another bottle of Prosecco from the fridge, which looks surprisingly well stocked, and hands it to me, apparently unfazed by what just happened.

'Here,' she says. 'Reckon we could all use some of this. Especially you.'

'Yeah, you may be right,' I laugh. With a swift twist, I strip off the wrapper and pop the cork, before filling a spare glass from the sideboard. I top each of theirs up to the rim.

'I'm so sorry,' Milly stammers awkwardly, her reaction comically delayed, as I hurriedly empty my glass. 'I'm sorry. Don't be mad at me. Please!'

'Hey, I'm not mad,' I assure her. 'Not by any length. Just surprised is all. But after the night I've had, honestly, who cares anymore?'

I refill my glass again. It, too, is emptied quickly.

'I couldn't help it,' she stammers, glancing back apologetically at Anabel. Turning to me, she stresses, 'I don't know why I did it.'

'Yeah, okay,' I reply absentmindedly as a third glass quickly follows the others.

'And you don't mind?' she enquires, bracing herself for the rejection she clearly still expects.

'You know,' I say, licking my lips with considered reflection. 'It actually kinda compliments you, this stuff does, like strawberries.'

Anabel takes the glass from me, has a long sip, hands it back and then turns to Milly, kissing her fully on the mouth.

'You're right,' she exclaims, pulling back. 'It does. Oh, wait. I already knew that.'

With a smirk, I toss the remaining sparkling wine into my mouth.

'I don't know about you two, but either I'm actually getting pissed, really quickly, or I'm getting the distinct feeling we're about to stumble headfirst into an interesting situation.'

'You sense it, too?' Anabel asks playfully, turning to me with a curious smile. She gazes questioningly into my eyes with an expression that bubbles with unspoken intent. The atmosphere shifts. And dramatically so. We all feel it, as if we've suddenly become connected by an invisible electric charge. I empty the last of the freshly opened bottle into my glass and quickly tip it back down my throat.

'I think I need another one of these.'

'Oh God,' Milly says, clearly taking her signal from Anabel. 'How the hell are we going to deal with this tomorrow morning?'

'Who gives a toss about tomorrow morning?' I mutter darkly, placing the glass with deliberate emphasis onto the sideboard. 'I figure every day that rolls around from now on is pretty much a gift. And I intend to live each like it's my last. So, screw next morning guilt-trips. Screw other people's rules. Screw all that crap!'

'You know, I was kind of hoping you'd say that,' Anabel says. Stepping in front of me, she gently pushes me by the shoulders, easing me down onto the edge of the bed.

'Jesus?' Milly whispers, wide-eyed. 'I thought you were joking!'

'Just having some fun, babe,' Anabel replies with a shrug. 'No harm done. Besides, she's right. Life's too short to be lived by other people's rules. Go with it. One night only, I promise.'

'Maybe best you get another bottle, then,' I mumble to Milly. 'Because this is going to be so wrong on so many levels.'

Evidently well practiced by now, she quickly has another one open and hurriedly takes a long series of gulps. We each drink heavily from it, before passing it on.

Bending forward at the hips, Anabel seductively pushes me down across the bed. I offer no resistance and fall backwards, watching them with interest as they both drink deeply from the bottle, before kissing, swilling the sparkling wine back and forth between their mouths before swallowing.

Smiling, Anabel tosses her head back, opens her enormous fluffy white bathrobe and lets it fall to the floor. She evidently wasn't planning on going out again tonight. I swallow hard, barely believing what is happening as she slowly climbs onto the bed and crawls towards me on all fours, all the while holding my gaze. My heart is hammering so hard it is almost impairing my ability to breathe properly.

Somewhere, deep in that most primal part of my brain, whatever still passes for rational thought scrambles to apply some logic to what is happening amidst the rapidly hazing fog of alcohol and its accompanying 'screw it' attitude. How can this possibly be okay? No good answer presents itself. And, frankly, the more I think about it and the more the alcohol takes effect, the less I care.

Grinning, Anabel begins drawing the tattered dark-blue silk dress slowly up my thighs. Behind her, Milly slips my silver high heels off and drops them with muffled thuds to the floor.

'Now what?' I ask, my voice choking awkwardly.

'I'm going to take your knickers off,' Anabel whispers matter-of-factly.

Instinctively, I reach down and blurt out, 'No, you're fucking not! That's way too fast.'

'Oh yes, I am,' she replies, calm and evenly. 'And I know you want me to. You've been intrigued ever since the flight over, haven't you?'

'How did you…?'

'She was watching?' Milly gasps in horror, flushing red with embarrassment.

'Of course she was,' says Anabel. 'And earlier, too, when we were in the shower.'

'But she's not –' Milly notes, cautiously taking Anabel's arm.

'Right now she is,' Anabel replies confidently. Her gaze doesn't waver from mine. In these few fleeting seconds, I realise how well she understands me.

'Curiosity's all she needs to get past whatever boundaries she has. And right now, she's seriously curious. Aren't you?' she whispers softly in my ear. 'She's craving something crazy. Name your cliché. A new lust for life. Maybe a desire for some boundary-expanding experience. Whatever. Maybe it's because of a history of crappy boyfriends, or bad sex. Just look at her. She's riding one big adrenaline high right now, and the booze isn't hurting, either. She'd probably go base-jumping off one of those silly tall towers out there if she could. I'll bet you this isn't even sexual for her. Just a massive rush, and right now that's what she needs. It'll keep the trauma of tonight at bay long enough for her coping mechanisms to kick in properly. Otherwise she's on her way to PTSD land. My professional opinion…' she concludes with a bemused smile. 'Just give in to it.'

'I don't even know how you came up with all that, half sloshed as you are,' I say. 'But it sounded good.'

'Sloshed maybe, but not ruined,' Anabel smirks. 'Not yet anyway.'

She reaches back for the bottle of Prosecco and takes several further glugs of it, all the while keeping her eyes locked firmly on mine. Licking her lips, she hands the bottle back to Milly, who quickly drains more of it.

'Besides, I want to see,' she says. 'So, last chance. Want to have some fun?'

'Yeah, I'm not a fucking nun, you know,' I counter, before taking a deep breath. 'Well, go on, then. Pull 'em off.'

Leaning forwards, Anabel embraces me with a deep, messy kiss that's tinged with sparkling wine. Both girls laugh.

'Oh my God, we're actually going to do this?' Milly exclaims with a hiccup. Despite her reservations, I detect a flicker of excitement in her eyes. 'This is such a bad idea,' she says, hiccupping again, which is then followed by a peel of laughter.

'*Please*,' I exclaim, grinning at Anabel. 'This is like so *way* beyond a bad idea!'

'Shall we stop?' Milly asks.

'No.'

'Why not?'

'Because it has no future.'

'So…?'

'So, we have nothing to lose.'

'Carpe diem, babe,' Anabel whispers.

Taking one last deep pull on the rapidly emptying bottle to steady her nerves, Milly curses in disbelief and then she, too, climbs onto the bed in her pyjamas. With hooked fingers, they snare the thin waist string on both sides of my underwear, and together they pull. Hoisting myself, I help them to drag the flimsy material down my legs, before Milly tosses it over her shoulder. Flipping the loose silk dress up past my hips, Anabel clasps my knees and slowly pries them apart with a wide grin. It would be futile to try to protect my modesty; there's none left.

Light-headed, mind spinning, almost dizzy, I close my eyes and flop my head back onto the bed. My heart pounds fiercely and I let out a short, involuntary gasp as I feel the first confident touch of someone's fingers. Fingers that clearly know what they are doing. With a sharp intake of breath, I grip the thick, down-filled duvet and sigh pleasurably with a release of tension.

'I know what'll make this more fun,' Anabel says with a smile as she slips nimbly off the bed. She pads across to check the blackout blinds are fully closed, then heads towards the front door to flick the master light switch, turning off the room's main lights, leaving just those in the bathroom on. Then she hurriedly returns to the bed, picks up one of the airline's blindfolds from the bedside table and turns off the lamp there. I feel the mattress dip as she climbs back onto the enormous king-size bed. At which point she slips the blindfold over my eyes, pitching me into a world of darkness, one where every sound and touch is amplified.

No longer able to tell who is doing what, I give in to wanton desire and abandon all my prior cares, hesitations and inhibitions as I am silently eased up into a sitting position. I feel someone unzip the dress behind me, slowly and with determination. Warm hands snake inside the fabric, grazing lightly across my skin and running down over my stomach. The ruined dress is quickly hauled up over my head and pulled from my outstretched arms. My lace bra is tugged up, freeing me from the constraints of the lingerie. Deft fingers unclip it, and I find myself suddenly exposed, more naked and vulnerable than I have ever felt before. But equally, I have never felt so excited or alive, either. My heart hammers as they embrace me hungrily with their wanting mouths.

'Jesus, are you both naked?'

Neither answers.

I can't help but smile. So this is how it's going to be, is it? Silent, anonymous and unattributable. On reflection, perhaps that may be for the best.

The girl sitting before me, whose identity I actually don't want to know, bends to kiss my bare chest again. At first, she just nuzzles, but then she comes in harder with her teeth. I gasp and let out small, appreciative moans. Emboldened, I reach out and pull her closer, relishing the feel of her warm, soft skin against mine. My hands stray over the unidentified body, exploring in tentative curiosity.

Any lingering doubts whether we should stop finally drift from my mind like the last faint wisps of smoke in a breeze. Instead, I give myself wholly to the experience.

Someone crawls behind me and edges in closer to wrap her legs around me. Feel alone is not enough to gauge who it is, but as she squashes herself up against my back, I try to dispel the suspicion that it could well be Anabel. Breathing softly millimetres from my neck, she gently blows against my ear and reaches around me with both hands. Her fingertips graze lightly across my skin and drift down over my stomach to come to a gentle rest cupping my groin. I am frozen, my entire focus on the sensuous touch of her hands and the light pressure of her fingertips. Their presence resonates through me as I realise that little else could quite so emphatically ram home just how far I have strayed from my comfort zone than the feel of another girl's hands between my legs. Mind blown, all I can think of is to reciprocate. So, with my right hand I tentatively reach back behind me. The reaction is electric and spontaneous, bringing an excited little gasp beside my ear.

'I'm so turned on.' I whisper, but again neither responds.

Rather, the girl behind me moves away and comes around to kneel before me, beside her girlfriend. Both lower themselves, straddling my outstretched thighs. I can sense what they are doing from their movements alone. The soft, wet sounds of their kissing and the gentle movement of their mutual masturbation simply fuels my own growing excitement.

Their bodies rub against mine. My tongue probes deeply into whoever's mouth presents itself and I suck hard on their tongues as they swirl around inside my mouth. Someone takes my right hand and places it between their legs.

Anabel was right. This is not explicitly sexual for me, even though it clearly is. But perhaps not on an identity level. Maybe that's just a newly liberated mind's way of thinking. But this feels grown-up and dangerous. Taboo and forbidden, even. An overwhelming urgency carries me along on the hedonistic headwinds and I increase the rhythmic movements of my right hand against whoever's genitals I've found myself caressing. More than anything, I want to know what it feels like to make someone climax.

It is not long before I'm rewarded by a low, muffled groan and a shivery tremble. For the first time, I realise just how similar they both sound when talking quietly. Perhaps it's good they are almost indistinguishable. The girl kissing me breaks off as her girlfriend's body jerks and bears down upon my hand, sandwiching it firmly against my thigh. Burying her face into my shoulder, she pants and moans hard against me as I increase my movements, bring her to a shuddering release. Powerful contractions grind down upon me as she rides the waves of pleasure convulsing through her.

I hold her tight as she heaves and gasps. Her breath is hot and urgent, her body noticeably sweaty. My heart pounds harder and faster, or is it hers? I can't tell. Taking my face in her hands, she bends to kiss me.

'God, that was amazing,' I moan softly.

'Our turn,' one of them whispers almost inaudibly into my ear. I am pushed backwards onto the bed as they reposition themselves on either side of me.

Someone's fingers move with a feather light touch down my forehead, tracing along the bridge of my nose, before brushing lightly over my lips and over the sensitive skin of my neck. From there they flitter down my sternum to my stomach and lower still, with a definite destination in mind. It's such a small distance, yet such a big journey – especially for me. The hand finally stops moving once it is cupping my quim. There it remains, still for a few seconds, as I find myself forgetting to breathe. Then, another hand is placed atop the first, and I feel their fingers entwine together, circling lightly for a moment, before one, then a second slip in, embarrassingly easily. Groaning, I arch my back, thrusting my hips forward invitingly, and my initially nervous gasps quickly turn to excited cries as four hands and at least one mouth find their target. Breathing deeply, I stop fighting the most incredible erotic sensation I've ever felt.

Time ceases to have relevance as each new experience tops the last. My chest heaves as one of them moves from between my legs to embrace me fully on the lips. I respond with equal vigour, deliberately not shrinking away from the taste in her mouth but, rather, eagerly savouring it. At the same time, my other friend moves in to scissor me. It feels good – really good – and within seconds I am writhing up against her equally sluiced groin in short, frenzied circular movements.

Laughing in wild abandonment, I roll onto my back and reach behind my knees to pull them to my chest, thrusting my groin obscenely upwards, like some kind of vulgar invitation for them to do whatever they want to me. Instantly, a hand moves in between my legs. Another comes in beneath my bottom, initially to support me. But a moment later, a daringly placed thumb elicits a deeper, more guttural groan and tips me further over the edge.

Pushing my hips higher, I maximise the potency, reach and sensation of their exploratory fingers. Someone bends forward to kiss me, while the other maintains her steady rhythm. Sensing the final stretch rapidly approaching, she pushes on, faster, harder, deeper, thrusting with genuine vigour.

'Awww, shit...' I grunt as they launch me towards my now inevitable climax, one which I can feel will be intense. They sense it, too, given the increasingly urgent bucking of my hips and my rapid panting. I can feel the predictable build-up welling inside me. Usually, it comes slowly, but this time it rises from within more explosively than normal. My hips grind involuntarily against one of their probing mouths and the other's fingers. Neither is forceful, but rather working in tandem. My pulse accelerates and my breath comes in ragged gasps. I can feel my whole body yearning for the release that is fast approaching. Suddenly, it's too late to stop. I am completely given to my impending orgasm and finally let go of my ankles, allowing my knees to bend into a more relaxed position.

'Yes... yes,' I repeatedly gasp, placing my hand on whoever's is circling between my legs, bringing their pace in line with the rhythm I need until, at last, it arrives and a raw, sexually charged cry bursts from my mouth.

'Oh *fuucckk, yes!*'

The girl kissing me giggles and pulls away as the power of my orgasm crashes through me, jerking my body with a release that is almost painful, rendering me momentarily unable to speak. I have never experienced anything so powerful, and lose all control of my body. An alarming, warm, sopping gush comes between my legs. It is unlike anything I have ever felt before, and my body shakes, locked up in a convulsion that racks me from head to foot. Shuddered, I groan into one of their panting, frantic, wanting mouths.

I love it and yet, at the same time, want it to stop. It's too much. I push an invasive hand away from between my legs, but not before my body is wracked by another intense explosion of pleasure. I shake and tremble and groan and roll away sideways into one of their bodies, still shuddering as the sensation pulses though me. They both hold me as I try to control the contractions within. One wraps their legs around me, hugging me tightly. The other does the same, but from behind. And there I lie, enveloped in their limbs until my climax finally subsides. For a lingering moment, I still feel as if it isn't finished, and as though I remain on the verge of the precipice, ready to fall right back in if only I were touched again. But thankfully no one moves, allowing my breathing to come back under control and my body to regain some degree of equilibrium as I feel the descent begin. We lie still, and I focus on the pounding of my heart – this time definitely mine – feeling more alive in this torrid, sweaty tangle than ever before.

Finally, I pull off the blindfold and lie, unmoving, for a long, drawn-out moment as rational thought slowly returns and the full realisation of what just happened comes crashing in around me. I blink a few times to acclimatise to the low light and laugh to see both girls smiling down at me.

I realise this is the decision point. Reciprocating now will take this on long into the early hours of the morning.

But something holds me back, and the critical seconds pass. Before I know it, the opportunity feels gone. And in a moment of curious introspection, I realise I don't mind.

'Are you okay?' Milly asks, her demeanour suddenly slightly less confident. Perhaps she feels the same. Anabel peers comically over her shoulder, also gauging my reaction.

'Yeah,' I pant. 'Yeah, I'm good.' Then, softening my expression, I laugh and add, 'Just feel fricking shattered is all. Maybe sleep isn't such a bad idea right now.'

'I think we're pretty shattered, too,' Milly says, glancing at Anabel. 'Just crash here.'

Too tired to argue, I slump back and lie splayed across the sheets, suddenly very self-conscious. Slowly, I pull the ruffled covers up and over me. While it's true that I am tired, I just want a moment alone to my own thoughts to reflect on and process the whirlwind of emotions that have suddenly begun battling for attention within my rapidly sobering mind. And, most important of all, I need to work out how to react come tomorrow morning – when the events of tonight will have either crystallised into a happy acceptance or a monumentally crushing regret.

At the same time, something else occurs to me. If any form of retribution is to come in response to the events of earlier tonight, I don't expect them to hang around and come like good little boys in the morning with a warrant and uniformed police in tow. If anything, it will be a knock at the door at three a.m. and a bullet to the head as I answer it. Or they'll simply let themselves into my room and put three rounds into the bed. Maybe it's better, then, if I stay put here rather than returning to my own room for the rest of the night.

As I ponder my options, the other two cheekily snuggle up behind me, and Milly shuffles forward to press her softness up against my back. I curse silently, for with the sensation goes all thought of reflective contemplation. Instead, the fire of desire bursts back to life within me. Sighing in defeat, I reach back to pull her closer. Craning my head around, I smile in the darkness and pull her into a deep kiss. Several pairs of hands immediately reach out for me, and Anabel comes in over the top to join the messy three-way snog.

'Damn you both,' I mutter.

*

The last of my dream dissipates into wispy mental puffs before disappearing completely as consciousness returns slowly, and painfully.

I gingerly open one eye a little and then hurriedly scrunch it shut again and pinch the bridge of my nose as the full force of the throbbing headache properly registers. For a moment, I dare not move, for fear it will just make the pain between my eyes even worse.

Finally, mustering all the effort I can, I peer blearily at the bedside clock. It is not even seven a.m. Slivers of bright light frame the blackout blinds on both sides, allowing just enough to see by. Looking over my shoulder, I see the other two are still asleep. With a groan, I ease myself up into a sitting position and scrunch up my face as I register a pinch of discomfort from my lower abdomen. Looking down, I am mortified to realise that I somehow managed to fall asleep with someone's sex toy still in place. Even more horrifying, it appears to have run out of batteries at some point in the night. Grimacing, I delicately ease the lifeless pink and black vibrator free, and for a moment I hold it out at arm's length, between thumb and forefinger, unsure what exactly to do with it. With a groan, I drop it onto the sheet beside me.

'Ugh, I am never drinking again,' I mutter dryly.

After slipping delicately out of bed, lest I wake them, I gather up a discarded bathrobe from the floor and tiptoe towards my friends' bathroom. There, I take a hydration tablet from Milly's washbag and let it dissolve in a glass of water. Appalled at the colour of my pee, I follow the first glass with several more from the tap.

Quietly, I poke my head back into the bedroom and see neither of them has moved, despite the refilling cistern. Both remain sprawled out, face down, legs entwined, with what little modesty they retain afforded only by some fortuitously strewn covers.

Mindful not to wake them, I collect my clothes, shoes, bag, watch and phone, all of which are littered around the room, and quietly let myself out. The Birkin I leave on the sideboard, near the TV. As I return to my room for a shower, I can't help but smile ruefully at how GC described this city. A morally corrosive environment. Guess that depends on what your moral baseline is. One thing's for sure, though, it is certainly boundary breaking.

*

'Jesus, at last…' I exclaim well over an hour later as my friends approach the breakfast table and sheepishly sit down.

'Hi,' Milly croaks weakly, removing her sunglasses, before quickly thinking better of it and replacing them. For a moment, neither speaks. Both shift awkwardly, unsure what to say.

'Wow, what's got into you two? Oh, wait, don't answer that,' I say, drumming my fingers emphatically on the tablecloth. Laughing at my own poor-taste joke, I reach for my coffee cup and drain it, before catching the waiter's attention and signalling my need for another refill.

'Oh, God, don't tell me you're embarrassed!'

Both look away evasively.

'You are! Wow, okay, so look... If I'm going to be honest, it's all I've been thinking about this morning, you know, like, since I woke up. And honestly, there's no other way to say this, but last night was fun. It was. So, relax. There's no recrimination coming from me, if that's what you're worried about. Same situation, I'd do it all over again. No regrets. Oh yeah, thanks,' I say, tapping the tabletop with two fingers as a waitress refills my coffee. 'See, you taught me to do that,' I say, looking at Anabel. 'The whole emperor's table tap thing.'

'You're serious, aren't you?' Milly whispers.

'Yes,' I reply, straight faced and earnest. 'Mills, why wouldn't I be? Trust me, I've had awkward mornings-after before – okay, well, maybe one – but believe me, this isn't one of them. Even if a few hours ago, my answer might have been seriously different.'

'Easy for you to say,' Anabel replies, finally revealing a properly glum expression. Frowning, she slumps in her chair, shoulders sagging. 'You didn't seduce one of your best friends and risk everything you treasure in the process.'

Pausing, she casts a wary, apologetic glance at Milly, who sits, fidgeting idly with her fingers, either upset or mortifyingly embarrassed. Possibly both.

'Okay, listen up, both of you,' I say softly, setting my coffee cup down with a sigh. 'Feel free to tell me I have absolutely no idea what I'm talking about. But I've got a pretty good imagination, so hear me out. Yeah, look, I get how you might feel this morning. Probably dreading that our friendship is ruined. That maybe your relationship is, too. And you know what? Under normal circumstances I should probably also be questioning my sexuality right about now. But I'm not. I don't regret anything that happened last night. And I don't think our friendship has been torpedoed by it, either.

'In fact,' I add as I raise my cup and take another long sip, 'I think it's actually strengthened it. I honestly don't think you could possibly care more for another person than someone with whom you've shared an experience like that. Ironically, if anyone should be dreading facing anyone today, it's probably me facing myself. But weirdly, no. Seriously, this shouldn't be causing you half the distress it clearly is. Now, I can't speak for what you both have, you know, like, as partners, but if you're beating yourselves up for giving in to something we all clearly wanted, alcohol aside, then it seems stupid to regret it now. I mean, sure, the booze probably didn't help, and if you want to say it's something you don't ever want to repeat again, well, that's fine. But don't let it spoil what you have.'

Leaning forward, I quietly add, 'Look, I don't know about you two, but last night was a crazy high unlike anything I've ever experienced. I have never felt so connected with anyone else as I did then. And I'm totally fine knowing it was a one-night-only kind of thing, if that's what it turns out to be. But if I can deal with it, then you both really should be able to, too.'

Sighing, they turn to face each other. With shrugs and sheepish smiles, they share a hug and turn to me with evident relief written all over their faces.

'Well, that was frickin' easy,' I exclaim, clapping my hands together. 'I thought I was going to have to employ some of Belle's psycho-babble talk to get you both over the line. But seriously, let's not be walking emotional clichés, shall we? It was incredible. But yeah, we move on. However, you,' I say, laughing at Milly, 'you're Catholic. So, you're definitely going to hell for last night.'

'Oh, shut up,' she giggles, coming around to smack me on the arm.

'Oh, meant to ask,' Anabel says. 'There's a Hermès handbag still in our room. That yours?'

'Ah, not exactly,' I reply with an evasive smile. 'Honestly, it's kind of inappropriate for me to keep it, so I don't want it, and I don't have the receipt, either, so I can't sell it. So, either of you want a Birkin?'

'As lovely as it is, it's not really my style,' Milly says.

'You being serious?' Anabel blurts out, biting her bottom lip in excitement.

'Absolutely. Consider it yours. Just don't ask where I got it, and you can't sell it, okay? Best pack it, and don't use it here in Honk on this trip, okay?'

'Okay. I can do that. Yeah, probably best I don't know where you got it. Don't want to spoil it.'

'Right, well, that's sorted, then. Best get yourselves some breakfast,' I add. 'We've got a mental day of espionage ahead of us, here in this crazy city. First, we need to go find GC as a matter of serious urgency.'

As they make their way towards the breakfast buffet, I slump back and exhale with relief. On balance, my performance met the needs of the hour. Having the team fall apart now would be a disaster. And frankly, I love them both too much to let a questionable drunk decision ruin everything. As they gather their food, my mind regresses to the introspective turmoil that has plagued me since I awoke. Sleeping with anyone, let alone my friends, was the absolute last thing on my mind, and yet somehow the unimaginable happened. Far from the calm air of indifference which I tried to project, I have no idea what to think now. Part of what I said wasn't a lie: it genuinely was fun... at the time. But in the clear light of morning, the ramifications of having sex with my two best friends threaten to overwhelm me, and that's the last thing I need right now.

It's amazing how every time I think I have myself sussed out, something happens that makes me realise everything I thought I knew was naïve rubbish, and that I actually have no idea what I am doing. Worse still is that with every perceived leap in maturity comes a spirit-crushing realisation of what an idiot I was beforehand. As I watch them return to the table, considerably more relaxed than when they first walked in, I know two things for sure. Firstly, I have a lot of soul-searching to do when this is all over. Because right now I feel like I know less about myself than ever before. And secondly, I am really never drinking again...

CHAPTER 14

AFFIRMATIVE ACTION
Hong Kong

As we meander along the mountainside road, I find myself curiously oblivious to our picturesque surroundings, so deep in thought am I about whether it was a subconscious decision of mine to sit in the taxi's front passenger seat rather than in the back with my friends. It perturbs me if it was. Suddenly, Anabel lunges forward, rousing me from my introspection, and points vigorously at the entrance which we are about to overshoot.

'*Ai yah! Hai lido, m'goy. Mm-ah-sam Sitúbá Dào!*' she exclaims in exasperation.

Sighing, the driver brakes hard, jams on his indicator and pulls aggressively across the other lane, to accelerate up the driveway of 53 Stubbs Road. Set majestically high up on the Peak, amidst the dense jungle overlooking the city, it affords a magnificent view of Hong Kong and the gleaming harbour in the distance, where choppy waves twinkle in the dazzling sunlight.

My phone rings. It is our headmaster.

'Morning, sir,' I answer.

'Well, someone sounds in a good mood. Just checking in. Seeing how you all are.'

Puzzled, I glance at my watch and rapidly do the time conversion.

'Sir, isn't it gone midnight there? This *really* just a social call?'

'Perhaps not. Up to anything fun today?'

'Well, we're on our way to see our man in Hong Kong. We need to tell him about last night. Things got a little sporty. He was understandably less than keen to hear it's the kind of stuff you just don't say over a telephone line.'

'Oh dear. That doesn't sound good. How *sporty* are we talking? Mildly offensive or really profane?'

'Probably more the latter.'

'Oh dear.'

'Yup. All got a little unpleasant.'

'My dear girl, welcome the sharp end of the spear. We excel in elegant unpleasantness. Truth be told, there's no one I would have rather sent.'

'Aw, thanks, sir, for those few kind words,' I gush in amusement. 'That's so sweet.'

'Hmm, indeed. Do give him my regards. And call if you need anything.'

'Thanks. Will do.'

I hang up and turn to my friends with a curious expression.

'Gambon. Checking in on us,' I explain, slipping my phone back into my cargo shorts pocket as we climb from the taxi.

The irritable driver pulls the rear self-closing passenger door shut with a bang and, with screeching tires, accelerates off back down the approach road, narrowly missing an oncoming BMW.

'What's up with him, huh?' Milly exclaims.

'Him personally?' Anabel replies with a smile. 'Nothing. They're all like that. Typical local taxi driver. Part of what gives Hong Kong it's enduring charm.'

'If that's what you want to call it,' I add with a raised eyebrow as I crane my neck to admire the impressive skyline-dominating condominium that is the Opus Hong Kong.

'Wow, would you look at this place!'

Vaguely reminiscent of white reeds swaying in the wind, the helical structure climbs, gently twisting and bending around on itself as it rises. The main columns rise with it, snaking up the exterior. Each floor appears to be sheathed in glass, which serves to lighten the façade with a translucent quality.

'Can you imagine how much a place here would cost?' Milly comments, whistling in wonder.

'Well, if I remember right,' says Anabel, 'I think the CG's pad is worth something like three hundred and eighty-odd million dollars. That's Hongky dollars, before you have a total heart attack. But still.'

'That's thirty-five million quid,' exclaims Milly.

'Yeah, but this is Hong Kong. The property market here is completely insane. Though that was back in 2013. Think it was ranked as one of the most expensive properties in the world, the building, I mean. Topped only by One Hyde Park in Knightsbridge.'

'Yeah, tells me all I need to know,' I joke with an amazed eye-roll. 'No wonder she doesn't want this posting to go tits-up.'

As Anabel heads for the lobby, Milly stops and turns with a concerned expression.

'Hey, you okay?'

'Not really,' I sigh, deflating slightly. Trying to hide my feelings from my best friend is pointless.

'Go on, talk to me,' she says. 'Is it last night?'

'Sort of. Well, yes and no. Honestly, I'm so conflicted right now, I don't know what to think.'

'Was it *that* bad?' she asks nervously.

'No,' I reply emphatically without pause. 'The opposite. It was amazing. I didn't want it to stop. I want more and more. I want to lose myself in it.'

'Are you lost?' she asks, fixing me with a quizzical look. 'Because I don't think you are.'

'I don't know. I mean, I was in half a mind to try and go back to that bar and see if I could find that pretty barmaid. So, you tell me, am I lost?'

'The chick with a…?' she giggles, eyeing me with newfound intrigue, before tossing her head back in laughter. 'Ha, does that excite you?' she cries, wiping tears from her eyes. 'Okay, I'm sorry. Seriously now. No, I don't think you're lost. I just think you're finally breaking out of all the expectations society has put on you. And you're starting to see it's fun, and that experimenting a bit is fine. Helps that the boundaries here are less clearly defined. Shame most people don't experience that. It's liberating, right?'

'Maybe a little too liberating. I mean –'

'Hey, you won't find any judgement coming from me. I kind of think this city is doing you some good,' she says, playfully patting me on the shoulder. 'And in case you were wondering, you always know where we are,' she sings airily, before skipping off happily behind Anabel towards the entrance. Smiling in disbelief at how this city is affecting all of us, I tail her into the lobby.

Nodding politely at the smartly uniformed doorman as he holds the door open, I thank him, before commenting under my breath to myself, 'See, not so hard to say thank you.'

Having only been here a few days, we quickly noticed how few people will ever acknowledge your having held a door open for them. And I'm not even a man.

After we sign the visitors' book at the plush reception, we are escorted through to the lift lobby, from where a member of building security escorts us up to the third floor. With a soft, melodic chime, the mirrored doors swish open to reveal a wonderfully lavish yet tastefully decorated whitewashed apartment.

'No way this place is less than five thousand square feet,' Anabel whistles with a hint of envy.

'So, wait, let me get this straight,' I say, holding her back. 'Our consul general lives in a multi-million-pound, five-thousand-square-foot apartment –'

'Might even be slightly bigger than that,' she says, peering into the living room with a scrutinising gaze.

'We are so in the wrong business,' Milly giggles. 'C'mon, you two. Look serious, and not like a bunch of gawping tourists.'

The apartment offers breath-taking views out across the city, the harbour and the New Territories beyond, which stretch on towards China, some thirty miles away to the north. Like each of the dozen or so four-bedroom apartments in the condo, the CG's occupies a single floor all to itself. From where we are standing, we can see left and right through into the adjacent living spaces, which gently curl back around on themselves to form an oblong-shaped layout. Lashings of wood trim complement the assorted sculptures and paintings which dot the apartment. Wrap-around floor-to-ceiling windows make it feel like the whole building is one huge viewing gallery. Each living space has its own balcony, all of which connect to encircle the condo.

I walk towards the nearest window and look down to see that directly below the consul general's are two duplex apartments, each with its own garden and pool.

'Damn. Would you look at this,' I mouth to my friends. 'Seriously, why would Styles not stay here if he had the option? I sure as hell would.'

'Is a bit far from Central,' Anabel suggests. 'Maybe he wanted to be closer to things.'

'Bars and clubs?' I ask dubiously. 'I mean, after what the girl last night said...'

'Yeah, maybe,' Milly says, looking past me. 'It's getting a little windy out there. Trees are swaying pretty badly up on the Peak.'

'Yeah,' Anabel notes casually. 'They think there's a storm on its way, later today most likely. But it's hard to predict. They can just veer off in another direction at the last minute. We can check again at lunch.'

Nodding, Milly picks up a newspaper from the dining room table and begins reading.

'What's gone wrong in the world?' I ask, peering back out the window.

'Loads, it seems.' She reads out a headline concerning the England football team's defeat in the European finals last night.

'Scenes of chaos were witnessed as hundreds of ticketless fans laid siege to the stadium in a bid to break through turnstiles and gain access to the match. Despite a heavy police presence, security was unprepared for the orgy of violence that ensued. Stewards were assaulted, barriers ripped open, and invaders surged into corporate boxes, evicting the well-heeled occupants into corridors and adjacent aisles.

'Once the match was all said and done, and England the victim, again, to an unfavourable penalty shoot-out, what followed was a sickening descent into outright racist abuse of England's ethnic players, on whose shoulders fans laid the blame for their side's defeat. The ensuing violence that spilled out into the streets of West London was nothing short of unprecedented as pitched street battles were fought with the police. Twenty-five officers and three horses were badly injured. The damage to property is expected to amount to hundreds of thousands to many millions of pounds. The damage to Britain's reputation and hopes of hosting the World Cup in years to come now look severely tarnished.

'It was delusional, wishful thinking that football might somehow unite a country so fundamentally divided along such glaring social and structural fault lines. Additionally, the winning of a sports tournament, no matter how close the sport to the nation's heart, could never be a substitute for education, decency and morality, not to mention the genuine leadership so glaringly lacking of late.

'Calls quickly followed from Westminster, where even members of the prime minister's own party called for him to take the necessary action,' she concludes. 'Oh, listen to what Forbes had to say. He's quoted as having said that the time has come for a reckoning of all those for whom racism and thuggery have become an everyday and accepted part of life. We must take a long, hard, careful look at ourselves as a nation, and ask what is wrong with us and –'

'Okay, what's this all about?' George says, interrupting Milly's flow as he enters the room, with the consul general following just behind him. She looks marginally less stressed than he does, but not by much.

'It's been a fairly interesting day so far,' she begins. 'Seems George has lost an intelligence officer, and that's only the half of it.'

'Yeah, well, I may be able to help you with that,' I reply, casually looking out the window at the breath-taking view. 'Because unless someone let him out of a certain industrial meat locker, I think it's safe to assume he's dead.'

George stops abruptly in the middle of the living room and stares at me.

'Excuse me? And why would he be in a freezer?'

'Because I locked him in there.'

'Care to explain?'

'Well, not to be too blunt about it, but he and his Chinese intelligence friends – for whom he's been working all along, you should know – thought it would be a laugh and a half to kidnap me and torture everything I know out of me.'

'Good Christ,' the CG splutters, her face going white as the damning ramifications of her favoured man being an enemy agent sink in. 'What did they want to know?'

'They seemed kind of keen to know what we knew about the dirty little plot they're hatching to bring this city to heel, Madam Consul General.'

'They...?' she enquires with a raised eyebrow.

'Yeah, Sam was working with Chinese intelligence and local Triads,' Anabel adds.

'Damn...' George mouths as he sinks onto a plush sitting room chair. 'That traitorous little turd.'

'When you say "his friends", who exactly are we talking about, and where are they now?' the CG asks, taking a seat beside George.

'Triads mostly, ma'am. Can't be sure. But one smelled like a handler. There was also a special ops guy we know is associated with the PLA. But anyway, they're all dead,' I reply, smothering an inappropriate little laugh. 'Well, all except for the PLA man. He left early.'

'How many of them were there?' she presses.

'Er, ten. Wait, no, sorry. Twelve, maybe. And Sam and his PLA girlfriend, too.'

'Fourteen!' she exclaims, casting a wary look at her colleague. 'And they are all dead? Who are you?'

'C told me not to ask that question,' George quips dryly.

'I think you should all take a seat,' the consul general suggests, a newfound gravitas in her voice. She gestures us to the sofa. There, we begin outlining what we have been up to since our arrival, only three days ago. We describe how we accidentally stumbled upon the clandestine meeting in the China Club, after Anabel recognised senior

PLA leadership figures. The adults, to their credit, remain silent, allowing us to cover everything that happened up until my arrival at the meat packaging warehouse late the previous night.

'Honestly, I think it's best you stop there,' the consul general advises. 'This is for George to handle now. He can decide when and on what to brief me. Till then, I and the consulate retain plausible deniability in this matter, which I expect to be very much of interest to the Hong Kong police.'

'If it was an intelligence operation, there's a good chance it'll get brushed under the carpet,' George ponders aloud. 'However, that one of their officers was involved could potentially make this a problem.'

'Well, the coroner would have to identify them first, which could be a little problematic, because I kind of piled all the bodies up and set fire to them,' I add with a shrug. 'That has to add at least a few days on to the identification process, right?'

'I don't know whether to laugh or cry,' the CG says. 'But regardless, I think it best that none of you remain in the city for any longer than you absolutely must. And especially you, Heather.'

'Styles has a day and a half left here,' Milly observes.

'Which is a day and a half longer than I'm comfortable,' the CG replies.

'Ma'am, perhaps best leave it with me,' George offers reassuringly.

'Excellent. Very happy with that idea. Now, could you all kindly sod off? I am expecting the consul general from Pakistan for Sunday brunch. Best he doesn't see my head of station and a bunch of teenagers camped out in my living room.'

Turning to face me, she adds, 'And by God, I have no desire to be seen socialising with you, my dear. Not after what I fear last night entailed.'

'Yeah, it's hard not to take that slightly personally.'

'Don't misunderstand me, I think you're lovely –'

'Princess Stephanie said much the same a few days ago,' Milly chimes in.

'Well, aren't you lucky. Most barely get noticed,' the CG notes, smiling as she shoos us from the room, just as the intercom buzzer goes.

'Lyn! Lyn, he's here,' she shouts at someone we can't see, presumably elsewhere in the apartment. 'My helper,' she explains. 'How did we ever survive without them? I wish you the best of luck. I really do. Let's just hope our paths don't cross again.' With that, she rushes off into the apartment.

*

'A right bloody mess this is shaping up to be,' George says, clearly bemused, as we take a seat on several loungers up on the thirteenth-floor pool level. Going up was preferable to going down, where we could have accidentally bumped into the Pakistani CG.

If the view from the third-floor apartment was impressive, then the vista of the sprawling city from up here is extraordinary. Besides us, there is no one else on the curving communal rooftop, nor in the several kidney-shaped infinity pools which are arranged around it.

'What do you think we should do?' Milly asks. 'If the authorities are aware of what happened, it's only a matter of time, right, before they come for us?'

'Well, look, don't forget,' says Anabel, 'even if they do know, this will be seen as a huge loss of face. They took one Western girl for questioning, and what? Somehow, she managed to lay waste to a dozen armed local Triads and cook them in a freezer. Now, I may be wrong, but I reckon that woman's boss may take a while to report this, to give him- or herself a bit of time to get their story to a better place.'

'You may well be right,' George nods. 'Or they'll simply lie and brush over the Triad bit. Either way, it's messy. But it buys us a bit of time... perhaps. Nevertheless, the CG's not wrong. It's best to assume that time is not on our side. We need to blow a hole in whatever their intentions are, and fast. I think you should go back and review whatever footage you have from the North Korean's room. Bring anything you find of interest to me. At the same time, we need to work out who these people are, the ones causing all the trouble. Look into the residence on the Peak. Start turning over stones. There must be something.'

'What about Styles?' asks Anabel.

'Him I don't know about,' George sighs. 'Don't suppose it would hurt to firm up what he's really up to here, given how he's been behaving. But this lot worry me more. Why meet at the China Club? It makes no sense. You have an entire garrison building or numerous government facilities at your disposal, any of which would be ideal for a clandestine meeting. The bit that worries me is if they met there deliberately so that no one from their *own* side would know. That puts this whole thing in a very different and far more concerning light. Because it would suggest that this little group have essentially gone rogue and are now writing their own tickets. The prospect of that kind of semi-rogue black ops group doing something stupid just to bring an end to all these protests and win favour from their masters back in Beijing trumps the potentially suspicious behaviour of a lone cabinet minister, whatever the minister of defence thinks. Any questions?'

None of us say anything.

'Good. I imagine this is not what you expected when they said, go to Hong Kong, follow a member of the cabinet, see what he's up to. But look, I honestly have no idea who you three really are – you especially, blondie. Apparently, the chief knows you personally. And by your account, you single-handedly neutralised a dozen Triads. A group whom, if you excuse my French, don't tend to fuck around. Now, I've met my fair share of Special Forces types. I've even met a few from E Squadron once. But I've never met someone who could take out that many heavily armed assailants without so match as a scratch. That puts you into what I'd call a rather niche bracket, if you don't mind my saying so. Now, I'm pretty sure I don't have the necessary clearance to know a whole lot more, but I sure am curious.'

I flick a glance at Milly and Anabel, both of whom look as incredulous as I am. Then we all burst into laughter.

'Don't worry, George,' I say consolingly. 'We'll be sure to give you a call as soon we know anything of interest.' Rising, I add, 'Just keep your phone on.'

*

Shoes and flip-flops kicked off in the hallway, we rush into my hotel room. Turning, I curse and dash back to the bathroom to wash my hands, like Anabel is doing.

'Mills, you gonna set up your computer?'

'Doing it now,' she calls back.

'Come wash your hands first,' Anabel shouts. 'You know how filthy this city is?'

'I know, I know,' Milly wails. 'Com-ing.'

With the laptop up and running, and hands all cleaned to Anabel's fastidious standards, Milly opens the secure-access portal and connects to the incoming feed from the device that's still transmitting from the side of the ICC.

'We've got all of last night, and then also this morning,' Milly says, scrolling back and forth across the accumulated footage. 'It's still running, but looks like he's checked out. They're doing the room up now. All his stuff's gone.'

'Let's see,' I say, bending to look over her shoulder. Sure enough, there are no personal effects on the bedside table, the floor or the sideboard. 'Okay, well, go back and see what we got last night.'

Milly swiftly rewinds the footage back to the beginning. It is slightly unsettling to be watching the goings-on in someone else's hotel room. I can't help but glance around at my own window, wary for any suspicious-looking marks on it that may suggest it, too, has been bugged. Scowling, I turn back to the computer, not reassured.

'Oh, you've got to be kidding,' we blurt out in unison only a few minutes into the footage, when a chambermaid enters the room and depresses a button on the bedside table. The microphone picks up a gentle whirring and an instant later the curtains track past the lens, hiding the room from sight.

'Yeah, that was a great idea,' Anabel exclaims sarcastically.

'Ugh,' I groan, sinking into the nearby armchair, head in hands. 'I don't believe it.'

'Yeah, we probably should have thought about that one,' Milly giggles, unable to keep a straight face.

Laughing in disbelief, I ask her to fast-forward to the morning. She presses play as the curtain ritual is repeated, albeit in reverse, at exactly seven a.m.

'Okay, so he's definitely Korean,' Anabel exclaims, peering closely. 'No doubt. Look at the book on the table. That's Korean.'

'How can you be so sure?' I ask.

'You're such a gwei-mui,' she laughs.

'What does that mean again?' I whisper, leaning over towards Milly. 'Coz Sam called me that last night, too.'

'Means ghost girl, if you're being literal,' Anabel explains. 'But basically it's just used to mean a Westerner in general. Between us, though, it's a term of endearment,' she grins playfully.

'Uh-huh, not so sure I believe that. Okay, so we need to figure out who this guy is. Sam insinuated an illness might be involved in their plans. Why else would he make the mask comment? Now, whether that's true or not, check out what's on his sideboard, there.' Reaching out, I turn the laptop around and zoom in. 'Tell me those don't look like biomedical magazines.' Cocking my head sideways, I look closer, to be sure. 'Coz they sure look like it. What's the bet this guy's some sort of virus expert.'

'An epidemiologist,' Milly offers.

'Exactly. He and Yang were totally focused on learning how we knew about this guy. Sounded like he is the lynchpin to their whole plan.'

'I don't buy the whole virus thing,' Anabel says sceptically. 'Who would be nuts enough to do that?'

'Well, what if it's just the threat of a virus?' I counter. 'Maybe you don't even have to release anything. Perhaps the threat is enough? All they want is people off the streets, and not protesting, right?'

'Hey, look, maybe. But either way, what would it be?' Anabel asks.

'Search me,' I sigh. 'But people always joke about some tool going and blending smallpox with the flu. Or that COVID came from a Chinese lab and just escaped prematurely. Imagine if someone went and weaponised Parkinson's or Alzheimer's? Everyone would stay home for fear of giving it to their parents, right? Now maybe I'm wrong, and I get we need to be aware of what Gambon said about trying not to let preconceived notions influence how we view facts, but just for a second, what if that's exactly what they intend to do?'

'I'd say,' Anabel replies seriously, 'that it means this plan of theirs may not be as mandated by the central government as we think. If at all. Think about it. The Chinese Academy of Sciences, who are headquartered in Beijing, operates facilities across China, right? In lots of cities, including Wuhan.'

'As in...?'

'Yes, as in where you think the Chinese was conspiring to develop some kind of pre-emptive modern-day Typhoid Mary strike capability which you call COVID. Hmm... not sold on that. But my point is, if there was any central plan here involving a virus, especially a real one – however unlikely – wouldn't you expect an expert, or a team of them, from either the Chinese military or something like the Wuhan Institute of Virology to be involved? I mean, wouldn't you? You would, right? Instead, we have this random North Korean bod...'

'Well,' Milly sighs, 'North Korea does have one of the most offensive biological weapons programmes on the planet.

Put bluntly, this stuff is oh so much worse than nuclear or chemical weapons, which have –'

'A natural limit to their impactful range?' I chip in.

'Oh, look who was secretly playing attention in class,' Anabel exclaims. 'Precisely. Did you know four litres of anthrax, that's four coke bottles' worth, would be enough to kill every person on the planet, assuming it's properly distributed? North Korea knows its nuclear threat is limited. Anti-missile missiles, space lasers, railguns, all that stuff make nuclear missiles look really expensive and pretty unreliable. Besides, launch one and some American or British nuclear sub lurking offshore will soon turn North Korea into an irradiated wasteland in retaliation. But bioweapons… uh, well, they're something wholly different, and way scarier.'

'Worth remembering,' Milly adds, 'that Porton Down is pretty sure North Korea has smallpox, despite it having technically been eradicated back in the eighties.'

'That wouldn't even be the worst of it,' Anabel continues, pointing at me. 'As we know, advances in genetic manipulation have taken some rather large steps forward of late. And despite what was achieved seventeen years ago –'

'As special as it was,' Milly laughs, leaning in to give me a hug.

'Yeah,' Anabel agrees. 'Newer advances in genetic manipulation and germ production make pathogens a cheaper, harder-to-detect weapon which can now be designer modified. So, you want to mix smallpox and rabies, or was it the flu? Go for it. Or you want to target a group of people with a pathogen specifically tailored to infect that group, ethnic minority or section of society? Go for it. You can also tweak a pathogen, making current vaccines useless.'

'South Korean intelligence has identified at least a dozen or so facilities in North Korea that could be involved in bio research,' Milly notes. 'And defectors talk about them testing stuff on political prisoners, so they know their stuff works.'

'How are they doing this?' I ask incredulously. 'There are, like, a crap-tonne of sanctions on them.'

'They evade them,' Anabel laughs. 'They use offshore front companies, money laundering, bribes, dodgy shipping companies. You name it. They can get the gear needed, and they have, frequently. They can build a pesticide plant, for all intents and purposes, and in weeks repurpose it to make anthrax spores, or worse. Or a fish processing plant, as the case may be.'

'Okay, wait, what's he doing now?' I say, peering at the screen. 'Can you zoom in on his computer?'

'It's only a digital zoom,' Milly says. 'But I can try.'

Pinching the screen, she expands her fingers out, enlarging the North Korean's laptop screen to fill most of her own.

'He's marking locations on a map,' Anabel quickly concludes. 'Wait, let me look closer.' Peering in beside Milly, she zooms the image in and out. 'It's definitely a map of Hong Kong. Looks like most of it's on the Kowloon side.'

'What's he putting those marker pins against?' Milly asks, pointing.

'I can't be sure,' Anabel replies, playing the scene back again. 'I could be wrong, but it looks like those could be metro stations.'

'So, I once met this woman. Friend of my dad's,' I explain as I take a seat on the other side of the room's glass-topped office desk. 'She used to work for the City of New York. Half American, half Greek, I think. Virus expert. And she was talking about how they had just run a disaster simulation of people smearing anthrax onto the bottom of the handrails on the stairs of several New York subway stations. Apparently, it's an epic way of spreading a pathogen.'

'I bet it is,' Anabel adds thoughtfully. 'Given how many people pass through them, heading to all corners of the city.'

'Too right,' says Milly. 'You think that's their plan?' she asks, casting a wary look at us both.

'Chimes with what tool-boy Sam said back at the meat place, wouldn't you agree? I mean, look outside,' I say. 'You tell me a better way to get people off the streets than news breaking of some funky new virus doing the rounds. And frankly, I agree, Bell. I'm not convinced they'd do it for real. But imagine the panic if rumours started spreading that it only affects old people, or something. None of the young protesters would risk going out, for the very reasons I mentioned earlier.'

'Yeah, lot of kids and young adults here still live with their parents and grandparents,' Anabel notes thoughtfully. 'That is true.'

'Precisely. Who takes the risk to go out and protest if returning to the family home risks infecting all of them? No one.'

'Chinese government would never be that nuts,' Anabel concludes. 'They like their over-the-top language as much as anyone, but no way would they take a punt on something that could unravel and make them look like a bunch of idiots, or worse, backfire and run rampant in their own country.'

'Okay, wait, hold on a second,' Milly says, perplexed. 'Why wouldn't Sam have just told you their plan?'

'I think he was about to but the Chinese girl gave him a right look, so he shut up,' I sigh. 'The guy was a prize twat, alright. Maybe he figured it would be funny to taunt me just before I was about to die that I failed to prevent a global pandemic or something. I mean, nothing quite like making someone you hate die an even more miserable and depressing death, huh? Add the taunt of epic failure to the mix.'

'I don't disagree,' Anabel comments. 'But even though that makes perfect sense, I think it's perhaps best we not let ourselves get lulled into a false sense of security.'

'Exactly,' adds Milly. 'We should proceed on the assumption they intend to go through with the plan. Just in case.'

'No issues from me,' I smile. 'How the hell did they even come up with this? That's what I don't get.'

'Well, put yourself in the shoes of the local commanders,' Anabel continues. 'You've been given what Beijing thinks is this super-simple task. Get little, obedient Hong Kong onside. But you arrive here only to find it's anything but simple. You've got hordes of pissed-off students, a press that isn't playing ball, courts that are far from towing the line. So, you set about instituting law after law to quash all of that. But it just drives people onto the streets even more. More protests. More unrest. And every day you have someone screaming down the phone at you. "You idiot, what are you people doing down there? How can you be screwing this up so badly?".

'So, how long before you begin to turn to some pretty questionable ideas, right? How long before you've watched one too many crappy Hollywood movies and an idea like this begins to sound convincing? So, they say let's find ourselves some kind of expert who can give us something we can use. Something to scare people off the streets. But they don't trust anyone who's Chinese for fear it will be leaked back to Beijing. And that's how they end up getting someone like this.

Mr North Korea. He gives them everything they need to know about a virus that could do what they're looking for. He shows them how it could be released. All of it. Who knows, maybe he even mocks up vials, or documents, or who the hell knows what. Stuff that can be left in MRT stations. I mean, that kind of stuff alone, even if it isn't real, is easily enough to freak people out. And it only needs to go viral. Who knows, maybe they have bots which can do that. And then let the rumour spread through WeChat. Perfect. Utter chaos. And in return, I bet the North Korean will get a nice fat payment into an offshore account somewhere.'

'How?' I exclaim. 'I mean, how could anyone think they could get away with something like this?'

'Because,' Milly says with a sigh, 'we're living in the age of impunity. If you want to do it, chances are you can get away with it. I mean, who's going to stop China? The US? They're in an even bigger mess with that twit in the White House. The UN? The UN Security Council has become completely useless –'

'Like the League of Nations, before it,' Anabel adds smugly.

'Exactly. Look at the members. They're at each other's throats all the time. Completely dysfunction. Who was it who said that where there's leadership there's no power, and where there's power there's no leadership?'

'Seriously, you can't remember a quote?' I joke.

'No, I'm too worked up. The point is, multilateral institutions like the UN have no teeth. And where they do, they're unwilling to use them. The US will block anything pro-China. China will counter-block anything pro-US. Britain and France barely matter. And Russia will do whatever is in the best interests of Russia, which is pretty much the opposite of whatever

the US and Europe want. They all just cripple themselves
with months of futile, squabbling discussions about whatever,
while the world marches boldly on. And it's just got worse
over time. In 2014, it took the Security Council one day to
agree a resolution on Ebola. In 2020, they spent three months
arguing over the wording of the COVID resolution because
the US didn't want a favourable comment in there about the
WHO. By the time it went through, twelve million people had
been infected and half a million were dead. So, the reason
these people think they can get away with it is because they
can. The law is for suckers nowadays.'

'Wow, that's even more cynical than me,' I joke dryly.

'But true,' Milly adds emphatically, getting into her stride.
'War crimes now go unpunished. Look at the mess in Syria,
where they openly used chemical weapons, a total violation
of international law. Nothing happened. Russia blocked humanitarian aid getting in something like fifteen or sixteen
times with their UN veto. I mean, are you kidding me? Or…
or Libya,' she exclaims, more and more worked up. 'A bloody
civil war since 2011. And despite an arms embargo, weapons
literally poured into that country. There is no accountability
anymore.

'Elections can almost be bought with social media interference and cyber-attacks alone. The voice of the people is
as good as dead. The war on fake news and objective journalism is a disgrace. Freedom of speech is under constant
attack. It's all just a bad joke. And don't even get me started
on the impending catastrophe that's going to be the collapse
of the planet's life-support systems. The individual stupidity
on display there from politicians and the heads of the major
corporations doing the most harm is criminally inexcusable.

'But whatever it is, political-military stuff, environmental issues, whatever, the response is always the same. They start with denial. Then there's distraction and then the media gets involved. The one part of society that should encourage discussion and communication now all too often scuppers it. It's all the same. Everything's completely geared against intellectualism. The hostility to anyone with a view or anything even slightly complex is astonishing. There is no serious focus on anything that matters anymore. Everyone is just obsessed, walking around like ostriches with their heads in their phone screens, checking out what the latest celebrity has done or what the newest consumer craze is.

'All the media does is peddle the views of the most self-obsessed members of society, if you can even call it that anymore. The one per cent have done such a good job of ensuring for themselves endless wealth and power that nothing can be done, certainly legally, anymore to dislodge them. Try to have a proper discussion with experts and the powers that be are more interested in the view of some plastic-riddled, grotesque celebrity than they are of real scientists. But that's what they want, right? Make the scientists mad with frustration at not being heard, and eventually they look mad as they resort to screaming from the rooftops. But by then it's too late. Oceans will have risen, half the animals and fish will be dead, famine, drought, ice and fire will be ravaging areas that have never had to contend with them. Chaos and pandemonium, the collapse of polite society. But, hey, don't worry, because by then the one per cent will have enough money and power that nothing will get them, coz they're far away on some base on Mars probably.'

'And you did that on almost a single breath.' I say with a smirk. 'Well, screw it, it's up to us, then.'

'Good,' Milly says. 'Because I'm so fricking sick and tired of the crap that old people shove in the way of progress. It's time for the senile old gits to piss off and let our generation sort all the mess out. It really is up to us, like, as a generation. It's time we stood up and were counted. Time we start tearing their walls down. We should be shoving them into jail in droves. All the heads of oil companies, all the polluters, the environment ministers, all of them. We're the generation without borders. We have weapons of mass mobilisation and social media at our disposal, weapons old people barely understand. It's time we used them to push back on the decrepit, senile seventy-year-old gits who've run the planet into the fricking ground.'

'Wow, I like it,' I exclaim, clapping. 'I have no idea where that all just came from. We were only talking about how they think they can get away with this, and then you came out, all guns blazing. Both Barrels Butterworth, that's what I'm going to call you from now on. You're kind of scary when you get all worked up,' I laugh. 'But I love it.'

'So, we're agreed?' Milly asks. 'It's up to us to stop whatever insane idea this lot have cooked up?'

'Yup,' nods Anabel.

'Too bloody right,' I add emphatically. 'Why should old people always be allowed to squish the hopes and dreams of young people?!'

'Cool,' Milly states. 'How?'

'I have no idea. Give me a bit of time to think.'

'Fine,' she replies, leaning back in the high-end office chair, her chest rising and falling rapidly. 'And while you do that, I might as well check that feed from Styles's room, too. You know, seeing as we're having a voyeuristic kind of morning,' she laughs.

My attention is distracted as Anabel glances up from her phone and turns on the TV to a local station.

'... are on alert as Hong Kongers brace themselves for the arrival of Typhoon Esmeralda,' the news anchor announces gravely. 'Organisers of this afternoon's pro-democracy march say they plan to go ahead with the demonstration, despite government authorities having banned the march on the grounds of health and safety concerns. In a statement, the Hong Kong Observatory said it expects the Category Eight typhoon, which is currently one hundred and forty kilometres south of Hong Kong, to make landfall at approximately eight o'clock this evening. The storm, which is now moving north at twenty kilometres an hour, may be upgraded to a Category Nine within the next few hours, as wind speeds increase to in excess of one hundred and twenty kilometres per hour. Police have warned they fear marchers will not have sufficient time to disperse before Esmeralda's arrival. Despite police calls for people to reconsider attending the march, protest leaders say people have had enough and not even a storm will deter them.'

The screen cuts away from the gaudy colours of the television studio to show a skinny, masked youth with thick glasses, messy black hair and a yellow T-shirt standing before a sea of protestors whose banners are billowing energetically in the wind.

'This march,' he says in heavily accented English, 'is to show the city authorities that we will never give up. This is our city, and even as a typhoon approaches, we will continue to make our views heard.'

'Do you expect the storm to make people stay at home?' an off-screen voice asks.

'No,' he replies. 'Our current projections indicate somewhere between five hundred thousand to a million marchers will join us today, making this one of the biggest events of its kind since the record-breaking June 2019 anti-extradition bill protest, which attracted nearly two million marchers.'

'Seriously,' I exclaim, pointing at a satellite image of a swirling mass of white cloud. 'That thing's bearing down on us, and they want to go out and march? Are they nuts?'

Milly whistles softly as she leans in towards her computer. 'I don't know about them, but you both might want to come check this out.'

'What have you found?' I ask casually without taking my eyes off the TV.

'Whoa! Holy cow,' she exclaims. 'Come over here.'

Seeing that neither of us is moving with anywhere near the urgency she clearly expects, Milly sighs and pulls her large over-ear headphones' plug from the computer. Deep sexual grunts and a furious wheezing boom from the small speakers.

'What the hell?' Anabel exclaims, leaping from the bed. Her eyes widen in astonishment the moment she steps in behind Milly's chair.

'What? What?' I call excitedly, finally hurrying over. 'What *are* you watching?'

'Christ, is that Styles's room?' Anabel gasps incredulously.

'Yup,' Milly says, nodding.

'When? What? Now?' I ask.

'No. Time stamp puts it late last night.'

'Go back to the beginning,' I urge. 'This we have to see.'

Scrolling rapidly backwards, Milly takes us through a blur of human movement. She presses play and the feed begins with a view from a camera mounted high in the far corner of the main bedroom, above the desk. The suite is in darkness. The bedside clock and the footage time-stamp correlate. It is just gone eleven p.m. the previous night.

A moment later, the door eases open and a beam of light spills across the length of the room. Three silhouetted figures enter. The door closes and a key card is inserted in the reader. Lights come on throughout the large suite.

'Right, what've we got here, then?' I laugh, barely believing what we are about to see.

'Looks like… yeah, I don't know,' Anabel begins, before falling silent as Styles's guests are quickly and unceremoniously revealed.

'Okay,' Milly says, leaning in. 'So, the fit-looking young guy is what?'

'Rent boy?' I suggest.

'Does kind of look it, right?' Anabel nods. 'And, oh my, what I thought was a pretty-looking girl with long hair is in fact –'

'Yup…' Milly says slowly, in stunned amazement. 'Sorry, but that I wasn't expecting.'

Both guests are small and effeminate, and their age is almost impossible to determine. But neither can be much older than us. Events unfold quickly, and it's soon clear this was not some carefully planned, delicate seduction.

'Now, that angle isn't exactly the best,' I laugh, cocking my head sideways to see into the bathroom. 'But tell me that isn't some ritualistic enema session going on there?'

'You are so gross at times,' Milly chides me, evidently equally appalled. 'You actually take pleasure in trying to shock people, don't you?'

I don't answer as the sordid encounter returns to the bedroom and the main show begins in earnest. What unfolds is a seemingly endless, torrid, sweaty, debauch-fest, fuelled by a heady cocktail of what is probably Viagra and cocaine, Red Bull and champagne.

Fast-forwarding just brings us to a different set-play. And as we flick through the footage, we are afforded the full spectrum of human sexual interaction: boy-on-girl-on-boy, boy-on-boy-on-girl, girl-on-boy-on-boy, boy-and-boy-on-girl and boy-and-girl-on-boy, all over again. Toys, hands, tongues and, last but by no means least, the one sexual organ they all have in common are put to good use. Around and around they go, switching places regularly, in one noisy, fluid-splattered, grunt-and cry-filled orgy that seems to go on and on, in nauseating high definition, long into the early morning. And by the end, the bin in the corner has become an unsavoury dumping ground for spent condom wrappers. Champagne bottles litter tabletops and sideboards.

When the drugs and alcohol finally run out, Styles leads them both back into the large bathroom, where they shower again. The rent boy departs first, before Styles and the now sexily redressed ladyboy leave together, possibly for a very early breakfast.

'Well, I don't know about you,' I comment, breaking the astonished silence which has lasted almost since the footage began, 'but I think it's fair to say I now have a slightly different view of the minister of ethics and morality than I did an hour ago.'

'You're such an understated ass,' Milly exclaims, leaning over to swat me on the arm. Then she laughs hard. 'Ew, I feel violated having just lived through that!'

'I guess people aren't always what they appear to be,' Anabel counters.

'And I get that. Everyone has a private side. And rightly so,' I argue. 'But you gotta admit, it's a whole other thing if they've put themselves out there to be something very different, don't you think?'

'Like morally whiter than white?' Anabel says, nodding. 'Yes, that's fair.'

'What's fair to say is the guy's no Snow White, that's for sure,' I note dryly as I turn on the room's coffee capsule machine. 'But troubling as that was to watch, I'm not sure it's our problem where he shoves his todger. We just needed to make sure he doesn't leak anything to another government.'

'I don't disagree,' Milly says. 'But what now? I mean, it effectively brings what we're out here for to a close, right?'

'Maybe. Search me. I guess we relay it back to London,' I suggest, dropping a capsule in and selecting a lungo-sized pour. 'That is kind of what Forbes requested, right?'

'Hev's right,' Anabel says. 'If this is his cup of tea, then chances are it explains that night when we lost him in London. Assuming nothing else crops up, I'd say the "Styles is an agent of China" issue is as good as closed. It would also pretty much explain his odd behaviour, or at least most of it. The leaks back home may have to wait till another time? Which just leaves the whole North Korean thing to suss out.'

'What should we say?' Milly asks, bringing up a secured e-mail program.

'Who are you sending it to?'

'I figured the personal private e-mail address which Forbes gave us. And the other contact he noted down. I think it's his permanent private secretary.'

'Personal mail addresses?' I note, sipping the hot, wonderfully aromatic brew with a raised eyebrow. 'Never seen that blow up before.'

'It is what he asked for.'

'I know. But hey, whatever.'

'What shall I say?'

'Maybe say that so far we've seen no evidence that Styles is spying for China,' Anabel suggests. 'That's because we haven't witnessed any clandestine contact with members of Chinese intelligence or any likely intermediaries. All observed contacts up to this point have been limited to social interactions or scheduled engagements.'

'That's it?'

'Yeah,' I add. 'Let's not go full tabloid at this point. Keep it objective.'

'Okay. Sending now.'

Barely has Milly sent the message when a reply pops back into her mailbox.

'Wow, that was fast,' she says, opening it.

'Forbes?' I ask.

'Yes.'

'You'd think he has nothing better to do,' Anabel jokes. 'And at this time of night, too. What'd he say?'

'He asks for supporting evidence for all the observed interactions. And he has underlined the word "all". He's sent a cloud storage link to dump it into. What shall I do?' she asks with obvious concern.

'I don't think there's much choice, is there?' Anabel concludes, shrugging resignedly.

'Agreed,' I say. 'We can't let principles dictate what we send and what we don't.'

'I have the photos from the China Club and the other

places. Shall I just take some screenshots? It's a massive video file to dump in there otherwise,' Milly notes.

'I'd take screenshots,' I suggest. 'It's not like he's going to watch the whole thing.'

'I suppose. Okay, but they always get a little grainy.'

'Somehow, I doubt he's going to care much. Do what you can. Just show Styles clearly, I guess.'

'Okay. How graphic do you want them to be?'

'Enough that the hypocrisy is made clear. But maybe leave the meat and potatoes shots out, though?'

'Okay, will do,' she says with a less than convinced look. A few minutes later, she turns and shrugs. 'Well, it's sent. God knows what happens now.'

'I know, right? But hey, we did our bit.'

'I suppose,' she says. 'Now what?'

'What do you think?' I ask Anabel. 'I reckon best we focus on the Chinese plan. Firm up what we know and then work on the black spots. Work it up to the point where we can hand it over to whoever it should go to.'

'Agreed,' Milly replies. 'Firm up what we *think* we know.'

'Quite,' Anabel laughs. 'So, we're effectively agreed, assuming there's credibility to what Sam said in Ap Lei Chau, which I get, okay, is anything but a sure thing, but if just for a moment we give it credibility, then this is an anthropogenic risk, meaning it's a man-made virus and –'

'Surely there must be people out there watching out for just this kind of thing, wouldn't you think?' I say, looking from one of them to the other.

'Are you kidding?' Milly replies, laughing grimly. 'Man-made viruses come from so many places nowadays, be it farming, markets, transportation of animals or just our tendency to huddle ever more closely into already overcrowded cities, this one being a classic in that regard. And that's not to mention what we're doing in labs all over the planet, half the time completely unmonitored. And as for the global body mandated to monitor bio-weaponry, they have an annual budget of something piddly like one point four million quid. Nail salons probably make more money.'

I laugh hard, but stop abruptly as the doorbell chimes.

'Er, anybody order room service?'

Both shake their heads.

Puzzled, I take a last sip of my coffee, get up and walk down the entry hall towards the front door. Keeping away from the peephole, I brace my foot on the floor, lest someone try to kick the door open, before opening it on the latch. As I peer cautiously through the gap, my heart misses a beat and my throat catches awkwardly mid-swallow. For there, standing in the corridor, barefoot but for shorts and a T-shirt and looking decidedly ashen faced, is none other than Robert Styles.

'Oh, turd!' I blurt out, almost coughing on a mouthful of unswallowed coffee. My first instinct is to slam the door and pretend it never happened. But a double take at his troubled expression makes me think twice. Straightening up, I say, 'Mr Styles, isn't it? Fancy meeting you here. Sure you have the right room?'

'Holy crap!' Anabel exclaims in a hissed whisper from somewhere close behind me. An uncomfortable silence falls over the room.

'I am not sure,' he replies finally. 'Who's in there?' he asks, peering suspiciously into the room.

'Nobodies,' I blurt out instinctively. 'Just two girls I picked up in Wan Chai last night.' Then I remember, with a horrible sinking feeling, that both were with me in the China Club when we met him. An embarrassed, guilty grin creeps onto my face.

For a second, Styles eyes me suspiciously, before Milly exclaims, 'We are *not*!'

'Oh, seriously,' I sigh, turning in defeat. 'How did you get this far?'

'I don't have time for this,' the politician mutters quietly. 'We need to talk. Be here in twenty minutes.'

He hands me a page of hotel notepaper with an address scribbled onto it in black biro. Without looking back, he turns and walks off down the corridor.

'What the hell was that?' Anabel calls as I hurriedly close the door. Both rush from the bedroom into the corridor.

'Tell me the man we were sent here to observe didn't just knock at the door?' Milly wails, head in her hands.

'Yeah, that's pretty much the sum of it,' I laugh, unsure what the appropriate response is. 'It's all so screwed up.'

'What did he give you?' Anabel asks, taking the slip of paper. 'Why'd he write the Queen Street Cooked Food Market on it?'

'He wants us to meet him there.'

'Is that such a great idea?' Milly says, taking her head from her hands.

'Who knows?'

'You don't think he knows about the surveillance, do you?' says Milly. 'Or what we just sent to Forbes?'

'I certainly hope not,' Anabel exclaims. 'Guy like that, he'd have busted in here to throw some kind of hissy fit if he did.'

'I agree. And something was definitely wrong,' I say, thinking aloud. 'He looked troubled. None of his arrogant strut from the tele. It was like he'd just been slapped by some kind of bad news. Like someone died.'

'Why'd he come to us, then?'

'Dunno, Mills. Only one way to find out. C'mon, grab your crap. Field trip time,' I announce, fetching my phone, purse and sunglasses.

'There's a sodding typhoon on its way and you take your *sunnies*?' Anabel comments in amusement.

'Always,' I laugh. 'Half protection, half disguise.'

'With that hairstyle, not sure it does much good,' Milly sniggers.

Scowling, I snatch up my MI13 baseball cap and flash her a disingenuous smile, before heading to the door.

'Oi, hold on,' she cries. 'We're not ready.'

*

The red-and-white local taxi drops us just behind the Ibis Central Hotel in the up-and-coming district of Sheung Wan. The air has become noticeably dense and sticky, the sky cloudy and broodingly overcast.

'Yup, storm's definitely on its way,' Anabel comments, glancing at her petite watch.

'When's that riot start?' I ask.

'It's a peaceful protest march,' she corrects me. 'And short-ly. We should try not to get caught up in it. The whole of Central usually gets completely congested, and all the traffic gets diverted.'

'You think the police will let it go ahead, given what's going on?' I ask, starting up the nondescript escalator. The building's pale-beige tiling looks old and tired and could do with a serious face-lift. But maybe that's part of its charm.

'Who knows?' Anabel replies, as we pass through a stainless-steel door and enter the relatively quiet food court. The décor is basic, with dozens of round tables surrounded by colourful plastic seats. Strip lights overhead bathe everything in a bright, garish glare. The various vendors are arranged around the fringe of the seating area. Each has a bold, brash backlit sign in English and Chinese above it. Glancing around, I see the signs suggest a wide variety of different cuisines on offer, including Indian and Nepalese, Vietnamese and Thai, French, assorted Chinese dishes and Beijing dumplings.

Spotting Robert Styles sitting alone at a small table in the far corner, we begin to walk towards him, but then I stop abruptly and hold my friends back. Warily, I cast my eye over the half dozen pre-lunch diners scattered across the food hall. While none look up at us, I can't be sure that no one is watching Styles.

'Hang on. Belle, you look local. Take this cup over to him, will you, and quietly ask if anyone's come in after him?'

Nodding, she hurriedly does so. As she bends forward across the table, a few words are shared. Slightly confused, Styles shakes his head. With an 'okay' hand gesture from Anabel, Milly and I follow her over to take seats opposite the scared-looking MP.

'So, who are you?' Styles asks, shivering uncomfortably in the overly enthusiastic air-conditioning that seems commonplace here in Hong Kong. That he is still just in shorts and a T-shirt probably doesn't help. 'I've met my fair share of spooks over the years, but you lot are different.'

'We can't tell you,' I reply neutrally and as unconfrontationally as I can. I set my cap down on the table. One glance at it, and he groans and rolls his eyes.

'Well, that's about as good an answer as one can expect in that world. Are we talking north or south of the river?'

'Technically speaking, neither,' I reply.

'Since when did you lot start announcing yourselves on your caps?'

'Told you it was a bad idea,' Milly hisses.

'And what are you lot doing in the city?' he asks leadingly.

'Afraid we can't tell you,' I reply flatly.

'Look, frankly I don't care which of the alphabet brigade you work for,' Styles sighs, 'nor how people as young as you could even be in their employ, because right now I have a problem and I see no one else from whom I could plausibly seek help.'

'What exactly was it that gave you the impression we were anything other than tourists?' I ask.

'Well, let's think. An English girl checks into the same hotel as I, and on the same day, too. And in Hong Kong of all places, during some of the worst riots this city has seen. Not exactly tourist country. That's chance. The subsequent appearance at the China Club became coincidence. But the approach at the bar in Wan Chai sealed it. I'm a politician. Which means if I'm not trying to persuade people of something, I'm trying to dissuade them of something else. Either way, reading people is rather key. I look at you, I see a girl who apparently lives fast, talks almost as quickly and clearly disrespects authority. The messy hair says carefree, the physique is not the result of a gym. And while the smile is captivating, the eyes are deceiving and dangerous,' he says.

'Now, tell me, which part of that would our intelligence services *not* be interested in?'

'I'd call that a bit of a stretch,' I counter. 'My guess is someone told you we were here. I'm betting it was your mate, the prime minister.'

'Well,' Milly chimes in, 'I expect he is made aware of all intelligence operations going on abroad. I'll wager that while he may not have known what we were up to, he knew to point you in our direction. Are we right?'

His demeanour deflates somewhat as his moment of mysteriousness is unravelled.

'Alright,' I sigh. 'What can we do for you, Mr Styles? And why not go seek help from staff at the consulate?'

'This is why,' he says, nervously placing a brown A4 envelope on the table. Without taking my eyes off him, I slowly reach out for it and slide it closer. When I pull the contents out, I barely believe what I am seeing. A hot, prickly flush washes over me. Photo after photo in grainy black and white of three figures cavorting on a messy bed during a sexual tryst. Somehow, the absence of colour makes the pictures look so much more sordid and seedier than the ones from the video. For a horrible second, I fear they *are* the photos we just sent to the minister of defence. But the angles seem wrong. These appear to have been taken from a totally different camera.

With my best poker face, I look up at the MP and pass the pictures casually to Milly and Anabel. Neither makes comment, and Anabel quickly slips them back into the envelope.

'Why are you showing these to us?' she asks.

'For the very reason I can't go to the consulate. I need people who know how to keep a secret. These bloody things get out, I am as good as ruined. And those bastards know it.'

I cast a wary look at Anabel. Leaning forward, she asks, 'Who?'

'The Chinese.'

'The Chinese? They gave these to you?'

'Yes.'

'When?'

'About fifteen minutes before I came up to find you.'

'How did you know what room number to go to?' I ask.

'Never you mind about that. Let's just say you don't get into my position without knowing how to grease a few poles.'

Fighting desperately not to snigger childishly, I nod slowly and let the pithy comment that is already on the tip of my tongue die.

'When did the events in those pictures occur?' I ask, realising, with an internal frown, that I have become a manipulative, pathological liar who only shares the truth when it is advantageous.

'Last night,' he replies, evidently unhappy to have to answer our questions.

Nodding, I remain silent, waiting, letting the awkward silence linger until, finally, he gives in to the innately human urge to fill silence with something. With a heavy sigh, Robert

Styles begins offering up a very sanitised version of events, recanting how he went to a bar in the Hyatt hotel to meet an old business colleague. Out of the corner of my eye, I spot the corner of Anabel's mouth curl up in amusement.

Undeterred, Styles continues, and it quickly becomes clear that he is a man so used to having his every word accepted by people that his lie detection filter is now well and truly broken. As his story veers into ever more implausible territory, in terms of how he was duped into taking the pair back to his room, Anabel leans forward and softly clears her throat.

'Sir, if I may?' she interjects. 'Without being crass, I think it's fair to say the pictures speak for themselves. Therefore, I suppose how you came to *being* in them is almost irrelevant at this point, wouldn't you agree? Perhaps if you just tell us how you came to be in *possession* of them and what your concern now is, then we can see how we might be of help. How's that sound?'

With a brief look of relief, his shoulders drop and he hunches forward.

'You absolutely swear this will go no further?' he implores sternly, though fear radiates through the bravado of confidence.

'We're not journalists, Mr Styles,' Milly says softly, easing him into a safer space.

With a heavy, resigned groan, he begins.

'I came to HK to look up a few old acquaintances and take a closer look at some of the programmes the Chinese are putting in place here. They're doing some fascinating stuff on education, re-education, national spirit building, corrections programmes, that sort of thing. Stuff which we might well not copy wholesale but could still offer some interesting ideas for the problems we are facing back in the UK with home-grown terrorism, civil

unrest, that sense of national dislocation some are feeling. But,'
he scowls, 'I also intended to... how shall I say, meet up... see...'

'I think we get the idea,' I say, noting his hesitancy. 'And
how were you going to arrange that?'

'Through a contact I used to know from back when we
lived here.'

'So, what happened?'

'Well, I messaged him, and I got a reply back that he had
since moved to Thailand, but that he was putting me in touch
with the person he had handed his business over to. And that
this chap would be able to sort me out. All very confidential.'

'Any chance that was the well-dressed, slick-looking guy
in the Captain's Bar a few nights ago?'

'You were there?' he comments neutrally. 'Suppose I shouldn't
be surprised.'

'Yeah, but by chance,' I add quickly.

'Either way, things went as they used to –'

'Photos, make a choice, text a number. Something like
that?' I suggest.

'Basically.'

'Okay. Then what? I assume the liaison went as planned?'

'You don't need to make it sound so, so tawdry,' he snaps,
a glimmer of the fiery politician from the television making
an appearance.

Fixing him with an uncompromising stare, I raise a questioning eyebrow and say, 'What happened then?'

Glancing at his watch, he scowls and shifts awkwardly in
his plastic garden chair. Sighing, I lean forward.

'Mr Styles. You came to us. What happened? What's so
important that you've dragged us out here just before a city-
wide protest kicks off and a sodding typhoon arrives?'

'Damn it, I'm getting to it,' he exclaims. Irked, he reaches for the envelope and clasps it protectively to his chest. 'Fine, bugger it,' he curses. 'Earlier today, I was approached in the hotel lobby by a man in a suit. Looked like a businessman. Local chap. He greeted me by name. Shook my hand. As if we were old friends. Then he handed me that envelope and said the contents could either disappear or become headline news. Which would I prefer?'

'Chinese intelligence?' I suggest, casting a glance at Anabel.

'Most likely,' she replies.

'And what did they ask for?'

Grinding his jaw resentfully, Robert Styles looks warily at each of us in turn. Then, cursing, he pulls a six-by-four photo of a young man and an effeminate-looking boy from his breast pocket and slides it across to me.

'Turn it over,' he instructs.

'These are the other people from the v… the photo?' I ask.

'Yes,' he nods.

I read the writing on the back of the picture quickly and lay it flat on the table again with a pursed look.

'What's it say?' Milly asks, unable to contain her curiosity.

'They want two documents,' I reply. 'The first being a confidential document drafted by the cabinet and the Foreign Office which sets out the British response plan should China breach the handover agreement.'

'Great. And the second?'

'That would be the classified US, UK and NATO response plans in the event that issues in the South China Sea deteriorate significantly.'

'Is there such a plan?' asks Milly.

'Probably,' the politician replies.

'What do you think?' I say, turning to Anabel.

'The presence of a camera suggests there was forethought behind all of this. But that means they knew you had vulnerabilities, Mr Styles. Personally, I wouldn't be surprised if they intercepted your communications with your original contact and set you up with one of their own. Maybe the room upgrade simply ensured you were moved to a suite they could monitor?'

'You're saying the man I met was actually a Chinese agent? God...' His head sinks slowly into his outstretched hands.

'Young, in his twenties, fit, lean and handsome,' Anabel notes, counting on her fingers. 'Would fit the bill. It's Darlington-Sorbet's classic honeytrap... just with a twist.'

'Did they say when they want these documents?'

'Tonight. He said they'd call late afternoon to arrange a meeting time.'

'Oh, really,' I laugh. 'Okay, well, loads of time, then.'

'I don't think you're taking this seriously,' he snaps.

'Mr Styles,' I reply calmly. 'I assure you I am. But I'm still amused by all this.'

'Well, I'm glad my predicament amuses you!'

'It isn't you,' I reply, surprising myself with my confidence in rebuffing someone so senior in government. 'I'm amused by how confident the Chinese are that you'll give them what they want. And how quickly. Question is, what do you intend to do?'

'I don't know. Nothing,' he splutters. But the desired conviction isn't quite there.

'You can't be thinking of giving it to them, can you?' Milly exclaims.

'No... no, of course not.'

'Okay, look,' I interrupt. 'We don't have a whole lot of time. So, we need to do a couple of things. First, we need to get back to the hotel. How about you both go check his room,' I suggest. 'See if the surveillance gear is still there. Its make and model might help us identify who put it there. Then we have two problems to solve: what to do about this plan of theirs to scupper these protests, and then what to do about this situation here. Anyone really want to eat, or should we just get going?'

'Let's go,' Milly says, rising.

'I came here deliberately,' Robert Styles protests nostalgically. 'They do exceptional wonton noodles at that stall.'

'Fine. Give me your spare room key card,' I demand, exasperated. 'Then come and find us the moment you get back to the Mandarin. You know where we are.'

The three of us rise and make for the exit.

'Do you get the feeling he isn't taking this as seriously as he probably should be?' Milly asks as we reach the bottom of the covered escalator which runs down the outside of the building.

Before I can answer, my phone rings.

'Hello, stranger,' I smile, answering it. 'Fancy meeting you here.'

'Oh God, who are you flirting with now?' Milly sighs.

'It's Hollis,' I whisper, cupping the microphone.

'The admiral. Oh great. This can't be good.'

'Literally just got off the phone with Jeremy Caines,' the admiral replies. 'He has an ask of you.'

'Sorry, the PM has an ask of us?' I repeat, laughing.

Both Milly and Anabel stare at me in amazed disbelief.

'Worryingly enough, yes.'

'Is it normal to receive orders directly from the PM?'

'Nowadays it seems to be,' the admiral replies flatly. 'Especially when one of his closest friends and ministers is about to get into a godawful mess over there.'

'I'm sorry,' I exclaim, stopping on the spot. 'How do you even know any of this?'

'You honestly think we haven't been keeping tabs on you lot out there?' he replies.

'Okay, that I get. But how could you possibly know any of this? We literally just left Styles.'

'He called the PM earlier. And because you lot leave your mobile phones on. You don't think it's that hard to turn the mike on and listen in, do you?'

Pulling the traitorous device from my ear, I hold it at arm's length and give it a deeply distrustful glare.

'Great, so who else knows?'

'Hopefully no one. Yet. Otherwise it means our secure comms channels are perilously at risk.'

'Okay, go on then,' I say. 'What's the ask?'

'Long and short of it is, the PM needs your help. We cannot have a close confidante of his, let alone a member of the cabinet, be caught up in anything that could cause embarrassment to HMG right now. Either domestically or anything that sours the Anglo–Chinese relationship, which is messy enough as it is. Sexual weakness is forgivable, but treason most certainly isn't. Ensure it doesn't come to that. Now, this cannot become formal, understand? And Styles cannot give them what they want. You watch him like a hawk. Make sure this does not develop into anything embarrassing for the prime minister or the country, either. Clear?'

'Got it. What about this other mess we've stumbled onto? I presume you know about that as well?'

'That I'm slightly less fussed about, unless you think the threat is real and not just nonsense. Clementine's number two sounded like a prize plonker, but I suppose if you think there's something of genuine concern there, and you can do something about it, then do it. If not, leave it be, focus on this Styles affair and get him out of there as fast as you can. Damned man's a liability.'

'Again, got it. We'll call if we need anything.'

'Good. Don't bugger it up.'

'Oh, wait. There is something, sir,' I say, lowering my voice and moving away from the others. 'Seems there's a pretty serious storm moving in. Likely they'll shut the airport. They always say, know your exits. Well, ours are closing fast. Rail links out of here only go to China. Ferries won't put out to sea in that kind of storm. And if it all kicks off, we can't hunker down and ride it out here, either. We only have a small window in which to get out of the city. So, I need a favour...'

'Let's hear it.'

With a deep breath, I launch into my idea. For a moment, the line goes silent.

'You don't make my life easy, do you?' he replies finally. 'Alright, I'll see what I can do.'

He hangs up. I turn to my friends with a rueful smile and begin to fill them in as we hail a taxi coming towards us on the other side of the road. It does a sharp U-turn and pulls up in front of us.

'There's got to be something deeply wrong,' Milly says, 'when people are so concerned about the world's reaction if it finds out you're homosexual that someone would actually consider betraying their country to keep that information secret, don't you think?'

'Yeah, pretty messed up,' Anabel sighs as we climb in. 'But he wouldn't be the first.'

'You're not wrong,' I say, glancing out the window at the dark, threatening clouds that have begun to swirl overhead. 'It's going to absolutely dump it down any minute now, isn't it? It's so fricking dark, it could be, like, eight p.m. And it's only lunchtime!'

'Strap in for your first typhoon,' Anabel says excitedly. 'I think this one's going to hit us face on.'

'Is that bad?' Milly asks as Anabel tells the driver where to go.

'What do you think?' I joke grimly. 'It's basically a hurricane.'

We ride the rest of the way back to the Mandarin in silence, each of us preoccupied with our own thoughts.

The driver is handing me my change when my phone rings again.

'Now what?' I groan, answering it.

'Hold for the personal private secretary to the minister of defence,' a dour woman's voice says the moment I accept the call. A second later, the line clicks and a man's voice comes on.

'Mr Forbes has asked me to inform you that the prime minister has just briefed him on what is unfolding out there. He says that it is of paramount importance that you get a confession.'

'A confession to what?'

'To being behind the leaked stories in the press. If this all blows up, we want to be on the right side of the narrative. We must be able to control the story. Do whatever you need to. But get that confession.'

'So, we pretend to be Styles's friend and help him, but we're really only trying to get him to confess?'

'Isn't that what espionage is all about?'

With that, the line goes dead.

'Do you get the sense,' I say pensively, turning to my friends, 'that the PM and Forbes aren't exactly... you know?'

'Singing off the same hymn sheet?' offers Milly.

'That's the one. According to OCS, Number Ten wants us to do whatever we can, without getting caught, to bail Styles's arse out of this mess, while Forbes makes it sound like the PM wants us to hang him out to dry.'

'Classic dysfunctional government,' Anabel sighs.

'Maybe. Or that they're not even speaking to each other.'

'Uh-oh,' Milly laughs. 'Here comes another Heather conspiracy theory.'

'Yeah, whatever,' I laugh. 'Honestly, who cares? We've got enough problems to deal with here without more dysfunctional adult crap to complicate it.

*

By the time Robert Styles returns from his lunch, we are well into our planning. The room is darkened, with the blackout curtains drawn, shutting out the early-afternoon glare coming off the harbour. From the news it is clear that the march will still proceed, even though the observatory has announced they will shortly raise the T3 warning flag. Every so often, Anabel checks an app on her phone for updates on the impending storm. A firm knock sounds on the room door.

'Yeah, this has all the hallmarks of a right royal mess,' Anabel comments, pulling the blinds aside for a peek at the street outside, as Milly peers through the peephole, before letting the errant politician in.

'My, what do we have here?' Robert Styles says, taking in the multiple projector screens being beamed onto the wall of the hotel room. On one screen we have Nigel, who has dialled in from the MI6's Q Branch country mansion, and Luther, who is in Cheltenham. I don't bother with introductions. We have no intention of telling Styles anyone's real name.

'Do you know what's been troubling me for a while now?' he says, calmly sitting in one of the corner armchairs. He lets the question hang and slowly crosses his legs. My dislike for him only increases at this thinly veiled attempt to gain some sort of upper hand and put us on the back foot. 'I'll tell you what it is,' he continues, wagging his finger reproachfully in the air. 'It is why you lot are actually here. Here in this hotel, I mean. If the Foreign Office sent you out here because of the troubles, I highly doubt they would put you up here. Similarly, SIS must have properties in the city which it uses. It got me thinking that perhaps your being here is not a coincidence after all. Perhaps you are actually here to spy on me.'

'You're absolutely right, Mr Styles,' I reply flatly, no longer in the mood for his games and power plays.

'And since when did British intelligence begin following prominent and senior members of the government?'

'Probably since government began,' I suggest with a wry smile.

'I'd say,' Milly interjects, 'since about 1949, when Clement Attlee instructed MI5 to inform him of MPs with subversive connections.'

'Really?' Robert Styles replies, trying to retain control of the conversation. 'Well, it was of course he who began the tradition after every general election for Millbank to present incoming PMs with a dossier concerning prospective ministers deemed to be a security concern. So, you are probably right. Well, this is all very interesting, but why would you be watching me?'

'Fact is, Mr Styles, you're the prime suspect behind all the recent tip-offs to the press about the conduct of cabinet colleagues of yours.'

From his instant reaction, that was clearly not what he was expecting. His face freezes and his calculating eyes suggest a rush of thoughts behind them.

'But… but that's preposterous,' he exclaims indignantly. 'Why would I do that?'

'Who knows? To get ahead maybe?' Milly suggests, seeing where I am going with my frontal attack. 'Remove those in your way.'

'Good God. Whoever thinks that clearly doesn't understand how politics works. Failure of the party means failure for me.'

'Perhaps in theory,' I reply. 'So, how is it that we have irrefutable evidence that you met the journalist behind each story in advance of each leak?'

'What tosh!'

'It's right there. The tech doesn't lie.'

'Show me,' he orders. 'Because I had nothing to do with any of those stories. Nothing, you hear!'

'Can you bring it up?' I ask Milly.

Projecting a map of London onto the wall, Milly explains the infographics as they appear.

'The map shows the movements over time of both parties, you and the journalist Jeffrey Pelt, based on the recorded geo-locational pings your respective phones made off mobile phone towers. The red dot is your newspaper reporter. The blue one is you. What we do now is speed time up until the dots come into proximity, and a flag goes up. Okay, so there's the first occasion. And interestingly, if we look at the date, it's not long before the press breaks the first story.'

'Where is that?' he demands. 'And when?'

He peers closer and then rounds on us angrily.

'Impossible,' he thunders, pointing at the time and location. 'I have never even been to that part of North London. And if I have, certainly not that recently. Perhaps years ago. And I barely know this Pelt fellow.'

'Well, let's see the next one,' Milly says hurriedly, a little unsure what to make of his strong denial. This is not the reaction I was expecting, either. A denial was almost certainly on the cards, but I was so sure that as Milly covered each subsequent meeting, his resolve would flounder, defeated by the sheer weight of evidence, and we would get the confession Guy Forbes is so dearly hoping for. Yet with each damning reveal, Styles checks his phone and his resolve strengthens, and so does his anger.

'This is the most appalling stitch-up,' he shouts. 'This is utter tampering with evidence.'

'The records don't lie, sir,' Milly states matter-of-factly.

'Then they must be wrong. I know exactly where I was on each of those evenings; I have it all here in my own calendar. And I was not with some bloody gutter press hack, of that I can assure you.'

'So, where were you?' I challenge.

'None of your bloody business,' he snaps.

'I think I know where you were, and why,' Milly says quietly. All eyes turn to her. She squirms at the attention.

'He went to meet men to have sex.'

'Good Christ,' Styles explodes, leaping from his chair. 'I think I have had quite enough of this insolent smearing of my good name. You take it back, you hear,' he cries.

'Sir, with all due respect, I don't think we have time for this,' I say calmly. 'If I had to take a punt, I'd say she's probably right. What do they call it? Cottaging?'

'Enough,' he bellows. 'I will not –'

'Okay, stop. Unhelpful, H,' Milly says more firmly. 'I don't think you understand what is happening here, sir. You say you didn't leak anything –'

'Other than from his –' I begin, only to be cut off by Milly's fierce look.

'Oh, will you stop,' she sighs. 'It's not funny anymore. We're not going to wind him up enough to get a confession. Fact is, sir, you know exactly where you were on each occasion. And you were probably meeting men to have sex. Am I wrong?'

'Must you be so crude about it?'

'Right now,' I note neutrally, 'we don't have time for delicacy, sir. Fact of the matter is, you need our help. Now, if you did leak those stories to the press, well, I don't know what to say. But if you didn't, because you were out socialising those nights, then that's a very different matter. Point is, we need to know because we only have a very small window in which to get you out of this country. If you don't give them the docs they want, who knows what their reaction might be? Arrest you, most likely. So right now, we need to explain how you could be in two places at the same time.'

'But,' Milly exclaims, 'we have all the data. It's right there! And the briefcase.'

'What briefcase?' Styles snaps defensively.

'You made what appeared to be a dead drop in a Chinese restaurant which just happens to be right next to the PRC's London embassy a few weeks back,' Milly says, bold-faced.

'I don't know what you mean.'

'You left your briefcase there unattended for a good while before you retrieved it. There are people back home who suspect that allowed them to copy documents you were giving them,' I say. 'They think you're working for the Chinese.'

'What utter tosh! I don't know what you're talking about. And yes, I often go to a very good takeaway there. We knew the son back when we were here. He moved to London, to take over his parents' place. So, I get my Chinese there. That's not a crime, is it?'

'Can you explain leaving the briefcase?' Anabel asks.

'Alright, wait, yes, there was a day when I got a call and left in a hurry. Someone was coming to fix the boiler. Had to be a weekend. And I walked out without it. But I remembered and hurried back not long after. It was nothing more than that, I assure you. Ended up missing the repair man, but got billed the call-out charge anyway.'

'Okay,' Anabel says, casting a questioning look across at us. We reply with uncertain shrugs. 'Fine, so that then leaves the bigger issue. How could you be in two places at once?'

'Well,' Milly sighs, 'that's the question, right?'

On the screen, Nigel clears his throat.

'You know, Milly's right that the tech doesn't lie. But that doesn't mean what we're seeing is what really happened.'

'What do you mean?' I ask.

'I have an idea. Remember the night you lost him in the Underground or wherever?'

'You lot were following me back in London? I should have known. Of course they'd then send you out here, too.'

'My point is,' Nigel continues, 'that you lost him because his mobile was turned off when he left his house.'

'You were outside my house?' Styles splutters.

'Yeah,' I say without looking at him. 'So what, Nigel?'

'Well, I'm just thinking, if he turned his phone off that night, why wouldn't he do it all the other nights?'

'Aye, makes sense,' Luther adds, before muting his line and cramming a large sandwich messily into his mouth. Glancing at the time, I try to fathom why he's eating so early in the morning.

'Well, of course I did,' Styles says, still less than keen to be having this discussion. 'So how did my phone end up in North London? Because I certainly did not lose it. Basic precaution I would have thought.'

'Okay, give me a moment,' Luther says, laying his sandwich down with a grimace. 'Share that data file with me. I cannae be sure, but if we have a wee rummage around…' he says, pursing his lips in concentration. We all wait silently as he taps away for a few moments. Then a wide smile forms on his face.

'Aye, get-tae, there it is. Okay. We need to go back a bit and we see what happened. Your flag only comes if both phones are in close range.'

'I see it now,' Nigel exclaims. 'It's so obvious. The way phones work is they ping the nearest tower to push and pull data. But it's not continuous, or your battery would die too quickly. So, it's periodic. Means you could expect the phone to have moved a little between pings, right? But not too far. See here, though. When a phone turns on or off, there's a handshake of sorts with the network. Like a "hi and bye" sort of thing. But look at the graphic I'm sharing. Mr Styles, when did you turn your phone off? In advance of leaving home, or right after you left?'

'If I recall, just as I left.'

'Cool. So, look here. His phone is pinging, alright? And we can see it in or about his home address. But then it goes off, which is when he's leaving. And then, like a minute later, it comes back on, but look where it is. It's in Westminster, near the Houses of Parliament.'

'Can you nail it down further?' I ask.

'He doesn't need to,' Styles says. 'I know where that is. Those buildings house our offices.'

'Exactly, and then the phone heads off towards North London, and shortly thereafter comes into proximity with the phone belonging to your journalist,' Nigel explains.

'Wait, so what? Someone had a clone of his phone?' I ask.

'That's definitely the most logical option, yes. And whoever it was took it and went to see this journalist each time, like a few days before each story leaked.'

'How would they know when to turn the cloned phone on?'

'Who knows?' Nigel replies. 'Maybe the house was under surveillance. Maybe they were monitoring his phone.'

'It's almost irrelevant at this point,' Milly says. 'But bear in mind, just because they were in proximity to this reporter doesn't mean they were the one who actually gave him the story. This merely incriminates you, Mr Styles, by way of suggesting you were there. The person with the phone only needed to ensure they were in the same bar or restaurant to be assured of being recorded as in the necessary proximity to the journalist. Which, by the way, then also tallies with that slip of the tongue when Pelt said his contact was female.'

'Exactly, but nonetheless it associated you with the newspapers, Mr Styles, and made you look like the prime candidate for the leaks to anyone who simply took the evidence on face value and didn't dig deeper,' adds Anabel.

'Which makes this a multi-person initiative,' I say.

'Conspiracy, I think you mean,' Styles grumbles.

'That too,' Milly says. 'But it means you were certainly under surveillance. It also suggests someone knew where you were going on these "social" occasions and what precautions you took. Specifically turning your phone off. Someone seems to have known when you were going out, or they simply watched and waited, and when you did, someone else got a call. Someone equipped with a clone of your phone, which could ping your location to Sentinel. At that point, whoever that was would turn the clone phone on and go to wherever the reporter was at that time. I'm speculating, but the story fits. And when the records were examined, as they surely would be eventually, it looked like it was you each time who spoke to the journalist. I'm sorry, but it does indeed look like someone is trying to set you up.'

'Don't apologise for being the smartest person here,' Styles says, turning to Milly.

Anabel smiles proudly. Then she asks Styles, 'Who could it have been? Is there anyone you can think of? Anyone who's behaved oddly? Anyone interested in your movements?'

'Anyone who also had a reason to be in Whitehall regularly, or in Notting Hill for that matter?' I add, observing the number of times the cloned phone was turned on in that neighbourhood.

'Christ, it's politics. It could have been half the opposition and *almost anyone* from my own party.'

'Can you think of anything odd that's happened recently?' I ask. 'Anything, no matter how small or trivial?'

'Strange things happen all the time in politics. One barely knows what to make of half of it. I mean, if I really have to think... Well, come to think of it now, I did lose a staffer a while back. Poor chap had an accident in his bath.'

'What kind of accident?' I ask, leaning closer.

'Coroner said it was death by misadventure. He dropped his hi-fi in the bath while he was in it.'

'Er, okay. Hell knows how you do that. And where did he live?'

'I don't know. Maybe in central London. Possibly Bayswater.'

'That's close enough to Notting Hill.'

'I don't recall. He was always at work early, though, so he can't have lived that far away. Tragic accident.'

'Yeah, I dunno about that,' I ponder suspiciously. 'Hey, look, accidents happen, right? But do you know how hard it is to electrocute yourself in a bath nowadays? With purified tap water? Okay, reasonably purified. It's, like, way harder than you'd think. I mean, forget the water quality, most bathrooms have trip switches. I'm not discounting what the coroner said, but... yeah, okay, look. Just saying it's hard, that's all.'

'How would you know this?' Styles asks in horror.

'Oh, don't ask,' Milly sighs.

With a grunt, Styles continues, 'Well, what is becoming abundantly clear is that someone is setting me up. And thereby, almost as importantly,' he adds ruefully, 'the PM as well.'

'You think Forbes knew before he gave us this?' I ask, turning to my friends.

'What's he got to do with this?' Styles snaps.

'Military intelligence, Mr Styles,' I say, pointing at my cap, which is sitting on the bed near him. 'Where do you think that reports into?'

'Christ, Forbes sent you?'

'Probably best we don't confirm or deny.'

'Which is a yes. What have you told him?'

'Definitely best we don't say.'

'Right,' he sighs, nodding in resigned acceptance. 'So, a few things you need to know about the man you lot seem to have got into bed with. He's a politician. His words aren't worth the air they're carried on. And don't think the irony isn't lost on me. What do you think Guy Forbes is if not a closet right-wing fanatic? Perhaps more accurately, Forbes sits just slightly to the right of Attila the Hun. He knows his agenda will never fly with the electorate, not in a million years, so he needs another way into Number Ten. He's been at it for ages. But he supposedly has some sort of leverage up his sleeve. I never managed to find out what it is, but it's sufficiently sensitive that no one has ever been able to get rid of him for fear he'd leak it. I think the question you need to ask yourselves is whether you aren't bloody giving him the key to Number Ten. Did he tell you this was all to protect the government and the PM? I bet he did. That's nothing more than a bad joke. With him, it'll be the complete bloody opposite. He will take anything you give him. He will take it and he will use it, and to hell with the collateral damage.'

'Great, it's Arcos all over again,' Milly sighs.

'Ar-what?' I repeat.

'So, Arcos is a story they tell you about at the very beginning. It's a cautionary tale about how dangerous it can be to give information to certain politicians, and how indiscreet some of them can be with that information if it suits their needs. Arcos was some kind of Russian co-operative society set up in the UK back in the day. It shared a building on Moorgate with the Russian trade mission. The place was a suspected base of operations for all sorts of espionage activities.

Then, in 1927, Sinclair, who was head of Six, passed the info to Kell, who headed Five – all names we know, right? He took it to Baldwin, who was PM. They raided the place, but it was a bust. The Russians had already burned everything out the back. The government got torn to pieces in Parliament, and desperate to save face, Baldwin released all sorts of secret intercepts to the House of Commons in his defence. All messy-messy.'

For a long, uncomfortable moment we remain silent, deep in our own personal reflections, Styles likely pondering how much we might already know and, critically, what we have communicated to Forbes back in London. It would be surprising if his mind was not already churning through political damage-limitation strategies. A quick, surreptitious glance at Anabel and Milly confirms a flash of guilt in both their eyes about what we have sent to London. Luther and Nigel look utterly confused in the wall-projected images.

'Okay look, advice noted,' I say. 'But perhaps better we'd deal with the issue at hand.'

'No disagreement from me,' Milly says, thankful the awkward, recrimination-filled silence is over. 'The fact that they've asked you for such sensitive documents presents us with an opportunity. One of the classic conundrums of espionage is that countries have traditionally viewed materials given to them willingly by foreign agents with suspicion. But when they think they have the agent over a barrel, either through intimidation or blackmail, they tend to trust the information they receive so much more.'

'So, you're saying we dupe them?' I ask.

'Precisely. It's a golden opportunity to hand them what we want them to believe will be our treaty breach response, not to mention the Pacific battle plan. I mean, can you imagine?

What an absolute coup that would be. We get to significantly influence Chinese thinking on a foreign policy matter, in line with our interests.'

'This is seriously ambitious,' Anabel laughs.

'True. But totally doable,' Milly exclaims excitedly, grabbing her phone. 'We need to make a call.' Turning to the concerned-looking politician, she says, 'Mr Styles, why don't you leave this to us? Maybe go back to your room. Get some rest. Have a nap. We need a few hours. The moment they contact you again, let us know. We need to know where you are told to meet them. And when.'

With an unconvincing nod, he rises and makes his way uncertainly to the door. There, he stops and turns.

'Please tell me you lot know what you're doing?'

'Mr Styles,' Milly says, fixing him with a calm, assured look. 'This is what we do. There is nothing to worry about. We'll speak shortly, yes?'

Whether satisfied or not, he merely nods resignedly and leaves.

For a moment, none of us say anything. Signalling they both remain silent, I pad quickly to the door to peep out and check he is not still there. Closing it again, I exclaim, 'Are you kidding me?! "We do this all the time!"'

'Yeah, what was that?' Anabel laughs. 'We have no idea what we're doing.'

'Shh, don't let him hear you say that,' Milly hisses, jabbing a thumb over her shoulder.

'So, smartest person in the room,' Anabel smiles. 'How are we going to get out of this fine mess?'

'It's not a mess, and don't remind me. That was kind of a cringey line, wasn't it?'

'Just a little. Not that it isn't true,' I laugh.

'We need to make a call,' Milly announces, smiling appreciatively. 'Here, give me your phone.'

She opens a commercially available end-to-end encrypted messaging app on it, selects the admiral's number and dials. He answers within three rings.

'All ears. What kind of a mess have you three got yourselves into now?'

'It's not that bad,' I reply. 'It's –'

'We need to ask you some questions,' Milly says, talking over me. 'Firstly, these documents they're squeezing Styles for, are they real? I mean, is there a NATO South China Sea Battle Plan?'

Silence.

'O-kay...' she says. 'How about a UK response plan in the event of a breach of the '97 Hong Kong handover?'

Again, silence.

'Alright, look,' I sigh. 'Whether they exist or not, China seems to think they do. So, either they know that as fact, right, or they simply suspect these plans exist. Either way, they don't have them, or else they wouldn't try to blackmail Styles for them.'

'I love it when you state the obvious,' Milly grins.

'Yeah, love you, too,' I reply sarcastically. 'The point is, Admiral, we've got an opportunity to sow some serious disinformation here. But it's a silly-small window of opportunity. We either get some fake versions of these documents in the next couple of hours or we lose the chance. I kinda doubt they'll give him an extension.'

'You realise what you're asking, don't you?' he says with a sigh. 'Do you have any idea of the kinds of approvals we need for a stunt like that?'

'Are you kidding? You've got the PM on speed dial!' I exclaim. 'Besides, surely there must be someone, like somewhere in the depths of Six, just churning this kind of stuff out all day long, just in case, right?'

'We'll see,' he replies. 'Just remember, whatever you do, don't get caught breaking the law over there. You are all associated with an organisation which theoretically doesn't exist. Let's leave it that way, shall we?'

'Hang on,' I reply, 'so if we see something bad about to go down and the only option is not entirely legal, then we're meant to just do nothing? Are you kidding me?! That can't be the official line?'

'My God, girl,' he replies, laughing hard. 'Read between the lines. It's not breaking the law if one doesn't get caught.'

'Okay, cool. Good to know.'

'I'll see what I can do. In exchange, there's something we'd like.'

'Uh-huh. Go on, then...'

'Take me off speaker phone.'

I do so and it doesn't take him long to outline his ask. I scowl and curse softly.

'You know that's not going to be easy, right?'

'If this was Mission Easy, I'd go call Tom bloody Cruise. What was the point of spending so much time with that French bastard Cabal if this is too hard? Think you can do it?'

'I'll give it a shot.'

'That's my girl. Bye then...'

'Hey, wait, how're you doing with that exit plan?'

'Give me a few hours.'

'Two tops,' I say, before he hangs up.

'What did he want?' Milly asks.

'You don't want to know. Hey, before I forget, remind me later to look at those pics I took at the China Club. I need to look at something...'

'Right,' Milly says with a disbelieving shake of her head. 'Think he'll come through?'

'Who knows? But if I had to put money on anyone to be sufficiently connected and nefarious, it'd be him. Guess we just wait and see.'

'You do know there's no way that Styles will leave here if he doesn't give them something which they fall for hook, line and sinker, right?' Anabel cautions.

'Yup,' I nod.

'Good, just checking,' she says. 'Now what?'

'I say we go back to the problem we were thinking about before he arrived,' Milly says, turning back to her laptop. Nodding, I retake my seat near the drawn curtains.

'Well,' she says, standing and advancing towards the projected image on the wall. 'To blow their plans we need to know who they are. We have lots of little bits. We have this car which followed you from the consulate when George gave you that little tour. Likely Chinese intelligence. Question is, how did they know we were here? They shouldn't have, right? George knew we were coming. C told him. Maybe he told Sam? What did you call him? An ambitious little turd? Well, he probably called it in anyway, just for the brownie points. You know, that London had sent someone out. He likely didn't know what for. But that's got to be the only way anyone could have known of your arrival. That therefore links whoever was in that car to the group Sam was in bed with, surely? But then again, we were nobodies to them at that point. Puzzling, then, that they bothered following you.'

'It depends on how many people they have working for them, though,' Anabel comments. 'Enough resources, not a problem, I guess.'

'True. We can come back to it. Then there's the white van that you followed up to the Peak, Hev. Who were they? PLA? Who knows? They didn't look like rental thugs.'

'That's for sure,' Anabel concludes.

'Right? And then we have the people from the China Club. And the woman Sam brought to Ap Lei Chau. The North Korean. That guy Styles met in the Captain's Bar. The question is, how much of it is connected? Or is half of it coincidence? What's actually going on here? And what ends is everyone working towards?'

'GC did say this place is an espionage hotbed at the moment,' I note. 'But wait, let's deal with them one by one. The guys at the China Club are all part of the plan that Sam and Yang were cooking up with the North Korean, right?'

'Agreed,' Anabel nods.

'So, let's just start running stuff and see what we can find. Maybe there's a connection we've missed? Something that ties some of those other loose ends in. I dunno.'

'Can you access anything from the Data Room back at school?' asks Anabel. 'Maybe run the photos and see what we get back?'

We try, but disappointment follows disappointment as attempt after attempt results in nothing more than a series of 'zero matches found' being displayed on the screen. That there is no information on Mr Sinister from the PLA is not a big surprise. But there is nothing on record for Sam's female associate, either.

Twenty minutes spent, with Luther's assistance, getting into the Mandarin's security camera back-up system for a face-on CCTV capture of the man Styles met in the bar proves to be a waste of time, too, when he also comes back as an unknown as far as Six's database is concerned.

'Well, I suppose it's fair to say the Chinese secret service takes the secret bit pretty seriously,' Anabel says with a peeved sigh. 'Now what?'

'Sod it, I dunno,' I frown despondently. 'Might as well try the number plates of those cars we got photos of.'

'We can try,' Milly says haltingly. 'But I can't believe getting into the local DVLA is going to be simple. Or quick.'

'Aye, right! Dinnae underestimate civil service tech,' Luther announces confidently from the screen. 'Or how shite it can be. Gonna need a few mins, lassies.'

'Do ya think he speaks like that just to piss us off?' I whisper under my breath. Shrugging, we stand, and Anabel opens the fridge to remove a can of beer. She offers one to Milly and me.

'Oh God, no,' I laugh, doubling over. 'After what happened the last time we went drinking and got absolutely bugger-blotted… yeah right, best I say no.'

'Do you regret it?' Anabel asks, completely straight-faced and with a disarmingly matter-of-fact tone. The bluntness takes me by surprise. For a moment I hesitate, aware both are watching me keenly.

'Funny, because she asked me the same question earlier on, too. Honest answer, no. But at the same time, I won't lie to you, I was seriously conflicted for a good while afterwards. Yeah, yeah, I know, despite what I said. But I didn't know how to process it or how I should react. So, I tried not to, I guess.

You know, play it all cool and the like. But I stick to what I said at the time.'

'I'm glad,' Anabel replies as she pops the ring pull with a sharp crack. 'Things are only uncomfortable if we make them uncomfortable. Besides, what happens in Hong Kong stays in Hong Kong, right?'

'Yeah,' I reply with a sheepish, embarrassed grin. 'That said, if this evening ends up going a bit pear-shaped, best I stick to a Coke or something.'

'Yeah, that's probably sensible,' Anabel giggles and swigs deeply from the beer can.

'I think your girlfriend's becoming an alcoholic.'

'Tell me something else that's new,' sighs Milly.

'They do have this,' Anabel suggests with a grin, holding up a green Heineken bottle from the fridge. 'Double-oh.'

'Yeah, that sounds appropriate,' I laugh as I reach out to take it. With a glance at the label, Heineken 0.0, I exclaim, 'Oh perfect. That'll do nicely.'

'Oh my God, you two are as bad as each other,' Milly scowls.

We turn as we finally notice Luther calling with growing irritation from the computer.

'Oi, is anyone still there?!'

'Yeah, we're coming,' laughs Milly as she takes her seat again in front of the laptop. Anabel and I hang back and listen, clinking our beers with wide grins.

'So, I'm in. What do you want to search for?'

'Wow, that was fast.'

'Aye, more than just a pretty face, huh?'

'Hey, guys, I've got to go,' Nigel says. 'We have a morning meeting which I need to prep for. Ping me if you need anything.'

We say goodbye and turn our attention back to Luther.

'Okay, I'm sending you the number plate of a car that Hev got a shot of on our first day here,' Milly says. 'Can you see what comes up for it?'

'Yeah, got it. Give me two... Er, yeah, so here we go. It's owned by a corporate entity –'

'Cover front perhaps?' theorises Milly.

'Possibly. All I can see is it's registered to an address on Middle Gap Road. Seems –'

'Hold on, stop a sec,' Anabel interrupts. 'Sorry, Luther. I know that road. It seems an odd place for commercial property. Way too expensive. It's just monster mansions up there as far as I know.'

'Just one more strange thing to add to this list of strange things,' Milly sighs. 'Okay, sending you another plate. This was from a transit van. Can you run it, too?'

'Yeah. Alright. Heh,' he chuckles a moment later. 'You ready for this? It's registered to the same address.'

'Kidding, right?' Anabel says, turning to us in surprise. 'What number? House number, I mean.'

'Twenty-four.'

'Let me find an aerial shot,' Milly says, typing quickly. On another screen she opens a series of satellite photos.

'Wait, wait,' I cry, quickly stepping forward, pointing excitedly. 'That's the house where the white van went. I'm positive. I just never saw a street sign or house number. What're the chances, right?' I laugh, fixing Milly with an amazed look.

'I don't believe in coincidence,' she says.

'I know, right? But that's exactly what this is,' I exclaim. 'Except maybe it isn't.'

'What do you mean?'

'I mean, maybe we shouldn't be surprised. Maybe we should have checked it way earlier. Like, why *wouldn't* they just use a big, isolated house? I mean, Chinese intelligence barely even has an official name, right? Why would they have set up an official public headquarters in the city? It makes me think of something C said, back in London. He said when they eventually flog Vauxhall Cross, people will be surprised what the building was really used for. Like it's not even for serving officers. I mean, you're the only one of us who's ever been there, right, Mills? And what did you really see? Not a whole lot, right? Certainly not tonnes of officers milling around. No black helicopters or counter-revolutionaries strolling around. Course not. That's all remote and decentralised. What if the Chinese don't have an official building here, either, but instead just based themselves out of that big mansion? Look at it. Buried in the jungle like that. It's perfect if you're up to no good.'

'True,' Milly adds. 'And if you don't want your comings and goings seen by nosey neighbours.'

'Hardly. Doubt there's a neighbour within several hundred metres of the place,' Anabel notes.

'Hang on. Luther, do us a favour, will you?' Milly says. 'Can you search the other way around? Do it by the address. How many cars are registered to the address?'

'Oh yeah, good one,' he replies, before whistling. 'Whoa, check this out...'

'Okay, look at this, you two,' Milly says as she receives the file from Luther. 'Oh wow, it's a busy place, alright. They have over two dozen cars up there and, er, thirty-four registered drivers. Sedans, vans, taxis. You name it. It's a proper fleet of vehicles. And, oh my God, look, we've got their photos and names as well. This is insane. Oh, it gets even worse. This is so sloppy. See, all the driving licences are in sequential order, meaning they were either miraculously all registered at once or more likely were "added" to the database at the same time by someone.'

'That's embarrassing, but it all fits, right?' Anabel comments, peering in closer to look over Milly's shoulder. 'They're all young, military-looking types, too.'

'Goes to show, right?' Milly says, looking in admiration at her girlfriend. 'Half of intelligence is tacit knowledge. That local expertise to know the difference between a building in Central and high society way up on the Peak.'

'Wait, that's it,' I say excitedly. 'That's how we beat them. Or certainly chuck a right spanner in their works. We just release their names, photos, licence plates, all of it to the local press, who can then publish it. We totally compromise their op-sec and blow the whole lot of them! It'll put their clandestine operations here back by months.'

'They'll think it's a hoax,' Milly scoffs. 'The press, I mean.'

'Maybe. But not necessarily. Done the right way, they might just buy it.'

'The Chinese are going to freaking freak out when this hits the fan,' Milly comments.

'Well, best we be long gone by then, don't you think?' says Anabel.

'How?' asks Milly. 'Time's not exactly on our side. We've also got to get Styles either off the hook or out of here within the next couple of hours. After that we have no idea how long we have before they suss out what's happened.'

'Mill's right,' Anabel says. 'Clock's ticking. We don't want to be here if they figure out the docs are fakes. Or when they trace the leak to the press. They'll lock this place down, iron clad.'

'Lock it down,' I say with a wry laugh. 'It already is! This storm's seen to that.'

'Hev's not wrong,' Milly groans. 'As much as it pains me to say it.'

'I bet it galls you when that happens,' I laugh. 'Point is, we're going to have to leg it the moment the handover is done. Which means if we're to release all this stuff and hopefully scupper whatever they intend to do, then we need to do it now. We wait any longer and the march will be over, and it'll be too late to do it after Styles does the handover.'

'Surely George must have contacts with the local press, wouldn't you think?' says Anabel. 'I'll deal with that. Meanwhile, you two figure out what we do to keep Styles out of jail.'

'You might be better off releasing the info to someone larger, maybe like the BBC or Associated Press. Reuters perhaps?' suggests Milly. 'Only because it'll spread faster than if you put it through the local press.'

'Perhaps, but here in Honk, local news spreads like wildfire. I'll see what contacts George has.' Then, after pausing for a moment, Anabel adds in a more cautionary tone, 'Something else to consider. Up till this point, we were simply watching Styles to assess whether he was here for nefarious reasons, right? Was there an espionage angle to his trip? But that was purely a United Kingdom problem. We weren't messing with the internal security of another sovereign nation. But what we're talking about here goes way beyond that, and right into Article 23 territory.'

'Okay, I'm fuzzy about what that means,' I reply, glancing at Milly to see if she is any the wiser.

'Point being, I assume,' says Milly, 'that given that none of us are here with any kind of diplomatic cover, we should be under no illusions about what will happen – should we get caught.'

'Exactly,' Anabel emphasises. 'To a large degree, this is what the protest outside is about. So, when we handed Honk back in '97, the government included something called Article 23 into Hong Kong's Basic Law which stated that a national security law was to be enacted in the Hong Kong Special Administrative Region. It was added partly because the existing law at the time was a bit woolly in this area. They'd tried to add the offences of subversion and secession in '96, but failed.

'They tried to pass it again in '03, but it got scuppered because of mass protests that summer. China pushed for it again several times, but it never happened. Then, in 2019, the city saw some major protests, which pissed Beijing off something chronic. So, they tried again to pass the law, but only managed to get a partial implementation which covered secession, subversion, terrorism and collusion with foreign powers. All that good stuff. But it didn't cover treason, theft of state secrets like through spying or anything to do with foreign meddling in Hong Kong's political affairs. Which is what China's after, let's face it.'

'What did it give them?' I ask. 'Like in terms of powers.'

'All your basics. Beijing got to set up a security office here, staffed with its own people. It allows the chief executive to appoint judges, so it hit the independence of the courts. It allows them to monitor the press, so it squashed free speech. They can try people out of sight and out of mind. The police can search someone's home without a warrant. They can ban people from leaving the territory. You get the drift, right?

But the real rub came in something called Article 38, which made the whole law applicable to anyone, regardless of whether they live in Hong Kong or not.'

'Wait,' I laugh. 'How can they make it extraterritorial?'

'Well, that's part of it, right? Not only does it criminalise criticism of the Chinese government here, but they essentially also asserted the legal right to enforce it against anyone in the world. No wonder, then, that shedloads of people fled HK. I mean, if you're going to be pedantic, it means eight billion people should've read that law to ensure they didn't violate it. But that's the joke interpretation, right? The reality is that it was only done that way to target local protestors and Hong Kong communities living abroad, to prevent them from stirring the pot and causing trouble back here. For some reason, they just used a really big paintbrush to achieve it.'

For a moment, she stops, momentarily lost in thought, before she suddenly gasps in realisation.

'But there's a real point here,' she stresses, holding a finger up in the air. 'One we haven't talked about yet. But perhaps it's the key to this entire thing. And I can't believe it only just occurred to me. Did you notice how each time they tried to pass this kind of legislation or clamp down on the city's liberties, it always seems to coincide with an outbreak of some kind of virus? SARS in '03, then COVID-19 in 2020.'

'Oh my God,' Milly cries. 'Tell me you aren't really being serious!? You can't honestly put faith in anything Sam said, can you? The traitorous little git. Besides, no one could be so stupid as to deliberately release a pathogen in the hope that it will prevent protests about a further clampdown on civil liberties, could they?'

I whistle. 'Wow, that's some serious conspiracy.'

'True, but not entirely beyond the realm of possibility,' Anabel cautions.

'Okay, but surely,' Milly ponders, 'if any further clamp-down on rights was coming, then someone – local politicians, the local government, whoever – would know? How would it stay secret?'

'Not necessarily,' says Anabel. 'Back in the summer of 2020, the details of the national security law were kept secret even from the then HK chief executive, Carrie Lam. First she knew about it was when the law was published in Chinese on the day it went live. I know it sounds a little far-fetched, but there are some pretty specialised corners of the clandestine services which have produced very sophisticated and insightful analysis into Chinese intent, and it's alarming.'

'Fine. Mills, call GC. Get the contacts he thinks the information should be leaked to. And figure out with him how best to leak it all very quickly. We should get it out before the march gets underway for real. Alright then, that's that,' I say, standing to look out the window, as Milly goes into the bathroom to make the call.

Turning to Anabel, I continue: 'Which brings us to Styles. What are the chances, you reckon, that the reason they want those documents is to see what the UK's reaction would be were they to rip the handover agreement up altogether? Which could be what their plan is, given what we were just discussing.'

'Makes sense,' nods Anabel. 'And securing the NATO plan is simply a play to see whether there's anything in it which alludes to a possible Western military or economic response to that kind of treaty violation with a standing NATO member. Like some kind of NATO pre-agreed pact thing.'

'Again, it would kind of be prudent to check that out first, right, if that's your plan?'

For a moment, neither of us say anything. A long, drawn-out silence grips the room as the full ramifications of our theory sink in.

'Fricking hell,' I say finally. 'We seriously need to call someone. George, the admiral, whoever. This we have to call in…'

'Okay, I have a mailing list from George,' Milly announces, reappearing from the bathroom. 'Let me get on to sending all this now. Give me a sec to get that VPN up and I can send it.'

'Remember to add the screenshot of the MTR stations the North Korean marked on the map.'

As she prepares the e-mail, which she formats to come from a sending account called Bunny410, we fill her in on our theory.

'As far as wild ideas go, you might not be wrong.'

'Who are you sending it to?' Anabel asks.

'Top of the list is the ICIJ, the International Consortium of Investigative Journalists, and then he added a bunch of local Asian news organisations. Guess we see who bites first. Okay, last check. Jeez, talk about pulling the pin on a grenade. Let's just hope it doesn't blow up in our faces.' With a deep breath, she cocks her head slightly, squints through one eye and winces as she emphatically presses send on her laptop.

CHAPTER 15

NO WAY OUT

Hong Kong

'Mr Styles, please sit down,' I stress, trying to conceal my mounting irritation as the agitated MP stalks nervously back and forth across the carpet of his hotel room. 'We get one shot at this, do you understand? One wrong move, one guilty look, and the game's up.'

'There has to be a better way,' he protests feebly.

'Trust us, ours is the best and, frankly, only option. The way I see it, besides this there were only three alternatives,' Milly explains, and counts on her fingers. 'One, you could have simply not told us anything, found a way to source the real documents – which I am still amazed actually exist – and betrayed your country to save yourself. Two, you could give them nothing and see what they do with those photos. Or three, you go to the press, tell them the Chinese are trying to blackmail a British cabinet minister, and again see what happens.'

'The way they'll likely spin that,' adds Anabel, 'before you know it, the Chinese will flip the story and make you the bad guy.'

'How? I haven't done anything wrong.'

'You're married,' I reply.

'Divorced,' he snaps bitterly.

'You're an MP,' Milly adds.

'You're the minister for ethics and morality,' Anabel concludes authoritatively and damningly. 'As much as I hate to say it, sir, the world is still not that accepting of homosexuality – especially for those who have taken a pretty big public stance around it constituting "moral rot", as you once put it. Those photos are one big, embarrassing target. As my friend said, this only works if you cooperate with HMG and give the Chinese these documents.' Glancing down, she pats the two thick stacks of paper lying beside her on the table.

Quite how the admiral managed to come through in such a short window with two entirely fabricated but wholly convincing protocols, none of us know. But come through he did, and in the nick of time, too, for George to print them on official paper and deliver them safely to the hotel within three hours of the initial ask going in.

'Because,' Milly adds pointedly, 'this gets out and you're right up there as another John Vassall.'

Styles's wounded look suggests he is all too aware of the ease with which men with his vulnerabilities have been sucked in and turned into an agent of a foreign power. And then publicly humiliated and imprisoned.

'What do they even say?' he asks, pointing at the documents.

'Basically,' Milly replies, as the only one of us to have perused the whole pack, 'that the UK will impose the harshest of economic sanctions on China, along with the US and a number of European countries. Just like with Russia and Ukraine. And that the UK will seek commitment from the US to revoke the HK special trading status and potentially ban Chinese companies from clearing dollars through US banks. The NATO plan calls for significantly increased right of passage trips by Western naval forces through the South China Sea, the establishment of a NATO APAC forward operating base in Singapore, and ultimately the establishment of a sister organisation in the Pacific to rival NATO, consisting of the US, UK, Japan, Australia, New Zealand, India and a few other countries.'

'That's preposterous,' Styles exclaims. 'They will never believe that. It's a complete overreaction. We probably wouldn't do that unless they went after Taiwan, and even that's questionable.'

'On the contrary, sir. The more far-fetched it is, the more likely they'll believe it,' Anabel replies, straight-faced. 'It'll feed into the level of paranoia they have. They think the West wants to do this anyway. Seeing it in black and white will simply confirm what they already suspect.'

'Okay, so we're agreed on the handover,' I note, concluding the discussion before Robert Styles can begin again with his tactic of deflecting and detracting from the topic at hand. 'And we have the handover address?'

'Agreed, and yes,' Milly chips in hurriedly, glancing at Styles. 'So, next question. What if they rumble the deception soon after we hand it over? How do we get out of here?'

'The admiral is working on a plan,' I reply.

'Would be so much easier if this storm wasn't bearing in on us,' she sighs.

'Well, the airport is definitely out,' Anabel says. 'Besides, they've become notorious for picking people up there just as they are about to leave. And they like to do it very publicly, too. The number of pro-democracy types who got lifted from the queue at immigration... I've lost count. That said, they only need to have photos of us from somewhere and we would immediately be picked out by their facial-recognition program,' she says, and turns to Robert Styles. 'Assuming that by the time we leg it, they'd be looking for you.'

'I don't know. It would almost be fun to try a typographic attack,' Milly laughs.

'I'm sorry, a what?' I say, looking confused.

'Okay, I get it that this is completely hypothetical now, but their surveillance system is just an AI programme which recognises things, right? In this case people. Facial recognition. But look, watch this,' she says, reaching for an apple from the complimentary bowl of fruit. 'Pass me my phone a sec. So, I open this app here called Real World ID, which is an object-recognition app but works just like all these programs, and watch.'

She points the camera at the apple and takes a photo.

'Okay, so it recognises it as a Granny Smith. Smart, huh? But now watch this. I take the hotel stationery and the pencil, and I tear a corner off and write on it the word "iPod", okay?'

Licking the small square, she sticks the paper to the side of the apple.

'Now watch what happens.'

She takes another photo, which elicits a small cry of triumph, and then places the phone on the table before doing a small celebratory dance.

'Are you kidding?' I exclaim, reading the AI's response. 'It really thinks that's a music player!'

'Yup,' Milly beams. 'I could paste a pound sign on a farmyard pig and it would say it was a child's piggy bank.'

'How does that even work?' Anabel asks in amazement.

'It's because people think these systems just do photo or image recognition. But that's not true. Their first-level ability, their bread and butter, is usually a pretty robust capability to read and comprehend text. When you show it a picture with really clear information on it, like words, the program sort of runs home to mummy, opts for the easiest answer and avoids the complex cross-referencing that would be required for something like facial recognition.'

'How can that help us?' I ask. 'Are you seriously saying we could just walk in there, right past all their cameras, and they wouldn't identify us if we held up a sign with someone else's name on it?'

'Yes,' she replies emphatically. 'Or written on a T-shirt or cap. The person probably needs to be alive. I mean, if you walked past with a sign saying "Marilyn Monroe", it might error the system, because she's, well...'

'Dead?'

'Yes. It would probably discount the answer which comes back because it knows she's dead. But choose someone alive and it will likely read that over identifying you.'

'How likely?' I ask, sitting forward.

'Pretty likely.'

'How come they haven't fixed it?'

'It's harder than it sounds. Like, back in 2015, Google's system was tagging black people as gorillas. Really embarrassing, right? But even years afterwards they still hadn't found why the AI was getting that error. They ended up having to manually untag everything that got tagged as a gorilla incorrectly by the AI. Fixing underlying issues in millions of lines of code isn't that easy. Same goes for this problem. Text recognition is a key part of these programs. You can't just turn it off. You can try to compensate, sure, so it gives higher percentage returns for the visual component, but that's not a fix.'

'Okay, so as cool as that sounds,' I reply, 'it only accounts for the tech side of things. Surely anyone stationed there physically – and I can't believe they wouldn't be, right? – they'd still spot us, assuming they were even looking for any of us?'

'Yes,' Anabel sighs. 'That is true.'

'What does that mean?' Robert Styles asks nervously.

'I think you know,' I say. 'I'm guessing it means we can't leave by the airport.'

'Right. But either way, it's all academic,' Anabel notes dryly. 'Because as I said earlier, we're not going anywhere in this storm. Not a chance. First thing they close is the airport.

And the storm will easily be here by the time we're done.'

'True,' I add ruefully. 'Don't worry, I'm sure the admiral will find another way out.'

'How?' Anabel implores. 'There is no other way!'

'There's always another way,' I reply calmly but without elaborating. 'Don't worry. We'll think of something.'

'That's not a plan,' Milly stresses, wide-eyed, her voice rising uncomfortably.

'Hey, no plan lasts once it's put into motion. Relax, we'll come up with something when the need arises.'

'Oh my God, you're so impulsive. You know it does my head in, right?'

'Yup,' I grin.

'And you know impulsiveness is a strong trait in psychopaths, right?'

'Yeah, we should probably get going,' I reply, flashing her an evasive smile. 'Not long till the handover meeting.'

'Hey, check your phones,' Milly exclaims excitedly. 'You see this? The story's out! George just pinged us a link to a news site that's run a piece about PLA agents operating in our midst. It's got all of it: their pictures, their cars, even the house where they're based. It's all blown!'

'No way,' Anabel gasps. 'That's awesome. Can't believe they did that.'

'Well, they're based in Taipei, so I guess they don't care too much about repercussions.'

'Do they mention the virus stuff?'

'Erm, only briefly, at the very bottom. And they only say the senior officers behind this unit were recently seen meeting with North Korean virology specialists, and the purpose of the meeting is currently unknown.'

'Well, that puts the cat amongst the pigeons,' I note dryly. 'We should get a move on.'

'Agreed. You good to go?' Anabel asks, turning to Robert Styles.

'If I must,' he replies reluctantly.

*

The near-empty streets of Central have a distinctly febrile atmosphere as we make the short trip from the hotel's rear exit, up the hill and towards the famous party district of Lan Kwai Fong. The very real chance that Robert Styles could be the target of surveillance teams the moment he leaves the hotel means we depart well before he does. The walk only takes a few minutes. Nonetheless, it's hot and humid enough that we are all sweating by the time we turn into LKF.

On the way, spotting what I have been looking for since we left the hotel, I turn to Anabel and ask a quick favour of her. With a puzzled look, she hurries off towards a Fortress electronics store on the other side of the wide crossroads.

'Worried you'll lose it?' Milly asks, nodding curiously at the iSpy I have clasped in my hand.

'Nah. Just planning ahead is all.'

'Didn't think you did that.'

'Shh, don't let anyone know,' I laugh. 'Our little secret...'

As far as clandestine meeting places go, Lan Kwai Fong turns out to be an inspired choice on the part of the Chinese intelligence officers. It is a tightly concentrated area, so typical of Hong Kong, full of narrow side-streets lined with garishly lit bars, clubs and restaurants, all of which are packed full with drinkers. Their chosen venue is an open-fronted bar-cum-restaurant straddling the corner of D'Aguilar Street and the L-shaped cobbled side street of Lan Kwai Fong itself. The raucous crowd of well-financed, drunken expats inside seems determined on riding out the impending storm to a heady cocktail of loud music and endless drinks. Few are likely to notice a quick slight-of-hand transfer of documents. Additionally, the constant movement within would make any surveillance team's ability to observe the handover incredibly difficult.

A crazy, carefree attitude holds sway inside as the rain starts to fall in earnest. Great surging gushes dump from the sky, quickly turning the sloping road beside the bar into a fast-flowing river. As we snake our way through the tightly pressed crowd, people smile and laugh with the wild abandonment that comes from being part of some huge, exclusive party.

A table set just in from the perimeter stands empty with a reserved sign on it. It corresponds to the instructions Robert Styles received earlier by instant message. Anabel and Milly nod and take up positions close by, while I head on towards the bar.

'Screw me,' I exclaim, rejoining them a few minutes later. 'It's bloody expensive!' Carefully, I hand them their drinks, both of which are already seeping with condensation in the sticky heat.

'Got to pay the insane rents around here somehow,' Anabel says with a resigned shrug. 'Hongky landlords are some of the biggest dicks going. Greedy bastards put the rents sky high. Then if a place does well and makes money, they just up the rent again. No wonder so many good places close. This area used to be so cool. But then they let Seven-Eleven open down the road, and it didn't need a liquor licence. It's little wonder all the bars struggle here when people can just buy booze from there super cheap and then drink on the streets.'

The force of her feelings surprises me. Still, I have the good sense to remain quiet as her face contorts in anger.

'Honestly, if people knew all the dodgy deals the government has made over the years with property developers, landlords and the uber rich, no government on earth would deal with them. Seriously. It's basically one massive criminal enterprise. Pocket lining on an industrial level. So sad, because I love this city, I really do, and they are just destroying it. Literally every decision the government makes, they make the wrong choice. Certainly not for the greater good, that's for sure.'

'Hey, you want to keep your drink cold?' Milly says, clearly looking to lighten the mood as Anabel falls silent. 'Wipe the condensation off it. Otherwise it actually warms the drink.'

'Really? I thought condensation works the other way round,' I laugh, putting a reassuring arm around Anabel's shoulders. 'Like sweat. Cools it, I thought.'

'Only in cool climates. Somewhere like this, it's the opposite. Weird, huh? It transfers the ambient heat *into* the drink. Gotta love science, right?' Milly smiles.

'Yeah,' I reply, giving the faintest nod of my head to draw her attention to Robert Styles's arrival. A waitress shows him to his table. But rather than order a drink, he merely sits still, glancing occasionally left and right, either intrigued by the rowdy crowds milling around him or nervously awaiting the arrival of the Chinese. His face betrays little, making it hard to be sure what he's thinking. As we talk, watching from afar, I can't help but wonder how much of his behaviour is the result of him having hidden his true self for so long.

Glancing at her Observatory app, Anabel announces that they have just raised the typhoon 8 signal. A minute later, a call goes out from the bar, announcing it, and the fact that happy hour prices are now in effect. A cheer goes up, and there's a surge of movement towards the bar. Yet still Styles sits and waits. Half an hour passes. Then forty-five minutes. And still no one shows up.

'You think anyone's coming?' I ask. 'Or you think the whole thing is just a set-up?'

'Your guess is as good as anyone's,' Anabel replies. 'I reckon the wait is a test. But who knows?'

Several people approach Styles, and for a moment we hold our breath, wondering if this is it. But each in turn gestures at the spare seats arranged around the table. Awkwardly, he replies, pointing outside, whilst consciously clasping the documents close to hand in a white plastic bag. Each nods, disappointed, and slips away again.

'Just wanted the seats, I guess,' Milly says, frowning. 'He doesn't exactly look optimistic that anyone's coming, does he?'

As we finish our first round, Anabel announces she'll get another one in, or else we'll begin to look odd standing here with nothing to drink.

Finally, after an hour's wait, three men arrive and make their way directly towards Styles's table. All are dressed in black military fatigues. None have any identifying badges or patches that we can see. Leading the way are two humourless-looking young men sporting universal military short-top-and-sides haircuts. Following behind them is the sinister-looking PLA Special Forces man from the China Club and the meat-packing factory. Gone is his calm, confident demeanour; a look of profound irritation has come over him. He scrolls his finger hurriedly across his phone's screen and his mood darkens the more he reads.

'I reckon that leak's chucked an almighty spanner into their plans,' I muse, failing to hide an amused little smile.

For a cold and calculating man – someone who, in all likelihood, is probably a ruthless piece of work – he can certainly still play the game. As he approaches Robert Styles, his irritation bleeds away. With a warm greeting, he shakes Styles's hand and takes a seat, as an old friend might. Once he does so, the others take their places as well. The leader orders a round of drinks from a passing waitress.

'Jeez, this guy is a piece of work, isn't he?' I mutter. 'You'd think they've known each other for years.'

'Tradecraft. Don't get where he is without breaking a few eggs,' Milly says.

'What does that even mean?' Anabel laughs.

Without a word, but with a less than willing look, Robert Styles slides the plastic bag across the table. In response, the PLA man nods at one of his foot soldiers, who reaches into a pocket and removes what could be a zip drive.

'The originals?' I ask.

'Probably,' replies Milly. 'Don't waste time, do they? You think that's it?'

'Sadly no,' I reply. 'Because now comes the hard part. Quite how I do this, I'm not quite sure.'

'Oh dear, what are you up to now?' Milly asks as I turn towards Styles's table.

'They want me to lift the phone of whoever turned up to meet him.'

'The admiral asked you to do that?' she exclaims in disbelief.

'Yup.'

'Bloody hell,' Anabel says. 'How are you going to do that?'

'Who knows? Fast hands, I suppose. We'll see.'

'You'll need a major distraction,' Milly says, thinking fast. 'They don't exactly look the types to fall asleep at the wheel.'

'Yup. Too right. Just no time for that. Reckon they're about to leave. Sod it. Back in a sec. Actually, see you by the door over there in about thirty secs...'

Milly bites her lip in deep, conflicted thought and nods. With an 'okay' gesture, I set off towards the huddled group, cursing silently to myself the closer I get. Milly was right, having a plan would be advantageous. Perhaps I can cause a bar brawl? Except the crowd doesn't feel the type for that. All alphas, for sure, but interestingly not the aggro alpha types one would find all too often back home.

I glance back for reassurance to see Milly has taken Anabel's hand and is quickly leading her towards the table nearest them, in the centre of the bar, where a group of young men are sitting, drinking and laughing. Delicately stepping on the edge of one of their chairs, she pulls Anabel up onto the tabletop, much to the consternation of the table's occupants. Their irritation is short lived, however. Curious, I pause for a moment, as puzzled as I am intrigued. Standing facing Anabel, Milly takes her waist and, with her free hand, pulls her into a passionate kiss. With a grin, I realise that if it's distraction that was needed, then it's distraction that I've got. The already charged atmosphere of the rowdy crowd erupts into a frenzied baying of excited wolf-whistles, whoops and cheers as people rise excitedly to their feet to clap.

'Only in fuckin' Hong Kong,' a nearby man in suit and tie shouts to his friend as I pass by his table. They, too, leap up clapping and shouting enthusiastically as I accelerate on towards Styles's table, approaching from behind in the hope that the PLA man won't look around and recognise me.

The spectacle from the centre of the bar is, thankfully, sufficiently unmissable that even he and his men have glanced around to see what the sudden commotion is all about. To his credit, he is disciplined enough not to leap up and cheer like almost everyone else has, but he is distracted nonetheless. The corner of his mouth curls up in mild amusement and he absentmindedly places his phone, with its screen still unlocked, on the table to his left.

It's the opportunity I need. Without a second thought, as my heart hammers inside my chest, I dart my hand out, swipe the handset and replace it in one swift movement with a similar-looking one which I asked Anabel to buy earlier in Fortress. Just another nondescript, black touch-screen slab of a phone, as close to what we saw he had from the China Club photos as possible. My hope was it is standard issue for all of them.

With several deep, calming breaths, I make a quick beeline back into the crowd, rolling my eyes in relieved disbelief at how men the world over all seem incapable of not gawping at two girls making out. Thankfully, it affords me the few extra seconds I need to escape and make my way outside.

Much to everyone's disappointment, Milly finally breaks for air, and giggles self-consciously atop the table. Taking Anabel's hand, she raises it triumphantly above them and shouts, 'I'm taking this one back to the hotel. Enjoy the typhoon lock-in, everyone!'

With a surprised yet intrigued look, Anabel jumps off the table, clearly a little shell-shocked, before helping Milly down. To much congratulatory back-patting, they make their way slowly through the tightly packed crowd towards the street. Glancing back, I see the PLA man irritably snatch his phone off the table and gesture to his men that it is time to leave. Now if only the torrential rain can serve as sufficient further distraction for him to not look at the phone again for a good few minutes, this might just work.

I hurriedly dart along the outside of the bar to intercept my friends as they break through the outer ring of drinkers and emerge with relief into the rain. I have never seen their smiles so big.

'Bloody hell, Mills,' I exclaim. 'Where did that come from?'

'I don't know,' she cries, alive and buzzing with excitement.

'I'd like to know, too,' says Anabel breathlessly.

'Whatever it was, it was brilliant!' I gush.

'One thing's for sure,' Anabel adds, wagging a reproachful finger with just enough humour not to come across as jealous or genuinely worried. 'No way are you two sharing a room anymore.'

'You don't have to worry about that,' I laugh. 'Upper-sixth next term, girlfriend. We all get our own studies.'

'That's true,' she grins with relief. 'Good!'

'You have nothing to worry about,' Milly says, turning to place a delicate kiss on her lips. 'I love you so much, nothing's getting in the way of that. I learnt that from royalty, you know,' she says with a laugh. 'Kissing like that.'

'Have some of them in your contacts, do you?' I ask.

'As a matter of fact, I do,' she giggles, lightening the moment. 'And well chuffed about it I am, too.'

'Besides, what happens in Hong Kong stays in Hong Kong, right?' I add.

'Absolutely,' they both reply, grinning.

'Right, I need your help,' I say, hurriedly handing Anabel the stolen handset, which I have been keeping awake with frequent taps of the screen. 'It's all in Chinese. Can you turn off all the security stuff? No password, nothing. We can't have it lock on us.'

'Yeah, that's easy enough,' she says, swiping quickly through various menus to disable several toggles. 'Okay, done. Now what?'

'Go into all his instant message apps and download all the chat histories onto the phone's memory. I don't want them deleting it all from the back end. And when you're done with that, can you save all the e-mails to the memory, too? Then remove the SIM card and turn it off. Can't imagine we have long before he finds the phone he's carrying is not his. And then it's just a matter of time before someone tries to locate it, block it or force-wipe the thing.'

'Knowing them, it'll have some sort of remote self-destruct,' Anabel half jokes.

'Yeah, so best it be turned off by then, and SIM free.'

'Okay, on it now.'

'Right, best we get back to the hotel,' I say, peering up at the rain. 'Anyone see where Styles went? He just upped and left.'

'Maybe he's also gone back to the hotel?' suggests Milly.

'In this?' Anabel asks, gesturing to the surging waves of water lashing down outside. The wind has also picked up noticeably since we arrived and is now gusting with real deter-mination, toppling anything not firmly held down, including the bright-orange rubbish bins on the street corners. Litter and debris are scattered across the street, and larger objects like branches and cardboard boxes are being tossed about outside by the wind with ease and impunity.

'C'mon,' I call. 'Let's just leg it. There's also no telling how quickly they could verify whether those docs are fake.'

'I doubt that's the real concern,' Anabel says as she furiously works the backups on the stolen phone. 'If they could conclude that, it means they have another source somewhere. Makes no sense. They wouldn't have needed Styles. No, the worry now is that they simply arrest him for spying. That's the real winner, right? They humiliate the UK something proper that way.'

'You think they'd do that? After he just gave them those documents?'

'I would, you know, if it were me,' she replies without looking up. 'You simply deny the exchange, or say he approached you to hand over documents for cash or for favours, whatever. Make up what you want. The more sordid, the better. Point being, everyone's having a go at them for spying and cyber-hacking day in, day out, right? How big a coup would it be to arrest someone coming here and offering to spy for them, or acting against *them*? Whichever.'

'Why would they arrest him?' I ask. 'Wouldn't they welcome such an approach?'

'Okay, maybe they wouldn't arrest him. But they could certainly go public with it, or they could have the local police arrest him instead. It's a show of, "See, we even turn spies away. You have us all wrong, international community. We aren't after all your secrets after all."'

'But no one will believe that,' I reply.

'You're missing the point. China, its military, all the muscle-flexing, the chest-thumping propaganda, all that stuff – it's not for us; it's for their own people. Don't you get it? China's basically built on three thousand years of rise and fall, empire after empire, armed insurrection, conquest and subjugation, then split and collapse, run and rerun, over and over again.

They have about three hundred million affluent citizens and the rest are still basically in paddy fields, whether they like to admit it or not. Those proportions are not too far off what France and Russia had before their revolutions. And when the peasants find out how the "let them eat cake" crowd are living, they tend to get pretty pissed, right?

'They have two million people monitoring the internet alone, just to ensure that no embarrassing story gets too much traction. All they need is one spark that hits the right note and before you know it... well, look how fast the Berlin Wall came down. And they didn't even have social media back then. Three quarters of what China does is for the consumption of their own population. And don't underestimate how important maintaining face is here. It's just massive, okay? It's all about respect and honour. Insult someone and they lose face with those around them, which is bad. Shower someone with respect and they gain face. Point being, with so much of the world having a go at China, saving face back home is a massive motivator at the moment. They have a huge mortgage crisis, runs on their banks, unrest from their silly Covid strategy, you name it. If arresting a foreign politician helps them save face at home, then it could be worth doing, especially with all the negative news coming out of Honk now.'

'Okay, let's just head back, then,' I suggest. 'We need to find Styles before this all starts unravelling. How's that phone coming?'

'IMs are almost done. WeChat is ninety per cent. Then I'll see what I can do with the e-mails. Probably need to flip the account from IMAP to POP3. We'll see. That's if he's even old school enough to use e-mail.'

'Good. Then let's go find the useless git and get out of here.'

'And how exactly are we supposed to do that?' Milly says with a raised eyebrow. 'Because that sounds great and all, but I don't see how it's possible now.'

'Oh, I don't know,' I reply blithely. 'Where there's a will there's a way.'

'Oh God, now what are you cooking up?' she sighs.

'Think!' I ponder aloud to myself. 'What would Bond do?'

'You idiot,' she exclaims, smacking me across the arm. 'We need a plan!'

'Oh wait, that's right, I already came up with one. C'mon, let's go. Don't worry, I have a plan.'

'Uh-huh. Why do I not find myself suddenly overcome with confidence and reassurance?' Milly groans reluctantly as we set off into the driving wind and rain. 'Besides, as far as I recall, Bond died, didn't he? Not exactly a positive benchmark.'

'*No Time to Die*?' I say.

'Was that the one?'

'Yeah. Not my favourite moment,' I reflect. 'I'd have done it differently, I think.'

'Oh, really?' she exclaims, already thoroughly drenched. 'Well, go on then, tell us, as we all get soaked through, how you'd have come up with a better ending than all the people who made that movie combined.'

'I dunno. Hey, don't get me wrong, it was a great film and all. And a cool way to say bye to Daniel Craig. I just think it was too blunt. Like, too permanent. I mean, what if you'd had him stumble off up that hill, away from the bunker, before the missiles landed? Kind of ambiguous. Like, did he or didn't he kick the bucket? And then you cut to that shot of the mum and daughter in the Aston Martin bombing along those mountain roads, and the mum turns to the kid and goes, "I'm going to tell you a story about a man named Bond, James Bond." And the girl grins in anticipation and then turns to look back behind her. And there, with his arms stretched out over the top of the rear seats, is Bond. Just relaxing. Chilling. And he just smiles all depreciatingly back at the girl. And that's it.'

'I don't get it,' Milly shouts in an effort to be heard over the driving wind. 'Is he there, or is he dead?'

'Well, that's the point, silly. You don't know. Maybe he made it and has just taken a back seat in life. All relaxed and chilled. Or maybe it's a ghost and he's just watching over that family of his.'

'Oh...'

'Either way, right, it's a neater ending than getting wasted on a hillside by some Royal Navy missile.'

'You give this stuff *way* too much thought,' Anabel laughs as we march on through the torrential rain and gusting wind.

'Yeah, I know,' I laugh. 'But it goes with the turf, right?'

It is a concerned-looking hotel doorman who rushes to open the taped-up glass door to let us in as we arrive back at the Mandarin. Five minutes outside might as well have been a plunge into a swimming pool. For a few comical moments, we stand laughing, wiping water and stray, matted hair from our faces as large puddles form beneath us on the gleaming marble of the hotel's back entrance corridor.

'You really shouldn't be out there in this,' the doorman says, peering out with wary trepidation as thick sheets of water lash across the glass outside. 'Would you like me to fetch you some towels?'

'That would be great,' Anabel says, wringing out the

bottom of her dress.

As the helpful staff member hurries off to find some towels, Milly turns to me and asks, 'Now what?'

'Best we check out,' I reply. 'At the same time, we need to find Styles and make a fast departure.'

'What about all our stuff?' asks Milly. 'I don't see us lugging it around in this – or whatever stupid plan you're cooking up.'

'Agreed,' Anabel adds. 'Let's leave it with the concierge and have George pick it up.'

'Like it,' I say. 'How's that phone doing?'

'Let me see,' she replies, taking it out from the relative dryness of her small clutch bag. 'It's done. It was only WeChat he used. I'll take out the SIM. Mills, you got a hairpin? Cool, thanks. Okay, and there we go, turning it off. Yay, all done,' she concludes, handing it to me.

'Ace. Why don't you both get our things? Here's my key. I'll settle everything for both rooms, okay?'

'And we really have to go back out in that?' Milly asks unhappily.

'Yeah, 'fraid so. It's just too risky to hang around here for any longer. I bet they're already going ape shit trying to figure out where all that info came from. Who knows what they could trace? And God help Styles if they suss out those documents were fake, too. Seriously, it's safest this way.'

'I'm just not convinced,' Anabel says, peering out towards the rain-lashed street with clear reluctance to venture out into it again. 'I mean, why leave now? How would they possibly think to look here? It's so public. So obvious. Even if they suss out who we are, chances are they'd assume that we'd be in some safe house somewhere, wouldn't they? Because that's where they'd put their people. It's like the PLA putting officers into the Dorchester. I mean, it's just not going to happen, like, ever. They'd squirrel them away in the depths of Chinatown or South Ken, as far away from anything public as possible. They'll expect HMG to do the same. In fact, staying here was about as good a cover as one could hope for.'

'Till now, yes,' I reply, growing tired of the debate. 'But you really want to take the chance? Who knows what Sam told that girl? Did he know we were here?'

'I don't even think he knew *we* were here,' Milly says, pointing to herself and Anabel. 'As in even in the city.'

'I don't disagree,' I reply. 'But they only need to have made me to make you. The longer we argue about this, the less time we have.'

'Why won't you tell us what the admiral's exit plan is?' Milly presses, changing tack.

'Because it's slightly mad.'

'Oh great, if you call it mad, I dread to imagine.'

'In fairness, it wasn't all his plan,' I add with a devilish smile. 'Most of it was mine. He just filled in the gaps. Anyway, like you say, best you don't know. Not yet anyway. Not until it's too late to say no,' I laugh. 'Okay, let's do this. Belle, I get your concern. You, too, Mills. But I just have a feeling. And you know I've learnt to trust them, right?'

'We are all quite mad,' Milly sighs, hanging her head. 'I swear, this goes tits up, I'm blaming you, you understand?'

'Yeah, that's fair. Belle, what about you?'

'Seriously not happy with this whole mess, either. But okay,' she agrees reluctantly.

'Awesome. What a team! Okay, can one of you call GC and tell him to come and collect all our stuff? Tell him we're leaving and getting Styles out of here, too. Orders from on high. Tell him I'm also leaving the personal encrypted mobile device of a senior Chinese intelligence officer, and it's unlocked and waiting for him to collect it at the front desk. Should have some interesting things on it.'

'Fine. We'll also pop by Styles's,' Milly says as they set off down the corridor. 'See if he's there. And then we'll pack. Anything we need to bring?'

'Maybe a waterproof jacket if you have one. And some sunnies. That kind of thing,' I call back. 'And we'll need those spare cheapy handsets you bought earlier on, too, Belle.'

'All of them?'

'Yeah. What we don't use, we bin later.'

They nod and make for the lift bank, off to the side of the main lobby. After pausing for a moment to consider if there is anything I am forgetting, I make my way into the hotel lobby and approach the front desk. After waiting for a Russian couple to finish, I reach the counter, just as my phone goes. Signalling for the clerk to give me a moment, I quickly answer it.

'Found Styles,' Milly says. 'He's in his room, showering. You wouldn't believe it. He's treating this like some kind of Sunday outing.'

'Tell him to move his arse. We need to leave now.'

'Yeah, he says he has no intention of leaving by any means other than the airport, and only once this storm has passed. He says he's not running from anyone with his tail between his legs.'

'Ironic that he would use that phrase. Okay, fine. Leave him for now. Go pack. We'll chase him down later, when you're done and we're ready to leg it. See how fast you can get back down here.'

'You sure?'

'Yup.'

'Okay. You want a change of clothes?' she asks. 'You know, while we're at it.'

'Just my Raid jacket. The black waterproof one. It's in the cupboard, I think. And my sunnies, please. Oh, and my baseball cap.'

'The grossly unsubtle one? The one that should have got you arrested the moment we arrived?'

'That's the one,' I laugh.

Hanging up the call, I turn to the patiently waiting staff member and request to settle the bills for both rooms. As he prepares these, I ask for an envelope and drop the stolen phone into it. After sealing the flap, I write 'GC' in big letters on the front and hand it back to the man for safekeeping until its collection.

'Miss Wright,' the clerk says. For a second, I am momentarily lost between the various names I am using here: one for immigration, another for the hotel and a third for the consulate.

'Sorry, yes,' I laugh. 'Miles away.'

'Would you like to use the same card from check-in or a different one?'

'Oh, right, let me see,' I reply, flicking through my purse to make sure I gave the right card. 'Let's use that one, please.'

It takes him a few minutes to combine the bills, which I then sign, again mindful to use the right name.

'My friends are bringing our bags down, and someone will come and collect them, either later today or tomorrow. Could you keep them safe till then?'

'Of course, miss,' he replies courteously. 'We'll give you a collection tag for them.'

'Sure, but best I slip it into that envelope, too.'

'Certainly. And would you like an envelope for the bill?'

'Sure, why not,' I reply, casting short, apprehensive glances left, right and then behind me.

With the bill finally in hand and my credit card returned, I fold the envelope in two and force it into one of my sodden thigh cargo pockets. With a snap of my wrist, I check the time, and then take a seat in the far corner of the raised waiting area set off to the side of the lobby. There I wait, tapping my foot impatiently, for my friends to arrive. For the first few minutes, I let my eyes roam over the heavily Chinese-influenced décor of the waiting area. But I bore quickly and soon find myself glancing at my watch with increased regularity. Five minutes soon becomes ten, and each minute thereafter drags with an almost deliberately drawn-out disregard for my mounting anxiety.

When Milly and Anabel finally reach the lobby, it's with the casual nonchalance of carefree tourists on holiday that they stroll towards me with their suitcases and assorted bags, laughing and joking. It's either remarkably good cover acting or they are genuinely not taking this seriously.

'Oh my God, what took you so long?' I exclaim in exasperation. 'I mean, did you stop off at the spa along the way? Get a massage or something?'

'Yeah, hah-hah, you're so funny,' Milly sighs. 'Isn't she funny?' she adds, turning to Anabel.

'Like a comedian. You do realise that packing that fast is a skill,' Anabel says, rebuffing the accusation with feigned seriousness. 'Especially when faced with the size of your cosmetics bag.'

'Oi, it's not that big. Milly's is way bigger than mine.'

'The difference is, I keep all my stuff neatly in the bag.

Yours was strewn all over your pigsty of a bathroom.'

'Hey, I'll have you both know I resent the insinuation that I live like a slob.'

'Fine. Doesn't mean it isn't true.'

As I cast a withering scowl at Milly, my eyes drift to a dark blur of movement in the taxi drop-off area, just beyond the glass front doors. The black delivery van that has just pulled to a halt outside is the first vehicle to arrive since I sat down here. Why it is out and about in this storm when barely any other vehicles seem to be is the first thing that piques my interest. More concerning, though, is the sight of four well-built men, all in similar black fatigues as those from the bar earlier, stepping from the van.

'Uh-oh, don't like the look of this,' I note quietly. 'You know those bad feelings I was talking about?'

'You think this is one of them?' Milly asks, glancing outside.

'Dunno. Maybe. Mills, do us a favour, will you? Go phone Styles from over there. Tell him to get out of his room, now. I'm calling the admiral, just in case. Belle, dump our bags with the front desk. Tell them to tape the tags to the envelope I left for GC. Make sure you watch them attach them.'

Milly's amused expression disappears as the men march into the lobby and follow a direct path towards the lifts.

'Yeah, those don't look like guests, or air-con engineers,' Anabel mumbles warily as she makes for the front desk with our luggage.

'No, they don't,' Milly says, hurrying after her.

Turning, I pull out my phone and redial London. Seconds tick by, yet no one answers.

'Come on, you've got to be kidding me,' I mutter, hanging up and switching to IM. The admiral was last online only two minutes ago. Fighting the surge of irritation that he isn't answering, I hurriedly tap out a message telling him to call me immediately. Pressing send, I cast an irked look towards Milly, who has the desk phone to her ear but isn't speaking. She shrugs with a pained look and hands the handset back to the desk clerk. Rolling my eyes, I redial. Again it rings and rings. Just as I am about to hang up in anger, he answers.

'Sorry. Nature called. What's up?'

Just as I begin to speak, the men reappear. With them is Robert Styles.

'It's about to go pear-shaped. I think they're arresting Styles.'

'Can you be sure?'

'Pretty sure.'

'For what?'

'Does it matter?'

The four men march the MP across the lobby. One man leads the way, very self-importantly. In his hand is a laptop computer. Another brings up the rear. And on either side, a man walks with Styles, keeping him in check. It's only when they get closer that I realise each has an arm interlocked with his. Going willingly he clearly isn't.

'This is outrageous,' he shouts to anyone who will listen. 'You have no authority to do this. I demand to speak to the prime minister this minute! I have no connection with any of these protestors, you hear?!'

But no one responds. Everyone in the lobby turns away, pretending not to hear. Milly approaches, feigning surprise at the disturbance.

'Now there's irony,' I mutter. 'Given that they wanted him to spy for them.'

'We need to get out of here, and fast,' Anabel exclaims,

hurrying up beside me, an edge of tension in her voice.

'Are they uniformed?' the admiral asks. 'The people taking him.'

'Nope.'

'Then it's a kidnapping. Technically. Not a formal arrest.'

'Yeah, that's kinda debatable around here. Question is, do we intervene?'

Milly fires me a wide-eyed look to enquire whether I have gone completely mad. She grips my arm in alarm.

'If you think you can,' he says. 'You tell me. Do what you feel you need to do. If not, walk away. But if they arrest him, this gets infinitely messier. At the same time, you owe this problem as much as you want to owe it. You three want to leave now, do. Technically, you've done what you were asked to do.'

'Yeah, but...'

'Yeah, well, your call. If you can get that damned liability of a man out of the country before they make a right bloody spectacle of him, then so much the better. We cannot afford to have pictures of the damned minister for morality copping off with bloody rent-boys going public. It's like a nun running a meth lab out of the chapel, for God's sake. He'll make the government, not to mention the PM, a laughing stock if it gets out.'

'Okay, let me see what I can do.'

'Foxton...'

'Yeah?'

'Whatever you do, don't bugger it up and cause some an even bigger diplomatic nightmare for us, understand?'

'Yup, copy. You just make sure to get that pick-up organised, alright? I'll deal with this.'

'Copy that,' he replies and hangs up.

'Crap,' I hiss, passing Milly my phone. 'Keep this. I can't afford to get it broken.'

'What the hell are you going to do?'

'I dunno yet.'

With that, I walk quickly towards the double swing doors at the front of the hotel, through which the five men have just left. As they reach the van, Styles struggles, digging his feet in, desperate not to be pushed inside it. With barely any effort, the two men holding him jerk forwards, pulling him off balance, and drag him around the far side of the van, towards what I presume must be an open sliding door.

Stepping from the lobby, I see the hotel's front entrance is deserted. The rain is driving even harder than before, and the wind is howling with an angry roar peppered intermittently by a high-pitched whistling, loud enough to ensure none of them hear me approaching. As I round the rear of the vehicle, I see Styles's feet being dragged inside, before the last man climbs in.

As I race for the side door, I realise that five on one, if I include the driver, makes for poor odds in such a small, confined space. My arrival and first impact, therefore, must carry sufficient shock and awe to ensure this doesn't go horribly wrong very quickly. And hitting a fully grown man hard enough in such a small space so that he stays down is no mean feat.

Just short of the door, I leap up, snatching at the edge of the roof runner, and swing, feet first, into the vehicle. That I connect with anyone at all is miracle enough. That it isn't Styles, even more so. But the impact sends the man slamming into the far side of the van with enough force to buckle the thin metal sheeting out into a convex pocket around him.

The van lurches violently from side to side on its soft suspension. Righting myself, I power forwards and upwards, catching two men who are crouched over Styles, binding his hands, unprepared. Neither has time to move away, and before they know it I have both their heads in my outstretched hands and I slam them together in an unforgiving clash. Whimpering in terror, Styles scrambles quickly away into the far corner, where he pulls his knees to his chest and cowers.

Two men are left in action: one in the back, near the rear doors, and the driver, up front. Snatching glances left, then right, I decide to go for the man at the rear first. The driver is cursing in Mandarin and wrestling furiously to undo his seatbelt, which appears to have jammed. It's the delay I need. The rear-most man fires a look at the back doors, weighs his options, fight or flight, and chooses the former. Rushing forwards, he hurriedly steps over the sprawled-out legs of his fallen teammates and advances on me. Options are limited, and he has the clear advantage now with momentum. Worse, time is not on my side. In seconds, the driver will have calmed enough to stop tugging on the seat belt buckle and will have freed himself. If he escapes the vehicle and gets back into the hotel lobby, this becomes a very different kind of problem. Whatever I do now must be fast and decisive.

Reaching for me, the man angrily grabs my vest top and makes to swing me around, probably with intent to get me in a choke hold. Without any resistance, I fall backwards towards the floor, which wasn't what he expected. It pulls him forwards and awkwardly off balance, enough for me to lash out with unhindered legs, catching his face with the soles of my shoes. Before he can slip away, I accelerate his head skyward into the van's roof. It impacts less dramatically than I had expected, with nothing more than a dull thud. But the effect is devastatingly effective as he sinks, groaning, to the wood-sheet flooring.

The five or so seconds that have passed since I vaulted into the van finally prove enough for the driver to undo his jammed seat belt. As he prises open the door, I grab him from behind around the neck and drag him kicking and shouting over the seat and into the back. As soon as I have sufficient grip on his collar and belt, I launch him like a sack of potatoes towards the rear doors with all the delicacy of an airport baggage handler tossing a suitcase towards a waiting dolly cart. He impacts with the left-hand door face first and collapses to the floor beside a visibly terrified Robert Styles.

Concussive each shot might have been, but conclusive they weren't. I snatch up a clump of black, heavy-duty nylon zip-ties from the floor and swiftly cuff the first two men's hands behind their backs as my hair whips about in the swirling wind. The third man is attempting to rise, but he gets no further than kneeling before I kick him sideways and cuff him before he can move again. Once I have them all bound, I use the remaining ties on their ankles and bundle them all towards the rear of the van, away from the prying eyes of any passers-by stupid enough to venture out in this weather.

'Still want to stay here, see what happens?' I fire at Robert Styles as I snatch a knife from a small pouch on the nearest man's belt. With a fast slice, the tie around his wrists comes apart. 'Maybe you wanna try your luck at the airport tomorrow?'

'Perhaps, on second thoughts,' he replies nervously, 'that might not be the safest option.'

'You think! Hell, if safe's what you want, I'm not sure you're gonna like what I have to offer, either. But it's a damned sight better, I reckon, than what this lot had in mind.'

He looks decidedly less than thrilled.

'Stay here,' I say. 'Do not move. Understand? Do not get out of the vehicle. Nothing. On second thoughts, the only thing I want you to do is to find all their mobile phones. And any one of these bastards so much as moves, you kick him as hard as you can in the face. Got it? And when I get back, you tell me who it was, and I'll break his fricking neck. So, sit tight, all of you, and you might just get out of this alive. Styles, I'll be back in a second.'

I jump from the van, slide the side door closed and run back towards the hotel. There I find Anabel and Milly coming out the main doors.

'You okay?' Anabel says with a mixture of concern, confusion and alarm. 'God, I hate being right.'

'Yup. All good.'

'Okay, we just dropped all the cases with reception,' Milly says, handing me my black waterproof jacket, cap and sunglasses.

'Cheers. I need those cheapy phones. You got them?'

'Here you go,' she says, passing me a small plastic bag.

'Do me a favour, Belle. Go find Styles. He'll have a bunch of mobile phones from the snatch squad guys. Bag 'em. Take the local SIMs from all of our phones, and Styles's, too, and put them into these cheapy Nokias, okay? Add them to the bag.'

'Sure,' she replies, a little confused. 'What are you going to do with all of them?'

'I'm working on that. We need to throw their mates off our scent. While you're at it, might as well shove our UK SIMs back into our handsets, okay? Milly's got mine,' I add.

'What shall I do?' asks Milly.

'Come help me,' Anabel beckons. 'We'll be faster that way.'

'Okay. Where are you going?' Milly asks as I turn to go back indoors again, where it is quiet enough to make a call.

'I need to get a grid reference from the admiral,' I reply with a cryptic smile.

The call does not take particularly long. I hurriedly note the critical grid reference down on my inner arm and as back-up on a piece of hotel letterheaded paper, which I tuck inside my purse. The admiral then takes a moment to cover a few key points to remember about the venture we are about to undertake. He does so in his usual no-nonsense manner, which begins to make me seriously question our escape plan.

By the time I return to the van, the phone swap is all done. Anabel and Milly are sitting near the sliding door, waiting nervously. Styles appears to be at a loose end, unsure what to do with himself. For the time being, inaction on his part is a welcome contribution to the effort.

'Now what?' Anabel asks, casting a wary glance towards the pile of struggling men at the back of the van.

'Almost there,' I reply as I slip my purse into a waterproof inner pocket in my jacket. 'Hand us that bag of phones, will you? Are they all on?'

Nodding, Anabel passes them across to me. As she does so, something else pops into my mind. I step from the van, duck low and peer into the front wheel arch on the driver's side. Nothing. Next, I try the rear wheel arch. Again, nothing. I slip around to the other side, in clear sight of the hotel lobby. As I check the third arch, I let out a small, triumphant cry. Reaching in, I pull a black, rubber-clad, rectangular block the size of a pack of playing cards from the arch's far wall. Without pause, I drop the vehicle's GPS tracker into the bag containing the various phone handsets.

A horn sounds from behind the van as a local taxi pulls into the covered pick-up and drop-off area.

'Mills, shift this thing around the corner, will you?' I call. 'I need to figure out what to do with these.'

Before she can reply, I slam the side door closed and quickly walk around the front of the van towards the hotel. Standing at the top of the hotel steps is the Russian couple who checked out before me. They appear to be in heated discussion with the uniformed Indian doorman. The husband looks particularly ill at ease, but is apparently unwilling to argue with his irate wife, whose arms are flapping in animated annoyance.

'But there will be no flights at this time,' the doorman stresses. 'Please, come back inside, where it is safe!'

'I think my wife is saying airport safer than here,' the husband counters, less than convinced by her idea.

'*Da*,' the wife concludes loudly, waving to the taxi. 'We go airport now, we get first flight out.'

'A ride to the airport will be very expensive,' the doorman says. 'I'm sure it will be –'

'I stay at Mandarin,' she fires back. 'I can afford taxi.'

'My apologies, I didn't mean to infer –'

'Better few hours at airport than here,' she adds. 'There, I can shop. Here, no shops.'

I dart amused glances from the woman, who clearly seems mad, to the waiting taxi, and then peer down, smiling, at the plastic bag in my hand as an idea occurs to me. Sighing, the husband looks back unenthusiastically at the collection of suitcases lined up just outside the main door.

'Would you like a hand?' I offer, hurrying forwards.

Unsure what to say, he merely shrugs in defeat and takes two of them. I snatch up the third suitcase and a holdall and follow him down the short flight of steps towards the waiting taxi, whose boot is already popped open. Up ahead, Milly starts the van's engine and slowly edges it forward in first gear, before turning the corner, where I hope she will park it.

The fuming Russian man deposits the two suitcases deep into the boot well and then nods stoically as he passes me by, heading for the side passenger door. His wife is already in the car, waiting impatiently. With the last suitcase squeezed into what space remains, I quickly double-check to ensure all the handsets are on, before slipping the plastic bag in behind an orange jerrycan of spare fuel. Slamming the boot with a resounding thud, I wave to the couple, and make my way around the corner of the hotel to the waiting van.

'You want the good news or the bad news?' Milly says, putting the van in gear, as I climb into the passenger side, careful to hold the door tightly against the gusting wind, which threatens to tear it from the hinges.

'Err, good?'

'Okay, George just called,' Anabel says from just behind me, where she is kneeling next to an uncomfortable-looking Robert Styles. 'So apparently, that PLA secret service compound up on the Peak seems to be completely abandoned. They've all gone. There are police and news crews there now, looking around. The Chinese spooks must be livid.'

'O-kay, well, that's positive, I guess. How about the bad, then?'

'He also says there's a police alert out for a certain British politician on the grounds of his being involved in espionage and interfering in Hong Kong's political situation.'

'Well, that didn't take long, did it?'

'It gets worse,' Milly adds, pulling out onto the nearly empty street. 'Apparently, it goes on to say he's travelling in the company of one or more adolescent girls.'

'Got to hand it to them. They're not incompetent, are they? Suppose the good news is, if they've really got their act together, they're going to be following a taxi to the airport.'

'True. On that subject, where are we going?' she asks.

'Head to Aberdeen. I'll direct you from there.'

'Why Aberdeen?' Anabel asks.

'Tell you when we get there. What else did GC have to say?'

'Not much,' Milly replies. 'Just that we have two options as far as he's concerned. Either flee now, before anyone can get organised, or hunker down for the long run in the consulate.'

'Interesting.'

'But the CG is seriously against the latter. He says she thinks it risks significant diplomatic problems.'

'And she probably isn't wrong,' I reply. 'Either way, it's something she doesn't have to worry about. We'll be long gone by morning.'

'Do wish you'd tell us what the plan is,' Milly sighs, fighting to see through the rain-lashed windscreen.

'Trust me, no, you don't,' I laugh. 'Best you see it when we arrive. Else you might prefer the "hunker down in the consulate" idea.'

'Best go via Pok Fu Lam and avoid Admiralty,' Anabel advises, pointing. 'I'm reading here there are still a tonne of protestors out on the streets. Apparently, it's all degenerating into some kind of pitched standoff between them and the police, who're now using tear gas on them.'

'Great, bet that works well in a typhoon,' I scoff.

The drive through the near-deserted streets of central Hong Kong soon becomes a sufficiently fraught experience that I seriously begin to question the sanity of our escape plan. Debris whips across the road, and in several places we find the streets obstructed by fallen branches and shredded foliage. Stopping, almost pointlessly, at a set of traffic lights, Milly peers dubiously up through the driving rain, against which the wipers are visibly struggling to cope.

'I might be wrong,' she says, 'but I'm pretty sure that building is actually swaying.'

'Probably not wrong,' Anabel replies. 'All the skyscrapers here are built to sway in typhoons.'

'Seriously?' I exclaim, turning in amazement.

'Yeah. They have to. Else they'd snap and collapse. Some of them can sway by, like, six feet at the top. Something like that.'

'So, what was all that glass back there on the road?'

'Well, the building can sway, but the windows sometimes just pop out, or get sucked off the building.'

'Jesus, you sure you want to be stopped here, waiting for the lights to change?' I ask Milly. 'With frickin' windows fallin' from the sky!'

'Let's try not to get arrested, shall we...'

'By what cops?' I laugh, peering searchingly out the windows for effect.

When she finally does pull away, it is not long before we find the road, which leads into Pok Fu Lam, completely blocked by a huge, tangled pile of broken bamboo poles and green mesh netting.

'It tore the sodding scaffolding off!' I observe in disbelief as I peer up at the tall residential tower block which looms high overhead.

The resulting detour takes us downhill towards Kennedy Town on a narrow, curving street which now resembles a river more than a road. As we near the bottom, great geysers of water shoot up from the overflowing roadside drains, pitter-pattering loudly on the van's roof as we pass by.

The longer route costs us, and by the time we finally park the van on a quiet side street in Aberdeen, just along from the Marina Club, what light there was in the sky is beginning to fade.

'Yeah, we're kind of running out of time,' I fret, glancing at my watch in irritation. 'Best we get moving, and fast.'

'Yeah,' Anabel says hesitantly, peering in consternation at her phone, 'I really don't know if getting out is such a great idea. Says here they've recorded winds clocking in at around a hundred and nine miles an hour in the city. Worse, there's a storm surge of up to eleven feet around most of the island's coastal areas.' Looking up at me, she adds, 'This is insane, Hev. Indoors is where we should be. Not out in this!'

'I agree,' Milly chimes in. 'I sure as hell hope that your hare-brained escape plan doesn't have anything to do with going out to sea! You know, us being in Aberdeen and all, and given that that building over there's a yacht club. Please tell me that isn't your master plan?'

'Does it say what conditions are like out at sea?' I ask Anabel as I open my door to climb from the air-conditioned comfort of the van out into the gusting maelstrom.

'Not explicitly. But I imagine that's because no one would be stupid enough to go out there and check.'

'Yeah, you're probably right. Which is kind of why we're betting on this plan. I doubt anyone will go out in this, either.

Police included. Well, how about you all stay here, then, and I'll ping you when it's safe to come. Or better yet, make your way to the marina on the other side of that building in about three minutes, okay?'

'I'm sorry,' Milly replies, her forehead furrowing, 'why are we here?'

'Okay, if you must know, because that building over there is the marine police base.'

'The grey one,' she says, looking nervously in the rear-view mirror. 'Where the road bends?'

'Yes.'

'Wait, so we're avoiding the police like the plague, yet we've come to a police station?'

'Yes. Because the police patrol division has some of the fastest go-fast boats on the island.' With that, I get out of the van.

'And you know this how?' Milly shouts, shielding her face with her hand, as she jumps out the driver's side.

'Coz one of them chased me across the harbour on the way back from ICC.'

'You never told us that.'

'Sorry, must have slipped my mind in all the excitement.'

'So, your plan does involve a boat! Are you mad?!'

'As much as it galls me to say this, I don't think we have a whole lot of choice now,' Anabel says grimly, emerging from the van's side door. 'Their mates,' she says, gesturing with her thumb to the men tied up inside the van, 'will be going nuts at finding their covers all got blown. They're going to be pissed! And if they don't already know Styles is on the run, then they soon will. I really think it's best we be long gone well before that.'

'Agreed. Stay here for two secs,' I urge, wiping rain from

my face. 'I want to scope the place out. Figure out how we are going to nick one of their boats without getting nicked ourselves in the process.'

After running through a narrow motorcycle parking area between the marine police headquarters and the Aberdeen Boat Club, I come upon a short flight of steps which lead down to a small embarkation point, likely for local sampan boats, where waves are relentlessly slapping up against the quayside. Access to the police pier is, unfortunately, blocked by a high wall to my left and a half-moon-shaped set of security bars designed to stop anyone from coming around the end of the perimeter wall. Off to my right, the usually sheltered harbour waters are noticeably choppier in the gusting winds.

Glancing up at the wall, I realise I may need to get the boat first and then collect my friends. Squinting through the near-horizontal rain, I see a group of figures clad all in black running along the raised concrete pier towards the safety of the main building. It looks like the last police rigid hull inflatable boat, or RHIBs as we call them, has just come back into port. As the paramilitary-looking passengers dash for shelter, a lone deckhand begins the unenviable task of refuelling the powerboat. He casts repeated apprehensive looks up at the brooding, ominous sky, and seems only too happy to flee back inside once the refuelling is complete.

'So, the good news is their security isn't great,' I explain to my friends, once I have returned to the van. 'Also, once I have a boat, I'll have to pick you all up at the small jetty at the far end of the car park, just over there,' I say, pointing. 'Maybe give me three minutes.'

'Fine, I know the way,' Anabel says reluctantly, before

opening the rear sliding door and taking one last glance into the relative comfort of the van. The bundle of men continue their struggling at the rear. Sighing, she reaches in and snatches Robert Styles's government-issue laptop from the floor.

'Yeah, best this doesn't fall into their hands,' she says, shaking her head as she hands the politician his computer. 'Come on, Mr Styles. Time to go. Of course, quite where we're going is anyone's guess.'

'Yeah, wait, so hang on,' Milly says, catching me by the arm. 'What exactly *is* the plan?'

'Ah, yes,' I reply. 'Almost forgot. Simple, really. We're going to take one of their wicked high-speed rigid inflatables, head out to sea and rendezvous with a Royal Navy vessel which is on its way to pick us up.'

For a comical moment, no one speaks. One by one, their faces crease in consternation and each looks skywards into the pouring rain.

'Are you completely out of your mind?' Milly hisses. 'That's completely insane. In case you missed the weather forecasts earlier, there's an absolute monster storm heading right for us!'

'Think it's already here,' Anabel shouts.

'Yes, I'm glad you're all taking it so well,' I laugh. 'Of course, in the absence of any better ideas, we kind of had to go with the options we had. Which means a departure by sea. And as ferries, sadly, aren't sailing today, well, it's time to improvise a little. Besides,' I exclaim, patting Milly on the shoulder, 'this could be fun.'

'Fun? *Fun!*' she shouts. 'Do you have any idea what it could be like out there? Do you? We're more likely to get swept overboard or crushed by some rogue wave than make any rendezvous. Did you never watch *The Perfect Storm*?'

'I have to agree with Mills,' murmurs Anabel glumly.

'Oh my God, could you two try to be slightly less glass-half-empty! Look on the bright side, will you? It'll have seat belts. And we all get a life jacket… most likely,' I reply blithely. 'And guess what? None of us get to go to jail in China. Woohoo.' I sigh deeply and then shrug, as if to ask what option we really have. While it isn't lost on me that they are scared – and rightfully so – this isn't helping. 'Quayside, three mins, okay?'

Fighting the gale and squinting against the eye-watering gusts, I make my way around the nearest building, leaning forwards at an acute angle so as not to be dumped unceremoniously onto the pavement by the force of the wind. I hurriedly adjust my cap's rear Velcro band as tightly as it will possibly go to stop it from being ripped off.

When I reach the small jetty, I run towards the high grey wall and launch myself off a stumpy, round mooring bollard up towards the top of the wall. Grabbing the edge, I vault over it and land deftly on the other side. Before me lies a harbourside path which leads alongside the police building. Two piers branch off it to the right. The nearest is a short jetty which zigzags out towards a boxy, dilapidated concrete outbuilding, beyond which is a narrow, rubber-clad pier where the pair of powerful go-fast boats are moored. Probably the exact same pair I saw a few days ago in the harbour. Exactly what the admiral and I hoped would be here now. The second pier, further along, plays host to the police's larger, battleship-grey offshore cruisers. But one of those would be too slow, too complicated and too troublesome to consider using. Even if taking one into a storm such as this might be a much more sensible option.

Crouching low, I plan out my approach, noting the most

likely dangers along the way. First to be dealt with is the security camera attached to the building's side corner. It affords a view of both jetties. A running leap gets me high enough up the wall to wrench it from its mounting. It trails severed cables as I toss it with disregard into the water.

After advancing cautiously along the zigzagging pier, I reach the boxy concrete building which straddles the jetty, and dart inside. The one uncertainty in this half-mad endeavour is whether these boats need keys or whether they have a push-to-start function. The admiral was all but convinced that as these are essentially paramilitary vessels there will be no key.

'Can't have some marine fumbling frantically in his thigh pockets for the key when tracer rounds come hissing overhead, now, can we?' he had laughed.

He might well be right, for I find no key rack in the outhouse. Scowling, I make the decision to run for the boat which I know has been refuelled. I jump down into it from the pier, duck into the open, tubular-framed housing protecting the helmsman's station and am rewarded by the sight of a large round start button on the console. Peering through the front windscreen, I realise the boat is a lot longer and bigger than I reckoned it would be. Looking down, I see the helmsman's console also appears a lot more complicated than I expected.

Both the driver's and co-pilot's bucket seats sit on a bed of shock-absorbing pneumatics. Set front and centre on the left-hand side of the console, directly in front of the pilot, is a large screen with multiple buttons set around its waterproof frame. Between the seats is the throttle column. A quick glance reassures me that it is just as I was told to expect: drive, neutral and reverse. Multiple dials are clustered on the dark-grey dashboard, displaying speed, fuel, engine oil and numerous other important pieces of information. Comically, a small battery-powered desk fan is affixed to the dash. We won't be needing that on this trip. On the roof overhead are all the electronics, including the radar, VHF radio and various assorted antennas.

I dart back to look over the twin three-hundred-horsepower outboard engine configuration set behind the crew station. Despite the gusting wind, I sniff deeply, just to check for any fuel seepage. It smells fine. A check of the under-seat locker there reveals an untidy pile of dark-grey life jackets. I quickly pull out enough for all of us, and hurriedly tug a medium-sized one over my head and fasten the side clips.

Returning to the driver's seat, I note the kill switch's lanyard is still attached to the red engine safety cut-off knob. That solves another major concern.

My first priority is to set the navigation. I turn the power switch and the electronic navigation screen and dials all spring to life. The local area's marine chart is immediately displayed. I click the option to create a new waypoint. Then, peering closely at the on-screen options, I use the touchscreen to plot in a few markers that will take us safely out of the Aberdeen approaches, through the outlying cluster of islands, mindful not to take us anywhere near their shorelines, before finally heading out into the open sea beyond. Not that I need to be particularly concerned about running aground; the draft of the boat is practically zero. This sleek black monster is made for two purposes and two purposes only. Agility and speed. And a lot of both, for that matter.

For the last waypoint, our final rendezvous location, it takes a few stressful moments to find the function to key in the specific GPS grid reference. Peering closely at the last message from the admiral on my phone, I very carefully key it in, and then reread it and save the waypoint. Finally, clicking 'set', I load the journey into the ChartPlotter. An egg timer spins for a second or two, before the route course is displayed on the screen. Remembering another pearl of wisdom from my earlier pep chat, I split the screen into two to see both the top-down sat-nav map screen on the left, and a compass heading and boat heading indication ticker tape on the right. Apparently, trying to navigate at sea using just the sat-nav map is notoriously unreliable, he informed me.

'Ha! Now how easy was that?' I exclaim excitedly to myself.

Glancing at my watch, I realise I need to hurry up. But just as I am about to press the large Engine Start button, I stop and curse, and then leap from the seat and rush to toss off the mooring ropes, both bow and stern. Back in the helmsman's seat, I quickly strap myself in with the tough nylon seat belt. Then, ensuring the throttle is in neutral, I take a last deep breath, cast a final wary look at the marine police's back door and press the on button. Behind me, the two huge outboards rumble to life, as do several sets of dashboard dials. The howling storm must mask it well, because even though the engines sound dreadfully unsubtle from where I am sitting, nothing happens. No doors fly open. No machine-gun-toting paramilitary police come charging out.

With the admiral's earlier warnings to maintain a proper lookout ringing in my ears, I carefully check my surroundings, wary of driving the boat into anything, and then depress the throttle release button and slip the jet-style lever into reverse. The boat slowly moves backwards, edging out, foot by foot, from behind its sleek sister vessel. Turning the chromed wheel, I bring the bow about, before slipping it back into neutral, pausing a second for the speed to slow and then pushing it up into drive. I put my sunglasses on, adjust my cap and pull the waterproof jacket's hood up and secure the drawstrings. Out of the corner of my eye, I see my friends and the politician appear at the top of the sampan jetty steps. Easing the throttle open, I head towards them. Unnecessary acceleration now could alert some sharp-eared member of the marine patrol to the unexpected departure of one of their boats. Slowly and carefully, given that I am still figuring out the boat's handling, I bring the speedboat around towards the jetty. As I come alongside, one after the other they leap from the bottom steps into the boat.

'We probably need two at the front and two at the back,' I shout. 'To balance it properly. Take the front two,' I call to Robert Styles and Anabel, throwing a pair of life jackets at their feet. 'They've got their own suspension, too.'

They glance at the two very exposed front seats, and then cautiously swing their legs over and begin working out how to do the unusual strap-like seatbelts. Milly hesitantly approaches the helmsman's station.

'Strap yourself in,' I call, patting the seat beside me. 'Time we put some serious distance between us and this place.'

Frowning with uncertainty, Milly slips into a life jacket and fastens the rear locker catch. Then she climbs into the right-hand seat and straps herself in.

'Cool, here we go,' I call, edging the throttle forwards a bit more. As we begin moving forwards between two large rows of huge flybridge motor yachts, we turn at the sound of shouting from behind us. There we see several police officers, as well as the men from the van, running along the pier-side towards the end of the jetty. All are clearly agitated.

'Well, didn't take them long to free themselves,' I sigh,

easing the throttle open. The boat responds immediately as the props bite, and we surge forwards as the bow raises noticeably. The acceleration pushes us all forcefully back into our seats.

'Oh my God,' I shout. 'What a rush!'

'You don't think they'll take the other boat, do you?' Milly calls.

'Sure hope not.'

'I don't suppose disabling it occurred to you, did it, super-agent?' she shouts derisively as the men arrive at the remaining pursuit boat. For a moment they look down at it, then back at us and then up at the sky.

'You may be in luck,' she notes sourly. 'Looks like they've decided against doing something as stupid as heading out into a hurricane in an inflatable boat!'

'You know what I love about this?' I shout. 'It's the sense of overwhelming camaraderie I get whenever we have adventures like this.'

'Yeah, I bet it is,' she replies with a bitter sideways scowl. 'You realise out there we can expect gusts of well over a hundred sodding miles an hour! Do you know what that'll do to a boat like this?' she screams. 'It'll flip us the first chance it gets. And then pound us into a thousand tiny pieces. And then sharks will eat us!'

'Yeah, you might not be wrong about that,' I shout excitedly, gunning the engine, accelerating the boat forwards over the first choppy waves.

'You should try to steer for where the sea will be the calmest,' Milly calls, gripping her seat with tangible trepidation. 'Where the waves will be the smallest.'

'Oh yeah, and where's that going to be in a hurricane?'

'Usually on the clean side of the storm, typically on the side counter-clockwise from the storm's leading edge.'

'Great, well, if you can find it, you just tell me where that is…'

'Just keep the front pointing into the waves,' she shouts, gesticulating furiously.

'The thought had occurred to me,' I yell back.

There is nothing to be gained by scaring her, but she's right: this boat is so light that if I don't get the angle of attack right on each wave, we have a very good chance of getting flipped. I take comfort from the fact that the admiral took a moment on our call earlier to walk me through some of the best practices learned, often the hard way, by the SBS about handling boats like this in stormy conditions. Apparently, charging straight at silly big waves is a bad idea. Key to it, he stressed, was to ensure that I approach waves at a forty-five-degree angle, and not to be afraid of reducing speed, either. His parting comment concerned the importance of gauging the time between crests just as much as I read the wave's steepness.

Even here, within the relative calm of the harbour walls, I can feel the wind and waves constantly trying to veer us off course. As we clear the first islands and turn towards our second waypoint, the conditions worsen considerably. Violent bursts of lightning fleck the distant, grim-looking skies. With a pursed expression, I look out at what we are powering towards, and the admiral's words of advice begin to feel less and less relevant. Each breached wave now sends the boat on a parabolic roller-coaster ride, first up the wave front, a nauseous, fear-inducing dread building in the bottom of the stomach the higher we climb, before we crest the top and accelerate down the far side in a stomach-churning descent towards the next trough.

For the most part, everyone stays silent. Which is good, and helpful, because it allows me to focus on the navigation, which is proving anything but easy, given the constant course corrections required between waves. As we begin our next leg, heading out to sea, we no longer have the outlying islands to offer any kind of shelter from the fierce wind, the driving rain or the growing waves. Before us lies the most inhospitable seascape imaginable. The entire horizon is one ominous, boiling mass of angry, frothing, dark-grey sea. Huge, rolling walls of water roam with impunity in all directions around us, merging and splitting unpredictably, with peaks and troughs so far apart that small buildings could fit within them. Great gusts of spray tear from the top of each raging white-crested peak that rolls past, drenching us with a shower of frigid water.

'This is insane,' Anabel screams, turning back to look at us as she wipes lashings of salt water from her ashen face. 'We're all going to die!'

'You know she can't swim very well,' Milly yells.

'Best she stays in the boat, then.'

'You know how much I hate you right now?'

'Yeah, pretty much,' I acknowledge as I ease the engines and drive us down the back of a particularly huge, swirling mass of water. 'Oh my God, that was frickin' awesome.'

'Glad you're finding this fun,' Milly cries, clutching the console's handle for dear life. 'How do we even know where we're going?'

'We're just aiming for that,' I call back, pointing at a marker on the sat-nav screen.

'And if it breaks?'

'Then we're buggered.'

'Oh great...'

Up front, barely visible anymore through the overwhelmed windshield wipers, the blurry shapes of Anabel and Robert Styles can be seen, lurching from side to side amidst the full force of the storm's embrace. Great sheets of spray and mist whip at the boat in the withering wind. Rivers of water run back along the decking to pour out from the side drains.

I glance around and see Milly has begun crying and is now praying beside me. With a heavy heart, it dawns on me how badly my friends are taking this. I reach out and give her arm a reassuring squeeze.

'Keep your hands on the wheel,' she screams as we lurch erratically sideways. Momentarily, both outboards rise free of the water and churn furiously at the air, before we tip over the crest of another colossal wave. For that brief instant, their noise changes alarmingly. A moment later, the props are thrust back into the churning sea, and again we race forwards into the unknown.

The repeated impacts of the hull slamming into the troughs between waves soon have Robert Styles vomiting violently into his lap. The wind whips the second hurl back up into his face. Presumably, it's the sight of that that triggers Anabel, who at least tries to aim over the side as a gush of vomit spews from her mouth. Some splatters across our windshield. I cast a wary glance sideways at Milly, who lurches forwards at the sight of it as it runs, globulously thick, across the Perspex, before being torn off in the wind. One retch, then two, and on the third pigeon-like head bob she heaves, too, and a blast of chunky sick splatters across the rubberised side of the boat beside her. The lashing rain washes it clean away in seconds.

'Well, that's just lovely,' I shout.

She looks at me, pale and drained, as she is tossed from side to side.

'All over soon,' I shout reassuringly, casting a wary glance at the erratically see-sawing bearing marker.

'Oh yeah,' she moans weakly, gesturing at the colossal towers of water sliding past us, before turning away to be sick again. 'See you at the Pearly Gates.'

'Yeah, I know. Anyway, hold on tight. Here we go again.'

Thrusting the throttle forwards, I accelerate the boat towards the lowest point between two oncoming waves. My aim is to zigzag us through without climbing over the top of such a massive swell and exposing the bottom of the hull to the amplified forces which would flip us before I could possibly do anything about it.

Employing the same strategy as much as possible, I push on farther out to sea. My eyes are constantly flitting from the ChartPlotter to the shifting horizon, and my brow furrows in concentration while my arms ache from the effort required to keep us heading towards the rendezvous point coordinates.

With every passing minute that gap closes, and I begin to believe we might actually make it. Even Milly begins to perk up at the prospect of reaching the RP and not being sunk by some freak, nightmarish wave. At one point, my pulse leaps at what I think sounds like a helicopter somewhere in the darkness behind us. But then it disappears, and I question whether I am now just hearing things. Would the Chinese be so desperate that they'd dispatch a helicopter in this? Being close to the surface is quite bad enough. What the wind must be like up there doesn't bear thinking about.

What little light remains is rapidly beginning to fade as we approach the final waypoint. Milly fires me a wary glance. I know what she's thinking, and she's not wrong. I just don't want to admit. If the light goes completely, our chances of finding whoever we are here to meet drop almost to zero. Our orders were vague and basic: simply to get here with maximum haste. And ideally within a set thirty-minute time window. Flicking my wrist, I see we are actually a few minutes ahead of schedule. Frowning, Milly takes a pair of binoculars from a hold-fast mounting and fights to keep them steady enough to scan the moving horizon.

'There's no ship here,' she shouts. 'You sure this is the right place?'

'It's what he told me.'

A wave of unease and concern grips me, and I ease off the throttle to bring the boat to a coast. A message flashes across the navigation screen: 'Waypoint Reached'.

'Great! Now what?' I mumble to myself, looking round in all directions. And yet no ship appears.

For a moment, I fear the sound I thought was a helicopter might have been one launched from a Royal Navy frigate. Could you even launch one in these conditions? What if they didn't see us? What if they gave up and returned to the ship? We must be about twenty miles offshore, easily. Would we even have enough fuel remaining to return to shore? My pulse quickens and I feel a prickly heat come over me, despite the driving cold wind tearing at us.

'Jesus Christ!' Milly suddenly screams, grabbing for my arm in alarm.

'What! *What?*' I scream back, darting half terrified glances in all directions in search of whatever could have so badly scared her. My eyes go wide, for there, barely thirty feet off our starboard bow, a mass of black is rising from the waves. Water pours from it in great torrents. And yet still it comes, growing bigger and then, suddenly, longer also. For a terrifying moment, my lizard brain is convinced that a colossal breaching whale is about to land on our boat and crush us. My hand instinctively flies for the throttle, and I am about to ram it to full ahead when my actual brain catches up and I realise what I am really looking at.

The black, weathered fin of what is clearly a nuclear submarine towers above us. Just visible amidst the rolling swells is the dark mass of the boat's hundred-metre-long hull.

'That's our ride?' Milly shouts in amazement.

'Don't ever say I don't show you a good time,' I yell back as I bring the powerboat's speed up to match that of the slowly moving nuclear boat.

'There's someone up there,' she calls, pointing.

Sure enough, peering low, I see someone in brightly coloured waterproofs appear at the top of the fin. A moment later, a rope ladder unravels down the side of it.

'Do they really expect us to climb up that?'

'Looks like it.'

'But look! That thing has a door at the base of the fin,' she protests. 'Can't we use that?'

'You want them to open it up in seas like this? Yeah, great way to send a two-billion-quid boat to the bottom real fast. Open the front door in a sodding typhoon. Duh, good one.'

'Suppose...' she replies grudgingly.

Up top, the lone figure waves for us to approach. But try as I might to bring the powerboat alongside the sub and then close enough that we could jump across, it proves almost impossible. The sub's bow wave alone sends us lurching six feet into the air. The curved flanks of the upper hull also means that if anyone's jump fell short they'd risk slipping off the side and into the waves. Cursing, I accelerate the RHIB forwards and veer twenty feet out to port. Then, easing off, I wait for the hull to come alongside us again. The massive sub rolls rhythmically from side to side in the surging seas as it slowly catches us up. I imagine getting back below the waves and into the relative calm of the depths must be the crew's top priority. From the look of it, I expect they're running out of sick bags below decks about now.

With my right hand on the throttle, I wait for a perfect moment when the sub's whole foredeck disappears beneath a particularly large swell. The seconds tick by and the buffeting continues unabated, slamming us from side to side, straining our seatbelts and exhausting our already fatigued muscles.

Suddenly, I see the break we need. The sub begins to dip, the bow wave crests its hull, washing backwards with alarming speed, just as a side-impacting wave rides up and over the foredeck. Gunning the engines, I shoot us aggressively forward, catching up with the fin in just a few seconds. Then I veer in hard to starboard, propelling us directly at the sub.

Milly screams, Anabel covers her eyes and Styles freezes, hands in his drenched hair, overcome with terror as the huge sub rockets towards us. At the last possible second, just as we reach it, I twist the wheel hard to port, jerking us sideways and aligning our bow in the same direction of travel as the sub. A moment later, as it rises again, a colossal thump comes from beneath our boat, almost throwing us from our seats, as eight thousand tonnes of nuclear-powered submarine impact us and violently propels our tiny boat from the sea, bringing it to a sudden stop, beached awkwardly at an angle on the foredeck, twelve feet from the fin.

'That's it,' I scream, cutting the engines and ripping my seatbelt off. 'Move!'

The others fumble with their restraints and then stagger unsteadily from the boat onto the hard casing of the sub's hull. I grab Milly and tug her forcefully the half dozen paces towards the left-hand side of the fin, where the flimsy ladder flaps wildly in the wind.

'Up,' I yell as I turn to reach for Anabel, who is staggering on poor sea legs towards us. Seeing she'll make it, I rush past her towards Robert Styles, who appears to have frozen half on and half off the powerboat as another colossal sideways-impacting wave breaks over the sub's bow and floods back over the flat foredeck towards us. Wiping a face-full of spray from my eyes, I curse and indelicately snatch him by the arm, sending his laptop clattering off across the deck, over the side and into the waiting waves.

'Forget it,' I shout, and tug him towards the rope ladder. Milly has just reached the top and is being pulled over the lip. Anabel is a few rungs behind her. Turning to Styles, I yell, 'Move your arse!'

Where he finds the speed to rush up the ladder, I don't know, but I am grateful that he does. Now, I just hope he doesn't slip and take me with him on the way down. Gripping the soaked ropes, I hurry up just beneath him. The fin's swaying motion makes the climb treacherous; it threatens to keel over heavily at any moment, which would leave us hanging precipitously over the churning water below. I cast constant wary glances left and right, on the lookout for any rogue wave that could potentially rip me from the ladder.

The RHIB is already some thirty feet away, drifting off in the tumultuous seas off the starboard bow. It takes Styles a few slips, each of which brings my heart into the back of my mouth, and some sudden panicked clutching of the ladder before he finally reaches the top, where a pair of indelicate hands drag him awkwardly to safety. I hurry upwards, scramble over the top and jostle Styles into the narrow bridge, which at best offers standing room for only a handful of people at any one time. Seeing where the girls have been directed, Styles tentatively begins the climb down through the hatch in the deck.

The decidedly anxious-looking sailor turns to me and shouts, 'Who are you people?'

'Don't ask,' I reply. 'Apparently, he pissed someone off. So, they called us to get him out.'

'Seriously? You're 'avin' a larf, aren't cha? Get yourself down into the control room,' he calls. 'Captain wants to get underway fast.'

Smiling, I duck down and descend the ladder as rapidly as I can, so the windswept sailor can close the conning tower hatch behind us. At the bottom of the ladder is a small space which has a reinforced door in the outer wall and another hatchway in the floor. Anabel, Milly and Styles have already begun to climb down the next ladder, which leads into the main pressurised hull below. A second or two behind me, the crewman arrives and takes the bridge line Stanaphone handset from a covered wall mounting and begins speaking into it.

'Fin – control room. Casing party has evac'd the deck. Casing is clear. Outer door locked and watertight.'

'Control room – fin, copy. The outer door is sealed, and leak check has been performed. Very well. Once you're done there, Barnsley, report to the wardroom on two deck, will you?'

'Aye, sir. On my way.'

Above me, the trailing sailor closes the final hatch and secures a very robust locking mechanism firmly in place. As I reach the bottom of the ladder, it's to find a very queasy and pale-looking Milly clinging to the ladder, equally soaked and dripping onto the linoleum flooring.

'Oh dear,' I say with a sympathetic laugh, brushing stray strands of sodden hair from her face. 'Hey, look on the bright side. It may not have been pleasant, but at least it was memorable.'

'Yeah, it'll be memorable in my sodding nightmares,' she groans, pressing her cheek against the ladder for comfort. I smile and turn to take in the incredibly complex command centre in which we find ourselves. Barely an inch of space is not covered by glowing screens, cables, pipes or other equipment. A roomful of curious-looking faces momentarily turns to stare at us, interested, I am sure, to see for themselves what kind of raging idiots would try a stunt like this.

'Permission to come aboard?' I venture with a playful grin as I wipe saltwater from my face. That makes even Milly giggle quietly behind me. Before us, standing authoritatively in the centre of the room, is a friendly-looking man in a blue naval uniform with a neatly trimmed ginger goatee. He smiles and turns to another senior crewmember.

'Officer of the Watch, submerge the boat. Take us to PD. Have a look around and then take us on down to sixty metres. Bring us about to a course of two-four-zero degrees, and make best speed to get us out of this bloody storm.'

'Aye, sir,' the OOW says, as the sub lurches violently, sending a few people stumbling backwards. Turning to the nearest junior rating sitting in front of a complex wall of screens, dials and gauges, he repeats the order.

'Helmsman, down planes. Take us to periscope depth. Sonar, take a look around. Make sure there is nothing in our baffles. Then, helm, take us on down to sixty metres. Steer in a course of two-four-zero degrees.'

'Aye, sir.'

'Crew, prepare to submerge the boat,' the commanding officer says, having taken the main internal communications system's handset from its ceiling mounting. 'Right, XO, you have the conn. Maintain EMCON plan Charlie and then lay in a course for Singapore.'

'Aye, Captain,' replies another officer, who is standing behind a group of men sitting before a wall of large, glowing monitors off to our left. The captain turns to us, smiles, and extends his hand in greeting.

'I'm Commander Leslie Garrick. Welcome aboard HMS *Audacious*. Now, what do you say we go find out what this little joy ride was all about, then? Perhaps my cabin, back that way,' he suggests, pointing aft towards a corridor at the rear of the command centre. 'But on second thoughts, I'm not sure we'd all fit. Better this way, then. We'll use the boat's office instead. Oh, Pete, see if the LO can't rustle up some dry clothes for our guests, will you?'

'Aye, Captain,' the executive officer replies with a knowing smile.

CHAPTER 16

TWISTING IN THE WIND

London

'I'm sorry,' I say with consternation as we pass the comforting familiarity of Boots and WH Smith's and round the corner to enter the immigration hall at Heathrow Terminal Five. 'But did we miss something, like, really fundamental while we were away?'

It has just gone eleven p.m., yet the airport is still busy and immigration queues are colossal.

'Isn't the eGate channel meant to be a fast-track route?' I observe, scowling at the torturously long queue ahead of us. 'Why so crowded, lah?'

'I don't know,' Milly says, laughing at my Asian joke. Frowning, she dives into her bag for her phone. 'I honestly haven't checked anything since we left Hong Kong.'

'Me neither,' says Anabel. 'Wow, how did we cope that long without social media?'

That any of us can even manage attempts at humour after the trip we've had is impressive. Even at full speed, it took just over two and a half days to travel the one thousand, eight hundred and sixty-two nautical miles to Singapore's Changi Naval Base. We were immediately escorted from the boat and driven straight to the ridiculously modern Changi airport, not far away. Clearly more important than us, Robert Styles was given a seat on the earliest BA flight and whisked back to the UK. For us, it was a further two hours' wait, albeit in a nice lounge, before we finally boarded our own flight to Heathrow.

Now, some thirteen hours later, we have arrived to find immigration a very different experience to when we left. Not only is it busier than usual, but there is also a dramatically increased armed police presence. But most concerning of all is the number of people being taken aside, and not particularly politely, either, as they reach the immigration booths.

'What happened?' I ask.

'Checking now,' Milly replies. As she taps, types and scrolls on her phone, her eyes widen into an expression of genuine shock.

'Well, go on,' I urge as the queue edges forward painfully slowly.

'I... I almost don't know where to start.'

'Try at the beginning,' Anabel suggests, laughing.

'Yeah, what the hell happened? Why's it turned into an armed cop convention here?'

'For starters,' Milly stammers, her voice dropping to a whisper, 'the PM's resigned.'

'I'm sorry, what?' I blurt out. 'Are you kidding me? How? Why?'

'Give me a second. I'm trying to figure it out. Jesus, this is bad. Erm, seems like right after we left HK, the story about Styles broke.'

'What story?' asks Anabel.

'The sex tape story, it seems. Oh dear, they've published photos and all. Oh, wait. Sorry, no, it gets worse. Seems first to break was a leaked story that the Chinese had tried to recruit Styles to hand over classified documents. Initial reports suggested they were blackmailing him. Looks like the PM came out all rah-rah, strongly defending Styles. Saying he'd known the man twenty years, blah, blah, blah, and there was nothing corrupt, immoral or traitorous about him. Really strong defence.'

'Oh God,' I sigh. 'You can almost see it coming, can't you?'

'Yup,' Milly says, rolling her eyes. 'Almost immediately, the press somehow found photos of Styles in Hong Kong. The media claimed these came from sources close to the government in Beijing. Apparently, the Chinese strongly denied that. And it all snowballed from there.'

'And that's it?' I ask incredulously. 'Why resign for that? He could've just, I dunno, fired Styles, right? Or said he was disappointed and let down.'

'Yeah, seems that wasn't the end of it. Hold on, I'm kind of jumping from story to story here. Okay, seems one of the tabloids then published claims by a government insider which suggested the PM had been fully aware of Styles's, how shall I say, interests all along. The story says he was told by the Security Service all about Styles before he appointed him. Sounds like there was some kind of feeble protest from Number Ten that the PM's dossier had been lost or stolen, but no one cared. The cat was out of the bag by that point. And, of course, when they pressed him on it, he couldn't deny it.'

'Jeez, what a mess,' I exclaim with a whistle.

'Oh, that's not the end of it. As they then dug for dirt, it was discovered that the government was aware that the recent press leaks all came from Styles, too. The press reported that he did it because he could not stand his peers' immoral behaviour.'

'Seriously! You buy that?' I ask. 'They're having a laugh, right?'

'Agreed,' Milly replies. 'We know that's untrue.'

'Oh dear,' I reply with a weary shake of my head. 'That's kind of awkward, isn't it?'

'You don't say,' scoffs Anabel.

'Of course, the press had an absolute field day,' Milly continues. 'They nailed the PM for poor judgement in appointing someone like Styles as minister for morality. Even the Church came out and slammed him. Lack of integrity, they said. Nepotism, poor judgement. Not fit for office. It goes on and on. And all the while, Styles was nowhere to be seen.'

'Duh, he was on a nuclear sub.'

'Yeah, but no one's going to explain that to the press, are they, Hev?' says Milly. 'Especially given the circumstances of his rushed departure from Hong Kong. Kind of screams "guilty", doesn't it? Hong Kong government's furious.'

'So, the PM resigned?'

'Yeah, apparently late yesterday afternoon, he went to the palace and tendered his resignation.'

'Well, who the hell's PM now?' I ask.

'You're not going to believe it,' Milly sighs, finally looking up from her phone. 'Our *buddy* Forbes.'

'No way,' I exclaim, snatching the handset from her. 'How the hell?'

'Seems he was the most credible member of the cabinet left. To be honest, I'm not surprised, right? He was, like, the only experienced one left. Half the others fricking resigned or got fired in the last few months for all those scandals.

Offshore tax dodges, bribes and corruption, favours for friends, extramarital affairs. I mean, no wonder the opposition labelled the government sleaze central. And now they're pinning all those leaks on Styles as well.'

'But we know that's not true,' Anabel protests. 'We know someone cloned his phone.'

'Reckon anyone gives a rat's toss about the details?' I ask.

'Exactly,' emphasises Milly. 'The headlines sell the story. Not the facts.'

'Sad, but true,' I reflect, scrolling through a linked article. 'Seems the party chairman recommended Forbes as immediate interim prime minister to the palace. He said there were too many problems now for any kind of vacuum at the top. Shocking, right?'

'Kills me to say this, because I have some major issues with Forbes,' Milly says, 'but it kind of makes sense. Just in a really wrong way. Maybe they're right, maybe they don't have the luxury of going through the usual process for the party to nominate a new leader. I guess the question is whether the PM also resigned as leader of the party?'

'Dunno. Doesn't say.'

'That might explain the caretaker role,' she says. 'The PM resigned in a personal capacity, right? He didn't resign on behalf of the government, otherwise the palace would've had to go to the opposition and ask them to form a government. Then again, maybe he did it to avoid a vote of no confidence, which was bound to happen. That would've been even messier, because then he'd trigger the fourteen-day period under the Fixed-term Parliaments Act, which would have required the government to find a successor. If they failed, it would trigger a general election.'

'How do you know all this shite?' I ask, passing her phone back.

'I read,' she says, sighing.

'You know,' I reply, wagging a reproachful finger at her, 'I resent the implication that I'm this lumbering, dense philistine. I read, too, you know!' Scowling, I gesture around the hall. 'So, what's all this about, then?'

'Looks like his first act was to respond to claims that the government has been soft on terror since the attacks,' she replies, peering again at her phone. 'Oh, listen to this. He goes, it's time to address the shocking and negligent lapse in national security during his predecessor's watch by enacting emergency legislation to immediately enhance security, contain known threats and move against those with known ill intent towards the United Kingdom.'

'Wow, even so, a little fast to get all this in place, don't you think?' I whisper.

'Not if you had the whole plan laid out well ahead of time,' Milly replies cynically.

'Yeah,' Anabel adds, slowly looking around. 'You might not be wrong about that.'

'So, where's Styles, then?' I ask. 'He must've got back an hour or two ago.'

'Fired, it seems,' Milly replies. 'First thing Forbes did, apparently, the moment his plane landed. Says he hasn't been seen since. Oh, wait. No. There's a quote saying he wants to spend time with his family amid this difficult and trying period. That was all he said when he arrived. Then some government car whisked him from the airport.'

'Yeah, right,' Anabel mumbles sarcastically. 'Fat chance.'

'Wow, would you listen to this article,' Milly whispers excitedly as we round the bend into the final stretch of the queue. '"Not since the heady days of 1963 has the United Kingdom had to witness immoral political debauchery like the conduct of the formerly, if ever, Right Honourable Robert Styles. But while history has tamed the antics of John Profumo, any such blessings are unlikely to save the self-styled minister of morality, or his steadfastly supportive ally the prime minister, from the inevitable fall from grace which is now destined to come. Damning echoes of hypocrisy have long been commonplace in Westminster's corridors of power, but the evidence that has been released by what many suspect are Chinese intelligence services doesn't just ring the bell of hypocrisy, it tears it from its mounting before setting the whole building on fire."'

'Well, they're clearly still on the fence, then,' I comment dryly.

We laugh, and the line edges forwards a little further. Within a few minutes, we are all standing before rather stressed-looking immigration officers. The system only has to scan our passports, and we are all immediately waved on. With no baggage to collect, given that GC hopefully had it all sent back directly to Vauxhall Cross a day or two ago, we pass through the huge, heaving baggage hall with relative speed. It's only once we are past customs that we see the full force of the British tabloid media's torching of Robert Styles. Glancing at my watch, I am surprised any of the shops are still open at this time.

'Holy sh...' Milly exclaims, covering her giggle with her hands as she rushes towards the rack outside the first newsagent we come across. She picks up several papers, both local and national.

'I'm sorry, Paedo Styles. Are they serious?'

'The *Standard*'s a bit tamer,' I laugh, pointing. On the front page, in large letters, are the words 'A New Style of Traitor'.

'Anything new there?' Anabel asks.

'Not that I can see,' Milly replies, speed-scanning the first few pages. Then she grabs the paper with the largest number of lurid photos and rushes inside the shop to buy it.

'Who'd have thought she was such a gossip-monger?'

'Don't I know it,' Anabel groans. 'Come on, Mills, hurry up, or we'll miss the train to Guilford. We need to get to Paddington first, don't forget.'

'When's the last train down?' I ask.

'Five past one in the morning from Waterloo,' Milly replies without thinking. 'Sorry, did that just pop out?' she asks, flushing red.

'You memorised the train timetable?'

'Not deliberately.'

'Well, either way, doesn't leave us a whole lot of time,' Anabel notes, glancing at her watch.

'Holy crap,' Milly whistles, seeing the time. 'I lost all track.'

'Yeah, we need to hurry,' Anabel says. 'Read that on the train.'

'Okay, fine,' Milly huffs, stuffing the paper into her Changi airport duty free carrier bag. We hurry on, slipping through the slow-moving crowds of recently arrived passengers. But as we pass by a colossal, glossy billboard advertising a new SLR camera, Milly stops dead in her tracks and pauses. Turning, she looks closer at the advert and then curses. Twisting, she rummages in her bag for the paper, hissing expletives and scolding herself for being so thick.

'Language?' I mock teasingly.

'It's a set-up!' she blurts out. 'The whole thing.'

'What do you mean?' Anabel and I both ask simultaneously.

'The Chinese didn't have anything to do with this,' she whispers. 'They can't have. The angle's all wrong.'

'What *are* you talking about?' I ask.

'Look,' she exclaims, pulling the paper out and flattening it on the floor. 'These surveillance shots which the Chinese supposedly leaked to the British press were taken from exactly where *our* camera was. The Chinese camera was on the other side of the lamp. Remember when we found it when we removed ours? They were watching him for sure, but theirs was up in the other corner of his hotel room. These pictures,' she hisses, flapping the newspaper aggressively at us, 'they're *our* shots, not the PLA's!'

'Gimme that, let me see,' I exclaim, snatching the paper. As I peer closer, she opens the video up on her phone. As it begins playing, we realise she is right.

'Jesus,' I mutter. 'These are what we sent to Forbes. We've been royally played!' Sighing, I smack my leg with the crumpled paper. 'Fark!'

'Language,' Milly mutters.

'Well, now what?' Anabel asks nervously. 'This is serious stuff.'

'It's worse than serious. I can't believe Forbes would do something like this,' Milly says darkly, pointing over to a large television set mounted on the wall. A BBC News headline flashes across the screen: 'Interim PM slams predecessor'. A journalist appears on the screen, standing outside the brightly illuminated Houses of Parliament.

'Questions are now being asked,' he reports gravely, 'about how the former prime minister could have given a key ministerial post to a man of such questionable judgement, and what other compromised decisions he made.'

The image switches to Guy Forbes, who is in the midst of giving a statement outside 10 Downing Street.

'... it is evident my predecessor was at best negligent,' he says, his expression one of stoic resignation, 'at worst clearly unfit for office. And many areas of government suffered as a result. Make no mistake, we have serious problems. Now is therefore the time for serious people, and serious action. That is what my interim government intends to take: serious action, across multiple fronts simultaneously, to bring safety and prosperity back to the United Kingdom of Great Britain. It may not be easy. But I am convinced that together, we can achieve this. And we start tonight.'

'You realise what this is, right?' Milly says, pointing accusingly. 'It's basically a silent coup. I can't believe it. Not in this country. Not in this day and age.'

'I love it that you still get surprised by stuff like this,' I laugh. 'But you're not wrong. We seriously gotta talk to Styles. He's the only one who can sort this mess out.'

'And I love it that you still have faith in the system,' Milly notes dryly. 'But I think this ship's already sailed. In fact, I'm surprised they haven't arrested Styles and locked him up to get him out of the way. Last thing they need is for him to go to the press. Easier to do him for treason and dump him in Belmarsh.'

'Dartmoor more like,' I say. 'And I love how bitterly cynical you are.'

'Ugh, hang on a second,' Milly sighs as she reaches into her bag for her mobile, which has just begun to ring.

'Yes, hello.' She listens for a moment. 'Well, no, that's very kind of him. Yes, please assure him that we got back safely.' She listens intently, but her brow furrows and a dark expression falls across her face. I glance with concern at Anabel, who reaches out to lay a hand on Milly's shoulder.

'That's right, straight back to school,' Milly says, nodding. 'In fact, sorry, we have to run or we'll miss the last train. Yes, thank you. No, that won't be necessary. We've already bought tickets. Okay, yes. Thank you. Goodnight, then.'

With pursed lips, she hangs up and gives us both an ominous look.

'Well, go on,' Anabel urges.

'That was the new cabinet secretary. Apparently, Forbes wanted to ensure we'd made it back safely, and to congratulate us on a job well done.'

'Amazing he'd even think of us,' Anabel says, urging us to hurry towards the train platform.

'That wasn't the bit that concerned me,' Milly adds, hurrying to keep up. 'It was the bit where he checked that we're heading back to school now.'

'Strange thing to ask, right?' I ponder aloud, stopping abruptly. 'Why do you think he'd bother to ask that?'

'Uh-oh,' Milly says. 'I know that look.'

'And you're not wrong. Seriously, why go fishing about that? You've just taken over the government. Why would you give a rat's arse about where we're going?'

'What are you thinking?' Anabel asks.

'I think we get this train. But then at Waterloo you head back to school.'

'Where are you going?' Milly says as we hurry towards the platform.

'Exactly where we planned. To Styles's house. Only possible reason I can fathom he'd check that we're going straight back to school is to make sure we aren't meeting Styles.'

'Bit of a stretch, don't you think?' Anabel says as we board the train and head down the centre of the carriage to find a set of four vacant seats.

There are too many people sitting close to us to talk privately, so we spend most of the journey in contemplative silence. Once at Paddington, we quickly distance ourselves from the throng of disembarking passengers and walk along the adjacent platform, away from any prying ears that could overhear our conversation.

'You know,' Milly says, 'I'm surprised Forbes's cabinet secretary didn't try to go fishing about what we thought of the Chinese leaking the pictures. Just to see our reactions.'

'I don't think it would even occur to them,' Anabel counters. 'I mean, the footage was almost the same, right? You'd have to be some kind of eagle-eyed rocket man to see the difference.'

'You're missing the point,' I interject. 'Only Styles and us three saw the photos the Chinese gave him. Forbes never actually saw them. They wouldn't even make the comparison.'

'Yeah, I suppose that's true,' Milly concedes.

'Okay, head back down to school. I'll take a taxi to his place. But subtle, yeah. See if I can get in to see him.'

'It's kind of late, don't you think?' Milly says.

'Would you sleep if you were in his position?' I ask.

'Okay, fair point.'

'I'll see what I see, if anything. But I need to speak to him. I mean, he got played as badly as we did, it seems.'

'Pay in cash,' Anabel suggests. 'They can't track the payment, then.'

'Exactly what I was thinking,' I reply with a smile. With no luggage, I give them both a quick hug and am about to set off towards the taxi rank when Milly catches my arm.

'Hey,' she says hesitantly, biting her lower lip. Her eyes dart left and right. 'Just checking we're... you know, all okay?'

Sighing, I stop and turn to her. I place a hand on her shoulder and stoop a little to look directly into her eyes.

'Mills, this is, like, the tenth time you've checked if we're cool since we left Honk. We're absolutely fine, I assure you. You don't need to keep asking, alright? Seriously. And don't overanalyse everything. If I was going to do it with anyone, I'm glad it was with you both.'

'But we took advantage.'

'Which is a skill any good spy needs to have. Don't beat yourself up for it. If I can deal with it, so can you. Some things just happen. Roll with it. Makes life a lot easier, right? It's not like I'm going to go shouting it from the rooftops. You know, like in some bid to up my flat-earth society LGBT woke credentials like half the world is. Besides, I have a reputation to maintain.'

'What's that?' she asks, hints of hurt evident on her face.

'Unlucky in love,' I reply, smiling in amusement at her instinctive assumption. 'Wouldn't want anyone thinking I actually got lucky and had some fun, now, would I?' I whisper.

A look of relief breaks across her face.

'It's fine,' I promise, smirking. 'I don't mind at all that you both took total advantage of me while I was inebriated and emotionally vulnerable.'

'Oh, please stop,' Anabel implores, laughing. 'You'll give her a complex.'

'I know. I'm sorry. I'm playing.'

'And I thought what happens in Hong Kong stays in Hong Kong.'

'Belle's right, what are we even talking about?'

'Nothing,' says Milly, grinning finally. 'We weren't talking about anything.'

'Exactly. Look, best you both head off,' I say. 'And take my phone. I don't trust these bastards as far as I could throw them. Wouldn't put it past them to track us heading back to school. Just to be sure. But I want to go see Styles. I don't particularly like the man, but he's been royally screwed, and not necessarily in the best interests of the country, either. He should at least know who screwed him. Coz it sure as hell wasn't the Chinese. I just don't want Forbes to know I went to see him.'

'What difference does it make?' Milly asks, taking my arm. 'Don't risk it. If they know you've been to see Styles, it'll raise all sorts of suspicions, don't you think?'

'I don't disagree, but we gave Forbes the rope with which to hang Styles. I have enough on my conscience from HK. And I'm not talking about *that*, okay? Let's just say there's red in my ledger,' I laugh. 'Sorry, I always wanted to use that line.'

Anabel smirks. 'Wow, would you believe it?' she giggles. 'Heather still has a conscience. After all this.'

'Hey, don't knock it. I have quite a strong conscience, I'll have you know. And if doing this eases the guilt trip a little, then all good, right?'

Handing her my phone, I nod and wave, before hurrying off across the station's concourse. As I go, I put my rather salt-stained MI13 cap on and pull my rain jacket's excessively-sized hood up. Getting spotted on CCTV cameras now is not what I need.

The black cab eventually drops me off, as requested, at the turning into Great College Street, just up from the Houses of Parliament. From here, I walk on cautiously, passing the turning into Little College Street. Thereafter, the road descends into near darkness, with just the original underpowered gas lamps to light the street. Without any moonlight, it gives the street an oddly sinister air of foreboding. All that's needed, I muse, is indeed a thick blanket of nineteenth-century London fog.

Staying close to the old cobblestone wall on the right, I approach the turn into Barton Street. As I take the corner, I spot a policeman just in sight at the far end of the street, where it turns the bend into Cowley Street. Without missing a beat, I continue along the road and follow it around until I join Great Peter Street. Without my phone – a decision I now regret – I must rely on judgement alone to gauge where the back of Styles's house is. Once past number fourteen, I stop at a long stretch of brick wall. Glancing up, I estimate this to be about right. Thankfully, there is no police presence here – the street is deserted – and two nearby streetlights give sufficient illumination to see what I am doing.

The back of Robert Styles's house sits flush with the rear garden wall. At its lowest point, the wall is about seven feet high. However, the left-hand side offers the best access, before it rises another few feet to accommodate an inbuilt black, slatted garage door. From there it looks a simple enough climb up the back wall to the second floor. Set against the rear of Styles's house is a road sign. Just beside that is a small, low-set window, presumably to the lower-ground floor. Unfortunately, a quick inspection reveals it to be latched and locked. Looking up, I see a burglar alarm higher up on the rear wall of the house.

Moving backwards, I decide the left-hand wall looks the easiest to scale. Sighing at the effort required to keep this visit secret, I approach it and step onto a square white planter, then pull myself up onto the narrow wall.

A wooden trellis is fixed to the top of the wall and it doesn't leave a lot of space to stand. Holding the trellis top for balance, I peer down into an enclosed drive-in parking space for the residents. Occupying most of it is a sleek-looking black Range Rover. Say one thing about Styles: the man has good taste.

Of course, entering at ground level, through either the white sash windows or the matching back door at the far end of the parking bay, would have been the easiest option, but it also carries a far greater chance of being seen by any guests Styles might have. And I don't need him calling the police, either, in some panic at the sight of movement outside.

Instead, gaining access from a higher floor seems preferable. I step up to the next level and carefully edge along it, holding the trellis, glad for the relative cover afforded by the shadow of a nearby tree. At the far end, the wall rises vertically. Very carefully, I step up onto the top of the trellis, wary as it wobbles precariously. Reaching up quickly, before it can snap sideways, I grab the top of the wall and shimmy up it, glad for the grip of my rubber-soled Palladium boots.

A waist-high wrought-iron railing runs around a flat roof-top area. Directly behind it is a far taller wooden fence, which affords greater privacy to the small garden within. Just as I am about to use the railing as a step up to scale the fence, the back door opens far below at the end of the parking bay. Freezing, I glance down, less than thrilled to be caught in the open like this, especially so high up.

A figure emerges from the house. Clearly male. The first thing that strikes me, though, is how different the figure's gait is to Robert Styles's. It is a stomping march, more reminiscent of a soldier on a parade ground than Styles's more casual amble. The light isn't good enough for me to make out any more detail. The man approaches the vehicle and removes a large holdall from the boot, before closing it quietly and returning to the house.

Intrigued to know who Styles is entertaining at this time of night, especially after the day he must have had, I scale the fence and drop down silently on the other side. I find myself in a small, enclosed second-floor rooftop garden, with actual grass, large pot planters running down either side and a set of patio garden furniture in the centre. In the far right-hand corner is a quaint little garden shed. It's a nice spot he has here, very quiet and secluded. Keeping to the shadows, I make my way towards the white sash garden door.

Looming over the second floor roof garden are the remaining upper two floors of the house, the top one set into the sloping roof. I have no lock-pick kit, and smashing the door's glass is out of the question if I am to maintain any semblance of operational subtlety. Hands on hips, I turn and ponder my options.

With nothing to lose, I bend down to peer beneath the door-mat, then sigh: I knew it would have been too good to be true. Undeterred, I tilt the nearest flowerpot sideways, just in case. That elicits another sigh. Then, with an irked scowl, I shrug and try the door's handle… and groan as it opens.

'Yeah, so much for security,' I mutter in amusement as I slip inside to find myself at the end of a long, dark corridor. With my first objective achieved without having been seen by anyone, I set my sights on finding Styles. The trick will be to do so without his guest knowing.

No lights are on in any of the rooms up here, either. Paint-ings of countryside hunting scenes and old sailboats adorn the hallway's walls. Just along the parquet-floored hallway, on the right, is the top of the curving stairs. Pausing there, I strain for any indication as to whether I should go down or up. Closing my eyes, I concentrate on the silence. Suddenly, there is a loud creak from somewhere down below. Freezing, I wait, barely breathing in the darkness, to see where the person is. And, critically, if they are coming out into the main hallway below.

But no one does.

Oddly, there are no voices, either. No talking. No laughter, or crying as the case might have been, given Styles has just lost his job, has been publicly disgraced and is now the laughing stock of the country. Nothing like one might expect to hear if someone has a guest around. Somewhere, buried deep in that wary, prehistoric warning centre of my brain, a small alarm goes off. Something does not feel right about this.

Ever so lightly, I put one foot onto the top stair and apply a little weight, bracing for any groan or creak of the wood, but none comes. Soundly built for sure. I feel more confident to add all my weight. Gripping the smooth, rounded wooden banister, I ease down onto the next step. There is a bit more give from this one, but still no telltale noise. Step by careful step, I creep down the darkened staircase until I turn the bend and the floor below finally comes into view. The hallway, which leads from the front door, past the bottom of the stairs and on towards the rear of the house, is also in darkness. A single, thin sliver of warm light stretches across the corridor, spilling from a room just beyond view.

I pause, somewhat confused, for below me is the ground floor. Which means the small window I saw at the back must be at basement level. The only explanations are that street level outside the front is higher than it is around the back, or the lower ground floor is set below street level. Either way, it concerns me not to fully understand the layout of the house. The variables are too unknown for my liking.

A noise from the rear of the house startles me. It sounds like a door being closed, or possibly kicked to rather than being closed by hand. Edging back into the gloom behind the banisters, I wait, heart hammering, to see who appears.

With heavy footsteps, the same dark-clothed figure from earlier comes into view, only this time he has a long black bag slung over his shoulder. For a moment, it looks like a mortician's body-bag, but the man is carrying it far too easily for there to be a person inside it. Effortlessly, he slips it from his shoulder and carries it in with one hand through the door.

A woman speaks as he enters. While her words are unintelligible from here, her accent is unmistakeable. That French bitch! My eyes go wide with realisation and my pulse quickens. What the hell is she doing here? Nothing good, I imagine. Her presence never bodes well for anyone. I now find myself equally concerned for Styles's wellbeing as I am angry – angry at being so close and yet unable to confront her. Cursing silently to myself in a long, drawn-out string of expletives, I strain to hear what is being said.

Her heels clack noisily across the bare wooden floor. Emerging into the hallway, she glances up, and for a second looks directly at me. Thankfully, the shadows must be sufficiently dark and masking, because she smiles privately to herself before turning on her obscenely high stilettos and continuing towards the rear of the house. She returns a moment later with a loose necktie swinging from her hand. One of Robert Styles's, I imagine. Quite what she intends to do with it is anyone's guess.

Despite loathing her with a visceral passion, I can't help but be struck by how effortlessly sophisticated her distinctly Parisian sense of style is: nonchalantly simple, yet capped off with some statement pieces, like tonight's brightly coloured Hermès silk scarf, a pair of elegant black leather gloves and a particularly nice pair of patent beige heels. I add it to the list of reasons I hate her.

'What is that?' the man asks from somewhere inside the room. 'Codeine? Diamorphine? Some kind of semi-synthetic heroin?'

'Something like zhat,' she relies in her irritatingly sing-songy accent, which makes me scowl, for as much as I am loath to admit it, there is something undeniably cool about how it sounds. My list grows longer again.

'It can't be this easy,' the man mutters darkly as something is dragged across the floor. A chair perhaps. 'Can it?'

'Oh, but eet ees, *mon chérrie*,' she exclaims. There's that laugh again. Whatever she's doing in there, she's clearly enjoying herself.

'Frankly, I am staggered it worked,' he says. 'Both Sanders and I told him the plan was far too complex. Had too many moving parts, all of which could have been derailed at any point. But I've got to hand it to him, the lucky son of a bitch. It worked. I'm still astonished they didn't see the pattern after you took that USB.'

'You presume 'ee even read eet,' Nicole replies. 'Locked away in a safe, all the way up zhere.'

As a string of light bulbs suddenly illuminate within my head, I realise I can't stay up here. I need to find Styles and figure out what is going on here. Are they robbing the place, or planting something? I finally see a chance when the man announces, 'Well, shall we go get him, then?'

'*Bon*,' she replies. 'Zhen let's get out of 'ere.'

As they both make their way to the rear of the house, I creep down the remainder of the stairs and hurry along the main hallway, before ducking hastily into a darkened study just beyond the living room. In the gloom, I sneak behind the desk and make room for myself to crouch in beneath it by moving the office chair back a fraction. From here, I am afforded a partial view into the brightly lit front living room. Nothing could have prepared me for what I see.

A half-naked, skinny young man dressed only in a pair of grey Y-front briefs lies slumped on the large Chesterfield sofa near the front window. Behind the sofa, the thick red velvet curtains are drawn. Up high, in the centre of the ornately decorated room, hanging from the ceiling fan's mounting, is the necktie from earlier. It has been tied to hang with a large noose at its end.

'Oh, that can't be good,' I mutter as the sound of heavy footsteps from outside in the hallway makes me freeze.

Nicole's accomplice reappears first, with the limp body of Robert Styles in his arms.

Now that I see the man properly, up close, a quiet sense of ill ease comes over me. While he is only of medium build, his footsteps are suggestive of someone far larger and heavier. His hair is marine short and slightly greying, reflecting his age, which I guess to be early forties. Running all the way down the left side of his face, from his hairline, over his eye and down to his jawline, is a raw, nasty-looking scar. Dressed in black hiking boots, blue jeans and a black jacket, he looks unremarkable. His appearance, however, belies a lurking, calculated menace to the man. Not only are his movements entirely purposeful, but the ease with which he then steps up onto the chair positioned directly beneath the ceiling fan and singlehandedly hefts Styles up and into the noose is unexpectedly alarming. The politician may not be a big man, but I can't believe he weighs much less than eighty kilos. Even the fittest, strongest men I have met in this strange, shadowy world of highly unusual people would not be able to manhandle that weight quite so effortlessly.

Holding Styles's limp body, he slips the noose over his head with the other hand. Stepping down, he gently releases the body to let it hang from the fan. Part of me wants to rush forward to intervene, but I am held back as it begins to dawn on me what is really happening here. The lack of response from Styles suggests he is already dead. Exposing myself now would serve no tactical purpose.

Stepping over to join him, Nicole looks up at the dangling figure with a quizzical expression.

'Mmm,' she ponders, stroking her chin thoughtfully. 'It needs... *je ne sais quoi*. Something more,' she exclaims with an artistic flourish of her hand. Reaching up, she undoes his belt and trousers, and swiftly pulls them, along with his underpants, down to his ankles.

'*Et voila!*'

'You are pretty sick,' her menacing companion notes dryly.

With an amused laugh, she walks to the sofa, beside which sits the holdall which the man brought in earlier. She removes a round mirrored plate, walks to the hanging body and forces the limp fingers to grip the edge of it. With his prints on it, she places the plate on the coffee table and tips a bag of white powder out onto it. Having retrieved Styles's wallet from his pocket, she then removes one of his metal credit cards, shapes up a neat line and places the card incriminatingly at the edge of the plate. She takes a clear plastic bag and a paper drinking straw from the bag and proceeds to carefully fill one end of the straw with the powder. Then, elegantly stepping up onto the chair, she inserts the drug-filled end into Styles's right nostril. She inhales deeply, puts her lips to the other end of the straw and blows hard, sending the drugs shooting high up into his nostril.

'Who's been a naughty boy,' she exclaims, pulling the bag down over his head.

'It has to be tight around his face,' the man cautions. 'Or it won't look like he suffocated.'

'You are so clever,' she gasps mockingly. 'Ze thought 'ad never occurred to me.' Smiling, she secures the bag around Styles's neck with help from a large elastic band. Then she slips the straw inside the seal from below and sucks deeply, emptying the air and forcing the plastic to pull tightly over Styles's contorted death grimace beneath.

'See, wasn't so hard, eh?' she laughs, removing the straw. Before the scarred man can comment, she moves over to the half-naked man on the sofa. Having set him upright with her gloved hands, she holds him still and ties a tourniquet around his left arm with a length of black rubber hosing taken from the holdall. After slapping the crease of his inner arm, she proceeds to inject him with a syringe which was lying on the coffee table set between the sofa and two matching armchairs. For effect, she leaves the empty syringe embedded in his arm.

Taking the holdall, as well as Styles's phone, wallet and house keys, she walks into the hallway and makes for what I presume to be the kitchen, at the rear of the house. Several loud thuds can be heard. A moment later, she returns with the empty bag folded under her arm. She no longer has Styles's belongings.

The man walks to the coffee table, picks up a remote control and turns on the wall-mounted flat-screen television. He scrolls through a few channels, until he reaches the news.

'And just like that, I give you plausible motive,' he says, laying the remote back down.

'... the scandal has culminated in the forced resignation of the prime minister. The recent emergence of the intelligence agency dossier, which many now speculate came into the possession of the PM's close friend and confidante and served as the source for the ensuing leaks concerning ministerial malpractice, has largely sealed public opinion. The leader of the opposition was fast to condemn what she described as damning hypocrisy and rampant rot at the heart of the government.'

A woman's voice replaces the reporter's.

'... it is the staggering hypocrisy of the former minister of morality who, unable to in good conscience work with colleagues of such questionable character, felt it was his public duty to inform the press of their conduct. And the recent leaks from Hong Kong illustrate just how ironic and hypocritical that double standard was. And now we discover that the PM was fully aware of his cabinet's questionable pasts when he came to power, including that of Robert Styles. This is just the latest damning indictment to emerge concerning the former prime minister's judgement.'

The programme misses a beat, before the original reporter comes back on air.

'Earlier this evening, Downing Street confirmed that newly appointed interim prime minister Guy Forbes has announced that a thorough clean-up of the government will be his first priority, commencing tomorrow.'

'And just like zhat,' Nicole says, 'you 'ave a front row seat to 'istory being made. Any minute, zhe press will arrive for a statement from zis irriot, only to find he died in a drug-fuelled sodomy session with some underage rent boy, and zhat's all zhe icing zhe cake needs.'

'Yeah, well, finally the adults get the country back,' the man replies.

'Isn't zhat what zhis was all about? All zhe effort. And zhat leetle zip-drive gave us the keys. Let's hope eet was all worth eet.'

'I'm sure he's grateful for it. Was a hell of a risk.'

'Meh, was seemple,' she sings airily. She walks to the door and flicks a switch on the wall, and the ceiling fan slowly begins to turn. The ghastly, torrid scene is finally complete. Anyone stumbling upon it will arrive at one conclusion and one conclusion only: a sexual deviancy gone wrong, with tonight's rent-boy overdosed on the sofa, leaving Styles hanging from the ceiling fan in a doomed bid for sexual asphyxia; an obscene sight, circling limply overhead, around and around, with his pants around his ankles.

'Proud of your work?' the man asks as Nicole opens a laptop and places it on the coffee table. She begins playing a film.

'*Bien sur,*' she gushes, gesturing at the scene. 'Zis makes 'ees boy in zee bath look amateur.'

My brow furrows as my brain races to try to work out what she means. The nagging discomfort of being folded awkwardly under the office desk is not helping. But then, with a startling moment of clarity, the final piece of the puzzle falls into place as I recall the story Styles told us in our darkened hotel room in Hong Kong about the staffer of his who had died by misadventure in his bathtub at home. I feel my heart pounding in excitement; not only at having been right, but at now finally seeing the whole picture. Of course there had to be more to all this than we could see. We just never knew enough to put the pieces together. But now, with these last elusive links, the whole conspiracy is clear to see.

Yet at each step, there has always been one constant. Nicole. Since the very beginning, all the way back to Pemberton-Smythe's... no wait, earlier in fact, I realise, as I recall my suspicions that she was present as far back as Marrakesh. The darting figure on the roof. The same, unmistakeable catlike litheness. There she's been, hiding in the shadows, manipulating, influencing everything all along.

And now, at last, the truth. But has it come too late? What I don't have, what I really need, is the missing link. Forbes has clearly been playing us. Of that there is no doubt. The question is can we find a solid connection between him, Nicole and her mysterious friend? We are certainly well beyond the point of random coincidence, that's for sure, but it's not enough. Not for the severity of the accusation. However, while we may not have enough evidence yet, I realise we finally hold the tactical advantage. We now know more than them. The question is, how can we make it count for something or give us an actual strategic advantage? In fact, I realise, the real question is whether it is wise now, with Forbes in place as the new PM, to even try.

With her holdall in hand, Nicole casts a final look around the living room. Nodding in satisfaction, she says, 'Make zhe call.'

The man takes his phone from his jacket pocket and dials a number as he walks towards the front window.

'Yes, police,' he says in a suddenly highly animated, clipped, upper-class accent. 'I have just seen the most dreadful thing whilst out walking my dog. A man seems to have hung himself. Yes, in his home. One doesn't have the best view, but from the street that's what it looks like. Twenty-one Cowley Street, Westminster.'

He quickly hangs up and tugs the curtains open a foot or two. He then dials a second number. This time when he speaks, it is with his normal heavy East End accent.

'The call's been made. Send your people now. They need to be here within a few minutes. Copy that. Yes, don't underestimate their response time once the penny drops who lives here.'

'*Bon,*' Nicole exclaims, clapping her hands as he hangs up. '*On se casse.*'

'Yup, let's move,' he replies, knocking the chair beneath Robert Styles over with a callous kick.

Together, they rush for the rear parking area and the waiting Range Rover. After a few seconds, once I am confident neither will return, I emerge stiffly from beneath the desk. Instinctively, I reach into my trouser pocket for my phone. For a dreadful second, I clutch furiously at both my pockets, fearful that I lost it in the taxi. But then I remember where it is, and groan. Cursing, I look around the room for another phone. Styles's will do. But it's nowhere to be seen.

I race to the hallway and am relieved to find Nicole has placed it on the sideboard, beside his house keys and wallet. Snatching it up, I rush into the living room and press his lifeless thumb to the screen's fingerprint reader, unlocking the phone. Berating myself for such poor planning, I realise I don't know the number to dial by heart. But I know Milly's. I step back towards the door to check the PC outside won't be able to see me. Thankfully, he is still standing where I last saw him, facing away, looking up the road, bored and oblivious to what's just happened right behind him.

I dial Milly's number and wait for it to begin ringing. But when it does, no one answers. The ringtone mocks me, and my frustration rises the longer I wait. I feel my hand tremble slightly as adrenaline surges into my bloodstream.

'Come on, Mills. Jesus, hurry up and answer, will you?' I huff. Finally, just as I am about to give up in desperation, she answers.

'Hello?'

'Mills, no time to speak. I need Gambon's number. Give me C's, too, if you have it.'

'You okay?' she asks. 'You sound stressed.'

'I am. But I haven't got time to explain. Styles is dead. I need those numbers.'

She gasps in shock, and I hurriedly note them down on a pad as she reads them out.

'Cheers. Tell you all later. Basically, it's a dog's breakfast here. Gotta go.'

I open an IM app, hurriedly create a new group chat, enter their numbers and then dial the group. Each step wastes precious time I don't have.

Gambon answers first. C's phone simply rings on.

'Evening, sir. It's Heather.'

'Ugh, Foxton, do you know what time it is?'

'Yes, sorry, sir.'

'Who's that?' a woman asks in the background.

'No one, dear,' Gambon replies softly. 'Someone from the orifice.'

'I do wish you wouldn't call it that,' she sighs. 'So vulgar.'

'Yes, dear. Sorry, dear. Go back to sleep now, dear,' he says soothingly. 'Right, Foxton, what's all this about? I presume you have seen the news?'

'Er, yes.'

'Pretty stunning turn of events, wouldn't you say? I can't believe this is over yet. It was not even a proper leadership transition. Unlikely your man Styles will take this sitting down.'

'Yeah, about that, sir, I don't think there's going to be any fightback. Things have gone a little pear-shaped,' I reply as I stare at the dreadful orchestrated scene.

'Miss Foxton. Pear-shaped is unhelpful as far as a sit-rep goes. A bit more detail, if you please?'

'We're screwed. How's that for detailed? I'm at Styles's. He's dead! They've strung him up from the fricking ceiling fan by his tie. His boxers are around his ankles, and he's got a plastic bag over his head. Coke's smeared all over his nose. Drugs everywhere. There's a porno playing on the laptop. Some skinny rent-boy in a pair of Y-fronts with a fricking ball gag in his mouth, dead from the looks of it, is on the living room sofa. OD'd. And it just gets worse in the kitchen,' I add as I walk into it. 'Oh, Christ, there's a sodding great pile of dildos in the sink –'

'Who did this?'

'Nicole. And some guy.'

'Okay. Well, we can clean it up. I can arrange for a team to come over.'

'Couldn't C send people who're closer? Why isn't he answering?'

'Haven't you heard?' Gambon asks. 'He was relieved of his position. Effective a couple of hours ago. Forbes has begun clearing the decks of anyone he feels is not wholeheartedly on his side. The new chief apparently walked him from the building. Now, admittedly they never got on, but I've never seen anything like it.'

'Fark!' I say, sighing as I turn back to the living room. 'What the hell am I supposed to do about this?'

'Was he alive when they brought him in?'

'Who?'

'Robert.'

'Honestly, no idea. Guess he could've been drugged. Pentobarbital or something. But I doubt it. That French cow sounded like she's done this before. Setting the scene, I mean. You wouldn't drug him. Any good autopsy would find it straightaway, right?'

'Agreed.'

'So, perhaps it would've been better to collect him from the airport, then strangle him on the way home. She could've hidden in the boot. Strangled him over the back seat. I mean, that's what I'd have done. If I intended to stage a hanging here.'

'And some of my staff say you scare them,' Gambon mutters. 'Can't imagine why.'

'Yeah, whatever,' I reply, before catching myself and apologising. 'Point is, sir, it all makes sense now. It was a set-up all along. And we gave it to them on a plate. The PM's USB was likely stolen by Nicole from his safe at Chequers. It gave whoever they are all the ammunition they needed to remove Forbes's competition. The goal must have been getting him into Downing Street.'

'That's a rather large leap, don't you think?'

'Maybe. But hear me out because it kinda makes sense. Using the stuff on the USB, they drip fed the press, causing resignation after resignation, weakening the PM. Sadly, Styles turned out to be the PM's Achilles' heel, the old friend with too many skeletons in the closet. They somehow got to one of his staffers and used him to set his boss up as the iron-clad source of the government leaks. Job done, he was taken out by Nicole. Yet by then the ball was already in motion for us to start digging into Styles at Forbes's behest. He must have known it was only a matter of time before we discovered the truth about the minister of morality. Of course, it would have all been for nothing had we not supplied Forbes with the evidence he needed, which could then be leaked and, ironically, attributed to the very people we had been led to assume Styles was potentially working for in the first place: the Chinese.'

'Look, I don't disagree, Foxton. But perhaps now is not the time to wildly speculate. It sounds like we have bigger problems.'

'You're right. So, what shall I do?' I ask, glancing nervously at my watch. 'They already called the police. Any second,

London Five-Oh are gonna remember they have a bobby standing right outside this place.'

'Oh dear, well, that changes things dramatically. I don't think there is much you can do. This thing is done, in that case. Heart of Westminster. A cabinet minister,' he declares. 'Doubt you have more than a minute or two. Smart, taking him out of the picture. It means they can pin whatever they want on him. And there'll be no pushback.'

'True, but there must be something we can do!'

'What? Ask London's finest not to come? This is just the way things go, Foxton. Sometimes we win, and sometimes we don't.'

In the background, Gambon turns on his TV; I recognise the news programme's introductory jingle.

'Here it is,' he says. 'Breaking story. Reports coming in of Styles's death.'

'How?' I exclaim. 'No one even knows yet. Sir, it's all bollocks. The whole story. Seriously, I swear they're linked. Forbes and these people, I mean. They have to be. It's the only logical conclusion. Pemberton and the Irish banker, they were the money. Which was then used to finance the attacks. But laundered and unattributable. Which undermined the government. The leaks were then intended to weaken the PM and discredit his cabinet colleagues, removing one after the other as Forbes's competition. And now they've served up the final nail, Styles and his Hong Kong antics, and Forbes is the only one left standing. It's a frickin' silent coup!'

'I don't know if you're right or mad,' he says. 'But if you're right, then we got played by a masterclass. We saw what we wanted to see. And we responded just how they hoped we'd respond. That said, this is the real world. Nothing's ever that neat, or that organised. I'm not fully sold on that theory, I must admit.'

'Sir, if the government was so riddled with problem people, why couldn't the opposition have just taken over?'

'My dear, the country is effectively at war after the attacks. Now is not the time to change government. Unless the PM was to call a snap general election, parliament has to follow its set course.'

'Clearly, Forbes isn't going to do that. Not after all that effort to get where he is.'

'Assuming you are right, that is,' he adds cautiously.

Spinning at the sound of approaching sirens, I swear and duck low to peer through the front windows, just as a pair of scooters pull up outside in the street. The PC on guard makes to approach them. Ignoring him, the two men race towards the front window, cameras in hand, helmets still on, as blue flashing lights appear at the far end of the road.

'Sounds like we're out of time,' Gambon notes dryly as I lurch backwards, out of sight. 'Get out of there before you get arrested and drop HMG in the proverbial.'

'What, and leave it all like this?' I exclaim. 'They set him up!'

'And very well, too, from the sound of it. Look, your instincts were spot on. That's good field craft. But we got played and we were too far behind them. It's an insurmountable lead. They won. The narrative is out of our hands. It will snowball from here. It already is. Scarper, Foxton! Get back here, fast, while you still can. There's nothing more you can do. As far as anyone's concerned, you're still in the green. Leave! Now's not the time to find yourself on the wrong side of things, twisting in the wind. Yes, of course action's required. But not now.

Not now, you hear! Regroup, strategise, and we act when the time's right. Do you understand?'

The photographers' flashguns go off through the front window, illuminating the scene with their blinding bursts before the police officer can intervene.

I curse and hang up. Ducking sideways, I hurriedly delete the two new contact numbers on Styles's handset and then remove the group chat, just as the first heavy thump slams into the solid front door. Heart hammering, throat dry, I frantically rub the handset down with the hem of my T-shirt. Another, far heavier bang shakes the front door, making me jump. The situation is now out of control.

Panting hard, I replace the handset, and sprint down the hallway and across the kitchen and let myself out into the now vacated parking area. A crash at the front of the house from what sounds like a breaching hammer only makes me move faster. Another loud bang and the front door must give, because I suddenly hear voices and movement. With the hem of my T-shirt, I quickly wipe the door handle and softly close it behind me. I run on, bent low, leap up onto the side wall at the far right-hand corner of the parking bay and scramble up. I perch momentarily atop the external wall and cast a wary glance down into the street to ensure I won't drop to the pavement only to find myself face to face with either the press or London's finest. Satisfied, I leap down and hurry off along the road, to disappear into the night.

Finally knowing the truth, I find myself hailing a black taxi, lost deep in thought as my mind whirls. This latest development certainly seals Styles's fate. But at the back of my mind is a niggling concern, not outright fear but sufficiently worrying to occupy my thinking.

Gambon says we're still in the green and above suspicion. But even if that's true, it doesn't make the bigger problem go away. If Guy Forbes, Nicole and whoever else is behind this plot have been involved since the very beginning, then surely they must see my friends and me as some kind of royal pain in the arse. Several times now we have scuppered or derailed their plans. How long, then, before they come for us? Revenge and underhand tactics seem to be Forbes's preferred choice for dealing with those who have crossed him. Once he is done clearing the decks of his main adversaries, like the former head of SIS, how long before he then turns his attention to us?

We have been sufficiently forewarned about what to expect from Guy Forbes. Yet at the same time I also feel a deep sense of injustice. Ignorance would be bliss, but now we know what Guy Forbes has done and how he played us. And soon he will realise this for himself, if indeed he hasn't already.

We have no option, therefore, but to ready ourselves. The trick will be to do so while remaining firmly in the shadows for as long as possible. But at some point we will have no choice but to fight back. And ideally before he comes for us. The question is when will that be? And, crucially, how?

M.N. SMITH

The End

675

Heather Foxton will return in
The Sons of Triton.

MY SINCERE THANKS...

To everyone who helps to bring Heather's world to its paper-and-ink reality:

To my editor, Charlie Wilson and my interior and cover designer, John Chandler – thank you for your hard work to make this a reality. It goes without saying that any remaining mistakes are entirely of my own making.

Sincere thanks, also, to my friend who has rejoined the muggles. Only you know who you are, and how much Heather and I owe you.

To Vanessa and Duncan, who gave their valuable time to plough through proofreading the manuscript and correcting my mistakes. Thank you for your help and suggestions; they were greatly appreciated.

To my friends who support and tolerate the compromise it takes to get Heather out the door each time and the number of nights out I need to abstain from, I am as appreciative as always.

To my family, for all your love and support, for which I am so fortunate and grateful.

And last but most decidedly not least, a special note of thanks to my amazing, fabulous wife for your rock-like support and good humour at the amount of time I spend in the company of a paper-and-ink teenage girl, without which none of this could or would ever happen.

I love you, my Bella Bambina!!!

Printed in Great Britain
by Amazon